JANE EYRE

JANE EYRE

Charlotte Brontë

edited by Richard Nemesvari

broadview editions

Canadian Cataloguing in Publication Data

Brontë Charlotte, 1816-1855
  Jane Eyre

(Broadview literary texts)
Includes bibliographical references
ISBN 1-55111-180-2

I. Nemesvari, Richard Andrew, 1959- . II. Title.   III. Series.

PR4167.J3 1998   823'.8   C99-930040-7

Broadview Press Ltd., is an independent, international publishing house, incorporated in
1985.

North America
PO Box 1243, Peterborough, Ontario, Canada K9J 7H5
Tel: (705) 743-8990; Fax: (705) 743-8353
email: customerservice@broadviewpress.com
3576 California Road, Orchard Park, NY, USA 14127

UK, Ireland, and continental Europe
NBN Plymbridge
Estover Road
Plymouth PL6 7PY UK
Tel: 44 (0) 1752 202 301
Fax: 44 (0) 1752 202 331
Fax Order Line: 44 (0) 1752 202 333
Customer Service: cserv@nbnplymbridge.com
Orders: orders@nbnplymbridge.com

Australia and New Zealand
UNIREPS, University of New South Wales
Sydney, NSW, 2052
Tel: 61 2 9664 0999; Fax: 61 2 9664 5420
email: info.press@unsw.edu.au
www.broadviewpress.com

Broadview Press gratefully acknowledges the support of the Ministry of Canadian Heritage.
We acknowledge the financial support of the Government of Canada through the Book
Publishing Industry Development Program for our publishing activities.

Broadview Press is grateful to Professor Eugene Benson for advice on
editorial matters for the Broadview Literary Texts series.

Text design and composition by George Kirkpatrick
PRINTED IN CANADA

Contents

Acknowledgements • 7

Introduction • 9

A Note on the Text • 50

Charlotte Brontë: A Brief Chronology • 56

Jane Eyre • 59

Appendix A: *Prefatory Material to Subsequent Editions
of Jane Eyre* • 557
1. Preface to the Second Edition of *Jane Eyre* • 557
2. Note to the Third Edition of *Jane Eyre* • 559

Appendix B: *Charlotte Brontë: Correspondence on
Being a Governess* • 560
1. To Emily Brontë, June 8, 1839 • 560
2. To Ellen Nussey, January 24, 1840 • 562
3. To Ellen Nussey, ?March 3, 1841 • 564

Appendix C: *Jane Eyre and the Governess Question* • 567
1. "Hints on the Modern Governess System"
(*Fraser's Magazine*) • 567
2. "Governesses' Benevolent Institution"
(*Punch*) • 578
3. Sarah Lewis, "On the Social Position of
Governesses" (*Fraser's Magazine*) • 579
4. Elizabeth Rigby, Review of *Vanity Fair, Jane Eyre,
Governesses' Benevolent Institution – Report for
1847* (*Quarterly Review*) • 585

Appendix D: *Jane Eyre and the Proper Young Woman* • 600
Sarah Stickney Ellis, *The Daughters of England:
Their Position in Society, Character and
Responsibilities* • 600

Appendix E: *Race, Empire, and the West Indies* • 607

    1. Thomas Carlyle, "Occasional Discourse on
      the Negro Question" (*Fraser's Magazine*) • 607

    2. John Stuart Mill, "The Negro Question"
      (*Fraser's Magazine*) • 625

Appendix F: *Jamaica and Governor Eyre* • 637

    1. Despatch from Edward John Eyre,
      "The Insurrection in Jamaica" (*The Times*) • 637

    2. "The Outbreak in Jamaica" *(The Times)* • 648

    3. Editorial (*The Times*) • 655

    4. Charles Buxton, Letter to the Editor
      (*The Times*) • 659

    5. "The Jamaica Question" (*Punch*) • 665

    6. "The Bold Governor Eyre and the Bulls
      of Exeter Hall" (*Punch*) • 666

    7. John Stuart Mill, "Statement of the Jamaica
      Committee" (*The Daily News*) • 668

    8. Thomas Carlyle, Letter to Hamilton Hume • 672

    9. John Ruskin, "A Speech in London"
      (*The Daily Telegraph*) • 674

Select Bibliography • 678

Acknowledgements

I would like to thank the following individuals and institutions for their help. I am grateful to Dr. Edward Langille for his translation of much of the French in *Jane Eyre*, and to the Department of English at St. Francis Xavier University for providing me with funding for photocopy expenses. I would also like to thank the Harry Ransom Humanities Research Center, University of Texas at Austin, for supplying me with a microfilm copy of the first edition of the novel, and Oxford University Press for its permission to reprint the three Brontë letters which appear in Appendix B. These were taken from the first volume of Dr. Margaret Smith's *The Letters of Charlotte Brontë*, and I must also acknowledge the Clarendon edition of *Jane Eyre* which she co-edited with Jane Jack. Their bibliographical research into the text was invaluable, and if I have not always agreed with their emendations the choice not to follow their decisions was never made lightly. The community of scholars on the VICTORIA-List discussion group were unfailingly generous in answering my questions on a wide range of topics, from statistics about governesses to details about nineteenth-century London buildings, and I thank all who responded to my queries. As well, my research assistants Ms. Josée Thibault and Ms. Carmel Purkis were instrumental in comparing the first edition of *Jane Eyre* with its subsequent versions, and in proofreading the entire text.

Finally I would like to thank my partner, Jane Strickler. Her constant support, both personal and intellectual, is, and always has been, more important than can adequately be acknowledged in such a brief note.

Introduction

"The business of a woman's life":
Charlotte Brontë, *alias* Currer Bell

When *Jane Eyre* appeared on the Victorian literary scene in October of 1847 it caused an immediate sensation. Almost as fascinating as its tale of childhood abuse, imprisoned lunacy, and cross-class courtship and marriage was the provocatively androgynous name of the text's supposed editor, "Currer Bell." Few contemporary readers were fooled by the first edition's claim that it was an edited autobiography; that convention of eighteenth-century novels must have seemed curiously quaint to a mid-nineteenth-century audience, and it was dropped for the second edition. The question of Currer Bell's true identity, however, remained, and as one reviewer put it, "various rumours, more or less romantic, have been current in Mayfair, the metropolis of gossip, as to the authorship."[1] None of the novel's detractors, or its equally staunch defenders, suspected that Currer Bell's initials provided the clue that identified this mysterious writer as the thirty-one-year-old daughter of a Yorkshire parson.

Charlotte Brontë would not have been complimented by their surprise. By now the myth that Brontë and her younger siblings were uncultivated "naturals," writing in isolation out of the primitive passion of their genius, has been thoroughly exploded, although the allure of this exotic vision remains. The reality was much more complex. Haworth, the Yorkshire town in which they were born (and in which most of them tragically died), although certainly on the geographical margins of England, was not a rural backwater. Juliet Barker notes that Haworth "was a township, a small, industrial town in the heart of a much larger chapelry, where politics and religion were hotly disputed and culture thrived."[2] Further, their father was not the stereotypical eccentric Irishman, famous mostly for sawing off the backs of chairs and firing his pistols out the back door in fits of Gaelic

---

1   Elizabeth Rigby, "Review of *Vanity Fair, Jane Eyre, Governesses' Benevolent Institution – Report for 1847*," *Quarterly Review* 84 (December 1848), 174. See Appendix C.4.

2   Juliet Barker, *The Brontës* (New York: St. Martin's P, 1994), xix.

temper, which some biographers have represented.[1] The Rev. Patrick Brontë had managed, through self-discipline and harsh economy, to graduate from Cambridge, achieving first-class honours during his career at St. John's College. He followed and had informed opinions on all the significant issues of the day, from Catholic Emancipation to the Reform Bills, and subscribed to such major journals as *Blackwood's Magazine* and *Fraser's Magazine*. Thus Brontë, along with her brother Branwell and sisters Emily and Anne, grew up in a setting and a household which provided them with more than sufficient opportunity for intellectual engagement with their world.

This is not, however, to deny their own unique imaginative gifts. Led originally by Charlotte and Branwell, the four children embarked early on an impressive narrative creation, much of it influenced by their awareness of both historic and current events. The Brontë juvenilia runs to hundreds of thousands of words, and moves from isolated plays about individual characters to the development of the city of Glasstown and eventually the fully realized kingdoms of Angria and Gondal.[2] Although it is not unusual for children to create imaginary worlds, or even for Victorian children to write stories about those imaginary worlds, the sheer detail of, and intense involvement with, their fiction marks this group of youngsters as particularly precocious. It also creates the possibility of writing as a source of potential income for a family of women with very few other reliable resources. Although Patrick Brontë did the best he could for his daughters, by sending them off to be educated at the Clergy's Daughters' School at Cowan Bridge, the opportunities for self-sufficiency available to women of the Brontës' class were painfully limited. As daughters of a clergyman, their status as middle-class ladies prevented them from undertaking any job involving physical labour or trade, no matter how economically desperate their situation might become. Yet the opportunities for any "higher" mode of employment were also few,

---

1   Elizabeth Gaskell, in her *The Life of Charlotte Brontë* (1857), is largely responsible for this caricature.

2   For more information on the Brontë juvenilia see T. J. Wise and J. A. Symington (eds.), *The Miscellaneous and Unpublished Writings of Charlotte and Patrick Branwell Brontë* (Oxford: Shakespeare Head P, 1936) and Christine Alexander, *An Edition of the Early Writings of Charlotte Brontë: 1826–1832* (Oxford: Shakespeare Head P, 1987).

leaving marriage as the most likely "salvation" from their lot. All of these tensions find their expression in *Jane Eyre*, for they were the bitter realities experienced by Brontë herself.

But there was more bitterness than this to endure at Cowan Bridge. Brontë's two older sisters had preceded her there, and she and Emily joined them in 1824. Both Maria and Elizabeth Brontë were in fragile health, and the harsh conditions of the school contributed to their decline. They died in 1825, and Brontë always blamed Cowan Bridge for her loss. In particular the death of Maria angered her, and she later took her revenge in the portrayal of Lowood Institution and its hypocritical administrator, Mr. Brocklehurst. Maria she idealized as the fictional Helen Burns, so although *Jane Eyre* is not an autobiography, there can be no doubt that it contains material from its author's life.

After her sisters' deaths Brontë was withdrawn from Cowan Bridge, and later enrolled at Roe Head School in 1831, where she eventually took a position as teacher in 1835. It was around this time that she also took the audacious step of testing the literary waters. She gathered together some of the poetry she had written for her Glasstown stories, and sent it off to Robert Southey, then Poet Laureate of England, asking for his evaluation. Southey's response has become almost legendary.

It is not my advice that you have asked as to the direction of your talents, but my opinion of them, and yet the opinion may be worth little, and the advice much....[T]here is a danger of which I would, with all kindness and all earnestness, warn you. The day dreams in which you habitually indulge are likely to induce a distempered state of mind; and in proportion as all the ordinary uses of the world seem to you flat and unprofitable, you will be unfitted for them without becoming fitted for anything else. Literature cannot be the business of a woman's life, and it ought not to be. The more she is engaged in her proper duties, the less leisure will she have for it, even as an accomplishment and a recreation.[1]

---

1   Quoted in Elizabeth Gaskell, *The Life of Charlotte Brontë* (Harmondsworth: Penguin, 1975), 172-73.

Such a bald statement about women's "proper place" can hardly be what Brontë hoped for, and it is to her credit that she replied to the Poet Laureate with a decorous but sharp letter intimating that she had no need to be informed of her female duties by *him*. Nonetheless, this lesson about conventional attitudes would shape her future tactics of gender camouflage when it came time to enter the world of literature he so brusquely attempted to deny her.

Eventually growing tired of her work at Roe Head, and having received this admonition from so prominent a source, Brontë decided that her next best option was to "go out" as a governess. The significance of governesses within mid-Victorian society will be returned to later; for now it is only necessary to note that Brontë found the position completely antithetical to her personality.[1] Leaving aside the potential for conflict with her employers, it was the sense of dependency and lack of privacy which most irked her, although in comparison with Anne, who had also become a governess, her situations (short-lived as they were) were relatively comfortable. Brontë was a governess in the household of John Sidgwick for less than three months, and in the household of John White for only ten months, but clearly the time seemed interminable. In reading her letters during this period it becomes clear that she is torn between her duty to accept her position, and the internal revolt which refuses to acknowledge that this is all life has to offer. The parallels with Jane Eyre are obvious. Having reached this impasse, however, Brontë came up with a new plan. Teaching seemed the only possible career available, and if teaching at someone else's school was wearisome, and teaching privately in someone else's home unbearable, then all that remained was to found one's own school. But in order to make such a scheme viable more training was required, and particularly training with a Continental flavour. Thus in 1842 Brontë, accompanied by her father and with Emily in tow, travelled to Belgium and the Pensionnat Heger to develop the familiarity with French culture and language necessary for establishing an attractive girl's school in England.

The directress of this school *"pour les jeunes Demoiselles"* was Madame Claire Zoë Heger, a formidable woman of thirty-eight,

---

1   See Appendix B.

mother of three daughters when she met the Brontës, and an experienced teacher herself. Patrick Brontë would have had no qualms about leaving his daughters with this picture of respectability. The figure who was to have the greatest impact on Brontë, however, was the directress' husband, Constantin Georges Romain Heger, who taught at the Athénée Royale, the adjacent boy's school. A charismatic and volatile man, Heger also gave literature lessons at his wife's institution, and he quickly recognized the intellectual qualities of the two new students from England. The Brontës had paid for six months' attendance at the school, and began with the usual exercises in grammar and syntax, dictation, and translation, but Monsieur Heger soon suggested they move on to a more advanced approach. He proposed that he would read aloud passages from French literature, discuss and analyze them with his pupils, and then have them write essays in the same style. Both sisters were originally reluctant, Emily especially, but eventually they agreed. Heger's dramatic readings were to fire Brontë's imagination, but perhaps even more important were his detailed criticisms of her essays. He imposed on her a discipline and economy of expression which she later transferred to her writings in English, and was thus instrumental in helping her develop the prose style of her novels. Although the two sisters fit in rather uncomfortably at the Pensionnat, Brontë seems to have enjoyed both the opportunity to learn it provided and, increasingly, the opportunity to be around Monsieur Heger.[1] Thus when their six months were over she convinced Madame Heger to keep them on as pupils for an additional half year in return for teaching at the school. They would not be paid a salary, but room and board would be free. Emily was less enthusiastic about this situation than Brontë herself, but the older sister carried the day. Within a few months, though, the arrangement foundered when their Aunt Branwell died late in October of 1842, and both felt dutybound to return to Haworth. Their aunt had been acting as housekeeper in the parsonage for years, and aside from mourning her loss it was necessary that they go back and see to the household situation.

Brontë was reluctant to return, Emily considerably less so, and

---

1 Brontë's increasing passion for Heger is fictionalized in the relationship between Lucy Snowe and Monsieur Paul Emanuel in *Villette* (1853).

when the appropriate time of mourning had passed she was pleased to stay in England as Brontë prepared to go back to Brussels. She again took her position at the Pensionnat as a teacher, but this time for a salary of sixteen pounds a year. Almost from the start, however, things went badly. She had underestimated how much she relied on Emily as company in the, for her, strange Catholic society of Belgium, and the time began to weigh heavily, especially during breaks in the teaching schedule. Perhaps worse, however, was her growing passion for Monsieur Heger. That this found expression in an actual affair is doubtful, but in her loneliness and growing sense of alienation from the world around her it is unsurprising that she developed an increasingly intense attachment to the only man who encouraged and obviously admired her intellectual gifts. This could result in nothing but trouble. Brontë had too strong a moral nature not to see her adulterous obsession with a married man as anything but completely reprehensible, and the sense of guilt this generated coloured her entire experience. She grew increasingly dissatisfied with her students, and more particularly with her employer, Madame Heger. This dissatisfaction with a woman who had treated her with real, if somewhat reserved, kindness, was probably a blend of guilt and jealousy, although it is at least possible Madame perceived her student-teacher was developing a questionable attitude towards her husband. Later Brontë would imply that her growing estrangement from Madame Heger was part of the older woman's attempt to force her to quit her position, and thus to separate her permanently from Monsieur Heger, but it is at least as likely that Brontë's own sense of the falseness of her position created the breach. In any case, by the end of 1843 the situation had become untenable, and she determined to leave, departing Brussels on December 31. Barker sums up the impact of this time on Brontë succinctly when she notes that the "experience of the last two years, both intellectually and emotionally, had marked her for life. She had successfully undergone the rigours of an academic discipline ... emerging as a better and more powerful writer. And she had fallen in love for the first time – with a man who was the antithesis of everything that she had previously valued. Monsieur Heger was ... small, ugly, [and] short-tempered....Her unrequited passion for him was to alter permanently and radically her vision of what the male hero should be. The future creator of Mr Rochester ... was born."[1]

The fulfillment of these experiences was still a few years away, however, and in the meantime Brontë's return to Haworth was rather grim. Her father's health, and particularly his eyesight, had deteriorated noticeably, and she herself felt listless and depressed. It was one thing to leave Brussels; it was quite another to forget the attachment she still felt for the man who remained there. Brontë wrote a number of letters, verging on the indiscreet, to Monsieur Heger, and although he responded it was quite clear that he did not reciprocate her feelings for him. There was little else she could do except pursue her idea of opening a school, although she did change the original plan so that instead of operating a separate establishment she would run the school out of the parsonage itself. This would prevent the need for buying or renting a building, and also allow Brontë and Emily to continue looking after their father. The main disadvantage was the relative remoteness of Haworth, and the consequent lack of potential students in the area. Nonetheless, in the late summer of 1844 an advertisement for "The Misses Brontë's [sic] Establishment for the Board and Education of a Limited Number of Young Ladies," appeared, and they attempted to secure some pupils from among the children of their friends and acquaintances. By the middle of October, however, not a single girl had materialized. It became clear that the idea of a girl's school at Haworth was impracticable, and reluctantly the plan was abandoned. Teaching and governessing had proven dead-ends. The time was now ripe for pursuing a different calling, and so in 1846 appeared the author Currer Bell.

"But women feel just as men": The Improper Feminine in *Jane Eyre*[2]

Brontë's original efforts to enter the world of Victorian literature were clearly failures,[3] but the success of *Jane Eyre* more than compen-

---

1   Barker, 427.
2   I owe my title for this section to Lyn Pykett's *The 'Improper' Feminine: The Women's Sensation Novel and the New Woman Writing* (London: Routledge, 1992).
3   See *A Note on the Text* (p. 50) for a brief discussion of *Poems by Currer, Ellis, and Acton Bell* and *The Professor*.

sated. It also, however, placed her at the centre of a controversy which was becoming increasingly intense. The choice of an ambiguous pen name, meant to defuse the question of her sex, instead became central to the book's reception, as numerous contemporary reviews demonstrated. The question of women's proper sphere and the characteristics of proper femininity were increasingly contested throughout the middle and later parts of the nineteenth century, and the novel was read as taking a decided stance on these issues. Thus Currer Bell found "himself" embroiled in what a contemporary writer, with obvious distaste, described as "that sickening clamour about the 'rights of women.'"[1]

Interestingly, the earliest reviews of the novel, most of which assumed that Currer Bell was a man, largely avoided this issue. For example the anonymous reviewer for *The Critic*, writing in the same month the novel was published, asserted "Our readers will probably remember a volume of poems, the joint production of three brothers, Bell, which ... took our fancy so much as seeming to be freighted with promise, that we dedicated several columns to a review....The performance before us, by one of the brothers, proves the justice of those anticipations. Currer Bell can write prose as well as poetry. He has fertile invention, great power of description, and a happy faculty for conceiving and sketching character."[2] Similarly, the reviewer for *Era*, after boldly stating "Although ladies have written histories, and travels, and warlike novels, to say nothing of books upon the different arts and sciences, no woman *could have* penned the 'Autobiography of Jane Eyre,'" provided the following glowing assessment:

> The apt, eloquent, elegant, and yet easy mode by which the writer engages you, is something altogether out of the common way. He fixes you at the commencement, and there is no flagging on his part – no getting away on yours – till the end....Such a work has no ordinary attractions, and it will be found that we have not overdrawn them. There is much to

---

1   "Hints on the Modern Governess Question," *Fraser's Magazine* 30 (November 1844), 573. See Appendix C.1.
2   Anonymous review, *The Critic*, October 30, 1847. Quoted in Miriam Allott (ed.), *The Brontës: The Critical Heritage* (London: Routledge & Kegan Paul, 1974), 73.

ponder over, rejoice over, and weep over, in its ably-written pages.[1]

Although not always quite as laudatory as this, early reviewers tended to focus on the text's powerful language and ability to enthrall the reader; in other words, they concentrated on the text's aesthetic success. As the rumour began to spread that Currer Bell was in fact female, however, this emphasis began to change, and what might be called the novel's "politics" came increasingly under attack.

Although not the first negative review, *The Christian Remembrancer*'s attitude towards *Jane Eyre* was fairly representative of those who found the novel objectionable. Stating unequivocally that "we, for our part, cannot doubt that the book is written by a female," its reviewer goes on to say that she/he "cannot wonder that the hypothesis of a male author should have been started....[f]or a book more unfeminine ... it would be hard to find in the annals of female authorship. Throughout there is a masculine power, breadth, and shrewdness, combined with masculine hardness, coarseness, and freedom of expression."[2] This is important because it demonstrates the way in which Brontë's femaleness could be acknowledged, while at the same time her femininity could be denied, so that the alleged impropriety of the author could be transferred to the novel. This review's literal "anxiety" about the text's potential influence is summed up in its conclusion: "To say that *Jane Eyre* is positively immoral or antichristian, would be to do its writer an injustice. Still, it wears a questionable aspect....We shall look with some anxiety for that second effort which is proverbially decisive of a writer's talent, and which, in this case, will probably be decisive of the moral question also."[3]

By far the most violent attack on the book, however, occurred a year after it first appeared. In *The Quarterly Review* of December 1848, Elizabeth Rigby clearly attempts to nullify what she sees as the serious threat posed by the novel's popularity. She takes *The Christian*

1 Anonymous review, *Era*, November 14, 1847. Quoted in Allott, 79.
2 Anonymous review, *The Christian Remembrancer* XV, April 1848. Quoted in Allot, 89.
3 Quoted in Allot, 91-92.

Remembrancer's concerns about morality and makes them much more specific.

> We have said that this was the picture of a natural heart. This, to our view, is the great and crying mischief of the book. Jane Eyre is throughout the personification of an unregenerate and undisciplined spirit, the more dangerous to exhibit from that prestige of principle and self-control which is liable to dazzle the eye too much for it to observe the inefficient and unsound foundation on which it rests. It is true Jane does right, and exerts great moral strength, but it is the strength of a mere heathen mind which is a law unto itself. No Christian grace is perceptible upon her. She has inherited in fullest measure the worst sin of our fallen nature – the sin of pride. Jane Eyre is proud, and therefore she is ungrateful too. It pleased God to make her an orphan, friendless, and penniless – yet she thanks nobody, and least of all Him, for the food and raiment, the friends, companions, and instructors of her helpless youth…. Altogether the autobiography of Jane Eyre is pre-eminently an anti-Christian composition. There is throughout it a murmuring against the comforts of the rich and against the privations of the poor, which, as far as each individual is concerned, is a murmuring against God's appointment – there is a proud and perpetual assertion of the rights of man, for which we find no authority either in God's word or in God's providence – there is that pervading tone of ungodly discontent which is at once the most prominent and the most subtle evil which the law and the pulpit, which all civilized society in fact has at the present day to contend with. We do not hesitate to say that the tone of mind and thought which has overthrown authority and violated every code human and divine abroad, and fostered Chartism and rebellion at home, is the same which has also written Jane Eyre.[1]

Obviously what Rigby finds most dangerous is Jane's refusal to

---

1   Rigby, 173-74.

accept, and keep, her "place." This is expressed on a number of levels, despite the apparent emphasis on morality and God's providence.

The mid-1840s was a time of radical political and labour unrest throughout England and Europe, so that for Rigby the novel's endorsement of individual assertion and self-worth takes on material as well as spiritual concerns. And this cannot be separated from questions of gender. Rigby's pejorative use of the term "rights of man" would immediately evoke in her readers' minds the "rights of woman" issue which was also shaking her society. The fundamental necessity for women to keep their place as subordinate inhabitants of the private sphere, in order to ensure social stability, was a standard Victorian idea, and to have a novel which manifestly supported a female character who refused to do so sent all the wrong messages. Even worse was to have such a novel written *by* a woman, for this indicated a personal investment which escaped the bounds of fiction, and thus presented an actual rejection of female constraint rather than a purely theoretical exploration of the topic.

Rigby's way of dealing with this is to return to the question of Currer Bell's sexual identity, but with a particular twist. She claims that she sees "no great interest in the question at all,"[1] because finally the book is simply reprehensible no matter whether written by a man or a woman. In this, however, she is being more than a little disingenuous, because by the time she wrote the piece Currer Bell's true sex was fairly well known. The following comments are therefore more than a little pointed.

> Without entering into the question whether the power of the writing be above her, or the vulgarity below her, there are, we believe, minutiæ of circumstantial evidence which at once acquit the feminine hand. No woman – a lady friend, whom we are always happy to consult, assures us – makes mistakes in her own *métier* – no woman *trusses game* and garnishes dessert-dishes with the same hands, or talks of so doing in the same breath. Above all, no woman attires another in such fancy dresses as Jane's ladies assume.... No lady, we understand, when suddenly roused in the night, would think of hurrying on '*a frock.*'

1   Rigby, 175.

They have garments more convenient for such occasions, and more becoming too. This evidence seems incontrovertible. Even granting that these incongruities were purposely assumed, for the sake of disguising the female pen, there is nothing gained; for if we ascribe the book to a woman at all, we have no alternative but to ascribe it to one who has, for some sufficient reason, long forfeited the society of her own sex.[1]

Such observations are obviously insulting. Rigby starts by suggesting that women authors in general need to be "acquitted" of writing such a vulgar book, implying that if this particular novelist does happen to be female she is guilty of a literary/gender crime. She then states that the text contains errors recognizable to a *lady*, thus suggesting that any woman who created such a text does not deserve that designation. Finally, this blow to Brontë's status is reinforced by the idea that only a woman who has been excluded from proper feminine circles ("for some sufficient reason") would be capable of such mistakes, or indeed of producing such a novel at all. This section of the review is a not very subtle effort at character assassination, and John G. Peters sums up Rigby's strategy well when he notes that "negative reviewers ... not only marginalize Jane but also Brontë herself and ... try to portray Jane, Brontë, and the novel as unnatural and something to be shunned."[2] It is fair to wonder what in the novel could provoke such a vehement reaction, and what in it seemed so dangerous to those who attacked it in this way.

Jane Eyre is a *Bildungsroman*, but the development of its female protagonist often seems less about a successful integration into society than about her resistance to society's coercive power. When the book opens we are introduced to a heroine who is without parents, without looks, without money, and most certainly without a docile temperament. To lack these things is, for a girl at least, to be worthless. As Jane's cousin, John Reed, puts it early in the text: "'You have no business to take our books: you are a dependant, mama says; you have no money; your father left you none; you ought to beg, and not to live

---

1   Rigby, 175–76.
2   John G. Peters, "Inside and Outside: *Jane Eyre* and Marginalization Through Labeling," *Studies in the Novel* 23:1 (Spring 1996): 68.

here with gentlemen's children like us, and eat the same meals we do, and wear clothes at our mamma's expense. Now, I'll teach you to rummage my book-shelves: for they *are* mine; all the house belongs to me, or will do in a few years'" (67). This brutal evaluation of Jane's position demonstrates her vulnerability in a world which values only what she does not possess. As important, however, is her cousin's claim to his masculine prerogative of ownership, and therefore to power. John Reed is the first in a long line of male figures who will attempt to impose their vision of her upon Jane, and it is her refusal to accept this patriarchal right which most marks Jane as improperly feminine. John Reed, Mr. Brocklehurst, Edward Fairfax Rochester, St. John Rivers, each in his own way tries to use his authority to make Jane conform to his idea of what she should be, and each of them is ultimately defeated by her. Further, it is Jane's "unwomanly" sense of self-worth which creates the ability to ward off masculine egotism.

In her influential conduct book *The Daughters of England: Their Position in Society, Character and Responsibilities*, published in 1842, Sarah Stickney Ellis declares "[a]s women, then, the first thing of importance is to be content to be inferior to men – inferior in mental power, in the same proportion that you are inferior in bodily strength."[1] This is utterly repudiated, both by Brontë and her character, in what is arguably the most famous and, for its Victorian audience, most controversial passage in *Jane Eyre*. Describing her restlessness Jane asserts,

> It is vain to say human beings ought to be satisfied with tranquility: they must have action; and they will make it if they cannot find it. Millions are condemned to a stiller doom than mine, and millions are in silent revolt against their lot. Nobody knows how many rebellions besides political rebellions ferment in the masses of life which people earth. Women are supposed to be very calm generally: but women feel just as men feel; they need exercise for their faculties, and a field for their efforts as much as their brothers do; they suffer from too rigid a restraint, too absolute a stagnation, precisely as men would suffer; and it

---

1 Sarah Stickney Ellis, *The Daughters of England: Their Position in Society, Character and Responsibilities* (New York: D. Appleton and Co., 1842), 8. See Appendix D.

is narrow-minded in their more privileged fellow-creatures to say they ought to confine themselves to making puddings and knitting stockings, to playing on the piano and embroidering bags. It is thoughtless to condemn them, or laugh at them, if they seek to do more or learn more than custom has pronounced necessary for their sex. (178)

These are manifestly not the words of a woman who accepts her inferiority to men, and what Elaine Showalter calls Jane's "drive to self-fulfillment"[1] worried many of the novel's readers. This was supposed to be a masculine characteristic, and directly contravened the self-sacrificing feminine ideal of the period. Thus for reviewers like Rigby, "the self-conscious heroine is an un-Christian and vulgar woman, a threat not only to the womanly ideal but to the values of Victorian society.... [and to] the mission laid out for women ... to exemplify Christian selflessness and resignation in a selfish male world."[2] That the text not only calls for the reader to sympathize with Jane, but in the end provides her with a husband, a successful marriage, and a home, clearly subverts the idea that only "proper" female characters deserve or can achieve these traditional novelistic rewards.

Unsurprisingly, what many nineteenth-century reviewers perceived as problematic in the book came to be esteemed by twentieth-century readers. In particular a number of feminist critics situated *Jane Eyre* at the centre of Victorian debates about gender, and analyzed the ways in which it embodied the conflicts of the time. For them Jane's status as "improper" is something to be admired, not condemned. Sandra M. Gilbert and Susan Gubar's important study *The Madwoman in the Attic: The Woman Writer and the Nineteenth-Century Literary Imagination* (1979) specifically invokes the novel's Bertha Mason in its title, and uses Brontë as a central illustration of its thesis. For Gilbert and Gubar Jane's "passionate drive toward freedom"[3] is representative of a growing recognition of gender oppression, and although they are not

---

1   Elaine Showalter, *A Literature of Their Own: British Women Novelists from Brontë to Lessing* (Princeton: Princeton UP, 1977), 123.
2   Elizabeth K. Helsinger, Robin Lauterbach Sheets, William Veeder, *The Woman Question: Literary Issues, 1837-1883* (New York: Garland, 1983), 101.
3   Sandra M. Gilbert and Susan Gubar, *The Madwoman in the Attic: The Woman Writer and the Nineteenth-Century Literary Imagination* (New Haven: Yale UP, 1979), 369.

sure that Brontë, or the text, is finally able "to envision viable solutions"[1] to the situation explored, they nonetheless celebrate what they see as its "rebellious feminism."[2] Similarly, Adrienne Rich in her 1979 essay "Jane Eyre: The Temptations of a Motherless Woman," sees Jane's movement towards maturity as the avoidance of a series of societal temptations which would lead her to betray her "Jane Eyre-ity."[3] Her successful navigation of these potential traps provides the opportunity for the character's final "creation of herself"[4] in such a way that she remains uncompromised by masculine values and assumptions. Such readings of the novel provide important and useful ways of understanding why the book created such a furor when it first appeared, and they continue to inform much of the writing on *Jane Eyre*.[5] It is possible, however, to suggest that the exclusive focus on gender, and the resultant emphasis on the text's subversive aspects, ignores some of its potentially more "conservative" tendencies. This is not to suggest that such approaches are invalid, only that in order to understand the full complexity of Brontë's representation of her heroine other elements need to be explored, most notably issues of class and imperialism. And one way to approach the first of these is to explore another controversial debate of the 1840s: the governess question.

"Half of them detestable and the rest ridiculous": The Governess and Class Hierarchy in *Jane Eyre*

Brontë's time as a governess has already been mentioned, but by placing Jane Eyre in that same position she was doing more than utilizing her own experience for fictional purposes. She was joining in a literary movement which reflected a growing social anxiety. As Kathryn Hughes notes, "[f]rom 1830 to 1865 there appeared in fiction every type of governess imaginable. From the panoramic sweep of Thacker-

---

1 Gilbert and Gubar, 369.

2 Gilbert and Gubar, 369.

3 Adrienne Rich, "Jane Eyre: The Temptations of a Motherless Woman," *On Lies, Secrets, and Silence: Selected Prose 1966-1978* (New York: W. W. Norton, 1979), 105.

4 Rich, 106.

5 Other examples of this approach include Showalter's *A Literature of Their Own*, already cited, and Ellen Moers, *Literary Women* (London: Women's Press, 1980).

ay to the domestic confines of Elizabeth Sewell, it sometimes seemed as if no novel of the period was complete without its governess."[1] It is no coincidence that "the governess question" became prominent at around the same time as "the woman question," for both are concerned with female status and female duties. For the Victorians the governess was a profoundly ambivalent figure, and Brontë's text cannot help but produce and re-produce those ambivalences.

On one level governesses were indicators of England's growing prosperity, and in particular its middle-class prosperity. M. Jeanne Peterson observes that

> The governess was a testimony to the economic power of the Victorian middle-class father, as were servants, carriages, and other "paraphernalia of gentility"....The governess was also an indicator of the extent to which a man's wife was truly a lady of leisure. The function of the mother had traditionally been, in addition to housewifely duties, that of educator of the children. Both boys and girls in the middle-class family began their education with their mother. Boys were later sent to school or a tutor was hired for them, but girls continued to learn their roles as women from their mothers. Unlike cooking, cleaning, and scrubbing, the education of children was hardly classifiable as manual labor. For this reason the employment of a governess was even more a symbol of the movement of wives and mothers from domestic to ornamental functions.[2]

The British aristocracy had a long tradition of hiring someone to educate its young, but the dynamics of such a relationship became very different when the social status of employer and employee was less clearly demarcated. Thus although the ability to employ a governess symbolized a middle-class family's economic success, and its aspirations to gentility, it also generated a number of tensions in the Victorian home. Most explicitly, the governess introduced into the

---

1 Kathryn Hughes, *The Victorian Governess* (London: Hambledon Press, 1993), xiii.
2 M. Jeanne Peterson, "The Victorian Governess: Status Incongruence in Family and Society," *Suffer and Be Still: Women in the Victorian Age*, ed. Martha Vicinus (Bloomington: Indiana UP, 1972), 5.

household what sociologists call "status incongruence."

Governesses were often drawn from the ranks of middle-class women in dire economic need; the highest qualification a governess could bring to the job was the fact that she was a "lady" (as defined by a bourgeois ethic). This clearly gave her a claim to be treated as the equal of the family for which she worked. But as a paid employee, such a claim could not be fully recognized, because that would reduce the family's prestige. Further, the very fact that she had entered the labour market seriously qualified the governess' position as a lady, since no "real" lady was forced to work for her living. She thus often found herself in a sort of class limbo. She might best be characterized as not quite a lady, but a lady nonetheless, and this ambiguous status has important gender implications. The ideology of "separate spheres" which came to dominate the period assigned the public, social sphere to men and the private, household sphere to women. But governesses were a symbol of this system's failure, for they "gave the lie to the construction of the home as a place beyond and above the market place and suggested that it too might be touched, if not over-whelmed, by ... social and material hungers.... In this context, the sight of middle-class women going out to work as governesses could not fail to mobilise a set of fears about the collapse of boundaries ... between men and women and the separate spheres that they were supposed to occupy."[1] The very woman hired to inculcate proper social/gender attributes into her charges, and especially into young girls, embodied the precarious foundations upon which those attributes rested, and demonstrated just how unstable a woman's status could be. It is no wonder that she felt uncomfortable in her position, and generated discomfort in those around her.

Almost as unsettling was the growing fear that women were becoming governesses in order to *advance* their class status. There is little evidence that this was actually happening, but the worry that it was is perhaps more important than the reality. In "Hints on the Modern Governess System" the anonymous writer for *Fraser's Maga-zine* notes that if "mothers would obey their highest calling, many who now fill their places would be safer and happier in their lower

---

1   Hughes, 143, 149.

vocation. Those tradespeople and yeomen who now send their daughters to bad schools, in order to fit them to be ill-paid governesses, would bring them up for housekeepers, were this office restored to respectability."[1] The implication of a statement like this is that lower class young women (for their own good) should aspire only to the position of an upper servant, and the reason for this is clear. If the attributes of a lady can be *learned* or, even worse, successfully *mimicked*, then the entire cultural capital of "ladyness" is demeaned. The scene in *Jane Eyre* which enacts this concern occurs just as Jane is preparing to leave Lowood to take up her position as governess at Thornfield Hall. Bessie, the servant from Gateshead who was closest to Jane as a child, comes to visit, and asks Jane to demonstrate her various accomplishments. This Jane does by playing the piano, showing Bessie one of her paintings, and asserting that she reads and speaks French as well as knows how to "work" both muslin and canvas. Indeed, Bessie observes, Jane does these things *better* than either Eliza or Georgiana Reed, her affluent cousins, and she concludes by stating "'Oh you are quite a lady, Miss Jane! I knew you would be'" (158). Of course it is possible to suggest that Bessie's status as a servant seriously undercuts her evaluation, for after all how can she be expected to recognize true gentility? But the point is that Brontë, and the text as a whole, endorse her assessment, so that by becoming a governess Jane has in effect escaped her "assigned" place as worthless orphan which the Reeds imposed on her at the start of the novel, and achieved an equal status with them. For a society as concerned about class hierarchy as the Victorians, such movement had seriously destabilizing possibilities, and this helps to explain one of the most humiliating scenes for Jane in the book.

Blanche Ingram, having been brought to Thornfield by Rochester to make Jane jealous, provides a short discourse on the topic of governesses. She is meant to be a completely unlikable character, and this commentary cements the reader's bad opinion of her, but there is more going on in what follows.

'You should hear mama on the chapter of governesses: Mary and I have had, I should think, a dozen at least in our day; half

---

1   "Hints on the Modern Governess Situation," 581.

of them detestable and the rest ridiculous.... I have just one word to say of the whole tribe: they are a nuisance. Not that I ever suffered much from them: I took care to turn the tables. What tricks Theodore and I used to play on our Miss Wilsons, and Mrs. Greys, and Madame Jouberts! Mary was always too sleepy to join in a plot with spirit. The best fun was with Madame Joubert: Miss Wilson was a poor sickly thing, lachrymose and low-spirited: not worth the trouble of vanquishing, in short; and Mrs. Grey was coarse and insensible: no blow took effect on her. But poor Madame Joubert! I see her yet in her raging passions, when we had driven her to extremities – spilt our tea, crumbled our bread and butter, tossed our books up to the ceiling, and played a charivari with the ruler and desk, the fender and fire-irons. Theodore, do you remember those merry days?' (255)

On one level this is purely a rude attempt to put Jane in her place, but it is also an attempt by Blanche to establish *her* own place. She explicitly describes her efforts to "vanquish" her governesses as a kind of battle, and it is not an overstatement to say that she is "battling" to confirm her class status and superiority. Jane's presence is a galling reminder not only of a childhood time when Blanche was nominally under the control of lower-status women, but also that, although lacking her wealth and birth, those women, and Jane herself, have "accomplishments" equal to hers. It is absolutely essential for Blanche to despise all governesses, because only in this way can she ensure (in her own mind and others') that there is no connection or potential relationship between them. Of course her boorish comments merely demonstrate what she is attempting to deny; in the value-system of the novel it is plain Jane Eyre who is the true lady, not the beautiful but vulgar Blanche Ingram. Characteristically, Jane does not mince words in evaluating Blanche and Rochester's "courtship": "There was nothing to cool or banish love in these circumstances; though much to create despair. Much too, you will think, reader, to engender jealousy.... But I was not jealous ... the nature of the pain I suffered could not be explained by that word. Miss Ingram was a mark beneath jealousy: she was too inferior to excite the feeling. Pardon the seeming paradox: I mean what I say" (264). The basis for this assertion of superiority is Jane's own sense of self-worth, and this shows the way in which her training problematizes female status. Hughes sums it up nicely when she observes that "the governess' presence ... unsettled the assumed relationship between genteel femininity and a life of leisure. For if, as her entry on the family's pay roll suggested, not all ladies were leisured, then might it not also follow that not all leisured women were necessarily ladies?"[1]

To this extent, then, Brontë's use of a governess as a central character reinforces the novel's gender subversion. She uses Jane to call into question Victorian ideologies about separate spheres, and to undercut assumptions about who is and who is not a "lady." But there is also in *Jane Eyre* a very real sense of privilege which defends middle-class interests, and the governess can be used to achieve this as well. As a child a good part of Jane's rage at the Reeds is based on their refusal to grant her the middle-class status which, as a cousin, she feels she deserves. Thus after her moment of explosive rebellion against John Reed, and after being told she should be ashamed of striking her "young master," Jane responds with "'Master! How is he my master? Am I a servant?'" (69). Even at the age of ten Jane is well aware of the stigma attached to servitude, and Terry Eagleton is right to observe that Jane's "smouldering hatred of [the Reeds'] snobbery is ... shot through with shared class-assumptions about the poor,"[2] something which is confirmed by her exchange with the apothecary Mr. Lloyd. Upon the young Jane being asked if she would be willing to go live with poor relations, we get the following:

> I reflected. Poverty looks grim to grown people; still more so to children: they have not much idea of industrious, working, respectable poverty; they think of the word only as connected with ragged clothes, scanty food, fireless grates, rude manners and debasing vices: poverty for me was synonymous with degradation.
>
> 'No; I should not like to belong to poor people,' was my reply. (82)

---

1 Hughes, 25.

2 Terry Eagleton, *Myths of Power: A Marxist Study of the Brontës*, 2nd ed., (London: Macmillan, 1988), 28.

The narrative structure is important here. The older Jane, looking back on herself as a child, seems to qualify and "correct" her younger self's unawareness of "respectable poverty." The implication is that the mature Jane Eyre narrating the story would have responded differently. But here is a much more experienced Jane Eyre, commenting on her situation at the village school at Morton, after her flight from Thornfield.

> Was I very gleeful, settled, content, during the hours I passed in yonder bare, humble school-room this morning and afternoon? Not to deceive myself, I must reply – No: I felt desolate to a degree. I felt – yes, idiot that I am – I felt degraded. I doubted I had taken a step which sank instead of raising me in the scale of social existence. I was weakly dismayed at the ignorance, the poverty, the coarseness of all I heard and saw round me. But let me not hate and despise myself too much for these feelings: I know them to be wrong – that is a great step gained; I shall strive to overcome them. To-morrow, I trust, I shall get the better of them partially, and in a few weeks, perhaps, they will be quite subdued. In a few months, it is possible, the happiness of seeing progress, and a change for the better in my scholars, may substitute gratification for disgust. (454–5)

This is a carefully qualified statement. Jane's very strong feelings of debasement and social regression are recognized as "wrong," but the best to be hoped for is that they can be overcome "partially," that they can be "subdued" (not eradicated), and that gratification "may" be substituted for disgust. Passages like this demonstrate how both Jane, and the text, accept her middle-class superiority even as they attempt to escape class-based evaluations of worth, and this tension "deftly defines petty-bourgeois consciousness which clings to real class-distinctions while spiritually rejecting them."[1]

Jane's training at Lowood, which prepares her to be a governess, is therefore important because it allows her to cultivate the accomplishments which will identify her "real" class status, even as her residence there supposedly confirms her lack of social worth. The example of

---

1   Eagleton, 28.

Miss Temple, as well as Helen Burns, teaches her how to behave so as to gain the acceptance, and even admiration, of those around her. In a kind of paradoxical reversal of what a governess represents for Blanche Ingram, Jane's attainment of "ladylike" characteristics as a governess *confirms* for her her own sense of merit, even though it may lead to her employment in a relatively lowly occupation. In a later passage of the novel, when Jane is wondering whether Rochester could have had an affair with Grace Poole, as a way of explaining the apparent liberties taken by this servant, her response to such an idea is once again disgust: "I hastened to drive from my mind the hateful notion I had been conceiving respecting Grace Poole: it disgusted me. I compared myself with her, and found we were different. Bessie Leaven had said I was quite a lady; and she spoke truth: I was a lady" (233). Jane, as a governess, is of a different kind than a servant such as Grace, and any comparison is odious.

Jane's Lowood education effectively neutralizes any serious questioning of class constructions within the novel. Despite the apparent opposition of Miss Temple's feminine, ladylike kindness to Mr. Brocklehurst's patriarchal, ungentlemanly hypocrisy, as the superintendent of Lowood she acts as his surrogate. By "[p]utting a kinder face on institutions such as Lowood, the proper lady allays suffering without seriously rebuffing it. She may even, by keeping discontent at a governable level, make it easier for the Brocklehursts to operate.... In short, [Miss Temple] softens the cruelty of ... class relations without fundamentally dissenting from them. By relating herself to Miss Temple, Jane does gain some personal power, but.... [a]spiring to middle-class womanhood, she is still governed by the ruling-class male, and now she concurs in the maintenance of class hierarchies."[1] This helps explain the relative lack of Victorian reaction to Jane and Rochester's courtship, and their eventual marriage. What at first might seem a serious transgression of class barriers, with the plain, poverty stricken governess loving and being loved by her aristocratic and wealthy master, received next to no attention in contemporary reviews. *Jane Eyre* effectively manages to present Jane and Rochester's union as a meeting of equals, while at the same time reassuring its predominantly

---

1   Susan Fraiman, "Jane Eyre's Fall from Grace," *Jane Eyre*, ed. Beth Newman (Boston: Bedford Books, 1996), 622.

middle-class audience that the merit of achieving such class mobility is safely contained within its own social ranks.

This is not to suggest that Rochester actually *treats* Jane as an equal for much of their relationship at Thornfield, an issue which will be returned to later. But because the text has successfully naturalized Jane's status as a lady by demonstrating that the qualities which make her a good governess are in fact an expression of her (middle-class) worthiness, the climactic moment of her declaration of love for Rochester seems completely appropriate. Having been pushed to the breaking point by his continued false assertions that he will marry Blanche, Jane finally cannot contain herself.

> 'Do you think I can stay to become nothing to you? Do you think I am an automaton? – a machine without feelings? And can bear to have my morsel of bread snatched from my lips, and my drop of living water dashed from my cup? Do you think, because I am poor, obscure, plain, and little, I am soulless and heartless? – You think wrong! – I have as much soul as you,– and full as much heart! And if God had gifted me with some beauty, and much wealth, I should have made it as hard for you to leave me, as it is now for me to leave you. I am not talking to you now through the medium of custom, conventionalities, nor even of mortal flesh: – it is my spirit that addresses your spirit; just as if both had passed through the grave, and we stood at God's feet, equal, – as we are!' (338)

On the face of it this ringing declaration of equality should be as potentially dangerous as Jane's earlier comments that men and women have the same feelings and desires. It rejects "customs" and "conventionalities" in the same way, but the significant difference is that this statement is thoroughly depoliticized. It takes place in the realm of the personal, as a direct challenge from Jane to Rochester, and in the realm of the metaphysical, as her spirit addresses his, but neatly escapes the realm of the social. By this point in the story any potential challenge the figure of the governess may have posed to the *status quo* is largely gone, because Brontë has subsumed "the economic necessity that drove Jane to work into the narrative of an elaborate courtship,"[1] and a courtship which has the potential to lift her once and for all out of any economic necessity whatsoever. It is telling, therefore, that in the face of Rochester's attempt to "possess" Jane after their engagement, she insists on maintaining her role as governess to Adèle, demonstrating that it has become a mark of self-reliance rather than of subordination. In this way the text demonstrates that Jane's position as a lady is fully secure, regardless of the tasks she performs, because her status has become essentially innate. But of course the text does not end here, and Jane's final trials confirm that she has earned the reward of her station.

There can be no doubt that Jane's lowest moments occur after her flight from Thornfield and Rochester. Ironically, her ladylike appearance and manner, bereft of any money to support them, or a position to explain them, provoke suspicion in the people she encounters. She is thus reduced to the ultimate degradation: begging. But this descent is only a prelude to her ultimate ascent. Although others may be unable to perceive her "true" social character, to the refined perceptions of Mary, Diana, and St. John Rivers it is obvious. Providence leads her to their door, and although she is almost turned away by the unperceptive servant Hannah, once inside everything becomes clear. The sisters immediately recognize "'she is not an uneducated person ... by her manner of speaking: her accent was quite pure; and the clothes she took off, though splashed and wet, were little worn, and fine'" (432). Similarly, St. John asserts that Jane has "'rather an unusual physiognomy: certainly, not indicative of vulgarity or degradation,'" and ventures the opinion that they "'will find she is some young lady who has had a misunderstanding with her friends, and has probably injudiciously left them'" (433). This is manifestly a matter of like calling to like, and the discovery that the Rivers are her cousins on her father's side simply confirms that Jane belongs in this class. Indeed, we are told that the Rivers have been members of the "gentry" for many years, so once again Jane's status is brought closely in line with an aristocracy of both birth and merit. When she actually inherits her uncle's fortune, therefore, the book presents this as an earned reward and a proper fulfillment. Nina Schwartz, playing on its main charac-

---

1   Mary Poovey, *Uneven Developments: The Ideological Work of Gender in Mid-Victorian England* (Chicago: U of Chicago P, 1988), 137.

ter's name, describes the movement of *Jane Eyre* as follows:"As a story about Jane's triumphing over adversity to arrive, finally, at her proper (that is, both *naturally* deserved and *familially* determined) social and domestic positions ... the novel could be read as working to bring together the apparently contradictory connotations of Jane's family name. She starts out a wanderer, cut off by bad luck from her proper origin, but through hard work and her natural superiority to the lowly contexts into which she is inappropriately displaced, Jane manages to find her way.... Ending up where she should have started off, Jane is thus, as her name implies, an *errant heiress*."[1] But the text brings this middle-class "heir" safely home.

Just as the governess was an ambivalent figure in Victorian society, so she is in *Jane Eyre*. On one hand the main character's employment at Thornfield emphasizes the potentially disruptive forces she embodies, but by the end of this part of the novel those forces have been largely absorbed into a plot which reinforces accepted constructions of class. And the fact that the fortune which secures Jane's social position comes from Madeira raises another fraught issue which appears within the text: colonialism.

"The very model of an eastern emir": Colonialism and Imperialism in *Jane Eyre*

Recent studies of *Jane Eyre* have emphasized the colonial and imperialist themes which run throughout Jane's narrative. In particular these are centred around the characters of Rochester, Bertha Mason, and St. John Rivers, so that a closer examination of their presentation helps understand Brontë's heroine. Each of the three is directly connected to colonialism and Britain's imperial holdings, as beneficiary, victim, or a strange mixture of the two, and the novel's fluctuating attitude towards them demonstrates its uncertainty about the Victorian imperialist project. Brontë's efforts to resolve that uncertainty achieve, at best, mixed results, and perhaps the most appropriate place to begin examining the text's ambiguities is with its putative hero, Edward Fairfax Rochester.

---

1   Nina Schwartz, "No Place Like Home: The Logic of the Supplement in *Jane Eyre*," *Jane Eyre*, ed. Beth Newman (Boston: Bedford Books, 1996), 552.

At his most basic Rochester is the kind of Byronic character which fascinated Brontë from her earliest juvenilia. The dark protagonist, a law unto himself, who wanders the world with an awful secret, had an enduring attraction for her. But what sets Rochester apart from his Romantic predecessors is the way in which his "darkness" takes on an overtly racial significance. Jane's portrayal of Rochester when she first sees him is clearly significant.

> I knew my traveller with his broad and jetty eyebrows; his square forehead, made squarer by the horizontal sweep of his black hair. I recognized his decisive nose, more remarkable for character than beauty; his full nostrils, denoting, I thought choler; his grim mouth, chin, and jaw – yes, all three were very grim, and no mistake. His shape, now divested of cloak, I perceived harmonized in squareness with his physiognomy: I suppose it was a good figure in the athletic sense of the term – broad chested and thin flanked; though neither tall nor graceful. (190)

Elsie Michie notes of this kind of description that "Rochester is represented, figuratively, as if he ... occupies an unsettling intermediate position between black and white.... from his first appearance onward, he is recurrently, almost obsessively, characterized in terms that suggest darkness, otherness, and simianization."[1] Constructing him in this way allows Brontë to provide her hero with the allure of the foreign and forbidden, while at the same time giving an indication of what within his personality needs to be reformed. More specifically, Rochester is presented as being "tainted" by his encounter with colonialism in such a way that he has adopted its excesses: excesses which in turn are reflected by his physical appearance. It is only after he has been "purified" that he can become an appropriate husband for Jane, and that purification takes the form of removing any vestiges of his colonial experience.

As the second son of an aristocratic family whose father is unwill-

---

[1] Elsie Michie, "White Chimpanzees and Oriental Despots: Racial Stereotyping and Edward Rochester," *Jane Eyre*, ed. Beth Newman (Boston: Bedford Books, 1996), 587.

ing to divide the estate, Rochester is encouraged to do what many a young man was in the same situation; go out and marry a rich colonial wife. The purpose of his voyage to Jamaica, therefore, is to complete an arrangement which has already been negotiated by his family. This might be called his first degradation, because he is clearly being bartered for economic advantage. And what he brings to the exchange is made clear when he notes that his prospective wife's "'family wished to secure me, because I was of good race'" (395). But it is just this "goodness of race" that is compromised by his union with Bertha Mason. In recalling his courtship of Bertha to Jane, Rochester describes his reaction to her in terms which suggest a failure of English (white) prudence and self-control. He thus manages to avoid acknowledging the benefits of sex, wealth, and social prestige she originally brings him by their union, and which are available to him for the asking because of his status in the colonial hierarchy.

> I found her a fine woman ... tall, dark, and majestic.... I seldom saw her alone, and had very little private conversation with her. She flattered me, and lavishly displayed for my pleasure her charms and accomplishments. All the men in her circle seemed to admire her and envy me. I was dazzled, stimulated: my senses were excited; and being ignorant, raw, and inexperienced, I thought I loved her.... Her relatives encouraged me; competitors piqued me; she allured me: a marriage was achieved almost before I knew where I was. Oh – I have no respect for myself when I think of that act! – an agony of inward contempt masters me. I never loved, I never esteemed, I did not even know her. I was not sure of the existence of one virtue in her nature: I had marked neither modesty, nor benevolence, nor candour, nor refinement in her mind or manners – and, I married her: – gross, grovelling, mole-eyed blockhead that I was! With less sin I might have – but let me remember to whom I am speaking. (395-6)

Bertha clearly appeals to the "dark" elements in Rochester, and by doing so draws him into the colonial darkness of the West Indies she represents. It seems appropriate, then, that after he discovers her hereditary madness, along with what he suggests are infidelities brought on by uncontrolled sexual appetite, it is a "sweet wind from Europe"(399) which whispers to Rochester what he should do to solve his dilemma with Bertha. He will "take the maniac with [him] to England; confine her with due attendance and precautions at Thornfield: then travel ... to what clime [he] will, and form what new tie [he] like[s]" (399). By locking Bertha up he attempts to "contain" not only her, but that part of him which she represents, and to reassert his European identity. In doing so, however, he actually reveals the 'imperious' tendency to treat women as chattel which the text identifies as the legacy of his colonial involvement.

The dating of events in *Jane Eyre* is kept intentionally ambiguous by Brontë,[1] but it is possible to do some general calculations, and Susan L. Meyers makes a convincing case that Rochester's experience in Jamaica occurs before the British emancipation of its slaves in 1833.[2] Her observations on what this suggests are important.

> When Rochester tells Jane, as he narrates the story of his life, 'hiring a mistress is the next worse thing to buying a slave: both are often by nature, and always by position, inferior: and to live familiarly with inferiors is degrading', his words take on a startling resonance in the context of the story he has just told. Rochester acquired a West Indian fortune by marrying a Jamaican wife and subsequently lived in Jamaica for four years. A wealthy white man living in Jamaica before emancipation would undoubtedly have had slaves to wait upon him, and his Jamaican fortune would of course have been the product of slave labor, so when Rochester discusses what it is like to buy and live with slaves he knows what he is talking about. When he compares his relationships with women to keeping slaves, then, the parallel is given a shocking vividness by his own history as a slave master.[3]

---

1 See "The Chronology of *Jane Eyre*" in *Jane Eyre*, eds. Jane Jack and Margaret Smith (Oxford: Clarendon, 1969), 610–14.
2 Susan L. Meyers, "Colonialism and the Figurative Strategy of *Jane Eyre*," *Victorian Studies* 33.2 (1990): 254–55.
3 Meyers, 259.

Rochester's willingness to simply lock up his wife and then move on to a succession of mistresses, not to mention his complete lack of guilt about manipulating Blanche Ingram in order to make Jane jealous, and indeed manipulating Jane herself in much the same way, indicates an attitude which, in nineteenth-century discourse, might best be described as "oriental." The idea that Rochester has had something very like a harem of females slaves, and that he therefore enacts the role of a Mahometan despot, is a recurring motif in the novel. This additional aspect of Rochester's "otherness" is made explicit in the game of charades at Thornfield, which is part of his strategy to play Blanche and Jane off one another. Jane describes the opening of the second charade as follows: "Seated on the carpet ... was seen Mr. Rochester, costumed in shawls, with a turban on his head. His dark eyes and swarth skin and Paynim features suited the costume exactly: he looked the very model of an eastern emir, an agent or a victim of the bowstring" (262). That Rochester's appearance can serve to identify him as "black" *and/or* "eastern" is telling, because although they are racially very different, within the economy of the novel they represent the same thing – an un-English, non-Christian imperiousness. The threat this poses to Jane's autonomy is made clear when, after she accepts his proposal, she reacts with anger to the suggestion that he "'would not exchange this one little English girl for the grand Turk's whole seraglio'" (355).

> The eastern allusion bit me again: 'I'll not stand you an inch in the stead of a seraglio,' I said: 'so don't consider me an equivalent for one: if you have a fancy for anything in that line, away with you, sir, to the bazaars of Stamboul without delay; and lay out in extensive slave-purchases some of that spare cash you seem at a loss to spend satisfactorily here.' (355)

Her refusal to be reduced to the level of a purchased slave indicates Jane's insistence on her rights as a Western, Christian woman, but the key point is that this can only be achieved by the expulsion of the "foreign" woman who both literally and symbolically is the barrier to successful union with the man she loves.

In presenting his story Rochester very clearly positions Bertha as the root cause of his flawed character, so that it is his marriage to Jane which will redeem him. As Joyce Zonana points out, the text appears to accept this shift of responsibility, and "to displace the blame for Rochester's Eastern tendencies on the intrusion of this 'Eastern' woman into his Western life."[1] It may seem strange to describe Bertha as "Eastern" when she is Jamaican, but Zonana elaborates on the way that the novel here, as with its presentation of Rochester, can have it both ways.

> Bertha, of course is West Indian, not 'Mahometan,' and she scarcely resembles the conventional image of an alluring harem inmate.... Yet, as Grosrichard points out, 'The West Indies can end by rejoining in the imagination, the East Indies'.... Bertha's characterization ... recalls the terms used ... to depict the fate of 'Mahometan' women: she is soulless, regarded as 'not ... a part of the human species,' and her all-too-real imprisonment at Thornfield invokes the root meaning of *seraglio*: a place where wild beasts are kept. One might say that Bertha's characterization as a 'clothed hyena' manifests the Western view of the underlying reality of the harem inmate.... Thus to note Bertha's 'blackness' and her birth in Jamaica need not preclude seeing that she is also, simultaneously, figured as an 'Eastern' woman.[2]

It is only after Bertha's fiery death, along with Rochester's mutilation and subsequent humbling, that her influence is cleansed from both him and the text, so that he and Jane can marry. From this perspective the novel can be seen as anti-colonialist, but in a very conservative way, since its successful conclusion depends on the destruction of the foreign "Other." What Brontë appears to be suggesting is that colonialism and imperialism are negative not because of the effect they have on those who have been *colonized*, but because of their effect on the *colonizers*. Using Rochester as its example, the novel thus implies "that the British have been sullied, 'darkened,' and made 'imperious'

---

1   Joyce Zonana, "The Sultan and the Slave: Feminist Orientalism and the Structure of *Jane Eyre*," *Revising the Word and the World: Essays in Feminist Literary Criticism*, eds. Vévé A. Clark, Ruth-Ellen B. Joeres, and Madelon Sprengnether (Chicago: U of Chicago P, 1993), 184.

2   Zonana, 184.

or oppressive by contact with the racial 'other,' and that such contact makes them arrogant oppressors.... The opposition to colonialism arises not out of concern for the well-being of the 'dark races' subject to British colonization – the African slaves in the West Indian colonies, the Indians whose economy was being destroyed under British rule – but primarily out of concern for the British who were ... being contaminated by their contact with the intrinsic despotism and oppressiveness of dark-skinned people."[1] This reading, which concentrates on Rochester and his relationship with Bertha, is, however, complicated by Brontë's presentation of Bertha herself. A view of the novel's action from the "madwoman's" perspective reveals a potentially different vision of its relationship to the idea of "the colonial."

In current criticism of *Jane Eyre* it is not much of an exaggeration to say that Bertha Mason has attracted almost as much attention as Jane herself. This focus received much of its impetus from Gilbert and Gubar, who see Bertha as the central expression of the novel's feminist rage at patriarchal oppression. Their demonstration that this "mad" figure intrudes into the text at moments when *Jane* feels anger and frustration was an antidote to earlier readings which suggested that Bertha was merely a negative expression of, for example, Jane's (or Brontë's) fear of passion and sexuality. By positioning Bertha as Jane's "dark double,"[2] Gilbert and Gubar give her character a symbolic significance which makes her essential to the text's gender protest. But what other critics have noted is that their emphasis on Bertha's "doubleness" obscures the question of her *darkness*, so that by eliding the issue of race Gilbert and Gubar avoid the more problematic aspects of her presentation.

Gayatri Chakravorty Spivak's influential article "Three Women's Texts and a Critique of Imperialism"[3] emphasizes this point. In it Spivak argues that *Jane Eyre* imposes the kind of characteristics upon Bertha that are so vital to the imperialist project. By constructing, and

---

1 Meyers, 260-61.

2 Gilbert and Gubar, 360.

3 Gayatri Chakravorty Spivak, "Three Women's Texts and a Critique of Imperialism," *Critical Inquiry* 12.1 (1985): 243-61. The other texts which Spivak discusses are Jean Rhys' *Wide Sargasso Sea* and Mary Shelley's *Frankenstein*.

then destroying, her as the not-yet-human Other, the novel allows Jane to establish her own identity in opposition to Bertha, thus replicating the way imperial powers construct their own identities and sense of superiority through applying the same process to "inferior" races. As Spivak notes, the text can therefore be read as "an allegory of the general epistemic violence of imperialism, the construction of a self-immolating colonial subject for the glorification of the social mission of the colonizer."[1] Jane's description of Bertha after the aborted wedding ceremony confirms the way in which the Jamaican woman is dehumanized in order to reinforce the "civilized" humanity of those gazing at her.

> In the deep shade, at the further end of the room, a figure ran backwards and forwards. What it was, whether beast or human being, one could not, at first sight, tell: it grovelled, seemingly, on all fours; it snatched and growled like some strange wild animal: but it was covered with clothing; and a quantity of dark, grizzled hair, wild as a mane, hid its head and face.... the clothed hyena rose up, and stood tall on its hind feet.... The maniac bellowed: she parted her shaggy locks from her visage, and gazed wildly at her visitors.... the lunatic sprang and grappled [Rochester's] throat viciously, and laid her teeth to his cheek. (380-1)

These qualities are presented as Bertha's "natural" state; that they might be the result of ten years' solitary incarceration in an attic never seems to occur to anyone.

Bertha's status as a "Creole" complicates matters even more. This thoroughly ambiguous and fluctuating designation has less to do with identifying an actual racial "type" than it does with expressing the discomfort that accompanies the possibility of inter-racial mixing, especially in the West Indies. Thus the "Creole is sometimes a white person born in the colonies – of European origin, not born in their own country.... However, a person of mixed European and Indian – native – or Black descent would also be classified as a Creole. The racial classification is based not on colour alone but on displacement

---

1   Spivak, 251.

from the place of origin."[1] Bertha therefore embodies the imperialist fear that at some point it will become impossible to discern who is racially "pure" and who is not. As the sister of the "singularly sallow" skinned Richard Mason (269), she must have been considered white "enough" to make Rochester an acceptable wife. Yet as the text proceeds she becomes literally and figuratively darker, so that when Rochester proclaims "'Her mother, the Creole, was both a madwoman and a drunkard!' he locates both madness and drunkenness in his wife's maternal line ... and....[b]y doing so he associates that line with two of the most common stereotypes associated with blacks in the nineteenth century."[2] The novel's blackening of Bertha, and the de-humanizing attributes which go along with that blackening, serve to reassure readers there can be no danger of mistaking who is really who in the racial hierarchies upon which colonialism depends. Her victimization is thus essential to neutralizing the threat she poses to English assumptions about racial identity, but that is not the only danger she represents.

If one thing becomes clear throughout *Jane Eyre*, it is that Bertha is singularly difficult to keep under control. She seems almost capable of getting loose at will, and when she does she obviously recognizes her enemies. Whether setting Rochester's bed on fire or tearing Jane's wedding veil in half, Bertha shows no sign of accepting her victimization quietly. Indeed, at the end of the book she succeeds in bringing down both Thornfield and its/her "master," although this can only be achieved through an act of "mad" self-destruction. But it is just this kind of "madness" born out of desperation which is one of the greatest fears of the colonizer, for it reveals that no matter how elaborate the system of control, if pushed far enough the colonized may rebel. In this way, when "Bertha escapes from her ten years' imprisonment to attempt periodically to stab and burn her oppressors ... she is symbolically enacting precisely the sort of revolt feared by the British colonists in Jamaica."[3] And this brings us to one of those coincidental moments in which history and literature intersect, for just under twenty years after the publication of Brontë's novel a rebellion did in

---

1 Firdous Azim, *The Colonial Rise of the Novel* (London: Routledge, 1993), 182.
2 Meyers, 253.
3 Meyers, 255.

fact break out in Jamaica, and was brutally suppressed by the colony's then-governor, Edward John *Eyre*.[1]

In his dispatch to England describing the insurrection, Eyre emphasized the barbarity of the rebels in order to justify the severity of his reprisals, and to once again demonstrate the inhuman "otherness" of their actions. But he cannot resist adding a further element to his report.

> The most frightful atrocities were perpetrated. The Island Curate of Bath, the Rev. V. Herschell, is said to have had his tongue cut out while still alive, and an attempt is said to have been made to skin him. One person ... was ripped open and his entrails taken out. One gentleman ... is said to have been pushed into an outbuilding, which was then set on fire, and kept there until he was literally roasted alive. Many are said to have had their eyes scooped out; heads were cleft open and the brains taken out....some bodies were half burst, others horribly battered. Indeed, the whole outrage could only be paralleled by the atrocities of the Indian mutiny. *The women, as usual on such occasions, were even more brutal and barbarous than the men.*[2] (emphasis added)

The status of these grisly details as pure hearsay is revealed by the repetition of "is said to have" and "are said to have," and indeed subsequent investigations suggested they were wildly exaggerated.[3] But there is no such qualifying phrase attached to the assertion that the woman are, "as usual," much worse than the men. This apparently indisputable fact helps explain Bertha's fearful potential for a Victorian

---

1   It is pushing the literary/historical congruences almost to the breaking point to note that Governor Eyre shares his first name with Jane's eventual husband, that he shares his second name with her uncle, and that he became governor of New Zealand the very year *Jane Eyre* was published.

2   Edward John Eyre, "The Insurrection in Jamaica," *The Times*, November 20, 1865, 6. See Appendix F.1.

3   Eyre's evocation of the Indian Mutiny is ironically appropriate. He recalls the most serious uprising to date in England's colonial experience to insinuate that the gravity of the situation is similar in Jamaica. But the account of Sepoy "atrocities" was likewise exaggerated, and revealed more about English anxieties and racism than it did about actual events.

audience; she unites in her person the double threat of gender and colonial rebellion, both of which represent the rejection of "proper" patriarchal authority. That in 1865 it fell to a governor named Eyre to suppress the outbreak of an actual Jamaican rebellion in order to reassert English superiority is eerily appropriate, for in many ways *Jane Eyre* foreshadows and enacts the same process. The novel provides a dark, fiery, female rebel whose self-immolation confirms Jane's humanity, and ensures the success of her white opposite: "[i]n this fictive England [Bertha] must play out her role, act out the transformation of her 'self' into that fictive Other, set fire to the house and kill herself, so that Jane Eyre can become the feminist individualist heroine of British fiction....the woman from the colonies is ... sacrificed as an insane animal for her sister's consolation."[1]

But there is one final twist in the relationship between Jane and Bertha which undercuts any idea that the book is a simple reinforcement of colonialist ideology. The fact that Jane's inheritance is entwined with British imperialism implicates *her* in its processes, so that despite the text's efforts to define her as essentially different, she cannot escape a kind of congruence with Bertha along these lines. Meyers notes that

> even if Rochester's tainted colonial wealth has been burned away, the wealth Jane is able to bring him, enabling her to meet him on equal terms ... has a colonial source. It comes from her uncle in Madeira, who is an agent for a Jamaican wine manufacturer, Bertha's brother. And the location of Jane's uncle John in Madeira, off Morocco, on the East Africa coast, where Richard Mason stops on his way home from England, also evokes, through Mason's itinerary, the triangular route of the British slave traders, and suggests that John Eyre's wealth is implicated in the slave trade.[2]

It is therefore possible to argue that Jane's "purity" is less secure than some of the other characters (and perhaps Jane herself) might wish to think. Firdous Azim pushes this idea even further when he argues that

---

1   Spivak, 251.
2   Meyers, 267.

"[c]olonial possessions and wealth, Creolise, as it were, the central figure, whose inscription within English society remains heterogeneous."[1] In other words, although on one level Jane appears to be successfully integrated into society at the end of the novel, on another she can never actually be so, any more than can Bertha. As a woman, and as a woman whose economic independence derives from colonial funds, Jane simply cannot fit into a world whose imperialism is so fully interconnected with patriarchal attitudes that there is no acceptable independent space she can inhabit. The novel's concluding scenes at Ferndean can therefore be seen as profoundly ambiguous. Although some readers see them as a positive statement of "happily ever after," the manor house's isolation, its unhealthy atmosphere of enclosure and perhaps even imprisonment, appear to indicate a retreat rather than a triumph. Thus in its closure *Jane Eyre* returns to a connection between Bertha and Jane by hinting that they "*share* a subject position marginalized through difference," and that they are "oppressed rather than opposed sisters."[2] Ultimately the novel recognizes that colonialism and imperialism are inescapably masculinist activities, and it represents that recognition in the character of St. John Rivers.

Brontë's introduction of St. John at first appears an exercise in contrasts. Jane's newly discovered, clergyman cousin is presented as a model of classical, Western male beauty, in obvious opposition to Rochester's dark, irregular, pagan looks. We are told that St. John is

> tall, slender; his face riveted the eye: it was like a Greek face, very pure in outline; quite a straight, classic nose; quite an Athenian mouth and chin. It is seldom, indeed, an English face comes so near the antique models as did his. He might well be a little shocked at the irregularity of my lineaments, his own being so harmonious. His eyes were large and blue, with brown lashes; his high forehead, colourless as ivory, was partially streaked over by careless locks of fair hair. (438-9)

---

1   Azim, 177.
2   Laura E. Donaldson, "The Miranda Complex: Colonialism and the Question of Feminist Reading," *Diacritics* 18.3 (1988): 75.

But Jane immediately qualifies this attractive description by noting that "there was something about his nostril, his mouth, his brow, which, to my perceptions, indicated elements within either restless, or hard, or eager" (439). St. John may be more like Rochester than one might initially think. Equally suggestive, however, is her later likening him to "a cold cumbrous column" (491), which provides a disconcerting echo of her first impression of Mr. Brocklehurst as "a black pillar" (90). That both men are Church of England ministers reinforces the connection. This is not to say that the text attacks St. John in the same way it does Brocklehurst, or that there is any suggestion of hypocrisy in the younger man's fervour. But it does hint that St. John fails to receive the novel's unqualified approval.

The most objectionable quality he shares with both Rochester and Brocklehurst is his authoritarian attitude towards women. St. John's patriarchal belief that women should conform to male expectations is as brutally coercive as that of either of his predecessors, so that he poses the same kind of challenge to Jane's autonomy. His attempt to force Jane to marry him relies on a kind of spiritual blackmail which closely echoes Rochester's attempt at emotional blackmail, and is in fact more difficult to resist. Rejecting Rochester's adulterous proposal to travel with him to France is a relatively "straightforward" moral choice; rejecting St. John's legitimate offer of marriage and their subsequent missionary journey to India is a different thing altogether, for it seems, as St. John puts it, "'to [number her] with those who have denied the faith and are worse than infidels!'" (509). Jane explicitly acknowledges the parallel nature of these situations when she says "'I was almost as hard beset by him now as I had been once before, in a different way, by another. I was a fool both times. To have yielded then would have been an error of principle; to have yielded now would have been an error of judgement'" (518), but the interesting thing is that while Rochester, as has already been discussed, needs to have his imperious attitude towards women reformed, the text does not require St. John to undergo a similar process. Although he does not succeed in getting Jane to marry him, he also does not experience the "purification" to which Rochester is subjected, and the reason for this is very much bound up in his imperialist drive.

At various points in the novel St. John confesses that the foundation of his missionary desire is ambition. He is simply unsatisfied with
the life of a country parson in an obscure parish, and Britain's colonial
holdings provide him with the opportunity for a much wider stage
upon which to enact both his faith and his egotism. Thus "India provides St. John with people to dominate and transform such as he
could never find in the land of his father, even if Jane had been willing to submit to his coercion."[1] The text is definitely uncomfortable
when this masculine will to domination is expressed *within* England,
so that both Rochester and St. John are criticized for the times they
direct it generally at those around them, and even more when they
direct it specifically at Jane. But when it becomes directed *externally*,
towards peoples and countries which "require" forceful reminders of
their own barbarity and Britain's civilization, then it becomes almost
sublime. In this way "St. John's ambition, domination, ruthlessness,
and aggression, seen as negative in England, become positive and
admirable when transported to India – Rochester, however, because
he remains in England, must be 'civilized' by Jane and have these
qualities exorcised."[2] Yet, even as the text supports St. John's religious
mission, it also makes clear that it will destroy him. He goes to India
with the full awareness that he will die, and so he both gains from, and
is victimized by, empire. His self-imposed martyrdom thus becomes a
strange echo of Bertha Mason's suicide, since through it she too gains
escape from an unbearable imprisonment. The difference, of course, is
that she can receive no empowerment from the colonial experience
which is even remotely accepted as legitimate. Empire thus provides a
conflicting set of potentialities in *Jane Eyre*. It is the site of temptation
and redemption, the sensual and the spiritual, the Other and the Us,
the black and the white; in other words, it is constructed in terms of
those binary oppositions which were essential for constructing nineteenth-century hierarchies of value. But the novel also demonstrates
just how shifting such constructions are, as characters slip from one
pole to the other in their complicated circling around Jane, whose
own anomalous and ambiguous position is thus emphasized.

Brontë's text evokes colonialism and imperialism, but never con-

---

1   Schwartz, 560.
2   Michie, 596.

fronts them directly. The power relations which such systems create are clearly antipathetic to the novel's desire for gender equality, but to extend that desire beyond gender and outside of England would subvert foundational assumptions about class and race upon which Brontë's own authority rests. Thus "the critique of colonialism which the novel promises to make ... finally collapses into a mere uneasiness.... That disquietude is the only remnant of Brontë's potentially radical revision of the analogy between white women and colonized races, and it is the only incomplete element in the ideological close of the novel."[1] This uneasiness is representative of the period in which *Jane Eyre* was published, and it tells us as much about that cultural moment as it does about its author. As the century proceeded Britain's attitude towards its colonial holdings hardened, so that Edward John Eyre and his supporters demonstrated none of the ambivalences of the book which contains his fictional namesake. The novel thus reveals a moment when the colonial experience could still provoke self-questioning, even if finally the text cannot achieve a significant challenge to the ideas which underlay the imperialist drive.

"Reader, I married him": *Jane Eyre* Past and Present

Both Jane Eyre the character and *Jane Eyre* the novel had a revolutionary impact on nineteenth-century fiction. The text rejects the standard female stereotypes of the period, so that "Brontë dispenses with the tomboy heroine who blossoms into womanhood, with the beauty who is punished for vanity and coquetry, with the less attractive woman whose sweet virtue endears her to all,"[2] and instead provides a narrator who refuses to be bound by anyone's expectations, novelistic or otherwise. Perhaps as significant is the power with which the reader is drawn to identify with and support Jane in her struggles and desires. This intensity of response, especially (but not only) in female readers was what generated so much comment at the time, both positive and negative. The book's success spawned a series of imitators whose plain, rebellious, and passionate heroines clearly owed

---

1   Meyers, 268.
2   Annette Federico, "'A cool observer of her own sex like me': Girl-Watching in *Jane Eyre,*" *Victorian Newsletter* 80 (Fall 1991): 32.

their personality to Jane;[1] but few of them matched her ability to draw the audience so deeply into her experience. Indeed, to feel something similar it was necessary to wait until the next works of "Currer Bell" appeared, for in the characters of Shirley Keeldar and, more especially, that of Lucy Snowe, could be detected the will and fire which made their earlier sister so fascinating.

But of course there were some who found the novel's influence anything but beneficial. Writing in *Blackwood's Magazine* twenty years almost to the month after the publication of *Jane Eyre*, and well after its author's death, Margaret Oliphant contemplated the state of English fiction.

> [T]here can be no doubt that a singular change has passed upon our light literature. It is not that its power has failed or its popularity diminished – much the reverse; it is because a new impulse has been given and a new current set in the flood of contemporary story-telling. We will not ask whence or from whom the influence is derived. It has been brought into being by society, and it naturally reacts upon society. The change perhaps began at the time when Jane Eyre made what advanced critics called her "protest" against the conventionalities in which the world clothes itself. We have had many "protests" since that time, but it is to be doubted how far they have been to our advantage. The point to which we have now arrived is certainly very far from satisfactory.[2]

Oliphant goes on to attack what were by then called "sensation" novels, and it is telling that she connects them to *Jane Eyre*, for the events of Brontë's story could certainly be described as "sensational." But more important is her contention that at the core of sensation fiction is a protest which can be traced back to this text. Brontë is seen as initiating a questioning of the *status quo* which, two decades later, has reached a dangerously extreme point, at least from *Blackwood's* conser-

---

1 For examples of novels that imitate significant elements of *Jane Eyre*, see Jane Warboise's *Thornycroft Hall* (1864), Florence Warden's *The House on the Marsh* (1877), and Rose Nouchette Carey's *The Old, Old Story* (1895).

2 Margaret Oliphant, "Novels," *Blackwood's Edinburgh Magazine*, September 1867, 258.

vative perspective. The calmly triumphant declaration "'Reader, I married him,'" which begins the final chapter, demonstrates the shift that has occurred. By creating a heroine "who *was* emphatically 'not an angel,' who combined the temperament of the strong-minded female with superior moral strength and yet wanted, and obtained, marriage and a home,"[1] Brontë changed the form and content of the Victorian novel. It was now possible to write stories which not only expected readers to sympathize with "improper" women, but which demonstrated that the *author* sympathized with them as well; the result was a challenge to the very ideas of what was proper and improper. Few pieces of fiction can claim such an impact, but *Jane Eyre* is one of them.

Brontë's novel remains provocative. The variety of readings which can be applied to the text are not always reconcilable, but they almost always bring new recognitions and perceptions. This complexity of reader response is the mark of the book's success, because it demonstrates the many levels on which it operates. *Jane Eyre* refuses to be constrained by any single or narrow interpretation, and in the process of coming to terms with it we are challenged to rethink questions about gender, class, and race which are as pertinent today as they were to a reader in 1847. The Victorians and their society are not so far "behind" us as some would like to think, and in the unique narrator of this text we hear a voice that confronts the world which created ours.

---

1   Helsinger, Sheets, Veeder, 101.

A Note on the Text

Charlotte Brontë began writing *Jane Eyre* under singularly inauspicious circumstances. The collection of poetry she had published with her sisters Emily and Anne, in the spring of 1846, had sold a grand total of two copies.[1] Her first novel, *The Professor*, had been rejected for publication twice, and in fact was not to appear in print until after Brontë's death. Added to these discouraging developments on the literary front, the family situation at Haworth Parsonage was also in disarray. Branwell Brontë, Charlotte's brother, had begun the rapid slide into self-pity and alcoholism which was to kill him a few years later. Of even more immediate concern, her father had recently been diagnosed with cataracts, an affliction which clearly threatened his livelihood as vicar in their Yorkshire parish. If he were to lose his eyesight the situation for his daughters, unless they could find some other source of income, looked very grim indeed. The family decided Brontë should accompany him to Manchester for the operation that would remove the blockage, and thus in the late summer of 1846 she found herself in a small lodging house caring for a man who was to rest in a dark room and be disturbed as little as possible. It was under these conditions that she began the book which was to make her famous.

Although the operation eventually proved to be a complete success, Brontë and her father were forced to stay in Manchester for five weeks as he recovered. During this time she appears to have worked steadily, if slowly, on the first draft of *Jane Eyre*, but it was with their return to Haworth at the end of September that the book caught fire in her imagination. Having gotten Jane to Thornfield, Brontë became swept up with her heroine's relationship with Rochester. Harriet Martineau, recording how Brontë described the intensity of this creative moment, states

---

1   This volume, entitled *Poems by Currer, Ellis, and Acton Bell*, established the pseudonyms under which the Brontës would write. Charlotte became "Currer Bell," Emily "Ellis," and Anne "Acton," all three thus keeping their initials while disguising their female identities.

On she went, writing incessantly for three weeks; by which time she had carried [Jane] away from Thornfield, and was herself in a fever, which compelled her to pause. The rest was written with less vehemence, and with more anxious care. The world adds, with less vigour and interest.[1]

The entire novel does not appear to have been completed until August of the following year, although Brontë began to make a fair copy of the opening chapters before finishing the text as a whole. This fair copy, from which the first edition of the novel was printed, is currently held by the British Museum, with its initial folio dated 16 March 1847, and its last 19 August 1847.[2]

Even as she was writing *Jane Eyre* Brontë continued to send *The Professor* out to various publishers, meeting with repeated and often curt rejection. Thus when the publishing house of Smith, Elder and Co. also turned it down she was hardly surprised. Along with the letter declining to publish the book for commercial reasons, however, came an "appreciative criticism"[3] encouraging "Currer Bell" to continue "his" attempts at writing fiction. This was certainly more than the abrupt dismissal Brontë was accustomed to receiving, and it led her to reply with the tentative suggestion that she had another novel under way which Messrs. Smith and Elder might find more interesting. They agreed to consider this newer work, and in a little over two weeks Brontë's carefully copied version of *Jane Eyre* was parceled out of Haworth and on its way to London. William Smith Williams, the same reader for Smith, Elder who had been so encouraging about *The Professor*, was immediately struck by the story's power, and encouraged George Smith, the company's owner, to look it over for himself. He, in turn, read the entire manuscript in a single day, and accepted it for publication the next. Realizing it had something unique, Smith, Elder wasted no time in preparing proofs, and Brontë was equally prompt in making the few adjustments required and

---

1   Quoted in Juliet Barker, *The Brontës* (New York: St. Martin's Press, 1994), 511.
2   See Jane Jack and Margaret Smith (eds.), *Jane Eyre* (Oxford: Clarendon Press, 1975), xii. All contemporary bibliographical discussions of this novel owe a large debt to the careful textual work of this edition, and anyone interested in a full collation of the relevant versions of *Jane Eyre* should refer to it.
3   Quoted in Barker, 525.

returning them. *Jane Eyre*, an "An Autobiography. Edited By Currer Bell," was published on 16 October 1847.

The relationship between Brontë's fair copy of the novel and Smith, Elder's three-volume first edition appears to be straightforward. Because they were working from such a clean source the compositors had no particular difficulty setting the text, and this helps explain why the proofs required so little authorial correction. The publisher's house-styling did, however, impose a heavier, more formal method of punctuation on the novel than had originally been provided by Brontë. This does not seem to have bothered her, and indeed she went out of her way to state her appreciation for their help. Thus in a letter dated 24 September 1847, commenting on the proofs she had received, Brontë says "I have to thank you for punctuating the sheets before sending them to me, as I found the task very puzzling, and, besides, I consider your mode of punctuation a great deal more correct and rational than my own."[1] In the face of such overt acceptance there is little doubt that the accidentals of the first edition should be taken as authoritative, even if they are not absolutely authorial.

Jane Eyre was, by any measure, a wildly successful book. Its original print run sold out in just under three months, thus requiring a second edition in something close to record time for a novel of the period. This gave Brontë the chance to provide both a dedication and a preface for the text, and she used the opportunity to compliment a writer she admired, and to confront her detractors. Therefore the second edition, also in three-volumes, carries the words: "To W. M. Thackeray, Esq. This Work is Respectfully Inscribed, by The Author." This is significant, for it shows Brontë fully accepting her role as "Author," a mark of confidence also reflected in the new title page, which drops the word "Edited" and now declares the work to be simply "By Currer Bell."

Thackeray had impressed Brontë by his willingness to confront social and religious hypocrisy in his novels, themes which obviously appear in her own text. Further, when Smith, Elder sent him a review copy of the novel, Thackeray responded with enthusiasm, declaring to Williams

---

1   Quoted in Jack and Smith, xiii.

It is a fine book...the man and the woman capital, the style very generous and upright so to speak....I don't know why I tell you this but that I have been exceedingly moved and pleased by *Jane Eyre*. It is a woman's writing, but whose? Give my respects and thanks to the author, whose novel is the first English one (and the French are only romances now) that I've been able to read for many a day.[1]

This is high praise, and Brontë was delighted. The dedication did have one unforeseen effect, however. Speculation about the true identity of "Currer Bell" had reached something of a frenzy, and the second edition added to the gossip circulating in London. Brontë was unaware that, only four years after he had married her, Thackeray's wife had gone insane, and in 1840 had been committed to an asylum. The coincidence of this echo of Rochester's relationship with Bertha encouraged rumours that the author of *Jane Eyre* had been a governess in the Thackeray household, and that the story was based on true events. When she was told of this unpleasant congruence Brontë was understandably upset, but there was little she could do once the edition had been published. And in some ways the preface which accompanied the dedication was equally unfortunate.

The first reviews of *Jane Eyre* were almost universally positive, and indeed many verged on extreme in their praise of the story and its mysterious author. There were, nonetheless, a few exceptions, most notably the *Spectator*, which questioned the "low tone of behaviour (rather than of morality) in the book." Brontë, as she was later to acknowledge, over-reacted to such negative comments, leading her in the Preface to characterize her critics as "the timorous or carping few," and to make the round declaration "Conventionality is not morality. Self-righteousness is not religion. To attack the first is not to assail the last. To pluck the mask from the face of the Pharisee, is not to lift an impious hand to the Crown of Thorns." The vehemence of the Preface is rather out of proportion to the provocation which generated it, and in a letter to her publishers after it appeared Brontë ruefully observes "I read my preface over with some pain – I do not

---

1   Quoted in Rebecca Fraser, *Charlotte Brontë* (London: Methuen, 1988), 278.

like it. I wrote it when I was a little enthusiastic....I wish I had written it in a cool moment; I should have said the same things, but in a different manner....I promise myself to take better care in future. *Still* I will *think* as I please."[1] Nonetheless, in some ways the Preface answered future criticisms, because as time went on more and more negative responses to the novel and its author appeared; perhaps, therefore, Brontë's first impulse was not quite so misplaced as she thought.

Textually, the second edition remedies a number of small errors which had crept into the first edition. As well, it provided Brontë with the opportunity to revise certain parts of the novel which had given her difficulty. As Jane Jack and Margaret Smith point out, however, "the second edition is on the whole less accurately printed than the first, with the result that numerous new printing errors make their appearance in it."[2] Thus the second edition introduces almost as many new problems as it corrects. This is particularly unfortunate since the second edition passes on many of its mistakes to the third edition, which appeared three months later. Here again Brontë takes the opportunity to adjust some minor elements of the story, and it is for this edition that she adds a "Note" asserting that her claim to authorship rests, to this point, on only one book. This is to counter insinuations that *Agnes Grey* (by "Acton Bell") and *Wuthering Heights* (by "Ellis Bell"), both of which had recently been published, were in fact by the same author as *Jane Eyre*.[3] Although the third edition is more carefully set than the second, it adds a new set of inaccuracies, including misquoting the opening lines of Sir Walter Scott's poem *Marmion*, which appear near the beginning of Chapter 33. Also, both the second and third editions increase the house-styling imposed on the text, thus moving even further away from the light punctuation of the MS. Brontë may have welcomed the more formal pointing of the first edition, but it is considerably less clear that subsequent layers of punc-

---

1   Quoted in Jack and Smith, xvi–xvii.
2   Jack and Smith, xv.
3   T. C. Newby, who had unscrupulously been withholding Anne and Emily's novels, rushed them into print as soon as the popularity of *Jane Eyre* became clear. Further, in advertising them he implied that all three texts were by the same author. Brontë, understandably angered by this shoddy treatment of her sisters, attempted to redress the dishonesty in her Note.

tuation received her approval. Thus while the substantive changes to the second and third editions must be taken into account, their overall authority is questionable.

Similarly the fourth, one-volume "cheap" edition of *Jane Eyre*, which Smith, Elder published in 1850, simply reproduces many of the errors, and all the accreted punctuation, of its immediate predecessor. Although it does correct some obvious misprints and mistakes which were generated in earlier versions of the novel, it does not appear to have been revised in any serious way. It is unlikely that Brontë, still reeling from the deaths of Branwell and Emily in 1848, of Anne in 1849, and from the negative reviews of her second novel *Shirley*, had either the time or the energy for a close reading of this six-shilling version of the text.

All of this being the case, I have chosen to return to the first edition of *Jane Eyre* for my copy text. Most modern editions of the novel base their texts on the third edition, since clearly it was the last version of the work which Brontë herself revised.[1] The first edition, however, was more carefully printed than any of those which followed it, and contains punctuation fully approved by the author. The goals of the present volume, then, are to retain the less obtrusive pointing of the text's first publication; to incorporate Brontë's later changes in wording; and to correct any mistakes introduced in the novel's printing. *Jane Eyre* provided a new and challenging fictional experience for its Victorian audience. Reproducing as closely as possible the rhythms and nuances of its original, distinctive narrative voice best serves to recreate the freshness of its appeal to both nineteenth- and twentieth-century readers.

---

1   In returning to the first edition I am, however, following the lead of Jane Jack and Margaret Smith, whose Clarendon edition also uses this early printing as its base text.

Charlotte Brontë: A Brief Chronology

1816	Born on April 21 at Thornton, Bradford, Yorkshire, third child of Patrick Brontë and Maria Branwell
1817	Patrick Branwell Brontë born on June 26
1818	Emily Jane Brontë born on July 30
1820	Anne Brontë born on January 17. Family moves to Haworth Parsonage, Yorkshire after father appointed curate
1821	Brontë's mother dies
1824	Brontë sent to Cowan Bridge school, later joined by Emily
1825	Brontë's two older sisters, Maria and Elizabeth, die. Emily and she return to Haworth from Cowan Bridge
1831	Enrolled at Miss Wooler's school, Roe Head
1832	Leaves Roe Head, but returns there in 1835 as teacher
1838	Gives up position as teacher at Roe Head
1839	Declines Henry Nussey's proposal of marriage. Becomes governess in household of John Sidgwick at Stonegappe. Gives up position of governess at Stonegappe after two-and-a-half months. Declines proposal of marriage from Rev. David Pryce
1840	Returns to Haworth
1841	Becomes governess in household of John White, Upperwood House. Leaves position at Upperwood House after ten months
1842	Brontë travels with Emily to Brussels to attend Mme. Heger's school. Both return to Haworth in October due to the death of their aunt
1843	Brontë returns to Brussels
1844	Leaves Brussels and returns to Haworth. Begins plans to establish school for girls at parsonage
1846	Publication of *Poems by Currer, Ellis, and Acton Bell*. Brontë's *The Professor* turned down by several publishers. Begins work on *Jane Eyre*
1847	*Jane Eyre* published in three volumes by Smith, Elder. Emily

Brontë's *Wuthering Heights* published. Anne Brontë's *Agnes Grey* published

1848 Anne Brontë's *The Tenant of Wildfell Hall* published. Death of Branwell and Emily Brontë

1849 Death of Anne Brontë. Brontë's *Shirley* published. Travels to London and meets Thackeray

1850 Brontë meets Elizabeth Gaskell

1851 Declines James Taylor's proposal of marriage

1853 Brontë publishes *Villette*

1854 Marries Rev. A. B. Nicholls

1855 Dies at Haworth on March 31

JANE EYRE

AN AUTOBIOGRAPHY

EDITED BY

CURRER BELL

IN THREE VOLUMES

VOLUME I

JANE EYRE

CHAPTER I

THERE was no possibility of taking a walk that day. We had been wandering, indeed, in the leafless shrubbery an hour in the morning; but since dinner (Mrs. Reed, when there was no company, dined early) the cold winter wind had brought with it clouds so sombre, and a rain so penetrating, that further out-door exercise was now out of the question.

I was glad of it: I never liked long walks, especially on chilly afternoons: dreadful to me was the coming home in the raw twilight, with nipped fingers and toes, and a heart saddened by the chidings of Bessie, the nurse, and humbled by the consciousness of my physical inferiority to Eliza, John, and Georgiana Reed.

The said Eliza, John, and Georgiana were now clustered round their mama in the drawing-room: she lay reclined on a sofa by the fire-side, and with her darlings about her (for the time neither quarrelling nor crying) looked perfectly happy. Me, she had dispensed from joining the group; saying, "She regretted to be under the necessity of keeping me at a distance; but that until she heard from Bessie, and could discover by her own observation that I was endeavouring in good earnest to acquire a more sociable and childlike disposition, a more attractive and sprightly manner; – something lighter, franker, more natural as it were – she really must exclude me from privileges intended only for contented, happy, little children."

"What does Bessie say I have done?" I asked.

"Jane, I don't like cavillers or questioners: besides, there is something truly forbidding in a child taking up her elders in that manner. Be seated somewhere; and until you can speak pleasantly, remain silent."

A small breakfast-room adjoined the drawing-room: I slipped in there. It contained a book-case: I soon possessed myself of a volume, taking care that it should be one stored with pictures. I mounted into the window-seat: gathering up my feet, I sat cross-legged, like a Turk;

and, having drawn the red moreen[1] curtain nearly close, I was shrined in double retirement.

Folds of scarlet drapery shut in my view to the right hand; to the left were the clear panes of glass, protecting, but not separating me from the drear November day. At intervals, while turning over the leaves of my book, I studied the aspect of that winter afternoon. Afar, it offered a pale blank of mist and cloud; near, a scene of wet lawn and storm-beat shrub, with ceaseless rain sweeping away wildly before a long and lamentable blast.

I returned to my book – Bewick's History of British Birds:[2] the letter-press[3] thereof I cared little for, generally speaking; and yet there were certain introductory pages that, child as I was, I could not pass quite as a blank. They were those which treat of the haunts of sea-fowl; of "the solitary rocks and promontories" by them only inhabit-ed; of the coast of Norway, studded with isles from its southern extremity, the Lindesness, or Naze, to the North Cape –

> "Where the Northern Ocean, in vast whirls
> Boils round the naked, melancholy isles
> Of farthest Thule; and the Atlantic surge
> Pours in among the stormy Hebrides."[4]

Nor could I pass unnoticed the suggestion of the bleak shores of Lapland, Siberia, Spitzbergen, Nova Zembla, Iceland, Greenland, with "the vast sweep of the Arctic Zone, and those forlorn regions of dreary space, – that reservoir of frost and snow, where firm fields of ice, the accumulation of centuries of winters, glazed in Alpine heights above heights, surround the pole, and concentre the multiplied rigours of extreme cold." Of these death-white realms I formed an idea of my own; shadowy, like all the half-comprehended notions that float dim through children's brains, but strangely impressive. The words in these introductory pages connected themselves with the

---

1   Ribbed woollen, or woollen and cotton, material.
2   A popular book of ornithology, in two volumes, published in 1797 and again in 1804. Brontë's references and quotations are from Vol. II, *Water Birds*.
3   i.e., the text.
4   James Thomson (1700-48) published his poem *Seasons* in four sections from 1726-30. This passage, which is quoted in *Bewick's*, consists of lines 862-65 from "Autumn."

succeeding vignettes, and gave significance to the rock standing up alone in a sea of billow and spray; to the broken boat stranded on a desolate coast; to the cold and ghastly moon glancing through bars of cloud at a wreck just sinking.

I cannot tell what sentiment haunted the quite solitary churchyard with its inscribed headstone; its gate, its two trees, its low horizon, girdled by a broken wall, and its newly-risen crescent, attesting the hour of even-tide.

The two ships becalmed on a torpid sea, I believed to be marine phantoms.

The fiend pinning down the thief's pack behind him, I passed over quickly: it was an object of terror.

So was the black, horned thing seated aloof on a rock, surveying a distant crowd surrounding a gallows.

Each picture told a story; mysterious often to my undeveloped understanding and imperfect feelings, yet ever profoundly interesting: as interesting as the tales Bessie sometimes narrated on winter evenings, when she chanced to be in good humour; and when, having brought her ironing-table to the nursery hearth, she allowed us to sit about it, and while she got up Mrs. Reed's lace frills, and crimped her night-cap borders, fed our eager attention with passages of love and adventure taken from old fairy tales and other ballads; or (as at a later period I discovered) from the pages of Pamela, and Henry, Earl of Moreland.[1]

With Bewick on my knee, I was then happy: happy at least in my way. I feared nothing but interruption, and that came too soon. The breakfast-room door opened.

"Boh! Madam Mope!" cried the voice of John Reed; then he paused: he found the room apparently empty.

"Where the dickens is she?" he continued. "Lizzy! Georgy!" (calling to his sisters) "Joan is not here: tell mama she is run out into the rain – bad animal!"

"It is well I drew the curtain," thought I; and I wished fervently he might not discover my hiding-place: nor would John Reed have found it out himself; he was not quick either of vision or conception:

---

1 Samuel Richardson (1689-1761) published his novel *Pamela* in 1740. *Henry, Earl of Moreland* (1781) was a popular abridgement of the novel *The Fool of Quality* (1766-72) by Henry Brooke (1703-83).

but Eliza just put her head in at the door, and said at once: –

"She is in the window-seat, to be sure, Jack."

And I came out immediately; for I trembled at the idea of being dragged forth by the said Jack.

"What do you want?" I asked, with awkward diffidence.

"Say, 'What do you want Master Reed;'" was the answer. "I want you to come here;" and seating himself in an arm-chair, he intimated by a gesture that I was to approach and stand before him.

John Reed was a schoolboy of fourteen years old: four years older than I, for I was but ten: large and stout for his age, with a dingy and unwholesome skin; thick lineaments in a spacious visage, heavy limbs and large extremities. He gorged himself habitually at table, which made him bilious, and gave him a dim and bleared eye and flabby cheeks. He ought now to have been at school; but his mama had taken him home for a month or two, "on account of his delicate health." Mr. Miles, the master, affirmed that he would do very well if he had fewer cakes and sweetmeats sent him from home; but the mother's heart turned from an opinion so harsh, and inclined rather to the more refined idea that John's sallowness was owing to over-application and, perhaps, to pining after home.

John had not much affection for his mother and sisters, and an antipathy to me. He bullied and punished me: not two or three times in the week, nor once or twice in the day, but continually: every nerve I had feared him, and every morsel of flesh in my bones shrank when he came near. There were moments when I was bewildered by the terror he inspired; because I had no appeal whatever against either his menaces or his inflictions: the servants did not like to offend their young master by taking my part against him, and Mrs. Reed was blind and deaf on the subject: she never saw him strike or heard him abuse me; though he did both now and then in her very presence: more frequently however behind her back.

Habitually obedient to John, I came up to his chair: he spent some three minutes in thrusting out his tongue at me as far as he could without damaging the roots: I knew he would soon strike, and while dreading the blow, I mused on the disgusting and ugly appearance of him who would presently deal it. I wonder if he read that notion in my face; for, all at once, without speaking, he struck suddenly and strongly. I tottered, and on regaining my equilibrium retired back a step or two from his chair.

"That is for your impudence in answering mama a while since," said he, "and for your sneaking way of getting behind curtains, and for the look you had in your eyes two minutes since, you rat!"

Accustomed to John Reed's abuse, I never had an idea of replying to it; my care was how to endure the blow which would certainly follow the insult.

"What were you doing behind the curtain?" he asked.

"I was reading."

"Shew the book."

I returned to the window and fetched it thence.

"You have no business to take our books: you are a dependant, mama says; you have no money; your father left you none; you ought to beg, and not to live here with gentlemen's children like us, and eat the same meals we do, and wear clothes at our mama's expense. Now, I'll teach you to rummage my book-shelves: for they *are* mine; all the house belongs to me, or will do in a few years. Go and stand by the door, out of the way of the mirror and the windows."

I did so, not at first aware what was his intention; but when I saw him lift and poise the book and stand in act to hurl it, I instinctively started aside with a cry of alarm: not soon enough, however; the volume was flung, it hit me, and I fell, striking my head against the door and cutting it. The cut bled, the pain was sharp: my terror had passed its climax; other feelings succeeded.

"Wicked and cruel boy!" I said. "You are like a murderer – you are like a slave-driver – you are like the Roman emperors!"

I had read Goldsmith's History of Rome,[1] and had formed my opinion of Nero, Caligula,[2] &c. Also I had drawn parallels in silence, which I never thought thus to have declared aloud.

"What! what!" he cried. "Did she say that to me? Did you hear her, Eliza and Georgiana? Won't I tell mama? but first —"

---

1   Oliver Goldsmith (1730?-74) published *The Roman History* in 1769.
2   Nero Claudius Caesar (37-68 CE) became Emperor of Rome in 54 CE. He was deposed and forced to commit suicide. Caligula Gaius Caesar (12-41 CE) became Emperor of Rome in 37 CE, and was assassinated four years later. Both men became famous for corruption and the misuse of power.

He ran headlong at me; I felt him grasp my hair and my shoulder: he had closed with a desperate thing. I really saw in him a tyrant: a murderer. I felt a drop or two of blood from my head trickle down my neck, and was sensible of somewhat pungent suffering: these sensations, for the time predominated over fear, and I received him in frantic sort. I don't very well know what I did with my hands, but he called me "Rat! rat!" and bellowed out aloud. Aid was near him: Eliza and Georgiana had run for Mrs. Reed, who was gone up stairs; she now came upon the scene, followed by Bessie and her maid Abbot. We were parted: I heard the words: –

"Dear! dear! What a fury to fly at Master John!"

"Did ever anybody see such a picture of passion!"

Then Mrs. Reed subjoined: –

"Take her away to the red-room, and lock her in there." Four hands were immediately laid upon me, and I was borne up stairs.

CHAPTER II

I RESISTED all the way: a new thing for me, and a circumstance which greatly strengthened the bad opinion Bessie and Miss Abbot were disposed to entertain of me. The fact is, I was a trifle beside myself; or rather *out* of myself, as the French would say: I was conscious that a moment's mutiny had already rendered me liable to strange penalties, and like any other rebel slave, I felt resolved, in my desperation, to go all lengths.

"Hold her arms, Miss Abbot; she's like a mad cat."

"For shame! for shame!" cried the lady's-maid. "What shocking conduct, Miss Eyre, to strike a young gentleman, your benefactress's son! Your young master!"

"Master! How is he my master? Am I a servant?"

"No; you are less than a servant, for you do nothing for your keep. There, sit down and think over your wickedness."

They had got me by this time into the apartment indicated by Mrs. Reed, and had thrust me upon a stool: my impulse was to rise from it like a spring; their two pairs of hands arrested me instantly.

"If you don't sit still, you must be tied down," said Bessie. "Miss Abbot, lend me your garters; she would break mine directly."

Miss Abbot turned to divest a stout leg of the necessary ligature. This preparation for bonds, and the additional ignominy it inferred, took a little of the excitement out of me.

"Don't take them off," I cried; "I will not stir."

In guarantee whereof I attached myself to my seat by my hands.

"Mind you don't," said Bessie; and when she had ascertained that I was really subsiding, she loosened her hold of me; then she and Miss Abbot stood with folded arms, looking darkly and doubtfully on my face, as incredulous of my sanity.

"She never did so before," at last said Bessie, turning to the Abigail.[1]

"But it was always in her," was the reply. "I've told Missis often my opinion about the child, and Missis agreed with me. She's an underhand little thing: I never saw a girl of her age with so much cover."

---

[1] Word denoting a lady's-maid or waiting-woman. The term derives from 1 Samuel 25, in which Abigail often refers to herself as a "handmaid."

Bessie answered not; but ere long, addressing me, she said,

"You ought to be aware, Miss, that you are under obligations to Mrs. Reed: she keeps you; if she were to turn you off, you would have to go to the poor-house."

I had nothing to say to these words: they were not new to me: my very first recollections of existence included hints of the same kind. This reproach of my dependence had become a vague sing-song in my ear; very painful and crushing, but only half intelligible. Miss Abbot joined in: –

"And you ought not to think yourself on an equality with the Misses Reed and Master Reed, because Missis kindly allows you to be brought up with them. They will have a great deal of money, and you will have none: it is your place to be humble, and to try to make yourself agreeable to them."

"What we tell you, is for your good," added Bessie, in no harsh voice: "you should try to be useful and pleasant, then perhaps you would always have a home here; but if you become passionate and rude, Missis will send you away, I am sure."

"Besides," said Miss Abbot, "God will punish her: he might strike her dead in the midst of her tantrums, and then where would she go? Come, Bessie, we will leave her: I wouldn't have her heart for any- thing. Say your prayers, Miss Eyre, when you are by yourself; for if you don't repent, something bad might be permitted to come down the chimney, and fetch you away."

They went, shutting the door, and locking it behind them.

The red-room was a spare chamber, very seldom slept in; I might say never, indeed; unless when a chance influx of visitors at Gateshead-hall rendered it necessary to turn to account all the accommodation it contained: yet it was one of the largest and stateliest chambers in the mansion. A bed supported on massive pillars of mahogany, hung with curtains of deep red damask,[1] stood out like a tabernacle in the centre; the two large windows, with their blinds always drawn down, were half shrouded in festoons and falls of similar drapery; the carpet was red; the table at the foot of the bed was cov- ered with a crimson cloth; the walls were a soft fawn colour, with a

---

1   Figured woven material with the pattern visible on both sides.

blush of pink in it; the wardrobe, the toilet-table, the chairs were of darkly polished old mahogany. Out of these deep surrounding shades rose high, and glared white, the piled-up mattresses and pillows of the bed, spread with a snowy Marseilles counterpane.[1] Scarcely less prominent was an ample, cushioned easy-chair near the head of the bed, also white, with a footstool before it; and looking, as I thought, like a pale throne.

This room was chill, because it seldom had a fire; it was silent, because remote from the nursery and kitchens; solemn, because it was known to be so seldom entered. The housemaid alone came here on Saturdays, to wipe from the mirrors and the furniture a week's quiet dust; and Mrs. Reed herself, at far intervals, visited it to review the contents of a certain secret drawer in the wardrobe, where were stored divers parchments, her jewel-casket, and a miniature of her deceased husband; and in those last words lies the secret of the red-room: – the spell which kept it so lonely in spite of its grandeur.

Mr. Reed had been dead nine years: it was in this chamber he breathed his last; here he lay in state; hence his coffin was borne by the undertaker's men; and, since that day, a sense of dreary consecration had guarded it from frequent intrusion.

My seat, to which Bessie and the bitter Miss Abbot had left me riveted, was a low ottoman[2] near the marble chimney-piece; the bed rose before me; to my right hand there was the high, dark wardrobe, with subdued, broken reflections varying the gloss of its pannels; to my left were the muffled windows; a great looking-glass between them repeated the vacant majesty of the bed and room. I was not quite sure whether they had locked the door; and, when I dared move, I got up, and went to see. Alas! yes: no jail was ever more secure. Returning, I had to cross before the looking-glass; my fascinated glance involuntarily explored the depth it revealed. All looked colder and darker in that visionary hollow than in reality; and the strange little figure there gazing at me, with a white face and arms specking the gloom, and glittering eyes of fear moving where all else was still, had the effect of a real spirit: I thought it like one of the tiny phantoms, half fairy, half imp, Bessie's evening stories represented as

---

1   Marseilles is a stiff cotton fabric; a counterpane is a bedspread.
2   A cushioned seat without arms or back.

coming up out of lone, ferny dells in moors, and appearing before the eyes of belated travellers. I returned to my stool.

Superstition was with me at that moment; but it was not yet her hour for complete victory: my blood was still warm; the mood of the revolted slave was still bracing me with its bitter vigour; I had to stem a rapid rush of retrospective thought before I quailed to the dismal present.

All John Reed's violent tyrannies, all his sisters' proud indifference, all his mother's aversion, all the servants' partiality, turned up in my disturbed mind like a dark deposit in a turbid well. Why was I always suffering, always brow-beaten, always accused, for ever condemned? Why could I never please? Why was it useless to try to win any one's favour? Eliza, who was headstrong and selfish, was respected. Georgiana, who had a spoiled temper, a very acrid spite, a captious and insolent carriage, was universally indulged. Her beauty, her pink cheeks and golden curls, seemed to give delight to all who looked at her, and to purchase indemnity for every fault. John, no one thwarted, much less punished; though he twisted the necks of the pigeons, killed the little pea-chicks,[1] set the dogs at the sheep, stripped the hothouse vines of their fruit, and broke the buds off the choicest plants in the conservatory: he called his mother "old girl," too; sometimes reviled her for her dark skin, similar to his own; bluntly disregarded her wishes; not unfrequently tore and spoiled her silk attire; and he was still "her own darling." I dared commit no fault: I strove to fulfil every duty; and I was termed naughty and tiresome, sullen and sneaking, from morning to noon, and from noon to night.

My head still ached and bled with the blow and fall I had received: no one had reproved John for wantonly striking me; and because I had turned against him to avert farther irrational violence, I was loaded with general opprobrium.

"Unjust! – unjust!" said my reason, forced by the agonizing stimulus into precocious though transitory power; and Resolve, equally wrought up, instigated some strange expedient to achieve escape from insupportable oppression – as running away, or, if that could not be effected, never eating or drinking more, and letting myself die.

---

1   Peacock or peahen chicks.

What a consternation of soul was mine that dreary afternoon! How all my brain was in tumult, and all my heart in insurrection! Yet in what darkness, what dense ignorance, was the mental battle fought! I could not answer the ceaseless inward question – *why* I thus suffered: now, at the distance of – I will not say how many years, I see it clearly.

I was a discord in Gateshead-hall: I was like nobody there: I had nothing in harmony with Mrs. Reed or her children, or her chosen vassalage. If they did not love me, in fact, as little did I love them. They were not bound to regard with affection a thing that could not sympathize with one amongst them; a heterogeneous thing, opposed to them in temperament, in capacity, in propensities; a useless thing, incapable of serving their interest, or adding to their pleasure; a noxious thing, cherishing the germs of indignation at their treatment, of contempt of their judgment. I know, that had I been a sanguine, brilliant, careless, exacting, handsome, romping child – though equally dependent and friendless – Mrs. Reed would have endured my presence more complacently; her children would have entertained for me more of the cordiality of fellow-feeling; the servants would have been less prone to make me the scape-goat of the nursery.

Daylight began to forsake the red-room; it was past four o'clock, and the beclouded afternoon was tending to drear twilight. I heard the rain still beating continuously on the staircase window, and the wind howling in the grove behind the hall; I grew by degrees cold as a stone, and then my courage sank. My habitual mood of humiliation, self-doubt, forlorn depression, fell damp on the embers of my decaying ire. All said I was wicked, and perhaps I might be so: what thought had I been but just conceiving of starving myself to death? That certainly was a crime: and was I fit to die? Or was the vault under the chancel of Gateshead church an inviting bourne? In such vault I had been told did Mr. Reed lie buried; and led by this thought to recall his idea,[1] I dwelt on it with gathering dread. I could not remember him; but I knew that he was my own uncle – my mother's brother – that he had taken me when a parentless infant to his house; and that in his last moments he had required a promise of Mrs. Reed that she

---

1 i.e., to recall the idea of him.

would rear and maintain me as one of her own children. Mrs. Reed probably considered she had kept this promise; and so she had, I dare say, as well as her nature would permit her: but how could she really like an interloper not of her race, and unconnected with her, after her husband's death, by any tie? It must have been most irksome to find herself bound by a hard-wrung pledge to stand in the stead of a parent to a strange child she could not love, and to see an uncongenial alien permanently intruded on her own family group.

A singular notion dawned upon me. I doubted not – had never doubted – that if Mr. Reed had been alive he would have treated me kindly; and now, as I sat looking at the white bed and overshadowed walls – occasionally also turning a fascinated eye towards the dimly gleaming mirror – I began to recall what I had heard of dead men, troubled in their graves by the violation of their last wishes, revisiting the earth to punish the perjured and avenge the oppressed; and I thought Mr. Reed's spirit, harassed by the wrongs of his sister's child, might quit its abode – whether in the church vault or in the unknown world of the departed – and rise before me in this chamber. I wiped my tears and hushed my sobs; fearful lest any sign of violent grief might waken a preternatural voice to comfort me, or elicit from the gloom some haloed face, bending over me with strange pity. This idea, consolatory in theory, I felt would be terrible if realized: with all my might I endeavoured to stifle it – I endeavoured to be firm. Shaking my hair from my eyes, I lifted my head and tried to look boldly round the dark room: at this moment a light gleamed on the wall. Was it, I asked myself, a ray from the moon penetrating some aperture in the blind? No; moonlight was still, and this stirred: while I gazed, it glided up to the ceiling and quivered over my head. I can now conjecture readily that this streak of light was, in all likelihood, a gleam from a lantern, carried by some one across the lawn; but then, prepared as my mind was for horror, shaken as my nerves were by agitation, I thought the swift-darting beam was a herald of some coming vision from another world. My heart beat thick, my head grew hot; a sound filled my ears, which I deemed the rushing of wings: something seemed near me; I was oppressed, suffocated: endurance broke down – I uttered a wild, involuntary cry – I rushed to the door and shook the lock in desperate effort. Steps came running along the outer passage; the key turned, Bessie and Abbot entered.

"Miss Eyre, are you ill?" said Bessie.

"What a dreadful noise! it went quite through me!" exclaimed Abbot.

"Take me out! Let me go into the nursery!" was my cry.

"What for? Are you hurt? Have you seen something?" again demanded Bessie.

"Oh! I saw a light, and I thought a ghost would come." I had now got hold of Bessie's hand, and she did not snatch it from me.

"She has screamed out on purpose;" declared Abbot in some disgust. "And what a scream! If she had been in great pain one would have excused it, but she only wanted to bring us all here: I know her naughty tricks."

"What is all this?" demanded another voice peremptorily; and Mrs. Reed came along the corridor, her cap flying wide, her gown rustling stormily. "Abbot and Bessie, I believe I gave orders that Jane Eyre should be left in the red-room till I came to her myself."

"Miss Jane screamed so loud, ma'am," pleaded Bessie.

"Let her go;" was the only answer. "Loose Bessie's hand, child: you cannot succeed in getting out by these means, be assured. I abhor artifice, particularly in children; it is my duty to show you that tricks will not answer: you will now stay here an hour longer, and it is only on condition of perfect submission and stillness that I shall liberate you then."

"Oh aunt, have pity! Forgive me! I cannot endure it – let me be punished some other way! I shall be killed if—"

"Silence! This violence is all most repulsive:" and so, no doubt, she felt it. I was a precocious actress in her eyes: she sincerely looked on me as a compound of virulent passions, mean spirit, and dangerous duplicity.

Bessie and Abbot having retreated, Mrs. Reed, impatient of my now frantic anguish and wild sobs, abruptly thrust me back and locked me in, without farther parley. I heard her sweeping away; and soon after she was gone, I suppose I had a species of fit: unconsciousness closed the scene.

CHAPTER III

THE next thing I remember is, waking up with a feeling as if I had had a frightful night-mare, and seeing before me a terrible red glare, crossed with thick black bars. I heard voices, too, speaking with a hollow sound, and as if muffled by a rush of wind or water: agitation, uncertainty, and an all predominating sense of terror confused my faculties. Ere long, I became aware that some one was handling me; lifting me up and supporting me in a sitting posture: and that more tenderly than I had ever been raised or upheld before. I rested my head against a pillow or an arm, and felt easy.

In five minutes more, the cloud of bewilderment dissolved: I knew quite well that I was in my own bed, and that the red glare was the nursery fire. It was night: a candle burnt on the table; Bessie stood at the bed-foot with a basin in her hand, and a gentleman sat in a chair near my pillow, leaning over me.

I felt an inexpressible relief, a soothing conviction of protection and security, when I knew that there was a stranger in the room; an individual not belonging to Gateshead, and not related to Mrs. Reed. Turning from Bessie (though her presence was far less obnoxious to me than that of Abbot, for instance, would have been), I scrutinised the face of the gentleman: I knew him; it was Mr. Lloyd, an apothecary, sometimes called in by Mrs. Reed when the servants were ailing: for herself and the children she employed a physician.

"Well, who am I?" he asked.

I pronounced his name, offering him at the same time my hand: he took it, smiling and saying, "We shall do very well by-and-by." Then he laid me down, and addressing Bessie, charged her to be very careful that I was not disturbed during the night. Having given some further directions, and intimated that he should call again the next day, he departed; to my grief: I felt so sheltered and befriended while he sat in the chair near my pillow; and as he closed the door after him, all the room darkened and my heart again sank: inexpressible sadness weighed it down.

"Do you feel as if you should sleep, Miss?" asked Bessie, rather softly.

Scarcely dared I answer her; for I feared the next sentence might be rough. "I will try."

"Would you like to drink, or could you eat anything?"

"No, thank you, Bessie."

"Then I think I shall go to bed, for it is past twelve o'clock; but you may call me if you want anything in the night."

Wonderful civility this! It emboldened me to ask a question.

"Bessie, what is the matter with me? Am I ill?"

"You fell sick, I suppose, in the red-room with crying; you'll be better soon, no doubt."

Bessie went into the housemaid's apartment which was near. I heard her say: —

"Sarah, come and sleep with me in the nursery; I daren't for my life be alone with that poor child to-night: she might die: it's such a strange thing she should have that fit: I wonder if she saw anything. Missis was rather too hard."

Sarah came back with her; they both went to bed; they were whispering together for half an hour before they fell asleep. I caught scraps of their conversation, from which I was able only too distinctly to infer the main subject discussed.

"Something passed her, all dressed in white, and vanished" – "A great black dog behind him" – "Three loud raps on the chamber door" – "A light in the church-yard just over his grave" &c. &c.

At last both slept: the fire and the candle went out. For me, the watches of that long night passed in ghastly wakefulness; ear, eye, and mind were alike strained by dread: such dread as children only can feel.

No severe or prolonged bodily illness followed this incident of the red-room: it only gave my nerves a shock; of which I feel the reverberation to this day. Yes, Mrs. Reed, to you I owe some fearful pangs of mental suffering. But I ought to forgive you, for you knew not what you did: while rending my heart-strings, you thought you were only up-rooting my bad propensities.

Next day, by noon, I was up and dressed, and sat wrapped in a shawl by the nursery hearth. I felt physically weak and broken down; but my worse ailment was an unutterable wretchedness of mind: a wretchedness which kept drawing from me silent tears; no sooner had I wiped one salt drop from my cheek than another followed. Yet, I thought, I ought to have been happy, for none of the Reeds were there; they were all gone out in the carriage with their mama: Abbot, too, was sewing in another room, and Bessie, as she moved hither and thither, putting away toys and arranging drawers, addressed to me every now and then a word of unwonted kindness. This state of things should have been to me a paradise of peace, accustomed as I was to a life of ceaseless reprimand and thankless fagging;[1] but, in fact, my racked nerves were now in such a state that no calm could soothe, and no pleasure excite them agreeably.

Bessie had been down into the kitchen, and she brought up with her a tart on a certain brightly painted china plate, whose bird of paradise, nestling in a wreath of convolvuli[2] and rosebuds, had been wont to stir in me a most enthusiastic sense of admiration; and which plate I had often petitioned to be allowed to take in my hand in order to examine it more closely, but had always hitherto been deemed unworthy of such a privilege. This precious vessel was now placed on my knee, and I was cordially invited to eat the circlet of delicate pastry upon it. Vain favour! coming, like most other favours long deferred and often wished for, too late! I could not eat the tart; and the plumage of the bird, the tints of the flowers, seemed strangely faded: I put both plate and tart away. Bessie asked if I would have a book: the word *book* acted as a transient stimulus, and I begged her to fetch Gulliver's Travels[3] from the library. This book I had again and again perused with delight; I considered it a narrative of facts, and discovered in it a vein of interest deeper than what I found in fairy tales: for as to the elves, having sought them in vain among foxglove leaves and bells, under mushrooms and beneath the ground-ivy mantling old wall-nooks, I had at length made up my mind to the sad truth that they were all gone out of England to some savage country, where the woods were wilder and thicker, and the population more scant; whereas, Lilliput and Brobdingnag being, in my creed, solid parts of the earth's surface, I doubted not that I might one day, by taking a long voyage, see with my own eyes the little fields, houses, and trees, the diminutive people, the tiny cows, sheep, and birds of the one realm; and the corn-fields forest-high, the mighty mastiffs, the monster cats, the tower-like men and women, of the

---

1 Tiresome work; drudgery.
2 A twining plant with trumpet-shaped flowers.
3 Jonathan Swift (1667-1745) published *Gulliver's Travels* in 1726.

other.[1] Yet, when this cherished volume was now placed in my hand – when I turned over its leaves, and sought in its marvellous pictures the charm I had, till now, never failed to find – all was eerie and dreary; the giants were gaunt goblins, the pigmies malevolent and fearful imps, Gulliver a most desolate wanderer in most dread and dangerous regions. I closed the book, which I dared no longer peruse, and put it on the table, beside the untasted tart.

Bessie had now finished dusting and tidying the room, and, having washed her hands, she opened a certain little drawer, full of splendid shreds of silk and satin, and began making a new bonnet for Georgiana's doll. Meantime she sang: her song was –

> "In the days when we were gipsying,
> A long time ago."[2]

I had often heard the song before, and always with lively delight; for Bessie had a sweet voice, – at least, I thought so. But now, though her voice was still sweet, I found in its melody an indescribable sadness. Sometimes, pre-occupied with her work, she sang the refrain very low, very lingeringly; "A long time ago" came out like the saddest cadence of a funeral hymn. She passed into another ballad, this time a really doleful one.

> "My feet they are sore, and my limbs they are weary;
> Long is the way, and the mountains are wild;
> Soon will the twilight close moonless and dreary
> Over the path of the poor orphan child.

> "Why did they send me so far and so lonely,
> Up where the moors spread and grey rocks are piled?
> Men are hard-hearted, and kind angels only
> Watch o'er the steps of a poor orphan child.

---

1   Lilliput, the first kingdom Gulliver visits, is scaled approximately one-twelfth the size of the real world. Brobdingnag, the realm he encounters on his second voyage, is approximately twelve times larger than reality.
2   A popular song by Edwin Ransford (1805-76), written in 1837.

"Yet distant and soft the night breeze is blowing,
   Clouds there are none, and clear stars beam mild;
God, in His mercy, protection is showing,
   Comfort and hope to the poor orphan child.

"Ev'n should I fall, o'er the broken bridge passing,
   Or stray in the marshes, by false lights beguiled,
Still will my Father, with promise and blessing,
   Take to His bosom the poor orphan child.

"There is a thought that for strength should avail me,
   Though both of shelter and kindred despoiled:
Heaven is a home, and a rest will not fail me;
   God is a friend to the poor orphan child."[1]

"Come, Miss Jane, don't cry," said Bessie, as she finished. She might as well have said to the fire "don't burn!" But how could she divine the morbid suffering to which I was a prey? In the course of the morning Mr. Lloyd came again.

"What, already up!" said he, as he entered the nursery. "Well, nurse, how is she?"

Bessie answered that I was doing very well.

"Then she ought to look more cheerful. Come here, Miss Jane; your name is Jane, is it not?"

"Yes, sir, Jane Eyre."

"Well, you have been crying, Miss Jane Eyre, can you tell me what about? Have you any pain?"

"No, sir."

"Oh! I daresay she is crying because she could not go out with Missis in the carriage," interposed Bessie.

"Surely not! why, she is too old for such pettishness."

I thought so too; and my self-esteem being wounded by the false charge, I answered promptly, "I never cried for such a thing in my life: I hate going out in the carriage. I cry because I am miserable."

"Oh, fie, Miss!" said Bessie.

---

1 This song was apparently written by Brontë.

The good apothecary appeared a little puzzled. I was standing before him; he fixed his eyes on me very steadily: his eyes were small and grey; not very bright, but I daresay I should think them shrewd now: he had a hard-featured yet good-natured looking face. Having considered me at leisure, he said, –

"What made you ill yesterday?"

"She had a fall," said Bessie, again putting in her word.

"Fall! why that is like a baby again! Can't she manage to walk at her age? She must be eight or nine years old."

"I was knocked down," was the blunt explanation jerked out of me by another pang of mortified pride: "but that did not make me ill," I added; while Mr. Lloyd helped himself to a pinch of snuff.

As he was returning the box to his waistcoat pocket, a loud bell rang for the servants' dinner; he knew what it was. "That's for you, nurse," said he; "you can go down; I'll give Miss Jane a lecture till you come back."

Bessie would rather have stayed; but she was obliged to go, because punctuality at meals was rigidly enforced at Gateshead Hall.

"The fall did not make you ill? what did, then?" pursued Mr. Lloyd, when Bessie was gone.

"I was shut up in a room where there is a ghost, till after dark."

I saw Mr. Lloyd smile and frown at the same time: "Ghost! What, you are a baby after all! You are afraid of ghosts?"

"Of Mr. Reed's ghost I am: he died in that room, and was laid out there. Neither Bessie nor any one else will go into it at night, if they can help it; and it was cruel to shut me up alone without a candle, – so cruel that I think I shall never forget it."

"Nonsense! And is it that makes you so miserable? Are you afraid now in daylight?"

"No; but night will come again before long: and besides, I am unhappy, – very unhappy, for other things."

"What other things? Can you tell me some of them?"

How much I wished to reply fully to this question! How difficult it was to frame any answer! Children can feel, but they cannot analyze their feelings; and if the analysis is partially effected in thought, they know not how to express the result of the process in words. Fearful, however, of losing this first and only opportunity of relieving my grief by imparting it, I, after a disturbed pause, contrived to frame a meagre, though as far as it went, true response.

"For one thing, I have no father or mother, brothers or sisters."

"You have a kind aunt and cousins."

Again I paused; then bunglingly enounced: –

"But John Reed knocked me down, and my aunt shut me up in the red-room."

Mr. Lloyd a second time produced his snuff-box.

"Don't you think Gateshead Hall a very beautiful house?" asked he. "Are you not very thankful to have such a fine place to live at?"

"It is not my house, sir; and Abbot says I have less right to be here than a servant."

"Pooh! you can't be silly enough to wish to leave such a splendid place?"

"If I had anywhere else to go I should be glad to leave it; but I can never get away from Gateshead till I am a woman."

"Perhaps you may – who knows? Have you any relations besides Mrs. Reed?"

"I think not, sir."

"None belonging to your father?"

"I don't know: I asked Aunt Reed once, and she said possibly I might have some poor, low relations called Eyre, but she knew nothing about them."

"If you had such, would you like to go to them?"

I reflected. Poverty looks grim to grown people; still more so to children: they have not much idea of industrious, working, respectable poverty; they think of the word only as connected with ragged clothes, scanty food, fireless grates, rude manners and debasing vices: poverty for me was synonymous with degradation.

"No; I should not like to belong to poor people," was my reply.

"Not even if they were kind to you?"

I shook my head: I could not see how poor people had the means of being kind; and then to learn to speak like them, to adopt their manners, to be uneducated, to grow up like one of the poor women I saw sometimes nursing their children or washing their clothes at the cottage doors of the village of Gateshead: no, I was not heroic enough to purchase liberty at the price of caste.

"But are your relatives so very poor? Are they working people?"

"I cannot tell; Aunt Reed says if I have any, they must be a beggarly set: I should not like to go a begging."

"Would you like to go to school?"

Again I reflected: I scarcely knew what school was; Bessie sometimes spoke of it as a place where young ladies sat in the stocks, wore back-boards,[1] and were expected to be exceedingly genteel and precise; John Reed hated his school, and abused his master: but John Reed's tastes were no rule for mine, and if Bessie's accounts of school-discipline (gathered from the young ladies of a family where she had lived before coming to Gateshead) were somewhat appalling, her details of certain accomplishments attained by these same young ladies were, I thought, equally attractive. She boasted of beautiful paintings of landscapes and flowers by them executed; of songs they could sing and pieces they could play, of purses they could net, of French books they could translate; till my spirit was moved to emulation as I listened. Besides, school would be a complete change: it implied a long journey, an entire separation from Gateshead, an entrance into a new life.

"I should indeed like to go to school," was the audible conclusion of my musings.

"Well, well; who knows what may happen?" said Mr. Lloyd, as he got up; "The child ought to have change of air and scene;" he added, speaking to himself, "nerves not in a good state."

Bessie now returned; at the same moment the carriage was heard rolling up the gravel-walk.

"Is that your mistress, nurse?" asked Mr. Lloyd, "I should like to speak to her before I go."

Bessie invited him to walk into the breakfast-room, and led the way out. In the interview which followed between him and Mrs. Reed, I presume, from after-occurrences, that the apothecary ventured to recommend my being sent to school; and the recommendation was no doubt readily enough adopted: for as Abbot said, in discussing the subject with Bessie when both sat sewing in the nursery one night, after I was in bed, and, as they thought, asleep, "Missis

---

1   A piece of board worn strapped to the back to correct posture.

was, she dared say, glad enough to get rid of such a tiresome, ill-con-
ditioned child, who always looked as if she were watching everybody,
and scheming plots underhand." Abbot I think gave me credit for
being a sort of infantine Guy Fawkes.[1]

On that same occasion I learned, for the first time, from Miss
Abbot's communications to Bessie, that my father had been a poor
clergyman; that my mother had married him against the wishes of her
friends, who considered the match beneath her; that my grandfather
Reed was so irritated at her disobedience, he cut her off without a
shilling; that after my mother and father had been married a year, the
latter caught the typhus fever while visiting among the poor of a large
manufacturing town where his curacy was situated, and where that
disease was then prevalent; that my mother took the infection from
him, and both died within a month of each other.

Bessie, when she heard this narrative, sighed and said, "Poor Miss
Jane is to be pitied, too, Abbot."

"Yes," responded Abbot, "if she were a nice, pretty child, one might
compassionate her forlornness; but one really cannot care for such a
little toad as that."

"Not a great deal, to be sure," agreed Bessie: "at any rate a beauty
like Miss Georgiana would be more moving in the same condition."

"Yes, I doat on Miss Georgiana!" cried the fervent Abbot. "Little
darling! – with her long curls and her blue eyes, and such a sweet
colour as she has; just as if she were painted! – Bessie, I could fancy a
Welsh rabbit[2] for supper."

"So could I – with a roast onion. Come, we'll go down." They
went.

---

1   Term for a dangerous rebel. Guy Fawkes (1570–1606) was chosen to execute the
    Gunpowder Plot of 1605, when a small group of Roman Catholics conspired to
    blow up the English Houses of Parliament. The plot failed, and Fawkes was tried
    and executed.
2   Melted cheese on toast.

CHAPTER IV

FROM my discourse with Mr. Lloyd, and from the above reported conference between Bessie and Abbot, I gathered enough of hope to suffice as a motive for wishing to get well: a change seemed near, – I desired and waited it in silence. It tarried, however: days and weeks passed: I had regained my normal state of health, but no new allusion was made to the subject over which I brooded. Mrs. Reed surveyed me at times with a severe eye, but seldom addressed me: since my illness she had drawn a more marked line of separation than ever between me and her own children; appointing me a small closet to sleep in by myself, condemning me to take my meals alone, and pass all my time in the nursery while my cousins were constantly in the drawing-room. Not a hint, however, did she drop about sending me to school: still I felt an instinctive certainty that she would not long endure me under the same roof with her; for her glance, now more than ever, when turned on me, expressed an insuperable and rooted aversion.

Eliza and Georgiana, evidently acting according to orders, spoke to me as little as possible: John thrust his tongue in his cheek whenever he saw me, and once attempted chastisement; but as I instantly turned against him, roused by the same sentiment of deep ire and desperate revolt which had stirred my corruption before, he thought it better to desist, and ran from me uttering execrations and vowing I had burst his nose. I had indeed levelled at that prominent feature as hard a blow as my knuckles could inflict; and when I saw that either that or my look daunted him, I had the greatest inclination to follow up my advantage to purpose; but he was already with his mama. I heard him in a blubbering tone commence the tale of how "that nasty Jane Eyre" had flown at him like a mad cat –: he was stopped rather harshly –

"Don't talk to me about her, John: I told you not to go near her; she is not worthy of notice; I do not choose that either you or your sisters should associate with her."

Here, leaning over the bannister, I cried out suddenly and without at all deliberating on my words, –

"They are not fit to associate with me."

Mrs. Reed was rather a stout woman, but, on hearing this strange and audacious declaration, she ran nimbly up the stair, swept me like a whirlwind into the nursery, and crushing me down on the edge of my crib, dared me in an emphatic voice to rise from that place or utter one syllable during the remainder of the day.

"What would Uncle Reed say to you if he were alive?" was my scarcely voluntary demand. I say scarcely voluntary, for it seemed as if my tongue pronounced words without my will consenting to their utterance: something spoke out of me over which I had no control.

"What?" said Mrs. Reed under her breath: her usually cold, composed grey eye became troubled with a look like fear; she took her hand from my arm and gazed at me as if she really did not know whether I were child or fiend. I was now in for it.

"My Uncle Reed is in heaven and can see all you do and think; and so can papa and mama: they know how you shut me up all day long, and how you wish me dead."

Mrs. Reed soon rallied her spirits: she shook me most soundly, she boxed both my ears,[1] and then left me without a word. Bessie supplied the hiatus by a homily of an hour's length, in which she proved beyond a doubt that I was the most wicked and abandoned child ever reared under a roof. I half believed her; for I felt indeed only bad feelings surging in my breast.

November, December, and half of January passed away. Christmas and the New Year had been celebrated at Gateshead with the usual festive cheer; presents had been interchanged, dinners and evening parties given. From every enjoyment I was, of course, excluded: my share of the gaiety consisted in witnessing the daily apparelling of Eliza and Georgiana, and seeing them descend to the drawing-room, dressed out in thin muslin frocks and scarlet sashes, with hair elaborately ringletted; and afterwards, in listening to the sound of the piano or the harp played below, to the passing to and fro of the butler and footmen, to the jingling of glass and china as refreshments were handed, to the broken hum of conversation as the drawing-room doors opened and closed. When tired of this occupation, I would retire from the stair-head to the solitary and silent nursery: there,

---

1   Slapped each side of her head.

though somewhat sad, I was not miserable. To speak truth, I had not the least wish to go into company, for in company I was very rarely noticed; and if Bessie had but been kind and companionable, I should have deemed it a treat to spend the evenings quietly with her, instead of passing them under the formidable eye of Mrs. Reed, in a room full of ladies and gentlemen. But Bessie, as soon as she had dressed her young ladies, used to take herself off to the lively regions of the kitchen and housekeeper's room, generally bearing the candle along with her: I then sat with my doll on my knee, till the fire got low, glancing round occasionally to make sure that nothing worse than myself haunted the shadowy room; and when the embers sank to a dull red, I undressed hastily, tugging at knots and strings as I best might, and sought shelter from cold and darkness in my crib. To this crib I always took my doll; human beings must love something, and, in the dearth of worthier objects of affection, I contrived to find a pleasure in loving and cherishing a faded graven image, shabby as a miniature scarecrow. It puzzles me now to remember with what absurd sincerity I doated on this little toy; half-fancying it alive and capable of sensation. I could not sleep unless it was folded in my night-gown; and when it lay there safe and warm, I was comparatively happy, believing it to be happy likewise.

Long did the hours seem while I waited the departure of the company, and listened for the sound of Bessie's step on the stairs: sometimes she would come up in the interval to seek her thimble or her scissors, or perhaps to bring me something by way of supper – a bun or a cheese-cake; – then she would sit on the bed while I ate it, and when I had finished, she would tuck the clothes round me, and twice she kissed me, and said, "Good night, Miss Jane." When thus gentle, Bessie seemed to me the best, prettiest, kindest being in the world; and I wished most intensely that she would always be so pleasant and amiable, and never push me about, or scold, or task me unreasonably, as she was too often wont to do. Bessie Lee must, I think, have been a girl of good natural capacity; for she was smart in all she did, and had a remarkable knack of narrative: so, at least, I judge from the impression made on me by her nursery tales. She was pretty, too, if my recollections of her face and person are correct. I remember her as a slim young woman, with black hair, dark eyes, very nice features, and good, clear complexion; but she had a capricious and hasty temper, and indifferent ideas of principle or justice: still, such as she was, I preferred her to any one else at Gateshead Hall.

It was the fifteenth of January, about nine o'clock in the morning: Bessie was gone down to breakfast; my cousins had not yet been summoned to their mama; Eliza was putting on her bonnet and warm garden-coat to go and feed her poultry, an occupation of which she was fond: and not less so of selling the eggs to the housekeeper and hoarding up the money she thus obtained. She had a turn for traffic,[1] and a marked propensity for saving; shown not only in the vending of eggs and chickens, but also in driving hard bargains with the gardener about flower-roots, seeds and slips of plants; that functionary having orders from Mrs. Reed to buy of his young lady all the products of her parterre[2] she wished to sell: and Eliza would have sold the hair off her head if she could have made a handsome profit thereby. As to her money, she first secreted it in odd corners, wrapped in a rag or an old curl-paper; but, some of these hoards having been discovered by the housemaid, Eliza, fearful of one day losing her valued treasure, consented to intrust it to her mother, at a usurious rate of interest – fifty or sixty per cent.: which interest she exacted every quarter, keeping her accounts in a little book with anxious accuracy.

Georgiana sat on a high stool, dressing her hair at the glass and interweaving her curls with artificial flowers and faded feathers, of which she had found a store in a drawer in the attic. I was making my bed; having received strict orders from Bessie to get it arranged before she returned (for Bessie now frequently employed me as a sort of under nursery-maid, to tidy the room, dust the chairs, &c.). Having spread the quilt and folded my night-dress, I went to the window-seat to put in order some picture books and doll's house furniture scattered there; an abrupt command from Georgiana to let her playthings alone (for the tiny chairs and mirrors, the fairy plates and cups were her property) stopped my proceedings; and then, for lack of other occupation, I fell to breathing on the frost-flowers with which the window was fretted, and thus clearing a space in the glass through which I might look out on the grounds, where all was still and petrified under the influence of a hard frost.

---

1 Trade, or bargaining.
2 Level space in a garden planted with flowers.

From this window were visible the porter's lodge and the carriage road, and just as I had dissolved so much of the silver-white foliage veiling the panes, as left room to look out, I saw the gates thrown open and a carriage roll through. I watched it ascending the drive with indifference: carriages often came to Gateshead, but none ever brought visitors in whom I was interested; it stopped in front of the house, the door-bell rang loudly, the newcomer was admitted. All this being nothing to me, my vacant attention soon found livelier attraction in the spectacle of a little hungry robin, which came and chirruped on the twigs of the leafless cherry-tree nailed against the wall near the casement. The remains of my breakfast of bread and milk stood on the table, and having crumbled a morsel of roll, I was tugging at the sash to put out the crumbs on the window-sill, when Bessie came running up stairs into the nursery.

"Miss Jane, take off your pinafore:[1] what are you doing there? Have you washed your hands and face this morning?" I gave another tug before I answered, for I wanted the bird to be secure of its bread: the sash yielded; I scattered the crumbs, some on the stone sill, some on the cherry-tree bough, then closing the window, I replied: –

"No, Bessie; I have only just finished dusting."

"Troublesome, careless child! and what are you doing now? You look quite red as if you have been about some mischief: what were you opening the window for?"

I was spared the trouble of answering, for Bessie seemed in too great a hurry to listen to explanations; she hauled me to the wash-stand, inflicted a merciless, but happily brief, scrub on my face and hands with soap, water, and a coarse towel; disciplined my head with a bristly brush, denuded me of my pinafore, and then hurrying me to the top of the stairs, bid me go down directly, as I was wanted in the breakfast-room.

I would have asked who wanted me: I would have demanded if Mrs. Reed was there; but Bessie was already gone, and had closed the nursery door upon me: I slowly descended. For nearly three months I had never been called to Mrs. Reed's presence; restricted so long to the nursery, the breakfast, dining and drawing-rooms were become for me awful regions on which it dismayed me to intrude.

---

1   Washable covering worn over clothing to protect it from dirt.

I now stood in the empty hall; before me was the breakfast-room door, and I stopped, intimidated and trembling. What a miserable little poltroon[1] had fear, engendered of unjust punishment, made of me in those days! I feared to return to the nursery; I feared to go forward to the parlour; ten minutes I stood in agitated hesitation: the vehement ringing of the breakfast-room bell decided me; I *must* enter.

"Who could want me?" I asked inwardly, as with both hands I turned the stiff door-handle which, for a second or two, resisted my efforts. "What should I see besides Aunt Reed in the apartment? – a man or a woman?" The handle turned, the door unclosed, and passing through and curtseying low, I looked up at – a black pillar! – such, at least, appeared to me, at first sight, the straight, narrow, sable-clad shape standing erect on the rug: the grim face at the top was like a carved mask, placed above the shaft by way of capital.

Mrs. Reed occupied her usual seat by the fireside: she made a signal to me to approach; I did so, and she introduced me to the stony stranger with the words: "This is the little girl respecting whom I applied to you."

He, for it was a man, turned his head slowly towards where I stood, and having examined me with the two inquisitive-looking grey eyes which twinkled under a pair of bushy brows, said solemnly, and in a bass voice: "Her size is small: what is her age?"

"Ten years."

"So much?" was the doubtful answer; and he prolonged his scrutiny for some minutes. Presently he addressed me: –

"Your name, little girl?"

"Jane Eyre, sir."

In uttering these words, I looked up: he seemed to me a tall gentleman; but then I was very little; his features were large, and they and all the lines of his frame were equally harsh and prim.

"Well, Jane Eyre, and are you a good child?"

Impossible to reply to this in the affirmative: my little world held a contrary opinion: I was silent. Mrs. Reed answered for me by an expressive shake of the head, adding soon, "Perhaps the less said on that subject the better, Mr. Brocklehurst."[2]

---

1   Coward.
2   Brocklehurst was apparently based on the Reverend William Carus Wilson, the founder of Cowan Bridge school, which in turn is the model for the novel's

"Sorry indeed to hear it! she and I must have some talk;" and bending from the perpendicular, he installed his person in the armchair, opposite Mrs. Reed's. "Come here," he said.

I stepped across the rug; he placed me square and straight before him. What a face he had, now that it was almost on a level with mine! what a great nose! and what a mouth! and what large prominent teeth!

"No sight so sad as that of a naughty child," he began, "especially a naughty little girl. Do you know where the wicked go after death?"

"They go to hell," was my ready and orthodox answer.

"And what is hell? Can you tell me that?"

"A pit full of fire."

"And should you like to fall into that pit and to be burning there for ever?"

"No, sir."

"What must you do to avoid it?"

I deliberated a moment; my answer when it did come, was objectionable: "I must keep in good health, and not die."

"How can you keep in good health? Children younger than you die daily. I buried a little child of five years old only a day or two since, – a good little child, whose soul is now in heaven. It is to be feared the same could not be said of you, were you to be called hence."

Not being in a condition to remove his doubt, I only cast my eyes down on the two large feet planted on the rug, and sighed; wishing myself far enough away.

"I hope that sigh is from the heart, and that you repent of ever having been the occasion of discomfort to your excellent benefactress."

"Benefactress! benefactress!" said I inwardly: "they all call Mrs. Reed my benefactress; if so, a benefactress is a disagreeable thing."

"Do you say your prayers night and morning?" continued my interrogator.

"Yes, sir."

"Do you read your bible?"

"Sometimes."

Lowood Institution. Brontë and her sisters attended the school, and her portrayal of both it and the Reverend Wilson caused some controversy.

"With pleasure? Are you fond of it?"

"I like Revelations and the book of Daniel, and Genesis and Samuel, and a little bit of Exodus, and some parts of Kings and Chronicles, and Job and Jonah."[1]

"And the Psalms? I hope you like them."

"No, Sir."

"No? oh, shocking! I have a little boy, younger than you, who knows six Psalms by heart; and when you ask him which he would rather have, a gingerbread-nut to eat, or a verse of a Psalm to learn, he says: 'Oh! the verse of a Psalm! angels sing Psalms;' says he, 'I wish to be a little angel here below;' he then gets two nuts in recompense for his infant piety."

"Psalms are not interesting," I remarked.

"That proves you have a wicked heart; and you must pray to God to change it: to give you a new and clean one: to take away your heart of stone and give you a heart of flesh."

I was about to propound a question, touching the manner in which that operation of changing my heart was to be performed, when Mrs. Reed interposed, telling me to sit down; she then proceeded to carry on the conversation herself.

"Mr. Brocklehurst, I believe I intimated in the letter which I wrote to you three weeks ago, that this little girl has not quite the character and disposition I could wish: should you admit her into Lowood school, I should be glad if the superintendent and teachers were requested to keep a strict eye on her, and, above all, to guard against her worst fault, a tendency to deceit. I mention this in your hearing, Jane, that you may not attempt to impose on Mr. Brocklehurst."

Well might I dread, well might I dislike Mrs. Reed; for it was her nature to wound me cruelly: never was I happy in her presence: however carefully I obeyed, however strenuously I strove to please her, my efforts were still repulsed and repaid by such sentences as the above. Now, uttered before a stranger, the accusation cut me to the heart: I dimly perceived that she was already obliterating hope from the new phase of existence which she destined me to enter; I felt, though I could not have expressed the feeling, that she was sowing

---

1 Jane demonstrates a preference for biblical texts which concentrate on narrative. The Psalms, with their more introspective focus, do not interest her.

aversion and unkindness along my future path; I saw myself transformed under Mr. Brocklehurst's eye into an artful, noxious child, and what could I do to remedy the injury?

"Nothing, indeed;" thought I, as I struggled to repress a sob, and hastily wiped away some tears, the impotent evidences of my anguish.

"Deceit is, indeed, a sad fault in a child," said Mr. Brocklehurst; "it is akin to falsehood, and all liars will have their portion in the lake burning with fire and brimstone: she shall, however, be watched, Mrs. Reed; I will speak to Miss Temple and the teachers."

"I should wish her to be brought up in a manner suiting her prospects," continued my benefactress; "to be made useful, to be kept humble: as for the vacations, she will, with your permission, spend them always at Lowood."

"Your decisions are perfectly judicious, madam," returned Mr. Brocklehurst. "Humility is a christian grace, and one peculiarly appropriate to the pupils of Lowood; I, therefore, direct that especial care shall be bestowed on its cultivation amongst them. I have studied how best to mortify in them the worldly sentiment of pride, and, only the other day, I had a pleasing proof of my success. My second daughter, Augusta, went with her mama to visit the school, and on her return she exclaimed: 'Oh, dear papa, how quiet and plain all the girls at Lowood look! with their hair combed behind their ears, and their long pinafores, and those little holland[1] pockets outside their frocks – they are almost like poor people's children! and,' said she, 'they looked at my dress and mama's, as if they had never seen a silk gown before.'"

"This is the state of things I quite approve," returned Mrs. Reed; "had I sought all England over, I could scarcely have found a system more exactly fitting a child like Jane Eyre. Consistency, my dear Mr. Brocklehurst; I advocate consistency in all things."

"Consistency, madam, is the first of Christian duties; and it has been observed in every arrangement connected with the establishment of Lowood: plain fare, simple attire, unsophisticated accommodations, hardy and active habits; such is the order of the day in the house and its inhabitants."

"Quite right, sir. I may then depend upon this child being received

---

1   A smooth, hard-wearing linen fabric.

as a pupil at Lowood, and there being trained in conformity to her position and prospects?"

"Madam, you may: she shall be placed in that nursery of chosen plants – and I trust she will shew herself grateful for the inestimable privilege of her election."

"I will send her then as soon as possible, Mr. Brocklehurst; for, I assure you, I feel anxious to be relieved of a responsibility that was becoming too irksome."

"No doubt, no doubt, madam: and now I wish you good morning. I shall return to Brocklehurst-hall in the course of a week or two: my good friend, the Archdeacon, will not permit me to leave him sooner. I shall send Miss Temple notice that she is to expect a new girl, so that there will be no difficulty about receiving her. Goodbye."

"Goodbye, Mr. Brocklehurst; remember me to Mrs. and Miss Brocklehurst, and to Augusta and Theodore, and Master Broughton Brocklehurst."

"I will, madam. Little girl, here is a book entitled the 'Child's Guide;' read it with prayer, especially that part containing 'an account of the awfully sudden death of Martha G——, a naughty child addicted to falsehood and deceit.'"[1]

With these words, Mr. Brocklehurst put into my hand a thin pamphlet sewn in a cover; and having rung for his carriage, he departed.

Mrs. Reed and I were left alone: some minutes passed in silence; she was sewing, I was watching her. Mrs. Reed might be, at that time, some six or seven-and-thirty; she was a woman of robust frame, square shouldered and strong-limbed, not tall, and though stout, not obese; she had a somewhat large face, the under-jaw being much developed and very solid; her brow was low, her chin large and prominent, mouth and nose sufficiently regular; under her light eyebrows glimmered an eye devoid of ruth; her skin was dark and opaque, her hair nearly flaxen; her constitution was sound as a bell – illness never came near her; she was an exact, clever manager, her household and tenantry were thoroughly under her control; her children, only, at times defied her authority and laughed it to scorn;

---

1   Religious conduct books for children were popular in the nineteenth century. Although meant to encourage a child's love of God, they tended to concentrate on the dangers of sin and its resulting punishment. William Carus Wilson produced a magazine called *The Children's Friend* which followed this format.

she dressed well, and had a presence and port calculated to set off handsome attire.

Sitting on a low stool, a few yards from her arm-chair, I examined her figure; I perused her features. In my hand I held the tract, containing the sudden death of the Liar; to which narrative my attention had been pointed as to an appropriate warning. What had just passed; what Mrs. Reed had said concerning me to Mr. Brocklehurst; the whole tenor of their conversation, was recent, raw and stinging in my mind: I had felt every word as acutely, as I had heard it plainly; and a passion of resentment fermented now within me.

Mrs. Reed looked up from her work; her eye settled on mine, her fingers at the same time suspended their nimble movements.

"Go out of the room: return to the nursery," was her mandate. My look or something else must have struck her as offensive, for she spoke with extreme, though suppressed, irritation. I got up, I went to the door; I came back again: I walked to the window, across the room, then close up to her.

Speak I must: I had been trodden on severely and *must* turn: but how? What strength had I to dart retaliation at my antagonist? I gathered my energies and launched them in this blunt sentence: —

"I am not deceitful: if I were, I should say I loved *you*; but I declare, I do not love you: I dislike you the worst of anybody in the world except John Reed; and this book about the liar, you may give to your girl, Georgiana, for it is she who tells lies, and not I."

Mrs. Reed's hands still lay on her work inactive: her eye of ice continued to dwell freezingly on mine: —

"What more have you to say?" she asked, rather in the tone in which a person might address an opponent of adult age than such as is ordinarily used to a child.

That eye of hers, that voice, stirred every antipathy I had. Shaking from head to foot, thrilled with ungovernable excitement, I continued: —

"I am glad you are no relation of mine: I will never call you aunt again so long as I live. I will never come to see you when I am grown up; and if any one asks me how I liked you, and how you treated me, I will say the very thought of you makes me sick, and that you treated me with miserable cruelty."

"How dare you affirm that, Jane Eyre?"

"How dare I, Mrs. Reed? How dare I? Because it is the *truth*. You think I have no feelings, and that I can do without one bit of love or kindness; but I cannot live so: and you have no pity. I shall remember how you thrust me back – roughly and violently thrust me back into the red-room, and locked me up there – to my dying day; though I was in agony; though I cried out, while suffocating with distress, 'Have mercy! Have mercy, Aunt Reed!' And that punishment you made me suffer because your wicked boy struck me – knocked me down for nothing. I will tell anybody who asks me questions, this exact tale. People think you a good woman, but you are bad; hard-hearted. *You* are deceitful!"

Ere I had finished this reply, my soul began to expand, to exult, with the strangest sense of freedom, of triumph, I ever felt. It seemed as if an invisible bond had burst, and that I had struggled out into unhoped-for liberty. Not without cause was this sentiment: Mrs. Reed looked frightened; her work had slipped from her knee; she was lifting up her hands, rocking herself to and fro, and even twisting her face as if she would cry.

"Jane, you are under a mistake: what is the matter with you? Why do you tremble so violently? Would you like to drink some water?"

"No, Mrs. Reed."

"Is there anything else you wish for, Jane? I assure you, I desire to be your friend."

"Not you. You told Mr. Brocklehurst I had a bad character, a deceitful disposition; and I'll let everybody at Lowood know what you are, and what you have done."

"Jane, you don't understand these things: children must be corrected for their faults."

"Deceit is not my fault!" I cried out in a savage, high voice.

"But you are passionate, Jane, that you must allow: and now return to the nursery – there's a dear – and lie down a little."

"I am not your dear; I cannot lie down: send me to school soon, Mrs. Reed, for I hate to live here."

"I will indeed send her to school soon," murmured Mrs. Reed, *sotto voce*;[1] and gathering up her work, she abruptly quitted the apartment.

---

1   In an undertone.

I was left there alone – winner of the field. It was the hardest battle I had fought, and the first victory I had gained: I stood awhile on the rug, where Mr. Brocklehurst had stood, and I enjoyed my conqueror's solitude. First, I smiled to myself and felt elate; but this fierce pleasure subsided in me as fast as did the accelerated throb of my pulses. A child cannot quarrel with its elders, as I had done; cannot give its furious feelings uncontrolled play, as I had given mine; without experiencing afterwards the pang of remorse and the chill of reaction. A ridge of lighted heath, alive, glancing, devouring, would have been a meet emblem of my mind when I accused and menaced Mrs. Reed: the same ridge, black and blasted after the flames are dead, would have represented as meetly my subsequent condition, when half an hour's silence and reflection had shewn me the madness of my conduct, and the dreariness of my hated and hating position.

Something of vengeance I had tasted for the first time; as aromatic wine it seemed on swallowing, warm and racy: its after-flavour, metallic and corroding, gave me a sensation as if I had been poisoned.- Willingly would I now have gone and asked Mrs. Reed's pardon; but I knew, partly from experience and partly from instinct, that was the way to make her repulse me with double scorn, thereby re-exciting every turbulent impulse of my nature.

I would fain exercise some better faculty than that of fierce speaking; fain find nourishment for some less fiendish feeling than that of sombre indignation. I took a book – some Arabian tales; I sat down and endeavoured to read. I could make no sense of the subject; my own thoughts swam always between me and the page I had usually found fascinating. I opened the glass-door in the breakfast-room; the shrubbery was quite still; the black frost reigned, unbroken by sun or breeze, through the grounds. I covered my head and arms with the skirt of my frock, and went out to walk in a part of the plantation which was quite sequestered; but I found no pleasure in the silent trees, the fallen fir-cones, the congealed relics of autumn, russet leaves, swept by past winds in heaps, and now stiffened together. I leaned against a gate, and looked into an empty field where no sheep were feeding, where the short grass was nipped and blanched. It was a very grey day; a most opaque sky, "onding on snaw,"[1] canopied all;

---

1   Dialect. "Threatening to snow."

thence flakes fell at intervals, which settled on the hard path and on the hoary lea without melting. I stood, a wretched child enough, whispering to myself over and over again, "What shall I do? – what shall I do?"

All at once I heard a clear voice call, "Miss Jane! where are you? Come to lunch!"

It was Bessie, I knew well enough; but I did not stir: her light step came tripping down the path.

"You naughty little thing!" she said. "Why don't you come when you are called?"

Bessie's presence, compared with the thoughts over which I had been brooding, seemed cheerful; even though, as usual, she was somewhat cross. The fact is, after my conflict with, and victory over, Mrs. Reed, I was not disposed to care much for the nursemaid's transitory anger; and I *was* disposed to bask in her youthful lightness of heart. I just put my two arms round her, and said, "Come, Bessie! don't scold."

The action was more frank and fearless than any I was habituated to indulge in: somehow it pleased her.

"You are a strange child, Miss Jane," she said, as she looked down at me: "a little roving, solitary thing: and you are going to school, I suppose?"

I nodded.

"And won't you be sorry to leave poor Bessie?"

"What does Bessie care for me? She is always scolding me."

"Because you're such a queer, frightened, shy little thing. You should be bolder."

"What! to get more knocks?"

"Nonsense! But you are rather put upon, that's certain. My mother said, when she came to see me last week, that she would not like a little one of her own to be in your place. – Now come in, and I've some good news for you."

"I don't think you have, Bessie."

"Child! What do you mean? What sorrowful eyes you fix on me! Well! but Missis and the young ladies and Master John are going out to tea this afternoon, and you shall have tea with me. I'll ask cook to bake you a little cake, and then you shall help me to look over your drawers; for I am soon to pack your trunk. Missis intends you to leave

Gateshead in a day or two, and you shall choose what toys you like to take with you."

"Bessie, you must promise not to scold me any more till I go."

"Well, I will: but mind you are a very good girl, and don't be afraid of me. Don't start when I chance to speak rather sharply: it's so provoking."

"I don't think I shall ever be afraid of you again, Bessie, because I have got used to you, and I shall soon have another set of people to dread."

"If you dread them they'll dislike you."

"As you do, Bessie?"

"I don't dislike you, miss; I believe I am fonder of you than of all the others."

"You don't show it."

"You little sharp thing! you've got quite a new way of talking. What makes you so venturesome and hardy?"

"Why, I shall soon be away from you, and besides" – I was going to say something about what had passed between me and Mrs. Reed; but on second thoughts I considered it better to remain silent on that head.

"And so you're glad to leave me?"

"Not at all, Bessie; indeed, just now I am rather sorry."

"Just now! and rather! How coolly my little lady says it! I daresay now if I were to ask you for a kiss you wouldn't give it me: you'd say you'd *rather* not."

"I'll kiss you and welcome: bend your head down." Bessie stooped; we mutually embraced, and I followed her into the house quite comforted. That afternoon lapsed in peace and harmony; and in the evening Bessie told me some of her most enchaining stories, and sung me some of her sweetest songs. Even for me life had its gleams of sunshine.

CHAPTER V

FIVE o'clock had hardly struck on the morning of the 19th of January, when Bessie brought a candle into my closet and found me already up and nearly dressed. I had risen half an hour before her entrance, and had washed my face and put on my clothes by the light of a half-moon just setting, whose rays streamed through the narrow window near my crib. I was to leave Gateshead that day by a coach which passed the lodge gates at six a.m. Bessie was the only person yet risen; she had lit a fire in the nursery, where she now proceeded to make my breakfast. Few children can eat when excited with the thoughts of a journey; nor could I. Bessie, having pressed me in vain to take a few spoonfuls of the boiled milk and bread she had prepared for me, wrapped up some biscuits in a paper and put them into my bag; then she helped me on with my pelisse[1] and bonnet, and wrapping herself in a shawl, she and I left the nursery. As we passed Mrs. Reed's bed-room, she said, "Will you go in and bid Missis good-bye?"

"No, Bessie: she came to my crib last night when you were gone down to supper, and said I need not disturb her in the morning, or my cousins either; and she told me to remember that she had always been my best friend, and to speak of her and be grateful to her accordingly."

"What did you say, miss?"

"Nothing: I covered my face with the bedclothes, and turned from her to the wall."

"That was wrong, Miss Jane."

"It was quite right, Bessie: your Missis has not been my friend; she has been my foe."

"Oh, Miss Jane! don't say so!"

"Good-bye to Gateshead!" cried I, as we passed through the hall and went out at the front door.

The moon was set, and it was very dark; Bessie carried a lantern, whose light glanced on wet steps and gravel road sodden by a recent thaw. Raw and chill was the winter morning; my teeth chattered as I

---

1   An ankle-length mantle with armholes or sleeves.

hastened down the drive. There was a light in the porter's lodge; when we reached it we found the porter's wife just kindling her fire: my trunk, which had been carried down the evening before, stood corded at the door. It wanted but a few minutes of six, and shortly after that hour had struck, the distant roll of wheels announced the coming coach; I went to the door and watched its lamps approach rapidly through the gloom.

"Is she going by herself?" asked the porter's wife.

"Yes."

"And how far is it?"

"Fifty miles."

"What a long way! I wonder Mrs. Reed is not afraid to trust her so far alone."

The coach drew up; there it was at the gates with its four horses and its top laden with passengers: the guard and coachman loudly urged haste; my trunk was hoisted up; I was taken from Bessie's neck, to which I clung with kisses.

"Be sure and take good care of her," cried she to the guard, as he lifted me into the inside.

"Aye, aye!" was the answer: the door was clapped to, a voice exclaimed "All right," and on we drove. Thus was I severed from Bessie and Gateshead: thus whirled away to unknown, and, as I then deemed, remote and mysterious regions.

I remember but little of the journey: I only know that the day seemed to me of a preternatural length, and that we appeared to travel over hundreds of miles of road. We passed through several towns, and in one, a very large one, the coach stopped; the horses were taken out, and the passengers alighted to dine. I was carried into an inn, where the guard wanted me to have some dinner; but, as I had no appetite, he left me in an immense room with a fire-place at each end, a chandelier pendant from the ceiling, and a little red gallery high up against the wall, filled with musical instruments. Here I walked about for a long time, feeling very strange, and mortally apprehensive of some one coming in and kidnapping me: for I believed in kidnappers; their exploits having frequently figured in Bessie's fire-side chronicles. At last the guard returned; once more I was stowed away in the coach, my protector mounted his own seat, sounded his hollow horn, and away we rattled over the "stony street"[1] of L——.

The afternoon came on wet and somewhat misty; as it waned into dusk, I began to feel that we were getting very far indeed from Gateshead: we ceased to pass through towns; the country changed; great grey hills heaved up round the horizon: as twilight deepened, we descended a valley, dark with wood, and long after night had over-clouded the prospect, I heard a wild wind rushing amongst trees.

Lulled by the sound, I at last dropped asleep: I had not long slum-bered when the sudden cessation of motion awoke me; the coach-door was open, and a person like a servant was standing at it: I saw her face and dress by the light of the lamps.

"Is there a little girl called Jane Eyre here?" she asked. I answered "Yes," and was then lifted out; my trunk was handed down, and the coach instantly drove away.

I was stiff with long sitting, and bewildered with the noise and motion of the coach: gathering my faculties, I looked about me. Rain, wind, and darkness filled the air; nevertheless, I dimly discerned a wall before me and a door open in it; through this door I passed with my new guide: she shut and locked it behind her. There was now visible a house or houses – for the building spread far – with many windows, and lights burning in some; we went up a broad, pebbly path, splash-ing wet, and were admitted at a door; then the servant led me through a passage into a room with a fire, where she left me alone.

I stood and warmed my numbed fingers over the blaze, then I looked round; there was no candle, but the uncertain light from the hearth showed by intervals, papered walls, carpet, curtains, shining mahogany furniture: it was a parlour, not so spacious or splendid as the drawing-room at Gateshead, but comfortable enough. I was puz-zling to make out the subject of a picture on the wall, when the door opened, and an individual carrying a light entered; another followed close behind.

The first was a tall lady with dark hair, dark eyes, and a pale and large forehead; her figure was partly enveloped in a shawl, her coun-

---

1   Brontë quotes from Canto III.xxii.2 of *Childe Harold's Pilgrimage*. The poem was published by Byron (1788–1824) between 1812 and 1818.

tenance was grave, her bearing erect.[1]

"The child is very young to be sent alone;" said she, putting her candle down on the table. She considered me attentively for a minute or two, then further added: –

"She had better be put to bed soon; she looks tired: are you tired?" she asked, placing her hand on my shoulder.

"A little, ma'am."

"And hungry, too, no doubt: let her have some supper before she goes to bed, Miss Miller. Is this the first time you have left your parents to come to school, my little girl?"

I explained to her that I had no parents. She inquired how long they had been dead; then how old I was, what was my name, whether I could read, write, and sew a little: then she touched my cheek gently with her forefinger, and saying, "She hoped I should be a good child," dismissed me along with Miss Miller.

The lady I had left might be about twenty-nine; the one who went with me appeared some years younger: the first impressed me by her voice, look, and air. Miss Miller was more ordinary; ruddy in complexion, though of a careworn countenance; hurried in gait and action like one who had always a multiplicity of tasks on hand: she looked indeed, what I afterwards found she really was, an under-teacher. Led by her, I passed from compartment to compartment, from passage to passage, of a large and irregular building; till, emerging from the total and somewhat dreary silence pervading that portion of the house we had traversed, we came upon the hum of many voices, and presently entered a wide, long room, with great deal tables, two at each end, on each of which burnt a pair of candles, and seated all round on benches, a congregation of girls of every age from nine or ten to twenty. Seen by the dim light of the dips,[2] their number to me appeared countless, though not in reality exceeding eighty; they were uniformly dressed in brown stuff frocks of quaint fashion, and long holland pinafores. It was the hour of study; they were engaged in conning over[3] their to-morrow's task, and the hum

---

1 The character of Miss Temple is apparently based on Ann Evans, the woman who was superintendent of Cowan Bridge school while the Brontës attended it.
2 Tallow candles.
3 Memorizing.

I had heard was the combined result of their whispered repetitions.

Miss Miller signed to me to sit on a bench near the door, then walking up to the top of the long room, she cried out: —

"Monitors, collect the lesson-books and put them away!"

Four tall girls arose from different tables, and going round, gathered the books and removed them. Miss Miller again gave the word of command: —

"Monitors, fetch the supper-trays!"

The tall girls went out and returned presently, each bearing a tray, with portions of something, I knew not what, arranged thereon, and a pitcher of water and mug in the middle of each tray. The portions were handed round; those who liked took a draught of the water, the mug being common to all. When it came to my turn, I drank, for I was thirsty, but did not touch the food; excitement and fatigue rendering me incapable of eating: I now saw, however, that it was a thin oaten cake, shared into fragments.

The meal over, prayers were read by Miss Miller, and the classes filed off — two and two, up stairs. Overpowered by this time with weariness, I scarcely noticed what sort of a place the bed-room was; except that, like the school-room, I saw it was very long. To-night I was to be Miss Miller's bed-fellow; she helped me to undress: when laid down I glanced at the long rows of beds, each of which was quickly filled with two occupants; in ten minutes the single light was extinguished; amidst silence and complete darkness, I fell asleep.

The night passed rapidly: I was too tired even to dream; I only once awoke to hear the wind rave in furious gusts, and the rain fall in torrents, and to be sensible that Miss Miller had taken her place by my side. When I again unclosed my eyes, a loud bell was ringing: the girls were up and dressing; day had not yet begun to dawn, and a rush light[1] or two burnt in the room. I too rose reluctantly; it was bitter cold, and I dressed as well as I could for shivering, and washed when there was a basin at liberty: which did not occur soon, as there was but one basin to six girls, on the stands down the middle of the room. Again the bell rung; all formed in file, two and two, and in that order descended the stairs and entered the cold and dimly lit school-room:

---

1   A cheap candle made by inserting the pith of a rush in tallow.

here prayers were read by Miss Miller; afterwards she called out: –

"Form classes!"

A great tumult succeeded for some minutes, during which Miss Miller repeatedly exclaimed, "Silence!" and "Order!" When it subsided, I saw them all drawn up in four semicircles, before four chairs, placed at the four tables; all held books in their hands, and a great book, like a bible, lay on each table, before the vacant seat. A pause of some seconds succeeded, filled up by the low, vague hum of numbers; Miss Miller walked from class to class, hushing this indefinite sound.

A distant bell tinkled: immediately three ladies entered the room, each walked to a table and took her seat; Miss Miller assumed the fourth vacant chair, which was that nearest the door, and around which the smallest of the children were assembled: to this inferior class I was called, and placed at the bottom of it.

Business now began: the day's Collect[1] was repeated, then certain texts of scripture were said, and to these succeeded a protracted reading of chapters in the Bible, which lasted an hour. By the time that exercise was terminated, day had fully dawned. The indefatigable bell now sounded for the fourth time: the classes were marshalled and marched into another room to breakfast: how glad I was to behold a prospect of getting something to eat! I was now nearly sick from inanition, having taken so little the day before.

The refectory was a great, low-ceiled gloomy room; on two long tables smoked basins of something hot, which, however, to my dismay, sent forth an odour far from inviting. I saw an universal manifestation of discontent when the fumes of the repast met the nostrils of those destined to swallow it: from the van of the procession, the tall girls of the first class, rose the whispered words: –

"Disgusting! The porridge is burnt again!"

"Silence!" ejaculated a voice; not that of Miss Miller, but of one of the upper teachers, a little and dark personage, smartly dressed but of somewhat morose aspect, who installed herself at the top of one table, while a more buxom lady presided at the other. I looked in vain for her I had first seen the night before; she was not visible: Miss Miller

---

1   The prayer in the Anglican church service which is said at morning and evening. Varying from day to day, it "collects" or summarizes the thought suggested by the day's devotions.

occupied the foot of the table where I sat, and a strange foreign-look-ing, elderly lady, the French teacher, as I afterwards found, took the corresponding seat at the other board. A long grace was said and a hymn sung; then a servant brought in some tea for the teachers and the meal began.

Ravenous, and now very faint, I devoured a spoonful or two of my portion without thinking of its taste; but the first edge of hunger blunted, I perceived I had got in hand a nauseous mess: burnt por-ridge is almost as bad as rotten potatoes; famine itself soon sickens over it. The spoons were moved slowly: I saw each girl taste her food and try to swallow it; but in most cases the effort was soon relin-quished. Breakfast was over and none had breakfasted. Thanks being returned for what we had not got, and a second hymn chanted, the refectory was evacuated for the school-room. I was one of the last to go out, and in passing the tables, I saw one teacher take a basin of the porridge and taste it; she looked at the others; all their countenances expressed displeasure, and one of them, the stout one, whispered: –

"Abominable stuff! How shameful!"

A quarter of an hour passed before lessons again begun, during which the school-room was in a glorious tumult; for that space of time, it seemed to be permitted to talk loud and more freely, and they used their privilege. The whole conversation ran on the breakfast, which one and all abused roundly. Poor things! it was the sole conso-lation they had. Miss Miller was now the only teacher in the room: a group of great girls standing about her, spoke with serious and sullen gestures. I heard the name of Mr. Brocklehurst pronounced by some lips; at which Miss Miller shook her head disapprovingly; but she made no great effort to check the general wrath: doubtless she shared in it.

A clock in the schoolroom struck nine; Miss Miller left her circle and standing in the middle of the room, cried: –

"Silence! To your seats!"

Discipline prevailed: in five minutes the confused throng was re-solved into order, and comparative silence quelled the Babel clamour of tongues. The upper-teachers now punctually resumed their posts; but still, all seemed to wait. Ranged on benches down the sides of the room, the eighty girls sat motionless and erect: a quaint assemblage they appeared, all with plain locks combed from their faces, not a curl visible; in brown dresses, made high and surrounded by a narrow tucker[1] about the throat, with little pockets of holland, (shaped something like a Highlander's purse) tied in front of their frocks and destined to serve the purpose of a work-bag: all too wearing woollen stockings and country-made shoes fastened with brass buckles. Above twenty of those clad in this costume were full-grown girls; or rather young women: it suited them ill, and gave an air of oddity even to the prettiest.

I was still looking at them, and also at intervals examining the teachers – none of whom precisely pleased me; for the stout one was a little coarse, the dark one not a little fierce, the foreigner harsh and grotesque, and Miss Miller, poor thing! looked purple, weather-beaten, and over-worked – when, as my eye wandered from face to face, the whole school rose simultaneously, as if moved by a common spring.

What was the matter? I had heard no order given: I was puzzled. Ere I had gathered my wits, the classes were again seated; but as all eyes were now turned to one point, mine followed the general direction, and encountered the personage who had received me last night. She stood at the bottom of the long room, on the hearth; for there was a fire at each end: she surveyed the two rows of girls silently and gravely. Miss Miller, approaching, seemed to ask her a question, and having received her answer, went back to her place, and said aloud, –

"Monitor of the first class, fetch the globes!"

While the direction was being executed, the lady consulted moved slowly up the room. I suppose I have a considerable organ of veneration,[2] for I retain yet the sense of admiring awe with which my eyes tracked her steps. Seen now, in broad daylight, she looked tall, fair, and shapely; brown eyes, with a benignant light in their irids, and a fine pencilling of long lashes round, relieved the whiteness of her large front; on each of her temples her hair, of a very dark brown, was

---

1 A piece of lace or linen material tucked in at the neck of a dress.
2 The first of a number of references to the pseudo-science of phrenology. Originated by the Austrian physician Franz Joseph Gall (1758-1828), it attempts to relate the mental and temperamental characteristics of an individual to the bumps and hollows of the skull.

clustered in round curls, according to the fashion of those times, when neither smooth bands nor long ringlets were in vogue; her dress, also in the mode of the day, was of purple cloth, relieved by a sort of Spanish trimming of black velvet; a gold watch (watches were not so common then as now) shone at her girdle. Let the reader add, to complete the picture, refined features; a complexion, if pale, clear; and a stately air and carriage, and he will have, at least as clearly as words can give it, a correct idea of the exterior of Miss Temple, – Maria Temple, as I afterwards saw the name written in a prayer-book entrusted to me to carry to church.

The superintendent of Lowood (for such was this lady) having taken her seat before a pair of globes placed on one of the tables, summoned the first class round her, and commenced giving a lesson in geography; the lower classes were called by the teachers: repetitions in history, grammar, &c. went on for an hour; writing and arithmetic succeeded, and music lessons were given by Miss Temple to some of the elder girls. The duration of each lesson was measured by the clock, which at last struck twelve. The superintendent rose: –

"I have a word to address to the pupils," said she.

The tumult of cessation from lessons was already breaking forth, but it sunk at her voice. She went on: –

"You had this morning a breakfast which you could not eat: you must be hungry: – I have ordered that a lunch of bread and cheese shall be served to all."

The teachers looked at her with a sort of surprise.

"It is to be done on my responsibility," she added, in an explanatory tone to them, and immediately afterwards left the room.

The bread and cheese was presently brought in and distributed, to the high delight and refreshment of the whole school. The order was now given "To the garden!" Each put on a coarse straw bonnet, with strings of coloured calico,[1] and a cloak of grey frieze.[2] I was similarly equipped, and, following the stream, I made my way into the open air.

The garden was a wide enclosure, surrounded with walls so high as to exclude every glimpse of prospect; a covered verandah ran down

---

1   Plain cotton cloth.
2   Coarse woollen cloth with a nap on only one side.

one side, and broad walks bordered a middle space divided into scores of little beds: these beds were assigned as gardens for the pupils to cultivate, and each bed had an owner. When full of flowers they would, doubtless, look pretty; but now, at the latter end of January, all was wintry blight and brown decay. I shuddered as I stood and looked round me: it was an inclement day for out-door exercise; not positively rainy, but darkened by a drizzling yellow fog; all underfoot was still soaking wet with the floods of yesterday. The stronger among the girls ran about and engaged in active games, but sundry pale and thin ones herded together for shelter and warmth in the verandah; and amongst these, as the dense mist penetrated to their shivering frames, I heard frequently the sound of a hollow cough.

As yet I had spoken to no one, nor did anybody seem to take notice of me; I stood lonely enough: but to that feeling of isolation I was accustomed; it did not oppress me much. I leant against a pillar of the verandah, drew my grey mantle close about me, and trying to forget the cold which nipped me without, and the unsatisfied hunger which gnawed me within, delivered myself up to the employment of watching and thinking. My reflections were too undefined and fragmentary to merit record: I hardly yet knew where I was; Gateshead and my past life seemed floated away to an immeasurable distance; the present was vague and strange, and of the future I could form no conjecture. I looked round the convent-like garden, and then up at the house; a large building, half of which seemed grey and old, the other half quite new. The new part, containing the school-room and dormitory, was lit by mullioned and latticed windows, which gave it a church-like aspect; a stone-tablet over the door bore this inscription: – "Lowood Institution. – This portion was rebuilt A.D. —, by Naomi Brocklehurst, of Brocklehurst Hall, in this county." "Let your light so shine before men that they may see your good works, and glorify your Father which is in heaven." – St. Matt. v. 16.

I read these words over and over again: I felt that an explanation belonged to them, and was unable fully to penetrate their import. I was still pondering the signification of "Institution," and endeavouring to make out a connection between the first words and the verse of scripture, when the sound of a cough close behind me, made me turn my head. I saw a girl sitting on a stone bench near;[1] she was bent over a book, on the perusal of which she seemed intent: from where I stood I could see the title – it was "Rasselas;"[2] a name that struck me as strange, and consequently attractive. In turning a leaf she happened to look up, and I said to her directly: –

"Is your book interesting?" I had already formed the intention of asking her to lend it to me some day.

"I like it," she answered, after a pause of a second or two, during which she examined me.

"What is it about?" I continued. I hardly know where I found the hardihood thus to open a conversation with a stranger; the step was contrary to my nature and habits: but I think her occupation touched a chord of sympathy somewhere; for I too liked reading, though of a frivolous and childish kind; I could not digest or comprehend the serious or substantial.

"You may look at it," replied the girl, offering me the book.

I did so; a brief examination convinced me that the contents were less taking than the title: "Rasselas" looked dull to my trifling taste; I saw nothing about fairies, nothing about genii; no bright variety seemed spread over the closely printed pages. I returned it to her; she received it quietly, and without saying anything, she was about to relapse into her former studious mood: again I ventured to disturb her: –

"Can you tell me what the writing on that stone over the door, means? What is Lowood Institution?"

"This house where you are come to live."

"And why do they call it Institution? Is it in any way different from other schools?"

"It is partly a charity-school: you and I, and all the rest of us are charity-children. I suppose you are an orphan: are not either your father or your mother dead?"

"Both died before I can remember."

---

1   The character of Helen Burns is based on Brontë's sister Maria, who died of tuberculosis at the age of eleven. Brontë at least partially blamed her death on the conditions at Cowan Bridge; she insisted that she did not exaggerate her sister's "saintly"
qualities in her portrayal of Helen.

2   Samuel Johnson (1709-84) published his didactic romance *The History of Rasselas,
Prince of Abyssinia* in 1759.

"Well, all the girls here have lost either one or both parents, and this is called an institution for educating orphans."

"Do we pay no money? Do they keep us for nothing?"

"We pay, or our friends pay, fifteen pounds a year for each."

"Then why do they call us charity-children?"

"Because fifteen pounds is not enough for board and teaching, and the deficiency is supplied by subscription."

"Who subscribes?"

"Different benevolent-minded ladies and gentlemen in this neighbourhood and in London."

"Who was Naomi Brocklehurst?"

"The lady who built the new part of this house as that tablet records, and whose son overlooks and directs everything here."

"Why?"

"Because he is treasurer and manager of the establishment."

"Then this house does not belong to that tall lady who wears a watch, and who said we were to have some bread and cheese?"

"To Miss Temple? Oh no! I wish it did: she has to answer to Mr. Brocklehurst for all she does. Mr. Brocklehurst buys all our food and all our clothes."

"Does he live here?"

"No – two miles off, at a large hall."

"Is he a good man?"

"He is a clergyman, and is said to do a great deal of good."

"Did you say that tall lady was called Miss Temple?"

"Yes."

"And what are the other teachers called?"

"The one with red cheeks is called Miss Smith; she attends to the work, and cuts out – for we make our own clothes, our frocks, and pelisses, and everything; the little one with black hair is Miss Scatcherd; she teaches history and grammar, and hears the second class repetitions; and the one who wears a shawl, and has a pocket-handkerchief tied to her side with a yellow ribband, is Madame Pierrot: she comes from Lisle, in France, and teaches French."

"Do you like the teachers?"

"Well enough."

"Do you like the little black one, and the Madame —? – I cannot pronounce her name as you do."

"Miss Scatcherd is hasty – you must take care not to offend her; Madame Pierrot is not a bad sort of person."

"But Miss Temple is the best – isn't she?"

"Miss Temple is very good, and very clever: she is above the rest, because she knows far more than they do."

"Have you been long here?"

"Two years."

"Are you an orphan?"

"My mother is dead."

"Are you happy here?"

"You ask rather too many questions. I have given you answers enough for the present; now I want to read."

But at that moment the summons sounded for dinner: all re-entered the house. The odour which now filled the refectory was scarcely more appetizing than that which had regaled our nostrils at breakfast: the dinner was served in two huge tin-plated vessels, whence rose a strong steam redolent of rancid fat. I found the mess to consist of indifferent potatoes and strange shreds of rusty[1] meat, mixed and cooked together. Of this preparation a tolerably abundant plateful was apportioned to each pupil. I ate what I could, and wondered within myself whether every day's fare would be like this.

After dinner we immediately adjourned to the schoolroom: lessons recommenced, and were continued till five o'clock.

The only marked event of the afternoon was, that I saw the girl with whom I had conversed in the verandah, dismissed in disgrace, by Miss Scatcherd, from a history class, and sent to stand in the middle of the large school-room. The punishment seemed to me in a high degree ignominious, especially for so great a girl – she looked thirteen or upwards. I expected she would show signs of great distress and shame; but to my surprise she neither wept nor blushed: composed, though grave, she stood, the central mark of all eyes. "How can she bear it so quietly – so firmly?" I asked of myself. "Were I in her place, it seems to me I should wish the earth to open and swallow me up. She looks as if she were thinking of something beyond her punish-

---

1 Rancid.

ment – beyond her situation: of something not round her nor before her. I have heard of day-dreams – is she in a day-dream now? Her eyes are fixed on the floor, but I am sure they do not see it – her sight seems turned in, gone down into her heart: she is looking at what she can remember, I believe; not at what is really present. I wonder what sort of a girl she is – whether good or naughty."

Soon after five p.m. we had another meal, consisting of a small mug of coffee, and half a slice of brown bread. I devoured my bread and drank my coffee with relish; but I should have been glad of as much more – I was still hungry. Half an hour's recreation succeeded, then study; then the glass of water and the piece of oat-cake, prayers, and bed. Such was my first day at Lowood.

CHAPTER VI

THE next day commenced as before, getting up and dressing by rush-light; but this morning we were obliged to dispense with the cere-mony of washing: the water in the pitchers was frozen. A change had taken place in the weather the preceding evening, and a keen north-east wind, whistling through the crevices of our bed-room windows all night long, had made us shiver in our beds, and turned the con-tents of the ewers to ice.

Before the long hour and a half of prayers and bible reading was over, I felt ready to perish with cold. Breakfast-time came at last, and this morning the porridge was not burnt; the quality was eatable, the quantity small: how small my portion seemed! I wished it had been doubled.

In the course of the day I was enrolled a member of the fourth class, and regular tasks and occupations were assigned me: hitherto, I had only been a spectator of the proceedings at Lowood, I was now to become an actor therein. At first, being little accustomed to learn by heart, the lessons appeared to me both long and difficult: the frequent change from task to task, too, bewildered me; and I was glad, when, about three o'clock in the afternoon, Miss Smith put into my hands a border of muslin two yards long, together with needle, thimble, &c., and sent me to sit in a quiet corner of the school-room, with direc-tions to hem the same. At that hour most of the others were sewing likewise; but one class still stood round Miss Scatcherd's chair reading, and as all was quiet, the subject of their lessons could be heard, together with the manner in which each girl acquitted herself, and the animadversions[1] or commendations of Miss Scatcherd on the per-formance. It was English history: among the readers, I observed my acquaintance of the verandah; at the commencement of the lesson, her place had been at the top of the class, but for some error of pro-nunciation or some inattention to stops, she was suddenly sent to the very bottom. Even in that obscure position, Miss Scatcherd continued to make her an object of constant notice; she was continually address-ing to her such phrases as the following: –

---

1   Criticisms.

"Burns, (such it seems was her name: the girls here, were all called by their surnames, as boys are elsewhere); Burns, you are standing on the side of your shoe, turn your toes out immediately." "Burns, you poke your chin most unpleasantly, draw it in." "Burns, I insist on your holding your head up: I will not have you before me in that attitude," &c. &c.

A chapter having been read through twice, the books were closed and the girls examined. The lesson had comprised part of the reign of Charles I.,[1] and there were sundry questions about tonnage and poundage, and ship-money, which most of them appeared unable to answer; still, every little difficulty was solved instantly when it reached Burns: her memory seemed to have retained the substance of the whole lesson, and she was ready with answers on every point. I kept expecting that Miss Scatcherd would praise her attention; but, instead of that, she suddenly cried out:

"You dirty, disagreeable girl! you have never cleaned your nails this morning!"

Burns made no answer: I wondered at her silence.

"Why," thought I, "does she not explain that she could neither clean her nails nor wash her face, as the water was frozen?"

My attention was now called off by Miss Smith, desiring me to hold a skein of thread: while she was winding it, she talked to me from time to time, asking, whether I had ever been at school before, whether I could mark, stitch, knit, &c.; till she dismissed me, I could not pursue my observations on Miss Scatcherd's movements. When I returned to my seat, that lady was just delivering an order, of which I did not catch the import; but Burns immediately left the class, and, going into the small inner room where the books were kept, returned in half a minute, carrying in her hand a bundle of twigs tied together at one end. This ominous tool she presented to Miss Scatcherd with a respectful curtsey; then she quietly, and without being told, unloosed her pinafore, and the teacher instantly and sharply inflicted on her neck a dozen strokes with the bunch of twigs. Not a tear rose to Burns's eye; and, while I paused from my sewing, because my fingers quivered at this spectacle with a sentiment of unavailing and impotent

---

1   Charles I (1600-49) became King of England in 1625.

anger, not a feature of her pensive face altered its ordinary expression.

"Hardened girl!" exclaimed Miss Scatcherd, "nothing can correct you of your slatternly habits: carry the rod away."

Burns obeyed: I looked at her narrowly as she emerged from the book-closet; she was just putting back her handkerchief into her pocket, and the trace of a tear glistened on her thin cheek.

The play-hour in the evening I thought the pleasantest fraction of the day at Lowood: the bit of bread, the draught of coffee swallowed at five o'clock had revived vitality, if it had not satisfied hunger; the long restraint of the day was slackened; the school-room felt warmer than in the morning: its fires being allowed to burn a little more brightly to supply, in some measure, the place of candles, not yet introduced; the ruddy gloaming, the licensed uproar, the confusion of many voices gave one a welcome sense of liberty.

On the evening of the day on which I had seen Miss Scatcherd flog her pupil, Burns, I wandered as usual among the forms and tables and laughing groups without a companion, yet not feeling lonely: when I passed the windows, I now and then lifted a blind and looked out; it snowed fast, a drift was already forming against the lower panes; putting my ear close to the window, I could distinguish from the gleeful tumult within, the disconsolate moan of the wind outside.

Probably, if I had lately left a good home and kind parents, this would have been the hour when I should most keenly have regretted the separation: that wind would then have saddened my heart; this obscure chaos would have disturbed my peace: as it was I derived from both a strange excitement, and reckless and feverish, I wished the wind to howl more wildly, the gloom to deepen to darkness, and the confusion to rise to clamour.

Jumping over forms and creeping under tables, I made my way to one of the fire-places: there, kneeling by the high wire fender, I found Burns, absorbed, silent, abstracted from all round her by the companionship of a book, which she read by the dim glare of the embers.

"Is it still Rasselas?" I asked, coming behind her.

"Yes;" she said, "and I have just finished it."

And in five minutes more she shut it up. I was glad of this.

"Now," thought I, "I can perhaps get her to talk." I sat down by her on the floor.

"What is your name besides Burns?"

"Helen."

"Do you come a long way from here?"

"I come from a place farther north; quite on the borders of Scotland."

"Will you ever go back?"

"I hope so; but nobody can be sure of the future."

"You must wish to leave Lowood?"

"No: why should I? I was sent to Lowood to get an education; and it would be of no use going away until I have attained that object."

"But that teacher, Miss Scatcherd, is so cruel to you?"

"Cruel? Not at all! She is severe: she dislikes my faults."

"And if I were in your place I should dislike her: I should resist her; if she struck me with that rod, I should get it from her hand; I should break it under her nose."

"Probably you would do nothing of the sort: but if you did, Mr. Brocklehurst would expel you from the school; that would be a great grief to your relations. It is far better to endure patiently a smart which nobody feels but yourself, than to commit a hasty action whose evil consequences will extend to all connected with you – and besides, the Bible bids us return good for evil."

"But then it seems disgraceful to be flogged, and to be sent to stand in the middle of a room full of people; and you are such a great girl: I am far younger than you and I could not bear it."

"Yet it would be your duty to bear it, if you could not avoid it: it is weak and silly to say you *cannot bear* what it is your fate to be required to bear."

I heard her with wonder: I could not comprehend this doctrine of endurance; and still less could I understand or sympathise with the forbearance she expressed for her chastiser. Still I felt that Helen Burns considered things by a light invisible to my eyes. I suspected she might be right and I wrong; but I would not ponder the matter deeply: like Felix, I put it off to a more convenient season.[1]

"You say you have faults, Helen: what are they? To me you seem very good."

---

1 See Acts 24:25.

"Then learn from me, not to judge by appearances: I am, as Miss Scatcherd said, slatternly; I seldom put, and never keep things in order; I am careless; I forget rules; I read when I should learn my lessons; I have no method; and sometimes I say, like you, I cannot *bear* to be subjected to systematic arrangements. This is all very provoking to Miss Scatcherd, who is naturally neat, punctual and particular."

"And cross and cruel," I added; but Helen Burns would not admit my addition: she kept silence.

"Is Miss Temple as severe to you as Miss Scatcherd?"

At the utterance of Miss Temple's name, a soft smile flitted over her grave face.

"Miss Temple is full of goodness; it pains her to be severe to any one, even the worst in the school: she sees my errors, and tells me of them gently; and, if I do anything worthy of praise, she gives me my meed[1] liberally. One strong proof of my wretchedly defective nature is, that even her expostulations, so mild, so rational, have no influence to cure me of my faults; and even her praise, though I value it most highly, cannot stimulate me to continued care and foresight."

"That is curious," said I: "it is so easy to be careful."

"For *you* I have no doubt it is. I observed you in your class this morning, and saw you were closely attentive: your thoughts never seemed to wander while Miss Miller explained the lesson and questioned you. Now, mine continually rove away: when I should be listening to Miss Scatcherd, and collecting all she says with assiduity, often I lose the very sound of her voice; I fall into a sort of dream. Sometimes I think I am in Northumberland, and that the noises I hear round me are the bubbling of a little brook which runs through Deepden, near our house; – then, when it comes to my turn to reply, I have to be wakened; and, having heard nothing of what was real for listening to the visionary brook, I have no answer ready."

"Yet how well you replied this afternoon!"

"It was mere chance: the subject on which we had been reading had interested me. This afternoon, instead of dreaming of Deepden, I was wondering how a man who wished to do right could act so unjustly and unwisely as Charles the First sometimes did; and

---

1 Reward by praise.

I thought what a pity it was that, with his integrity and con-
scientiousness, he could see no farther than the prerogatives of the
crown. If he had but been able to look to a distance, and see how
what they call the spirit of the age was tending! Still, I like Charles –
I respect him – I pity him, poor murdered king! Yes, his enemies
were the worst: they shed blood they had no right to shed. How
dared they kill him!"[1]

Helen was talking to herself now: she had forgotten I could not
very well understand her – that I was ignorant, or nearly so, of the
subject she discussed. I recalled her to my level.

"And when Miss Temple teaches you, do your thoughts wander
then?"

"No, certainly, not often; because Miss Temple has generally something to say which is newer than my own reflections: her language is
singularly agreeable to me, and the information she communicates is
often just what I wished to gain."

"Well, then, with Miss Temple you are good?"

"Yes, in a passive way: I make no effort; I follow as inclination
guides me. There is no merit in such goodness."

"A great deal: you are good to those who are good to you. It is all
I ever desire to be. If people were always kind and obedient to those
who are cruel and unjust, the wicked people would have it all their
own way: they would never feel afraid, and so they would never alter,
but would grow worse and worse. When we are struck at without a
reason, we should strike back again very hard; I am sure we should –
so hard as to teach the person who struck us never to do it again."

"You will change your mind, I hope, when you grow older: as yet
you are but a little untaught girl."

"But I feel this, Helen: I must dislike those who, whatever I do to
please them, persist in disliking me; I must resist those who punish
me unjustly. It is as natural as that I should love those who show me
affection, or submit to punishment when I feel it is deserved."

"Heathens and savage tribes hold that doctrine, but Christians and
civilised nations disown it."

"How? I don't understand."

1   Charles I was executed by the Puritan parliament on January 30, 1649.

"It is not violence that best overcomes hate – nor vengeance that most certainly heals injury."

"What then?"

"Read the New Testament, and observe what Christ says, and how he acts – make his word your rule, and his conduct your example."

"What does he say?"

"Love your enemies; bless them that curse you; do good to them that hate you and despitefully use you."[1]

"Then I should love Mrs. Reed, which I cannot do; I should bless her son John, which is impossible."

In her turn, Helen Burns asked me to explain; and I proceeded forthwith to pour out in my own way the tale of my sufferings and resentments. Bitter and truculent when excited, I spoke as I felt, without reserve or softening.

Helen heard me patiently to the end: I expected she would then make a remark, but she said nothing.

"Well," I asked impatiently, "Is not Mrs. Reed a hard-hearted, bad woman?"

"She has been unkind to you, no doubt; because, you see, she dislikes your cast of character, as Miss Scatcherd does mine: but how minutely you remember all she has done and said to you! What a singularly deep impression her injustice seems to have made on your heart! No ill usage so brands its record on my feelings. Would you not be happier if you tried to forget her severity, together with the passionate emotions it excited? Life appears to me too short to be spent in nursing animosity, or registering wrongs. We are and must be, one and all, burdened with faults in this world: but the time will soon come when, I trust, we shall put them off in putting off our corruptible bodies;[2] when debasement and sin will fall from us with this cumbrous frame of flesh, and only the spark of the spirit will remain, – the impalpable principle of life and thought, pure as when it left the Creator to inspire the creature: whence it came it will return; perhaps again to be communicated to some being higher than man – perhaps to pass through gradations of glory, from the pale human

---

1   Matthew 5:44.
2   See 1 Corinthians 15:52-53.

soul to brighten to the seraph![1] Surely it will never, on the contrary, be suffered to degenerate from man to fiend? No; I cannot believe that: I hold another creed; which no one ever taught me, and which I seldom mention; but in which I delight, and to which I cling; for it extends hope to all: it makes Eternity a rest — a mighty home, not a terror and an abyss. Besides, with this creed, I can so clearly distinguish between the criminal and his crime; I can so sincerely forgive the first while I abhor the last: with this creed revenge never worries my heart, degradation never too deeply disgusts me, injustice never crushes me too low: I live in calm, looking to the end."

Helen's head, always drooping, sank a little lower as she finished this sentence. I saw by her look she wished no longer to talk to me, but rather to converse with her own thoughts. She was not allowed much time for meditation: a monitor, a great rough girl, presently came up, exclaiming in a strong Cumberland accent: –

"Helen Burns, if you don't go and put your drawer in order, and fold up your work this minute, I'll tell Miss Scatcherd to come and look at it!"

Helen sighed as her reverie fled, and getting up, obeyed the monitor without reply as without delay.

---

1 A seraph is one of the highest beings in the hierarchy of heaven. For the idea of "gradations of glory" see 2 Corinthians 3:18.

CHAPTER VII

My first quarter at Lowood seemed an age; and not the golden age either: it comprised an irksome struggle with difficulties in habituating myself to new rules and unwonted tasks. The fear of failure in these points harassed me worse than the physical hardships of my lot; though these were no trifles.

During January, February, and part of March, the deep snows, and after their melting, the almost impassable roads prevented our stirring beyond the garden walls, except to go to church; but within these limits we had to pass an hour every day in the open air. Our clothing was insufficient to protect us from the severe cold: we had no boots, the snow got into our shoes and melted there; our ungloved hands became numbed and covered with chilblains, as were our feet:[1] I remember well the distracting irritation I endured from this cause, every evening when my feet inflamed; and the torture of thrusting the swelled, raw and stiff toes into my shoes in the morning. Then the scanty supply of food was distressing: with the keen appetites of growing children, we had scarcely sufficient to keep alive a delicate invalid. From this deficiency of nourishment resulted an abuse, which pressed hardly on the younger pupils: whenever the famished great girls had an opportunity, they would coax or menace the little ones out of their portion. Many a time I have shared between two claimants the precious morsel of brown bread distributed at tea-time; and after relinquishing to a third, half the contents of my mug of coffee, I have swallowed the remainder with an accompaniment of secret tears, forced from me by the exigency of hunger.

Sundays were dreary days in that wintry season. We had to walk two miles to Brocklebridge church,[2] where our patron officiated: we set out cold, we arrived at church colder; during the morning service we became almost paralyzed. It was too far to return to dinner, and an allowance of cold meat and bread, in the same penurious proportion observed in our ordinary meals, was served round between the services.

---

1 Chilblains are itchy swellings which result from exposure to cold and poor blood circulation.

2 Tunstall church, which Brontë and the other girls from Cowan Bridge school attended.

At the close of the afternoon service, we returned by an exposed and hilly road, where the bitter winter wind, blowing over a range of snowy summits to the north, almost flayed the skin from our faces.

I can remember Miss Temple walking lightly and rapidly along our drooping line, her plaid cloak, which the frosty wind fluttered, gathered close about her, and encouraging us, by precept and example, to keep up our spirits, and march forward, as she said, "like stalwart soldiers." The other teachers, poor things, were generally themselves too much dejected to attempt the task of cheering others.

How we longed for the light and heat of a blazing fire when we got back! But, to the little ones at least, this was denied: each hearth in the school-room was immediately surrounded by a double row of great girls, and behind them the younger children crouched in groups, wrapping their starved[1] arms in their pinafores.

A little solace came at tea-time, in the shape of a double ration of bread – a whole, instead of a half- slice – with the delicious addition of a thin scrape of butter: it was the hebdomadal[2] treat to which we all looked forward from Sabbath to Sabbath. I generally contrived to reserve a moiety[3] of this bounteous repast for myself; but the remainder I was invariably obliged to part with.

The Sunday evening was spent in repeating, by heart, the Church Catechism, and the fifth, sixth, and seventh chapters of St. Matthew;[4] and in listening to a long sermon, read by Miss Miller, whose irrepressible yawns attested her weariness. A frequent interlude of these performances was the enactment of the part of Eutychus[5] by some half dozen of little girls; who, overpowered with sleep, would fall down, if not out of the third loft, yet off the fourth form, and be taken up half dead. The remedy was to thrust them forward into the centre of the school-room, and oblige them to stand there till the sermon was finished. Sometimes their feet failed them, and they sank together in a heap; they were then propped up with the monitors' high stools.

I have not yet alluded to the visits of Mr. Brocklehurst; and indeed

---

1   "Starved" for warmth; i.e., numb with cold.
2   Weekly.
3   Half.
4   The Sermon on the Mount.
5   See Acts 20:9.

that gentleman was from home during the greater part of the first month after my arrival; perhaps prolonging his stay with his friend the archdeacon: his absence was a relief to me. I need not say that I had my own reasons for dreading his coming: but come he did at last.

One afternoon (I had then been three weeks at Lowood), as I was sitting with a slate in my hand, puzzling over a sum in long division, my eyes, raised in abstraction to the window, caught sight of a figure just passing: I recognised almost instinctively that gaunt outline; and when, two minutes after, all the school, teachers included, rose *en masse*, it was not necessary for me to look up in order to ascertain whose entrance they thus greeted. A long stride measured the school-room, and presently beside Miss Temple, who herself had risen, stood the same black column which had frowned on me so ominously from the hearth-rug of Gateshead. I now glanced sideways at this piece of architecture. Yes, I was right: it was Mr. Brocklehurst, buttoned up in a surtout,[1] and looking longer, narrower, and more rigid than ever.

I had my own reasons for being dismayed at this apparition: too well I remembered the perfidious hints given by Mrs. Reed about my disposition, &c.; the promise pledged by Mr. Brocklehurst to apprize Miss Temple and the teachers of my vicious nature. All along I had been dreading the fulfilment of this promise, – I had been looking out daily for the "Coming Man," whose information respecting my past life and conversation was to brand me as a bad child for ever: now there he was. He stood at Miss Temple's side; he was speaking low in her ear: I did not doubt he was making disclosures of my villainy; and I watched her eye with painful anxiety, expecting every moment to see its dark orb turn on me a glance of repugnance and contempt. I listened too; and as I happened to be seated quite at the top of the room, I caught most of what he said: its import relieved me from immediate apprehension.

"I suppose, Miss Temple, the thread I bought at Lowton will do; it struck me that it would be just of the quality for the calico chemises, and I sorted the needles to match. You may tell Miss Smith that I for-got to make a memorandum of the darning needles, but she shall have some papers sent in next week; and she is not, on any account, to give

---

1   A tight overcoat.

out more than one at a time to each pupil: if they have more, they are apt to be careless and lose them. And, oh, ma'am! I wish the woollen stockings were better looked to! – when I was here last I went into the kitchen-garden and examined the clothes drying on the line; there was a quantity of black hose in a very bad state of repair: from the size of the holes in them I was sure they had not been well mended from time to time."

He paused.

"Your directions shall be attended to, sir," said Miss Temple.

"And, ma'am," he continued, "the laundress tells me some of the girls have two clean tuckers in the week; it is too much: the rules limit them to one."

"I think I can explain that circumstance, sir. Agnes and Catherine Johnstone were invited to take tea with some friends at Lowton last Thursday, and I gave them leave to put on clean tuckers for the occasion."

Mr. Brocklehurst nodded.

"Well, for once it may pass; but please not to let the circumstance occur too often. And there is another thing which surprised me: I find, in settling accounts with the housekeeper, that a lunch, consisting of bread and cheese, has twice been served out to the girls during the past fortnight. How is this? I looked over the regulations, and I find no such meal as lunch mentioned. Who introduced this innovation? and by what authority?"

"I must be responsible for the circumstance, sir," replied Miss Temple: "the breakfast was so ill prepared that the pupils could not possibly eat it; and I dared not allow them to remain fasting till dinner time."

"Madam, allow me an instant! – You are aware that my plan in bringing up these girls is, not to accustom them to habits of luxury and indulgence, but to render them hardy, patient, self-denying. Should any little accidental disappointment of the appetite occur, such as the spoiling of a meal, the under or the over dressing of a dish, the incident ought not to be neutralized by replacing with something more delicate the comfort lost, thus pampering the body and obviating the aim of this institution; it ought to be improved to the spiritual edification of the pupils, by encouraging them to evince fortitude under the temporary privation. A brief address on those occasions would not be mistimed, wherein a judicious instructor would take the opportunity of referring to the sufferings of the primitive Christians; to the torments of martyrs; to the exhortations of our blessed Lord himself, calling upon his disciples to take up their cross and follow him; to his warnings that man shall not live by bread alone, but by every word that proceedeth out of the mouth of God; to his divine consolations, 'if ye suffer hunger or thirst for my sake, happy are ye.'[1] Oh, madam, when you put bread and cheese, instead of burnt porridge into these children's mouths, you may indeed feed their vile bodies, but you little think how you starve their immortal souls!"

Mr. Brocklehurst again paused – perhaps overcome by his feelings. Miss Temple had looked down when he first began to speak to her; but she now gazed straight before her, and her face, naturally pale as marble, appeared to be assuming also the coldness and fixity of that material: especially her mouth closed as if it would have required a sculptor's chisel to open it, and her brow settled gradually into petrified severity.

Meantime, Mr. Brocklehurst, standing on the hearth with his hands behind his back, majestically surveyed the whole school. Suddenly his eye gave a blink, as if it had met something that either dazzled or shocked its pupil; turning, he said in more rapid accents than he had hitherto used: –

"Miss Temple, Miss Temple, what – *what* is that girl with curled hair? Red hair, ma'am, curled – curled all over?" And extending his cane he pointed to the awful object, his hand shaking as he did so.

"It is Julia Severn," replied Miss Temple very quietly.

"Julia Severn, ma'am! And why has she, or any other, curled hair? Why, in defiance of every precept and principle of this house, does she conform to the world so openly – here in an evangelical, charitable establishment – as to wear her hair one mass of curls?"

"Julia's hair curls naturally," returned Miss Temple, still more quietly.

"Naturally! Yes but we are not to conform to nature: I wish these girls to be the children of Grace: and why that abundance? I have again and again intimated that I desire the hair to be arranged closely,

---

1   See Matthew 4:4 and 5:6; Luke 6:21; 1 Peter 3:14.

modestly, plainly. Miss Temple, that girl's hair must be cut off entirely; I will send a barber to-morrow: and I see others who have far too much of the excrescence – that tall girl, tell her to turn round. Tell all the first form to rise up and direct their faces to the wall."

Miss Temple passed her handkerchief over her lips, as if to smooth away the involuntary smile that curled them; she gave the order, however, and when the first class could take in what was required of them, they obeyed. Leaning a little back on my bench, I could see the looks and grimaces with which they commented on this manœuvre: it was a pity Mr. Brocklehurst could not see them too; he would perhaps have felt that, whatever he might do with the outside of the cup and platter, the inside was further beyond his interference than he imagined.[1]

He scrutinised the reverse of these living medals some five minutes, then pronounced sentence. These words fell like the knell of doom: –

"All those top-knots[2] must be cut off."

Miss Temple seemed to remonstrate.

"Madam," he pursued, "I have a Master to serve whose kingdom is not of this world: my mission is to mortify in these girls the lusts of the flesh; to teach them to clothe themselves with shame-facedness and sobriety, not with braided hair and costly apparel; and each of the young persons before us has a string of hair twisted in plaits which vanity itself might have woven: these, I repeat, must be cut off; think of the time wasted, of —"

Mr. Brocklehurst was here interrupted: three other visitors, ladies, now entered the room. They ought to have come a little sooner to have heard his lecture on dress, for they were splendidly attired in velvet, silk, and furs. The two younger of the trio (fine girls of sixteen and seventeen) had grey beaver hats, then in fashion, shaded with ostrich plumes, and from under the brim of this graceful head-dress fell a profusion of light tresses, elaborately curled; the elder lady was enveloped in a costly velvet shawl, trimmed with ermine, and she wore a false front of French curls.[3]

---

1   See Matthew 23:25.
2   Hair on the crown of the head, in this case gathered together with a ribbon or bow.
3   A hair-piece worn over the forehead. Jane calls attention to Brocklehurst's hypocrisy.

These ladies were deferentially received by Miss Temple, as Mrs. and the Misses Brocklehurst, and conducted to seats of honour at the top of the room. It seems they had come in the carriage with the reverend relative, and had been conducting a rummaging scrutiny of the room up stairs, while he transacted business with the house-keeper, questioned the laundress and lectured the superintendent. They now proceeded to address divers remarks and reproofs to Miss Smith, who was charged with the care of the linen and the inspection of the dormitories: but I had no time to listen to what they said; other matters called off and enchained my attention.

Hitherto, while gathering up the discourse of Mr. Brocklehurst and Miss Temple, I had not, at the same time, neglected precautions to secure my personal safety; which I thought would be effected, if I could only elude observation. To this end, I had sat well back on the form, and while seeming to be busy with my sum, had held my slate in such a manner as to conceal my face: I might have escaped notice, had not my treacherous slate somehow happened to slip from my hand, and falling with an obtrusive crash, directly drawn every eye upon me; I knew it was all over now, and, as I stooped to pick up the two fragments of slate, I rallied my forces for the worst. It came.

"A careless girl!" said Mr. Brocklehurst, and immediately after – "It is the new pupil, I perceive." And before I could draw breath, "I must not forget I have a word to say respecting her." Then aloud: how loud it seemed to me! "Let the child who broke her slate, come forward!"

Of my own accord, I could not have stirred; I was paralysed: but the two great girls who sat on each side of me, set me on my legs and pushed me towards the dread judge, and then Miss Temple gently assisted me to his very feet, and I caught her whispered counsel, –

"Don't be afraid, Jane, I saw it was an accident; you shall not be punished."

The kind whisper went to my heart like a dagger.

"Another minute, and she will despise me for a hypocrite," thought I; and an impulse of fury against Reed, Brocklehurst, and Co., bounded in my pulses at the conviction. I was no Helen Burns.

"Fetch that stool," said Mr. Brocklehurst, pointing to a very high one from which a monitor had just risen: it was brought.

"Place the child upon it."

And I was placed there, by whom I don't know: I was in no condition to note particulars; I was only aware that they had hoisted me up to the height of Mr. Brocklehurst's nose, that he was within a yard of me, and that a spread of shot orange and purple silk pelisses, and a cloud of silvery plumage extended and waved below me.

Mr. Brocklehurst hemmed.

"Ladies," said he, turning to his family; "Miss Temple, teachers, and children, you all see this girl?"

Of course they did; for I felt their eyes directed like burning-glasses against my scorched skin.

"You see she is yet young; you observe she possesses the ordinary form of childhood; God has graciously given her the shape that he has given to all of us; no signal deformity points her out as a marked character. Who would think that the Evil One had already found a servant and agent in her? Yet such, I grieve to say, is the case."

A pause – in which I began to steady the palsy of my nerves, and to feel that the rubicon was passed;[1] and that the trial, no longer to be shirked, must be firmly sustained.

"My dear children," pursued the black marble clergyman, with pathos, "this is a sad, a melancholy occasion; for it becomes my duty to warn you, that this girl, who might be one of God's own lambs, is a little castaway: not a member of the true flock, but evidently an interloper and an alien. You must be on your guard against her; you must shun her example: if necessary, avoid her company, exclude her from your sports, and shut her out from your converse. Teachers, you must watch her: keep your eyes on her movements, weigh well her words, scrutinise her actions, punish her body to save her soul; if, indeed, such salvation be possible, for (my tongue falters while I tell it) this girl, this child, the native of a Christian land, worse than many a little heathen who says its prayers to Brahma and kneels before Juggernaut[2] – this girl is – a liar!"

Now came a pause of ten minutes; during which I, by this time in

---

1 A boundary which, once crossed, commits you to proceeding. The Rubicon was a stream which marked the boundaries of Julius Caesar's province. When he crossed it in 49 CE the action began his war with Pompey.

2 Brahma is the supreme god in the Hindu pantheon. Juggernaut is another name for Krishna, the eighth "avatar," or manifestation, of the Hindu god Vishnu.

perfect possession of my wits, observed all the female Brocklehursts produce their pocket-handkerchiefs and apply them to their optics, while the elderly lady swayed herself to and fro, and the two younger ones whispered, "How shocking!"

Mr. Brocklehurst resumed.

"This I learned from her benefactress; from the pious and charitable lady who adopted her in her orphan state, reared her as her own daughter, and whose kindness, whose generosity, the unhappy girl repaid by an ingratitude so bad, so dreadful, that at last her excellent patroness was obliged to separate her from her own young ones, fearful lest her vicious example should contaminate their purity: she has sent her here to be healed, even as the Jews of old sent their diseased to the troubled pool of Bethesda;[1] and, teachers, superintendent, I beg of you not to allow the waters to stagnate round her."

With this sublime conclusion, Mr. Brocklehurst adjusted the top button of his surtout, muttered something to his family, who rose, bowed to Miss Temple, and then all the great people sailed in state from the room. Turning at the door, my judge said: –

"Let her stand half an hour longer on that stool, and let no one speak to her during the remainder of the day."

There I was, then, mounted aloft: I, who had said I could not bear the shame of standing on my natural feet in the middle of the room, was now exposed to general view on a pedestal of infamy. What my sensations were, no language can describe; but just as they all rose, stifling my breath and constricting my throat, a girl came up and passed me: in passing, she lifted her eyes. What a strange light inspired them! What an extraordinary sensation that ray sent through me! How the new feeling bore me up! It was as if a martyr, a hero, had passed a slave or victim, and imparted strength in the transit. I mastered the rising hysteria, lifted up my head, and took a firm stand on the stool. Helen Burns asked some slight questions about her work of Miss Smith, was chidden for the triviality of the inquiry, returned to her place, and smiled at me as she again went by. What a smile! I remember it now, and I know that it was the effluence of fine intellect, of true courage; it lit up her marked lineaments, her thin face, her

---

1 See John 5:2-4.

sunken grey eye, like a reflection from the aspect of an angel. Yet at that moment Helen Burns wore on her arm "the untidy badge;" scarcely an hour ago I had heard her condemned by Miss Scatcherd to a dinner of bread and water on the morrow, because she had blotted an exercise in copying it out. Such is the imperfect nature of man! such spots are there on the disc of the clearest planet; and eyes like Miss Scatcherd's can only see those minute defects, and are blind to the full brightness of the orb.

CHAPTER VIII

ERE the half-hour ended, five o'clock struck; school was dismissed, and all were gone into the refectory to tea. I now ventured to descend: it was deep dusk: I retired into a corner and sat down on the floor. The spell by which I had been so far supported began to dissolve; reaction took place, and soon, so overwhelming was the grief that seized me, I sank prostrate with my face to the ground. Now I wept: Helen Burns was not here; nothing sustained me: left to myself I abandoned myself, and my tears watered the boards. I had meant to be so good, and to do so much at Lowood; to make so many friends, to earn respect, and win affection. Already I had made visible progress: that very morning I had reached the head of my class; Miss Miller had praised me warmly; Miss Temple had smiled approbation; she had promised to teach me drawing, and to let me learn French, if I continued to make similar improvement two months longer: and then I was well received by my fellow-pupils; treated as an equal by those of my own age, and not molested by any: now, here I lay again crushed and trodden on: and could I ever rise more?

"Never," I thought; and ardently I wished to die. While sobbing out this wish in broken accents, some one approached: I started up – again Helen Burns was near me; the fading fires just showed her coming up the long, vacant room; she brought my coffee and bread.

"Come, eat something," she said; but I put both away from me, feeling as if a drop or a crumb would have choked me in my present condition. Helen regarded me, probably with surprise: I could not now abate my agitation, though I tried hard; I continued to weep aloud. She sat down on the ground near me, embraced her knees with her arms, and rested her head upon them; in that attitude she remained silent as an Indian. I was the first who spoke: –

"Helen, why do you stay with a girl whom everybody believes to be a liar?"

"Everybody, Jane? Why, there are only eighty people who have heard you called so, and the world contains hundreds of millions."

"But what have I to do with millions? The eighty I know despise me."

"Jane, you are mistaken: probably not one in the school either despises or dislikes you: many, I am sure, pity you much."

"How can they pity me after what Mr. Brocklehurst said?"

"Mr. Brocklehurst is not a god; nor is he even a great and admired man: he is little liked here; he never took steps to make himself liked. Had he treated you as an especial favourite, you would have found enemies, declared or covert, all around you; as it is, the greater number would offer you sympathy if they dared. Teachers and pupils may look coldly on you for a day or two, but friendly feelings are concealed in their hearts; and if you persevere in doing well, these feelings will ere long appear so much the more evidently for their temporary suppression. Besides, Jane," — she paused.

"Well, Helen?" said I, putting my hand into hers: she chafed my fingers gently to warm them, and went on: —

"If all the world hated you, and believed you wicked, while your own conscience approved you, and absolved you from guilt, you would not be without friends."

"No; I know I should think well of myself; but that is not enough: if others don't love me, I would rather die than live — I cannot bear to be solitary and hated, Helen. Look here; to gain some real affection from you, or Miss Temple, or any other whom I truly love, I would willingly submit to have the bone of my arm broken, or to let a bull toss me, or to stand behind a kicking horse, and let it dash its hoof at my chest, —"

"Hush, Jane! you think too much of the love of human beings; you are too impulsive, too vehement: the sovereign hand that created your frame, and put life into it, has provided you with other resources than your feeble self, or than creatures feeble as you. Besides this earth, and besides the race of men, there is an invisible world and a kingdom of spirits: that world is round us, for it is everywhere; and those spirits watch us, for they are commissioned to guard us; and if we were dying in pain and shame, if scorn smote us on all sides, and hatred crushed us, angels see our tortures, recognise our innocence (if innocent we be: as I know you are of this charge which Mr. Brocklehurst has weakly and pompously repeated at second hand from Mrs. Reed; for I read a sincere nature in your ardent eyes and on your clear front), and God waits only the separation of spirit from flesh to crown us with a full reward. Why, then, should we ever sink overwhelmed with distress, when life is so soon over, and death is so certain an entrance to happiness: to glory?"

I was silent: Helen had calmed me; but in the tranquillity she imparted there was an alloy of inexpressible sadness. I felt the impression of woe as she spoke, but I could not tell whence it came; and when, having done speaking, she breathed a little fast and coughed a short cough, I momentarily forgot my own sorrows to yield to a vague concern for her.

Resting my head on Helen's shoulder, I put my arms round her waist; she drew me to her, and we reposed in silence. We had not sat long thus, when another person came in. Some heavy clouds, swept from the sky by a rising wind, had left the moon bare; and her light, streaming in through a window near, shone full both on us and on the approaching figure, which we at once recognised as Miss Temple.

"I came on purpose to find you, Jane Eyre," said she; "I want you in my room; and as Helen Burns is with you, she may come too."

We went; following the superintendent's guidance, we had to thread some intricate passages, and mount a staircase before we reached her apartment; it contained a good fire, and looked cheerful. Miss Temple told Helen Burns to be seated in a low arm-chair on one side of the hearth, and herself taking another, she called me to her side.

"Is it all over?" she asked, looking down at my face. "Have you cried your grief away?"

"I am afraid I never shall do that."

"Why?"

"Because I have been wrongly accused; and you, ma'am, and everybody else will now think me wicked."

"We shall think you what you prove yourself to be, my child. Continue to act as a good girl, and you will satisfy me."

"Shall I, Miss Temple?"

"You will," said she, passing her arm round me. "And now tell me who is the lady whom Mr. Brocklehurst called your benefactress?"

"Mrs. Reed, my uncle's wife. My uncle is dead, and he left me to her care."

"Did she not, then, adopt you of her own accord?"

"No, ma'am; she was sorry to have to do it: but my uncle, as I have often heard the servants say, got her to promise, before he died, that she would always keep me."

"Well now, Jane, you know, or at least I will tell you, that when a criminal is accused, he is always allowed to speak in his own defence. You have been charged with falsehood: defend yourself to me as well as you can. Say whatever your memory suggests as true; but add nothing and exaggerate nothing."

I resolved in the depth of my heart that I would be most moderate: most correct; and, having reflected a few minutes in order to arrange coherently what I had to say, I told her all the story of my sad childhood. Exhausted by emotion, my language was more subdued than it generally was when it developed that sad theme; and mindful of Helen's warnings against the indulgence of resentment, I infused into the narrative far less of gall and wormwood than ordinary. Thus restrained and simplified, it sounded more credible: I felt as I went on that Miss Temple fully believed me.

In the course of the tale I had mentioned Mr. Lloyd as having come to see me after the fit; for I never forgot the, to me, frightful episode of the red room; in detailing which, my excitement was sure, in some degree, to break bounds; for nothing could soften in my recollection the spasm of agony which clutched my heart when Mrs. Reed spurned my wild supplication for pardon, and locked me a second time in the dark and haunted chamber.

I had finished: Miss Temple regarded me a few minutes in silence; she then said: —

"I know something of Mr. Lloyd; I shall write to him; if his reply agrees with your statement, you shall be publicly cleared from every imputation: to me, Jane, you are clear now."

She kissed me, and still keeping me at her side (where I was well contented to stand, for I derived a child's pleasure from the contemplation of her face, her dress, her one or two ornaments, her white forehead, her clustered and shining curls, and beaming dark eyes), she proceeded to address Helen Burns.

"How are you to-night, Helen? Have you coughed much to-day?"

"Not quite so much I think, ma'am."

"And the pain in your chest?"

"It is a little better."

Miss Temple got up, took her hand and examined her pulse; then she returned to her own seat: as she resumed it, I heard her sigh low.

She was pensive a few minutes, then rousing herself, she said cheerfully: –

"But you two are my visitors to-night; I must treat you as such." She rang her bell.

"Barbara," she said to the servant who answered it, "I have not yet had tea; bring the tray, and place cups for these two young ladies."

And a tray was soon brought. How pretty to my eyes, did the china cups and bright teapot look, placed on the little round table near the fire! How fragrant was the steam of the beverage, and the scent of the toast! of which, however, I, to my dismay (for I was beginning to be hungry), discerned only a very small portion: Miss Temple discerned it too: –

"Barbara," said she, "can you not bring a little more bread and butter? There is not enough for three."

Barbara went out; she returned soon: –

"Madam, Mrs. Harden says she has sent up the usual quantity."

Mrs. Harden, be it observed, was the house-keeper: a woman after Mr. Brocklehurst's own heart, made up of equal parts whalebone and iron.

"Oh, very well!" returned Miss Temple; "we must make it do, Barbara, I suppose." And as the girl withdrew, she added, smiling, "Fortunately, I have it in my power to supply deficiencies for this once."

Having invited Helen and me to approach the table, and placed before each of us a cup of tea with one delicious but thin morsel of toast, she got up, unlocked a drawer, and taking from it a parcel wrapped in paper, disclosed presently to our eyes a good-sized seed-cake.

"I meant to give each of you some of this to take with you," said she; "but as there is so little toast you must have it now," and she proceeded to cut slices with a generous hand.

We feasted that evening as on nectar and ambrosia;[1] and not the least delight of the entertainment was the smile of gratification with which our hostess regarded us, as we satisfied our famished appetites on the delicate fare she liberally supplied. Tea over and the tray removed, she again summoned us to the fire; we sat one on each side

---

1   The food of the gods in Greek mythology.

of her, and now a conversation followed between her and Helen, which it was indeed a privilege to be admitted to hear.

Miss Temple had always something of serenity in her air, of state in her mien, of refined propriety in her language, which precluded deviation into the ardent, the excited, the eager: something which chastened the pleasure of those who looked on her and listened to her, by a controlling sense of awe; and such was my feeling now: but as to Helen Burns, I was struck with wonder.

The refreshing meal, the brilliant fire, the presence and kindness of her beloved instructress, or perhaps more than all these, something in her own unique mind, had roused her powers within her. They woke, they kindled: first, they glowed in the bright tint of her cheek, which till this hour I had never seen but pale and bloodless; then they shone in the liquid lustre of her eyes, which had suddenly acquired a beauty more singular than that of Miss Temple's – a beauty neither of fine colour nor long eyelash, nor pencilled brow, but of meaning, of movement, of radiance. Then her soul sat on her lips, and language flowed, from what source I cannot tell: has a girl of fourteen a heart large enough, vigorous enough to hold the swelling spring of pure, full, fervid eloquence? Such was the characteristic of Helen's discourse on that, to me, memorable evening: her spirit seemed hastening to live within a very brief span as much as many live during a protracted existence.

They conversed of things I had never heard of; of nations and times past; of countries far away; of secrets of nature discovered or guessed at: they spoke of books: how many they had read! What stores of knowledge they possessed! Then they seemed so familiar with French names and French authors: but my amazement reached its climax when Miss Temple asked Helen if she sometimes snatched a moment to recall the Latin her father had taught her, and taking a book from a shelf, bade her read and construe a page of "Virgil;" and Helen obeyed, my organ of Veneration expanding at every sounding line. She had scarcely finished ere the bell announced bed-time! no delay could be admitted; Miss Temple embraced us both, saying as she drew us to her heart: –

"God bless you, my children!"

Helen she held a little longer than me: she let her go more reluctantly; it was Helen her eye followed to the door; it was for her she a second time breathed a sad sigh; for her she wiped a tear from her cheek.

On reaching the bed-room, we heard the voice of Miss Scatcherd: she was examining drawers; she had just pulled out Helen Burns's, and when we entered Helen was greeted with a sharp reprimand, and told that to-morrow she should have half a dozen of untidily folded articles pinned to her shoulder.

"My things were indeed in shameful disorder," murmured Helen to me, in a low voice, "I intended to have arranged them, but I forgot."

Next morning, Miss Scatcherd wrote in conspicuous characters on a piece of pasteboard the word "Slattern," and bound it like a phylactery[1] round Helen's large, mild, intelligent, and benign-looking forehead. She wore it till evening, patient, unresentful, regarding it as a deserved punishment. The moment Miss Scatcherd withdrew after afternoon-school, I ran to Helen, tore it off, and thrust it into the fire: the fury of which she was incapable had been burning in my soul all day, and tears, hot and large, had continually been scalding my cheek; for the spectacle of her sad resignation gave me an intolerable pain at the heart.

About a week subsequently to the incidents above narrated, Miss Temple, who had written to Mr. Lloyd, received his answer: it appeared that what he said went to corroborate my account. Miss Temple, having assembled the whole school, announced that inquiry had been made into the charges alleged against Jane Eyre, and that she was most happy to be able to pronounce her completely cleared from every imputation. The teachers then shook hands with me and kissed me, and a murmur of pleasure ran through the ranks of my companions.

Thus relieved of a grievous load, I from that hour set to work afresh, resolved to pioneer[2] my way through every difficulty: I toiled hard, and my success was proportionate to my efforts; my memory, not naturally tenacious, improved with practice; exercise sharpened

---

1 A small leather box containing a scrap of text, worn by Jewish men at morning weekday prayer to remind them to keep the law.
2 Dig or tunnel.

my wits; in a few weeks I was promoted to a higher class; in less than two months I was allowed to commence French and drawing. I learned the first two tenses of the verb *Etre*,[1] and sketched my first cottage (whose walls, by-the-by, outrivalled in slope those of the leaning tower of Pisa), on the same day. That night, on going to bed, I forgot to prepare in imagination the Barmecide supper[2] of hot roast potatoes, or white bread and new milk, with which I was wont to amuse my inward cravings: I feasted instead on the spectacle of ideal drawings, which I saw in the dark; all the work of my own hands: freely pencilled houses and trees, picturesque rocks and ruins, Cuyp-like[3] groups of cattle, sweet paintings of butterflies hovering over unblown roses, of birds pecking at ripe cherries, of wrens' nests enclosing pearl-like eggs, wreathed about with young ivy sprays. I examined, too, in thought, the possibility of my ever being able to translate currently[4] a certain little French story-book which Madame Pierrot had that day shewn me; nor was that problem solved to my satisfaction ere I fell sweetly asleep.

Well has Solomon said: – "Better is a dinner of herbs where love is, than a stalled ox and hatred therewith."[5]

I would not now have exchanged Lowood with all its privations, for Gateshead and its daily luxuries.

---

1   "To be" in French.
2   Imaginary meal. In *The Arabian Nights* a starving beggar is invited to a meal of empty dishes by a prince of the Barmecide family.
3   Resembling the landscapes of Dutch painter Albert Cuyp (1620-91).
4   Fluently.
5   Proverbs 15:17.

CHAPTER IX

BUT the privations, or rather the hardships of Lowood lessened. Spring drew on: she was indeed already come; the frosts of winter had ceased; its snows were melted; its cutting winds ameliorated. My wretched feet, flayed and swollen to lameness by the sharp air of January, began to heal and subside under the gentler breathings of April; the nights and mornings no longer by their Canadian temperature froze the very blood in our veins; we could now endure the play-hour passed in the garden: sometimes on a sunny day it began even to be pleasant and genial, and a greenness grew over those brown beds which, freshening daily, suggested the thought that Hope traversed them at night, and left each morning brighter traces of her steps. Flowers peeped out amongst the leaves; snowdrops, crocuses, purple auriculas, and golden-eyed pansies. On Thursday afternoons (half-holidays) we now took walks, and found still sweeter flowers opening by the way-side, under the hedges.

I discovered, too, that a great pleasure, an enjoyment which the horizon only bounded, lay all outside the high and spike-guarded walls of our garden: this pleasure consisted in a prospect of noble summits girdling a great hill-hollow, rich in verdure and shadow; in a bright beck,[1] full of dark stones and sparkling eddies. How different had this scene looked when I viewed it laid out beneath the iron sky of winter, stiffened in frost, shrouded with snow! – When mists as chill as death wandered to the impulse of east winds along those purple peaks, and rolled down 'ing' and holm[2] till they blended with the frozen fog of the beck! That beck itself was then a torrent, turbid and curbless: it tore asunder the wood, and sent a raving sound through the air, often thickened with wild rain or whirling sleet; and for the forest on its banks, *that* showed only ranks of skeletons.

April advanced to May: a bright, serene May it was; days of blue sky, placid sunshine, and soft western or southern gales filled up its duration. And now vegetation matured with vigour; Lowood shook loose its tresses; it became all green, all flowery; its great elm, ash, and oak skeletons were restored to majestic life; woodland plants sprang up profusely in its recesses; unnumbered varieties of moss filled its

---

1 Brook.
2 Dialect words for a meadow or piece of flat land subject to flooding.

hollows, and it made a strange ground-sunshine out of the wealth of its wild primrose plants: I have seen their pale gold gleam in over-shadowed spots like scatterings of the sweetest lustre. All this I enjoyed often and fully, free, unwatched, and almost alone: for this unwonted liberty and pleasure, there was a cause, to which it now becomes my task to advert.

Have I not described a pleasant site for a dwelling, when I speak of it as bosomed in hill and wood, and rising from the verge of a stream? Assuredly, pleasant enough: but whether healthy or not is another question.

That forest-dell, where Lowood lay, was the cradle of fog and fog-bred pestilence; which, quickening with the quickening spring, crept into the Orphan Asylum, breathed typhus[1] through its crowded school-room and dormitory, and, ere May arrived, transformed the seminary into an hospital.

Semi-starvation and neglected colds had predisposed most of the pupils to receive infection: forty-five out of the eighty girls lay ill at one time. Classes were broken up, rules relaxed. The few who continued well were allowed almost unlimited license; because the medical attendant insisted on the necessity of frequent exercise to keep them in health: and had it been otherwise, no one had leisure to watch or restrain them. Miss Temple's whole attention was absorbed by the patients: she lived in the sick-room; never quitting it except to snatch a few hours' rest at night. The teachers were fully occupied with packing up and making other necessary preparations for the departure of those girls who were fortunate enough to have friends and relations able and willing to remove them from the seat of contagion. Many, already smitten, went home only to die: some died at the school, and were buried quietly and quickly; the nature of the malady forbidding delay.

While disease had thus become an inhabitant of Lowood, and death its frequent visitor; while there was gloom and fear within its walls; while its rooms and passages steamed with hospital smells: the drug and the pastille[2] striving vainly to overcome the effluvia of mortality; that bright May shone unclouded over the bold hills and

1 An infectious fever characterized by delirium and the eruption of purple spots on the skin.
2 A small roll of aromatic paste burned as a fumigator.

beautiful woodland out of doors. Its garden, too, glowed with flowers: hollyhocks had sprung up tall as trees, lilies had opened, tulips and roses were in bloom; the borders of the little beds were gay with pink thrift and crimson double-daisies; the sweet-briars gave out, morning and evening, their scent of spice and apples; and these fragrant treasures were all useless for most of the inmates of Lowood: except to furnish now and then a handful of herbs and blossoms to put in a coffin.

But I, and the rest who continued well, enjoyed fully the beauties of the scene and season: they let us ramble in the wood, like gipsies, from morning till night; we did what we liked, went where we liked: we lived better too. Mr. Brocklehurst and his family never came near Lowood now: household matters were not scrutinized into; the cross housekeeper was gone, driven away by the fear of infection; her successor, who had been matron at the Lowton Dispensary, unused to the ways of her new abode, provided with comparative liberality. Besides, there were fewer to feed: the sick could eat little; our breakfast-basins were better filled: when there was no time to prepare a regular dinner, which often happened, she would give us a large piece of cold pie, or a thick slice of bread and cheese, and this we carried away with us to the wood, where we each chose the spot we liked best, and dined sumptuously.

My favourite seat was a smooth and broad stone, rising white and dry from the very middle of the beck, and only to be got at by wading through the water; a feat I accomplished barefoot. The stone was just broad enough to accommodate, comfortably, another girl and me, at that time my chosen comrade – one Mary Ann Wilson; a shrewd observant personage, whose society I took pleasure in, partly because she was witty and original, and partly because she had a manner which set me at my ease. Some years older than I, she knew more of the world, and could tell me many things I liked to hear: with her my curiosity found gratification: to my faults also she gave ample indulgence; never imposing curb or rein on anything I said. She had a turn for narrative, I for analysis; she liked to inform, I to question; so we got on swimmingly together, deriving much entertainment, if not much improvement, from our mutual intercourse.

And where, meantime, was Helen Burns? Why did I not spend these sweet days of liberty with her? Had I forgotten her; or was I so worthless as to have grown tired of her pure society? Surely the Mary Ann Wilson I have mentioned was inferior to my first acquaintance: she could only tell me amusing stories, and reciprocate any racy and pungent gossip I chose to indulge in; while, if I have spoken truth of Helen, she was qualified to give those who enjoyed the privilege of her converse, a taste of far higher things.

True, reader; and I knew and felt this: and though I am a defective being, with many faults and few redeeming points, yet I never tired of Helen Burns; nor ever ceased to cherish for her a sentiment of attachment as strong, tender, and respectful as any that ever animated my heart. How could it be otherwise, when Helen, at all times and under all circumstances, evinced for me a quiet and faithful friendship, which ill-humour never soured nor irritation ever troubled? But Helen was ill at present: for some weeks she had been removed from my sight to I knew not what room up-stairs. She was not, I was told, in the hospital portion of the house with the fever patients; for her complaint was consumption,[1] not typhus: and by consumption I, in my ignorance, understood something mild, which time and care would be sure to alleviate.

I was confirmed in this idea by the fact of her once or twice coming down stairs on very warm sunny afternoons, and being taken by Miss Temple into the garden: but, on these occasions, I was not allowed to go and speak to her; I only saw her from the school-room window, and then not distinctly; for she was much wrapped up, and sat at a distance under the verandah.

One evening in the beginning of June, I had stayed out very late with Mary Ann in the wood; we had, as usual, separated ourselves from the others, and had wandered far: so far that we lost our way, and had to ask it at a lonely cottage, where a man and woman lived, who looked after a herd of half-wild swine that fed on the mast[2] in the wood. When we got back, it was after moon-rise: a pony, which we knew to be the surgeon's, was standing at the garden-door. Mary Ann remarked that she supposed some one must be very ill, as Mr. Bates

---

1   Tuberculosis. This disease devastated Brontë's family, killing her older sisters Maria and Elizabeth, as well as her brother Branwell, and her younger sisters Emily and Anne.
2   Fruit from beech, oak, and chestnut trees.

had been sent for at that time of the evening. She went into the house; I stayed behind a few minutes to plant in my garden a handful of roots I had dug up in the forest, and which I feared would wither if I left them till the morning. This done, I lingered yet a little longer: the flowers smelt so sweet as the dew fell; it was such a pleasant evening, so serene, so warm; the still glowing west promised so fairly another fine day on the morrow; the moon rose with such majesty in the grave east. I was noting these things and enjoying them as a child might, when it entered my mind, as it had never done before: –

"How sad to be lying now on a sick-bed, and to be in danger of dying! This world is pleasant – it would be dreary to be called from it, and to have to go who knows where?"

And then my mind made its first earnest effort to comprehend what had been infused into it concerning heaven and hell: and for the first time it recoiled, baffled; and for the first time, glancing behind, on each side, and before it, it saw all round an unfathomed gulf: it felt the one point where it stood – the present; all the rest was formless cloud and vacant depth; and it shuddered at the thought of tottering, and plunging amid that chaos. While pondering this new idea, I heard the front door open; Mr. Bates came out, and with him was a nurse. After she had seen him mount his horse and depart, she was about to close the door, but I ran up to her.

"How is Helen Burns?"

"Very poorly," was the answer.

"Is it her Mr. Bates has been to see?"

"Yes."

"And what does he say about her?"

"He says she'll not be here long."

This phrase, uttered in my hearing yesterday, would have only conveyed the notion that she was about to be removed to Northumberland, to her own home. I should not have suspected that it meant she was dying; but I knew instantly now: it opened clear on my comprehension that Helen Burns was numbering her last days in this world, and that she was going to be taken to the region of spirits, if such region there were. I experienced a shock of horror, then a strong thrill of grief; then a desire – a necessity to see her; and I asked in what room she lay.

"She is in Miss Temple's room," said the nurse.

"May I go up and speak to her?"

"Oh, no, child! It is not likely:[1] and now it is time for you to come in; you'll catch the fever if you stop out when the dew is falling."

The nurse closed the front door; I went in by the side entrance which led to the school-room: I was just in time; it was nine o'clock, and Miss Miller was calling the pupils to go to bed.

It might be two hours later, probably near eleven, when I – not having been able to fall asleep, and deeming, from the perfect silence of the dormitory, that my companions were all wrapt in profound repose – rose softly, put on my frock over my night-dress, and, without shoes, crept from the apartment, and set off in quest of Miss Temple's room. It was quite at the other end of the house; but I knew my way; and the light of the unclouded summer moon, entering here and there at passage windows, enabled me to find it without difficulty. An odour of camphor and burnt vinegar[2] warned me when I came near the fever room; and I passed its door quickly, fearful lest the nurse who sat up all night should hear me. I dreaded being discovered and sent back; for I *must* see Helen, – I must embrace her before she died, – I must give her one last kiss, exchange with her one last word.

Having descended a staircase, traversed a portion of the house below, and succeeded in opening and shutting, without noise, two doors, I reached another flight of steps; these I mounted, and then just opposite to me was Miss Temple's room. A light shone through the key-hole and from under the door: a profound stillness pervaded the vicinity. Coming near, I found the door slightly ajar; probably to admit some fresh air into the close abode of sickness. Indisposed to hesitate, and full of impatient impulses – soul and senses quivering with keen throes – I put it back and looked in. My eye sought Helen, and feared to find death.

Close by Miss Temple's bed, and half covered with its white curtains, there stood a little crib. I saw the outline of a form under the clothes, but the face was hid by the hangings: the nurse I had spoken to in the garden sat in an easychair, asleep; an unsnuffed candle burnt

---

1   Proper.

2   Camphor is a white, crystalline substance. Both it and vinegar were burned in sick-rooms as disinfectants.

dimly on the table. Miss Temple was not to be seen: I knew afterwards that she had been called to a delirious patient in the fever-room. I advanced; then paused by the crib side: my hand was on the curtain, but I preferred speaking before I withdrew it. I still recoiled at the dread of seeing a corpse.

"Helen!" I whispered softly; "are you awake?"

She stirred, herself put back the curtain, and I saw her face, pale, wasted, but quite composed: she looked so little changed that my fear was instantly dissipated.

"Can it be you, Jane?" she asked in her own gentle voice.

"Oh!" I thought, "she is not going to die; they are mistaken: she could not speak and look so calmly if she were."

I got on to her crib and kissed her: her forehead was cold, and her cheek both cold and thin, and so were her hand and wrist; but she smiled as of old.

"Why are you come here, Jane? It is past eleven o'clock: I heard it strike some minutes since."

"I came to see you, Helen: I heard you were very ill, and I could not sleep till I had spoken to you."

"You came to bid me good-bye, then: you are just in time probably."

"Are you going somewhere, Helen? Are you going home?"

"Yes; to my long home – my last home."

"No, no, Helen:" I stopped, distressed. While I tried to devour my tears, a fit of coughing seized Helen; it did not, however, wake the nurse: when it was over, she lay some minutes exhausted; then she whispered: –

"Jane, your little feet are bare; lie down and cover yourself with my quilt."

I did so: she put her arm over me, and I nestled close to her. After a long silence, she resumed, still whispering —

"I am very happy, Jane; and when you hear that I am dead you must be sure and not grieve: there is nothing to grieve about. We all must die one day, and the illness which is removing me is not painful; it is gentle and gradual: my mind is at rest. I leave no one to regret me much: I have only a father; and he is lately married, and will not miss me. By dying young I shall escape great sufferings. I had not qualities or talents to make my way very well in the world: I should have been continually at fault."

"But where are you going to, Helen? Can you see? Do you know?"

"I believe; I have faith: I am going to God."

"Where is God? What is God?"

"My Maker and yours; who will never destroy what he created. I rely implicitly on his power, and confide wholly in his goodness: I count the hours till that eventful one arrives which shall restore me to him, reveal him to me."

"You are sure, then, Helen, that there is such a place as heaven; and that our souls can get to it when we die?"

"I am sure there is a future state; I believe God is good: I can resign my immortal part to him without any misgiving. God is my father; God is my friend: I love him; I believe he loves me."

"And shall I see you again, Helen, when I die?"

"You will come to the same region of happiness: be received by the same mighty, universal Parent, no doubt, dear Jane."

Again I questioned; but this time only in thought. "Where is that region? Does it exist?" And I clasped my arms closer around Helen: she seemed dearer to me than ever; I felt as if I could not let her go; I lay with my face hidden on her neck. Presently she said in the sweetest tone: −

"How comfortable I am! That last fit of coughing has tired me a little; I feel as if I could sleep: but don't leave me, Jane; I like to have you near me."

"I'll stay with you, *dear* Helen: no one shall take me away."

"Are you warm, darling?"

"Yes."

"Good-night, Jane."

"Good-night, Helen."

She kissed me, and I her; and we both soon slumbered.

When I awoke it was day: an unusual movement roused me; I looked up; I was in somebody's arms; the nurse held me; she was carrying me through the passage back to the dormitory. I was not reprimanded for leaving my bed; people had something else to think about: no explanation was afforded then to my many questions; but a day or two afterwards I learned that Miss Temple, on returning to her own room at dawn, had found me laid in the little crib; my face against Helen Burns's shoulder, my arms round her neck. I was asleep, and Helen was – dead.

Her grave is in Brocklebridge churchyard: for fifteen years after her death it was only covered by a grassy mound; but now a grey marble tablet marks the spot, inscribed with her name, and the word "Resurgam."[1]

---

1   Latin. "I shall rise again."

CHAPTER X

HITHERTO I have recorded in detail the events of my insignificant existence: to the first ten years of my life, I have given almost as many chapters. But this is not to be a regular autobiography: I am only bound to invoke memory where I know her responses will possess some degree of interest; therefore I now pass a space of eight years almost in silence: a few lines only are necessary to keep up the links of connection.

When the typhus fever had fulfilled its mission of devastation at Lowood, it gradually disappeared from thence; but not till its virulence and the number of its victims had drawn public attention on the school. Inquiry was made into the origin of the scourge, and by degrees various facts came out which excited public indignation in a high degree. The unhealthy nature of the site; the quantity and quality of the children's food; the brackish, fetid water used in its preparation; the pupils' wretched clothing and accommodations: – all these things were discovered; and the discovery produced a result mortifying to Mr. Brocklehurst, but beneficial to the institution.

Several wealthy and benevolent individuals in the county subscribed largely for the erection of a more convenient building in a better situation; new regulations were made; improvements in diet and clothing introduced; the funds of the school were entrusted to the management of a committee. Mr. Brocklehurst, who, from his wealth and family connections, could not be overlooked, still retained the post of treasurer; but he was aided in the discharge of his duties by gentlemen of rather more enlarged and sympathizing minds: his office of inspector, too, was shared by those who knew how to combine reason with strictness, comfort with economy, compassion with uprightness. The school, thus improved, became in time a truly useful and noble institution. I remained an inmate of its walls, after its regeneration, for eight years: six as pupil, and two as teacher; and in both capacities I bear my testimony to its value and importance.

During these eight years my life was uniform; but not unhappy, because it was not inactive. I had the means of an excellent education placed within my reach; a fondness for some of my studies and a desire to excel in all, together with a great delight in pleasing my teachers, especially such as I loved, urged me on: I availed myself fully of the advantages offered me. In time I rose to be the first girl of the first class; then I was invested with the office of teacher; which I discharged with zeal for two years: but at the end of that time I altered.

Miss Temple, through all changes, had thus far continued superintendent of the seminary: to her instruction I owed the best part of my acquirements; her friendship and society had been my continual solace; she had stood me in the stead of mother, governess, and, latterly, companion. At this period she married, removed with her husband (a clergyman, an excellent man, almost worthy of such a wife) to a distant county, and consequently was lost to me.

From the day she left I was no longer the same: with her was gone every settled feeling, every association that had made Lowood in some degree a home to me. I had imbibed from her something of her nature and much of her habits: more harmonious thoughts, what seemed better regulated feelings had become the inmates of my mind. I had given in allegiance to duty and order; I was quiet; I believed I was content: to the eyes of others, usually even to my own, I appeared a disciplined and subdued character.

But destiny, in the shape of the Rev. Mr. Nasmyth, came between me and Miss Temple: I saw her in her travelling dress step into a postchaise, shortly after the marriage ceremony, I watched the chaise mount the hill and disappear beyond its brow; and then retired to my own room; and there spent in solitude the greatest part of the halfholiday granted in honour of the occasion.

I walked about the chamber most of the time. I imagined myself only to be regretting my loss and thinking how to repair it; but when my reflections were concluded, and I looked up and found that the afternoon was gone, and evening far advanced, another discovery dawned on me: namely, that in the interval I had undergone a transforming process; that my mind had put off all it had borrowed of Miss Temple – or rather that she had taken with her the serene atmosphere I had been breathing in her vicinity – and that now I was left in my natural element; and beginning to feel the stirring of old emotions. It did not seem as if a prop were withdrawn, but rather as if a motive were gone: it was not the power to be tranquil which had failed me, but the reason for tranquillity was no more. My world had for some years been in Lowood: my experience had been of its rules and systems; now I remembered that the real world was wide, and that a varied field of hopes and fears, of sensations and excitements, awaited those who had courage to go forth into its expanse, to seek real knowledge of life amidst its perils.

I went to my window, opened it, and looked out. There were the two wings of the building; there was the garden; there were the skirts of Lowood; there was the hilly horizon. My eye passed all other objects to rest on those most remote, the blue peaks: it was those I longed to surmount; all within their boundary of rock and heath seemed prison-ground, exile limits. I traced the white road winding round the base of one mountain, and vanishing in a gorge between two: how I longed to follow it further! I recalled the time when I had travelled that very road in a coach; I remembered descending that hill at twilight: an age seemed to have elapsed since the day which brought me first to Lowood; and I had never quitted it since. My vacations had all been spent at school: Mrs. Reed had never sent for me to Gateshead; neither she nor any of her family had ever been to visit me. I had had no communication by letter or message with the outer world: school-rules, school-duties, school-habits and notions, and voices, and faces, and phrases, and costumes, and preferences, and antipathies: such was what I knew of existence. And now I felt that it was not enough: I tired of the routine of eight years in one afternoon. I desired liberty; for liberty I gasped; for liberty I uttered a prayer; it seemed scattered on the wind then faintly blowing. I abandoned it, and framed a humbler supplication; for change, stimulus: that petition, too, seemed swept off into vague space; "Then," I cried, half desperate, "Grant me at least a new servitude!"

Here, a bell, ringing the hour of supper, called me down stairs.

I was not free to resume the interrupted chain of my reflections till bedtime: even then a teacher who occupied the same room with me kept me from the subject to which I longed to recur, by a prolonged effusion of small talk. How I wished sleep would silence her! It seemed as if, could I but go back to the idea which had last entered my mind as I stood at the window, some inventive suggestion would rise for my relief.

Miss Gryce snored at last: she was a heavy Welshwoman, and till now her habitual nasal strains had never been regarded by me in any other light than as a nuisance; to-night I hailed the first deep notes with satisfaction; I was debarrassed[1] of interruption; my half-effaced thought instantly revived.

"A new servitude! There is something in that," I soliloquized (mentally, be it understood; I did not talk aloud). "I know there is, because it does not sound too sweet; it is not like such words as Liberty, Excitement, Enjoyment: delightful sounds truly; but no more than sounds for me; and so hollow and fleeting that it is mere waste of time to listen to them. But Servitude! That must be matter of fact. Any one may serve: I have served here eight years; now all I want is to serve elsewhere. Can I not get so much of my own will? Is not the thing feasible? Yes – yes – the end is not so difficult; if I had only a brain active enough to ferret out the means of attaining it."

I sat up in bed by way of arousing this said brain: it was a chilly night; I covered my shoulders with a shawl, and then I proceeded *to think* again with all my might.

"What do I want? A new place, in a new house, amongst new faces, under new circumstances: I want this because it is of no use wanting anything better. How do people do to get a new place? They apply to friends, I suppose: I have no friends. There are many others who have no friends, who must look about for themselves and be their own helpers; and what is their resource?"

I could not tell: nothing answered me; I then ordered my brain to find a response, and quickly. It worked and worked faster: I felt the pulses throb in my head and temples; but for nearly an hour it worked in chaos, and no result came of its efforts. Feverish with vain labour, I got up and took a turn in the room; undrew the curtain, noted a star or two, shivered with cold, and again crept to bed.

A kind fairy, in my absence, had surely dropped the required suggestion on my pillow; for as I lay down it came quietly and naturally to my mind: – "Those who want situations advertise: you must advertise in the —shire Herald."

"How? I know nothing about advertising."

Replies rose smooth and prompt now: –

"You must enclose the advertisement and the money to pay for it under a cover directed to the Editor of the Herald; you must put it,

---

1 Relieved of.

the first opportunity you have, into the post at Lowton; answers must be addressed to J. E. at the post-office there: you can go and inquire in about a week after you send your letter, if any are come, and act accordingly."

This scheme I went over twice, thrice; it was then digested in my mind: I had it in a clear practical form; I felt satisfied, and fell asleep.

With earliest day, I was up: I had my advertisement written, enclosed, and directed before the bell rang to rouse the school; it ran thus: –

"A young lady accustomed to tuition (had I not been a teacher two years?) is desirous of meeting with a situation in a private family where the children are under fourteen (I thought that as I was barely eighteen, it would not do to undertake the guidance of pupils nearer my own age). She is qualified to teach the usual branches of a good English education, together with French, Drawing, and Music (in those days, reader, this now narrow catalogue of accomplishments, would have been held tolerably comprehensive). Address J. E. Post-office, Lowton, —shire."

This document remained locked in my drawer all day: after tea, I asked leave of the new Superintendent to go to Lowton, in order to perform some small commissions for myself and one or two of my fellow-teachers; permission was readily granted; I went. It was a walk of two miles, and the evening was wet, but the days were still long; I visited a shop or two, slipped the letter into the post-office, and came back through heavy rain, with streaming garments, but with a relieved heart.

The succeeding week seemed long: it came to an end at last, however, like all sublunary[1] things, and once more, towards the close of a pleasant autumn day, I found myself afoot on the road to Lowton. A picturesque track it was, by the way; lying along the side of the beck and through the sweetest curves of the dale: but that day I thought more of the letters, that might or might not be awaiting me at the little burgh whither I was bound, than of the charms of lea and water.

My ostensible errand on this occasion was to get measured for a pair of shoes; so I discharged that business first, and when it was done,

---

1   Literally "under the moon;" i.e. earthly.

I stepped across the clean and quiet little street from the shoemaker's to the post-office: it was kept by an old dame, who wore horn spectacles on her nose, and black mittens on her hands.

"Are there any letters for J. E.?" I asked.

She peered at me over her spectacles, and then she opened a drawer, and fumbled among its contents for a long time; so long that my hopes began to falter. At last, having held a document before her glasses for nearly five minutes, she presented it across the counter; accompanying the act by another inquisitive and mistrustful glance – it was for J. E.

"Is there only one?" I demanded.

"There are no more," said she; and I put it in my pocket and turned my face homeward: I could not open it then; rules obliged me to be back by eight, and it was already half-past seven.

Various duties awaited me on my arrival: I had to sit with the girls during their hour of study; then it was my turn to read prayers; to see them to bed: afterwards I supped with the other teachers. Even when we finally retired for the night, the inevitable Miss Gryce was still my companion: we had only a short end of candle in our candlestick, and I dreaded lest she should talk till it was all burnt out; fortunately, however, the heavy supper she had eaten produced a soporific effect: she was already snoring, before I had finished undressing. There still remained an inch of candle: I now took out my letter; the seal was an initial, F.; I broke it; the contents were brief.

"If J.E., who advertised in the —shire *Herald* of last Thursday, possesses the acquirements mentioned, and if she is in a position to give satisfactory references as to character and competency; a situation can be offered her where there is but one pupil, a little girl, under ten years of age; and where the salary is thirty pounds per annum. J. E. is requested to send references, name, address, and all particulars to the direction:

"Mrs. Fairfax, Thornfield, near Millcote, —shire."

I examined the document long: the writing was oldfashioned and rather uncertain, like that of an elderly lady. This circumstance was satisfactory: a private fear had haunted me, that in thus acting for myself and by my own guidance, I ran the risk of getting into some scrape; and above all things, I wished the result of my endeavours to be respectable, proper, *en règle*.[1] I now felt that an elderly lady was no bad ingredient in the business I had on hands. Mrs. Fairfax! I saw her in a black gown and widow's cap; frigid, perhaps, but not uncivil: a model of elderly English respectability. Thornfield! that, doubtless, was the name of her house: a neat, orderly spot, I was sure; though I failed in my efforts to conceive a correct plan of the premises. Millcote, —shire: I brushed up my recollections of the map of England; yes, I saw it; both the shire and the town. —shire was seventy miles nearer London than the remote county where I now resided: that was a recommendation to me. I longed to go where there was life and movement: Millcote was a large manufacturing town on the banks of the A—; a busy place enough, doubtless: so much the better, it would be a complete change at least. Not that my fancy was much captivated by the idea of long chimnies and clouds of smoke – "but" – I argued, "Thornfield will, probably, be a good way from the town."

Here the socket of the candle dropped, and the wick went out.

Next day new steps were to be taken: my plans could no longer be confined to my own breast; I must impart them in order to achieve their success. Having sought and obtained an audience of the Superintendent during the noontide recreation, I told her I had a prospect of getting a new situation where the salary would be double what I now received (for, at Lowood, I only got 15 *l.* per annum); and requested she would break the matter for me to Mr. Brocklehurst or some of the committee, and ascertain whether they would permit me to mention them as references. She obligingly consented to act as mediatrix in the matter. The next day she laid the affair before Mr. Brocklehurst; who said that Mrs. Reed must be written to, as she was my natural guardian. A note was accordingly addressed to that lady, who returned for answer, that "I might do as I pleased: she had long relinquished all interference in my affairs." This note went the round of the committee, and at last, after what appeared to me most tedious delay, formal leave was given me to better my condition if I could; and an assurance added, that as I had always conducted myself well, both as teacher and pupil, at Lowood, a testimonial of character and capacity signed by the inspectors of that institution, should forthwith be furnished me.

---

1 By the rule.

This testimonial I accordingly received in about a week; forwarded a copy of it to Mrs. Fairfax, and got that lady's reply, stating that she was satisfied, and fixing that day fortnight as the period for my assuming the post of governess in her house.

I now busied myself in preparations: the fortnight passed rapidly. I had not a very large wardrobe, though it was adequate to my wants; and the last day sufficed to pack my trunk, – the same I had brought with me eight years ago from Gateshead.

The box was corded, the card nailed on. In half an hour the carrier was to call for it to take it to Lowton, whither I myself was to repair at an early hour the next morning to meet the coach. I had brushed my black stuff travelling dress, prepared my bonnet, gloves, and muff; sought in all my drawers to see that no article was left behind; and now, having nothing more to do, I sat down and tried to rest. I could not: though I had been on foot all day, I could not now repose an instant; I was too much excited. A phase of my life was closing to-night, a new one opening to-morrow: impossible to slumber in the interval; I must watch feverishly while the change was being accomplished.

"Miss," said a servant who met me in the lobby, where I was wandering like a troubled spirit, "a person below wishes to see you."

"The carrier, no doubt," I thought, and ran downstairs without inquiry. I was passing the back parlour, or teachers' sitting-room, the door of which was half open, to go to the kitchen, when some one ran out: –

"It's her, I am sure! – I could have told her anywhere!" cried the individual who stopped my progress and took my hand.

I looked: I saw a woman attired like a well-dressed servant, matronly, yet still young; very good-looking, with black hair and eyes, and lively complexion.

"Well, who is it?" she asked in a voice and with a smile I half recognised; "you've not quite forgotten me, I think, Miss Jane?"

In another second I was embracing and kissing her rapturously: "Bessie! Bessie! Bessie!" that was all I said; whereat she half laughed, half cried, and we both went into the parlour. By the fire stood a little fellow of three years old, in plaid frock and trousers.

"That is my little boy," said Bessie, directly.

"Then you are married, Bessie?"

"Yes: nearly five years since, to Robert Leaven, the coachman; and I've a little girl besides Bobby there, that I've christened Jane."

"And you don't live at Gateshead?"

"I live at the Lodge: the old porter has left."

"Well, and how do they all get on? Tell me everything about them, Bessie: but sit down first; and, Bobby, come and sit on my knee, will you?" but Bobby preferred sidling over to his mother.

"You're not grown so very tall, Miss Jane, nor so very stout," continued Mrs. Leaven. "I dare say they've not kept you too well at school: Miss Reed is the head and shoulders taller than you are; and Miss Georgiana would make two of you in breadth."

"Georgiana is handsome, I suppose, Bessie?"

"Very. She went up to London last winter with her mama, and there everybody admired her, and a young lord fell in love with her: but his relations were against the match; and – what do you think? – he and Miss Georgiana made it up to run away: but they were found out and stopped. It was Miss Reed that found them out: I believe she was envious; and now she and her sister lead a cat and dog life together: they are always quarrelling."

"Well, and what of John Reed?"

"Oh, he is not doing so well as his mama could wish. He went to college, and he got – plucked,[1] I think they call it; and then his uncles wanted him to be a barrister, and study the law: but he is such a dissipated young man, they will never make much of him, I think."

"What does he look like?"

"He is very tall: some people call him a fine looking young man; but he has such thick lips."

"And Mrs. Reed?"

"Missis looks stout and well enough in the face, but I think she's not quite easy in her mind: Mr. John's conduct does not please her – he spends a deal of money."

"Did she send you here, Bessie?"

"No, indeed: but I have long wanted to see you, and when I heard that there had been a letter from you, and that you were going to another part of the country, I thought I'd just set off and get a look at you before you were quite out of my reach."

---

1   John Reed has been expelled from university for failing his examinations.

"I am afraid you are disappointed in me, Bessie." I said this laughing: I perceived that Bessie's glance, though it expressed regard, did in no shape denote admiration.

"No, Miss Jane, not exactly: you are genteel enough; you look like a lady, and it is as much as ever I expected of you: you were no beauty as a child."

I smiled at Bessie's frank answer: I felt that it was correct, but I confess I was not quite indifferent to its import: at eighteen most people wish to please, and the conviction that they have not an exterior likely to second that desire brings anything but gratification.

"I daresay you are clever, though," continued Bessie, by way of solace. "What can you do? Can you play on the piano?"

"A little."

There was one in the room; Bessie went and opened it, and then asked me to sit down and give her a tune: I played a waltz or two and she was charmed.

"The Miss Reeds could not play as well!" said she exultingly. "I always said you would surpass them in learning: and can you draw?"

"That is one of my paintings over the chimney-piece." It was a landscape in water colours, of which I had made a present to the Superintendent, in acknowledgment of her obliging mediation with the committee on my behalf; and which she had had framed and glazed.

"Well, that is beautiful, Miss Jane! It is as fine a picture as any Miss Reed's drawing-master could paint, let alone the young ladies themselves, who could not come near it: and have you learnt French?"

"Yes, Bessie, I can both read it and speak it."

"And you can work on muslin and canvas?"

"I can."

"Oh you are quite a lady, Miss Jane! I knew you would be: you will get on whether your relations notice you or not. There was something I wanted to ask you. – Have you ever heard anything from your father's kinsfolk, the Eyres?"

"Never in my life."

"Well, you know Missis always said they were poor and quite despicable: and they may be poor; but I believe they are as much gentry as the Reeds are; for one day, nearly seven years ago, a Mr. Eyre came to Gateshead and wanted to see you; Missis said you were at school fifty miles off; he seemed so much disappointed, for he could not stay: he was going on a voyage to a foreign country, and the ship was to sail from London in a day or two. He looked quite a gentleman, and I believe he was your father's brother."

"What foreign country was he going to, Bessie?"

"An island thousands of miles off, where they make wine – the butler did tell me —"

"Madeira?"[1] I suggested.

"Yes, that is it – that is the very word."

"So he went?"

"Yes; he did not stay many minutes in the house: Missis was very high with him; she called him afterwards a 'sneaking tradesman.' My Robert believes he was a wine-merchant."

"Very likely," I returned; "or perhaps clerk or agent to a wine-merchant."

Bessie and I conversed about old times an hour longer, and then she was obliged to leave me: I saw her again for a few minutes the next morning at Lowton, while I was waiting for the coach. We parted finally at the door of the Brocklehurst Arms there: each went her separate way; she set off for the brow of Lowood Fell to meet the conveyance which was to take her back to Gateshead, I mounted the vehicle which was to bear me to new duties and a new life in the unknown environs of Millcote.

---

1   Madeira, an island located off the coast of Morocco, was famous for its wine.

CHAPTER XI

A NEW chapter in a novel is something like a new scene in a play; and when I draw up the curtain this time, reader, you must fancy you see a room in the George Inn at Millcote, with such large-figured papering on the walls as inn rooms have: such a carpet, such furniture, such ornaments on the mantel-piece, such prints; including a portrait of George the Third,[1] and another of the Prince of Wales,[2] and a representation of the death of Wolfe.[3] All this is visible to you by the light of an oil-lamp hanging from the ceiling, and by that of an excellent fire, near which I sit in my cloak and bonnet; my muff and umbrella lie on the table, and I am warming away the numbness and chill contracted by sixteen hours' exposure to the rawness of an October day: I left Lowton at four o'clock p.m., and the Millcote town clock is now just striking eight.

Reader, though I look comfortably accommodated, I am not very tranquil in my mind: I thought when the coach stopped here there would be some one to meet me; I looked anxiously round as I descended the wooden steps the "boots"[4] placed for my convenience, expecting to hear my name pronounced and to see some description of carriage waiting to convey me to Thornfield. Nothing of the sort was visible; and when I asked a waiter if any one had been to inquire after a Miss Eyre, I was answered in the negative; so I had no resource but to request to be shown into a private room: and here I am, waiting, while all sorts of doubts and fears are troubling my thoughts.

It is a very strange sensation to inexperienced youth to feel itself quite alone in the world: cut adrift from every connection; uncertain whether the port to which it is bound can be reached, and prevented by many impediments from returning to that it has quitted. The charm of adventure sweetens that sensation, the glow of pride warms it: but then the throb of fear disturbs it; and fear with me became

---

1   George III (1738-1820) became King of England in 1760.
2   The future George IV (1762-1830) became King of England in 1820, but was made Prince Regent in 1810 because of his father's insanity.
3   Major-general James Wolfe (1727-59) was killed fighting French forces on the Plains of Abraham in Quebec. His victory secured British control over Canada.
4   A hotel servant who cleans boots and shoes, carries luggage, and does other odd jobs.

predominant, when half an hour elapsed and still I was alone. I bethought myself to ring the bell.

"Is there a place in this neighbourhood called Thornfield?" I asked of the waiter who answered the summons.

"Thornfield? I don't know, ma'am; I'll inquire at the bar." He vanished, but reappeared instantly: –

"Is your name Eyre, Miss?"

"Yes."

"Person here waiting for you."

I jumped up, took my muff and umbrella, and hastened into the inn-passage: a man was standing by the open door, and in the lamplit street, I dimly saw a one horse conveyance.

"This will be your luggage, I suppose?" said the man rather abruptly when he saw me, pointing to my trunk in the passage.

"Yes." He hoisted it on to the vehicle, which was a sort of car, and then I got in: before he shut me up, I asked him how far it was to Thornfield.

"A matter of six miles."

"How long shall we be before we get there?"

"Happen an hour and a half."

He fastened the car door, climbed to his own seat outside, and we set off. Our progress was leisurely, and gave me ample time to reflect: I was content to be at length so near the end of my journey; and as I leaned back in the comfortable though not elegant conveyance, I meditated much at my ease.

"I suppose," thought I, "judging from the plainness of the servant and carriage, Mrs. Fairfax is not a very dashing person: so much the better; I never lived amongst fine people but once, and I was very miserable with them. I wonder if she lives alone except this little girl; if so, and if she is in any degree amiable, I shall surely be able to get on with her; I will do my best: it is a pity that doing one's best does not always answer. At Lowood, indeed, I took that resolution, kept it, and succeeded in pleasing; but with Mrs. Reed, I remember my best was always spurned with scorn. I pray God Mrs. Fairfax may not turn out a second Mrs. Reed; but if she does, I am not bound to stay with her: let the worst come to the worst, I can advertise again. How far are we on our road now, I wonder?"

I let down the window and looked out: Millcote was behind us; judging by the number of its lights, it seemed a place of considerable magnitude, much larger than Lowton. We were now, as far as I could see, on a sort of common; but there were houses scattered all over the district: I felt we were in a different region to Lowood, more populous, less picturesque; more stirring, less romantic.

The roads were heavy, the night misty; my conductor let his horse walk all the way, and the hour and a half extended, I verily believe, to two hours; at last he turned in his seat and said: –

"You're noan so far fro' Thornfield now."

Again I looked out: we were passing a church; I saw its low broad tower against the sky, and its bell was tolling a quarter; I saw a narrow galaxy of lights too, on a hill-side, marking a village or hamlet. About ten minutes after, the driver got down and opened a pair of gates: we passed through, and they clashed to behind us. We now slowly ascended a drive, and came upon the long front of a house: candle-light gleamed from one curtained bow-window; all the rest were dark. The car stopped at the front door; it was opened by a maid-servant; I alighted and went in.

"Will you walk this way, ma'am," said the girl; and I followed her across a square hall with high doors all round: she ushered me into a room, whose double illumination of fire and candle at first dazzled me, contrasting as it did with the darkness to which my eyes had been for two hours inured; when I could see, however, a cozy and agreeable picture presented itself to my view.

A snug, small room; a round table by a cheerful fire; an arm-chair high-backed and old-fashioned, wherein sat the neatest imaginable little elderly lady, in widow's cap, black silk gown and snowy muslin apron: exactly like what I had fancied Mrs. Fairfax, only less stately and milder looking. She was occupied in knitting; a large cat sat demurely at her feet; nothing in short was wanting to complete the beau ideal of domestic comfort. A more reassuring introduction for a new governess could scarcely be conceived: there was no grandeur to overwhelm, no stateliness to embarrass; and then, as I entered, the old lady got up, and promptly and kindly came forward to meet me.

"How do you do, my dear? I am afraid you have had a tedious ride; John drives so slowly: you must be cold, come to the fire."

"Mrs. Fairfax, I suppose?" said I.

"Yes, you are right: do sit down."

She conducted me to her own chair, and then began to remove my shawl and untie my bonnet-strings: I begged she would not give herself so much trouble.

"Oh, it is no trouble; I dare say your own hands are almost numbed with cold. Leah, make a little hot negus[1] and cut a sandwich or two: here are the keys of the store-room."

And she produced from her pocket a most housewifely bunch of keys, and delivered them to the servant.

"Now, then, draw nearer to the fire;" she continued. "You've brought your luggage with you, haven't you, my dear?"

"Yes, ma'am."

"I'll see it carried into your room," she said, and bustled out.

"She treats me like a visitor," thought I. "I little expected such a reception; I anticipated only coldness and stiffness: this is not like what I have heard of the treatment of governesses; but I must not exult too soon."

She returned; with her own hands cleared her knitting apparatus and a book or two from the table, to make room for the tray which Leah now brought, and then herself handed me the refreshments. I felt rather confused at being the object of more attention than I had ever before received, and, that too, shewn by my employer and superior; but as she did not herself seem to consider she was doing anything out of her place, I thought it better to take her civilities quietly.

"Shall I have the pleasure of seeing Miss Fairfax to-night?" I asked, when I had partaken of what she offered me.

"What did you say, my dear? I am a little deaf," returned the good lady, approaching her ear to my mouth.

I repeated the question more distinctly.

"Miss Fairfax? Oh, you mean Miss Varens! Varens is the name of your future pupil."

"Indeed! Then she is not your daughter?"

"No, – I have no family."

I should have followed up my first inquiry, by asking in what way

---

1 Sweetened wine mixed with hot water.

Miss Varens was connected with her; but I recollected it was not polite to ask too many questions: besides, I was sure to hear in time.

"I am so glad −" she continued, as she sat down opposite to me, and took the cat on her knee: "I am so glad you are come; it will be quite pleasant living here now with a companion. To be sure it is pleasant at any time; for Thornfield is a fine old hall, rather neglected of late years perhaps, but still it is a respectable place: yet you know in winter time, one feels dreary quite alone, in the best quarters. I say alone − Leah is a nice girl to be sure, and John and his wife are very decent people; but then you see they are only servants, and one can't converse with them on terms of equality: one must keep them at due distance, for fear of losing one's authority. I'm sure last winter (it was a very severe one, if you recollect, and when it did not snow, it rained and blew), not a creature but the butcher and postman came to the house, from November till February; and I really got quite melancholy with sitting night after night alone; I had Leah in to read to me sometimes; but I don't think the poor girl liked the task much: she felt it confining. In spring and summer one got on better: sunshine and long days make such a difference; and then, just at the commencement of this autumn, little Adela Varens came and her nurse: a child makes a house alive all at once; and now you are here I shall be quite gay."

My heart really warmed to the worthy lady as I heard her talk; and I drew my chair a little nearer to her, and expressed my sincere wish that she might find my company as agreeable as she anticipated.

"But I'll not keep you sitting up late to-night," said she; "it is on the stroke of twelve now, and you have been travelling all day: you must feel tired. If you have got your feet well warmed I'll shew you your bed-room. I've had the room next to mine prepared for you; it is only a small apartment, but I thought you would like it better than one of the large front chambers: to be sure they have finer furniture, but they are so dreary and solitary, I never sleep in them myself."

I thanked her for her considerate choice, and as I really felt fatigued with my long journey, expressed my readiness to retire. She took her candle, and I followed her from the room. First she went to see if the hall-door was fastened; having taken the key from the lock, she led the way up stairs. The steps and bannisters were of oak; the staircase window was high and latticed: both it and the long gallery into which the bed-room doors opened, looked as if they belonged to a church rather than a house. A very chill and vault-like air pervaded the stairs and gallery, suggesting cheerless ideas of space and solitude; and I was glad when finally ushered into my chamber, to find it of small dimensions and furnished in ordinary modern style.

When Mrs. Fairfax had bidden me a kind good night, and I had fastened my door, gazed leisurely round, and in some measure effaced the eerie impression made by that wide hall, that dark and spacious staircase, and that long, cold gallery, by the livelier aspect of my little room, I remembered that after a day of bodily fatigue and mental anxiety, I was now at last in safe haven. The impulse of gratitude swelled my heart, and I knelt down at the bed-side, and offered up thanks where thanks were due; not forgetting, ere I rose, to implore aid on my further path, and the power of meriting the kindness which seemed so frankly offered me before it was earned. My couch had no thorns in it that night; my solitary room no fears. At once weary and content, I slept soon and soundly: when I awoke it was broad day.

The chamber looked such a bright little place to me as the sun shone in between the gay blue chintz[1] window curtains, showing papered walls and a carpeted floor, so unlike the bare planks and stained plaster of Lowood, that my spirits rose at the view. Externals have a great effect on the young: I thought that a fairer era of life was beginning for me, – one that was to have its flowers and pleasures, as well as its thorns and toils. My faculties, roused by the change of scene, the new field offered to hope, seemed all astir. I cannot precisely define what they expected, but it was something pleasant: not perhaps that day or that month, but at an indefinite future period.

I rose; I dressed myself with care: obliged to be plain – for I had no article of attire that was not made with extreme simplicity – I was still by nature solicitous to be neat. It was not my habit to be disregardful of appearance, or careless of the impression I made: on the contrary, I ever wished to look as well as I could, and to please as much as my want of beauty would permit. I sometimes regretted that I was not

---

1 Printed cotton cloth.

handsomer: I sometimes wished to have rosy cheeks, a straight nose, and small cherry mouth; I desired to be tall, stately, and finely developed in figure; I felt it a misfortune that I was so little, so pale, and had features so irregular and so marked. And why had I these aspirations and these regrets? It would be difficult to say: I could not then distinctly say it to myself; yet I had a reason, and a logical, natural reason too. However, when I had brushed my hair very smooth, and put on my black frock – which, Quaker-like as it was, at least had the merit of fitting to a nicety – and adjusted my clean white tucker, I thought I should do respectably enough to appear before Mrs. Fairfax; and that my new pupil would not at least recoil from me with antipathy. Having opened my chamber window, and seen that I left all things straight and neat on the toilet table, I ventured forth.

Traversing the long and matted gallery, I descended the slippery steps of oak; then I gained the hall: I halted there a minute; I looked at some pictures on the walls (one I remember represented a grim man in a cuirass,[1] and one a lady with powdered hair and a pearl necklace), at a bronze lamp pendent from the ceiling, at a great clock whose case was of oak curiously carved, and ebon black with time and rubbing. Everything appeared very stately and imposing to me: but then I was so little accustomed to grandeur. The hall-door, which was half of glass, stood open; I stepped over the threshold. It was a fine Autumn morning; the early sun shone serenely on embrowned groves and still green fields: advancing on to the lawn, I looked up and surveyed the front of the mansion. It was three stories high, of proportions not vast, though considerable; a gentleman's manor-house, not a nobleman's seat: battlements round the top gave it a picturesque look. Its grey front stood out well from the back-ground of a rookery, whose cawing tenants were now on the wing: they flew over the lawn and grounds to alight in a great meadow, from which these were separated by a sunk fence, and where an array of mighty old thorn trees, strong, knotty, and broad as oaks, at once explained the etymology of the mansion's designation. Farther off were hills: not so lofty as those round Lowood, nor so craggy, nor so like barriers of separation from the living world; but yet quiet and lonely hills enough, and seeming

---

1   A piece of body armour reaching to the waist.

to embrace Thornfield with a seclusion I had not expected to find existent so near the stirring locality of Millcote. A little hamlet, whose roofs were blent with trees, straggled up the side of one of these hills; the church of the district stood nearer Thornfield: its old tower-top looked over a knoll between the house and gates.

I was yet enjoying the calm prospect and pleasant fresh air, yet listening with delight to the cawing of the rooks, yet surveying the wide, hoary front of the hall, and thinking what a great place it was for one lonely little dame like Mrs. Fairfax to inhabit, when that lady appeared at the door.

"What! out already?" said she. "I see you are an early riser." I went up to her, and was received with an affable kiss and shake of the hand.

"How do you like Thornfield?" she asked. I told her I liked it very much.

"Yes," she said, "it is a pretty place; but I fear it will be getting out of order, unless Mr. Rochester should take it into his head to come and reside here permanently; or, at least, visit it rather oftener: great houses and fine grounds require the presence of the proprietor."

"Mr. Rochester!" I exclaimed. "Who is he?"

"The owner of Thornfield," she responded quietly. "Did you not know he was called Rochester?"

Of course I did not – I had never heard of him before; but the old lady seemed to regard his existence as an universally understood fact, with which everybody must be acquainted by instinct.

"I thought," I continued, "Thornfield belonged to you."

"To me? Bless you child! what an idea! To me? I am only the housekeeper – the manager. To be sure I am distantly related to the Rochesters by the mother's side; or, at least, my husband was: he was a clergyman, incumbent of Hay – that little village yonder on the hill – and that church near the gates was his. The present Mr. Rochester's mother was a Fairfax, and second cousin to my husband; but I never presume on the connection – in fact, it is nothing to me; I consider myself quite in the light of an ordinary housekeeper: my employer is always civil, and I expect nothing more."

"And the little girl – my pupil?"

"She is Mr. Rochester's ward; he commissioned me to find a governess for her. He intends to have her brought up in —shire, I believe.

Here she comes, with her 'bonne,' as she calls her nurse." The enigma then was explained: this affable and kind little widow was no great dame, but a dependent like myself. I did not like her the worse for that; on the contrary, I felt better pleased than ever. The equality between her and me was real; not the mere result of condescension on her part: so much the better – my position was all the freer.

As I was meditating on this discovery, a little girl, followed by her attendant, came running up the lawn. I looked at my pupil, who did not at first appear to notice me: she was quite a child, perhaps seven or eight years old, slightly built, with a pale small-featured face, and a redundancy of hair falling in curls to her waist.

"Good morning, Miss Adela," said Mrs. Fairfax. "Come and speak to the lady who is to teach you, and to make you a clever woman some day." She approached.

"C'est là ma gouvernante?"[1] said she, pointing to me, and addressing her nurse; who answered:

"Mais oui, certainement."[2]

"Are they foreigners?" I inquired, amazed at hearing the French language.

"The nurse is a foreigner, and Adela was born on the continent; and, I believe, never left it till within six months ago. When she first came here she could speak no English; now she can make shift to talk it a little: I don't understand her, she mixes it so with French; but you will make out her meaning very well, I daresay."

Fortunately I had had the advantage of being taught French by a French lady; and as I had always made a point of conversing with Madame Pierrot, as often as I could, and had, besides, during the last seven years, learnt a portion of French by heart daily – applying myself to take pains with my accent, and imitating as closely as possible the pronunciation of my teacher – I had acquired a certain degree of readiness and correctness in the language, and was not likely to be much at a loss with Mademoiselle Adela. She came and shook hands with me when she heard that I was her governess; and as I led her in to breakfast, I addressed some phrases to her in her own tongue: she replied briefly at first, but after we were seated at the table, and she

1   "Is that my governess?"
2   "Why yes, certainly."

had examined me some ten minutes with her large hazel eyes, she suddenly commenced chattering fluently.

"Ah!" cried she in French, "you speak my language as well as Mr. Rochester does: I can talk to you as I can to him, and so can Sophie. She will be glad: nobody here understands her: Madame Fairfax is all English. Sophie is my nurse; she came with me over the sea in a great ship with a chimney that smoked – how it did smoke! – and I was sick, and so was Sophie, and so was Mr. Rochester. Mr. Rochester lay down on a sofa in a pretty room called the salon, and Sophie and I had little beds in another place. I nearly fell out of mine; it was like a shelf. And, Mademoiselle — what is your name?"

"Eyre – Jane Eyre."

"Aïre? Bah! I cannot say it. Well: our ship stopped in the morning, before it was quite daylight, at a great city – a huge city, with very dark houses and all smoky; not at all like the pretty clean town I came from; and Mr. Rochester carried me in his arms over a plank to the land, and Sophie came after, and we all got into a coach, which took us to a beautiful large house, larger than this and finer, called an hotel. We stayed there nearly a week: I and Sophie used to walk every day in a great green place full of trees, called the Park; and there were many children there besides me, and a pond with beautiful birds on it, that I fed with crumbs."

"Can you understand her when she runs on so fast?" asked Mrs. Fairfax.

I understood her very well, for I had been accustomed to the fluent tongue of Madame Pierrot.

"I wish," continued the good lady, "you would ask her a question or two about her parents: I wonder if she remembers them?"

"Adèle," I inquired, "with whom did you live when you were in that pretty clean town you spoke of?"

"I lived long ago with mama; but she is gone to the Holy Virgin. Mama used to teach me to dance and sing, and to say verses. A great many gentlemen and ladies came to see mama, and I used to dance before them, or to sit on their knees and sing to them: I liked it. Shall I let you hear me sing now?"

She had finished her breakfast, so I permitted her to give a specimen of her accomplishments. Descending from her chair, she came and placed herself on my knee; then, folding her little hands demurely before her, shaking back her curls and lifting her eyes to the ceiling, she commenced singing a song from some opera. It was the strain of a forsaken lady, who, after bewailing the perfidy of her lover, calls pride to her aid; desires her attendant to deck her in her brightest jewels and richest robes, and resolves to meet the false one that night at a ball, and prove to him by the gaiety of her demeanour how little his desertion has affected her.

The subject seemed strangely chosen for an infant singer; but I suppose the point of the exhibition lay in hearing the notes of love and jealousy warbled with the lisp of childhood; and in very bad taste that point was: at least I thought so.

Adèle sang the canzonette tunefully enough, and with the naiveté of her age. This achieved, she jumped from my knee and said, "Now, mademoiselle, I will repeat you some poetry."

Assuming an attitude, she began "La Ligue des Rats; fable de La Fontaine."[1] She then declaimed the little piece with an attention to punctuation and emphasis, a flexibility of voice and an appropriateness of gesture, very unusual indeed at her age; and which proved she had been carefully trained.

"Was it your mama who taught you that piece?" I asked.

"Yes, and she just used to say it in this way: 'Qu'avez vous donc? lui dit un de ces rats; parlez!'[2] She made me lift my hand – so – to remind me to raise my voice at the question. Now shall I dance for you?"

"No, that will do: but after your mama went to the Holy Virgin, as you say, with whom did you live then?"

"With Madame Frédéric and her husband: she took care of me, but she is nothing related to me. I think she is poor, for she had not so fine a house as mama. I was not long there; Mr. Rochester asked me if I would like to go and live with him in England, and I said yes; for I knew Mr. Rochester before I knew Madame Frédéric, and he was always kind to me and gave me pretty dresses and toys: but you see he

---

1 "The League of Rats: A Fable by Fontaine." Jean de la Fontaine (1621-95), French poet, dramatist, and satirist, was perhaps most famous for his "Fables," published in 1668, 1678-9, and 1694. This particular story is from *Dernières Fables,* XXV.22.

2 "What's the matter with you? said one of the rats; speak!"

has not kept his word, for he has brought me to England, and now he is gone back again himself, and I never see him."

After breakfast, Adèle and I withdrew to the library; which room, it appears, Mr. Rochester had directed should be used as the school-room. Most of the books were locked up behind glass doors; but there was one book-case left open, containing everything that could be needed in the way of elementary works, and several volumes of light literature, poetry, biography, travels, a few romances, &c. I sup-pose he had considered that these were all the governess would require for her private perusal; and, indeed, they contented me amply for the present: compared with the scanty pickings I had now and then been able to glean at Lowood, they seemed to offer an abundant harvest of entertainment and information. In this room, too, there was a cabinet piano, quite new and of superior tone; also an easel for painting, and a pair of globes.

I found my pupil sufficiently docile, though disinclined to apply: she had not been used to regular occupation of any kind. I felt it would be injudicious to confine her too much at first; so, when I had talked to her a great deal, and got her to learn a little, and when the morning had advanced to noon, I allowed her to return to her nurse. I then proposed to occupy myself till dinner-time in drawing some little sketches for her use.

As I was going up-stairs to fetch my portfolio and pencils, Mrs. Fairfax called to me: "Your morning school-hours are over now, I suppose," said she. She was in a room the folding-doors of which stood open: I went in when she addressed me. It was a large, stately apartment, with purple chairs and curtains, a Turkey carpet, walnut-panelled walls, one vast window rich in stained glass, and a lofty ceil-ing, nobly moulded. Mrs. Fairfax was dusting some vases of fine purple spar,[1] which stood on a side-board.

"What a beautiful room!" I exclaimed, as I looked round: for I had never before seen any half so imposing.

"Yes; this is the dining-room. I have just opened the window, to let in a little air and sunshine; for everything gets so damp in apart-ments that are seldom inhabited: the drawing-room yonder feels like a vault."

---

1   Crystal.

She pointed to a wide arch corresponding to the window, and hung like it with a Tyrian-dyed[1] curtain, now looped up. Mounting to it by two broad steps and looking through, I thought I caught a glimpse of a fairy place; so bright to my novice-eyes appeared the view beyond. Yet it was merely a very pretty drawing-room, and within it a boudoir, both spread with white carpets, on which seemed laid brilliant garlands of flowers; both ceiled with snowy mouldings of white grapes and vine-leaves, beneath which glowed in rich contrast crimson couches and ottomans; while the ornaments on the pale Parian[2] mantel-piece were of sparkling Bohemian glass, ruby red; and between the windows large mirrors repeated the general blending of snow and fire.

"In what order you keep these rooms, Mrs. Fairfax!" said I. "No dust, no canvas coverings: except that the air feels chilly, one would think they were inhabited daily."

"Why, Miss Eyre, though Mr. Rochester's visits here are rare, they are always sudden and unexpected; and as I observed that it put him out to find everything swathed up, and to have a bustle of arrangement on his arrival, I thought it best to keep the rooms in readiness."

"Is Mr. Rochester an exacting, fastidious sort of man?"

"Not particularly so; but he has a gentleman's tastes and habits, and he expects to have things managed in conformity to them."

"Do you like him? Is he generally liked?"

"Oh, yes; the family have always been respected here. Almost all the land in this neighbourhood, as far as you can see, has belonged to the Rochesters time out of mind."

"Well, but, leaving his land out of the question, do you like him? Is he liked for himself?"

"*I* have no cause to do otherwise than like him; and I believe he is considered a just and liberal landlord by his tenants: but he has never lived much amongst them."

"But has he no peculiarities? What, in short, is his character?"

"Oh! his character is unimpeachable, I suppose. He is rather peculiar, perhaps: he has travelled a great deal, and seen a great deal of the world, I should think. I dare say he is clever: but I never had much conversation with him."

---

1 Purple.
2 White marble.

"In what way is he peculiar?"

"I don't know – it is not easy to describe – nothing striking, but you feel it when he speaks to you: you cannot be always sure whether he is in jest or earnest, whether he is pleased or the contrary; you don't thoroughly understand him, in short – at least, I don't: but it is of no consequence, he is a very good master."

This was all the account I got from Mrs. Fairfax, of her employer and mine. There are people who seem to have no notion of sketching a character, or observing and describing salient points, either in persons or things: the good lady evidently belonged to this class; my queries puzzled, but did not draw her out. Mr. Rochester was Mr. Rochester in her eyes; a gentleman, a landed proprietor – nothing more: she inquired and searched no further, and evidently wondered at my wish to gain a more definite notion of his identity.

When we left the dining-room, she proposed to show me over the rest of the house; and I followed her up-stairs and down-stairs, admiring as I went: for all was well-arranged and handsome. The large front chambers I thought especially grand; and some of the third story rooms, though dark and low, were interesting from their air of antiquity. The furniture once appropriated to the lower apartments had from time to time been removed here, as fashions changed; and the imperfect light entering by their narrow casements showed bedsteads of a hundred years old; chests in oak or walnut, looking, with their strange carvings of palm branches and cherubs' heads, like types of the Hebrew ark;[1] rows of venerable chairs, high-backed and narrow; stools still more antiquated, on whose cushioned tops were yet apparent traces of half-effaced embroideries, wrought by fingers that for two generations had been coffin-dust. All these relics gave to the third story of Thornfield Hall the aspect of a home of the past: a shrine of memory. I liked the hush, the gloom, the quaintness of these retreats in the day; but I by no means coveted a night's repose on one of those wide and heavy beds: shut in, some of them, with doors of oak; shaded, others, with wrought old English hangings crusted with thick work, pourtraying effigies of strange flowers, and stranger birds, and strangest human beings, – all which would have looked strange, indeed, by the pallid gleam of moon-light.

---

1   The elaborately carved cabinent which held the tablets of the Ten Commandments.

"Do the servants sleep in these rooms?" I asked.

"No; they occupy a range of smaller apartments to the back; no one ever sleeps here: one would almost say that, if there were a ghost at Thornfield Hall, this would be its haunt."

"So I think: you have no ghost then?"

"None that I ever heard of," returned Mrs. Fairfax, smiling.

"Nor any traditions of one? no legends or ghost stories?"

"I believe not. And yet it is said, the Rochesters have been rather a violent than a quiet race in their time: perhaps, though, that is the reason they rest tranquilly in their graves now."

"Yes – 'after life's fitful fever they sleep well,'"[1] I muttered. "Where are you going now, Mrs. Fairfax?" for she was moving away.

"On to the leads: will you come and see the view from thence?" I followed still, up a very narrow staircase to the attics, and thence by a ladder and through a trap-door to the roof of the hall. I was now on a level with the crow-colony, and could see into their nests. Leaning over the battlements and looking far down, I surveyed the grounds laid out like a map: the bright and velvet lawn closely girdling the grey base of the mansion; the field, wide as a park, dotted with its ancient timber; the wood, dun and sere, divided by a path visibly overgrown, greener with moss than the trees were with foliage; the church at the gates, the road, the tranquil hills all reposing in the autumn day's sun; the horizon bounded by a propitious sky, azure, marbled with pearly white. No feature in the scene was extraordinary, but all was pleasing. When I turned from it and repassed the trap-door, I could scarcely see my way down the ladder: the attic seemed black as a vault compared with that arch of blue air to which I had been looking up, and to that sunlit scene of grove, pasture and green hill of which the hall was the centre, and over which I had been gazing with delight.

Mrs. Fairfax stayed behind a moment to fasten the trap-door; I, by dint of groping, found the outlet from the attic, and proceeded to descend the narrow garret staircase. I lingered in the long passage to which this led, separating the front and back rooms of the third story: narrow, low, and dim, with only one little window at the far

1 See *Macbeth* III.ii.23.

end, and looking, with its two rows of small black doors all shut, like a corridor in some Bluebeard's castle.[1]

While I paced softly on, the last sound I expected to hear in so still a region, a laugh, struck my ear. It was a curious laugh; distinct, formal, mirthless. I stopped: the sound ceased, only for an instant; it began again, louder: for at first, though distinct, it was very low. It passed off in a clamorous peal that seemed to wake an echo in every lonely chamber; though it originated but in one, and I could have pointed out the door whence the accents issued.

"Mrs. Fairfax!" I called out: for I now heard her descending the garret stairs. "Did you hear that loud laugh? Who is it?"

"Some of the servants very likely," she answered: "perhaps Grace Poole."

"Did you hear it?" I again inquired.

"Yes, plainly: I often hear her; she sews in one of these rooms. Sometimes Leah is with her: they are frequently noisy together."

The laugh was repeated in its low, syllabic tone, and terminated in an odd murmur.

"Grace!" exclaimed Mrs. Fairfax.

I really did not expect any Grace to answer; for the laugh was as tragic, as preternatural a laugh as any I ever heard; and, but that it was high noon, and that no circumstance of ghostliness accompanied the curious cachination;[2] but that neither scene nor season favoured fear, I should have been superstitiously afraid. However, the event showed me I was a fool for entertaining a sense even of surprise.

The door nearest me opened, and a servant came out, – a woman of between thirty and forty; a set, square-made figure, red-haired, and with a hard plain face: any apparition less romantic or less ghostly could scarcely be conceived.

"Too much noise, Grace," said Mrs. Fairfax. "Remember directions!" Grace curtseyed silently and went in.

---

1   Charles Perrault (1628-1703) collected and published a group of French fairy tales under the title *Histoires et Contes du Temps Passé* in 1697. It was eventually translated into English, and contains such standards as "Sleeping Beauty," "Cinderella," and "Red Riding Hood." "Blue Beard" is the story of a man who murders a series of wives and locks their bodies in a room in his castle.

2   Loud laughter.

"She is a person we have to sew and assist Leah in her housemaid's work," continued the widow; "not altogether unobjectionable in some points, but she does well enough. By-the-by, how have you got on with your new pupil this morning?"

The conversation, thus turned on Adèle, continued till we reached the light and cheerful region below. Adèle came running to meet us in the hall, exclaiming: –

"Mesdames, vous êtes servies!" adding "J'ai bien faim, moi!"[1]

We found dinner ready and waiting for us in Mrs. Fairfax's room.

---

1 "Ladies, you are served!...I'm famished, I am!"

CHAPTER XII

THE promise of a smooth career, which my first calm introduction to
Thornfield-Hall seemed to pledge, was not belied on a longer
acquaintance with the place and its inmates. Mrs. Fairfax turned out
to be what she appeared, a placid-tempered, kind-natured woman, of
competent education and average intelligence. My pupil was a lively
child, who had been spoilt and indulged, and therefore was sometimes wayward; but as she was committed entirely to my care, and no
injudicious interference from any quarter ever thwarted my plans for
her improvement, she soon forgot her little freaks, and became obedient and teachable. She had no great talents, no marked traits of character, no peculiar development of feeling or taste which raised her
one inch above the ordinary level of childhood; but neither had she
any deficiency or vice which sunk her below it. She made reasonable
progress, entertained for me a vivacious, though perhaps not very
profound affection, and by her simplicity, gay prattle, and efforts to
please, inspired me, in return, with a degree of attachment sufficient
to make us both content in each other's society.

This, *par parenthèse*,[1] will be thought cool language by persons who
entertain solemn doctrines about the angelic nature of children, and
the duty of those charged with their education to conceive for them
an idolatrous devotion: but I am not writing to flatter parental egotism, to echo cant, or prop up humbug; I am merely telling the truth.
I felt a conscientious solicitude for Adèle's welfare and progress, and
a quiet liking to her little self; just as I cherished towards Mrs. Fairfax
a thankfulness for her kindness, and a pleasure in her society propor-
tionate to the tranquil regard she had for me, and the moderation of
her mind and character.

Anybody may blame me who likes, when I add further, that, now
and then, when I took a walk by myself in the grounds; when I went
down to the gates and looked through them along the road; or when,
while Adèle played with her nurse, and Mrs. Fairfax made jellies in
the store-room, I climbed the three staircases, raised the trap-door of
the attic, and having reached the leads, looked out afar over

---

1 Parenthetically.

sequestered field and hill, and along dim skyline: that then I longed for a power of vision which might overpass that limit; which might reach the busy world, towns, regions full of life I had heard of but never seen: that then I desired more of practical experience than I possessed; more of intercourse with my kind, of acquaintance with variety of character, than was here within my reach. I valued what was good in Mrs. Fairfax, and what was good in Adèle; but I believed in the existence of other and more vivid kinds of goodness, and what I believed in I wished to behold.

Who blames me? Many no doubt; and I shall be called discontented. I could not help it: the restlessness was in my nature; it agitated me to pain sometimes. Then my sole relief was to walk along the corridor of the third story, backwards and forwards, safe in the silence and solitude of the spot, and allow my mind's eye to dwell on whatever bright visions rose before it – and certainly they were many and glowing; to let my heart be heaved by the exultant movement which, while it swelled it in trouble, expanded it with life; and, best of all, to open my inward ear to a tale that was never ended – a tale my imagination created, and narrated continuously; quickened with all of incident, life, fire, feeling, that I desired and had not in my actual existence.

It is in vain to say human beings ought to be satisfied with tranquillity: they must have action; and they will make it if they cannot find it. Millions are condemned to a stiller doom than mine, and millions are in silent revolt against their lot. Nobody knows how many rebellions besides political rebellions ferment in the masses of life which people earth. Women are supposed to be very calm generally: but women feel just as men feel; they need exercise for their faculties, and a field for their efforts as much as their brothers do; they suffer from too rigid a restraint, too absolute a stagnation, precisely as men would suffer; and it is narrow-minded in their more privileged fellow-creatures to say that they ought to confine themselves to making puddings and knitting stockings, to playing on the piano and embroidering bags. It is thoughtless to condemn them, or laugh at them, if they seek to do more or learn more than custom has pronounced necessary for their sex.

When thus alone, I not unfrequently heard Grace Poole's laugh: the same peal, the same low, slow ha! ha! which, when first heard, had thrilled me: I heard, too, her eccentric murmurs; stranger than her laugh. There were days when she was quite silent; but there were others when I could not account for the sounds she made. Sometimes I saw her: she would come out of her room with a basin, or a plate, or a tray in her hand, go down to the kitchen and shortly return, generally (oh romantic reader, forgive me for telling the plain truth!) bearing a pot of porter.[1] Her appearance always acted as a damper to the curiosity raised by her oral oddities: hard-featured and staid, she had no point to which interest could attach. I made some attempts to draw her into conversation, but she seemed a person of few words: a monosyllabic reply usually cut short every effort of that sort.

The other members of the household, viz. John and his wife, Leah the housemaid, and Sophie the French nurse, were decent people; but in no respect remarkable: with Sophie I used to talk French, and sometimes I asked her questions about her native country; but she was not of a descriptive or narrative turn, and generally gave such vapid and confused answers as were calculated rather to check than encourage inquiry.

October, November, December passed away. One afternoon in January, Mrs. Fairfax had begged a holiday for Adèle, because she had a cold; and, as Adèle seconded the request with an ardour that reminded me how precious occasional holidays had been to me in my own childhood, I accorded it; deeming that I did well in shewing pliability on the point. It was a fine, calm day, though very cold; I was tired of sitting still in the library through a whole long morning: Mrs. Fairfax had just written a letter which was waiting to be posted, so I put on my bonnet and cloak and volunteered to carry it to Hay; – the distance, two miles, would be a pleasant winter afternoon walk. Having seen Adèle comfortably seated in her little chair by Mrs. Fairfax's parlour fireside, and given her her best wax doll (which I usually kept enveloped in silver paper in a drawer) to play with, and a story-book for change of amusement; and having replied to her "Revenez bientôt ma bonne amie, ma chère Mdlle. Jeannette"[2] with a kiss, I set out.

The ground was hard, the air was still, my road was lonely; I walked fast till I got warm, and then I walked slowly to enjoy and

---

1 A dark brown beer.
2 "Come again soon, my good friend, my dear Miss Jane."

analyze the species of pleasure brooding for me in the hour and situation. It was three o'clock; the church bell tolled as I passed under the belfry: the charm of the hour lay in its approaching dimness, in the low-gliding and pale-beaming sun. I was a mile from Thornfield, in a lane noted for wild roses in summer, for nuts and blackberries in autumn, and even now possessing a few coral treasures in hips and haws;[1] but whose best winter delight lay in its utter solitude and leafless repose. If a breath of air stirred, it made no sound here; for there was not a holly, not an evergreen to rustle, and the stripped hawthorn and hazel bushes were as still as the white, worn stones which causewayed the middle of the path. Far and wide, on each side, there were only fields, where no cattle now browsed; and the little brown birds which stirred occasionally in the hedge, looked like single russet leaves that had forgotten to drop.

This lane inclined up-hill all the way to Hay: having reached the middle, I sat down on a stile which led thence into a field. Gathering my mantle about me and sheltering my hands in my muff, I did not feel the cold, though it froze keenly; as was attested by a sheet of ice covering the causeway, where a little brooklet, now congealed, had overflowed after a rapid thaw some days since. From my seat I could look down on Thornfield: the grey and battlemented hall was the principal object in the vale below me; its woods and dark rookery rose against the west. I lingered till the sun went down amongst the trees, and sank crimson and clear behind them. I then turned eastward.

On the hill-top above me sat the rising moon; pale yet as a cloud, but brightening momently: she looked over Hay, which, half lost in trees, sent up a blue smoke from its few chimneys; it was yet a mile distant, but in the absolute hush I could hear plainly its thin murmurs of life. My ear too felt the flow of currents; in what dales and depths I could not tell: but there were many hills beyond Hay, and doubtless many becks threading their passes. That evening calm betrayed alike the tinkle of the nearest streams, the sough of the most remote.

A rude noise broke on these fine ripplings and whisperings, at once so far away and so clear: a positive tramp, tramp; a metallic

---

1 Hips are the fruit of wild rose bushes; haws are the small red berries of hawthorn shrubs.

clatter, which effaced the soft wave-wanderings; as, in a picture, the solid mass of a crag, or the rough boles of a great oak, drawn in dark and strong on the foreground, efface the aërial distance of azure hill, sunny horizon and blended clouds, where tint melts into tint.

The din was on the causeway: a horse was coming; the windings of the lane yet hid it, but it approached. I was just leaving the stile; yet as the path was narrow, I sat still to let it go by. In those days I was young, and all sorts of fancies bright and dark tenanted my mind: the memories of nursery stories were there amongst other rubbish; and when they recurred, maturing youth added to them a vigour and vividness beyond what childhood could give. As this horse approached, and as I watched for it to appear through the dusk, I remembered certain of Bessie's tales wherein figured a North-of-England spirit, called a "Gytrash;" which, in the form of horse, mule, or large dog, haunted solitary ways, and sometimes came upon belated travellers, as this horse was now coming upon me.

It was very near, but not yet in sight; when, in addition to the tramp, tramp, I heard a rush under the hedge, and close down by the hazel stems glided a great dog, whose black and white colour made him a distinct object against the trees. It was exactly one mask[1] of Bessie's Gytrash, – a lion-like creature with long hair and a huge head: it passed me, however, quietly enough; not staying to look up, with strange pretercanine eyes, in my face, as I half expected it would. The horse followed, – a tall steed, and on its back a rider. The man, the human being, broke the spell at once. Nothing ever rode the Gytrash: it was always alone; and goblins, to my notions, though they might tenant the dumb carcasses of beasts, could scarce covet shelter in the common-place human form. No Gytrash was this, – only a traveller taking the short cut to Millcote. He passed, and I went on; a few steps, and I turned: a sliding sound and an exclamation of "What the deuce is to do now?" and a clattering tumble, arrested my attention. Man and horse were down; they had slipped on the sheet of ice which glazed the causeway. The dog came bounding back, and seeing his master in a predicament, and hearing the horse groan, barked till the evening hills echoed the sound; which was deep in proportion to

---

1 Manifestation.

his magnitude. He snuffed round the prostrate group, and then he ran up to me; it was all he could do, – there was no other help at hand to summon. I obeyed him, and walked down to the traveller, by this time struggling himself free of his steed. His efforts were so vigorous, I thought he could not be much hurt; but I asked him the question: –

"Are you injured, sir?"

I think he was swearing, but am not certain; however, he was pronouncing some formula which prevented him from replying to me directly.

"Can I do anything?" I asked again.

"You must just stand on one side," he answered as he rose, first to his knees, and then to his feet. I did; whereupon began a heaving, stamping, clattering process, accompanied by a barking and baying which removed me effectually some yards distance: but I would not be driven quite away till I saw the event. This was finally fortunate; the horse was re-established, and the dog was silenced with a "Down, Pilot!" The traveller now, stooping, felt his foot and leg, as if trying whether they were sound; apparently something ailed them, for he halted to the stile whence I had just risen, and sat down.

I was in the mood for being useful, or at least officious, I think, for I now drew near him again.

"If you are hurt, and want help, sir, I can fetch some one, either from Thornfield Hall or from Hay."

"Thank you; I shall do: I have no broken bones, – only a sprain;" and again he stood up and tried his foot, but the result extorted an involuntary "Ugh!"

Something of daylight still lingered, and the moon was waxing bright; I could see him plainly. His figure was enveloped in a riding cloak, fur collared, and steel clasped; its details were not apparent, but I traced the general points of middle height, and considerable breadth of chest. He had a dark face, with stern features and a heavy brow; his eyes and gathered eyebrows looked ireful and thwarted just now; he was past youth, but had not reached middle age: perhaps he might be thirty-five. I felt no fear of him, and but little shyness. Had he been a handsome, heroic-looking young gentleman, I should not have dared to stand thus questioning him against his will, and offering my services unasked. I had hardly ever seen a handsome youth: never in my life spoken to one. I had a theoretical reverence and homage for beauty, elegance, gallantry, fascination; but had I met those qualities incarnate in masculine shape, I should have known instinctively that they neither had nor could have sympathy with anything in me, and should have shunned them as one would fire, lightning, or anything else that is bright but antipathetic.

If even this stranger had smiled and been good-humoured to me when I addressed him; if he had put off my offer of assistance gaily and with thanks, I should have gone on my way and not felt any vocation to renew inquiries; but the frown, the roughness of the traveller set me at my ease: I retained my station when he waved to me to go, and announced: –

"I cannot think of leaving you, sir, at so late an hour, in this solitary lane, till I see you are fit to mount your horse."

He looked at me when I said this: he had hardly turned his eyes in my direction before.

"I should think you ought to be at home yourself," said he, "if you have a home in this neighbourhood: where do you come from?"

"From just below; and I am not at all afraid of being out late when it is moonlight: I will run over to Hay for you with pleasure, if you wish it – indeed, I am going there to post a letter."

"You live just below – do you mean at that house with the battlements?" pointing to Thornfield Hall, on which the moon cast a hoary gleam, bringing it out distinct and pale from the woods, that, by contrast with the western sky, now seemed one mass of shadow.

"Yes, sir."

"Whose house is it?"

"Mr. Rochester's."

"Do you know Mr. Rochester?"

"No, I have never seen him."

"He is not resident then?"

"No."

"Can you tell me where he is?"

"I cannot."

"You are not a servant at the hall, of course? You are —." He stopped, ran his eye over my dress, which, as usual, was quite simple: a black merino[1] cloak, a black beaver bonnet; neither of them half fine

---

1   Soft wool or wool-and-cotton material.

enough for a lady's maid. He seemed puzzled to decide what I was: I helped him.

"I am the governess."

"Ah, the governess!" he repeated; "deuce take me if I had not forgotten! The governess!" and again my raiment underwent scrutiny. In two minutes he rose from the stile: his face expressed pain, when he tried to move.

"I cannot commission you to fetch help," he said, "but you may help me a little yourself, if you will be so kind."

"Yes, sir."

"You have not an umbrella that I can use as a stick?"

"No."

"Try to get hold of my horse's bridle and lead him to me: you are not afraid?"

I should have been afraid to touch a horse when alone, but when told to do it, I was disposed to obey. I put down my muff on the stile, and went up to the tall steed; I endeavoured to catch the bridle, but it was a spirited thing, and would not let me come near its head; I made effort on effort, though in vain: meantime, I was mortally afraid of its trampling fore-feet. The traveller waited and watched for some time, and at last he laughed.

"I see," he said, "the mountain will never be brought to Mahomet, so all you can do is to aid Mahomet to go to the mountain; I must beg of you to come here."

I came – "Excuse me;" he continued, "necessity compels me to make you useful." He laid a heavy hand on my shoulder, and leaning on me with some stress, limped to his horse. Having once caught the bridle, he mastered it directly, and sprang to his saddle; grimacing grimly as he made the effort, for it wrenched his sprain.

"Now," said he, releasing his under lip from a hard bite, "just hand me my whip; it lies there under the hedge."

I sought it and found it.

"Thank you; now make haste with the letter to Hay, and return as fast as you can."

A touch of a spurred heel made his horse first start and rear, and then bound away; the dog rushed in his traces: all three vanished

"Like heath that in the wilderness
The wild wind whirls away."[1]

I took up my muff and walked on. The incident had occurred and
was gone for me: it was an incident of no moment, no romance, no
interest in a sense; yet it marked with change one single hour of a
monotonous life. My help had been needed and claimed; I had given
it: I was pleased to have done something; trivial, transitory though the
deed was, it was yet an active thing, and I was weary of an existence
all passive. The new face, too, was like a new picture introduced to the
gallery of memory; and it was dissimilar to all the others hanging
there: firstly, because it was masculine; and secondly, because it was
dark, strong and stern. I had it still before me when I entered Hay, and
slipped the letter into the post-office; I saw it as I walked fast down
hill all the way home. When I came to the stile I stopped a minute,
looked round and listened; with an idea that a horse's hoofs might
ring on the causeway again, and that a rider in a cloak, and a Gytrash-
like Newfoundland dog, might be again apparent: I saw only the
hedge and a pollard willow[2] before me, rising up still and straight to
meet the moonbeams; I heard only the faintest waft of wind, roaming
fitful among the trees round Thornfield, a mile distant; and when I
glanced down in the direction of the murmur, my eye, traversing the
hall-front, caught a light kindling in a window: it reminded me that I
was late, and I hurried on.

I did not like re-entering Thornfield. To pass its threshold was to
return to stagnation: to cross the silent hall, to ascend the darksome
staircase, to seek my own lonely little room, and then to meet tranquil
Mrs. Fairfax, and spend the long winter evening with her and her
only, was to quell wholly the faint excitement wakened by my walk, –
to slip again over my faculties the viewless fetters of an uniform and
too still existence; of an existence whose very privileges of security
and ease I was becoming incapable of appreciating. What good it
would have done me at that time to have been tossed in the storms of
an uncertain struggling life, and to have been taught by rough and

---

1 A quotation from the poem "Fallen is thy Throne" by Thomas Moore (1779-1852).
2 The tree has been trimmed to produce a close, round head of branches.

bitter experience to long for the calm amidst which I now repined! Yes, just as much good as it would do a man tired of sitting still in a "too easy chair"[1] to take a long walk: and just as natural was the wish to stir, under my circumstances, as it would be under his.

I lingered at the gates; I lingered on the lawn; I paced backwards and forwards on the pavement: the shutters of the glass door were closed; I could not see into the interior; and both my eyes and spirit seemed drawn from the gloomy house – from the grey hollow filled with rayless cells, as it appeared to me – to that sky expanded before me, – a blue sea absolved from taint of cloud; the moon ascending it in solemn march; her orb seeming to look up as she left the hill tops, from behind which she had come, far and farther below her, and aspired to the zenith, midnight-dark in its fathomless depth and measureless distance: and for those trembling stars that followed her course, they made my heart tremble, my veins glow when I viewed them. Little things recall us to earth: the clock struck in the hall; that sufficed; I turned from moon and stars, opened a side-door and went in.

The hall was not dark, nor yet was it lit only by the high-hung bronze lamp: a warm glow suffused both it and the lower steps of the oak staircase. This ruddy shine issued from the great dining-room, whose two-leaved door stood open and showed a genial fire in the grate, glancing on marble hearth and brass fire-irons, and revealing purple draperies and polished furniture in the most pleasant radiance. It revealed, too, a group near the mantelpiece: I had scarcely caught it, and scarcely become aware of a cheerful mingling of voices, amongst which I seemed to distinguish the tones of Adèle, when the door closed.

I hastened to Mrs. Fairfax's room: there was a fire there, too; but no candle, and no Mrs. Fairfax. Instead, all alone, sitting upright on the rug and gazing with gravity at the blaze, I beheld a great black and white long-haired dog, just like the Gytrash of the lane. It was so like it that I went forward and said –

"Pilot," and the thing got up and came to me and snuffed me. I caressed him, and he wagged his great tail: but he looked an eerie

---

1   A reference to *The Dunciad* IV.342 by Alexander Pope (1688-1744).

creature to be alone with, and I could not tell whence he had come. I rung the bell, for I wanted a candle; and I wanted too to get an account of this visitant. Leah entered.

"What dog is this?"

"He came with master."

"With whom?"

"With master – Mr. Rochester – he is just arrived."

"Indeed – and is Mrs. Fairfax with him?"

"Yes, and Miss Adela; they are in the dining-room, and John is gone for a surgeon: for master has had an accident; his horse fell and his ancle is sprained."

"Did the horse fall in Hay-lane?"

"Yes, coming down hill; it slipped on some ice."

"Ah! Bring me a candle, will you, Leah?"

Leah brought it: she entered followed by Mrs. Fairfax, who repeated the news; adding that Mr. Carter the surgeon was come and was now with Mr. Rochester: then she hurried out to give orders about tea, and I went up stairs to take off my things.

CHAPTER XIII

MR. ROCHESTER, it seems, by the surgeon's orders, went to bed early that night; nor did he rise soon next morning. When he did come down it was to attend to business: his agent and some of his tenants were arrived, and waiting to speak with him.

Adèle and I had now to vacate the library: it would be in daily requisition as a reception-room for callers. A fire was lit in an apartment up stairs, and there I carried our books, and arranged it for the future school-room. I discerned in the course of the morning that Thornfield Hall was a changed place: no longer silent as a church, it echoed every hour or two to a knock at the door or a clang of the bell; steps, too, often traversed the hall, and new voices spoke in different keys below: a rill from the outer world was flowing through it; it had a master: for my part, I liked it better.

Adèle was not easy to teach that day; she could not apply: she kept running to the door and looking over the bannisters to see if she could get a glimpse of Mr. Rochester; then she coined pretexts to go down stairs, in order, as I shrewdly suspected, to visit the library, where I knew she was not wanted; then, when I got a little angry, and made her sit still, she continued to talk incessantly of her "ami, Monsieur Edouard Fairfax *de* Rochester," as she dubbed him (I had not before heard his prenomens), and to conjecture what presents he had brought her: for it appears he had intimated the night before that when his luggage came from Millcote, there would be found amongst it a little box in whose contents she had an interest.

"Et cela doit signifier," said she, "qu'il y aura là dedans un cadeau pour moi, et peutêtre pour vous aussi Mademoiselle. Monsieur a parlé de vous: il m'a demandé le nom de ma gouvernante, et si elle n'était pas une petite personne, assez mince et un peu pâle. J'ai dit qu'oui: car c'est vrai, n'est-ce pas, Mademoiselle?"[1]

I and my pupil dined as usual in Mrs. Fairfax's parlour; the afternoon was wild and snowy, and we passed it in the school-room. At

---

1   "And that must mean...that there will be a present for me inside, and perhaps for you too, Miss. The gentleman spoke about you: he asked me the name of my governess, and if she wasn't a small person, rather slim and slightly pale. I said yes, for it's true, isn't it Miss?"

dark I allowed Adèle to put away books and work, and to run down-stairs; for, from the comparative silence below, and from the cessation of appeals to the door-bell, I conjectured that Mr. Rochester was now at liberty. Left alone, I walked to the window, but nothing was to be seen thence: twilight and snow-flakes together thickened the air and hid the very shrubs on the lawn. I let down the curtain and went back to the fireside.

In the clear embers I was tracing a view, not unlike a picture I remembered to have seen of the castle of Heidelberg, on the Rhine;[1] when Mrs. Fairfax came in: breaking up by her entrance the fiery mosaic I had been piecing together, and scattering too some heavy, unwelcome thoughts that were beginning to throng on my solitude.

"Mr. Rochester would be glad if you and your pupil would take tea with him in the drawing-room this evening," said she: "he has been so much engaged all day that he could not ask to see you before."

"When is his tea-time?" I inquired.

"Oh – at six o'clock: he keeps early hours in the country. You had better change your frock now; I will go with you and fasten it. Here is a candle."

"Is it necessary to change my frock?"

"Yes, you had better: I always dress for the evening when Mr. Rochester is here."

This additional ceremony seemed somewhat stately: however, I repaired to my room, and, with Mrs. Fairfax's aid, replaced my black stuff dress by one of black silk; the best and the only additional one I had, except one of light grey, which, in my Lowood notions of the toilette, I thought too fine to be worn, except on first-rate occasions.

"You want a brooch," said Mrs. Fairfax. I had a single little pearl ornament which Miss Temple gave me as a parting keepsake: I put it on, and then we went down stairs. Unused as I was to strangers, it was rather a trial to appear thus formally summoned in Mr. Rochester's presence. I let Mrs. Fairfax precede me into the dining-room, and kept in her shade as we crossed that apartment; and, passing the arch, whose curtain was now dropped, entered the elegant recess beyond.

---

1   Heidelberg is not actually on the Rhine; it is on the Neckar.

Two wax candles stood lighted on the table, and two on the mantelpiece; basking in the light and heat of a superb fire, lay Pilot – Adèle knelt near him. Half reclined on a couch appeared Mr. Rochester, his foot supported by the cushion; he was looking at Adèle and the dog: the fire shone full on his face. I knew my traveller with his broad and jetty eyebrows; his square forehead, made squarer by the horizontal sweep of his black hair. I recognised his decisive nose, more remarkable for character than beauty; his full nostrils, denoting, I thought, choler; his grim mouth, chin, and jaw – yes, all three were very grim, and no mistake. His shape, now divested of cloak, I perceived harmonized in squareness with his physiognomy: I suppose it was a good figure in the athletic sense of the term – broad chested and thin flanked; though neither tall nor graceful.

Mr. Rochester must have been aware of the entrance of Mrs. Fairfax and myself: but it appeared he was not in the mood to notice us, for he never lifted his head as we approached.

"Here is Miss Eyre, sir," said Mrs. Fairfax, in her quiet way. He bowed; still not taking his eyes from the group of the dog and child.

"Let Miss Eyre be seated," said he: and there was something in the forced stiff bow, in the impatient, yet formal tone, which seemed further to express, "What the deuce is it to me whether Miss Eyre be there or not? At this moment I am not disposed to accost her."

I sat down quite disembarrassed. A reception of finished politeness would probably have confused me: I could not have returned or repaid it by answering grace and elegance on my part; but harsh caprice laid me under no obligation; on the contrary, a decent quiescence, under the freak of manner, gave me the advantage. Besides, the eccentricity of the proceeding was piquant: I felt interested to see how he would go on.

He went on as a statue would: that is, he neither spoke nor moved. Mrs. Fairfax seemed to think it necessary that some one should be amiable, and she began to talk. Kindly, as usual – and, as usual, rather trite – she condoled with him on the pressure of business he had had all day; on the annoyance it must have been to him with that painful sprain: then she commended his patience and perseverance in going through with it.

"Madam, I should like some tea," was the sole rejoinder she got. She hastened to ring the bell; and, when the tray came, she proceeded

to arrange the cups, spoons, &c., with assiduous celerity. I and Adèle
went to the table; but the master did not leave his couch.

"Will you hand Mr. Rochester's cup?" said Mrs. Fairfax to me;
"Adèle might perhaps spill it."

I did as requested. As he took the cup from my hand, Adèle,
thinking the moment propitious for making a request in my favour,
cried out: –

"N'est-ce pas, Monsieur, qu'il y a un cadeau pour Mademoiselle
Eyre, dans votre petit coffre?"[1]

"Who talks of cadeaux?" said he gruffly: "did you expect a present,
Miss Eyre? Are you fond of presents?" and he searched my face with
eyes that I saw were dark, irate and piercing.

"I hardly know, sir; I have little experience of them: they are generally thought pleasant things."

"Generally thought! But what do *you* think?"

"I should be obliged to take time, sir, before I could give you an
answer worthy of your acceptance: a present has many faces to it, has
it not? and one should consider all, before pronouncing an opinion as
to its nature."

"Miss Eyre, you are not so unsophisticated as Adèle: she demands a
'cadeau,' clamorously, the moment she sees me; you beat about the
bush."

"Because I have less confidence in my deserts than Adèle has: she
can prefer the claim of old acquaintance, and the right too of custom;
for she says you have always been in the habit of giving her playthings; but if I had to make out a case I should be puzzled, since I am
a stranger and have done nothing to entitle me to an acknowledgment."

"Oh, don't fall back on over-modesty! I have examined Adèle, and
find you have taken great pains with her: she is not bright, she has no
talents, yet in a short time she has made much improvement."

"Sir, you have now given me my 'cadeau;' I am obliged to you: it is
the meed teachers most covet; – praise of their pupils' progress."

"Humph!" said Mr. Rochester, and he took his tea in silence.

"Come to the fire," said the master, when the tray was taken away
and Mrs. Fairfax had settled into a corner with her knitting; while

---

1   "Isn't it true, Sir, that there is a gift for Miss Eyre in your small chest?"

Adèle was leading me by the hand round the room, showing me the beautiful books and ornaments on the consoles and chiffonnières. We obeyed, as in duty bound: Adèle wanted to take a seat on my knee, but she was ordered to amuse herself with Pilot.

"You have been resident in my house three months?"

"Yes, sir."

"And you came from —?"

"From Lowood school in ——shire."

"Ah! a charitable concern. – How long were you there?"

"Eight years."

"Eight years! you must be tenacious of life. I thought half the time in such a place would have done up any constitution! No wonder you have rather the look of another world. I marvelled where you had got that sort of face. When you came on me in Hay Lane last night, I thought unaccountably of fairy tales, and had half a mind to demand whether you had bewitched my horse: I am not sure yet. Who are your parents?"

"I have none."

"Nor ever had, I suppose: do you remember them?"

"No."

"I thought not. And so you were waiting for your people when you sat on that stile?"

"For whom, sir?"

"For the men in green:[1] it was a proper moonlight evening for them. Did I break through one of your rings, that you spread that damned ice on the causeway?"[2]

I shook my head. "The men in green all forsook England a hundred years ago," said I, speaking as seriously as he had done. "And not even in Hay Lane or the fields about it, could you find a trace of them. I don't think either summer or harvest, or winter moon will ever shine on their revels more."

Mrs. Fairfax had dropped her knitting, and with raised eyebrows, seemed wondering what sort of talk this was.

---

1 Fairies. This is the first in a number of times Rochester associates Jane with the supernatural.

2 Intruding on a fairy "ring," an enchanted circle in which fairies dance, was said to make them angry enough to punish the intruder.

"Well," resumed Mr. Rochester, "if you disown parents, you must have some sort of kinsfolk: uncles and aunts?"

"No; none that I ever saw."

"And your home?"

"I have none."

"Where do your brothers and sisters live?"

"I have no brothers or sisters."

"Who recommended you to come here?"

"I advertised, and Mrs. Fairfax answered my advertisement."

"Yes;" said the good lady who now knew what ground we were upon, "and I am daily thankful for the choice Providence led me to make. Miss Eyre has been an invaluable companion to me, and a kind and careful teacher to Adèle."

"Don't trouble yourself to give her a character," returned Mr. Rochester: "eulogiums will not bias me; I shall judge for myself. She began by felling my horse."

"Sir?" said Mrs. Fairfax.

"I have to thank her for this sprain."

The widow looked bewildered.

"Miss Eyre, have you ever lived in a town?"

"No, sir."

"Have you seen much society?"

"None but the pupils and teachers of Lowood; and now the inmates of Thornfield."

"Have you read much?"

"Only such books as came in my way; and they have not been numerous or very learned."

"You have lived the life of a nun: no doubt you are well drilled in religious forms; – Brocklehurst, who I understand directs Lowood, is a parson, is he not?"

"Yes, sir."

"And you girls probably worshipped him, as a convent full of religieuses[1] would worship their director."

"Oh no."

"You are very cool! No! What! a novice not worship her priest?

---

1   Young nuns.

That sounds blasphemous."

"I disliked Mr. Brocklehurst; and I was not alone in the feeling. He is a harsh man; at once pompous and meddling: he cut off our hair; and, for economy's sake, bought us bad needles and thread, with which we could hardly sew."

"That was very false economy," remarked Mrs. Fairfax, who now again caught the drift of the dialogue.

"And was that the head and front of his offending?"[1] demanded Mr. Rochester.

"He starved us when he had the sole superintendence of the provision department, before the committee was appointed; and he bored us with long lectures once a week, and with evening readings from books of his own inditing, about sudden deaths and judgments, which made us afraid to go to bed."

"What age were you when you went to Lowood?"

"About ten."

"And you stayed there eight years: you are now, then, eighteen?"

I assented.

"Arithmetic, you see, is useful: without its aid, I should hardly have been able to guess your age. It is a point difficult to fix where the features and countenance are so much at variance as in your case. And now, what did you learn at Lowood? Can you play?"

"A little."

"Of course: that is the established answer. Go into the library – I mean, if you please. – (Excuse my tone of command; I am used to say 'Do this,' and it is done:[2] I cannot alter my customary habits for one new inmate.) – Go, then, into the library; take a candle with you; leave the door open; sit down to the piano, and play a tune."

I departed, obeying his directions.

"Enough!" he called out in a few minutes. "You play a *little*, I see; like any other English school-girl: perhaps rather better than some, but not well."

I closed the piano, and returned. Mr. Rochester continued.

"Adèle showed me some sketches this morning, which she said

---

1   See *Othello* I.iii.80.

2   See Matthew 8:9.

were yours. I don't know whether they were entirely of your doing: probably a master aided you?"

"No, indeed!" I interjected.

"Ah! that pricks pride. Well, fetch me your portfolio, if you can vouch for its contents being original; but don't pass your word unless you are certain: I can recognise patch-work."

"Then I will say nothing, and you shall judge for yourself, sir."

I brought the portfolio from the library.

"Approach the table," said he; and I wheeled it to his couch. Adèle and Mrs. Fairfax drew near to see the pictures.

"No crowding," said Mr. Rochester: "take the drawings from my hand as I finish with them; but don't push your faces up to mine."

He deliberately scrutinized each sketch and painting. Three he laid aside; the others, when he had examined them, he swept from him.

"Take them off to the other table, Mrs. Fairfax," said he, "and look at them with Adèle; – you" (glancing at me), "resume your seat, and answer my questions. I perceive these pictures were done by one hand: was that hand yours?"

"Yes."

"And when did you find time to do them? They have taken much time, and some thought."

"I did them in the last two vacations I spent at Lowood, when I had no other occupation."

"Where did you get your copies?"

"Out of my head."

"That head I see now on your shoulders?"

"Yes, sir."

"Has it other furniture of the same kind within?"

"I should think it may have: I should hope – better."

He spread the pictures before him, and again surveyed them alternately.

While he is so occupied, I will tell you, reader, what they are: and first, I must premise that they are nothing wonderful. The subjects had indeed risen vividly on my mind. As I saw them with the spiritual eye, before I attempted to embody them, they were striking; but my hand would not second my fancy, and in each case it had wrought out but a pale portrait of the thing I had conceived.

These pictures were in water colours. The first represented clouds low and livid, rolling over a swollen sea: all the distance was in eclipse; so, too, was the foreground; or rather, the nearest billows, for there was no land. One gleam of light lifted into relief a half-submerged mast, on which sat a cormorant, dark and large, with wings flecked with foam; its beak held a gold bracelet, set with gems, that I had touched with as brilliant tints as my palette could yield, and as glittering distinctness as my pencil could impart. Sinking below the bird and mast, a drowned corse glanced through the green water; a fair arm was the only limb clearly visible, whence the bracelet had been washed or torn.

The second picture contained for foreground only the dim peak of a hill, with grass and some leaves slanted as if by a breeze. Beyond and above spread an expanse of sky, dark-blue as at twilight: rising into the sky, was a woman's shape to the bust, portrayed in tints as dusk and soft as I could combine. The dim forehead was crowned with a star; the lineaments below were seen as through the suffusion of vapour; the eyes shone dark and wild; the hair streamed shadowy, like a beamless cloud torn by storm or by electric travail. On the neck lay a pale reflection like moonlight; the same faint lustre touched the train of thin clouds from which rose and bowed this vision of the Evening Star.

The third showed the pinnacle of an iceberg piercing a polar winter sky: a muster of northern lights reared their dim lances, close serried, along the horizon. Throwing these into distance, rose, in the foreground, a head, – a colossal head, inclined towards the iceberg, and resting against it. Two thin hands, joined under the forehead, and supporting it, drew up before the lower features a sable veil; a brow quite bloodless, white as bone, and an eye hollow and fixed, blank of meaning but for the glassiness of despair, alone were visible. Above the temples, amidst wreathed turban folds of black drapery, vague in its character and consistency as cloud, gleamed a ring of white flame, gemmed with sparkles of a more lurid tinge. This pale crescent was "The likeness of a Kingly Crown;" what it diademed was "the shape which shape had none."[1]

---

[1] Brontë is quoting from the description of Death in *Paradise Lost*. See Book II.666-676.

"Were you happy when you painted these pictures?" asked Mr. Rochester, presently.

"I was absorbed, sir: yes, and I was happy. To paint them, in short, was to enjoy one of the keenest pleasures I have ever known."

"That is not saying much. Your pleasures, by your own account, have been few; but I daresay you did exist in a kind of artist's dreamland while you blent and arranged these strange tints. Did you sit at them long each day?"

"I had nothing else to do, because it was the vacation, and I sat at them from morning till noon, and from noon till night: the length of the Midsummer days favoured my inclination to apply."

"And you felt self-satisfied with the result of your ardent labours?"

"Far from it. I was tormented by the contrast between my idea and my handiwork: in each case I had imagined something which I was quite powerless to realize."

"Not quite: – you have secured the shadow of your thought; but no more, probably. You had not enough of the artist's skill and science to give it full being: yet the drawings are, for a school girl, peculiar. As to the thoughts, they are elfish. These eyes in the Evening Star you must have seen in a dream. How could you make them look so clear, and yet not at all brilliant? for the planet above quells their rays. And what meaning is that in their solemn depth? And who taught you to paint wind? There is a high gale in that sky, and on this hilltop. Where did you see Latmos? – for that is Latmos.[1] There, – put the drawings away!"

I had scarce tied the strings of the portfolio, when, looking at his watch, he said abruptly –

"It is nine o'clock: what are you about, Miss Eyre, to let Adèle sit up so long? Take her to bed."

Adèle went to kiss him before quitting the room: he endured the caress, but scarcely seemed to relish it more than Pilot would have done, nor so much.

"I wish you all good-night, now," said he, making a movement of the hand towards the door, in token that he was tired of our company, and wished to dismiss us. Mrs. Fairfax folded up her knitting: I took

---

1   A mountain from Greek mythology.

my portfolio: we curtseyed to him, received a frigid bow in return, and so withdrew.

"You said Mr. Rochester was not strikingly peculiar, Mrs. Fairfax," I observed, when I rejoined her in her room, after putting Adèle to bed.

"Well, is he?"

"I think so: he is very changeful and abrupt."

"True: no doubt he may appear so to a stranger, but I am so accustomed to his manner, I never think of it; and then, if he has peculiarities of temper, allowance should be made."

"Why?"

"Partly, because it is his nature – and we can none of us help our nature; and partly, he has painful thoughts, no doubt, to harass him, and make his spirits unequal."

"What about?"

"Family troubles, for one thing."

"But he has no family."

"Not now; but he has had – or, at least, relatives. He lost his elder brother a few years since."

"His *elder* brother?"

"Yes. The present Mr. Rochester has not been very long in possession of the property: only about nine years."

"Nine years is a tolerable time. Was he so very fond of his brother as to be still inconsolable for his loss?"

"Why, no – perhaps not. I believe there were some misunderstandings between them. Mr. Rowland Rochester was not quite just to Mr. Edward; and perhaps he prejudiced his father against him. The old gentleman was fond of money, and anxious to keep the family estate together. He did not like to diminish the property by division, and yet he was anxious that Mr. Edward should have wealth, too, to keep up the consequence of the name; and, soon after he was of age, some steps were taken that were not quite fair, and made a great deal of mischief. Old Mr. Rochester and Mr. Rowland combined to bring Mr. Edward into what he considered a painful position, for the sake of making his fortune: what the precise nature of that position was I never clearly knew, but his spirit could not brook what he had to suffer in it. He is not very forgiving: he broke with his family, and now for many years he has led an unsettled kind of life. I don't think he has ever been resident at Thornfield for a fortnight together, since the death of his brother without a will, left him master of the estate: and, indeed, no wonder he shuns the old place."

"Why should he shun it?"

"Perhaps he thinks it gloomy."

The answer was evasive – I should have liked something clearer; but Mrs. Fairfax either could not, or would not, give me more explicit information of the origin and nature of Mr. Rochester's trials. She averred they were a mystery to herself, and that what she knew was chiefly from conjecture. It was evident, indeed, that she wished me to drop the subject; which I did accordingly.

CHAPTER XIV

For several subsequent days I saw little of Mr. Rochester. In the mornings he seemed much engaged with business, and in the afternoons, gentlemen from Millcote or the neighbourhood called, and sometimes stayed to dine with him. When his sprain was well enough to admit of horse exercise, he rode out a good deal; probably to return these visits, as he generally did not come back till late at night.

During this interval, even Adèle was seldom sent for to his presence, and all my acquaintance with him was confined to an occasional rencontre in the hall, on the stairs, or in the gallery; when he would sometimes pass me haughtily and coldly, just acknowledging my presence by a distant nod or a cool glance, and sometimes bow and smile with gentlemanlike affability. His changes of mood did not offend me, because I saw that I had nothing to do with their alternation: the ebb and flow depended on causes quite disconnected with me.

One day he had had company to dinner, and had sent for my portfolio; in order, doubtless, to exhibit its contents: the gentlemen went away early, to attend a public meeting at Millcote, as Mrs. Fairfax informed me; but the night being wet and inclement, Mr. Rochester did not accompany them. Soon after they were gone, he rung the bell: a message came that I and Adèle were to go down stairs. I brushed Adèle's hair and made her neat, and having ascertained that I was myself in my usual Quaker trim, where there was nothing to retouch – all being too close and plain, braided locks included, to admit of disarrangement – we descended; Adèle wondering whether the *petite coffre*[1] was at length come: for owing to some mistake, its arrival had hitherto been delayed. She was gratified: there it stood, a little carton, on the table when we entered the dining-room. She appeared to know it by instinct.

"Ma boîte! ma boîte!"[2] exclaimed she, running towards it.

"Yes – there is your 'boîte' at last: take it into a corner, you genuine daughter of Paris, and amuse yourself with disembowelling it," said the deep and rather sarcastic voice of Mr. Rochester, proceeding from the depths of an immense easy-chair at the fire-side. "And mind," he

---

1   Small chest.
2   "My box! My box!"

continued, "don't bother me with any details of the anatomical process, or any notice of the condition of the entrails: let your operation be conducted in silence – tiens-toi tranquille, enfant; comprends-tu?"[1]

Adèle seemed scarcely to need the warning; she had already retired to a sofa with her treasure, and was busy untying the cord which secured the lid. Having removed this impediment, and lifted certain silvery envelopes of tissue paper, she merely exclaimed: –

"Oh, Ciel! Que c'est beau!"[2] and then remained absorbed in ecstatic contemplation.

"Is Miss Eyre there?" now demanded the master, half rising from his seat to look round to the door, near which I still stood.

"Ah! well; come forward: be seated here." He drew a chair near his own. "I am not fond of the prattle of children," he continued; "for, old bachelor as I am, I have no pleasant associations connected with their lisp. It would be intolerable to me to pass a whole evening *tête-à-tête* with a brat. Don't draw that chair further off, Miss Eyre; sit down exactly where I placed it – if you please, that is. Confound these civilities! I continually forget them. Nor do I particularly affect simple-minded old ladies. By-the-by, I must have in mine; it won't do to neglect her: she is a Fairfax, or wed to one; and blood is said to be thicker than water."

He rung, and dispatched an invitation to Mrs. Fairfax, who soon arrived, knitting-basket in hand.

"Good evening, madam; I sent to you for a charitable purpose: I have forbidden Adèle to talk to me about her presents, and she is bursting with repletion; have the goodness to serve her as auditress and interlocutrice: it will be one of the most benevolent acts you ever performed."

Adèle, indeed, no sooner saw Mrs. Fairfax, than she summoned her to her sofa, and there quickly filled her lap with the porcelain, the ivory, the waxen contents of her "boîte;" pouring out, meantime, explanations and raptures in such broken English as she was mistress of.

"Now I have performed the part of a good host," pursued Mr.

---

1 "Be still, child; do you understand?"
2 "Oh heavens! How lovely!"

Rochester; "put my guests into the way of amusing each other, I ought to be at liberty to attend to my own pleasure. Miss Eyre, draw your chair still a little further forward: you are yet too far back; I cannot see you without disturbing my position in this comfortable chair, which I have no mind to do."

I did as I was bid; though I would much rather have remained somewhat in the shade: but Mr. Rochester had such a direct way of giving orders, it seemed a matter of course to obey him promptly.

We were, as I have said, in the dining-room: the lustre,[1] which had been lit for dinner, filled the room with a festal breadth of light; the large fire was all red and clear; the purple curtains hung rich and ample before the lofty window and loftier arch: everything was still, save the subdued chat of Adèle (she dared not speak loud), and, filling up each pause, the beating of winter rain against the panes.

Mr. Rochester, as he sat in his damask-covered chair, looked different to what I had seen him look before, – not quite so stern; much less gloomy. There was a smile on his lips, and his eyes sparkled, whether with wine or not, I am not sure; but I think it very probable. He was, in short, in his after-dinner mood; more expanded and genial, and also more self-indulgent than the frigid and rigid temper of the morning: still, he looked preciously grim, cushioning his massive head against the swelling back of his chair, and receiving the light of the fire on his granite-hewn features, and in his great, dark eyes – for he had great, dark eyes, and very fine eyes, too; not without a certain change in their depths sometimes, which, if it was not softness, reminded you, at least, of that feeling.

He had been looking two minutes at the fire, and I had been looking the same length of time at him, when, turning suddenly, he caught my gaze fastened on his physiognomy.

"You examine me, Miss Eyre," said he: "do you think me handsome?"

I should, if I had deliberated, have replied to this question by something conventionally vague and polite; but the answer somehow slipped from my tongue before I was aware: –

"No, sir."

---

1   Chandelier.

"Ah! By my word! there is something singular about you," said he: "you have the air of a little nonnette;[1] quaint, quiet, grave, and simple, as you sit with your hands before you, and your eyes generally bent on the carpet (except, by-the-by, when they are directed piercingly to my face; as just now, for instance); and when one asks you a question, or makes a remark to which you are obliged to reply, you rap out a round rejoinder, which, if not blunt, is at least brusque. What do you mean by it?"

"Sir, I was too plain: I beg your pardon. I ought to have replied that it was not easy to give an impromptu answer to a question about appearances; that tastes differ; that beauty is of little consequence, or something of that sort."

"You ought to have replied no such thing. Beauty of little consequence, indeed! And so, under pretence of softening the previous outrage, of stroking and soothing me into placidity, you stick a sly penknife under my ear! Go on: what fault do you find with me, pray? I suppose I have all my limbs and all my features like any other man?"

"Mr. Rochester, allow me to disown my first answer: I intended no pointed repartee; it was only a blunder."

"Just so: I think so; and you shall be answerable for it. Criticize me: does my forehead not please you?"

He lifted up the sable waves of hair which lay horizontally over his brow, and showed a solid enough mass of intellectual organs; but an abrupt deficiency where the suave sign of benevolence should have risen.[2]

"Now, ma'am, am I a fool?"

"Far from it, sir. You would perhaps think me rude if I inquired in return whether you are a philanthropist?"

"There again! Another stick of the penknife, when she pretended to pat my head: and that is because I said I did not like the society of children and old women (low be it spoken!). No, young lady, I am not a general philanthropist; but I bear a conscience;" and he pointed to the prominences which are said to indicate that faculty – and which, fortunately for him, were sufficiently conspicuous; giving, indeed, a marked breadth to the upper part of his head: "and besides, I once had

---

1   Young nun.
2   Another reference to phrenology.

a kind of rude tenderness of heart. When I was as old as you, I was a feeling fellow enough; partial to the unfledged, unfostered, and unlucky; but fortune has knocked me about since: she has even kneaded me with her knuckles, and now I flatter myself I am hard and tough as an Indian-rubber ball; pervious, though, through a chink or two still, and with one sentient point in the middle of the lump. Yes: does that leave hope for me?"

"Hope of what, sir?"

"Of my final re-transformation from India-rubber back to flesh?"

"Decidedly he has had too much wine," I thought; and I did not know what answer to make to his queer question: how could I tell whether he was capable of being re-transformed?

"You look very much puzzled, Miss Eyre; and though you are not pretty any more than I am handsome, yet a puzzled air becomes you: besides, it is convenient, for it keeps those searching eyes of yours away from my physiognomy, and busies them with the worsted flowers of the rug; so puzzle on. Young lady, I am disposed to be gregarious and communicative to-night."

With this announcement he rose from his chair, and stood, leaning his arm on the marble mantel-piece: in that attitude his shape was seen plainly as well as his face; his unusual breadth of chest, disproportionate almost to his length of limb. I am sure most people would have thought him an ugly man; yet there was so much unconscious pride in his port; so much ease in his demeanour; such a look of complete indifference to his own external appearance; so haughty a reliance on the power of other qualities, intrinsic or adventitious, to atone for the lack of mere personal attractiveness, that in looking at him, one inevitably shared the indifference; and even in a blind, imperfect sense, put faith in the confidence.

"I am disposed to be gregarious and communicative to-night," he repeated; "and that is why I sent for you: the fire and the chandelier were not sufficient company for me; nor would Pilot have been, for none of these can talk. Adèle is a degree better, but still far below the mark; Mrs. Fairfax ditto; you, I am persuaded, can suit me if you will: you puzzled me the first evening I invited you down here. I have almost forgotten you since: other ideas have driven yours from my head; but to-night I am resolved to be at ease; to dismiss what importunes, and recall what pleases. It would please me now to draw you out: to learn more of you – therefore speak —"

Instead of speaking, I smiled: and not a very complacent or submissive smile either.

"Speak," he urged.

"What about, sir?"

"Whatever you like. I leave both the choice of subject and the manner of treating it, entirely to yourself."

Accordingly I sat and said nothing: "If he expects me to talk for the mere sake of talking and showing off, he will find he has addressed himself to the wrong person," I thought.

"You are dumb, Miss Eyre."

I was dumb still. He bent his head a little towards me and with a single hasty glance seemed to dive into my eyes.

"Stubborn?" he said, "and annoyed. Ah, it is consistent. I put my request in an absurd, almost insolent form. Miss Eyre, I beg your pardon. The fact is, once for all, I don't wish to treat you like an inferior: that is (correcting himself), I claim only such superiority as must result from twenty years' difference in age and a century's advance in experience. This is legitimate, et j'y tiens,[1] as Adèle would say; and it is by virtue of this superiority and this alone that I desire you to have the goodness to talk to me a little now, and divert my thoughts, which are galled with dwelling on one point: cankering as a rusty nail."

He had deigned an explanation; almost an apology: and I did not feel insensible to his condescension, and would not seem so.

"I am willing to amuse you if I can, sir: quite willing; but I cannot introduce a topic, because how do I know what will interest you? Ask me questions, and I will do my best to answer them."

"Then, in the first place, do you agree with me that I have a right to be a little masterful, abrupt; perhaps exacting, sometimes, on the grounds I stated: namely, that I am old enough to be your father, and that I have battled through a varied experience with many men of many nations, and roamed over half the globe, while you have lived quietly with one set of people in one house?"

"Do as you please, sir."

---

1 "And I insist on it."

"That is no answer: or rather it is a very irritating, because a very evasive one – reply clearly."

"I don't think, sir, you have a right to command me, merely because you are older than I, or because you have seen more of the world than I have – your claim to superiority depends on the use you have made of your time and experience."

"Humph! Promptly spoken. But I won't allow that, seeing that it would never suit my case; as I have made an indifferent, not to say, a bad use of both advantages. Leaving superiority out of the question then, you must still agree to receive my orders now and then, without being piqued or hurt by the tone of command – will you?"

I smiled: I thought to myself, "Mr. Rochester *is* peculiar – he seems to forget that he pays me 30*l.* per annum for receiving his orders."

"The smile is very well," said he, catching instantly the passing expression; "but speak too."

"I was thinking, sir, that very few masters would trouble themselves to inquire whether or not their paid subordinates were piqued and hurt by their orders."

"Paid subordinates! What, you are my paid subordinate, are you? Oh yes, I had forgotten the salary! Well then, on that mercenary ground, will you agree to let me hector a little?"

"No, sir, not on that ground: but on the ground that you did forget it, and that you care whether or not a dependent is comfortable in his dependency, I agree heartily."

"And will you consent to dispense with a great many conventional forms and phrases, without thinking that the omission arises from insolence?"

"I am sure, sir, I should never mistake informality for insolence: one I rather like, the other nothing free-born would submit to, even for a salary."

"Humbug! Most things free-born will submit to anything for a salary; therefore, keep to yourself and don't venture on generalities of which you are intensely ignorant. However, I mentally shake hands with you for your answer, despite its inaccuracy; and as much for the manner in which it was said, as for the substance of the speech: the manner was frank and sincere; one does not often see such a manner:

no, on the contrary, affectation, or coldness, or stupid, coarse-minded misapprehension of one's meaning are the usual rewards of candour. Not three in three thousand raw school-girl-governesses would have answered me as you have just done. But I don't mean to flatter you: if you are cast in a different mould to the majority, it is no merit of yours: Nature did it. And then, after all, I go too fast in my conclusions: for what I yet know, you may be no better than the rest; you may have intolerable defects to counterbalance your few good points."

"And so may you," I thought. My eye met his as the idea crossed my mind: he seemed to read the glance, answering as if its import had been spoken as well as imagined: –

"Yes, yes, you are right," said he; "I have plenty of faults of my own: I know it, and I don't wish to palliate them, I assure you. God wot[1] I need not be too severe about others; I have a past existence, a series of deeds, a colour of life to contemplate within my own breast, which might well call my sneers and censures from my neighbours to myself. I started, or rather (for like other defaulters, I like to lay half the blame on ill fortune and adverse circumstances) was thrust on to a wrong tack at the age of one and twenty, and have never recovered the right course since: but I might have been very different; I might have been as good as you, – wiser, – almost as stainless. I envy you your peace of mind, your clean conscience, your unpolluted memory. Little girl, a memory without blot or contamination must be an exquisite treasure – an inexhaustible source of pure refreshment: is it not?"

"How was your memory when you were eighteen, sir?"

"All right then; limpid, salubrious: no gush of bilge water had turned it to fetid puddle. I was your equal at eighteen – quite your equal. Nature meant me to be, on the whole, a good man, Miss Eyre: one of the better end, and you see I am not so. You would say you don't see it: at least I flatter myself I read as much in your eye (beware, by-the-bye, what you express with that organ, I am quick at interpreting its language). Then take my word for it, – I am not a villain: you are not to suppose that – not to attribute to me any such bad

---

1 God knows.

eminence;[1] but, owing, I verily believe, rather to circumstances than to my natural bent, I am a trite common-place sinner, hackneyed in all the poor petty dissipations with which the rich and worthless try to put on life. Do you wonder that I avow this to you? Know, that in the course of your future life you will often find yourself elected the involuntary confidant of your acquaintances' secrets: people will instinctively find out, as I have done, that it is not your forte to talk of yourself, but to listen while others talk of themselves; they will feel, too, that you listen with no malevolent scorn of their indiscretion, but with a kind of innate sympathy; not the less comforting and encouraging because it is very unobtrusive in its manifestations."

"How do you know? – how can you guess all this, sir?"

"I know it well; therefore I proceed almost as freely as if I were writing my thoughts in a diary. You would say, I should have been superior to circumstances: so I should – so I should; but you see I was not. When fate wronged me, I had not the wisdom to remain cool: I turned desperate; then I degenerated. Now, when any vicious simpleton excites my disgust by his paltry ribaldry, I cannot flatter myself that I am better than he: I am forced to confess that he and I are on a level. I wish I had stood firm – God knows I do! Dread remorse when you are tempted to err, Miss Eyre: remorse is the poison of life."

"Repentance is said to be its cure, sir."

"It is not its cure. Reformation may be its cure; and I could reform – I have strength yet for that – if – but where is the use of thinking of it, hampered, burdened, cursed as I am? Besides, since happiness is irrevocably denied me, I have a right to get pleasure out of life: and I *will* get it, cost what it may."

"Then you will degenerate still more, sir."

"Possibly: yet why should I, if I can get sweet fresh pleasure? And I may get it as sweet and fresh as the wild honey the bee gathers on the moor."

"It will sting – it will taste bitter, sir."

"How do you know? – you never tried it. How very serious – how very solemn you look; and you are as ignorant of the matter as this cameo head (taking one from the mantelpiece)! You have no right to preach to me; you Neophyte, that have not passed the porch of life,

---

1   "Bad eminence" is used to describe Satan in *Paradise Lost*. See Book II.6.

and are absolutely unacquainted with its mysteries."

"I only remind you of your own words, sir: you said error brought remorse, and you pronounced remorse the poison of existence."

"And who talks of error now? I scarcely think the notion that flitted across my brain was an error. I believe it was an inspiration rather than a temptation: it was very genial, very soothing, – I know that. Here it comes again! It is no devil, I assure you: or if it be, it has put on the robes of an angel of light. I think I must admit so fair a guest when it asks entrance to my heart."

"Distrust it, sir; it is not a true angel."

"Once more, how do you know? By what instinct do you pretend to distinguish between a fallen seraph of the abyss, and a messenger from the eternal throne – between a guide and a seducer?"

"I judged by your countenance, sir; which was troubled, when you said the suggestion had returned upon you. I feel sure it will work you more misery if you listen to it."

"Not at all – it bears the most gracious message in the world: for the rest, you are not my conscience keeper, so don't make yourself uneasy. Here, come in, bonny wanderer!"

He said this as if he spoke to a vision, viewless to any eye but his own; then folding his arms, which he had half extended, on his chest, he seemed to enclose in their embrace the invisible being.

"Now," he continued, again addressing me, "I have received the pilgrim – a disguised deity, as I verily believe. Already it has done me good: my heart was a sort of charnel; it will now be a shrine."

"To speak truth, sir, I don't understand you at all: I cannot keep up the conversation, because it has got out of my depth. Only one thing I know: you said you were not as good as you should like to be, and that you regretted your own imperfection – one thing I can comprehend: you intimated that to have a sullied memory was a perpetual bane. It seems to me, that if you tried hard, you would in time find it possible to become what you yourself would approve; and that if from this day you began with resolution to correct your thoughts and actions, you would in a few years have laid up a new and stainless store of recollections, to which you might revert with pleasure."

"Justly thought; rightly said, Miss Eyre; and at this moment, I am paving hell with energy."

"Sir?"

"I am laying down good intentions,[1] which I believe durable as flint. Certainly, my associates and pursuits shall be other than they have been."

"And better?"

"And better – as much better as pure ore is than foul dross. You seem to doubt me; I don't doubt myself: I know what my aim is, what my motives are; and at this moment I pass a law, unalterable as that of the Medes and Persians,[2] that both are right."

"They cannot be, sir, if they require a new statute to legalize them."

"They are, Miss Eyre, though they absolutely require a new statute: unheard-of combinations of circumstances demand unheard-of rules."

"That sounds a dangerous maxim, sir; because one can see at once that it is liable to abuse."

"Sententious sage! so it is: but I swear by my household gods not to abuse it."

"You are human and fallible."

"I am: so are you – what then?"

"The human and fallible should not arrogate a power with which the divine and perfect alone can be safely entrusted."

"What power?"

"That of saying of any strange, unsanctioned line of action, – 'Let it be right.'"

"'Let it be right' – the very words: you have pronounced them."

"*May* it be right then," I said, as I rose; deeming it useless to continue a discourse which was all darkness to me; and, besides, sensible that the character of my interlocutor was beyond my penetration: at least, beyond its present reach; and feeling the uncertainty, the vague sense of insecurity, which accompanies a conviction of ignorance.

---

1 Proverbial: "The road to hell is paved with good intentions." Rochester is promising himself to reform his life.

2 A possible allusion to Esther 1:19, in which King Ahasuerus is advised to "let it be written among the laws of the Persians and the Medes, that it be not altered," that his disobedient wife Vashti be put aside in favour of "another who is better than she." The image of an imperious man rejecting a rebellious wife and replacing her with one more to his taste foreshadows later events in the novel. Brontë alludes to Vashti again in her last novel, *Villette* (1853).

"Where are you going?"

"To put Adèle to bed: it is past her bed-time."

"You are afraid of me, because I talk like a Sphynx."[1]

"Your language is enigmatical, sir: but though I am bewildered, I am certainly not afraid."

"You *are* afraid – your self-love dreads a blunder."

"In that sense I do feel apprehensive – I have no wish to talk nonsense."

"If you did, it would be in such a grave, quiet manner, I should mistake it for sense. Do you never laugh, Miss Eyre? Don't trouble yourself to answer – I see, you laugh rarely; but you can laugh very merrily: believe me, you are not naturally austere, any more than I am naturally vicious. The Lowood constraint still clings to you somewhat; controlling your features, muffling your voice, and restricting your limbs; and you fear in the presence of a man and a brother – or father, or master, or what you will – to smile too gaily, speak too freely, or move too quickly: but in time, I think you will learn to be natural with me, as I find it impossible to be conventional with you; and then your looks and movements will have more vivacity and variety than they dare offer now. I see, at intervals, the glance of a curious sort of bird through the close-set bars of the cage: a vivid, restless, resolute captive is there; were it but free, it would soar cloud-high. You are still bent on going?"

"It has struck nine, sir."

"Never mind, – wait a minute: Adèle is not ready to go to bed yet. My position, Miss Eyre, with my back to the fire, and my face to the room, favours observation. While talking to you, I have also occasionally watched Adèle; (I have my own reasons for thinking her a curious study, – reasons that I may: nay that I shall, impart to you some day;) she pulled out of her box, about ten minutes ago, a little pink silk frock; rapture lit her face as she unfolded it: coquetry runs in her blood, blends with her brains, and seasons the marrow of her bones. "Il faut que je l'essaie!' cried she; 'et à l'instant même!'[2] and she rushed out of the room. She is now with Sophie, undergoing a robing process: in a few minutes she will re-enter; and I know what I shall

---

1   i.e., in riddles.

2   "I must try it on!...and this very minute!"

see, – a miniature of Céline Varens, as she used to appear on the boards at the rising of —: but never mind that. However, my tenderest feelings are about to receive a shock: such is my presentiment; stay now, to see whether it will be realized."

Ere long, Adèle's little foot was heard tripping across the hall. She entered, transformed as her guardian had predicted. A dress of rose-coloured satin, very short, and as full in the skirt as it could be gathered, replaced the brown frock she had previously worn; a wreath of rosebuds circled her forehead; her feet were dressed in silk stockings and small white satin sandals.

"Est-ce que ma robe va bien?" cried she, bounding forwards; "et mes souliers? et mes bas? Tenez, je crois que je vais danser!"[1]

And spreading out her dress, she chasséed across the room; till having reached Mr. Rochester, she wheeled lightly round before him on tip-toe, then dropped on one knee at his feet, exclaiming: –

"Monsieur, je vous remercie mille fois de votre bonté;" then rising, she added, "C'est comme cela que maman faisait, n'est-ce pas, Monsieur?"[2]

"Pre–cise–ly!" was the answer; "and 'comme cela,' she charmed my English gold out of my British breeches' pocket. I have been green, too, Miss Eyre, – aye, grass-green: not a more vernal tint freshens you now than once freshened me. My Spring is gone, however: but it has left me that French floweret on my hands; which, in some moods, I would fain be rid of. Not valuing now the root whence it sprung; having found that it was of a sort which nothing but gold dust could manure, I have but half a liking to the blossom: especially when it looks so artificial as just now. I keep it and rear it rather on the Roman Catholic principle of expiating numerous sins, great or small, by one good work. I'll explain all this some day. Good night."

---

1   "Does my dress suit me?...and my slippers? and my stockings? Wait! I think I shall dance!"

2   "Sir, I thank you a thousand times over for your kindness....That's how mama would have done it, isn't that so, sir?"

CHAPTER XV

Mr. Rochester did, on a future occasion, explain it.

It was one afternoon, when he chanced to meet me and Adèle in the grounds; and while she played with Pilot and her shuttlecock,[1] he asked me to walk up and down a long beech avenue within sight of her.

He then said that she was the daughter of a French opera dancer, Céline Varens; towards whom he had once cherished what he called a "grande passion." This passion Céline had professed to return with even superior ardour. He thought himself her idol, ugly as he was: he believed, as he said, that she preferred his "taille d'athlète"[2] to the elegance of the Apollo Belvidere.[3]

"And, Miss Eyre, so much was I flattered by this preference of the Gallic sylph for her British gnome, that I installed her in an hotel;[4] gave her a complete establishment of servants, a carriage, cashmeres, diamonds, dentelles,[5] &c. In short, I began the process of ruining myself in the received style; like any other spoonie.[6] I had not, it seems, the originality to chalk out a new road to shame and destruction, but trode the old track with stupid exactness not to deviate an inch from the beaten centre. I had – as I deserved to have – the fate of all other spoonies. Happening to call one evening, when Céline did not expect me, I found her out; but it was a warm night, and I was tired with strolling through Paris, so I sat down in her boudoir; happy to breathe the air consecrated so lately by her presence. No, – I exaggerate; I never thought there was any consecrating virtue about her: it was rather a sort of pastile[7] perfume she had left; a scent of musk and amber, than an odour of sanctity. I was just beginning to stifle with the fumes of conservatory flowers and sprinkled essences, when I

---

1   The "birdie" used in badminton. Later we are told that Jane and Adèle play a game of "battledore and shuttlecock." A battledore is the racket used to strike the shuttlecock.
2   Athlete's build.
3   A famous statue of Apollo housed in the Belvedere section of the Vatican.
4   A town house.
5   Lace clothing.
6   Slang for someone foolishly in love.
7   Aromatic.

bethought myself to open the window and step out on to the balcony. It was moonlight, and gas-light besides, and very still and serene. The balcony was furnished with a chair or two; I sat down, took out a cigar, – I will take one now, if you will excuse me."

Here ensued a pause, filled up by the producing and lighting of a cigar; having placed it to his lips and breathed a trail of Havannah incense on the freezing and sunless air, he went on: –

"I liked bonbons too, in those days, Miss Eyre, and I was *croquant*[1] – (overlook the barbarism) *croquant* chocolate comfits, and smoking alternately, watching meantime the equipages that rolled along the fashionable street towards the neighbouring opera-house, when in an elegant close carriage drawn by a beautiful pair of English horses, and distinctly seen in the brilliant city-night, I recognized the 'voiture'[2] I had given Céline. She was returning: of course my heart thumped with impatience against the iron rails I leant upon. The carriage stopped, as I had expected, at the hotel door; my flame (that is the very word for an opera inammorata) alighted: though muffled in a cloak – an unnecessary incumbrance, by the bye, on so warm a June evening – I knew her instantly by her little foot, seen peeping from the skirt of her dress, as she skipped from the carriage-step. Bending over the balcony I was about to murmur, 'Mon Ange'[3] – in a tone, of course, which should be audible to the ear of love alone – when a figure jumped from the carriage after her; cloaked also: but that was a spurred heel which had rung on the pavement, and that was a hatted head which now passed under the arched *porte cochère*[4] of the hotel.

"You never felt jealousy did you, Miss Eyre? Of course not: I need not ask you; because you never felt love. You have both sentiments yet to experience: your soul sleeps; the shock is yet to be given which shall waken it. You think all existence lapses in as quiet a flow as that in which your youth has hitherto slid away. Floating on with closed eyes and muffled ears, you neither see the rocks bristling not far off in the bed of the flood, nor hear the breakers boil at their base. But I tell you – and you may mark my words – you will come some day to a

1 Crunching.
2 Carriage.
3 My angel.
4 Carriage entrance.

craggy pass of the channel, where the whole of life's stream will be broken up into whirl and tumult, foam and noise: either you will be dashed to atoms on crag-points, or lifted up and borne on by some master wave into a calmer current – as I am now.

"I like this day: I like that sky of steel; I like the sternness and stillness of the world under this frost. I like Thornfield; its antiquity; its retirement; its old crow-trees and thorn-trees; its grey façade, and lines of dark windows reflecting that metal welkin:[1] and yet how long have I abhorred the very thought of it; shunned it like a great plaguehouse! How I do still abhor —"

He ground his teeth and was silent: he arrested his step and struck his boot against the hard ground. Some hated thought seemed to have him in its grip, and to hold him so tightly that he could not advance.

We were ascending the avenue when he thus paused; the hall was before us. Lifting his eye to its battlements, he cast over them a glare such as I never saw before or since. Pain, shame, ire – impatience, disgust, detestation – seemed momentarily to hold a quivering conflict in the large pupil dilating under his ebon eyebrow. Wild was the wrestle which should be paramount; but another feeling rose and triumphed: something hard and cynical; self-willed and resolute: it settled his passion and petrified his countenance: he went on: –

"During the moment I was silent, Miss Eyre, I was arranging a point with my destiny. She stood there, by that beech-trunk – a hag like one of those who appeared to Macbeth on the heath of Forres.[2] 'You like Thornfield?' she said, lifting her finger; and then she wrote in the air a memento, which ran in lurid hieroglyphics all along the house-front, between the upper and lower row of windows, 'Like it if you can! Like it if you dare!'

"'I will like it,' said I. 'I dare like it;' and (he subjoined moodily) I will keep my word: I will break obstacles to happiness, to goodness – yes, goodness; I wish to be a better man than I have been; than I am – as Job's leviathan broke the spear the dart and the habergeon;[3] hindrances which others count as iron and brass, I will esteem but straw and rotten wood."

---

1   Sky.
2   See *Macbeth* I.iii.37-47.
3   See Job 41:24-27.

Adèle here ran before him with her shuttle-cock. "Away!" he cried harshly; "keep at a distance, child; or go in to Sophie!" Continuing then to pursue his walk in silence, I ventured to recall him to the point whence he had abruptly diverged: –

"Did you leave the balcony, sir," I asked, "when Mdlle. Varens entered?"

I almost expected a rebuff for this hardly well-timed question: but, on the contrary, waking out of his scowling abstraction, he turned his eyes towards me, and the shade seemed to clear off his brow.

"Oh, I had forgotten Céline! Well, to resume. When I saw my charmer thus come in accompanied by a cavalier, I seemed to hear a hiss, and the green snake of jealousy, rising on undulating coils from the moonlit balcony, glided within my waistcoat and eat its way in two minutes to my heart's core. Strange!" he exclaimed, suddenly starting again from the point. "Strange that I should choose you for the confidant of all this, young lady: passing strange that you should listen to me quietly, as if it were the most usual thing in the world for a man like me to tell stories of his opera-mistresses to a quaint, inexperienced girl like you! But the last singularity explains the first, as I intimated once before: you, with your gravity, considerateness, and caution were made to be the recipient of secrets. Besides, I know what sort of a mind I have placed in communication with my own; I know it is one not liable to take infection: it is a peculiar mind; it is a unique one. Happily I do not mean to harm it: but if I did it would not take harm from me. The more you and I converse, the better; for while I cannot blight you, you may refresh me." After this digression, he proceeded: –

"I remained in the balcony. 'They will come to her boudoir no doubt,' thought I: 'let me prepare an ambush.' So putting my hand in through the open window, I drew the curtain over it, leaving only an opening through which I could take observations; then I closed the casement, all but a chink just wide enough to furnish an outlet to 'lovers' whispered vows':[1] then I stole back to my chair; and as I resumed it the pair came in. My eye was quickly at the aperture. Céline's chambermaid entered, lit a lamp, left it on the table and

---

1   See Byron's *Parisina* I.3-4.

withdrew. The couple were thus revealed to me clearly: both removed their cloaks, and there was 'the Varens' shining in satin and jewels, – my gifts of course, – and there was her companion in an officer's uniform; and I knew him for a young roué of a vicomte – a brainless and vicious youth whom I had sometimes met in society, and had never thought of hating because I despised him so absolutely. On recognizing him, the fang of the snake, – jealousy, was instantly broken; because at the same moment my love for Céline sank under an extinguisher. A woman who could betray me for such a rival was not worth contending for: she deserved only scorn; less, however, than I, who had been her dupe.

"They began to talk; their conversation eased me completely: frivolous, mercenary, heartless, and senseless, it was rather calculated to weary than enrage a listener. A card of mine lay on the table; this being perceived brought my name under discussion. Neither of them possessed energy or wit to belabour me soundly; but they insulted me as coarsely as they could in their little way: especially Céline; who even waxed rather brilliant on my personal defects – deformities she termed them. Now it had been her custom to launch out into fervent admiration of what she called my 'beauté mâle:'[1] wherein she differed diametrically from you, who told me point-blank at the second interview, that you did not think me handsome. The contrast struck me at the time, and —"

Adèle here came running up again.

"Monsieur, John has just been to say that your agent has called and wishes to see you."

"Ah! in that case I must abridge. Opening the window, I walked in upon them; liberated Céline from my protection; gave her notice to vacate her hotel; offered her a purse for immediate exigencies; disregarded screams, hysterics, prayers, protestations, convulsions; made an appointment with the Vicomte for a meeting at the bois de Boulogne. Next morning I had the pleasure of encountering him; left bullet in one of his poor, etiolated arms, feeble as the wing of a chicken in the pip,[2] and then thought I had done with the whole crew. But

---

1 Manly beauty.
2 A sick chicken. The "pip" is a common poultry disease.

unluckily the Varens, six months before, had given me this fillette Adèle; who she affirmed was my daughter: and perhaps she may be; though I see no proofs of such grim paternity written in her countenance: Pilot is more like me than she. Some years after I had broken with the mother, she abandoned her child and ran away to Italy with a musician, or singer. I acknowledged no natural claim on Adèle's part to be supported by me; nor do I now acknowledge any, for I am not her father; but hearing that she was quite destitute, I e'en took the poor thing out of the slime and mud of Paris, and transplanted it here, to grow up clean in the wholesome soil of an English country garden. Mrs. Fairfax found you to train it; but now you know that it is the illegitimate offspring of a French opera-girl, you will perhaps think differently of your post and protégée: you will be coming to me some day with notice that you have found another place – that you beg me to look out for a new governess, &c. – eh?"

"No – Adèle is not answerable for either her mother's faults or yours: I have a regard for her, and now that I know she is, in a sense, parentless – forsaken by her mother and disowned by you, sir, – I shall cling closer to her than before. How could I possibly prefer the spoilt pet of a wealthy family, who would hate her governess as a nuisance, to a lonely little orphan, who leans towards her as a friend?"

"Oh, that is the light in which you view it! Well, I must go in now; and you too: it darkens."

But I stayed out a few minutes longer with Adèle and Pilot – ran a race with her, and played a game of battledore and shuttlecock. When we went in and I had removed her bonnet and coat, I took her on my knee; kept her there an hour, allowing her to prattle as she liked: not rebuking even some little freedoms and trivialities into which she was apt to stray when much noticed; and which betrayed in her a superficiality of character, inherited probably from her mother, hardly congenial to an English mind. Still she had her merits; and I was disposed to appreciate all that was good in her to the utmost. I sought in her countenance and features a likeness to Mr. Rochester, but found none: no trait, no turn of expression announced relationship. It was a pity: if she could but have been proved to resemble him, he would have thought more of her.

It was not till after I had withdrawn to my own chamber for the night, that I steadily reviewed the tale Mr. Rochester had told me. As he had said, there was probably nothing at all extraordinary in the substance of the narrative itself: a wealthy Englishman's passion for a French dancer, and her treachery to him, were every-day matters enough, no doubt, in society; but there was something decidedly strange in the paroxysm of emotion which had suddenly seized him, when he was in the act of expressing the present contentment of his mood, and his newly revived pleasure in the old Hall and its environs. I meditated wonderingly on this incident; but gradually quitting it, as I found it for the present inexplicable, I turned to the consideration of my master's manner to myself. The confidence he had thought fit to repose in me seemed a tribute to my discretion: I regarded and accepted it as such. His deportment had now for some weeks been more uniform towards me than at the first. I never seemed in his way; he did not take fits of chilling hauteur: when he met me unexpectedly the encounter seemed welcome; he had always a word and sometimes a smile for me: when summoned by formal invitation to his presence, I was honoured by a cordiality of reception that made me feel I really possessed the power to amuse him, and that these evening conferences were sought as much for his pleasure as for my benefit.

I, indeed, talked comparatively little; but I heard him talk with relish. It was his nature to be communicative; he liked to open to a mind unacquainted with the world, glimpses of its scenes and ways (I do not mean its corrupt scenes and wicked ways, but such as derived their interest from the great scale on which they were acted, the strange novelty by which they were characterized); and I had a keen delight in receiving the new ideas he offered, in imaging the new pictures he portrayed, and following him in thought through the new regions he disclosed; never startled or troubled by one noxious allusion.

The ease of his manner freed me from painful restraint: the friendly frankness, as correct as cordial, with which he treated me, drew me to him. I felt at times, as if he were my relation, rather than my master: yet he was imperious sometimes still; but I did not mind that; I saw it was his way. So happy, so gratified did I become with this new interest added to life, that I ceased to pine after kindred: my thin crescent-destiny seemed to enlarge; the blanks of existence were filled up; my bodily health improved; I gathered flesh and strength.

And was Mr. Rochester now ugly in my eyes? No, reader: gratitude, and many associations, all pleasurable and genial, made his face
the object I best liked to see; his presence in a room was more cheering than the brightest fire. Yet I had not forgotten his faults: indeed, I
could not; for he brought them frequently before me. He was proud,
sardonic, harsh to inferiority of every description: in my secret soul I
knew that his great kindness to me was balanced by unjust severity to
many others. He was moody, too; unaccountably so: I more than
once, when sent for to read to him, found him sitting in his library
alone, with his head bent on his folded arms; and, when he looked up,
a morose, almost a malignant, scowl blackened his features. But I
believed that his moodiness, his harshness, and his former faults of
morality (I say *former*, for now he seemed corrected of them) had their
source in some cruel cross of fate. I believed he was naturally a man of
better tendencies, higher principles, and purer tastes than such as circumstances had developed, education instilled, or destiny encouraged.
I thought there were excellent materials in him; though for the present they hung together somewhat spoiled and tangled. I cannot deny
that I grieved for his grief, whatever that was, and would have given
much to assuage it.

Though I had now extinguished my candle and was laid down in
bed, I could not sleep for thinking of his look when he paused in the
avenue, and told how his destiny had risen up before him and dared
him to be happy at Thornfield.

"Why not?" I asked myself: "what alienates him from the house?
Will he leave it again soon? Mrs. Fairfax said he seldom stayed here
longer than a fortnight at a time; and he has now been resident eight
weeks. If he does go, the change will be doleful. Suppose he should be
absent, spring, summer, and autumn: how joyless sunshine and fine
days will seem!"

I hardly know whether I had slept or not after this musing; at any
rate I started wide awake on hearing a vague murmur, peculiar and
lugubrious, which sounded, I thought, just above me. I wished I had
kept my candle burning: the night was drearily dark; my spirits were
depressed. I rose and sat up in bed, listening. The sound was hushed.

I tried again to sleep; but my heart beat anxiously: my inward tranquillity was broken. The clock, far down in the hall, struck two. Just

then it seemed my chamber-door was touched; as if fingers had swept the pannels in groping a way along the dark gallery outside. I said, "Who is there?" Nothing answered. I was chilled with fear.

All at once I remembered that it might be Pilot; who, when the kitchen-door chanced to be left open, not unfrequently found his way up to the threshold of Mr. Rochester's chamber: I had seen him lying there myself, in the mornings. The idea calmed me somewhat: I lay down. Silence composes the nerves; and as an unbroken hush now reigned again through the whole house, I began to feel the return of slumber. But it was not fated that I should sleep that night. A dream had scarcely approached my ear, when it fled affrighted, scared by a marrow-freezing incident enough.

This was a demoniac laugh – low, suppressed, and deep – uttered, as it seemed, at the very key-hole of my chamber-door. The head of my bed was near the door, and I thought at first, the goblin-laugher stood at my bedside – or rather, crouched by my pillow: but I rose, looked round, and could see nothing; while, as I still gazed, the unnatural sound was reiterated: and I knew it came from behind the panels. My first impulse was to rise and fasten the bolt; my next, again to cry out, "Who is there?"

Something gurgled and moaned. Ere long, steps retreated up the gallery towards the third story staircase: a door had lately been made to shut in that staircase; I heard it open and close, and all was still.

"Was that Grace Poole? and is she possessed with a devil?" thought I. Impossible now to remain longer by myself: I must go to Mrs. Fairfax. I hurried on my frock and a shawl; I withdrew the bolt and opened the door with a trembling hand. There was a candle burning just outside, left on the matting in the gallery. I was surprised at this circumstance: but still more was I amazed to perceive the air quite dim, as if filled with smoke; and, while looking to the right hand and left, to find whence these blue wreaths issued, I became further aware of a strong smell of burning.

Something creaked: it was a door ajar; and that door was Mr. Rochester's, and the smoke rushed in a cloud from thence. I thought no more of Mrs. Fairfax; I thought no more of Grace Poole or the laugh: in an instant, I was within the chamber. Tongues of flame darted round the bed: the curtains were on fire. In the midst of blaze and vapour, Mr. Rochester lay stretched motionless, in deep sleep.

"Wake! wake!" I cried – I shook him, but he only murmured and turned: the smoke had stupefied him. Not a moment could be lost: the very sheets were kindling. I rushed to his basin and ewer; fortunately, one was wide and the other deep, and both were filled with water. I heaved them up, deluged the bed and its occupant, flew back to my own room, brought my own water-jug, baptised the couch afresh, and by God's aid, succeeded in extinguishing the flames which were devouring it.

The hiss of the quenched element, the breakage of a pitcher which I flung from my hand when I had emptied it, and above all, the splash of the shower-bath I had liberally bestowed, roused Mr. Rochester at last. Though it was now dark, I knew he was awake; because I heard him fulminating strange anathemas at finding himself lying in a pool of water.

"Is there a flood?" he cried.

"No, sir," I answered; "but there has been a fire: get up, do, you are quenched now; I will fetch you a candle."

"In the name of all the elves in Christendom, is that Jane Eyre?" he demanded. "What have you done with me, witch, sorceress? Who is in the room besides you? Have you plotted to drown me?"

"I will fetch you a candle, sir; and in Heaven's name, get up. Somebody has plotted something: you cannot too soon find out who and what it is."

"There – I am up now; but at your peril you fetch a candle yet: wait two minutes till I get into some dry garments, if any dry there be – yes, here is my dressing-gown, now run!"

I did run; I brought the candle which still remained in the gallery. He took it from my hand, held it up, and surveyed the bed, all blackened and scorched, the sheets drenched, the carpet round swimming in water.

"What is it? and who did it?" he asked.

I briefly related to him what had transpired: the strange laugh I had heard in the gallery; the step ascending to the third story; the smoke, – the smell of fire which had conducted me to his room; in what state I had found matters there, and how I had deluged him with all the water I could lay hands on.

He listened very gravely; his face, as I went on, expressed more concern than astonishment: he did not immediately speak when I had concluded.

"Shall I call Mrs. Fairfax?" I asked.

"Mrs. Fairfax? No: – what the deuce would you call her for? What can she do? Let her sleep unmolested."

"Then I will fetch Leah, and wake John and his wife."

"Not at all: just be still. You have a shawl on: if you are not warm enough, you may take my cloak yonder; wrap it about you, and sit down in the arm-chair: there, – I will put it on. Now place your feet on the stool, to keep them out of the wet. I am going to leave you a few minutes. I shall take the candle. Remain where you are till I return: be as still as a mouse. I must pay a visit to this third story. Don't move, remember, or call any one."

He went: I watched the light withdraw. He passed up the gallery very softly, unclosed the staircase door with as little noise as possible, shut it after him, and the last ray vanished. I was left in total darkness. I listened for some noise, but heard nothing. A very long time elapsed. I grew weary: it was cold, in spite of the cloak; and then I did not see the use of staying, as I was not to rouse the house. I was on the point of risking Mr. Rochester's displeasure, by disobeying his orders, when the light once more gleamed dimly on the gallery-wall, and I heard his unshod feet tread the matting. "I hope it is he," thought I, "and not something worse."

He re-entered pale and very gloomy. "I have found it all out," said he, setting his candle down on the wash-stand; "it is as I thought."

"How, sir?"

He made no reply, but stood with his arms folded, looking on the ground. At the end of a few minutes he enquired in rather a peculiar tone: –

"I forget whether you said you saw anything when you opened your chamber door."

"No, sir, only the candlestick on the ground."

"But you heard an odd laugh? You have heard that laugh before I should think, or something like it?"

"Yes, sir: there is a woman who sews here, called Grace Poole, – she laughs in that way. She is a singular person."

"Just so. Grace Poole: – you have guessed it. She is as you say, singular, – very. Well I shall reflect on the subject. Meantime, I am glad that you are the only person, besides myself, acquainted with the precise details of to-night's incident. You are no talking fool: say nothing about it. I will account for this state of affairs (pointing to the bed): and now return to your own room. I shall do very well on the sofa in the library for the rest of the night. It is near four; – in two hours the servants will be up."

"Good night then, sir," said I, departing.

He seemed surprised, – very inconsistently so, as he had just told me to go.

"What!" he exclaimed, "are you quitting me already: and in that way?"

"You said I might go, sir."

"But not without taking leave; not without a word or two of acknowledgment and good will: not, in short, in that brief, dry fashion. Why, you have saved my life! – snatched me from a horrible and excruciating death! – and you walk past me as if we were mutual strangers! At least shake hands."

He held out his hand; I gave him mine: he took it first in one, then in both his own.

"You have saved my life: I have a pleasure in owing you so immense a debt. I cannot say more. Nothing else that has being would have been tolerable to me in the character of creditor for such an obligation: but you; it is different; – I feel your benefits no burden, Jane."

He paused; gazed at me: words almost visible trembled on his lips, – but his voice was checked.

"Good night again, sir. There is no debt, benefit, burden, obligation, in the case."

"I knew," he continued, "you would do me good in some way, at some time; – I saw it in your eyes when I first beheld you: their expression and smile did not – (again he stopped) – did not (he proceeded hastily) strike delight to my very inmost heart so for nothing. People talk of natural sympathies; I have heard of good genii: – there are grains of truth in the wildest fable. My cherished preserver, good night!"

Strange energy was in his voice, strange fire in his look.

"I am glad I happened to be awake," I said; and then I was going.

"What! you *will* go?"

"I am cold, sir."

"Cold? Yes, – and standing in a pool! Go, then, Jane; go!" But he still retained my hand, and I could not free it. I bethought myself of an expedient.

"I think I hear Mrs. Fairfax move, sir," said I.

"Well, leave me:" he relaxed his fingers, and I was gone.

I regained my couch, but never thought of sleep. Till morning dawned I was tossed on a buoyant but unquiet sea, where billows of trouble rolled under surges of joy. I thought sometimes I saw beyond its wild waters a shore, sweet as the hills of Beulah;[1] and now and then a freshening gale, wakened by hope, bore my spirit triumphantly towards the bourne: but I could not reach it, even in fancy, – a counteracting breeze blew off land, and continually drove me back. Sense would resist delirium: judgment would warn passion. Too feverish to rest, I rose as soon as day dawned.

END OF VOLUME I.

---

1   See Isaiah 62:4

VOLUME II

CHAPTER XVI

I BOTH wished and feared to see Mr. Rochester on the day which followed this sleepless night: I wanted to hear his voice again, yet feared to meet his eye. During the early part of the morning, I momentarily expected his coming: he was not in the frequent habit of entering the school-room; but he did step in for a few minutes sometimes, and I had the impression that he was sure to visit it that day.

But the morning passed just as usual: nothing happened to interrupt the quiet course of Adèle's studies; only, soon after breakfast, I heard some bustle in the neighbourhood of Mr. Rochester's chamber, Mrs. Fairfax's voice, and Leah's, and the cook's – that is, John's wife – and even John's own gruff tones. There were exclamations of "What a mercy master was not burnt in his bed!" "It is always dangerous to keep a candle lit at night." "How providential that he had presence of mind to think of the water-jug!" "I wonder he waked nobody!" "It is to be hoped he will not take cold with sleeping on the library sofa," &c.

To much confabulation succeeded a sound of scrubbing and setting to rights; and when I passed the room, in going down stairs to dinner, I saw through the open door that all was again restored to complete order: only the bed was stripped of its hangings. Leah stood up in the window-seat, rubbing the panes of glass, dimmed with smoke. I was about to address her; for I wished to know what account had been given of the affair: but, on advancing, I saw a second person in the chamber – a woman sitting on a chair by the bed-side, and sewing rings to new curtains. That woman was no other than Grace Poole.

There she sat, staid and taciturn-looking, as usual; in her brown stuff gown, her check apron, white handkerchief, and cap. She was intent on her work, in which her whole thoughts seemed absorbed: on her hard forehead, and in her common-place features, was nothing either of the paleness or desperation one would have expected to see marking the countenance of a woman who had attempted murder; and whose intended victim had followed her last night to her lair, and (as I believed) charged her with the crime she wished to perpetrate. I was amazed – confounded. She looked up while I still gazed at her:

no start, no increase or failure of colour betrayed emotion, conscious-ness of guilt, or fear of detection. She said, "Good morning, Miss," in her usual phlegmatic and brief manner; and taking up another ring and more tape, went on with her sewing.

"I will put her to some test," thought I: "such absolute impenetra-bility is past comprehension."

"Good morning, Grace," I said. "Has anything happened here? I thought I heard the servants all talking together a while ago."

"Only, master had been reading in his bed last night; he fell asleep with his candle lit, and the curtains got on fire: but, fortunately, he awoke before the bed-clothes or the wood-work caught, and con-trived to quench the flame with the water in the ewer."

"A strange affair!" I said, in a low voice: then, looking at her fixed-ly, – "Did Mr. Rochester wake nobody? Did no one hear him move?"

She again raised her eyes to me; and this time there was something of consciousness in their expression. She seemed to examine me war-ily; then she answered, –

"The servants sleep so far off, you know, Miss, they would not be likely to hear. Mrs. Fairfax's room and yours are the nearest to mas-ter's; but Mrs. Fairfax said she heard nothing: when people get elderly, they often sleep heavy." She paused, and then added, with a sort of assumed indifference, but still in a marked and significant tone, "But you are young, Miss; and I should say a light sleeper: perhaps you may have heard a noise?"

"I did," said I, dropping my voice, so that Leah, who was still pol-ishing the panes, could not hear me, "and at first I thought it was Pilot: but Pilot cannot laugh; and I am certain I heard a laugh, and a strange one."

She took a new needleful of thread, waxed it carefully, threaded her needle with a steady hand, and then observed, with perfect com-posure, –

"It is hardly likely master would laugh, I should think, Miss, when he was in such danger: you must have been dreaming."

"I was not dreaming," I said, with some warmth: for her brazen coolness provoked me. Again she looked at me; and with the same scrutinizing and conscious eye.

"Have you told master that you heard a laugh?" she inquired.

"I have not had the opportunity of speaking to him this morning."

"You did not think of opening your door and looking out into the gallery?" she further asked.

She appeared to be cross-questioning me; attempting to draw from me information unawares: the idea struck me that if she discovered I knew or suspected her guilt, she would be playing off some of her malignant pranks on me; I thought it advisable to be on my guard.

"On the contrary," said I, "I bolted my door."

"Then you are not in the habit of bolting your door every night before you get into bed?"

"Fiend! she wants to know my habits that she may lay her plans accordingly!" Indignation again prevailed over prudence; I replied sharply: "Hitherto I have often omitted to fasten the bolt: I did not think it necessary. I was not aware any danger or annoyance was to be dreaded at Thornfield-Hall: but in future (and I laid marked stress on the words) I shall take good care to make all secure before I venture to lie down."

"It will be wise so to do;" was her answer: "this neighbourhood is as quiet as any I know, and I never heard of the hall being attempted by robbers since it was a house; though there are hundreds of pounds' worth of plate[1] in the plate-closet, as is well known. And you see, for such a large house there are very few servants, because master has never lived here much; and when he does come, being a bachelor, he needs little waiting on: but I always think it best to err on the safe side; a door is soon fastened, and it is as well to have a drawn bolt between one and any mischief that may be about. A deal of people, Miss, are for trusting all to Providence; but I say Providence will not dispense with the means, though he often blesses them when they are used discreetly." And here she closed her harangue: a long one for her, and uttered with the demureness of a Quakeress.

I still stood absolutely dumfounded at what appeared to me her miraculous self-possession and most inscrutable hypocrisy; when the cook entered.

"Mrs. Poole," said she, addressing Grace, "the servants' dinner will soon be ready: will you come down?"

---

1   Silver-plated table settings.

"No; just put my pint of porter and bit of pudding on a tray, and I'll carry it up-stairs."

"You'll have some meat?"

"Just a morsel, and a taste of cheese, that's all."

"And the sago?"[1]

"Never mind it, at present: I shall be coming down before tea-time: I'll make it myself."

The cook here turned to me, saying that Mrs. Fairfax was waiting for me; so I departed.

I hardly heard Mrs. Fairfax's account of the curtain conflagration during dinner, so much was I occupied in puzzling my brains over the enigmatical character of Grace Poole; and still more in pondering the problem of her position at Thornfield: in questioning why she had not been given into custody that morning; or at the very least dismissed from her master's service. He had almost as much as declared his conviction of her criminality last night: what mysterious cause withheld him from accusing her? Why had he enjoined me too to secrecy? It was strange: a bold, vindictive and haughty gentleman seemed somehow in the power of one of the meanest of his dependents; so much in her power, that even when she lifted her hand against his life, he dared not openly charge her with the attempt, much less punish her for it.

Had Grace been young and handsome, I should have been tempted to think that tenderer feelings than prudence or fear influenced Mr. Rochester in her behalf; but hard-favoured and matronly as she was, the idea could not be admitted. "Yet," I reflected, "she has been young once; her youth would be contemporary with her master's: Mrs. Fairfax told me once, she had lived here many years. I don't think she can ever have been pretty; but for aught I know she may possess originality and strength of character to compensate for the want of personal advantages. Mr. Rochester is an amateur of the decided and eccentric: Grace is eccentric at least. What if a former caprice (a freak very possible to a nature so sudden and headstrong as his) has delivered him into her power, and she now exercises over his actions a secret influence, the result of his own indiscretion, which he

---

1 A kind of cereal or gruel.

cannot shake off and dare not disregard?" But, having reached this point of conjecture, Mrs. Poole's square, flat figure, and uncomely, dry, even coarse face, recurred so distinctly to my mind's eye, that I thought "No; impossible! my supposition cannot be correct. Yet," suggested the secret voice which talks to us in our own hearts, "*you are not beautiful either, and perhaps Mr. Rochester approves you: at any rate you have often felt as if he did; and last night – remember his words; remember his look; remember his voice!*"

I well remembered all: language, glance and tone seemed at the moment vividly renewed. I was now in the school-room; Adèle was drawing; I bent over her and directed her pencil. She looked up with a sort of start.

"Qu'avez-vous, Mademoiselle?" said she; "Vos doigts tremblent comme la feuille, et vos joues sont rouges: mais, rouges comme des cerises!"[1]

"I am hot, Adèle, with stooping!" She went on sketching, I went on thinking.

I hastened to drive from my mind the hateful notion I had been conceiving respecting Grace Poole: it disgusted me. I compared myself with her, and found we were different. Bessie Leaven had said I was quite a lady; and she spoke truth: I was a lady. And now I looked much better than I did when Bessie saw me: I had more colour and more flesh; more life, more vivacity; because I had brighter hopes and keener enjoyments.

"Evening approaches," said I, as I looked towards the window. "I have never heard Mr. Rochester's voice or step in the house to-day; but surely I shall see him before night: I feared the meeting in the morning; now I desire it, because expectation has been so long baffled that it is grown impatient."

When dusk actually closed, and when Adèle left me to go and play in the nursery with Sophie, I did most keenly desire it. I listened for the bell to ring below; I listened for Leah coming up with a message; I fancied sometimes I heard Mr. Rochester's own tread, and I turned to the door, expecting it to open and admit him. The door remained shut: darkness only came in through the window. Still it was not late:

---

[1] "What's the matter miss?...Your fingers quiver like a leaf, and your cheeks are red: red like cherries!"

he often sent for me at seven and eight o'clock, and it was yet but six. Surely I should not be wholly disappointed to-night, when I had so many things to say to him! I wanted again to introduce the subject of Grace Poole, and to hear what he would answer; I wanted to ask him plainly if he really believed it was she who had made last night's hideous attempt; and if so, why he kept her wickedness a secret. It little mattered whether my curiosity irritated him; I knew the pleasure of vexing and soothing him by turns; it was one I chiefly delighted in, and a sure instinct always prevented me from going too far: beyond the verge of provocation I never ventured; on the extreme brink I liked well to try my skill. Retaining every minute form of respect, every propriety of my station, I could still meet him in argument without fear or uneasy restraint: this suited both him and me.

A tread creaked on the stairs at last; Leah made her appearance: but it was only to intimate that tea was ready in Mrs. Fairfax's room. Thither I repaired, glad at least to go down-stairs; for that brought me, I imagined, nearer to Mr. Rochester's presence.

"You must want your tea," said the good lady as I joined her; "you ate so little at dinner. I am afraid," she continued, "you are not well to-day: you look flushed and feverish."

"Oh, quite well! I never felt better."

"Then you must prove it by evincing a good appetite; will you fill the tea-pot while I knit off this needle?" Having completed her task, she rose to draw down the blind which she had hitherto kept up; by way, I suppose, of making the most of daylight: though dusk was now fast deepening into total obscurity.

"It is fair to-night," said she, as she looked through the panes, "though not starlight: Mr. Rochester has, on the whole, had a favourable day for his journey."

"Journey! – Is Mr. Rochester gone anywhere? I did not know he was out."

"Oh, he set off the moment he had breakfasted! He is gone to the Leas; Mr. Eshton's place, ten miles on the other side Millcote: I believe there is quite a party assembled there; Lord Ingram, Sir George Lynn, Colonel Dent and others."

"Do you expect him back to-night?"

"No – nor to-morrow either; I should think he is very likely to stay a week or more: when these fine, fashionable people get together, they are so surrounded by elegance and gaiety; so well provided with all that can please and entertain, they are in no hurry to separate. Gentlemen, especially, are often in request on such occasions; and Mr. Rochester is so talented and so lively in society, that I believe he is a general favourite: the ladies are very fond of him; though you would not think his appearance calculated to recommend him particularly in their eyes: but I suppose his acquirements and abilities, perhaps his wealth and good blood, make amends for any little fault of look."

"Are there ladies at the Leas?"

"There are Mrs. Eshton and her three daughters – very elegant young ladies indeed; and there are the honourable Blanche and Mary Ingram; most beautiful women, I suppose: indeed I have seen Blanche, six or seven years since, when she was a girl of eighteen. She came here to a Christmas ball and party Mr. Rochester gave. You should have seen the dining-room that day – how richly it was decorated, how brilliantly lit up! I should think there were fifty ladies and gentlemen present – all of the first county-families; and Miss Ingram was considered the belle of the evening."

"You saw her, you say, Mrs. Fairfax: what was she like?"

"Yes, I saw her. The dining-room doors were thrown open; and, as it was Christmas-time, the servants were allowed to assemble in the hall, to hear some of the ladies sing and play. Mr. Rochester would have me to come in, and I sat down in a quiet corner and watched them. I never saw a more splendid scene: the ladies were magnificently dressed; most of them – at least most of the younger ones – looked handsome; but Miss Ingram was certainly the queen."

"And what was she like?"

"Tall, fine bust, sloping shoulders; long, graceful neck; olive complexion, dark and clear; noble features; eyes rather like Mr. Rochester's: large and black, and as brilliant as her jewels. And then she had such a fine head of hair; raven-black, and so becomingly arranged: a crown of thick plaits behind, and in front the longest, the glossiest curls I ever saw. She was dressed in pure white; an amber-coloured scarf was passed over her shoulder and across her breast, tied at the side, and descending in long, fringed ends below her knee. She wore an amber-coloured flower, too, in her hair: it contrasted well with the jetty mass of her curls."

"She was greatly admired, of course?"

"Yes, indeed: and not only for her beauty, but for her accomplishments. She was one of the ladies who sang: a gentleman accompanied her on the piano. She and Mr. Rochester sung a duet."

"Mr. Rochester! I was not aware he could sing."

"Oh! he has a fine bass voice, and an excellent taste for music."

"And Miss Ingram: what sort of a voice had she?"

"A very rich and powerful one: she sang delightfully; it was a treat to listen to her; – and she played afterwards. I am no judge of music, but Mr. Rochester is; and I heard him say her execution was remarkably good."

"And this beautiful and accomplished lady is not yet married?"

"It appears not: I fancy neither she nor her sister have very large fortunes. Old Lord Ingram's estates were chiefly entailed, and the eldest son came in for everything almost."

"But I wonder no wealthy nobleman or gentleman has taken a fancy to her: Mr. Rochester, for instance. He is rich, is he not?"

"Oh! yes. But, you see, there is a considerable difference in age: Mr. Rochester is nearly forty; she is but twenty-five."

"What of that? More unequal matches are made every day."

"True: yet I should scarcely fancy Mr. Rochester would entertain an idea of the sort. – But you eat nothing: you have scarcely tasted since you began tea."

"No: I am too thirsty to eat. Will you let me have another cup?"

I was about again to revert to the probability of a union between Mr. Rochester and the beautiful Blanche: but Adèle came in, and the conversation was turned into another channel.

When once more alone, I reviewed the information I had got; looked into my heart, examined its thoughts and feelings, and endeavoured to bring back with a strict hand such as had been straying through imagination's boundless and trackless waste, into the safe fold of common sense.

Arraigned at my own bar, Memory having given her evidence of the hopes, wishes, sentiments I had been cherishing since last night – of the general state of mind in which I had indulged for nearly a fortnight past; Reason having come forward and told, in her own quiet way, a plain, unvarnished tale, showing how I had rejected the real and rabidly devoured the ideal; – I pronounced judgment to this effect: –

That a greater fool than Jane Eyre had never breathed the breath of life: that a more fantastic idiot had never surfeited herself on sweet lies, and swallowed poison as if it were nectar.

"*You*," I said, "a favourite with Mr. Rochester? *You* gifted with the power of pleasing him? *You* of importance to him in any way? Go! your folly sickens me. And you have derived pleasure from occasional tokens of preference – equivocal tokens, shown by a gentleman of family, and a man of the world, to a dependent and a novice. How dared you? Poor stupid dupe! – Could not even self-interest make you wiser? You repeated to yourself this morning the brief scene of last night? – Cover your face and be ashamed! He said something in praise of your eyes, did he? Blind puppy! Open their bleared lids and look on your own accursed senselessness! It does good to no woman to be flattered by her superior, who cannot possibly intend to marry her; and it is madness in all women to let a secret love kindle within them, which, if unreturned and unknown, must devour the life that feeds it; and, if discovered and responded to, must lead, *ignis-fatuus-* like,[1] into miry wilds whence there is no extrication.

"Listen, then, Jane Eyre, to your sentence: to-morrow, place the glass before you, and draw in chalk your own picture, faithfully; without softening one defect: omit no harsh line, smooth away no displeasing irregularity; write under it, 'Portrait of a Governess, disconnected, poor, and plain.'

"Afterwards, take a piece of smooth ivory – you have one prepared in your drawing-box: take your palette, mix your freshest, finest, clearest tints; choose your most delicate camel-hair pencils; delineate carefully the loveliest face you can imagine; paint it in your softest shades and sweetest hues, according to the description given by Mrs. Fairfax of Blanche Ingram: remember the raven ringlets, the oriental eye; – what! you revert to Mr. Rochester's as a model! Order!

---

1   Will-o'-the-wisp-like. This describes a phosphorescent light which appears on marshy ground due to the combustion of methane, and which may mislead travellers into becoming trapped in a bog.

No snivel! – no sentiment! – no regret! I will endure only sense and resolution. Recall the august yet harmonious lineaments, the Grecian neck and bust: let the round and dazzling arm be visible, and the delicate hand; omit neither diamond ring nor gold bracelet; portray faithfully the attire, aërial lace and glistening satin, graceful scarf and golden rose: call it 'Blanche, an accomplished lady of rank.'

"Whenever, in future, you should chance to fancy Mr. Rochester thinks well of you, take out these two pictures and compare them: say, 'Mr. Rochester might probably win that noble lady's love, if he chose to strive for it; is it likely he would waste a serious thought on this indigent and insignificant plebeian?'"

"I'll do it," I resolved: and having framed this determination, I grew calm, and fell asleep.

I kept my word. An hour or two sufficed to sketch my own portrait in crayons; and in less than a fortnight I had completed an ivory miniature of an imaginary Blanche Ingram. It looked a lovely face enough, and when compared with the real head in chalk, the contrast was as great as self-control could desire. I derived benefit from the task: it had kept my head and hands employed, and had given force and fixedness to the new impressions I wished to stamp indelibly on my heart.

Ere long I had reason to congratulate myself on the course of wholesome discipline to which I had thus forced my feelings to submit: thanks to it, I was able to meet subsequent occurrences with a decent calm; which, had they found me unprepared, I should probably have been unequal to maintain even externally.

CHAPTER XVII

A WEEK passed, and no news arrived of Mr. Rochester: ten days; and still he did not come. Mrs. Fairfax said she should not be surprised if he were to go straight from the Leas to London, and thence to the continent, and not show his face again at Thornfield for a year to come: he had not unfrequently quitted it in a manner quite as abrupt and unexpected. When I heard this I was beginning to feel a strange chill and failing at the heart. I was actually permitting myself to experience a sickening sense of disappointment: but rallying my wits, and recollecting my principles, I at once called my sensations to order; and it was wonderful how I got over the temporary blunder – how I cleared up the mistake of supposing Mr. Rochester's movements a matter in which I had any cause to take a vital interest. Not that I humbled myself by a slavish notion of inferiority: on the contrary, I just said: –

"You have nothing to do with the master of Thornfield, further than to receive the salary he gives you for teaching his protégée, and to be grateful for such respectful and kind treatment as, if you do your duty, you have a right to expect at his hands. Be sure that is the only tie he seriously acknowledges between you and him: so don't make him the object of your fine feelings, your raptures, agonies, and so forth. He is not of your order: keep to your caste; and be too self-respecting to lavish the love of the whole heart, soul, and strength, where such a gift is not wanted and would be despised."

I went on with my day's business tranquilly; but ever and anon, vague suggestions kept wandering across my brain of reasons why I should quit Thornfield; and I kept involuntarily framing advertisements and pondering conjectures about new situations: these thoughts I did not think it necessary to check; they might germinate and bear fruit if they could.

Mr. Rochester had been absent upwards of a fortnight, when the post brought Mrs. Fairfax a letter.

"It is from the master," said she, as she looked at the direction. "Now I suppose we shall know whether we are to expect his return or not."

And while she broke the seal and perused the document, I went on taking my coffee (we were at breakfast): it was hot, and I attributed to that circumstance a fiery glow which suddenly rose to my face. Why my hand shook, and why I involuntarily spilt half the contents of my cup into my saucer, I did not choose to consider.

"Well – I sometimes think we are too quiet; but we run a chance of being busy enough now: for a little while at least," said Mrs. Fairfax, still holding the note before her spectacles.

Ere I permitted myself to request an explanation, I tied the string of Adèle's pinafore which happened to be loose: having helped her also to another bun and refilled her mug with milk, I said nonchalantly: –

"Mr. Rochester is not likely to return soon, I suppose?"

"Indeed, he is – in three days, he says; that will be next Thursday; and not alone either. I don't know how many of the fine people at the Leas are coming with him: he sends directions for all the best bedrooms to be prepared; and the library and drawing-rooms are to be cleaned out; and I am to get more kitchen hands from the George Inn, at Millcote, and from wherever else I can; and the ladies will bring their maids and the gentlemen their valets: so we shall have a full house of it." And Mrs. Fairfax swallowed her breakfast and hastened away to commence operations.

The three days were, as she had foretold, busy enough. I had thought all the rooms at Thornfield beautifully clean and well-arranged: but it appears I was mistaken. Three women were got to help; and such scrubbing, such brushing, such washing of paint and beating of carpets, such taking down and putting up of pictures, such polishing of mirrors and lustres, such lighting of fires in bed-rooms, such airing of sheets and feather-beds on hearths, I never beheld, either before or since. Adèle ran quite wild in the midst of it: the preparations for company and the prospect of their arrival, seemed to throw her into ecstasies. She would have Sophie to look over all her "toilettes" as she called frocks; to furbish up any that were "passées,"[1] and to air and arrange the new. For herself, she did nothing but caper about in the front chambers, jump on and off the bedsteads, and lie on the mattresses and piled-up bolsters and pillows before the enormous fires roaring in the chimneys. From school duties she was exon-

---

1 Out of date.

erated: Mrs. Fairfax had pressed me into her service, and I was all day in the store-room, helping (or hindering) her and the cook; learning to make custards and cheesecakes and French pastry, to truss game and garnish dessert-dishes.

The party were expected to arrive on Thursday afternoon, in time for dinner at six. During the intervening period I had no time to nurse chimeras;[1] and I believe I was as active and gay as anybody – Adèle excepted. Still, now and then, I received a damping check to my cheerfulness; and was, in spite of myself, thrown back on the region of doubts and portents, and dark conjectures. This was when I chanced to see the third story staircase door (which of late had always been kept locked) open slowly, and give passage to the form of Grace Poole, in prim cap, white apron, and handkerchief: when I watched her glide along the gallery, her quiet tread muffled in a list slipper;[2] when I saw her look into the bustling, topsy-turvy bed-rooms, – just say a word, perhaps, to the charwomen about the proper way to polish a grate, or clean a marble mantelpiece, or take stains from papered walls, and then pass on. She would thus descend to the kitchen once a day, eat her dinner, smoke a moderate pipe on the hearth, and go back, carrying her pot of porter with her, for her private solace, in her own gloomy upper haunt. Only one hour in the twenty-four did she pass with her fellow-servants below; all the rest of her time was spent in some low-ceiled, oaken chamber of the third story: there she sat and sewed – and probably laughed drearily to herself, – as companionless as a prisoner in his dungeon.

The strangest thing of all was, that not a soul in the house, except me, noticed her habits, or seemed to marvel at them: no one discussed her position or employment; no one pitied her solitude or isolation. I once, indeed, overheard part of a dialogue between Leah and one of the charwomen, of which Grace formed the subject. Leah had been saying something I had not caught, and the charwoman remarked: –

"She gets good wages, I guess?"

"Yes," said Leah; "I wish I had as good: not that mine are to complain of, – there's no stinginess at Thornfield; but they're not one-fifth

---

1 Fanciful, unrealistic ideas. The Chimera was a monster in Greek mythology with a lion's head, goat's body, and serpent's tail.

2 Cloth slipper.

of the sum Mrs. Poole receives. And she is laying by: she goes every quarter to the bank at Millcote. I should not wonder but she has saved enough to keep her independent if she liked to leave; but I suppose she's got used to the place: and then she's not forty yet, and strong and able for anything. It is too soon for her to give up business."

"She is a good hand, I daresay," said the charwoman.

"Ah! – she understands what she has to do, – nobody better," rejoined Leah, significantly; "and it is not every one could fill her shoes: not for all the money she gets."

"That it is not!" was the reply. "I wonder whether master —"

The charwoman was going on; but here Leah turned and perceived me, and she instantly gave her companion a nudge.

"Doesn't she know?" I heard the woman whisper.

Leah shook her head, and the conversation was of course dropped. All I had gathered from it amounted to this, – that there was a mystery at Thornfield; and that from participation in that mystery, I was purposely excluded.

Thursday came: all work had been completed the previous evening; carpets were laid down, bed-hangings festooned, radiant white counterpanes spread, toilet tables arranged, furniture rubbed, flowers piled in vases: both chambers and saloons looked as fresh and bright as hands could make them. The hall, too, was scoured; and the great carved clock, as well as the steps and bannisters of the staircase, were polished to the brightness of glass: in the dining-room, the sideboard flashed resplendent with plate; in the drawing-room and boudoir, vases of exotics bloomed on all sides.

Afternoon arrived: Mrs. Fairfax assumed her best black satin gown, her gloves, and her gold watch; for it was her part to receive the company, – to conduct the ladies to their rooms, &c. Adèle, too, would be dressed; though I thought she had little chance of being introduced to the party, that day at least. However, to please her, I allowed Sophie to apparel her in one of her short, full muslin frocks. For myself, I had no need to make any change; I should not be called upon to quit my sanctum of the school-room; for a sanctum it was now become to me, – "a very pleasant refuge in time of trouble."[1]

---

1   See Psalms 46:1.

It had been a mild, serene spring day: – one of those days which towards the end of March or the beginning of April, rise shining over the earth as heralds of summer. It was drawing to an end now; but the evening was even warm, and I sat at work in the school-room with the window open.

"It gets late;" said Mrs. Fairfax, entering in rustling state. "I am glad I ordered dinner an hour after the time Mr. Rochester mentioned; for it is past six now. I have sent John down to the gates to see if there is anything on the road: one can see a long way from thence in the direction of Millcote." She went to the window. "Here he is!" said she. "Well, John," (leaning out) "any news?"

"They're coming, ma'am," was the answer. "They'll be here in ten minutes."

Adèle flew to the window. I followed; taking care to stand on one side, so that, screened by the curtain, I could see without being seen.

The ten minutes John had given seemed very long, but at last wheels were heard; four equestrians galloped up the drive, and after them came two open carriages. Fluttering veils and waving plumes filled the vehicles; two of the cavaliers were young, dashing looking gentlemen; the third was Mr. Rochester on his black horse, Mesrour;[1] Pilot bounding before him: at his side rode a lady, and he and she were the first of the party. Her purple riding-habit almost swept the ground, her veil streamed long on the breeze; mingling with its transparent folds, and gleaming through them, shone rich raven ringlets.

"Miss Ingram!" exclaimed Mrs. Fairfax, and away she hurried to her post below.

The cavalcade, following the sweep of the drive, quickly turned the angle of the house, and I lost sight of it. Adèle now petitioned to go down; but I took her on my knee and gave her to understand that she must not on any account think of venturing in sight of the ladies, either now or at any other time, unless expressly sent for: that Mr. Rochester would be very angry, &c. "Some natural tears she shed"[2] on being told this; but as I began to look very grave, she consented at last to wipe them.

A joyous stir was now audible in the hall: gentlemen's deep tones,

---

1 Rochester's horse is named for an executioner who appears in *The Arabian Nights*.
2 See *Paradise Lost*, Book XII.645.

and ladies' silvery accents blent harmoniously together, and distinguishable above all, though not loud, was the sonorous voice of the master of Thornfield Hall, welcoming his fair and gallant guests under its roof. Then light steps ascended the stairs; and there was a tripping through the gallery, and soft, cheerful laughs, and opening and closing doors, and, for a time, a hush.

"Elles changent de toilettes,"[1] said Adele; who, listening attentively, had followed every movement; and she sighed.

"Chez maman," said she, "quand il y avait du monde, je les suivais partout, au salon et à leurs chambres; souvent je regardais les femmes de chambre coiffer et habiller les dames, et c'était si amusant: comme cela on apprend."[2]

"Don't you feel hungry, Adèle?"

"Mais oui, mademoiselle: voilà cinq ou six heures que nous n'avons pas mangé."[3]

"Well now, while the ladies are in their rooms, I will venture down and get you something to eat."

And issuing from my asylum with precaution, I sought a back-stairs which conducted directly to the kitchen. All in that region was fire and commotion; the soup and fish were in the last stage of projection, and the cook hung over her crucibles in a frame of mind and body threatening spontaneous combustion. In the servants' hall two coachmen and three gentlemen's gentlemen stood or sat round the fire; the Abigails I suppose were up-stairs with their mistresses: the new servants that had been hired from Millcote, were bustling about everywhere. Threading this chaos, I at last reached the larder; there I took possession of a cold chicken, a roll of bread, some tarts, a plate or two and a knife and fork: with this booty I made a hasty retreat. I had regained the gallery, and was just shutting the back-door behind me, when an accelerated hum warned me that the ladies were about to issue from their chambers. I could not proceed to the school-room without passing some of their doors, and running the risk of being

---

1   "They're changing their dresses."
2   "At mama's…when there were people about, I followed them everywhere, to the drawing-room and to their bed chambers; often I watched the maids dress the ladies and do their hair, it was such fun: that's how one learns."
3   "But of course, Miss: it's been five or six hours since we've eaten."

surprised with my cargo of victuallage; so I stood still at this end, which, being windowless, was dark: quite dark now, for the sun was set and twilight gathering.

Presently the chambers gave up their fair tenants one after another: each came out gaily and airily, with dress that gleamed lustrous through the dusk. For a moment they stood grouped together at the other extremity of the gallery, conversing in a key of sweet subdued vivacity: they then descended the staircase, almost as noiselessly as a bright mist rolls down a hill. Their collective appearance had left on me an impression of high-born elegance, such as I had never before received.

I found Adèle peeping through the school-room door, which she held ajar. "What beautiful ladies!" cried she in English. "Oh I wish I might go to them! Do you think Mr. Rochester will send for us by-and-by, after dinner?"

"No, indeed, I don't; Mr. Rochester has something else to think about. Never mind the ladies to-night; perhaps you will see them to-morrow: here is your dinner."

She was really hungry, so the chicken and tarts served to divert her attention for a time. It was well I secured this forage; or both she, I and Sophie, to whom I conveyed a share of our repast, would have run a chance of getting no dinner at all: every one down stairs was too much engaged to think of us. The dessert was not carried out till after nine, and at ten, footmen were still running to and fro with trays and coffee-cups. I allowed Adèle to sit up much later than usual; for she declared she could not possibly go to sleep while the doors kept opening and shutting below, and people bustling about. Besides, she added, a message might possibly come from Mr. Rochester when she was undressed; "et alors quel dommage!"[1]

I told her stories as long as she would listen to them; and then for a change, I took her out into the gallery. The hall lamp was now lit, and it amused her to look over the balustrade and watch the servants passing backwards and forwards. When the evening was far advanced, a sound of music issued from the drawing-room, whither the piano had been removed; Adèle and I sat down on the top step of the stairs

---

1   "And that would be most unfortunate!"

to listen. Presently a voice blent with the rich tones of the instrument: it was a lady who sang, and very sweet her notes were. The solo over, a duet followed, and then a glee: a joyous conversational murmur filled up the intervals. I listened long: suddenly I discovered that my ear was wholly intent on analyzing the mingled sounds, and trying to discriminate amidst the confusion of accents those of Mr. Rochester; and when it caught them, which it soon did, it found a further task in framing the tones, rendered by distance inarticulate, into words.

The clock struck eleven. I looked at Adèle, whose head leant against my shoulder; her eyes were waxing heavy, so I took her up in my arms and carried her off to bed. It was near one before the gentlemen and ladies sought their chambers.

The next day was as fine as its predecessor; it was devoted by the party to an excursion to some site in the neighbourhood. They set out early in the forenoon, some on horseback, the rest in carriages; I witnessed both the departure and the return. Miss Ingram, as before, was the only lady equestrian; and as before, Mr. Rochester galloped at her side: the two rode a little apart from the rest. I pointed out this circumstance to Mrs. Fairfax, who was standing at the window with me: –

"You said it was not likely they should think of being married," said I, "but you see Mr. Rochester evidently prefers her to any of the other ladies."

"Yes; I daresay: no doubt he admires her."

"And she him," I added; "look how she leans her head towards him as if she were conversing confidentially! I wish I could see her face: I have never had a glimpse of it yet."

"You will see her this evening;" answered Mrs. Fairfax. "I happened to remark to Mr. Rochester how much Adèle wished to be introduced to the ladies, and he said: 'Oh! let her come into the drawing-room after dinner; and request Miss Eyre to accompany her.'"

"Yes – he said that from mere politeness: I need not go, I am sure," I answered.

"Well – I observed to him that as you were unused to company, I did not think you would like appearing before so gay a party – all strangers; and he replied, in his quick way: 'Nonsense! If she objects, tell her it is my particular wish; and if she resists, say I shall come and fetch her in case of contumacy.'"

"I will not give him that trouble;" I answered. "I will go, if no better may be: but I don't like it. Shall you be there, Mrs. Fairfax?"

"No; I pleaded off, and he admitted my plea. I'll tell you how to manage so as to avoid the embarrassment of making a formal entrance, which is the most disagreeable part of the business. You must go into the drawing-room while it is empty, before the ladies leave the dinner-table; choose your seat in any quiet nook you like; you need not stay long after the gentlemen come in, unless you please: just let Mr. Rochester see you are there and then slip away – nobody will notice you."

"Will these people remain long, do you think?"

"Perhaps two or three weeks; certainly not more. After the Easter recess,[1] Sir George Lynn, who was lately elected member for Millcote, will have to go up to town and take his seat; I daresay Mr. Rochester will accompany him: it surprises me that he has already made so protracted a stay at Thornfield."

It was with some trepidation that I perceived the hour approach when I was to repair with my charge to the drawing-room. Adèle had been in a state of ecstasy all day, after hearing she was to be presented to the ladies in the evening; and it was not till Sophie commenced the operation of dressing her, that she sobered down. Then the importance of the process quickly steadied her; and by the time she had her curls arranged in well-smoothed, drooping clusters, her pink satin frock put on, her long sash tied, and her lace mittens adjusted, she looked as grave as any judge. No need to warn her not to disarrange her attire: when she was dressed, she sat demurely down in her little chair, taking care previously to lift up the satin skirt for fear she should crease it, and assured me she would not stir thence till I was ready. This I quickly was: my best dress (the silver-grey one, purchased for Miss Temple's wedding and never worn since) was soon put on; my hair was soon smoothed; my sole ornament, the pearl brooch, soon assumed. We descended.

Fortunately there was another entrance to the drawing-room than

---

1   The spring break for Parliament.

that through the saloon where they were all seated at dinner. We found the apartment vacant; a large fire burning silently on the marble hearth, and wax candles shining in bright solitude, amid the exquisite flowers with which the tables were adorned. The crimson curtain hung before the arch: slight as was the separation this drapery formed from the party in the adjoining saloon, they spoke in so low a key that nothing of their conversation could be distinguished beyond a soothing murmur.

Adèle, who appeared to be still under the influence of a most solemnizing impression, sat down without a word on the footstool I pointed out to her. I retired to a window seat, and taking a book from a table near, endeavoured to read. Adèle brought her stool to my feet; ere long she touched my knee.

"What is it, Adèle?"

"Est-ce que je ne puis pas prendre une seule de ces fleurs magnifiques, Mademoiselle? Seulement pour compléter ma toilette."[1]

"You think too much of your 'toilette,' Adèle: but you may have a flower." And I took a rose from a vase and fastened it in her sash. She sighed a sigh of ineffable satisfaction, as if her cup of happiness were now full. I turned my face away to conceal a smile I could not suppress: there was something ludicrous as well as painful in the little Parisienne's earnest and innate devotion to matters of dress.

A soft sound of rising now became audible; the curtain was swept back from the arch; through it appeared the dining-room, with its lit lustre pouring down light on the silver and glass of a magnificent dessert-service covering a long table; a band of ladies stood in the opening; they entered, and the curtain fell behind them.

There were but eight; yet somehow as they flocked in, they gave the impression of a much larger number. Some of them were very tall; many were dressed in white; and all had a sweeping amplitude of array that seemed to magnify their persons as a mist magnifies the moon. I rose and curtseyed to them: one or two bent their heads in return; the others only stared at me.

They dispersed about the room; reminding me, by the lightness and buoyancy of their movements, of a flock of white plumy birds.

---

1   "May I not take just one of these magnificent flowers, Miss? Just to set off my dress."

Some of them threw themselves in half-reclining positions on the sofas and ottomans; some bent over the tables and examined the flowers and books; the rest gathered in a group round the fire: all talked in a low but clear tone which seemed habitual to them. I knew their names afterwards, and may as well mention them now.

First, there was Mrs. Eshton and two of her daughters. She had evidently been a handsome woman, and was well preserved still. Of her daughters, the eldest, Amy, was rather little; naïve, and child-like in face and manner, and piquant in form: her white muslin dress and blue sash became her well. The second, Louisa, was taller and more elegant in figure; with a very pretty face, of that order the French term "minois chiffonné:"[1] both sisters were fair as lilies.

Lady Lynn was a large and stout personage of about forty; very erect, very haughty-looking, richly dressed in a satin robe of changeful sheen: her dark hair shone glossily under the shade of an azure plume, and within the circlet of a band of gems.

Mrs. Colonel Dent was less showy; but, I thought, more lady-like. She had a slight figure, a pale, gentle face, and fair hair. Her black satin dress, her scarf of rich foreign lace, and her pearl ornaments, pleased me better than the rainbow radiance of the titled dame.

But the three most distinguished – partly perhaps, because the tallest figures of the band – were the Dowager Lady Ingram and her daughters, Blanche and Mary. They were all three of the loftiest stature of woman. The dowager might be between forty and fifty: her shape was still fine; her hair (by candle light at least) still black; her teeth, too, were still apparently perfect. Most people would have termed her a splendid woman of her age: and so she was, no doubt, physically speaking; but then there was an expression of almost insupportable haughtiness in her bearing and countenance. She had Roman features and a double chin, disappearing into a throat like a pillar: these features appeared to me not only inflated and darkened, but even furrowed with pride; and the chin was sustained by the same principle, in a position of almost preternatural erectness. She had, likewise, a fierce and a hard eye: it reminded me of Mrs. Reed's; she mouthed her words in speaking; her voice was deep, its inflexions

---

1 Sweet but somewhat petulant.

very pompous, very dogmatical, – very intolerable, in short. A crimson velvet robe, and a shawl turban of some gold-wrought Indian fabric, invested her (I suppose she thought) with a truly imperial dignity.

Blanche and Mary were of equal stature, – straight and tall as poplars. Mary was too slim for her height; but Blanche was moulded like a Dian.[1] I regarded her, of course, with special interest. First, I wished to see whether her appearance accorded with Mrs. Fairfax's description; secondly, whether it at all resembled the fancy miniature I had painted of her; and thirdly – it will out! – whether it were such as I should fancy likely to suit Mr. Rochester's taste.

As far as person went, she answered point for point, both to my picture and Mrs. Fairfax's description. The noble bust, the sloping shoulders, the graceful neck, the dark eyes and black ringlets were all there: – but her face? – Her face was like her mother's; a youthful, unfurrowed likeness: the same low brow, the same high features, the same pride. It was not, however, so saturnine a pride: she laughed continually; her laugh was satirical, and so was the habitual expression of her arched and haughty lip.

Genius is said to be self-conscious: I cannot tell whether Miss Ingram was a genius, but she was self-conscious – remarkably self-conscious indeed. She entered into a discourse on botany with the gentle Mrs. Dent. It seemed Mrs. Dent had not studied that science: though, as she said, she liked flowers, "especially wild ones;" Miss Ingram had, and she ran over its vocabulary with an air. I presently perceived she was (what is vernacularly termed) *trailing* Mrs. Dent; that is, playing on her ignorance: her *trail* might be clever, but it was decidedly not good-natured. She played: her execution was brilliant; she sang: her voice was fine; she talked French apart to her mama; and she talked it well, with fluency and with a good accent.

Mary had a milder and more open countenance than Blanche; softer features too, and a skin some shades fairer (Miss Ingram was dark as a Spaniard) – but Mary was deficient in life: her face lacked expression, her eye lustre; she had nothing to say, and having once taken her seat, remained fixed like a statue in its niche. The sisters were both attired in spotless white.

---

1 i.e., like Diana, goddess of the hunt in Greek mythology.

And did I now think Miss Ingram such a choice as Mr. Rochester would be likely to make? I could not tell – I did not know his taste in female beauty. If he liked the majestic, she was the very type of majesty: then she was accomplished, sprightly. Most gentlemen would admire her, I thought; and that he *did* admire her, I already seemed to have obtained proof: to remove the last shade of doubt, it remained but to see them together.

You are not to suppose, reader, that Adèle has all this time been sitting motionless on the stool at my feet: no; when the ladies entered, she rose, advanced to meet them, made a stately reverence, and said, with gravity, –

"Bon jour, mesdames."

And Miss Ingram had looked down at her with a mocking air, and exclaimed, "Oh, what a little puppet!"

Lady Lynn had remarked, "It is Mr. Rochester's ward, I suppose – the little French girl he was speaking of."

Mrs. Dent had kindly taken her hand, and given her a kiss. Amy and Louisa Eshton had cried out simultaneously, –

"What a love of a child!"

And then they had called her to a sofa, where she now sat, ensconced between them, chattering alternately in French and broken English; absorbing not only the young ladies' attention, but that of Mrs. Eshton and Lady Lynn, and getting spoilt to her heart's content.

At last coffee is brought in, and the gentlemen are summoned. I sit in the shade – if any shade there be in this brilliantly lit apartment; the window-curtain half hides me. Again the arch yawns: they come. The collective appearance of the gentlemen, like that of the ladies, is very imposing: they are all costumed in black; most of them are tall, some young. Henry and Frederick Lynn are very dashing sparks, indeed; and Colonel Dent is a fine soldierly man. Mr. Eshton, the magistrate of the district, is gentleman-like: his hair is quite white, his eyebrows and whiskers still dark, which gives him something of the appearance of a "père noble de théâtre."[1] Lord Ingram, like his sisters, is very tall; like them, also, he is handsome; but he shares Mary's apathetic and listless look: he seems to have more length of limb than vivacity of blood or vigour of brain.

---

1   "An imposing father such as you might see on stage."

And where is Mr. Rochester?

He comes in last: I am not looking at the arch, yet I see him enter. I try to concentrate my attention on these netting-needles, on the meshes of the purse I am forming – I wish to think only of the work I have in my hands, to see only the silver beads and silk threads that lie in my lap; whereas, I distinctly behold his figure, and I inevitably recall the moment when I last saw it: just after I had rendered him, what he deemed, an essential service – and he, holding my hand, and looking down on my face, surveyed me with eyes that revealed a heart full and eager to overflow; in whose emotions I had a part. How near had I approached him at that moment! What had occurred since, calculated to change his and my relative positions? Yet now, how distant, how far estranged we were! So far estranged, that I did not expect him to come and speak to me. I did not wonder, when, without looking at me, he took a seat at the other side of the room, and began conversing with some of the ladies.

No sooner did I see that his attention was riveted on them, and that I might gaze without being observed, than my eyes were drawn involuntarily to his face: I could not keep their lids under control: they would rise, and the irids would fix on him. I looked, and had an acute pleasure in looking, – a precious, yet poignant pleasure; pure gold, with a steely point of agony: a pleasure like what the thirst-perishing man might feel who knows the well to which he has crept is poisoned, yet stoops and drinks divine draughts nevertheless.

Most true is it that "beauty is in the eye of the gazer." My master's colourless, olive face, square, massive brow, broad and jetty eyebrows, deep eyes, strong features, firm, grim mouth, – all energy, decision, will, – were not beautiful, according to rule; but they were more than beautiful to me: they were full of an interest, an influence that quite mastered me, – that took my feelings from my own power and fettered them in his. I had not intended to love him: the reader knows I had wrought hard to extirpate from my soul the germs of love there detected; and now, at the first renewed view of him, they spontaneously revived, green and strong! He made me love him without looking at me.

I compared him with his guests. What was the gallant grace of the Lynns, the languid elegance of Lord Ingram, – even the military distinction of Colonel Dent contrasted with his look of native pith and genuine power? I had no sympathy in their appearance, their expression: yet I could imagine that most observers would call them attractive, handsome, imposing; while they would pronounce Mr. Rochester at once harsh-featured and melancholy-looking. I saw them smile, laugh – it was nothing: the light of the candles had as much soul in it as their smile; the tinkle of the bell as much significance as their laugh. I saw Mr. Rochester smile: – his stern features softened; his eye grew both brilliant and gentle, its ray both searching and sweet. He was talking, at the moment, to Louisa and Amy Eshton. I wondered to see them receive with calm that look which seemed to me so penetrating: I expected their eyes to fall, their colour to rise under it; yet I was glad when I found they were in no sense moved. "He is not to them what he is to me," I thought: "he is not of their kind. I believe he is of mine; – I am sure he is, – I feel akin to him, – I understand the language of his countenance and movements: though rank and wealth sever us widely, I have something in my brain and heart, in my blood and nerves, that assimilates me mentally to him. Did I say, a few days since, that I had nothing to do with him but to receive my salary at his hands? Did I forbid myself to think of him in any other light than as a paymaster? Blasphemy against nature! Every good, true, vigorous feeling I have, gathers impulsively round him. I know I must conceal my sentiments: I must smother hope; I must remember that he cannot care much for me. For when I say that I am of his kind, I do not mean that I have his force to influence, and his spell to attract: I mean only that I have certain tastes and feelings in common with him. I must, then, repeat continually that we are for ever sundered: – and yet, while I breathe and think, I must love him."

Coffee is handed. The ladies, since the gentlemen entered, have become lively as larks: conversation waxes brisk and merry. Colonel Dent and Mr. Eshton argue on politics; their wives listen. The two proud dowagers, Lady Lynn and Lady Ingram, confabulate together. Sir George – whom, by-the-by, I have forgotten to describe, – a very big, and very fresh-looking country gentleman, stands before their sofa, coffee-cup in hand, and occasionally puts in a word. Mr. Frederick Lynn has taken a seat beside Mary Ingram, and is showing her the engravings of a splendid volume: she looks, smiles now and then, but apparently says little. The tall and phlegmatic Lord Ingram leans with folded arms on the chair-back of the little and lively Amy Eshton; she glances up at him, and chatters like a wren: she likes him better than she does Mr. Rochester. Henry Lynn has taken possession of an ottoman at the feet of Louisa; Adèle shares it with him: he is trying to talk French with her, and Louisa laughs at his blunders. With whom will Blanche Ingram pair? She is standing alone at the table, bending gracefully over an album. She seems waiting to be sought; but she will not wait too long: she herself selects a mate.

Mr. Rochester, having quitted the Eshtons, stands on the hearth as solitary as she stands by the table; she confronts him, taking her station on the opposite side of the mantelpiece.

"Mr. Rochester, I thought you were not fond of children?"

"Nor am I."

"Then, what induced you to take charge of such a little doll as that? (pointing to Adèle). Where did you pick her up?"

"I did not pick her up, she was left on my hands."

"You should have sent her to school."

"I could not afford it: schools are so dear."

"Why, I suppose you have a governess for her: I saw a person with her just now – is she gone? Oh, no! there she is still behind the window-curtain. You pay her, of course: I should think it quite as expensive, – more so; for you have them both to keep in addition."

I feared – or should I say, hoped? – the allusion to me would make Mr. Rochester glance my way; and I involuntarily shrunk farther into the shade: but he never turned his eyes.

"I have not considered the subject," said he indifferently, looking straight before him.

"No – you men never do consider economy and common sense. You should hear mama on the chapter of governesses: Mary and I have had, I should think, a dozen at least in our day; half of them detestable and the rest ridiculous, and all incubi[1] – were they not, mama?"

"Did you speak, my own?"

The young lady thus claimed as the Dowager's special property, reiterated her question with an explanation.

---

1 Oppressive nightmares.

"My dearest, don't mention governesses: the word makes me nervous. I have suffered a martyrdom from their incompetency and caprice: I thank Heaven I have now done with them!"

Mrs. Dent here bent over to the pious lady, and whispered something in her ear: I suppose from the answer elicited, it was a reminder that one of the anathematized race was present.

"Tant pis!"[1] said her ladyship, "I hope it may do her good!" Then, in a lower tone, but still loud enough for me to hear, "I noticed her: I am a judge of physiognomy, and in hers I see all the faults of her class."

"What are they, Madam?" inquired Mr. Rochester aloud.

"I will tell you in your private ear," replied she, wagging her turban three times with portentous significancy.

"But my curiosity will be past its appetite: it craves food now."

"Ask Blanche: she is nearer you than I."

"Oh, don't refer him to me, mama! I have just one word to say of the whole tribe: they are a nuisance. Not that I ever suffered much from them: I took care to turn the tables. What tricks Theodore and I used to play on our Miss Wilsons, and Mrs. Greys, and Madame Jouberts! Mary was always too sleepy to join in a plot with spirit. The best fun was with Madame Joubert: Miss Wilson was a poor sickly thing, lachrymose and low-spirited: not worth the trouble of vanquishing, in short; and Mrs. Grey was coarse and insensible: no blow took effect on her. But poor Madame Joubert! I see her yet in her raging passions, when we had driven her to extremities – spilt our tea, crumbled our bread and butter, tossed our books up to the ceiling, and played a charivari[2] with the ruler and desk, the fender and fire-irons. Theodore, do you remember those merry days?"

"Yaas, to be sure I do," drawled Lord Ingram: "and the poor old stick used to cry out 'Oh you villains childs!' – and then we sermonized her on the presumption of attempting to teach such clever blades as we were, when she was herself so ignorant."

"We did: and Tedo, you know, I helped you in prosecuting (or persecuting) your tutor, whey-faced Mr. Vining – the parson in the pip,[3]

---

1   "Too bad!"
2   Loud, dissonant noise used to mock and express disapproval of an unpopular person.
3   The sick parson.

as we used to call him. He and Miss Wilson took the liberty of falling in love with each other – at least Tedo and I thought so: we surprised sundry tender glances and sighs which we interpreted as tokens of 'la belle passion,' and I promise you the public soon had the benefit of our discovery: we employed it as a sort of lever to hoist our dead-weights from the house. Dear mama there, as soon as she got an inkling of the business, found out that it was of an immoral tendency. Did you not, my lady-mother?"

"Certainly, my best. And I was quite right; depend on that: there are a thousand reasons why liaisons between governesses and tutors should never be tolerated a moment in any well-regulated house; firstly –"

"Oh gracious, mama! Spare us the enumeration! Au reste,[1] we all know them: danger of bad example to innocence of childhood; dis-tractions and consequent neglect of duty on the part of the attached; – mutual alliance and reliance; confidence thence resulting – inso-lence accompanying – mutiny and general blow-up. Am I right, Baroness Ingram of Ingram Park?"

"My lily-flower, you are right now as always."

"Then no more need be said: change the subject."

Amy Eshton, not hearing or not heeding this dictum, joined in with her soft, infantine tone: "Louisa and I used to quiz[2] our gov-erness too; but she was such a good creature, she would bear any-thing: nothing put her out. She was never cross with us; was she, Louisa?"

"No, never: we might do what we pleased; ransack her desk and her workbox, and turn her drawers inside out; and she was so good-natured, she would give us anything we asked for."

"I suppose now," said Miss Ingram, curling her lip sarcastically, "we shall have an abstract of the memoirs of all the governesses extant: in order to avert such a visitation, I again move the introduction of a new topic. Mr. Rochester, do you second my motion?"

"Madam, I support you on this point as on every other."

"Then on me be the onus of bringing it forward. Signior Eduardo, are you in voice to-night?"

---

1   Besides.
2   Mock.

"Donna Bianca, if you command it, I will be."

"Then Signior, I lay on you my sovereign behest to furbish up your lungs and other vocal organs, as they will be wanted on my royal service."

"Who would not be the Rizzio of so divine a Mary?"

"A fig for Rizzio!" cried she, tossing her head with all its curls, as she moved to the piano. "It is my opinion the fiddler David must have been an insipid sort of fellow; I like black Bothwell better: to my mind a man is nothing without a spice of the devil in him; and history may say what it will of James Hepburn, but I have a notion, he was just the sort of wild, fierce, bandit-hero whom I could have consented to gift with my hand."[1]

"Gentlemen, you hear! Now which of you most resembles Bothwell?" cried Mr. Rochester.

"I should say the preference lies with you," responded Colonel Dent.

"On my honour, I am much obliged to you," was the reply.

Miss Ingram, who had now seated herself with proud grace at the piano, spreading out her snowy robes in queenly amplitude, commenced a brilliant prelude; talking meantime. She appeared to be on her high horse to-night; both her words and her air seemed intended to excite not only the admiration, but the amazement of her auditors: she was evidently bent on striking them as something very dashing and daring indeed.

"Oh, I am so sick of the young men of the present day!" exclaimed she, rattling away at the instrument. "Poor, puny things not fit to stir a step beyond papa's park-gates: nor to go even so far without mama's permission and guardianship! Creatures so absorbed in care about their pretty faces and their white hands, and their small feet; as if a man had anything to do with beauty! As if loveliness were not the special prerogative of woman – her legitimate appanage and heritage! I grant an ugly *woman* is a blot on the fair face of creation;

1   A series of allusions to English history. David Rizzio was an Italian singer at the court of Mary Queen of Scots. He was assassinated, probably on the order of Darnley, Mary's second husband, because he was suspected of being her lover. Darnley was, in turn, murdered by James Hepburn, Earl of Bothwell, who himself married Mary in 1567. Rochester is not complimented by Colonel Dent's subsequent assertion that he most closely resembles Bothwell.

but as to the *gentlemen*, let them be solicitous to possess only strength and valour: let their motto be: – Hunt, shoot and fight: the rest is not worth a filip. Such should be my device, were I a man."

"Whenever I marry," she continued, after a pause which none interrupted, "I am resolved my husband shall not be a rival, but a foil to me. I will suffer no competitor near the throne; I shall exact an undivided homage: his devotions shall not be shared between me and the shape he sees in his mirror. Mr. Rochester, now sing, and I will play for you."

"I am all obedience," was the response.

"Here then is a Corsair-song. Know that I doat on Corsairs;[1] and for that reason, sing it 'con spirito.'"[2]

"Commands from Miss Ingram's lips would put spirit into a mug of milk and water."

"Take care, then: if you don't please me, I will shame you by show-ing how such things *should* be done."

"That is offering a premium on incapacity: I shall now endeavour to fail."

"Gardez-vous en bien![3] If you err wilfully, I shall devise a propor-tionate punishment."

"Miss Ingram ought to be clement, for she has it in her power to inflict a chastisement beyond mortal endurance."

"Ha! explain!" commanded the lady.

"Pardon me, madam: no need of explanation; your own fine sense must inform you that one of your frowns would be a sufficient substi-tute for capital punishment."

"Sing!" said she, and again touching the piano, she commenced an accompaniment in spirited style.

"Now is my time to slip away," thought I: but the tones that then severed the air arrested me. Mrs. Fairfax had said Mr. Rochester pos-sessed a fine voice: he did – a mellow, powerful bass, into which he threw his own feeling, his own force; finding a way through the ear to the heart and there waking sensation strangely. I waited till the last

---

1 Byron's poem *The Corsair* (1814) gave a popular appeal to pirates, brigands, and other "romantic" outcasts.
2 With spirit.
3 Mind you don't!

deep and full vibration had expired – till the tide of talk, checked an instant, had resumed its flow; I then quitted my sheltered corner and made my exit by the side-door, which was fortunately near. Thence a narrow passage led into the hall: in crossing it, I perceived my sandal was loose; I stopped to tie it, kneeling down for that purpose on the mat at the foot of the staircase. I heard the dining-room door unclose; a gentleman came out; rising hastily, I stood face to face with him: it was Mr. Rochester.

"How do you do?" he asked.

"I am very well, sir."

"Why did you not come and speak to me in the room?"

I thought I might have retorted the question on him who put it: but I would not take that freedom. I answered: –

"I did not wish to disturb you, as you seemed engaged, sir."

"What have you been doing during my absence?"

"Nothing particular: teaching Adèle as usual."

"And getting a good deal paler than you were – as I saw at first sight. What is the matter?"

"Nothing at all, sir."

"Did you take any cold that night you half drowned me?"

"Not the least."

"Return to the drawing-room: you are deserting too early."

"I am tired, sir."

He looked at me for a minute.

"And a little depressed;" he said. "What about? Tell me."

"Nothing – nothing, sir. I am not depressed."

"But I affirm that you are: so much depressed that a few more words would bring tears to your eyes – indeed, they are there now, shining and swimming; and a bead has slipped from the lash and fallen on to the flag.[1] If I had time, and was not in mortal dread of some prating prig of a servant passing, I would know what all this means. Well, to-night I excuse you; but understand that so long as my visitors stay, I expect you to appear in the drawing-room every evening: it is my wish; don't neglect it. Now go, and send Sophie for Adèle. Good-night, my —" He stopped, bit his lip, and abruptly left me.

---

1 i.e., the flagstone in the passage.

CHAPTER XVIII

Merry days were these at Thornfield Hall; and busy days too: how different from the first three months of stillness, monotony, and solitude I had passed beneath its roof! All sad feelings seemed now driven from the house, all gloomy associations forgotten: there was life everywhere, movement all day long. You could not now traverse the gallery, once so hushed, nor enter the front chambers, once so tenantless, without encountering a smart lady's maid or a dandy valet.

The kitchen, the butler's pantry, the servants' hall, the entrance hall, were equally alive; and the saloons were only left void and still, when the blue sky and halcyon sunshine of the genial spring weather called their occupants out into the grounds. Even when that weather was broken, and continuous rain set in for some days, no damp seemed cast over enjoyment: in-door amusements only became more lively and varied, in consequence of the stop put to out-door gaiety.

I wondered what they were going to do the first evening a change of entertainment was proposed: they spoke of "playing charades," but in my ignorance I did not understand the term. The servants were called in, the dining-room tables wheeled away, the lights otherwise disposed, the chairs placed in a semicircle opposite the arch. While Mr. Rochester and the other gentlemen directed these alterations, the ladies were running up and down stairs ringing for their maids. Mrs. Fairfax was summoned to give information respecting the resources of the house in shawls, dresses, draperies of any kind; and certain wardrobes of the third story were ransacked, and their contents, in the shape of brocaded and hooped petticoats, satin sacques, black modes, lace lappets, &c.,[1] were brought down in armfuls by the Abigails; then a selection was made, and such things as were chosen were carried to the boudoir within the drawing-room.

Meantime, Mr. Rochester had again summoned the ladies round him, and was selecting certain of their number to be of his party. "Miss Ingram is mine, of course," said he: afterwards he named the two Misses Eshton, and Mrs. Dent. He looked at me: I happened to be near him, as I had been fastening the clasp of Mrs. Dent's bracelet, which had got loose.

---

1   Sacques are loose-fitting dresses which were fashionable in the eighteenth century. Mode is a type of glossy silk. Lappets are streamers attached to ladies' headwear.

"Will you play?" he asked. I shook my head. He did not insist, which I rather feared he would have done: he allowed me to return quietly to my usual seat.

He and his aids now withdrew behind the curtain: the other party, which was headed by Colonel Dent, sat down on the crescent of chairs. One of the gentlemen, Mr. Eshton, observing me, seemed to propose that I should be asked to join them; but Lady Ingram instantly negatived the notion.

"No," I heard her say; "she looks too stupid for any game of the sort."

Ere long, a bell tinkled, and the curtain drew up. Within the arch, the bulky figure of Sir George Lynn, whom Mr. Rochester had likewise chosen, was seen enveloped in a white sheet: before him, on a table, lay open a large book; and at his side stood Amy Eshton, draped in Mr. Rochester's cloak, and holding a book in her hand. Somebody, unseen, rung the bell merrily; then Adèle (who had insisted on being one of her guardian's party) bounded forward, scattering round her the contents of a basket of flowers she carried on her arm. Then appeared the magnificent figure of Miss Ingram, clad in white, a long veil on her head, and a wreath of roses round her brow: by her side walked Mr. Rochester, and together they drew near the table. They knelt; while Mrs. Dent and Louisa Eshton, dressed also in white, took up their stations behind them. A ceremony followed, in dumb show, in which it was easy to recognize the pantomime of a marriage. At its termination, Colonel Dent and his party consulted in whispers for two minutes, then the Colonel called out, –

"Bride!" Mr. Rochester bowed, and the curtain fell.

A considerable interval elapsed before it again rose. Its second rising displayed a more elaborately prepared scene than the last. The drawing-room, as I have before observed, was raised two steps above the dining-room, and on the top of the upper step, placed a yard or two back within the room, appeared a large marble basin, which I recognized as an ornament of the conservatory – where it usually stood surrounded by exotics,[1] and tenanted by gold fish – and whence it must have been transported with some trouble, on account of its size and weight.

---

1   Exotic flowers.

Seated on the carpet, by the side of this basin, was seen Mr. Rochester, costumed in shawls, with a turban on his head. His dark eyes and swarth skin and Paynim[1] features suited the costume exactly: he looked the very model of an eastern emir, an agent or a victim of the bowstring.[2] Presently advanced into view Miss Ingram. She, too, was attired in oriental fashion: a crimson scarf tied sash-like round the waist; an embroidered handkerchief knotted about her temples; her beautifully-moulded arms bare, one of them upraised in the act of supporting a pitcher, poised gracefully on her head. Both her cast of form and feature, her complexion and her general air, suggested the idea of some Israelitish princess of the patriarchal days; and such was doubtless the character she intended to represent.

She approached the basin, and bent over it as if to fill her pitcher; she again lifted it to her head. The personage on the well-brink now seemed to accost her; to make some request: – "She hasted, let down her pitcher on her hand and gave him to drink." From the bosom of his robe, he then produced a casket, opened it and showed magnificent bracelets and ear rings; she acted astonishment and admiration; kneeling, he laid the treasure at her feet; incredulity and delight were expressed by her looks and gestures; the stranger fastened the bracelets on her arms, and the rings in her ears. It was Eliezer and Rebecca: the camels only were wanting.[3]

The divining party again laid their heads together: apparently they could not agree about the word or syllable the scene illustrated. Colonel Dent, their spokesman, demanded "the tableau of the Whole";[4] whereupon the curtain again descended.

On its third rising only a portion of the drawing-room was disclosed; the rest being concealed by a screen, hung with some sort of dark and coarse drapery. The marble basin was removed; in its place stood a deal table and a kitchen chair: these objects were visible by a very dim light proceeding from a horn lantern, the wax candles being all extinguished.

---

1 Pagan, non-Christian.
2 It was popularly believed that in the Orient bowstrings were sometimes used, as instruments of assassination or execution, to strangle rivals or criminals.
3 See Genesis 24. The quotation in the preceding sentence is from Genesis 24:18.
4 In the game of charades, after the various syllables of the word to be guessed had been acted out, it was allowable to demand a scene representing the entire word.

Amidst this sordid scene, sat a man with his clenched hands resting on his knees, and his eyes bent on the ground. I knew Mr. Rochester; though the begrimed face, the disordered dress (his coat hanging loose from one arm, as if it had been almost torn from his back in a scuffle), the desperate and scowling countenance, the rough, bristling hair might well have disguised him. As he moved, a chain clanked: to his wrists were attached fetters.

"Bridewell!"[1] exclaimed Colonel Dent, and the charade was solved.

A sufficient interval having elapsed for the performers to re-sume their ordinary costume, they re-entered the dining-room. Mr. Rochester led in Miss Ingram; she was complimenting him on his acting.

"Do you know," said she, "that, of the three characters, I liked you in the last best? Oh, had you but lived a few years earlier, what a gal-lant gentleman-highwayman you would have made!"

"Is all the soot washed from my face?" he asked, turning it towards her.

"Alas! yes; the more's the pity! Nothing could be more becoming to your complexion than that ruffian's rouge."

"You would like a hero of the road then?"

"An English hero of the road would be the next best thing to an Italian bandit; and that could only be surpassed by a Levantine pirate."

"Well, whatever I am, remember you are my wife: we were mar-ried an hour since, in the presence of all these witnesses." She giggled, and her colour rose.

"Now, Dent," continued Mr. Rochester, "it is your turn." And as the other party withdrew, he and his band took the vacated seats. Miss Ingram placed herself at her leader's right hand; the other diviners filled the chairs on each side of him and her. I did not now watch the actors; I no longer waited with interest for the curtain to rise: my attention was absorbed by the spectators; my eyes, ere-while fixed on the arch, were now irresistibly attracted to the semi-circle of chairs. What charade Colonel Dent and his party played, what word they chose, how they acquitted themselves, I no longer

---

1   Originally a royal palace in London, Bridewell was later turned into a hospital, and then into a prison.

remember; but I still see the consultation which followed each scene: I see Mr. Rochester turn to Miss Ingram, and Miss Ingram to him; I see her incline her head towards him, till the jetty curls almost touch his shoulder and wave against his cheek; I hear their mutual whisperings; I recall their interchanged glances; and something even of the feeling roused by the spectacle returns in memory at this moment.

I have told you reader, that I had learnt to love Mr. Rochester: I could not unlove him now, merely because I found that he had ceased to notice me – because I might pass hours in his presence, and he would never once turn his eyes in my direction – because I saw all his attentions appropriated by a great lady, who scorned to touch me with the hem of her robes as she passed; who, if ever her dark and imperious eye fell on me by chance, would withdraw it instantly as from an object too mean to merit observation. I could not unlove him, because I felt sure he would soon marry this very lady – because I read daily in her a proud security in his intentions respecting her – because I witnessed hourly in him a style of courtship which, if careless and choosing rather to be sought than to seek, was yet, in its very carelessness, captivating, and in its very pride, irresistible.

There was nothing to cool or banish love in these circumstances; though much to create despair. Much too, you will think, reader, to engender jealousy: if a woman, in my position, could presume to be jealous of a woman in Miss Ingram's. But I was not jealous: or very rarely; – the nature of the pain I suffered could not be explained by that word. Miss Ingram was a mark beneath jealousy: she was too inferior to excite the feeling. Pardon the seeming paradox: I mean what I say. She was very showy, but she was not genuine: she had a fine person, many brilliant attainments; but her mind was poor, her heart barren by nature: nothing bloomed spontaneously on that soil; no unforced natural fruit delighted by its freshness. She was not good; she was not original: she used to repeat sounding phrases from books; she never offered, nor had, an opinion of her own. She advocated a high tone of sentiment; but she did not know the sensations of sympathy and pity: tenderness and truth were not in her. Too often she betrayed this, by the undue vent she gave to a spiteful antipathy she had conceived against little Adèle: pushing her away with some con-

tumelious[1] epithet if she happened to approach her; sometimes ordering her from the room, and always treating her with coldness and
acrimony. Other eyes besides mine watched these manifestations
of character – watched them closely, keenly, shrewdly. Yes: the future
bridegroom, Mr. Rochester himself, exercised over his intended a
ceaseless surveillance: and it was from this sagacity – this guardedness
of his – this perfect, clear consciousness of his fair one's defects – this
obvious absence of passion in his sentiments towards her, that my
ever-torturing pain arose.

I saw he was going to marry her, for family, perhaps political reasons; because her rank and connexions suited him; I felt he had not
given her his love, and that her qualifications were ill adapted to win
from him that treasure. This was the point – this was where the nerve
was touched and teazed – this was where the fever was sustained and
fed: *she could not charm him.*

If she had managed the victory at once, and he had yielded and
sincerely laid his heart at her feet, I should have covered my face,
turned to the wall, and (figuratively) have died to them. If Miss
Ingram had been a good and noble woman, endowed with force, fervour, kindness, sense, I should have had one vital struggle with two
tigers – jealousy and despair: then, my heart torn out and devoured, I
should have admired her – acknowledged her excellence, and been
quiet for the rest of my days: and the more absolute her superiority,
the deeper would have been my admiration – the more truly tranquil
my quiescence. But as matters really stood, to watch Miss Ingram's
efforts at fascinating Mr. Rochester; to witness their repeated failure –
herself unconscious that they did fail; vainly fancying that each shaft
launched, hit the mark, and infatuatedly pluming herself on success,
when her pride and self-complacency repelled further and further
what she wished to allure – to witness *this*, was to be at once under
ceaseless excitation and ruthless restraint.

Because, when she failed, I saw how she might have succeeded.
Arrows that continually glanced off from Mr. Rochester's breast and
fell harmless at his feet, might, I knew, if shot by a surer hand, have
quivered keen in his proud heart – have called love into his stern eye,

---

1   Insolent, reproachful.

and softness into his sardonic face or, better still, without weapons, a silent conquest might have been won.

"Why can she not influence him more, when she is privileged to draw so near to him?" I asked myself. "Surely she cannot truly like him; or not like him with true affection! If she did, she need not coin her smiles so lavishly; flash her glances so unremittingly; manufacture airs so elaborate, graces so multitudinous. It seems to me, that she might, by merely sitting quietly at his side, saying little and looking less, get nigher his heart. I have seen in his face a far different expression from that which hardens it now while she is so vivaciously accosting him; but then it came of itself: it was not elicited by meretricious arts and calculated manœuvres; and one had but to accept it – to answer what he asked, without pretension, to address him when needful without grimace – and it increased, and grew kinder and more genial, and warmed one like a fostering sunbeam. How will she manage to please him when they are married? I do not think she will manage it: and yet it might be managed; and his wife might, I verily believe, be the very happiest woman the sun shines on."

I have not yet said anything condemnatory of Mr. Rochester's project of marrying for interest and connexions. It surprised me when I first discovered that such was his intention: I had thought him a man unlikely to be influenced by motives so common-place in his choice of a wife; but the longer I considered the position, education, &c., of the parties, the less I felt justified in judging and blaming either him or Miss Ingram, for acting in conformity to ideas and principles instilled into them, doubtless, from their childhood. All their class held these principles: I supposed, then, they had reasons for holding them such as I could not fathom. It seemed to me that, were I a gentleman like him, I would take to my bosom only such a wife as I could love; but the very obviousness of the advantages to the husband's own happiness, offered by this plan, convinced me that there must be arguments against its general adoption of which I was quite ignorant: otherwise I felt sure all the world would act as I wished to act.

But in other points, as well as this, I was growing very lenient to my master: I was forgetting all his faults, for which I had once kept a sharp look-out. It had formerly been my endeavour to study all sides of his character: to take the bad with the good; and from the just weighing of both, to form an equitable judgment. Now I saw no bad. The sarcasm that had repelled, the harshness that had startled me once, were only like keen condiments in a choice dish: their presence was pungent, but their absence would be felt as comparatively insipid. And as for the vague something – was it a sinister or a sorrowful, a designing or a desponding expression? – that opened upon a careful observer, now and then, in his eye, and closed again before one could fathom the strange depth partially disclosed; that something which used to make me fear and shrink, as if I had been wandering amongst volcanic-looking hills, and had suddenly felt the ground quiver and seen it gape: that something, I, at intervals, beheld still; and with throbbing heart, but not with palsied nerves. Instead of wishing to shun, I longed only to dare – to divine it; and I thought Miss Ingram happy, because one day she might look into the abyss at her leisure, explore its secrets and analyze their nature.

Meantime, while I thought only of my master and his future bride – saw only them, heard only their discourse, and considered only their movements of importance – the rest of the party were occupied with their own separate interests and pleasures. The ladies Lynn and Ingram continued to consort in solemn conferences; where they nodded their two turbans at each other, and held up their four hands in confronting gestures of surprise, or mystery, or horror, according to the theme on which their gossip ran, like a pair of magnified puppets. Mild Mrs. Dent talked with good-natured Mrs. Eshton; and the two sometimes bestowed a courteous word or smile on me. Sir George Lynn, Colonel Dent, and Mr. Eshton, discussed politics, or county affairs, or justice business. Lord Ingram flirted with Amy Eshton; Louisa played and sang to and with one of the Messrs. Lynn; and Mary Ingram listened languidly to the gallant speeches of the other. Sometimes all, as with one consent, suspended their by-play to observe and listen to the principal actors: for, after all, Mr. Rochester, and – because closely connected with him – Miss Ingram, were the life and soul of the party. If he was absent from the room an hour, a perceptible dulness seemed to steal over the spirits of his guests; and his re-entrance was sure to give a fresh impulse to the vivacity of conversation.

The want of his animating influence appeared to be peculiarly felt one day that he had been summoned to Millcote on business, and was not likely to return till late. The afternoon was wet: a walk the party had proposed to take to see a gipsy camp, lately pitched on a common beyond Hay, was consequently deferred. Some of the gentlemen were gone to the stables: the younger ones, together with the younger ladies, were playing billiards in the billiard-room. The dowagers Ingram and Lynn sought solace in a quiet game at cards. Blanche Ingram, after having repelled, by supercilious taciturnity, some efforts of Mrs. Dent and Mrs. Eshton to draw her into conversation, had first murmured over some sentimental tunes and airs on the piano, and then, having fetched a novel from the library, had flung herself in haughty listlessness on a sofa, and prepared to beguile, by the spell of fiction, the tedious hours of absence. The room and the house were silent: only now and then the merriment of the billiard players was heard from above.

It was verging on dusk, and the clock had already given warning of the hour to dress for dinner, when little Adèle, who knelt by me in the drawing-room window seat, suddenly exclaimed: –

"Voilà Monsieur Rochester, qui revient!"[1]

I turned, and Miss Ingram darted forwards from her sofa: the others, too, looked up from their several occupations; for at the same time a crunching of wheels, and a splashing tramp of horse-hoofs became audible on the wet gravel. A post-chaise was approaching.

"What can possess him to come home in that style?" said Miss Ingram. "He rode Mesrour (the black horse) did he not, when he went out? and Pilot was with him: – what has he done with the animals?"

As she said this, she approached her tall person and ample garments so near the window, that I was obliged to bend back almost to the breaking of my spine: in her eagerness she did not observe me at first, but when she did, she curled her lip and moved to another casement. The post-chaise stopped; the driver rang the door-bell, and a gentleman alighted, attired in travelling garb: but it was not Mr. Rochester; it was a tall, fashionable-looking man, a stranger.

---

1 "Here's Mr. Rochester coming back!"

"Provoking!" exclaimed Miss Ingram: "you tiresome monkey!" (apostrophizing Adèle) "who perched you up in the window to give false intelligence?" and she cast on me an angry glance, as if I were in fault.

Some parleying was audible in the hall, and soon the new-comer entered. He bowed to Lady Ingram, as deeming her the eldest lady present.

"It appears I come at an inopportune time, madam," said he, "when my friend, Mr. Rochester, is from home; but I arrive from a very long journey, and I think I may presume so far on old and intimate acquaintance as to install myself here till he returns."

His manner was polite; his accent, in speaking, struck me as being somewhat unusual, – not precisely foreign, but still not altogether English; his age might be about Mr. Rochester's, – between thirty and forty; his complexion was singularly sallow: otherwise he was a fine-looking man, at first sight especially. On closer examination, you detected something in his face that displeased: or rather, that failed to please. His features were regular, but too relaxed: his eye was large and well cut, but the life looking out of it was a tame, vacant life – at least so I thought.

The sound of the dressing-bell dispersed the party. It was not till after dinner that I saw him again: he then seemed quite at his ease. But I liked his physiognomy even less than before: it struck me as being, at the same time, unsettled and inanimate. His eye wandered, and had no meaning in its wandering: this gave him an odd look, such as I never remembered to have seen. For a handsome and not an unamiable-looking man, he repelled me exceedingly: there was no power in that smooth-skinned face of a full oval shape; no firmness in that aquiline nose, and small, cherry mouth; there was no thought on the low, even forehead; no command in that blank, brown eye.

As I sat in my usual nook, and looked at him with the light of the girandoles[1] on the mantelpiece beaming full over him – for he occupied an arm-chair, drawn close to the fire, and kept shrinking still nearer, as if he were cold – I compared him with Mr. Rochester. I think (with deference be it spoken) the contrast could not be much

---

1   Branched candlesticks.

greater between a sleek gander and a fierce falcon: between a meek sheep and the rough-coated keen-eyed dog, its guardian.

He had spoken of Mr. Rochester as an old friend. A curious friendship theirs must have been: a pointed illustration, indeed, of the old adage that "extremes meet."

Two or three of the gentlemen sat near him, and I caught at times scraps of their conversation across the room. At first I could not make much sense of what I heard; for the discourse of Louisa Eshton and Mary Ingram, who sat nearer to me, confused the fragmentary sentences that reached me at intervals. These last were discussing the stranger: they both called him "a beautiful man." Louisa said he was "a love of a creature," and she "adored him;" and Mary instanced his "pretty little mouth, and nice nose," as her ideal of the charming.

"And what a sweet-tempered forehead he has!" cried Louisa, – "so smooth – none of those frowning irregularities I dislike so much: and such a placid eye and smile!"

And then, to my great relief, Mr. Henry Lynn summoned them to the other side of the room, to settle some point about the deferred excursion to Hay Common.

I was now able to concentrate my attention on the group by the fire, and I presently gathered that the new-comer was called Mr. Mason: then I learned that he was but just arrived in England, and that he came from some hot country; which was the reason, doubtless, his face was so sallow, and that he sat so near the hearth, and wore a surtout in the house. Presently the words Jamaica, Kingston, Spanish Town, indicated the West Indies as his residence; and it was with no little surprise I gathered, ere long, that he had there first seen and become acquainted with Mr. Rochester. He spoke of his friend's dislike of the burning heats, the hurricanes, and rainy seasons of that region. I knew Mr. Rochester had been a traveller: Mrs. Fairfax had said so; but I thought the continent of Europe had bounded his wanderings: till now I had never heard a hint given of visits to more distant shores.

I was pondering these things, when an incident, and a somewhat unexpected one, broke the thread of my musings. Mr. Mason, shivering as some one chanced to open the door, asked for more coal to be put on the fire, which had burnt out its flame, though its mass of cinder still shone hot and red. The footman who brought the coal, in going out, stopped near Mr. Eshton's chair, and said something to him in a low voice, of which I heard only the words, "old woman" – "quite troublesome."

"Tell her she shall be put in the stocks, if she does not take herself off," replied the magistrate.

"No – stop!" interrupted Colonel Dent. "Don't send her away, Eshton; we might turn the thing to account: better consult the ladies." And speaking aloud, he continued, – "Ladies, you talked of going to Hay Common to visit the gipsy camp; Sam, here, says that one of the old Mother Bunches[1] is in the servants' hall at this moment, and insists upon being brought in before 'the quality,' to tell them their fortunes. Would you like to see her?"

"Surely, Colonel," cried Lady Ingram, "you would not encourage such a low impostor? Dismiss her, by all means, at once!"

"But I cannot persuade her to go away, my lady," said the footman; "nor can any of the servants: Mrs. Fairfax is with her just now, entreating her to be gone; but she has taken a chair in the chimney-corner, and says nothing shall stir her from it till she gets leave to come in here."

"What does she want?" asked Mrs. Eshton.

"'To tell the gentry their fortunes,' she says, ma'am: and she swears she must and will do it."

"What is she like?" inquired the Misses Eshton in a breath.

"A shockingly ugly old creature, Miss; almost as black as a crock."

"Why, she's a real sorceress!" cried Frederick Lynn. "Let us have her in, of course."

"To be sure," rejoined his brother; "it would be a thousand pities to throw away such a chance of fun."

"My dear boys, what are you thinking about?" exclaimed Lady Lynn.

"I cannot possibly countenance any such inconsistent proceeding," chimed in the Dowager Ingram.

"Indeed, mama, but you can – and will," pronounced the haughty voice of Blanche, as she turned round on the piano-stool; where till now she had sat silent, apparently examining sundry sheets of music.

---

1   Wise-woman. Mother Bunch was a well-known alewife in sixteenth-century London. Her name was later attached to a number of seventeenth-century collections of lore and folk-wisdom.

"I have a curiosity to hear my fortune told: therefore, Sam, order the beldame forward."

"My darling Blanche! recollect —"

"I do — I recollect all you can suggest; and I must have my will — quick, Sam!"

"Yes — yes — yes!" cried all the juveniles, both ladies and gentlemen. "Let her come — it will be excellent sport!"

The footman still lingered. "She looks such a rough one," said he.

"Go!" ejaculated Miss Ingram, and the man went.

Excitement instantly seized the whole party: a running fire of raillery and jests was proceeding when Sam returned.

"She won't come now," said he. "She says it's not her mission to appear before the 'vulgar herd' (them's her words). I must show her into a room by herself, and then those who wish to consult her must go to her one by one."

"You see now, my queenly Blanche," began Lady Ingram, "she encroaches. Be advised, my angel-girl — and —"

"Show her into the library, of course," cut in the "angel-girl." "It is not my mission to listen to her before the vulgar herd either: I mean to have her all to myself. Is there a fire in the library?"

"Yes, ma'am — but she looks such a tinkler."[1]

"Cease that chatter, blockhead! and do my bidding."

Again Sam vanished; and mystery, animation, expectation rose to full flow once more.

"She's ready now," said the footman as he re-appeared. "She wishes to know who will be her first visitor."

"I think I had better just look in upon her before any of the ladies go," said Colonel Dent. "Tell her, Sam, a gentleman is coming."

Sam went and returned.

"She says, sir, that she'll have no gentlemen; they need not trouble themselves to come near her: nor," he added, with difficulty suppressing a titter, "any ladies either, except the young and single."

"By Jove, she has taste!" exclaimed Henry Lynn.

Miss Ingram rose solemnly: "I go first," she said, in a tone which might have befitted the leader of a forlorn hope, mounting a breach in the van of his men.

---

1 i.e., a tinker; someone with a rough appearance and personality.

"Oh, my best! oh, my dearest! pause – reflect!" was her mama's cry; but she swept past her in stately silence, passed through the door which Colonel Dent held open, and we heard her enter the library.

A comparative silence ensued. Lady Ingram thought it "le cas"[1] to wring her hands; which she did accordingly. Miss Mary declared she felt, for her part, she never dared venture. Amy and Louisa Eshton tittered under their breath, and looked a little frightened.

The minutes passed very slowly: fifteen were counted before the library-door again opened. Miss Ingram returned to us through the arch.

Would she laugh? Would she take it as a joke? – All eyes met her with a glance of eager curiosity, and she met all eyes with one of rebuff and coldness: she looked neither flurried nor merry; she walked stiffly to her seat, and took it in silence.

"Well, Blanche?" said Lord Ingram.

"What did she say, sister?" asked Mary.

"What did you think? How do you feel? Is she a real fortune-teller?" demanded the Misses Eshton.

"Now, now, good people," returned Miss Ingram, "don't press upon me. Really your organs of wonder and credulity are easily excited: you seem by the importance you all – my good mama included – ascribe to this matter, – absolutely to believe we have a genuine witch in the house, who is in close alliance with the old gentleman.[2] I have seen a gipsy-vagabond; she has practised in hackneyed fashion the science of palmistry, and told me what such people usually tell. My whim is gratified; and now I think Mr. Eshton will do well to put the hag in the stocks to-morrow morning, as he threatened."

Miss Ingram took a book, leant back in her chair, and so declined further conversation. I watched her for nearly half an hour: during all that time she never turned a page, and her face grew momently darker, more dissatisfied, and more sourly expressive of disappointment. She had obviously not heard anything to her advantage; and it seemed to me, from her prolonged fit of gloom and taciturnity, that she herself, notwithstanding her professed indifference, attached undue importance to whatever revelations had been made her.

---

1   Appropriate, suitable.

2   The devil.

Meantime, Mary Ingram, Amy and Louisa Eshton, declared they dared not go alone; and yet they all wished to go. A negociation was opened through the medium of the ambassador, Sam; and after much pacing to and fro, till, I think, the said Sam's calves must have ached with the exercise, permission was at last, with great difficulty, extorted from the rigorous Sibyl,[1] for the three to wait upon her in a body.

Their visit was not so still as Miss Ingram's had been: we heard hysterical giggling and little shrieks proceeding from the library; and at the end of about twenty minutes they burst the door open, and came running across the hall, as if they were half-scared out of their wits.

"I'm sure she is something not right!" they cried, one and all. "She told us such things! She knows all about us!" and they sank breathless into the various seats the gentlemen hastened to bring them.

Pressed for further explanation, they declared she had told them of things they had said and done when they were mere children; described books and ornaments they had in their boudoirs at home: keepsakes that different relations had presented to them. They affirmed that she had even divined their thoughts, and had whispered in the ear of each the name of the person she liked best in the world, and informed them of what they most wished for.

Here the gentlemen interposed with earnest petitions to be further enlightened on these two last-named points; but they got only blushes, ejaculations, tremors and titters, in return for their importunity. The matrons, meantime, offered vinaigrettes[2] and wielded fans; and again and again reiterated the expression of their concern that their warning had not been taken in time; and the elder gentlemen laughed, and the younger urged their services on the agitated fair ones.

In the midst of the tumult, and while my eyes and ears were fully engaged in the scene before me, I heard a hem close at my elbow: I turned, and saw Sam.

"If you please, Miss, the gipsy declares that there is another young single lady in the room who has not been to her yet, and she swears she will not go till she has seen all. I thought it must be you: there is no one else for it. What shall I tell her?"

---

1 Prophetess.
2 Smelling salts.

"Oh, I will go by all means," I answered; and I was glad of the unexpected opportunity to gratify my much excited curiosity. I slipped out of the room, unobserved by any eye – for the company were gathered in one mass about the trembling trio just returned – and I closed the door quietly behind me.

"If you like, Miss," said Sam, "I'll wait in the hall for you; and if she frightens you, just call and I'll come in."

"No, Sam, return to the kitchen: I am not in the least afraid." Nor was I; but I was a good deal interested and excited.

CHAPTER XIX

THE Library looked tranquil enough as I entered it, and the Sibyl – if Sibyl she were, – was seated snugly enough in an easy chair at the chimney-corner. She had on a red cloak and a black bonnet; or rather, a broad-brimmed gipsy hat, tied down with a striped handkerchief under her chin. An extinguished candle stood on the table; she was bending over the fire, and seemed reading in a little black book, like a prayer-book, by the light of the blaze: she muttered the words to herself, as most old women do, while she read; she did not desist immediately on my entrance: it appeared she wished to finish a paragraph.

I stood on the rug and warmed my hands, which were rather cold with sitting at a distance from the drawing-room fire. I felt now as composed as ever I did in my life: there was nothing indeed in the gipsy's appearance to trouble one's calm. She shut her book and slowly looked up; her hat-brim partially shaded her face, yet I could see, as she raised it, that it was a strange one. It looked all brown and black: elf-locks[1] bristled out from beneath a white band which passed under her chin, and came half over her cheeks or rather jaws; her eye confronted me at once, with a bold and direct gaze.

"Well, and you want your fortune told?" she said in a voice as decided as her glance, as harsh as her features.

"I don't care about it, mother; you may please yourself: but I ought to warn you, I have no faith."

"It's like your impudence to say so: I expected it of you; I heard it in your step as you crossed the threshold."

"Did you? You've a quick ear."

"I have; and a quick eye, and a quick brain."

"You need them all in your trade."

"I do; especially when I've customers like you to deal with. Why don't you tremble?"

"I'm not cold."

"Why don't you turn pale?"

"I am not sick."

---

1   Tangled masses of hair.

"Why don't you consult my art?"

"I'm not silly."

The old crone "nichered"[1] a laugh under her bonnet and bandage: she then drew out a short black pipe, and lighting it, began to smoke. Having indulged a while in this sedative, she raised her bent body, took the pipe from her lips, and while gazing steadily at the fire, said very deliberately: —

"You are cold; you are sick; and you are silly."

"Prove it," I rejoined.

"I will, in few words. You are cold; because you are alone: no contact strikes the fire from you that is in you. You are sick; because the best of feelings, the highest and the sweetest given to man, keeps far away from you. You are silly; because, suffer as you may, you will not beckon it to approach; nor will you stir one step to meet it where it waits you."

She again put her short, black pipe to her lips and renewed her smoking with vigour.

"You might say all that to almost any one who, you knew, lived as a solitary dependant in a great house."

"I might say it to almost any one; but would it be true of almost any one?"

"In my circumstances."

"Yes; just so, in *your* circumstances: but find me another precisely placed as you are."

"It would be easy to find you thousands."

"You could scarcely find me one. If you knew it, you are peculiarly situated: very near happiness; yes; within reach of it. The materials are all prepared; there only wants a movement to combine them. Chance laid them somewhat apart: let them be once approached and bliss results."

"I don't understand enigmas. I never could guess a riddle in my life."

"If you wish me to speak more plainly, show me your palm."

"And I must cross it with silver, I suppose?"

"To be sure."

---

1 Dialect. Snickered.

I gave her a shilling: she put it into an old stocking-foot which she took out of her pocket, and having tied it round and returned it, she told me to hold out my hand. I did. She approached her face to the palm, and pored over it without touching it.

"It is too fine;" said she. "I can make nothing of such a hand as that; almost without lines: besides, what is in a palm? Destiny is not written there."

"I believe you," said I.

"No;" she continued, "it is in the face: on the forehead, about the eyes, in the eyes themselves, in the lines of the mouth. Kneel, and lift up your head."

"Ah! Now you are coming to reality," I said as I obeyed her. "I shall begin to put some faith in you presently."

I knelt within half a yard of her. She stirred the fire, so that a ripple of light broke from the disturbed coal: the glare, however, as she sat, only threw her face into deeper shadow: mine, it illumined.

"I wonder with what feelings you came to me to-night," she said, when she had examined me awhile. "I wonder what thoughts are busy in your heart during all the hours you sit in yonder room with the fine people flitting before you like shapes in a magic-lantern:[1] just as little sympathetic communion passing between you and them, as if they were really mere shadows of human forms and not the actual substance."

"I feel tired often, sleepy sometimes; but seldom sad."

"Then you have some secret hope to buoy you up and please you with whispers of the future?"

"Not I. The utmost I hope is, to save money enough out of my earnings to set up a school some day in a little house rented by myself."

"A mean nutriment for the spirit to exist on: and sitting in that window-seat (you see I know your habits) –."

"You have learned them from the servants."

"Ah! You think yourself sharp. Well – perhaps I have: to speak truth, I have an acquaintance with one of them – Mrs. Poole ——"

I started to my feet when I heard the name.

---

1   An early form of slide projector.

"You have – have you?" thought I; "there is diablerie in the business after all, then!"

"Don't be alarmed," continued the strange being; "she's a safe hand, is Mrs. Poole: close and quiet: any one may repose confidence in her. But, as I was saying: sitting in that window-seat, do you think of nothing but your future school? Have you no present interest in any of the company who occupy the sofas and chairs before you? Is there not one face you study? One figure whose movements you follow with, at least, curiosity?"

"I like to observe all the faces, and all the figures."

"But do you never single one from the rest – or it may be, two?"

"I do frequently; when the gestures or looks of a pair seem telling a tale: it amuses me to watch them."

"What tale do you like best to hear?"

"Oh, I have not much choice! They generally run on the same theme – courtship; and promise to end in the same catastrophe – marriage."

"And do you like that monotonous theme?"

"Positively I don't care about it: it is nothing to me."

"Nothing to you? When a lady, young and full of life and health, charming with beauty and endowed with the gifts of rank and fortune, sits and smiles in the eyes of a gentleman you —"

"I what?"

"You know – and, perhaps, think well of."

"I don't know the gentlemen here. I have scarcely interchanged a syllable with one of them; and as to thinking well of them, I consider some respectable and stately, and middle-aged, and others young, dashing, handsome and lively: but certainly they are all at liberty to be the recipients of whose smiles they please, without my feeling disposed to consider the transaction of any moment to me."

"You don't know the gentlemen here? You have not exchanged a syllable with one of them? Will you say that of the master of the house?"

"He is not at home."

"A profound remark! A most ingenious quibble! He went to Millcote this morning, and will be back here to-night, or to-morrow: does that circumstance exclude him from the list of your acquaintance – blot him, as it were, out of existence?"

"No: but I can scarcely see what Mr. Rochester has to do with the theme you had introduced."

"I was talking of ladies smiling in the eyes of gentlemen; and of late so many smiles have been shed into Mr. Rochester's eyes that they overflow like two cups filled above the brim: have you never remarked that?"

"Mr. Rochester has a right to enjoy the society of his guests."

"No question about his right: but have you never observed that, of all the tales told here about matrimony, Mr. Rochester has been favoured with the most lively and the most continuous?"

"The eagerness of a listener quickens the tongue of a narrator." I said this rather to myself than to the gipsy; whose strange talk, voice, manner had by this time wrapped me in a kind of dream. One unexpected sentence came from her lips after another, till I got involved in a web of mystification; and wondered what unseen spirit had been sitting for weeks by my heart, watching its workings, and taking record of every pulse.

"Eagerness of a listener!" repeated she: "yes; Mr. Rochester has sat by the hour, his ear inclined to the fascinating lips that took such delight in their task of communicating; and Mr. Rochester was so willing to receive, and looked so grateful for the pastime given him: you have noticed this?"

"Grateful! I cannot remember detecting gratitude in his face."

"Detecting! You have analyzed, then. And what did you detect, if not gratitude?"

I said nothing.

"You have seen love: have you not? – and, looking forward, you have seen him married, and beheld his bride happy?"

"Humph! Not exactly. Your witch's skill is rather at fault sometimes."

"What the devil have you seen, then?"

"Never mind: I came here to inquire, not to confess. Is it known that Mr. Rochester is to be married?"

"Yes; and to the beautiful Miss Ingram."

"Shortly?"

"Appearances would warrant that conclusion; and, no doubt (though, with an audacity that wants chastising out of you, you seem to question it), they will be a superlatively happy pair. He must love such a handsome, noble, witty, accomplished lady; and probably she loves him: or, if not his person, at least his purse. I know she considers the Rochester estate eligible to the last degree; though (God pardon me!) I told her something on that point about an hour ago, which made her look wondrous grave: the corners of her mouth fell half an inch. I would advise her blackaviced[1] suitor to look out: if another comes, with a longer or clearer rent-roll, – he's dished —"

"But, mother, I did not come to hear Mr. Rochester's fortune: I came to hear my own; and you have told me nothing of it."

"Your fortune is yet doubtful: when I examined your face, one trait contradicted another. Chance has meted you a measure of happiness: that I know. I knew it before I came here this evening. She has laid it carefully on one side for you. I saw her do it. It depends on yourself to stretch out your hand, and take it up: but whether you will do so, is the problem I study. Kneel again on the rug."

"Don't keep me long; the fire scorches me."

I knelt. She did not stoop towards me, but only gazed, leaning back in her chair. She began muttering:

"The flame flickers in the eye; the eye shines like dew; it looks soft and full of feeling; it smiles at my jargon: it is susceptible; impression follows impression through its clear sphere; when it ceases to smile, it is sad; an unconscious lassitude weighs on the lid: that signifies melancholy resulting from loneliness. It turns from me; it will not suffer farther scrutiny; it seems to deny, by a mocking glance, the truth of the discoveries I have already made, – to disown the charge both of sensibility and chagrin: its pride and reserve only confirm me in my opinion. The eye is favourable.

"As to the mouth, it delights at times in laughter: it is disposed to impart all that the brain conceives; though I dare say it would be silent on much the heart experiences. Mobile and flexible, it was never intended to be compressed in the eternal silence of solitude: it is a mouth which should speak much and smile often, and have human affection for its interlocutor. That feature, too, is propitious.

"I see no enemy to a fortunate issue but in the brow; and that brow professes to say, – 'I can live alone, if self-respect and circum-

---

1   Dark countenanced.

stances require me so to do. I need not sell my soul to buy bliss. I have an inward treasure, born with me, which can keep me alive if all extraneous delights should be withheld; or offered only at a price I cannot afford to give.' The forehead declares, 'Reason sits firm and holds the reins, and she will not let the feelings burst away and hurry her to wild chasms. The passions may rage furiously, like true hea-thens,[1] as they are; and the desires may imagine all sorts of vain things: but judgment shall still have the last word in every argument, and the casting vote in every decision. Strong wind, earthquake-shock, and fire may pass by: but I shall follow the guiding of that still small voice[2] which interprets the dictates of conscience.'

"Well said, forehead; your declaration shall be respected. I have formed my plans — right plans I deem them — and in them I have attended to the claims of conscience, the counsels of reason. I know how soon youth would fade and bloom perish, if, in the cup of bliss offered, but one dreg of shame, or one flavour of remorse were detected; and I do not want sacrifice, sorrow, dissolution — such is not my taste. I wish to foster, not to blight — to earn gratitude, not to wring tears of blood — no, nor of brine: my harvest must be in smiles, in endearments, in sweet — that will do. I think I rave in a kind of exquisite delirium. I should wish now to protract this moment *ad infinitum*; but I dare not. So far I have governed myself thoroughly. I have acted as I inwardly swore I would act; but farther might try me beyond my strength. Rise, Miss Eyre: leave me; 'the play is played out.'"[3]

Where was I? Did I wake or sleep? Had I been dreaming? Did I dream still? The old woman's voice had changed: her accent, her ges-ture, and all, were familiar to me as my own face in the glass — as the speech of my own tongue. I got up, but did not go. I looked; I stirred the fire, and I looked again: but she drew her bonnet and her bandage closer about her face, and again beckoned me to depart. The flame illuminated her hand stretched out: roused now, and on the alert for discoveries, I at once noticed that hand. It was no more the withered limb of eld[4] than my own: it was a rounded supple member, with

---

1   See Psalms 2:1.
2   See I Kings 19:11-12.
3   See *I Henry IV*, II, iv.460.
4   Old age.

smooth fingers, symmetrically turned; a broad ring flashed on the little finger, and stooping forward, I looked at it, and saw a gem I had seen a hundred times before. Again I looked at the face; which was no longer turned from me – on the contrary, the bonnet was doffed, the bandage displaced, the head advanced.

"Well, Jane, do you know me?" asked the familiar voice.

"Only take off the red cloak, sir, and then —"

"But the string is in a knot – help me."

"Break it, sir."

"There, then – 'Off, ye lendings!'"[1] And Mr. Rochester stepped out of his disguise.

"Now, sir, what a strange idea!"

"But well carried out, eh? Don't you think so?"

"With the ladies you must have managed well."

"But not with you?"

"You did not act the character of a gipsy with me."

"What character did I act? My own?"

"No; some unaccountable one. In short, I believe you have been trying to draw me out – or in: you have been talking nonsense to make me talk nonsense. It is scarcely fair, sir."

"Do you forgive me, Jane?"

"I cannot tell till I have thought it all over. If, on reflection, I find I have fallen into no great absurdity, I shall try to forgive you: but it was not right."

"Oh! you have been very correct – very careful, very sensible."

I reflected, and thought, on the whole, I had. It was a comfort: but, indeed, I had been on my guard almost from the beginning of the interview. Something of masquerade I suspected. I knew gipsies and fortune-tellers did not express themselves as this seeming old woman had expressed herself: besides, I had noted her feigned voice, her anxiety to conceal her features. But my mind had been running on Grace Poole – that living enigma, that mystery of mysteries, as I considered her: I had never thought of Mr. Rochester.

"Well," said he, "what are you musing about? What does that grave smile signify?"

"Wonder and self-congratulation, sir. I have your permission to retire now, I suppose?"

---

1   See *King Lear* III.iv.103.

"No: stay a moment; and tell me what the people in the drawing-room yonder are doing."

"Discussing the gipsy, I daresay."

"Sit down, sit down! – Let me hear what they said about me."

"I had better not stay long, sir: it must be near eleven o'clock. Oh! are you aware, Mr. Rochester, that a stranger has arrived here since you left this morning?"

"A stranger! – no: who can it be? I expected no one: is he gone?"

"No: he said he had known you long, and that he could take the liberty of installing himself here till you returned."

"The devil he did! Did he give his name?"

"His name is Mason, sir; and he comes from the West Indies: from Spanish Town, in Jamaica, I think."

Mr. Rochester was standing near me: he had taken my hand, as if to lead me to a chair. As I spoke, he gave my wrist a convulsive grip; the smile on his lips froze: apparently a spasm caught his breath.

"Mason! – the West Indies!" he said, in the tone one might fancy a speaking automaton to enounce its single words; "Mason! – the West Indies!" he reiterated; and he went over the syllables three times, growing, in the intervals of speaking, whiter than ashes: he hardly seemed to know what he was doing.

"Do you feel ill, sir?" I inquired.

"Jane, I've got a blow; – I've got a blow, Jane!"

He staggered.

"Oh! – lean on me, sir."

"Jane, you offered me your shoulder once before; let me have it now."

"Yes, sir, yes; and my arm."

He sat down, and made me sit beside him. Holding my hand in both his own, he chafed it; gazing on me, at the same time, with the most troubled and dreary look.

"My little friend!" said he, "I wish I were in a quiet island with only you; and trouble, and danger, and hideous recollections removed from me."

"Can I help you, sir? – I'd give my life to serve you."

"Jane, if aid is wanted, I'll seek it at your hands: I promise you that."

"Thank you, sir: tell me what to do, – I'll try, at least, to do it."

"Fetch me now, Jane, a glass of wine from the dining-room: they will be at supper there; and tell me if Mason is with them, and what he is doing."

I went. I found all the party in the dining-room at supper, as Mr. Rochester had said: they were not seated at table, – the supper was arranged on the sideboard; each had taken what he chose, and they stood about here and there in groups, their plates and glasses in their hands. Every one seemed in high glee; laughter and conversation were general and animated. Mr. Mason stood near the fire, talking to Colonel and Mrs. Dent, and appeared as merry as any of them. I filled a wine-glass (I saw Miss Ingram watch me frowningly as I did so: she thought I was taking a liberty, I dare say), and I returned to the library.

Mr. Rochester's extreme pallor had disappeared, and he looked once more firm and stern. He took the glass from my hand.

"Here is to your health, ministrant spirit!" he said: he swallowed the contents and returned it to me. "What are they doing, Jane?"

"Laughing and talking, sir."

"They don't look grave and mysterious, as if they had heard something strange?"

"Not at all: – they are full of jests and gaiety."

"And Mason?"

"He was laughing too."

"If all these people came in a body and spat at me, what would you do, Jane?"

"Turn them out of the room, sir, if I could."

He half smiled. "But if I were to go to them, and they only looked at me coldly, and whispered sneeringly amongst each other, and then dropt off and left me one by one, what then? Would you go with them?"

"I rather think not, sir: I should have more pleasure in staying with you."

"To comfort me?"

"Yes, sir, to comfort you, as well as I could."

"And if they laid you under a ban for adhering to me?"

"I, probably, should know nothing about their ban; and if I did, I should care nothing about it."

"Then, you could dare censure for my sake?"

"I could dare it for the sake of any friend who deserved my adherence; as you, I am sure do."

"Go back now into the room; step quietly up to Mason, and whisper in his ear that Mr. Rochester is come and wishes to see him: show him in here, and then leave me."

"Yes, sir."

I did his behest. The company all stared at me as I passed straight among them. I sought Mr. Mason, delivered the message, and preceded him from the room: I ushered him into the library, and then I went up stairs.

At a late hour, after I had been in bed some time, I heard the visitors repair to their chambers: I distinguished Mr. Rochester's voice, and heard him say, "This way, Mason; this is your room."

He spoke cheerfully: the gay tones set my heart at ease. I was soon asleep.

CHAPTER XX

I HAD forgotten to draw my curtain,[1] which I usually did; and also to let down my window-blind. The consequence was, that when the moon, which was full and bright, (for the night was fine) came in her course to that space in the sky opposite my casement, and looked in at me through the unveiled panes, her glorious gaze roused me. Awaking in the dead of night, I opened my eyes on her disk – silver-white and crystal-clear. It was beautiful, but too solemn: I half rose, and stretched my arm to draw the curtain.

Good God! What a cry!

The night – its silence – its rest, was rent in twain by a savage, a sharp, a shrilly sound that ran from end to end of Thornfield-Hall.

My pulse stopped: my heart stood still; my stretched arm was paralyzed. The cry died, and was not renewed. Indeed, whatever being uttered that fearful shriek could not soon repeat it: not the widest-winged condor on the Andes could, twice in succession, send out such a yell from the cloud shrouding his eyry. The thing delivering such utterance must rest ere it could repeat the effort.

It came out of the third story; for it passed overhead. And overhead – yes, in the room just above my chamber-ceiling – I now heard a struggle: a deadly one it seemed from the noise; and a half-smothered voice shouted: –

"Help! help! help;" three times rapidly. "Will no one come?" it cried; and then while the staggering and stamping went on wildly, I distinguished through plank and plaster: – "Rochester! Rochester! For God's sake, come!"

A chamber-door opened: some one ran, or rushed, along the gallery. Another step stamped on the flooring above, and something fell; and there was silence.

I had put on some clothes, though horror shook all my limbs: I issued from my apartment. The sleepers were all aroused: ejaculations, terrified murmurs sounded in every room; door after door unclosed; one looked out and another looked out; the gallery filled. Gentlemen and ladies alike had quitted their beds; and "Oh! What is it?" – "Who

---

1   i.e., the curtain to her poster bed.

is hurt?" – "What has happened?" – "Fetch a light!" – "Is it fire?" – "Are there robbers?" – "Where shall we run?" was demanded confusedly on all hands. But for the moonlight they would have been in complete darkness. They ran to and fro; they crowded together: some sobbed, some stumbled: the confusion was inextricable.

"Where the devil is Rochester?" cried Colonel Dent. "I cannot find him in his bed."

"Here! here!" was shouted in return. "Be composed, all of you: I'm coming."

And the door at the end of the gallery opened, and Mr. Rochester advanced with a candle: he had just descended from the upper story. One of the ladies ran to him directly; she seized his arm: it was Miss Ingram.

"What awful event has taken place?" said she. "Speak! let us know the worst at once!"

"But don't pull me down or strangle me," he replied: for the Misses Eshton were clinging about him now; and the two dowagers, in vast white wrappers, were bearing down on him like ships in full sail.

"All's right! – all's right!" he cried. "It's a mere rehearsal of Much Ado about Nothing. Ladies, keep off; or I shall wax dangerous."

And dangerous he looked: his black eyes darted sparks. Calming himself by an effort, he added:

"A servant has had the nightmare; that is all. She's an excitable, nervous person: she construed her dream into an apparition, or something of that sort, no doubt; and has taken a fit with fright. Now, then, I must see you all back into your rooms; for, till the house is settled, she cannot be looked after. Gentlemen, have the goodness to set the ladies the example. Miss Ingram, I am sure you will not fail in evincing superiority to idle terrors. Amy and Louisa, return to your nests like a pair of doves, as you are. Mesdames" (to the dowagers) "you will take cold to a dead certainty, if you stay in this chill gallery any longer."

And so, by dint of alternate coaxing and commanding, he contrived to get them all once more enclosed in their separate dormitories. I did not wait to be ordered back to mine; but retreated unnoticed: as unnoticed I had left it. Not, however, to go to bed: on the contrary, I began and dressed myself carefully. The sounds I had heard after the scream, and the words that had been uttered, had probably been heard only by me; for they had proceeded from the room above mine: but they assured me that it was not a servant's dream which had thus struck horror through the house; and that the explanation Mr. Rochester had given was merely an invention framed to pacify his guests. I dressed, then, to be ready for emergencies. When dressed, I sat a long time by the window, looking out over the silent grounds and silvered fields, and waiting for I knew not what. It seemed to me that some event must follow the strange cry, struggle, and call.

No: stillness returned: each murmur and movement ceased gradually, and in about an hour Thornfield Hall was again as hushed as a desert. It seemed that sleep and night had resumed their empire. Meantime the moon declined: she was about to set. Not liking to sit in the cold and darkness, I thought I would lie down on my bed, dressed as I was. I left the window, and moved with little noise across the carpet; as I stooped to take off my shoes, a cautious hand tapped low at the door.

"Am I wanted?" I asked.

"Are you up?" asked the voice I expected to hear, viz., my master's.

"Yes, sir."

"And dressed?"

"Yes."

"Come out, then, quietly."

I obeyed. Mr. Rochester stood in the gallery, holding a light.

"I want you," he said: "come this way: take your time, and make no noise."

My slippers were thin: I could walk the matted floor as softly as a cat. He glided up the gallery and up the stairs, and stopped in the dark, low corridor of the fateful third story: I had followed and stood at his side.

"Have you a sponge in your room?" he asked in a whisper.

"Yes, sir."

"Have you any salts – volatile salts?"

"Yes."

"Go back and fetch both."

I returned, sought the sponge on the wash-stand, the salts in my drawer, and once more retraced my steps. He still waited; he held a key in his hand: approaching one of the small, black doors, he put it in the lock; he paused, and addressed me again.

"You don't turn sick at the sight of blood?"

"I think I shall not: I have never been tried yet."

I felt a thrill while I answered him; but no coldness, and no faintness.

"Just give me your hand;" he said, "it will not do to risk a fainting fit."

I put my fingers into his. "Warm and steady," was his remark: he turned the key and opened the door.

I saw a room I remembered to have seen before, the day Mrs. Fairfax showed me over the house: it was hung with tapestry; but the tapestry was now looped up in one part, and there was a door apparent, which had then been concealed. This door was open; a light shone out of the room within: I heard thence a snarling, snatching sound, almost like a dog quarrelling. Mr. Rochester, putting down his candle, said to me, "wait a minute," and he went forward to the inner apartment. A shout of laughter greeted his entrance; noisy at first, and terminating in Grace Poole's own goblin ha! ha! *She* then was there. He made some sort of arrangement, without speaking; though I heard a low voice address him: he came out and closed the door behind him.

"Here, Jane!" he said; and I walked round to the other side of a large bed, which with its drawn curtains concealed a considerable portion of the chamber. An easy-chair was near the bed-head: a man sat in it, dressed with the exception of his coat; he was still; his head leant back; his eyes were closed. Mr. Rochester held the candle over him; I recognized in his pale and seemingly lifeless face – the stranger, Mason: I saw too that his linen on one side, and one arm, was almost soaked in blood.

"Hold the candle," said Mr. Rochester, and I took it; he fetched a basin of water from the washstand: "hold that," said he. I obeyed. He took the sponge, dipped it in and moistened the corpse-like face: he asked for my smelling-bottle, and applied it to the nostrils. Mr. Mason shortly unclosed his eyes; he groaned. Mr. Rochester opened the shirt of the wounded man, whose arm and shoulder were bandaged: he sponged away blood, trickling fast down.

"Is there immediate danger?" murmured Mr. Mason.

"Pooh! No – a mere scratch. Don't be so overcome, man: bear up! I'll fetch a surgeon for you now, myself: you'll be able to be removed by morning, I hope. Jane –" he continued.

"Sir?"

"I shall have to leave you in this room with this gentleman, for an hour, or perhaps two hours; you will sponge the blood as I do when it returns: if he feels faint, you will put the glass of water on that stand, to his lips, and your salts to his nose. You will not speak to him on any pretext – and – Richard – it will be at the peril of your life if you speak to her: open your lips – agitate yourself – and I'll not answer for the consequences."

Again the poor man groaned: he looked as if he dared not move: fear, either of death or of something else, appeared almost to paralyze him. Mr. Rochester put the now bloody sponge into my hand, and I proceeded to use it as he had done. He watched me a second, then saying, "remember! – No conversation," he left the room. I experienced a strange feeling as the key grated in the lock, and the sound of his retreating step ceased to be heard.

Here then I was in the third story, fastened into one of its mystic[1] cells; night around me; a pale and bloody spectacle under my eyes and hands; a murderess hardly separated from me by a single door: yes – that was appalling – the rest I could bear; but I shuddered at the thought of Grace Poole bursting out upon me.

I must keep to my post, however. I must watch this ghastly countenance – these blue, still lips forbidden to unclose – these eyes now shut, now opening, now wandering through the room, now fixing on me, and ever glazed with the dulness of horror. I must dip my hand again and again in the basin of blood and water, and wipe away the trickling gore. I must see the light of the unsnuffed candle wane on my employment; the shadows darken on the wrought, antique tapestry round me, and grow black under the hangings of the vast old bed, and quiver strangely over the doors of a great cabinet opposite –

---

1   Mysterious.

whose front, divided into twelve panels, bore in grim design, the heads of the twelve apostles, each inclosed in its separate panel as in a frame; while above them at the top rose an ebon crucifix and a dying Christ.

According as the shifting obscurity and flickering gleam hovered here or glanced there, it was now the bearded physician, Luke, that bent his brow; now St. John's long hair that waved; and anon the devilish face of Judas, that grew out of the panel and seemed gathering life and threatening a revelation of the arch-traitor – of Satan himself – in his subordinate's form.

Amidst all this, I had to listen as well as watch: to listen for the movements of the wild beast or the fiend in yonder side den. But since Mr. Rochester's visit it seemed spell-bound: all the night I heard but three sounds at three long intervals, – a step creak, a momentary renewal of the snarling, canine noise, and a deep, human groan.

Then my own thoughts worried me. What crime was this, that lived incarnate in this sequestered mansion, and could neither be expelled nor subdued by the owner? – What mystery, that broke out, now in fire and now in blood, at the deadest hours of night? – What creature was it, that, masked in an ordinary woman's face and shape, uttered the voice, now of a mocking demon, and anon of a carrion-seeking bird of prey?

And this man I bent over – this common-place, quiet stranger – how had he become involved in the web of horror? and why had the Fury flown at him? What made him seek this quarter of the house at an untimely season, when he should have been asleep in bed? I had heard Mr. Rochester assign him an apartment below – what brought him here? And why, now, was he so tame under the violence or treachery done him? Why did he so quietly submit to the concealment Mr. Rochester enforced? Why *did* Mr. Rochester enforce this concealment? His guest had been outraged, his own life on a former occasion had been hideously plotted against; and both attempts he smothered in secresy and sunk in oblivion! Lastly, I saw Mr. Mason was submissive to Mr. Rochester; that the impetuous will of the latter held complete sway over the inertness of the former: the few words which had passed between them assured me of this. It was evident that in their former intercourse, the passive disposition of the one had been habitually influenced by the active energy of the other: whence then had arisen Mr. Rochester's dismay when he heard of Mr. Mason's arrival? Why had the mere name of this unresisting individual – whom his word now sufficed to control like a child – fallen on him, a few hours since, as a thunderbolt might fall on an oak?

Oh! I could not forget his look and his paleness when he whispered: "Jane, I have got a blow – I have got a blow, Jane." I could not forget how the arm had trembled which he rested on my shoulder: and it was no light matter which could thus bow the resolute spirit and thrill the vigorous frame of Fairfax Rochester.

"When will he come? When will he come?" I cried inwardly, as the night lingered and lingered – as my bleeding patient drooped, moaned, sickened: and neither day nor aid arrived. I had, again and again, held the water to Mason's white lips; again and again offered him the stimulating salts: my efforts seemed ineffectual: either bodily or mental suffering, or loss of blood, or all three combined, were fast prostrating his strength. He moaned so, and looked so weak, wild and lost, I feared he was dying; and I might not even speak to him.

The candle, wasted at last, went out; as it expired, I perceived streaks of grey light edging the window curtains: dawn then was approaching. Presently I heard Pilot bark far below, out of his distant kennel in the courtyard: hope revived. Nor was it unwarranted: in five minutes more the grating key, the yielding lock, warned me my watch was relieved. It could not have lasted more than two hours: many a week has seemed shorter.

Mr. Rochester entered, and with him the surgeon he had been to fetch.

"Now, Carter, be on the alert;" he said to this last: "I give you but half an hour for dressing the wound, fastening the bandages, getting the patient down stairs and all."

"But is he fit to move, sir?"

"No doubt of it; it is nothing serious: he is nervous, his spirits must be kept up. Come, set to work."

Mr. Rochester drew back the thick curtain, drew up the holland blind, let in all the daylight he could; and I was surprised and cheered to see how far dawn was advanced: what rosy streaks were beginning to brighten the East. Then he approached Mason, whom the surgeon was already handling.

"Now, my good fellow, how are you?" he asked.

"She's done for me, I fear," was the faint reply.

"Not a whit! – courage! This day fortnight you'll hardly be a pin the worse of it: you've lost a little blood; that's all. Carter, assure him there's no danger."

"I can do that conscientiously," said Carter, who had now undone the bandages; "only I wish I could have got here sooner: he would not have bled so much – but how is this? The flesh on the shoulder is torn as well as cut? This wound was not done with a knife: there have been teeth here?"

"She bit me," he murmured. "She worried me like a tigress, when Rochester got the knife from her."

"You should not have yielded: you should have grappled with her at once," said Mr. Rochester.

"But under such circumstances, what could one do?" returned Mason. "Oh it was frightful!" he added, shuddering. "And I did not expect it: she looked so quiet at first."

"I warned you," was his friend's answer; "I said – be on your guard when you go near her. Besides, you might have waited till tomorrow, and had me with you: it was mere folly to attempt the interview to-night, and alone."

"I thought I could have done some good."

"You thought! you thought! Yes; it makes me impatient to hear you: but, however, you have suffered, and are likely to suffer enough for not taking my advice; so I'll say no more. Carter – hurry! hurry! The sun will soon rise, and I must have him off."

"Directly, sir; the shoulder is just bandaged. I must look to this other wound in the arm: she has had her teeth here too, I think."

"She sucked the blood: she said she'd drain my heart," said Mason.

I saw Mr. Rochester shudder: a singularly marked expression of disgust, horror, hatred, warped his countenance almost to distortion; but he only said: –

"Come, be silent, Richard, and never mind her gibberish: don't repeat it."

"I wish I could forget it," was the answer.

"You will when you are out of the country: when you get back to Spanish Town you may think of her as dead and buried – or rather you need not think of her at all."

"Impossible to forget this night!"

"It is not impossible: have some energy, man. You thought you were as dead as a herring two hours since, and you are all alive and talking now. There! – Carter has done with you or nearly so; I'll make you decent in a trice. Jane," (he turned to me for the first time since his re-entrance) "take this key: go down into my bed-room, and walk straight forward into my dressing-room; open the top drawer of the wardrobe and take out a clean shirt and neck-handkerchief; bring them here: and be nimble."

I went; sought the repository he had mentioned, found the articles named, and returned with them.

"Now," said he, "go to the other side of the bed while I order his toilet; but don't leave the room: you may be wanted again."

I retired as directed.

"Was anybody stirring below when you went down, Jane?" enquired Mr. Rochester, presently.

"No, sir; all was very still."

"We shall get you off cannily, Dick: and it will be better, both for your sake, and for that of the poor creature in yonder. I have striven long to avoid exposure, and I should not like it to come at last. Here, Carter, help him on with his waistcoat. Where did you leave your furred cloak? You can't travel a mile without that, I know, in this damned cold climate. In your room? – Jane, run down to Mr. Mason's room, – the one next mine, – and fetch a cloak you will see there."

Again I ran, and again returned, bearing an immense mantle, lined and edged with fur.

"Now I've another errand for you," said my untiring master; "you must away to my room again. What a mercy you are shod with velvet, Jane! – a clod-hopping messenger would never do at this juncture. You must open the middle drawer of my toilet-table and take out a little phial and a little glass you will find there, – quick!"

I flew thither and back, bringing the desired vessels.

"That's well! Now, doctor, I shall take the liberty of administering a dose myself; on my own responsibility. I got this cordial[1] at Rome, of an Italian charlatan,[2] – a fellow you would have kicked, Carter. It is

---

1   Stimulant.
2   Travelling vendor of drugs and folk remedies.

not a thing to be used indiscriminately, but it is good upon occasion: as now for instance. Jane, a little water."

He held out the tiny glass, and I half filled it from the water bottle on the wash-stand.

"That will do: – now wet the lip of the phial."

I did so: he measured twelve drops of a crimson liquid, and presented it to Mason.

"Drink, Richard: it will give you the heart you lack, for an hour or so."

"But will it hurt me? – is it inflammatory?"

"Drink! drink! drink!"

Mr. Mason obeyed, because it was evidently useless to resist. He was dressed now: he still looked pale, but he was no longer gory and sullied. Mr. Rochester let him sit three minutes after he had swallowed the liquid; he then took his arm: –

"Now I am sure you can get on your feet," he said; – "try."

The patient rose.

"Carter, take him under the other shoulder. Be of good cheer, Richard; step out: – that's it!"

"I do feel better," remarked Mr. Mason.

"I am sure you do. Now, Jane, trip on before us away to the back-stairs; unbolt the side passage door, and tell the driver of the post-chaise you will see in the yard – or just outside, for I told him not to drive his rattling wheels over the pavement – to be ready; we are coming: and Jane, if any one is about, come to the foot of the stairs and hem."[1]

It was by this time half-past five, and the sun was on the point of rising; but I found the kitchen still dark and silent. The side-passage door was fastened; I opened it with as little noise as possible: all the yard was quiet; but the gates stood wide open, and there was a post-chaise, with horses ready harnessed, and driver seated on the box, stationed outside. I approached him, and said the gentlemen were coming; he nodded: then I looked carefully round and listened. The stillness of early morning slumbered everywhere; the curtains were yet drawn over the servants' chamber windows; little birds were just

---

1   i.e., clear her throat as a warning.

twittering in the blossom-blanched orchard trees, whose boughs drooped like white garlands over the wall enclosing one side of the yard; the carriage horses stamped from time to time in their closed stables: all else was still.

The gentlemen now appeared. Mason, supported by Mr. Rochester and the surgeon, seemed to walk with tolerable ease: they assisted him into the chaise; Carter followed.

"Take care of him," said Mr. Rochester to the latter, "and keep him at your house till he is quite well: I shall ride over in a day or two to see how he gets on. Richard, how is it with you?"

"The fresh air revives me, Fairfax."

"Leave the window open on his side, Carter; there is no wind – good-bye, Dick."

"Fairfax —"

"Well, what is it?"

"Let her be taken care of; let her be treated as tenderly as may be: let her —" he stopped and burst into tears.

"I do my best; and have done it, and will do it," was the answer: he shut up the chaise door, and the vehicle drove away.

"Yet would to God there was an end of all this!" added Mr. Rochester, as he closed and barred the heavy yard-gates. This done, he moved with slow step and abstracted air, towards a door in the wall bordering the orchard. I, supposing he had done with me, prepared to return to the house; again, however, I heard him call "Jane!" He had opened the portal and stood at it, waiting for me.

"Come where there is some freshness, for a few moments," he said; "that house is a mere dungeon: don't you feel it so?"

"It seems to me a splendid mansion, sir."

"The glamour of inexperience is over your eyes," he answered; "and you see it through a charmed medium: you cannot discern that the gilding is slime and the silk draperies cobwebs; that the marble is sordid slate, and the polished woods mere refuse chips and scaly bark. Now *here* (he pointed to the leafy enclosure we had entered) all is real, sweet, and pure."

He strayed down a walk edged with box; with apple trees, pear trees, and cherry trees on one side, and a border on the other, full of all sorts of old-fashioned flowers, stocks, sweet-williams, primroses, pansies, mingled with southernwood, sweet-briar, and various fragrant herbs. They were fresh now as a succession of April showers and gleams, followed by a lovely spring morning, could make them: the sun was just entering the dappled east, and his light illumined the wreathed and dewy orchard trees and shone down the quiet walks under them.

"Jane, will you have a flower?"

He gathered a half-blown rose, the first on the bush, and offered it to me.

"Thank you, sir."

"Do you like this sunrise, Jane? That sky with its high and light clouds which are sure to melt away as the day waxes warm – this placid and balmy atmosphere?"

"I do, very much."

"You have passed a strange night, Jane."

"Yes, sir."

"And it has made you look pale – were you afraid when I left you alone with Mason?"

"I was afraid of some one coming out of the inner room."

"But I had fastened the door – I had the key in my pocket: I should have been a careless shepherd if I had left a lamb – my pet lamb – so near a wolf's-den, unguarded: you were safe."

"Will Grace Poole live here still, sir?"

"Oh, yes! don't trouble your head about her – put the thing out of your thoughts."

"Yet it seems to me your life is hardly secure while she stays."

"Never fear – I will take care of myself."

"Is the danger you apprehended last night gone by now, sir?"

"I cannot vouch for that till Mason is out of England: nor even then. To live, for me, Jane, is to stand on a crater-crust which may crack and spue fire any day."

"But Mr. Mason seems a man easily led. Your influence, sir, is evidently potent with him: he will never set you at defiance, or wilfully injure you."

"Oh, no! Mason will not defy me; nor knowing it, will he hurt me – but, unintentionally, he might in a moment, by one careless word, deprive me, if not of life, yet for ever of happiness."

"Tell him to be cautious, sir: let him know what you fear, and show him how to avert the danger."

He laughed sardonically, hastily took my hand, and as hastily threw it from him.

"If I could do that, simpleton, where would the danger be? Annihilated in a moment. Ever since I have known Mason, I have only had to say to him 'Do that,' and the thing has been done. But I cannot give him orders in this case: I cannot say 'Beware of harming me, Richard;' for it is imperative that I should keep him ignorant that harm to me is possible. Now you look puzzled; and I will puzzle you farther. You are my little friend, are you not?"

"I like to serve you, sir, and to obey you in all that is right."

"Precisely: I see you do. I see genuine contentment in your gait and mien, your eye and face, when you are helping me and pleasing me – working for me, and with me, in, as you characteristically say, 'all that is right:' for if I bid you do what you thought wrong, there would be no light-footed running, no neat-handed alacrity, no lively glance and animated complexion. My friend would then turn to me, quiet and pale, and would say, 'No, sir; that is impossible: I cannot do it, because it is wrong;' and would become immutable as a fixed star. Well, you too have power over me, and may injure me: yet I dare not show you where I am vulnerable, lest, faithful and friendly as you are, you should transfix me at once."

"If you have no more to fear from Mr. Mason than you have from me, sir, you are very safe."

"God grant it may be so! Here, Jane, is an arbour; sit down."

The arbour was an arch in the wall, lined with ivy; it contained a rustic seat. Mr. Rochester took it, leaving room, however, for me: but I stood before him.

"Sit," he said; "the bench is long enough for two. You don't hesitate to take a place at my side, do you? Is that wrong, Jane?"

I answered him by assuming it: to refuse would, I felt, have been unwise.

"Now, my little friend, while the sun drinks the dew – while all the flowers in this old garden awake and expand, and the birds fetch their young ones' breakfast out of the Thorn-field, and the early bees do their first spell of work – I'll put a case to you; which you must endeavour to suppose your own: but first, look at me, and tell me you are at ease, and not fearing that I err in detaining you, or that you err in staying."

"No, sir; I am content."

"Well then, Jane, call to aid your fancy: – suppose you were no longer a girl well reared and disciplined, but a wild boy, indulged from childhood upwards; imagine yourself in a remote foreign land; conceive that you there commit a capital error, no matter of what nature or from what motives, but one whose consequences must follow you through life and taint all your existence. Mind, I don't say a *crime*; I am not speaking of shedding of blood or any other guilty act, which might make the perpetrator amenable to the law: my word is *error*. The results of what you have done become in time to you utterly insupportable; you take measures to obtain relief: unusual measures, but neither unlawful nor culpable. Still you are miserable; for hope has quitted you on the very confines of life: your sun at noon darkens in an eclipse,[1] which you feel will not leave it till the time of setting. Bitter and base associations have become the sole food of your memory: you wander here and there, seeking rest in exile, happiness in pleasure – I mean in heartless, sensual pleasure – such as dulls intellect and blights feeling. Heart-weary and soul-withered, you come home after years of voluntary banishment: you make a new acquaintance – how or where no matter: you find in this stranger much of the good and bright qualities which you have sought for twenty years, and never before encountered; and they are all fresh, healthy, without soil and without taint. Such society revives, regenerates: you feel better days come back – higher wishes, purer feelings; you desire to recommence your life, and to spend what remains to you of days in a way more worthy of an immortal being. To attain this end, are you justified in overleaping an obstacle of custom – a mere conventional impediment, which neither your conscience sanctifies nor your judgment approves?"

He paused for an answer: and what was I to say? Oh, for some good spirit to suggest a judicious and satisfactory response! Vain aspiration! The west wind whispered in the ivy round me; but no gentle

---

1   See lines 80-82 of *Samson Agonistes* (1671) by John Milton (1608-74).

Ariel borrowed its breath as a medium of speech: the birds sang in the tree-tops; but their song, however sweet, was inarticulate.

Again Mr. Rochester propounded his query:

"Is the wandering and sinful, but now rest-seeking and repentant man, justified in daring the world's opinion, in order to attach to him for ever, this gentle, gracious, genial stranger: thereby securing his own peace of mind and regeneration of life?"

"Sir," I answered, "a Wanderer's repose or a Sinner's reformation should never depend on a fellow-creature. Men and women die; philosophers falter in wisdom, and Christians in goodness: if any one you know has suffered and erred, let him look higher than his equals for strength to amend, and solace to heal."

"But the instrument – the instrument! God, who does the work, ordains the instrument. I have myself – I tell it you without parable – been a worldly, dissipated, restless man; and I believe I have found the instrument for my cure, in —"

He paused: the birds went on carolling, the leaves lightly rustling. I almost wondered they did not check their songs and whispers to catch the suspended revelation: but they would have had to wait many minutes – so long was the silence protracted. At last I looked up at the tardy speaker: he was looking eagerly at me.

"Little friend," said he, in quite a changed tone – while his face changed too; losing all its softness and gravity, and becoming harsh and sarcastic, – "you have noticed my tender penchant for Miss Ingram: don't you think if I married her she would regenerate me with a vengeance?"

He got up instantly, went quite to the other end of the walk, and when he came back he was humming a tune.

"Jane, Jane," said he, stopping before me, "you are quite pale with your vigils: don't you curse me for disturbing your rest?"

"Curse you? No, sir."

"Shake hands in confirmation of the word. What cold fingers! They were warmer last night when I touched them at the door of the mysterious chamber. Jane, when will you watch with me again?"

"Whenever I can be useful, sir."

"For instance, the night before I am married? I am sure I shall not be able to sleep. Will you promise to sit up with me to bear me company? To you I can talk of my lovely one; for now you have seen her and know her."

"Yes, sir."

"She's a rare one, is she not, Jane?"

"Yes, sir."

"A strapper – a real strapper, Jane: big, brown, and buxom; with hair just such as the ladies of Carthage[1] must have had. Bless me! there's Dent and Lynn in the stables! Go in by the shrubbery, through that wicket."

As I went one way, he went another, and I heard him in the yard, saying cheerily: –

"Mason got the start of you all this morning; he was gone before sunrise: I rose at four to see him off."

---

1   City in North Africa destroyed by Rome in 146 BCE. Rochester is playing on Blanche's "barbaric" beauty.

CHAPTER XXI

PRESENTIMENTS are strange things! and so are sympathies; and so are signs: and the three combined make one mystery to which humanity has not yet found the key. I never laughed at presentiments in my life; because I have had strange ones of my own. Sympathies I believe exist (for instance, between far-distant, long-absent, wholly estranged relatives; asserting, notwithstanding their alienation, the unity of the source to which each traces his origin) whose workings baffle mortal comprehension. And signs, for aught we know, may be but the sympathies of Nature with man.

When I was a little girl, only six years old, I, one night, heard Bessie Leaven say to Martha Abbot that she had been dreaming about a little child; and that to dream of children was a sure sign of trouble, either to one's self or one's kin. The saying might have worn out of my memory, had not a circumstance immediately followed which served indelibly to fix it there. The next day Bessie was sent for home to the deathbed of her little sister.

Of late I had often recalled this saying and this incident; for during the past week scarcely a night had gone over my couch that had not brought with it a dream of an infant: which I sometimes hushed in my arms, sometimes dandled on my knee, sometimes watched playing with daisies on a lawn; or again, dabbling its hands in running water. It was a wailing child this night, and a laughing one the next: now it nestled close to me, and now it ran from me; but whatever mood the apparition evinced, whatever aspect it wore, it failed not for seven successive nights to meet me the moment I entered the land of slumber.

I did not like this iteration of one idea – this strange recurrence of one image; and I grew nervous as bed-time approached, and the hour of the vision drew near. It was from companionship with this baby-phantom I had been roused on that moonlight night when I heard the cry; and it was on the afternoon of the day following I was summoned down stairs by a message that some one wanted me in Mrs. Fairfax's room. On repairing thither, I found a man waiting for me, having the appearance of a gentleman's servant: he was dressed in deep mourning, and the hat he held in his hand was surrounded with a crape band.

"I daresay you hardly remember me, Miss," he said, rising as I entered; "but my name is Leaven: I lived coachman with Mrs. Reed when you were at Gateshead eight or nine years since, and I live there still."

"Oh, Robert! how do you do? I remember you very well: you used to give me a ride sometimes on Miss Georgiana's bay pony. And how is Bessie? You are married to Bessie?"

"Yes, Miss: my wife is very hearty, thank you; she brought me another little one about two months since – we have three now – and both mother and child are thriving."

"And are the family well at the House, Robert?"

"I am sorry I can't give you better news of them, Miss: they are very badly at present – in great trouble."

"I hope no one is dead," I said, glancing at his black dress. He too looked down at the crape round his hat and replied: –

"Mr. John died yesterday was a week, at his chambers in London."

"Mr. John?"

"Yes."

"And how does his mother bear it?"

"Why you see, Miss Eyre, it is not a common mishap: his life has been very wild: these last three years he gave himself up to strange ways; and his death was shocking."

"I heard from Bessie he was not doing well."

"Doing well! He could not do worse: he ruined his health and his estate amongst the worst men and the worst women. He got into debt and into jail: his mother helped him out twice, but as soon as he was free he returned to his old companions and habits. His head was not strong: the knaves he lived amongst fooled him beyond anything I ever heard. He came down to Gateshead about three weeks ago and wanted Missis to give up all to him. Missis refused: her means have long been much reduced by his extravagance; so he went back again, and the next news was that he was dead. How he died, God knows! – they say he killed himself."

I was silent: the tidings were frightful. Robert Leaven resumed: –

"Missis had been out of health herself for some time: she had got very stout, but was not strong with it; and the loss of money and fear of poverty were quite breaking her down. The information about Mr. John's death and the manner of it came too suddenly: it brought on a stroke. She was three days without speaking; but last Tuesday she seemed rather better: she appeared as if she wanted to say something, and kept making signs to my wife and mumbling. It was only yesterday morning, however, that Bessie understood she was pronouncing your name; and at last she made out the words, 'Bring Jane – fetch Jane Eyre: I want to speak to her.' Bessie is not sure whether she is in her right mind, or means anything by the words; but she told Miss Reed and Miss Georgiana, and advised them to send for you. The young ladies put it off at first: but their mother grew so restless and said, 'Jane, Jane,' so many times, that at last they consented. I left Gateshead yesterday; and if you can get ready, Miss, I should like to take you back with me early to-morrow morning."

"Yes, Robert, I shall be ready: it seems to me that I ought to go."

"I think so too, Miss. Bessie said she was sure you would not refuse: but I suppose you will have to ask leave before you can get off?"

"Yes; and I will do it now;" and having directed him to the servants' hall, and recommended him to the care of John's wife, and the attentions of John himself, I went in search of Mr. Rochester.

He was not in any of the lower rooms; he was not in the yard, the stables, or the grounds. I asked Mrs. Fairfax if she had seen him; – yes; she believed he was playing billiards with Miss Ingram. To the billiard room I hastened: the click of balls and the hum of voices resounded thence; Mr. Rochester, Miss Ingram, the two Misses Eshton and their admirers, were all busied in the game. It required some courage to disturb so interesting a party; my errand, however, was one I could not defer, so I approached the master where he stood at Miss Ingram's side. She turned as I drew near, and looked at me haughtily: her eyes seemed to demand, "What can the creeping creature want now?" and when I said, in a low voice, "Mr. Rochester," she made a movement as if tempted to order me away. I remember her appearance at the moment, – it was very graceful and very striking: she wore a morning robe of sky-blue crape; a gauzy azure scarf was twisted in her hair. She had been all animation with the game, and irritated pride did not lower the expression of her haught[1] lineaments.

---

1   Haughty.

"Does that person want you?" she inquired of Mr. Rochester; and Mr. Rochester turned to see who the "person" was. He made a curious grimace, – one of his strange and equivocal demonstrations – threw down his cue and followed me from the room.

"Well, Jane?" he said, as he rested his back against the school-room door, which he had shut.

"If you please, sir, I want leave of absence for a week or two."

"What to do? – Where to go?"

"To see a sick lady who has sent for me."

"What sick lady? – Where does she live?"

"At Gateshead, in ——shire."

"——shire? That is a hundred miles off! Who may she be that sends for people to see her that distance?"

"Her name is Reed, sir, – Mrs. Reed."

"Reed of Gateshead? There was a Reed of Gateshead, a magistrate."

"It is his widow, sir."

"And what have you to do with her? How do you know her?"

"Mr. Reed was my uncle, – my mother's brother."

"The deuce he was! You never told me that before: you always said you had no relations."

"None that would own me, sir. Mr. Reed is dead, and his wife cast me off."

"Why?"

"Because I was poor, and burdensome, and she disliked me."

"But Reed left children? – you must have cousins? Sir George Lynn was talking of a Reed of Gateshead, yesterday – who he said was one of the veriest rascals on town; and Ingram was mentioning a Georgiana Reed of the same place, who was much admired for her beauty, a season or two ago, in London."

"John Reed is dead, too, sir: he ruined himself and half ruined his family, and is supposed to have committed suicide. The news so shocked his mother that it brought on an apoplectic attack."

"And what good can you do her? Nonsense, Jane! I would never think of running a hundred miles to see an old lady who will, perhaps, be dead before you reach her: besides, you say she cast you off."

"Yes, sir, but that is long ago; and when her circumstances were very different: I could not be easy to neglect her wishes now."

"How long will you stay?"

"As short a time as possible, sir."

"Promise me only to stay a week —"

"I had better not pass my word: I might be obliged to break it."

"At all events you *will* come back: you will not be induced under any pretext to take up a permanent residence with her?"

"Oh, no! I shall certainly return if all be well."

"And who goes with you? You don't travel a hundred miles alone?"

"No, sir; she has sent her coachman."

"A person to be trusted?"

"Yes, sir, he has lived ten years in the family."

Mr. Rochester meditated. "When do you wish to go?"

"Early to-morrow morning, sir."

"Well, you must have some money; you can't travel without money, and I daresay you have not much: I have given you no salary yet. How much have you in the world, Jane?" he asked, smiling.

I drew out my purse; a meagre thing it was. "Five shillings, sir." He took the purse, poured the hoard into his palm and chuckled over it as if its scantiness pleased him. Soon he produced his pocket-book: "Here," said he, offering me a note: it was fifty pounds, and he owed me but fifteen. I told him I had no change.

"I don't want change: you know that. Take your wages."

I declined accepting more than was my due. He scowled at first; then, as if recollecting something, he said: –

"Right, right! Better not give you all now: you would, perhaps, stay away three months if you had fifty pounds. There are ten: is it not plenty?"

"Yes, sir, but now you owe me five."

"Come back for it then: I am your banker for forty pounds."

"Mr. Rochester, I may as well mention another matter of business to you while I have the opportunity."

"Matter of business? I'm curious to hear it."

"You have as good as informed me, sir, that you are going shortly to be married?"

"Yes: what then?"

"In that case, sir, Adèle ought to go to school: I am sure you will perceive the necessity of it."

"To get her out of my bride's way; who might otherwise walk over her rather too emphatically. There's sense in the suggestion; not a doubt of it: Adèle, as you say, must go to school; and you, of course, must march straight to – the devil?"

"I hope not, sir: but I must seek another situation somewhere."

"In course!"[1] he exclaimed, with a twang of voice and a distortion of features equally fantastic and ludicrous. He looked at me some minutes.

"And old Madam Reed, or the Misses, her daughters, will be solicited by you to seek a place, I suppose?"

"No sir; I am not on such terms with my relatives as would justify me in asking favours of them – but I shall advertise."

"You shall walk up the pyramids of Egypt!" he growled. "At your peril you advertise! I wish I had only offered you a sovereign instead of ten pounds. Give me back nine pounds, Jane; I've a use for it."

"And so have I, sir," I returned, putting my hands and my purse behind me. "I could not spare the money on any account."

"Little niggard!" said he, "refusing me a pecuniary request! Give me five pounds, Jane."

"Not five shillings, sir; nor five pence."

"Just let me look at the cash."

"No, sir; you are not to be trusted."

"Jane!"

"Sir?"

"Promise me one thing."

"I'll promise you anything, sir, that I think I am likely to perform."

"Not to advertise: and to trust this quest of a situation to me. I'll find you one in time."

"I shall be glad so to do, sir; if you, in your turn, will promise that I and Adèle shall be both safe out of the house before your bride enters it."

"Very well! very well! I'll pledge my word on it. You go to-morrow, then?"

---

1   Of course.

"Yes, sir; early."

"Shall you come down to the drawing-room after dinner?"

"No, sir, I must prepare for the journey."

"Then you and I must bid good-bye for a little while?"

"I suppose so, sir."

"And how do people perform that ceremony of parting, Jane? Teach me: I'm not quite up to it."

"They say farewell; or any other form they prefer."

"Then say it."

"Farewell, Mr. Rochester, for the present."

"What must I say?"

"The same, if you like, sir."

"Farewell, Miss Eyre, for the present: is that all?"

"Yes."

"It seems stingy, to my notions, and dry, and unfriendly. I should like something else: a little addition to the rite. If one shook hands, for instance; but no, – that would not content me either. So you'll do no more than say 'farewell,' Jane?"

"It is enough, sir: as much good-will may be conveyed in one hearty word as in many."

"Very likely; but it is blank and cool – 'farewell.'"

"How long is he going to stand with his back against that door?" I asked myself; "I want to commence my packing." The dinner-bell rang, and suddenly away he bolted, without another syllable: I saw him no more during the day, and was off before he had risen in the morning.

I reached the lodge at Gateshead about five o'clock in the afternoon of the first of May: I stepped in there before going up to the hall. It was very clean and neat; the ornamental windows were hung with little white curtains; the floor was spotless; the grate and fire-irons were burnished bright, and the fire burnt clear. Bessie sat on the hearth, nursing her last-born, and Robert and his sister played quietly in a corner.

"Bless you! – I knew you would come!" exclaimed Mrs. Leaven, as I entered.

"Yes, Bessie," said I, after I had kissed her; "and I trust I am not too late. How is Mrs. Reed? – Alive still, I hope."

"Yes, she is alive; and more sensible and collected than she was. The doctor says she may linger a week or two yet: but he hardly thinks she will finally recover."

"Has she mentioned me lately?"

"She was talking of you only this morning, and wishing you would come: but she is sleeping now; or was ten minutes ago, when I was up at the house. She generally lies in a kind of lethargy all the afternoon, and wakes up about six or seven. Will you rest yourself here an hour, Miss; and then I will go up with you?"

Robert here entered, and Bessie laid her sleeping child in the cradle and went to welcome him: afterwards she insisted on my taking off my bonnet and having some tea; for she said I looked pale and tired. I was glad to accept her hospitality; and I submitted to be relieved of my travelling garb just as passively as I used to let her undress me when a child.

Old times crowded fast back on me as I watched her bustling about – setting out the tea-tray with her best china, cutting bread and butter, toasting a tea-cake, and, between whiles, giving little Robert or Jane an occasional tap or push, just as she used to give me in former days. Bessie had retained her quick temper as well as her light foot and good looks.

Tea ready, I was going to approach the table; but she desired me to sit still, quite in her old, peremptory tones. I must be served at the fire-side, she said; and she placed before me a little round stand with my cup and a plate of toast, absolutely as she used to accommodate me with some privately purloined dainty on a nursery chair: and I smiled and obeyed her as in bygone days.

She wanted to know if I was happy at Thornfield Hall, and what sort of a person the mistress was; and when I told her there was only a master, whether he was a nice gentleman, and if I liked him. I told her he was rather an ugly man, but quite a gentleman; and that he treated me kindly, and I was content. Then I went on to describe to her the gay company that had lately been staying at the house; and to these details Bessie listened with interest: they were precisely of the kind she relished.

In such conversation an hour was soon gone: Bessie restored to me my bonnet, &c. and, accompanied by her, I quitted the lodge for the hall. It was also accompanied by her that I had, nearly nine years ago, walked down the path I was now ascending. On a dark, misty, raw morning in January, I had left a hostile roof with a desperate and embittered heart – a sense of outlawry and almost of reprobation – to seek the chilly harbourage of Lowood: that bourne so far away and unexplored. The same hostile roof now again rose before me: my prospects were doubtful yet; and I had yet an aching heart. I still felt as a wanderer on the face of the earth: but I experienced firmer trust in myself and my own powers, and less withering dread of oppression. The gaping wound of my wrongs, too, was now quite healed; and the flame of resentment extinguished.

"You shall go into the breakfast-room first," said Bessie, as she preceded me through the hall; "the young ladies will be there."

In another moment I was within that apartment. There was every article of furniture looking just as it did on the morning I was first introduced to Mr. Brocklehurst: the very rug he had stood upon still covered the hearth. Glancing at the book-cases, I thought I could distinguish the two volumes of Bewick's British Birds occupying their old place on the third shelf, and Gulliver's Travels and the Arabian Nights ranged just above. The inanimate objects were not changed: but the living things had altered past recognition.

Two young ladies appeared before me; one very tall, almost as tall as Miss Ingram, – very thin too, with a sallow face and severe mien. There was something ascetic in her look, which was augmented by the extreme plainness of a strait-skirted, black, stuff dress, a starched linen collar, hair combed away from the temples, and the nun-like ornament of a string of ebony beads and a crucifix. This I felt sure was Eliza, though I could trace little resemblance to her former self in that elongated and colourless visage.

The other was as certainly Georgiana; but not the Georgiana I remembered – the slim and fairy-like girl of eleven. This was a full-blown, very plump damsel, fair as wax-work; with handsome and regular features, languishing blue eyes, and ringleted yellow hair. The hue of her dress was black too; but its fashion was so different from her sister's – so much more flowing and becoming – it looked as stylish as the other's looked puritanical.

In each of the sisters there was one trait of the mother – and only one: the thin and pallid elder daughter had her parent's Cairngorm[1] eye; the blooming and luxuriant younger girl had her contour of jaw and chin, – perhaps a little softened, but still imparting an indescribable hardness to the countenance, otherwise so voluptuous and buxom.

Both ladies, as I advanced, rose to welcome me, and both addressed me by the name of "Miss Eyre." Eliza's greeting was delivered in a short, abrupt voice, without a smile; and then she sat down again, fixed her eyes on the fire, and seemed to forget me. Georgiana added to her "How d' ye do?" several commonplaces about my journey, the weather, and so on, uttered in rather a drawling tone; and accompanied by sundry side-glances that measured me from head to foot – now traversing the folds of my drab merino pelisse, and now lingering on the plain trimming of my cottage bonnet. Young ladies have a remarkable way of letting you know that they think you a "quiz,"[2] without actually saying the words. A certain superciliousness of look, coolness of manner, nonchalance of tone, express fully their sentiments on the point, without committing them by any positive rudeness in word or deed.

A sneer, however, whether covert or open, had now no longer that power over me it once possessed: as I sat between my cousins, I was surprised to find how easy I felt under the total neglect of the one and the semi-sarcastic attentions of the other – Eliza did not mortify, nor Georgiana ruffle me. The fact was, I had other things to think about; within the last few months feelings had been stirred in me so much more potent than any they could raise – pains and pleasures so much more acute and exquisite had been excited, than any it was in their power to inflict or bestow – that their airs gave me no concern either for good or bad.

"How is Mrs. Reed?" I asked soon, looking calmly at Georgiana, who thought fit to bridle at the direct address, as if it were an unexpected liberty.

"Mrs. Reed? Ah! mama you mean; she is extremely poorly: I doubt if you can see her to-night."

"If," said I, "you would just step up stairs and tell her I am come, I should be much obliged to you."

---

1   Flinty. Cairngorm is a semi-precious mineral found in Scotland.
2   Odd or ridiculous person.

Georgiana almost started, and she opened her blue eyes "wild and wide."[1] "I know she had a particular wish to see me," I added, "and I would not defer attending to her desire longer than is absolutely necessary."

"Mama dislikes being disturbed in an evening," remarked Eliza. I soon rose, quietly took off my bonnet and gloves, uninvited, and said I would just step out to Bessie – who was, I dared say, in the kitchen – and ask her to ascertain whether Mrs. Reed was disposed to receive me or not to-night. I went, and having found Bessie and despatched her on my errand, I proceeded to take further measures. It had heretofore been my habit always to shrink from arrogance: received as I had been to-day, I should, a year ago, have resolved to quit Gateshead the very next morning; now, it was disclosed to me all at once, that that would be a foolish plan. I had taken a journey of a hundred miles to see my aunt, and I must stay with her till she was better – or dead: as to her daughters' pride or folly, I must put it on one side: make myself independent of it. So I addressed the housekeeper; asked her to show me a room, told her I should probably be a visitor here for a week or two, had my trunk conveyed to my chamber, and followed it thither myself: I met Bessie on the landing.

"Missis is awake," said she; "I have told her you are here: come and let us see if she will know you."

I did not need to be guided to the well-known room: to which I had so often been summoned for chastisement or reprimand in former days. I hastened before Bessie; I softly opened the door: a shaded light stood on the table, for it was now getting dark. There was the great four-post bed with amber hangings as of old; there the toilet-table, the arm-chair and the footstool: at which I had a hundred times been sentenced to kneel, to ask pardon for offences, by me, uncommitted. I looked into a certain corner near, half-expecting to see the slim outline of a once dreaded switch; which used to lurk there, waiting to leap out imp-like and lace my quivering palm or shrinking neck. I approached the bed; I opened the curtains and leant over the high-piled pillows.

Well did I remember Mrs. Reed's face, and I eagerly sought the

---

1   See Byron's *Parasina*, XIV.46.

familiar image. It is a happy thing that time quells the longings of vengeance, and hushes the promptings of rage and aversion: I had left this woman in bitterness and hate, and I came back to her now with no other emotion than a sort of ruth for her great sufferings, and a strong yearning to forget and forgive all injuries – to be reconciled, and clasp hands in amity.

The well-known face was there: stern, relentless as ever – there was that peculiar eye which nothing could melt; and the somewhat raised, imperious, despotic eyebrow. How often had it lowered on me menace and hate! and how the recollection of childhood's terrors and sorrows revived as I traced its harsh line now! And yet I stooped down and kissed her: she looked at me.

"Is this Jane Eyre?" she said.

"Yes, Aunt Reed. How are you, dear aunt?"

I had once vowed that I would never call her aunt again: I thought it no sin to forget and break that vow, now. My fingers had fastened on her hand which lay outside the sheet: had she pressed mine kindly, I should at that moment have experienced true pleasure. But unimpressionable natures are not so soon softened, nor are natural antipathies so readily eradicated: Mrs. Reed took her hand away, and turning her face rather from me, she remarked that the night was warm. Again she regarded me, so icily, I felt at once that her opinion of me – her feeling towards me – was unchanged, and unchangeable. I knew by her stony eye – opaque to tenderness, indissoluble to tears – that she was resolved to consider me bad to the last; because to believe me good, would give her no generous pleasure: only a sense of mortification.

I felt pain, and then I felt ire; and then I felt a determination to subdue her – to be her mistress in spite both of her nature and her will. My tears had risen, just as in childhood: I ordered them back to their source. I brought a chair to the bed-head: I sat down and leaned over the pillow.

"You sent for me," I said, "and I am here; and it is my intention to stay till I see how you get on."

"Oh, of course! You have seen my daughters?"

"Yes."

"Well, you may tell them I wish you to stay, till I can talk some things over with you I have on my mind: to-night it is too late; and I have a difficulty in recalling them. But there was something I wished to say – let me see —"

The wandering look and changed utterance told what wreck had taken place in her once vigorous frame. Turning restlessly, she drew the bed-clothes round her; my elbow, resting on a corner of the quilt, fixed it down: she was at once irritated.

"Sit up!" said she, "don't annoy me with holding the clothes fast – are you Jane Eyre?"

"I am Jane Eyre."

"I have had more trouble with that child than any one would believe. Such a burden to be left on my hands – and so much annoy-ance as she caused me, daily and hourly, with her incomprehensible disposition, and her sudden starts of temper, and her continual, unnat-ural watchings of one's movements! I declare she talked to me once like something mad, or like a fiend – no child ever spoke or looked as she did: I was glad to get her away from the house. What did they do with her at Lowood? The fever broke out there, and many of the pupils died. She, however, did not die: but I said she did – I wish she had died!"

"A strange wish, Mrs. Reed: why do you hate her so?"

"I had a dislike to her mother always; for she was my husband's only sister, and a great favourite with him: he opposed the family's disowning her when she made her low marriage; and when news came of her death, he wept like a simpleton. He would send for the baby; though I entreated him rather to put it out to nurse and pay for its maintenance. I hated it the first time I set my eyes on it – a sickly, whining, pining thing! It would wail in its cradle all night long – not screaming heartily like any other child, but whimpering and moan-ing. Reed pitied it; and he used to nurse it and notice it as if it had been his own: more, indeed, than he ever noticed his own at that age. He would try to make my children friendly to the little beggar: the darlings could not bear it, and he was angry with them when they showed their dislike. In his last illness, he had it brought continually to his bedside; and but an hour before he died, he bound me by a vow to keep the creature. I would as soon have been charged with a pau-per brat out of a work-house: but he was weak, naturally weak. John does not at all resemble his father, and I am glad of it: John is like me and like my brothers – he is quite a Gibson. Oh, I wish he would cease tormenting me with letters for money! I have no more money to give him: we are getting poor. I must send away half the servants and shut up part of the house; or let it off. I can never submit to do that – yet how are we to get on? Two-thirds of my income goes in paying the interest of mortgages. John gambles dreadfully, and always loses – poor boy! He is beset by sharpers: John is sunk and degraded – his look is frightful – I feel ashamed for him when I see him."

She was getting much excited. "I think I had better leave her now," said I to Bessie, who stood on the other side of the bed.

"Perhaps you had, Miss: but she often talks in this way towards night – in the morning she is calmer."

I rose. "Stop!" exclaimed Mrs. Reed. "There is another thing I wished to say. He threatens me – he continually threatens me with his own death, or mine: and I dream sometimes that I see him laid out with a great wound in his throat, or with a swollen and blackened face. I am come to a strange pass: I have heavy troubles. What is to be done? How is the money to be had?"

Bessie now endeavoured to persuade her to take a sedative draught: she succeeded with difficulty. Soon after, Mrs. Reed grew more composed, and sank into a dozing state. I then left her.

More than ten days elapsed before I had again any conversation with her. She continued either delirious or lethargic; and the doctor forbade everything which could painfully excite her. Meantime, I got on as well as I could with Georgiana and Eliza. They were very cold, indeed, at first. Eliza would sit half the day sewing, reading, or writing, and scarcely utter a word either to me or her sister. Georgiana would chatter nonsense to her canary bird by the hour, and take no notice of me. But I was determined not to seem at a loss for occupation or amusement: I had brought my drawing materials with me, and they served me for both.

Provided with a case of pencils, and some sheets of paper, I used to take a seat apart from them, near the window, and busy myself in sketching fancy vignettes, representing any scene that happened momentarily to shape itself in the ever-shifting kaleidoscope of imagination: a glimpse of sea between two rocks; the rising moon, and a ship crossing its disk; a group of reeds and water-flags, and a naiad's head,[1] crowned with lotus-flowers, rising out of them; an

---

1   A naiad is a water-nymph in Greek mythology.

elf sitting in a hedge-sparrow's nest, under a wreath of hawthorn-bloom.

One morning I fell to sketching a face: what sort of a face it was to be I did not care or know. I took a soft black pencil, gave it a broad point, and worked away. Soon I had traced on the paper a broad and prominent forehead, and a square lower outline of visage: that contour gave me pleasure; my fingers proceeded actively to fill it with features. Strongly marked horizontal eyebrows must be traced under that brow; then followed, naturally, a well-defined nose, with a straight ridge and full nostrils; then a flexible-looking mouth, by no means narrow; then a firm chin, with a decided cleft down the middle of it: of course, some black whiskers were wanted, and some jetty hair, tufted on the temples, and waved above the forehead. Now for the eyes: I had left them to the last, because they required the most careful working. I drew them large; I shaped them well: the eyelashes I traced long and sombre; the irids lustrous and large. "Good! but not quite the thing," I thought, as I surveyed the effect: "They want more force and spirit;" and I wrought the shades blacker, that the lights might flash more brilliantly – a happy touch or two secured success. There, I had a friend's face under my gaze: and what did it signify that those young ladies turned their backs on me? I looked at it; I smiled at the speaking likeness: I was absorbed and content.

"Is that a portrait of some one you know?" asked Eliza, who had approached me unnoticed. I responded that it was merely a fancy head, and hurried it beneath the other sheets. Of course, I lied: it was, in fact, a very faithful representation of Mr. Rochester. But what was that to her; or to any one but myself? Georgiana also advanced to look. The other drawings pleased her much, but she called that "an ugly man." They both seemed surprised at my skill. I offered to sketch their portraits; and each, in turn, sat for a pencil outline. Then Georgiana produced her album. I promised to contribute a water-colour drawing: this put her at once into good humour. She proposed a walk in the grounds. Before we had been out two hours, we were deep in a confidential conversation: she had favoured me with a description of the brilliant winter she had spent in London two seasons ago – of the admiration she had there excited – the attention she had received; and I even got hints of the titled conquest she had made. In the course of the afternoon and evening these hints were enlarged on: various soft conversations were reported, and sentimental scenes represented; and, in short, a volume of a novel of fashionable life was that day improvised by her for my benefit. The communications were renewed from day to day: they always ran on the same theme – herself, her loves, and woes. It was strange she never once adverted either to her mother's illness, or her brother's death, or the present gloomy state of the family prospects. Her mind seemed wholly taken up with reminiscences of past gaiety, and aspirations after dissipations to come. She passed about five minutes each day in her mother's sick-room, and no more.

Eliza still spoke little: she had evidently no time to talk. I never saw a busier person than she seemed to be; yet it was difficult to say what she did: or rather, to discover any result of her diligence. She had an alarum to call her up early. I know not how she occupied herself before breakfast, but after that meal she divided her time into regular portions; and each hour had its allotted task. Three times a day she studied a little book, which I found, on inspection, was a Common Prayer Book. I asked her once what was the great attraction of that volume, and she said, "the Rubric."[1] Three hours she gave to stitching, with gold thread, the border of a square of crimson cloth, almost large enough for a carpet. In answer to my inquiries after the use of this article, she informed me it was a covering for the altar of a new church lately erected near Gateshead. Two hours she devoted to her diary; two to working by herself in the kitchen-garden; and one to the regulation of her accounts. She seemed to want no company; no conversation. I believe she was happy in her way: this routine sufficed to her; and nothing annoyed her so much as the occurrence of any incident which forced her to vary its clock-work regularity.

She told me one evening, when more disposed to be communicative than usual, that John's conduct, and the threatened ruin of the family, had been a source of profound affliction to her: but she had now, she said, settled her mind, and formed her resolution. Her own fortune she had taken care to secure; and when her mother died, – and it was wholly improbable, she tranquilly remarked, that she should either recover or linger long – she would execute a long-cherished project: seek a retirement where punctual habits would be

---

1   The directions for divine service printed, usually in red, in the Anglican Book of Common Prayer.

permanently secured from disturbance, and place safe barriers between herself and a frivolous world. I asked if Georgiana would accompany her.

"Of course not. Georgiana and she had nothing in common: they never had had. She would not be burdened with her society for any consideration. Georgiana should take her own course; and she, Eliza, would take hers."

Georgiana, when not unburdening her heart to me, spent most of her time in lying on the sofa, fretting about the dulness of the house, and wishing over and over again that her Aunt Gibson would send her an invitation up to town. "It would be so much better," she said, "if she could only get out of the way for a month or two, till all was over." I did not ask what she meant by "all being over," but I suppose she referred to the expected decease of her mother, and the gloomy sequel of funeral rites. Eliza generally took no more notice of her sister's indolence and complaints than if no such murmuring, lounging object had been before her. One day, however, as she put away her account-book, and unfolded her embroidery, she suddenly took her up thus: —

"Georgiana, a more vain and absurd animal than you, was certainly never allowed to cumber the earth. You had no right to be born; for you make no use of life. Instead of living for, in, and with yourself, as a reasonable being ought, you seek only to fasten your feebleness on some other person's strength: if no one can be found willing to burden her or himself with such a fat, weak, puffy, useless thing, you cry out that you are ill-treated, neglected, miserable. Then, too, existence for you must be a scene of continual change and excitement, or else the world is a dungeon: you must be admired, you must be courted, you must be flattered — you must have music, dancing, and society — or you languish, you die away. Have you no sense to devise a system which will make you independent of all efforts, and all wills, but your own? Take one day; share it into sections; to each section apportion its task: leave no stray unemployed quarters of an hour, ten minutes, five minutes, — include all; do each piece of business in its turn with method, with rigid regularity. The day will close almost before you are aware it has begun; and you are indebted to no one for helping you to get rid of one vacant moment: you have had to seek no one's company, conversation, sympathy, forbearance: you have lived, in short, as an independent being ought to do. Take this advice: the first and last I shall offer you; then you will not want me or any one else, happen what may. Neglect it – go on as heretofore, craving, whining, and idling – and suffer the results of your idiocy: however bad and insufferable they may be. I tell you this plainly; and listen: for though I shall no more repeat what I am now about to say, I shall steadily act on it. After my mother's death, I wash my hands of you: from the day her coffin is carried to the vault in Gateshead church, you and I will be as separate as if we had never known each other. You need not think that because we chanced to be born of the same parents, I shall suffer you to fasten me down by even the feeblest claim: I can tell you this – if the whole human race, ourselves excepted, were swept away, and we two stood alone on the earth, I would leave you in the old world, and betake myself to the new."

She closed her lips.

"You might have spared yourself the trouble of delivering that tirade," answered Georgiana. "Everybody knows you are the most selfish, heartless creature in existence; and *I* know your spiteful hatred towards me: I have had a specimen of it before in the trick you played me about Lord Edwin Vere: you could not bear me to be raised above you, to have a title, to be received into circles where you dare not show your face, and so you acted the spy and informer, and ruined my prospects for ever." Georgiana took out her handkerchief and blew her nose for an hour afterwards; Eliza sat cold, impassible, and assiduously industrious.

True, generous feeling is made small account of by some: but here were two natures rendered, the one intolerably acrid, the other despicably savourless for the want of it. Feeling without judgment is a washy draught indeed; but judgment untempered by feeling is too bitter and husky a morsel for human deglutition.[1]

It was a wet and windy afternoon: Georgiana had fallen asleep on the sofa over the perusal of a novel; Eliza was gone to attend a saint's-day service at the new church – for in matters of religion she was a rigid formalist: no weather ever prevented the punctual discharge of

---

1   Swallowing.

what she considered her devotional duties; fair or foul she went to church thrice every Sunday, and as often on week-days as there were prayers.

I bethought myself to go up stairs and see how the dying woman sped, who lay there almost unheeded: the very servants paid her but a remittent attention; the hired nurse, being little looked after, would slip out of the room whenever she could. Bessie was faithful; but she had her own family to mind, and could only come occasionally to the Hall. I found the sick-room unwatched, as I had expected: no nurse was there; the patient lay still, and seemingly lethargic; her livid face sunk in the pillows: the fire was dying in the grate. I renewed the fuel, re-arranged the bedclothes, gazed awhile on her who could not now gaze on me, and then I moved away to the window.

The rain beat strongly against the panes, the wind blew tempestuously: "One lies there," I thought, "who will soon be beyond the war of earthly elements. Whither will that spirit – now struggling to quit its material tenement – flit when at length released?"

In pondering the great mystery, I thought of Helen Burns: recalled her dying words – her faith – her doctrine of the equality of disembodied souls. I was still listening in thought to her well-remembered tones – still picturing her pale and spiritual aspect, her wasted face and sublime gaze, as she lay on her placid deathbed, and whispered her longing to be restored to her divine Father's bosom – when a feeble voice murmured from the couch behind: "Who is that?"

I knew Mrs. Reed had not spoken for days: was she reviving? I went up to her.

"It is I, Aunt Reed."

"Who – I?" was her answer. "Who are you?" looking at me with surprise and a sort of alarm, but still not wildly. "You are quite a stranger to me – where is Bessie?"

"She is at the lodge, Aunt."

"Aunt!" she repeated. "Who calls me Aunt? You are not one of the Gibsons; and yet I know you – that face, and the eyes and forehead are quite familiar to me: you are like – why, you are like Jane Eyre!"

I said nothing: I was afraid of occasioning some shock by declaring my identity.

"Yet," said she, "I am afraid it is a mistake: my thoughts deceive me.

I wished to see Jane Eyre, and I fancy a likeness where none exists: besides in eight years she must be so changed." I now gently assured her that I was the person she supposed and desired me to be; and seeing that I was understood, and that her senses were quite collected, I explained how Bessie had sent her husband to fetch me from Thornfield.

"I am very ill, I know," she said ere long; "I was trying to turn myself a few minutes since, and find I cannot move a limb. It is as well I should ease my mind before I die: what we think little of in health, burdens us at such an hour as the present is to me. Is the nurse here? or is there no one in the room but you?"

I assured her we were alone.

"Well, I have twice done you a wrong which I regret now. One was in breaking the promise which I gave my husband to bring you up as my own child; the other —" she stopped. "After all, it is of no great importance perhaps," she murmured to herself: "and then I may get better; and to humble myself so to her is painful."

She made an effort to alter her position, but failed: her face changed; she seemed to experience some inward sensation – the precursor, perhaps, of the last pang.

"Well: I must get it over. Eternity is before me: I had better tell her. Go to my dressing-case, open it, and take out a letter you will see there."

I obeyed her directions. "Read the letter," she said.

It was short, and thus conceived: –

"MADAM,

"Will you have the goodness to send me the address of my niece, Jane Eyre, and to tell me how she is: it is my intention to write shortly and desire her to come to me at Madeira. Providence has blessed my endeavours to secure a competency; and as I am unmarried and childless, I wish to adopt her during my life, and bequeath her at my death whatever I may have to leave."

"I am, Madam, &c. &c.

"JOHN EYRE, Madeira."

It was dated three years back.

"Why did I never hear of this?" I asked.

"Because I disliked you too fixedly and thoroughly ever to lend a hand in lifting you to prosperity. I could not forget your conduct to me, Jane – the fury with which you once turned on me; the tone in which you declared you abhorred me the worst of anybody in the world; the unchildlike look and voice with which you affirmed that the very thought of me made you sick, and asserted that I had treated you with miserable cruelty. I could not forget my own sensations when you thus started up and poured out the venom of your mind: I felt fear, as if an animal that I had struck or pushed had looked up at me with human eyes and cursed me in a man's voice. – Bring me some water! Oh, make haste!"

"Dear Mrs. Reed," said I, as I offered her the draught she required, "think no more of all this, let it pass away from your mind. Forgive me for my passionate language: I was a child then; eight, nine years have passed since that day."

She heeded nothing of what I said; but when she had tasted the water and drawn breath, she went on thus: –

"I tell you I could not forget it; and I took my revenge: for you to be adopted by your uncle and placed in a state of ease and comfort was what I could not endure. I wrote to him; I said I was sorry for his disappointment, but Jane Eyre was dead: she had died of typhus fever at Lowood. Now act as you please: write and contradict my assertion – expose my falsehood as soon as you like. You were born, I think, to be my torment: my last hour is racked by the recollection of a deed which, but for you, I should never have been tempted to commit."

"If you could but be persuaded to think no more of it, aunt, and to regard me with kindness and forgiveness —"

"You have a very bad disposition," said she, "and one, to this day I feel it impossible to understand: how for nine years you could be patient and quiescent under any treatment, and in the tenth break out all fire and violence, I can never comprehend."

"My disposition is not so bad as you think: I am passionate, but not vindictive. Many a time, as a little child, I should have been glad to love you if you would have let me; and I long earnestly to be reconciled to you now: kiss me, aunt."

I approached my cheek to her lips: she would not touch it. She said I oppressed her by leaning over the bed; and again demanded water. As I laid her down – for I raised her and supported her on my arm while she drank – I covered her ice-cold and clammy hand with mine: the feeble fingers shrank from my touch – the glazing eyes shunned my gaze.

"Love me, then, or hate me, as you will," I said at last, "you have my full and free forgiveness: ask now for God's; and be at peace."

Poor, suffering woman! it was too late for her to make now the effort to change her habitual frame of mind: living, she had ever hated me – dying, she must hate me still.

The nurse now entered, and Bessie followed. I yet lingered half an hour longer, hoping to see some sign of amity: but she gave none. She was fast relapsing into stupor; nor did her mind again rally: at twelve o'clock that night she died. I was not present to close her eyes; nor were either of her daughters. They came to tell us the next morning that all was over. She was by that time laid out. Eliza and I went to look at her: Georgiana, who had burst out into loud weeping, said she dared not go. There was stretched Sarah Reed's once robust and active frame, rigid and still: her eye of flint was covered with its cold lid; her brow and strong traits wore yet the impress of her inexorable soul. A strange and solemn object was that corpse to me. I gazed on it with gloom and pain: nothing soft, nothing sweet, nothing pitying, or hopeful, or subduing did it inspire; only a grating anguish for *her* woes – not *my* loss – and a sombre tearless dismay at the fearfulness of death in such a form.

Eliza surveyed her parent calmly. After a silence of some minutes she observed: –

"With her constitution she should have lived to a good old age: her life was shortened by trouble." And then a spasm constricted her mouth for an instant: as it passed away she turned and left the room, and so did I. Neither of us had dropt a tear.

CHAPTER XXII

Mr. Rochester had given me but one week's leave of absence: yet a month elapsed before I quitted Gateshead. I wished to leave immediately after the funeral; but Georgiana entreated me to stay till she could get off to London: whither she was now at last invited by her uncle, Mr. Gibson; who had come down to direct his sister's interment, and settle the family affairs. Georgiana said she dreaded being left alone with Eliza: from her she got neither sympathy in her dejection, support in her fears, nor aid in her preparations; so I bore with her feeble-minded quailings, and selfish lamentations, as well as I could, and did my best in sewing for her and packing her dresses. It is true, that while I worked, she would idle; and I thought to myself, "If you and I were destined to live always together, cousin, we would commence matters on a different footing. I should not settle tamely down into being the forbearing party; I should assign you your share of labour, and compel you to accomplish it, or else it should be left undone: I should insist, also, on your keeping some of those drawling, half insincere complaints hushed in your own breast. It is only because our connection happens to be very transitory, and comes at a peculiarly mournful season, that I consent thus to render it so patient and compliant on my part."

At last I saw Georgiana off: but now it was Eliza's turn to request me to stay another week. Her plans required all her time and attention, she said: she was about to depart for some unknown bourne; and all day long she stayed in her own room, her door bolted within, filling trunks, emptying drawers, burning papers, and holding no communication with any one. She wished me to look after the house, to see callers, and answer notes of condolence.

One morning she told me I was at liberty. "And," she added, "I am obliged to you for your valuable services and discreet conduct. There is some difference between living with such a one as you, and with Georgiana: you perform your own part in life, and burden no one. To-morrow," she continued, "I set out for the continent. I shall take up my abode in a religious house, near Lisle[1] – a nunnery you would

---

1   A city in northern France.

call it: there I shall be quiet and unmolested. I shall devote myself for a time to the examination of the Roman Catholic dogmas, and to a careful study of the workings of their system: if I find it to be, as I half suspect it is, the one best calculated to ensure the doing of all things decently and in order, I shall embrace the tenets of Rome and probably take the veil."

I neither expressed surprise at this resolution nor attempted to dissuade her from it. "The vocation will fit you to a hair," I thought: "much good may it do you!"

When we parted, she said: "Good-bye, cousin Jane Eyre; I wish you well: you have some sense."

I then returned: "You are not without sense, cousin Eliza; but what you have, I suppose in another year will be walled up alive in a French convent. However, it is not my business, and so it suits you – I don't much care."

"You are in the right," said she: and with these words we each went our separate way. As I shall not have occasion to refer either to her or her sister again I may as well mention here, that Georgiana made an advantageous match with a wealthy worn-out man of fashion, and that Eliza actually took the veil, and is at this day superior of the convent where she passed the period of her novitiate: and which she endowed with her fortune.

How people feel when they are returning home from an absence, long or short, I did not know: I had never experienced the sensation. I had known what it was to come back to Gateshead, when a child, after a long walk – to be scolded for looking cold or gloomy; and later, what it was to come back from church to Lowood – to long for a plenteous meal and a good fire, and to be unable to get either. Neither of these returnings was very pleasant or desirable: no magnet drew me to a given point, increasing in its strength of attraction the nearer I came. The return to Thornfield was yet to be tried.

My journey seemed tedious – very tedious: fifty miles one day, a night spent at an inn; fifty miles the next day. During the first twelve hours I thought of Mrs. Reed in her last moments: I saw her disfigured and discoloured face, and heard her strangely altered voice. I mused on the funeral day, the coffin, the hearse, the black train of tenants and servants – few was the number of relatives – the gaping vault, the silent church, the solemn service. Then I thought of Eliza and Georgiana: I beheld one the cynosure[1] of a ball-room, the other the inmate of a convent cell; and I dwelt on and analyzed their separate peculiarities of person and character. The evening arrival at the great town of — scattered these thoughts; night gave them quite another turn: laid down on my traveller's bed, I left reminiscence for anticipation.

I was going back to Thornfield: but how long was I to stay there? Not long: of that I was sure. I had heard from Mrs. Fairfax in the interim of my absence: the party at the hall was dispersed; Mr. Rochester had left for London three weeks ago, but he was then expected to return in a fortnight. Mrs. Fairfax surmised that he was gone to make arrangements for his wedding, as he had talked of purchasing a new carriage: she said the idea of his marrying Miss Ingram still seemed strange to her; but from what everybody said, and from what she had herself seen, she could no longer doubt that the event would shortly take place. "You would be strangely incredulous if you did doubt it," was my mental comment. "I don't doubt it."

The question followed, "Where was I to go?" I dreamt of Miss Ingram all the night: in a vivid morning dream I saw her closing the gates of Thornfield against me and pointing me out another road; and Mr. Rochester looked on with his arms folded – smiling sardonically, as it seemed, at both her and me.

I had not notified to Mrs. Fairfax the exact day of my return; for I did not wish either car or carriage to meet me at Millcote. I proposed to walk the distance quietly by myself; and very quietly, after leaving my box in the ostler's care, did I slip away from the George Inn, about six o'clock of a June evening, and take the old road to Thornfield: a road which lay chiefly through fields, and was now little frequented.

It was not a bright or splendid summer evening, though fair and soft: the hay-makers were at work all along the road; and the sky, though far from cloudless, was such as promised well for the future: its blue – where blue was visible – was mild and settled, and its cloud strata high and thin. The west, too, was warm: no watery gleam chilled it – it seemed as if there was a fire lit, an altar burning behind its

---

1   Centre of attraction.

screen of marbled vapour, and out of apertures shone a golden redness.

I felt glad as the road shortened before me: so glad that I stopped
once to ask myself what that joy meant; and to remind reason that
it was not to my home I was going, or to a permanent resting-place,
or to a place where fond friends looked out for me and waited
my arrival. "Mrs. Fairfax will smile you a calm welcome, to be sure,"
said I; "and little Adèle will clap her hands and jump to see you: but
you know very well you are thinking of another than they; and that
he is not thinking of you."

But what is so headstrong as youth? What so blind as inexperience? These affirmed that it was pleasure enough to have the
privilege of again looking on Mr. Rochester, whether he looked on
me or not; and they added – "Hasten! hasten! be with him while
you may: but a few more days or weeks, at most, and you are parted
from him for ever!" And then I strangled a new-born agony – a
deformed thing which I could not persuade myself to own and rear –
and ran on.

They are making hay, too, in Thornfield meadows: or rather, the
labourers are just quitting their work, and returning home with their
rakes on their shoulders; now, at the hour I arrive. I have but a field or
two to traverse, and then I shall cross the road and reach the gates.
How full the hedges are of roses! But I have no time to gather any; I
want to be at the house. I pass a tall briar, shooting leafy and flowery
branches across the path; I see the narrow stile with stone steps; and I
see – Mr. Rochester sitting there, a book and a pencil in his hand: he
is writing.

Well, he is not a ghost; yet every nerve I have is unstrung: for a
moment I am beyond my own mastery. What does it mean? I did not
think I should tremble in this way when I saw him – or lose my voice
or the power of motion in his presence. I will go back as soon as I can
stir: I need not make an absolute fool of myself. I know another way
to the house. It does not signify if I knew twenty ways; for he has seen
me.

"Hillo!" he cries; and he puts up his book and his pencil. "There
you are! Come on, if you please."

I suppose I do come on; though in what fashion I know not: being scarcely cognizant of my movements, and solicitous only to appear calm; and, above all, to control the working muscles of my face — which I feel rebel insolently against my will, and struggle to express what I had resolved to conceal. But I have a veil — it is down: I may make shift yet to behave with decent composure.

"And this is Jane Eyre? Are you coming from Millcote, and on foot? Yes — just one of your tricks: not to send for a carriage, and come clattering over street and road like a common mortal, but to steal into the vicinage of your home along with twilight, just as if you were a dream or a shade. What the deuce have you done with yourself this last month?"

"I have been with my aunt, sir, who is dead."

"A true Janian reply! Good angels be my guard! She comes from the other world — from the abode of people who are dead; and tells me so when she meets me alone here in the gloaming! If I dared, I'd touch you, to see if you are substance or shadow, you elf! — but I'd as soon offer to take hold of a blue *ignis fatuus* light in a marsh. Truant! truant!" he added, when he had paused an instant. "Absent from me a whole month: and forgetting me quite, I'll be sworn!"

I knew there would be pleasure in meeting my master again; even though broken by the fear that he was so soon to cease to be my master, and by the knowledge that I was nothing to him: but there was ever in Mr. Rochester (so at least I thought) such a wealth of the power of communicating happiness, that to taste but of the crumbs he scattered to stray and stranger birds like me, was to feast genially. His last words were balm: they seemed to imply that it imported something to him whether I forgot him or not. And he had spoken of Thornfield as my home — would that it were my home!

He did not leave the stile, and I hardly liked to ask to go by. I inquired soon if he had not been to London.

"Yes: I suppose you found that out by second-sight."

"Mrs. Fairfax told me in a letter."

"And did she inform you what I went to do?"

"Oh, yes, sir! Everybody knew your errand."

"You must see the carriage, Jane, and tell me if you don't think it will suit Mrs. Rochester exactly; and whether she won't look like

Queen Boadicea,[1] leaning back against those purple cushions. I wish, Jane, I were a trifle better adapted to match with her externally. Tell me now, fairy as you are, – can't you give me a charm, or a philter,[2] or something of that sort, to make me a handsome man?"

"It would be past the power of magic, sir;" and, in thought, I added, "A loving eye is all the charm needed: to such you are handsome enough; or rather, your sternness has a power beyond beauty."

Mr. Rochester had sometimes read my unspoken thoughts with an acumen to me incomprehensible: in the present instance he took no notice of my abrupt vocal response; but he smiled at me with a certain smile he had of his own, and which he used but on rare occasions. He seemed to think it too good for common purposes: it was the real sunshine of feeling – he shed it over me now.

"Pass, Janet," said he, making room for me to cross the stile: "go up home, and stay your weary little wandering feet at a friend's threshold."

All I had now to do was to obey him in silence: no need for me to colloquize further. I got over the stile without a word, and meant to leave him calmly. An impulse held me fast, – a force turned me round: I said – or something in me said for me, and in spite of me: –

"Thank you, Mr. Rochester, for your great kindness. I am strangely glad to get back again to you; and wherever you are is my home, – my only home."

I walked on so fast that even he could hardly have overtaken me had he tried. Little Adèle was half wild with delight when she saw me. Mrs. Fairfax received me with her usual plain friendliness. Leah smiled; and even Sophie bid me "bon soir" with glee. This was very pleasant: there is no happiness like that of being loved by your fellow-creatures, and feeling that your presence is an addition to their comfort.

I, that evening, shut my eyes resolutely against the future: I stopped my ears against the voice that kept warning me of near separation and

---

1 Boadicea, or more correctly Boudicca, was a British warrior-queen who led an uprising against Rome. After her forces sacked several Roman towns, including Londinium (London), she was finally defeated by Seutonius Paulinus in 61 CE. She is reputed to have then taken poison.
2 Love potion.

coming grief. When tea was over, and Mrs. Fairfax had taken her knitting, and I had assumed a low seat near her, and Adèle, kneeling on the carpet, had nestled close up to me, and a sense of mutual affection seemed to surround us with a ring of golden peace, I uttered a silent prayer that we might not be parted far or soon; but when, as we thus sat, Mr. Rochester entered, unannounced, and looking at us, seemed to take pleasure in the spectacle of a group so amicable – when he said he supposed the old lady was all right now that she had got her adopted daughter back again, and added that he saw Adèle was "prête à croquer sa petite maman Anglaise"[1] – I half ventured to hope that he would, even after his marriage, keep us together somewhere under the shelter of his protection, and not quite exiled from the sunshine of his presence.

A fortnight of dubious calm succeeded my return to Thornfield Hall. Nothing was said of the master's marriage, and I saw no preparation going on for such an event. Almost every day I asked Mrs. Fairfax if she had yet heard anything decided: her answer was always in the negative. Once, she said, she had actually put the question to Mr. Rochester as to when he was going to bring his bride home; but he had answered her only by a joke, and one of his queer looks, and she could not tell what to make of him.

One thing specially surprised me, and that was, there were no journeyings backward and forward, no visits to Ingram Park: to be sure it was twenty miles off, on the borders of another county; but what was that distance to an ardent lover? To so practised and indefatigable a horseman as Mr. Rochester, it would be but a morning's ride. I began to cherish hopes I had no right to conceive: that the match was broken off; that rumour had been mistaken; that one or both parties had changed their minds. I used to look at my master's face to see if it were sad or fierce; but I could not remember the time when it had been so uniformly clear of clouds or evil feelings. If, in the moments I and my pupil spent with him, I lacked spirits and sank into inevitable dejection, he became even gay. Never had he called me more frequently to his presence; never been kinder to me when there – and, alas! never had I loved him so well.

---

1   "Ready to devour her little English mother."

CHAPTER XXIII

A SPLENDID Midsummer shone over England: skies so pure, suns so radiant as were then seen in long succession, seldom favour, even singly, our wave-girt land. It was as if a band of Italian days had come from the South, like a flock of glorious passenger birds, and lighted to rest them on the cliffs of Albion. The hay was all got in; the fields round Thornfield were green and shorn; the roads white and baked; the trees were in their dark prime: hedge and wood, full-leaved and deeply tinted, contrasted well with the sunny hue of the cleared meadows between.

On Midsummer-eve, Adèle, weary with gathering wild strawberries in Hay-Lane half the day, had gone to bed with the sun. I watched her drop asleep, and when I left her I sought the garden.

It was now the sweetest hour of the twenty-four: – "Day its fervid fires had wasted,"[1] and dew fell cool on panting plain and scorched summit. Where the sun had gone down in simple state – pure of the pomp of clouds – spread a solemn purple, burning with the light of red jewel and furnace flame at one point, on one hill-peak, and extending high and wide, soft and still softer, over half heaven. The east had its own charm of fine, deep blue, and its own modest gem, a rising and solitary star: soon it would boast the moon; but she was yet beneath the horizon.

I walked awhile on the pavement; but a subtle, well-known scent – that of a cigar – stole from some window; I saw the library casement open a handbreadth; I knew I might be watched thence; so I went apart into the orchard. No nook in the grounds more sheltered and more Eden-like; it was full of trees, it bloomed with flowers: a very high wall shut it out from the court, on one side; on the other, a beech avenue screened it from the lawn. At the bottom was a sunk fence; its sole separation from lonely fields: a winding walk, bordered with laurels and terminating in a giant horse-chestnut, circled at the base by a seat, led down to the fence. Here one could wander unseen. While such honey-dew fell, such silence reigned, such gloaming gathered, I felt as if I could haunt such shade for ever: but in threading the

---

1   From the poem "The Turkish Lady" by Thomas Campbell (1777-1844).

flower and fruit-parterres at the upper part of the enclosure, enticed there by the light the now-rising moon casts on this more open quarter, my step is stayed – not by sound, not by sight, but once more by a warning fragrance.

Sweet-briar and southern-wood, jasmine, pink, and rose have long been yielding their evening sacrifice of incense: this new scent is neither of shrub nor flower; it is – I know it well – it is Mr. Rochester's cigar. I look round and I listen. I see trees laden with ripening fruit. I hear a nightingale warbling in a wood half a mile off; no moving form is visible, no coming step audible; but that perfume increases: I must flee. I make for the wicket leading to the shrubbery, and I see Mr. Rochester entering. I step aside into the ivy recess; he will not stay long: he will soon return whence he came, and if I sit still he will never see me.

But no – eventide is as pleasant to him as to me, and this antique garden as attractive; and he strolls on, now lifting the gooseberry-tree branches to look at the fruit, large as plums, with which they are laden; now taking a ripe cherry from the wall; now stooping towards a knot of flowers, either to inhale their fragrance or to admire the dew-beads on their petals. A great moth goes humming by me; it alights on a plant at Mr. Rochester's foot: he sees it, and bends to examine it.

"Now, he has his back towards me," thought I, "and he is occupied too; perhaps, if I walk softly, I can slip away unnoticed."

I trode on an edging of turf that the crackle of the pebbly gravel might not betray me: he was standing among the beds at a yard or two distant from where I had to pass; the moth apparently engaged him. "I shall get by very well," I meditated. As I crossed his shadow, thrown long over the garden by the moon, not yet risen high, he said quietly without turning: –

"Jane, come and look at this fellow."

I had made no noise: he had not eyes behind – could his shadow feel? I started at first, and then I approached him.

"Look at his wings," said he, "he reminds me rather of a West Indian insect; one does not often see so large and gay a night-rover in England: there! he is flown."

The moth roamed away; I was sheepishly retreating also: but Mr.

Rochester followed me, and when we reached the wicket, he said: –

"Turn back: on so lovely a night it is a shame to sit in the house; and surely no one can wish to go to bed while sunset is thus at meeting with moonrise."

It is one of my faults, that though my tongue is sometimes prompt enough at an answer, there are times when it sadly fails me in framing an excuse; and always the lapse occurs at some crisis, when a facile word or plausible pretext is specially wanted to get me out of painful embarrassment. I did not like to walk at this hour alone with Mr. Rochester in the shadowy orchard; but I could not find a reason to allege for leaving him. I followed with lagging step, and thoughts busily bent on discovering a means of extrication; but he himself looked so composed and so grave also, I became ashamed of feeling any confusion: the evil – if evil existent or prospective there was – seemed to lie with me only; his mind was unconscious and quiet.

"Jane," he recommenced, as we entered the laurel-walk, and slowly strayed down in the direction of the sunk fence and the horse-chestnut, "Thornfield is a pleasant place in summer, is it not?"

"Yes, sir."

"You must have become in some degree attached to the house, – you, who have an eye for natural beauties, and a good deal of the organ of Adhesiveness?"[1]

"I am attached to it, indeed."

"And, though I don't comprehend how it is, I perceive you have acquired a degree of regard for that foolish little child Adèle, too; and even for simple dame Fairfax?"

"Yes, sir; in different ways, I have an affection for both."

"And would be sorry to part with them?"

"Yes."

"Pity!" he said, and sighed and paused. "It is always the way of events in this life," he continued presently: "no sooner have you got settled in a pleasant resting-place, than a voice calls out to you to rise and move on, for the hour of repose is expired."

"Must I move on, sir?" I asked. "Must I leave Thornfield?"

"I believe you must, Jane. I am sorry Janet, but I believe indeed you must."

---

1 Yet another reference to phrenology.

This was a blow: but I did not let it prostrate me.

"Well, sir, I shall be ready when the order to march comes."

"It is come now – I must give it to-night."

"Then you are going to be married, sir?"

"Ex-act-ly – pre-cise-ly: with your usual acuteness, you have hit the nail straight on the head."

"Soon, sir?"

"Very soon, my — that is, Miss Eyre: and you'll remember, Jane, the first time I, or Rumour, plainly intimated to you that it was my intention to put my old bachelor's neck into the sacred noose, to enter into the holy estate of matrimony – to take Miss Ingram to my bosom, in short, (she's an extensive armful: but that's not to the point – one can't have too much of such a very excellent thing as my beautiful Blanche): well, as I was saying – listen to me Jane! You're not turning your head to look after more moths, are you? That was only a lady-clock,[1] child, 'flying away home.' I wish to remind you that it was you who first said to me, with that discretion I respect in you – with that foresight, prudence, and humility which befit your responsible and dependent position – that in case I married Miss Ingram, both you and little Adèle had better trot forthwith. I pass over the sort of slur conveyed in this suggestion on the character of my beloved; indeed, when you are far away, Janet, I'll try to forget it: I shall notice only its wisdom; which is such that I have made it my law of action. Adèle must go to school; and you, Miss Eyre, must get a new situation."

"Yes, sir, I will advertise immediately: and meantime, I suppose —" I was going to say, "I suppose I may stay here, till I find another shelter to betake myself to:" but I stopped, feeling it would not do to risk a long sentence, for my voice was not quite under command.

"In about a month I hope to be a bridegroom," continued Mr. Rochester; "and in the interim, I shall myself look out for employment and an asylum for you."

"Thank you, sir; I am sorry to give —"

"Oh – no need to apologize! I consider that when a dependant does her duty as well as you have done yours, she has a sort of claim

---

1   Lady bug. Rochester recalls the nursery rhyme beginning "Lady bug, lady bug, fly away home."

\

upon her employer for any little assistance he can conveniently render her; indeed I have already, through my future mother-in-law, heard of a place that I think will suit: it is to undertake the education of the five daughters of Mrs. Dionysius O'Gall of Bitternutt Lodge, Connaught, Ireland. You'll like Ireland, I think: they're such warm-hearted people there, they say."

"It is a long way off, sir."

"No matter – a girl of your sense will not object to the voyage or the distance."

"Not the voyage, but the distance: and then the sea is a barrier —"

"From what, Jane?"

"From England; and from Thornfield: and —"

"Well?"

"From *you*, sir."

I said this almost involuntarily; and with as little sanction of free will, my tears gushed out. I did not cry so as to be heard, however; I avoided sobbing. The thought of Mrs. O'Gall and Bitternutt Lodge struck cold to my heart; and colder the thought of all the brine and foam, destined, as it seemed, to rush between me and the master, at whose side I now walked; and coldest the remembrance of the wider ocean – wealth, caste, custom intervened between me and what I naturally and inevitably loved.

"It is a long way," I again said.

"It is, to be sure; and when you get to Bitternutt Lodge, Connaught, Ireland, I shall never see you again, Jane: that's morally certain. I never go over to Ireland, not having myself much of a fancy for the country. We have been good friends, Jane, have we not?"

"Yes, sir."

"And when friends are on the eve of separation, they like to spend the little time that remains to them close to each other. Come – we'll talk over the voyage and the parting quietly, half an hour or so, while the stars enter into their shining life up in heaven yonder: here is the chestnut tree; here is the bench at its old roots. Come, we will sit there in peace to-night, though we should never more be destined to sit there together." He seated me and himself.

"It is a long way to Ireland, Janet, and I am sorry to send my little friend on such weary travels: but if I can't do better, how is it to be helped? Are you anything akin to me, do you think, Jane?"

I could risk no sort of answer by this time: my heart was full.

"Because," he said, "I sometimes have a queer feeling with regard to you – especially when you are near me, as now: it is as if I had a string somewhere under my left ribs, tightly and inextricably knotted to a similar string situated in the corresponding quarter of your little frame. And if that boisterous channel, and two hundred miles or so of land come broad between us, I am afraid that cord of communion will be snapt; and then I've a nervous notion I should take to bleeding inwardly. As for you, – you'd forget me."

"That I *never* should, sir: you know —" impossible to proceed.

"Jane, do you hear that nightingale singing in the wood? – Listen!"

In listening, I sobbed convulsively; for I could repress what I endured no longer: I was obliged to yield; and I was shaken from head to foot with acute distress. When I did speak, it was only to express an impetuous wish that I had never been born, or never come to Thornfield.

"Because you are sorry to leave it?"

The vehemence of emotion, stirred by grief and love within me, was claiming mastery, and struggling for full sway; and asserting a right to predominate: to overcome, to live, rise, and reign at last; yes, – and to speak.

"I grieve to leave Thornfield: I love Thornfield: – I love it, because I have lived in it a full and delightful life, – momentarily at least. I have not been trampled on. I have not been petrified. I have not been buried with inferior minds, and excluded from every glimpse of communion with what is bright, and energetic, and high. I have talked, face to face, with what I reverence; with what I delight in, – with an original, a vigorous, an expanded mind. I have known you, Mr. Rochester; and it strikes me with terror and anguish to feel I absolutely must be torn from you for ever. I see the necessity of departure; and it is like looking on the necessity of death."

"Where do you see the necessity?" he asked, suddenly.

"Where? You, sir, have placed it before me."

"In what shape?"

"In the shape of Miss Ingram; a noble and beautiful woman, – your bride."

"My bride! What bride? I have no bride!"

"But you will have."

"Yes; – I will! – I will!" He set his teeth.

"Then I must go: – you have said it yourself."

"No: you must stay! I swear it – and the oath shall be kept."

"I tell you I must go!" I retorted, roused to something like passion. "Do you think I can stay to become nothing to you? Do you think I am an automaton? – a machine without feelings? and can bear to have my morsel of bread snatched from my lips, and my drop of living water dashed from my cup? Do you think, because I am poor, obscure, plain, and little, I am soulless and heartless? – You think wrong! – I have as much soul as you, – and full as much heart! And if God had gifted me with some beauty, and much wealth, I should have made it as hard for you to leave me, as it is now for me to leave you. I am not talking to you now through the medium of custom, conventionalities, nor even of mortal flesh: – it is my spirit that addresses your spirit; just as if both had passed through the grave, and we stood at God's feet, equal, – as we are!"

"As we are!" repeated Mr. Rochester – "so," he added, enclosing me in his arms, gathering me to his breast, pressing his lips on my lips: "so, Jane!"

"Yes, so, sir," I rejoined: "and yet not so; for you are a married man – or as good as a married man, and wed to one inferior to you – to one with whom you have no sympathy – whom I do not believe you truly love; for I have seen and heard you sneer at her. I would scorn such a union; therefore I am better than you – let me go!"

"Where, Jane? To Ireland?"

"Yes – to Ireland. I have spoken my mind, and can go anywhere now."

"Jane, be still; don't struggle so, like a wild, frantic bird that is rending its own plumage in its desperation."

"I am no bird; and no net ensnares me: I am a free human being with an independent will; which I now exert to leave you."

Another effort set me at liberty, and I stood erect before him.

"And your will shall decide your destiny," he said: "I offer you my hand, my heart, and a share of all my possessions."

"You play a farce, which I merely laugh at."

"I ask you to pass through life at my side – to be my second self, and best earthly companion."

"For that fate you have already made your choice, and must abide by it."

"Jane, be still a few moments; you are over-excited: I will be still too."

A waft of wind came sweeping down the laurel-walk, and trembled through the boughs of the chestnut: it wandered away – away – to an indefinite distance – it died. The nightingale's song was then the only voice of the hour: in listening to it, I again wept. Mr. Rochester sat quiet, looking at me gently and seriously. Some time passed before he spoke; he at last said: –

"Come to my side, Jane, and let us explain, and understand one another."

"I will never again come to your side: I am torn away now, and cannot return."

"But, Jane, I summon you as my wife: it is you only I intend to marry."

I was silent: I thought he mocked me.

"Come, Jane – come hither."

"Your bride stands between us."

He rose, and with a stride reached me.

"My bride is here," he said, again drawing me to him, "because my equal is here, and my likeness. Jane, will you marry me?"

Still I did not answer; and still I writhed myself from his grasp: for I was still incredulous.

"Do you doubt me, Jane?"

"Entirely."

"You have no faith in me?"

"Not a whit."

"Am I a liar in your eyes?" he asked passionately. "Little sceptic, you *shall* be convinced. What love have I for Miss Ingram? None: and that you know. What love has she for me? None; as I have taken pains to prove: I caused a rumour to reach her that my fortune was not a third of what was supposed, and after that I presented myself to see the result: it was coldness both from her and her mother. I would not – I could not – marry Miss Ingram. You – you strange – you almost unearthly thing! – I love as my own flesh. You – poor and obscure, and small and plain as you are – I entreat to accept me as a husband."

"What, me!" I ejaculated: beginning in his earnestness – and especially in his incivility – to credit his sincerity; "me, who have not a friend in the world but you – if you are my friend: not a shilling but what you have given me?"

"You, Jane. I must have you for my own – entirely my own. Will you be mine? Say yes, quickly."

"Mr. Rochester, let me look at your face: turn to the moonlight."

"Why?"

"Because I want to read your countenance: – turn!"

"There: you will find it scarcely more legible than a crumpled, scratched page. Read on: only make haste, for I suffer."

His face was very much agitated and very much flushed, and there were strong workings in the features, and strange gleams in the eyes.

"Oh, Jane, you torture me!" he exclaimed. "With that searching and yet faithful and generous look, you torture me!"

"How can I do that? If you are true, and your offer real, my only feelings to you must be gratitude and devotion – they cannot torture."

"Gratitude!" he ejaculated; and added wildly – "Jane, accept me quickly. Say, Edward – give me my name – Edward, I will marry you."

"Are you in earnest? – Do you truly love me? – Do you sincerely wish me to be your wife?"

"I do; and if an oath is necessary to satisfy you, I swear it."

"Then, sir, I will marry you."

"Edward – my little wife!"

"Dear Edward!"

"Come to me – come to me entirely now," said he; and added, in his deepest tone, speaking in my ear as his cheek was laid on mine, "Make my happiness – I will make yours."

"God, pardon me!" he subjoined ere long; "and man, meddle not with me: I have her, and will hold her."

"There is no one to meddle, sir. I have no kindred to interfere."

"No – that is the best of it," he said. And if I had loved him less I should have thought his accent and look of exultation savage: but, sitting by him, roused from the nightmare of parting – called to the paradise of union – I thought only of the bliss given me to drink in so abundant a flow. Again and again he said, "Are you happy, Jane?" And again and again I answered, "Yes." After which he murmured, "It will atone – it will atone. Have I not found her friendless, and cold, and comfortless? Will I not guard, and cherish, and solace her? Is there not love in my heart, and constancy in my resolves? It will expiate at God's tribunal. I know my Maker sanctions what I do. For the world's judgment – I wash my hands thereof. For man's opinion – I defy it."

But what had befallen the night? The moon was not yet set, and we were all in shadow: I could scarcely see my master's face, near as I was. And what ailed the chestnut tree? it writhed and groaned; while wind roared in the laurel walk, and came sweeping over us.

"We must go in," said Mr. Rochester: "the weather changes. I could have sat with thee till morning, Jane."

"And so," thought I, "could I with you." I should have said so, per-haps, but a livid, vivid spark leapt out of a cloud at which I was look-ing, and there was a crack, a crash, and a close rattling peal; and I thought only of hiding my dazzled eyes against Mr. Rochester's shoulder. The rain rushed down. He hurried me up the walk, through the grounds, and into the house; but we were quite wet before we could pass the threshold. He was taking off my shawl in the hall, and shaking the water out of my loosened hair, when Mrs. Fairfax emerged from her room. I did not observe her at first, nor did Mr. Rochester. The lamp was lit. The clock was on the stroke of twelve.

"Hasten to take off your wet things," said he; "and before you go, good-night – good-night, my darling!"

He kissed me repeatedly. When I looked up, on leaving his arms, there stood the widow, pale, grave, and amazed. I only smiled at her, and ran up stairs. "Explanation will do for another time," thought I. Still, when I reached my chamber, I felt a pang at the idea she should even temporarily misconstrue what she had seen. But joy soon effaced every other feeling; and loud as the wind blew, near and deep as the thunder crashed, fierce and frequent as the lightning gleamed, cataract-like as the rain fell during a storm of two hours' duration, I experienced no fear, and little awe. Mr. Rochester came thrice to my door in the course of it, to ask if I was safe and tranquil: and that was comfort, that was strength for anything.

Before I left my bed in the morning, little Adèle came running in to tell me that the great horse-chestnut at the bottom of the orchard had been struck by lightning in the night, and half of it split away.

CHAPTER XXIV

As I rose and dressed, I thought over what had happened, and wondered if it were a dream. I could not be certain of the reality till I had seen Mr. Rochester again, and heard him renew his words of love and promise.

While arranging my hair, I looked at my face in the glass, and felt it was no longer plain: there was hope in its aspect, and life in its colour; and my eyes seemed as if they had beheld the fount of fruition, and borrowed beams from the lustrous ripple. I had often been unwilling to look at my master, because I feared he could not be pleased at my look; but I was sure I might lift my face to his now, and not cool his affection by its expression. I took a plain but clean and light summer dress from my drawer and put it on: it seemed no attire had ever so well become me; because none had I ever worn in so blissful a mood.

I was not surprised, when I ran down into the hall, to see that a brilliant June morning had succeeded to the tempest of the night; and to feel, through the open glass door, the breathing of a fresh and fragrant breeze. Nature must be gladsome when I was so happy. A beggar-woman and her little boy – pale, ragged objects both – were coming up the walk, and I ran down and gave them all the money I happened to have in my purse – some three or four shillings: good or bad, they must partake of my jubilee. The rooks cawed, and blither birds sang; but nothing was so merry or so musical as my own rejoicing heart.

Mrs. Fairfax surprised me by looking out of the window with a sad countenance, and saying gravely: – "Miss Eyre, will you come to breakfast?" During the meal she was quiet and cool: but I could not undeceive her then. I must wait for my master to give explanations; and so must she. I ate what I could, and then I hastened up stairs. I met Adèle leaving the school-room.

"Where are you going? It is time for lessons."

"Mr. Rochester has sent me away to the nursery."

"Where is he?"

"In there," pointing to the apartment she had left; and I went in, and there he stood.

"Come and bid me good-morning," said he. I gladly advanced; and it was not merely a cold word now, or even a shake of the hand that I received, but an embrace and a kiss. It seemed natural: it seemed genial to be so well-loved, so caressed by him.

"Jane, you look blooming, and smiling, and pretty," said he: "truly pretty this morning. Is this my pale, little elf? Is this my Mustard-Seed?[1] This little sunny-faced girl with the dimpled cheek and rosy lips; the satin-smooth hazel hair, and the radiant hazel eyes?" (I had green eyes, reader; but you must excuse the mistake: for him they were new-dyed, I suppose.)

"It is Jane Eyre, sir."

"Soon to be Jane Rochester," he added: "in four weeks, Janet; not a day more. Do you hear that?"

I did; and I could not quite comprehend it: it made me giddy. The feeling, the announcement sent through me, was something stronger than was consistent with joy – something that smote and stunned: it was, I think, almost fear.

"You blushed, and now you are white, Jane: what is that for?"

"Because you gave me a new name – Jane Rochester; and it seems so strange."

"Yes; Mrs. Rochester," said he; "young Mrs. Rochester – Fairfax Rochester's girl-bride."

"It can never be, sir; it does not sound likely. Human beings never enjoy complete happiness in this world. I was not born for a different destiny to the rest of my species: to imagine such a lot befalling me, is a fairy tale – a day-dream."

"Which I can and will realize. I shall begin to-day. This morning I wrote to my banker in London to send me certain jewels he has in his keeping, – heir-looms for the ladies of Thornfield. In a day or two I hope to pour them into your lap: for every privilege, every attention shall be yours, that I would accord a peer's daughter, if about to marry her."

"Oh, sir! – never mind jewels! I don't like to hear them spoken of. Jewels for Jane Eyre sounds unnatural and strange: I would rather not have them."

---

1   One of the fairies in *A Midsummer Night's Dream*.

"I will myself put the diamond chain round your neck, and the circlet on your forehead, – which it will become: for nature, at least, has stamped her patent of nobility on this brow, Jane; and I will clasp the bracelets on these fine wrists, and load these fairy-like fingers with rings."

"No, no, sir! think of other subjects, and speak of other things; and in another strain. Don't address me as if I were a beauty: I am your plain, Quakerish governess."

"You are a beauty, in my eyes; and a beauty just after the desire of my heart, – delicate and aërial."

"Puny and insignificant, you mean. You are dreaming, sir – or you are sneering. For God's sake, don't be ironical!"

"I will make the world acknowledge you a beauty, too," he went on, while I really became uneasy at the strain he had adopted; because I felt he was either deluding himself, or trying to delude me. "I will attire my Jane in satin and lace, and she shall have roses in her hair; and I will cover the head I love best with a priceless veil."

"And then you won't know me, sir; and I shall not be your Jane Eyre any longer, but an ape in a harlequin's jacket, – a jay in borrowed plumes. I would as soon see you, Mr. Rochester, tricked out in stage-trappings, as myself clad in a court-lady's robe; and I don't call you handsome, sir, though I love you most dearly: far too dearly to flatter you. Don't flatter me."

He pursued his theme, however, without noticing my deprecation. "This very day I shall take you in the carriage to Millcote, and you must choose some dresses for yourself. I told you we shall be married in four weeks. The wedding is to take place quietly, in the church down below yonder; and then I shall waft you away at once to town. After a brief stay there, I shall bear my treasure to regions nearer the sun: to French vineyards and Italian plains; and she shall see whatever is famous in old story and in modern record: she shall taste, too, of the life of cities; and she shall learn to value herself by just comparison with others."

"Shall I travel? – and with you, sir?"

"You shall sojourn at Paris, Rome, and Naples; at Florence, Venice, and Vienna: all the ground I have wandered over shall be re-trodden by you: wherever I stamped my hoof, your sylph's foot shall step also.

Ten years since, I flew through Europe half mad; with disgust, hate, and rage, as my companions: now I shall revisit it healed and cleansed, with a very angel as my comforter."

I laughed at him as he said this. "I am not an angel," I asserted; "and I will not be one till I die: I will be myself. Mr. Rochester, you must neither expect nor exact anything celestial of me, – for you will not get it, any more than I shall get it of you; which I do not at all anticipate."

"What do you anticipate of me?"

"For a little while you will perhaps be as you are now, – a very little while; and then you will turn cool; and then you will be capricious; and then you will be stern, and I shall have much ado to please you: but when you get well used to me, you will perhaps like me again, – *like* me, I say, not *love* me. I suppose your love will effervesce in six months, or less. I have observed in books written by men, that period assigned as the farthest to which a husband's ardour extends. Yet, after all, as a friend and companion, I hope never to become quite distasteful to my dear master."

"Distasteful! and like you again! I think I shall like you again and yet again: and I will make you confess I do not only *like*, but *love* you – with truth, fervour, constancy."

"Yet are you not capricious, sir?"

"To women who please me only by their faces, I am the very devil when I find out they have neither souls nor hearts – when they open to me a perspective of flatness, triviality, and perhaps imbecility, coarseness, and ill-temper: but to the clear eye and eloquent tongue, to the soul made of fire, and the character that bends but does not break – at once supple and stable, tractable and consistent – I am ever tender and true."

"Had you ever experience of such a character, sir? Did you ever love such a one?"

"I love it now."

"But before me: if I, indeed, in any respect come up to that difficult standard?"

"I never met your likeness, Jane: you please me, and you master me – you seem to submit, and I like the sense of pliancy you impart; and while I am twining the soft, silken skein round my finger, it sends a thrill up my arm to my heart. I am influenced – conquered; and the influence is sweeter than I can express; and the conquest I undergo has a witchery beyond any triumph I can win. Why do you smile, Jane? What does that inexplicable, that uncanny turn of countenance mean?"

"I was thinking, sir (you will excuse the idea; it was involuntary), I was thinking of Hercules and Samson with their charmers –"[1]

"You were, you little, elfish —"

"Hush, sir! You don't talk very wisely just now; any more than those gentlemen acted very wisely. However, had they been married, they would no doubt by their severity as husbands have made up for their softness as suitors: and so will you, I fear. I wonder how you will answer me a year hence, should I ask a favour it does not suit your convenience or pleasure to grant."

"Ask me something now, Janet – the least thing: I desire to be entreated —"

"Indeed, I will sir; I have my petition all ready."

"Speak! But if you look up and smile with that countenance, I shall swear concession before I know to what, and that will make a fool of me."

"Not at all, sir; I ask only this: don't send for the jewels, and don't crown me with roses: you might as well put a border of gold lace round that plain pocket handkerchief you have there."

"I might as well 'gild refined gold.'[2] I know it: your request is granted then – for the time. I will remand the order I despatched to my banker. But you have not yet asked for anything; you have prayed a gift to be withdrawn: try again."

"Well, then, sir; have the goodness to gratify my curiosity, which is much piqued on one point."

He looked disturbed. "What? what?" he said hastily. "Curiosity is a dangerous petitioner: it is well I have not taken a vow to accord every request —"

"But there can be no danger in complying with this, sir."

---

1   Both Hercules and Samson are "conquered" by women. Deianira inadvertently poisons Hercules when she dips his garments in what she thinks is a love potion. Delilah seduces Samson into revealing the secret of his strength, and then reveals it to his enemies.

2   *King John* IV.ii.11.

"Utter it, Jane: but I wish that instead of a mere inquiry into, perhaps, a secret, it was a wish for half my estate."

"Now, king Ahasuerus![1] What do I want with half your estate? Do you think I am a Jew-usurer, seeking good investment in land? I would much rather have all your confidence. You will not exclude me from your confidence, if you admit me to your heart?"

"You are welcome to all of my confidence that is worth having, Jane: but for God's sake, don't desire a useless burden! Don't long for poison – don't turn out a downright Eve on my hands!"[2]

"Why not, sir? You have just been telling me how much you like to be conquered, and, how pleasant overpersuasion is to you. Don't you think I had better take advantage of the confession, and begin and coax, and entreat – even cry and be sulky if necessary – for the sake of a mere essay of my power?"

"I dare you to any such experiment. Encroach, presume, and the game is up."

"Is it, sir? You soon give in. How stern you look now! Your eyebrows have become as thick as my finger, and your forehead resembles, what, in some very astonishing poetry, I once saw styled, 'a blue-piled thunder-loft.'[3] That will be your married look, sir, I suppose?"

"If that will be *your* married look, I, as a Christian, will soon give up the notion of consorting with a mere sprite or salamander.[4] But what had you to ask, thing? – out with it!"

"There, you are less than civil now; and I like rudeness a great deal better than flattery. I had rather be a *thing* than an angel. This is what I have to ask, – Why did you take such pains to make me believe you wished to marry Miss Ingram?"

"Is that all? Thank God, it is no worse!" And now he unknit his black brows; looked down, smiling at me, and stroked my hair, as if well pleased at seeing a danger averted. "I think I may confess," he continued, "even although I should make you a little indignant, Jane –

---

1   See Esther 5:3.
2   i.e., someone who will destroy their paradise by insisting on the "forbidden fruit" of knowledge.
3   See Milton's "At a Vacation Exercise in the College," 42.
4   In mythology a salamander was an elemental fire-spirit. Rochester makes this characterization of Jane explicit in his next speech.

and I have seen what a fire-spirit you can be when you are indignant. You glowed in the cool moonlight last night, when you mutinied against fate, and claimed your rank as my equal. Janet, by-the-by, it was you who made me the offer."

"Of course I did. But to the point if you please, sir – Miss Ingram?"

"Well, I feigned courtship of Miss Ingram, because I wished to render you as madly in love with me as I was with you; and I knew jealousy would be the best ally I could call in for the furtherance of that end."

"Excellent! Now you are small – not one whit bigger than the end of my little finger. It was a burning shame, and a scandalous disgrace to act in that way. Did you think nothing of Miss Ingram's feelings, sir?"

"Her feelings are concentrated in one – pride; and that needs humbling. Were you jealous, Jane?"

"Never mind, Mr. Rochester: it is in no way interesting to you to know that. Answer me truly once more. Do you think Miss Ingram will not suffer from your dishonest coquetry? Won't she feel forsaken and deserted?"

"Impossible! – when I told you how she, on the contrary, deserted me: the idea of my insolvency cooled, or rather extinguished, her flame in a moment."

"You have a curious designing mind, Mr. Rochester. I am afraid your principles on some points are eccentric."

"My principles were never trained, Jane: they may have grown a little awry for want of attention."

"Once again, seriously; may I enjoy the great good that has been vouchsafed to me, without fearing that any one else is suffering the bitter pain I myself felt a while ago?"

"That you may, my good little girl: there is not another being in the world has the same pure love for me as yourself – for I lay that pleasant unction to my soul,[1] Jane, a belief in your affection."

I turned my lips to the hand that lay on my shoulder. I loved him very much – more than I could trust myself to say – more than words had power to express.

---

1 See *Hamlet* III.iv.146.

"Ask something more," he said presently; "it is my delight to be entreated, and to yield."

I was again ready with my request. "Communicate your intentions to Mrs. Fairfax, sir: she saw me with you last night in the hall, and she was shocked. Give her some explanation before I see her again. It pains me to be misjudged by so good a woman."

"Go to your room, and put on your bonnet," he replied. "I mean you to accompany me to Millcote this morning; and while you prepare for the drive, I will enlighten the old lady's understanding. Did she think, Janet, you had given the world for love, and considered it well lost?"[1]

"I believe she thought I had forgotten my station; and yours, sir."

"Station! station! – your station is in my heart, and on the necks of those who would insult you, now or hereafter. – Go."

I was soon dressed; and when I heard Mr. Rochester quit Mrs. Fairfax's parlour, I hurried down to it. The old lady had been reading her morning portion of Scripture – the lesson for the day: her Bible lay open before her, and her spectacles were upon it. Her occupation, suspended by Mr. Rochester's announcement, seemed now forgotten: her eyes, fixed on the blank wall opposite, expressed the surprise of a quiet mind, stirred by unwonted tidings. Seeing me, she roused herself: she made a sort of effort to smile, and framed a few words of congratulation; but the smile expired, and the sentence was abandoned unfinished. She put up her spectacles, shut the Bible, and pushed her chair back from the table.

"I feel so astonished," she began, "I hardly know what to say to you, Miss Eyre. I have surely not been dreaming, have I? Sometimes I half fall asleep when I am sitting alone, and fancy things that have never happened. It has seemed to me more than once, when I have been in a doze, that my dear husband, who died fifteen years since, has come in and sat down beside me; and that I have even heard him call me by my name, Alice, as he used to do. Now, can you tell me whether it is actually true that Mr. Rochester has asked you to marry him? Don't laugh at me. But I really thought he came in here five minutes ago, and said, that in a month you would be his wife."

"He has said the same thing to me," I replied.

---

1   John Dryden (1631-1700) published his play *All for Love, or The World Well Lost* in 1678.

"He has! Do you believe him? Have you accepted him?"

"Yes."

She looked at me bewildered.

"I could never have thought it. He is a proud man: all the Rochesters were proud: and his father, at least, liked money. He, too, has always been called careful. He means to marry you?"

"He tells me so."

She surveyed my whole person: in her eyes I read that they had there found no charm powerful enough to solve the enigma.

"It passes me!"[1] she continued: "but no doubt it is true, since you say so. How it will answer, I cannot tell: I really don't know. Equality of position and fortune is often advisable in such cases; and there are twenty years of difference in your ages. He might almost be your father."

"No, indeed, Mrs. Fairfax!" exclaimed I, nettled; "he is nothing like my father! No one, who saw us together, would suppose it for an instant. Mr. Rochester looks as young, and is as young as some men at five-and-twenty."

"Is it really for love he is going to marry you?" she asked.

I was so hurt by her coldness and scepticism, that the tears rose to my eyes.

"I am sorry to grieve you," pursued the widow; "but you are so young, and so little acquainted with men, I wished to put you on your guard. It is an old saying that 'all is not gold that glitters;' and in this case I do fear there will be something found to be different to what either you or I expect."

"Why? – am I a monster?" I said: "is it impossible that Mr. Rochester should have a sincere affection for me?"

"No: you are very well; and much improved of late; and Mr. Rochester, I daresay, is fond of you. I have always noticed that you were a sort of pet of his. There are times when, for your sake, I have been a little uneasy at his marked preference, and have wished to put you on your guard: but I did not like to suggest even the possibility of wrong. I knew such an idea would shock, perhaps offend you; and you were so discreet, and so thoroughly modest and sensible, I hoped you might be trusted to protect yourself. Last night I cannot tell you

---

1   Dialect: "It is beyond my understanding!"

what I suffered when I sought all over the house, and could find you nowhere, nor the master either; and then, at twelve o'clock, saw you come in with him."

"Well, never mind that now," I interrupted, impatiently: "it is enough that all was right."

"I hope all will be right in the end," she said: "but, believe me, you cannot be too careful. Try and keep Mr. Rochester at a distance: distrust yourself as well as him. Gentlemen in his station are not accustomed to marry their governesses."

I was growing truly irritated: happily, Adèle ran in.

"Let me go, – let me go to Millcote, too!" she cried. "Mr. Rochester won't: though there is so much room in the new carriage. Beg him to let me go, mademoiselle."

"That I will, Adèle;" and I hastened away with her, glad to quit my gloomy monitress. The carriage was ready: they were bringing it round to the front, and my master was pacing the pavement, Pilot following him backwards and forwards.

"Adèle may accompany us, may she not, sir?"

"I told her no. I'll have no brats! – I'll have only you."

"Do let her go, Mr. Rochester, if you please: it would be better."

"Not it: she will be a restraint."

He was quite peremptory, both in look and voice. The chill of Mrs. Fairfax's warnings, and the damp of her doubts, were upon me: something of unsubstantiality and uncertainty had beset my hopes. I half lost the sense of power over him. I was about mechanically to obey him, without further remonstrance; but as he helped me into the carriage, he looked at my face.

"What is the matter?" he asked; "all the sunshine is gone. Do you really wish the bairn to go? Will it annoy you if she is left behind?"

"I would far rather she went, sir."

"Then off for your bonnet, and back, like a flash of lightning!" cried he to Adèle.

She obeyed him with what speed she might.

"After all, a single morning's interruption will not matter much," said he, "when I mean shortly to claim you – your thoughts, conversation, and company – for life."

Adèle, when lifted in, commenced kissing me, by way of expressing her gratitude for my intercession: she was instantly stowed away into a corner on the other side of him. She then peeped round to where I sat; so stern a neighbour was too restrictive: to him, in his present fractious mood, she dared whisper no observations, nor ask of him any information.

"Let her come to me," I entreated; "she will, perhaps, trouble you, sir: there is plenty of room on this side."

He handed her over as if she had been a lap-dog: "I'll send her to school yet," he said, but now he was smiling.

Adèle heard him, and asked if she was to go to school "sans mademoiselle?"[1]

"Yes," he replied, "absolutely 'sans mademoiselle'; for I am going to take mademoiselle to the moon, and there I shall seek a cave in one of the white valleys among the volcano-tops, and mademoiselle shall live with me there, and only me."

"She will have nothing to eat: you will starve her," observed Adèle.

"I shall gather manna for her morning and night: the plains and hill-sides in the moon are bleached with manna, Adèle."

"She will want to warm herself; what will she do for a fire?"

"Fire rises out of the lunar mountains: when she is cold, I'll carry her up to a peak and lay her down on the edge of a crater."

"Oh, qu'elle y sera mal – peu confortable![2] And her clothes, they will wear out: how can she get new ones?"

Mr. Rochester professed to be puzzled. "Hem!" said he. "What would you do, Adèle? Cudgel your brains for an expedient. How would a white or a pink cloud answer for a gown, do you think? And one could cut a pretty enough scarf out of a rainbow."

"She is far better as she is," concluded Adèle, after musing some time: "besides, she would get tired of living with only you in the moon. If I were mademoiselle, I would never consent to go with you."

"She has consented: she has pledged her word."

"But you can't get her there: there is no road to the moon: it is all air; and neither you nor she can fly."

"Adèle, look at that field." We were now outside Thornfield gates, and bowling lightly along the smooth road to Millcote, where the

---

1   Without Miss [Eyre].
2   Oh, she won't be very comfortable there!

dust was well laid by the thunder-storm, and where the low hedges and lofty timber trees on each side glistened green, and rain-refreshed.

"In that field, Adèle, I was walking late one evening about a fortnight since – the evening of the day you helped me to make hay in the orchard meadows; and as I was tired with raking swaths, I sat down to rest me on a stile; and there I took out a little book and a pencil, and began to write about a misfortune that befell me long ago, and a wish I had for happy days to come: I was writing away very fast, though daylight was fading from the leaf, when something came up the path and stopped two yards off me. I looked at it. It was a little thing with a veil of gossamer on its head. I beckoned it to come near me: it stood soon at my knee. I never spoke to it, and it never spoke to me, in words: but I read its eyes, and it read mine; and our speechless colloquy was to this effect: –

"It was a fairy, and come from Elf-land, it said; and its errand was to make me happy: I must go with it out of the common world to a lonely place – such as the moon, for instance – and it nodded its head towards her horn, rising over Hay-hill: it told me of the alabaster cave and silver vale where we might live. I said I should like to go; but reminded it, as you did me, that I had no wings to fly.

"'Oh,' returned the fairy, 'that does not signify! Here is a talisman will remove all difficulties;' and she held out a pretty gold ring. 'Put it,' she said, 'on the fourth finger of my left hand, and I am yours, and you are mine; and we shall leave earth, and make our own heaven yonder.' She nodded again at the moon. The ring, Adèle, is in my breeches-pocket, under the disguise of a sovereign: but I mean soon to change it to a ring again."

"But what has mademoiselle to do with it? I don't care for the fairy: you said it was mademoiselle you would take to the moon —?"

"Mademoiselle is a fairy," he said, whispering mysteriously. Whereupon I told her not to mind his badinage;[1] and she, on her part, evinced a fund of genuine French scepticism: denominating Mr. Rochester "un vrai menteur,"[2] and assuring him that she made no account whatever of his "Contes de fée,"[3] and that "du reste, il n'y

---

1   Humorous ridicule.
2   A real liar.
3   Fairy tales.

avait pas de fées, et quand même il y en avait,"[1] she was sure they would never appear to him, nor ever give him rings, or offer to live with him in the moon.

The hour spent at Millcote was a somewhat harassing one to me. Mr. Rochester obliged me to go to a certain silk warehouse: there I was ordered to choose half a dozen dresses. I hated the business, I begged leave to defer it: no – it should be gone through with now. By dint of entreaties expressed in energetic whispers, I reduced the half-dozen to two: these, however, he vowed he would select himself. With anxiety I watched his eye rove over the gay stores: he fixed on a rich silk of the most brilliant amethyst dye, and a superb pink satin. I told him in a new series of whispers, that he might as well buy me a gold gown and a silver bonnet at once: I should certainly never venture to wear his choice. With infinite difficulty, (for he was stubborn as a stone) I persuaded him to make an exchange in favour of a sober black satin and pearl-grey silk. "It might pass for the present," he said; "but he would yet see me glittering like a parterre."

Glad was I to get him out of the silk warehouse, and then out of a jeweller's shop: the more he bought me, the more my cheek burned with a sense of annoyance and degradation. As we re-entered the carriage, and I sat back feverish and fagged, I remembered what in the hurry of events, dark and bright, I had wholly forgotten – the letter of my uncle, John Eyre, to Mrs. Reed: his intention to adopt me and make me his legatee. "It would, indeed, be a relief," I thought, "if I had ever so small an independency; I never can bear being dressed like a doll by Mr. Rochester, or sitting like a second Danae with the golden shower falling daily round me.[2] I will write to Madeira the moment I get home, and tell my uncle John I am going to be married, and to whom: if I had but a prospect of one day bringing Mr. Rochester an accession of fortune, I could better endure to be kept by him now." And somewhat relieved by this idea (which I failed not to execute that day), I ventured once more to meet my master's and lover's eye; which most pertinaciously sought mine, though I averted both face and gaze. He smiled; and I thought his smile was such as a sultan

---

1   "Besides, there were no fairies, and even if there had been."
2   In Greek mythology Danae was visited by Zeus as a shower of gold. The resulting offspring was Perseus.

might, in a blissful and fond moment, bestow on a slave his gold and gems had enriched: I crushed his hand, which was ever hunting mine, vigorously, and thrust it back to him red with the passionate pressure —

"You need not look in that way," I said: "if you do, I'll wear nothing but my old Lowood frocks to the end of the chapter. I'll be married in this lilac gingham – you may make a dressing-gown for yourself out of the pearl-grey silk, and an infinite series of waistcoats out of the black satin."

He chuckled; he rubbed his hands: "Oh, it is rich to see and hear her!" he exclaimed. "Is she original? Is she piquant? I would not exchange this one little English girl for the grand Turk's whole seraglio,[1] gazelle-eyes, houri[2] forms, and all!"

The eastern allusion bit me again: "I'll not stand you an inch in the stead of a seraglio," I said; "so don't consider me an equivalent for one: if you have a fancy for anything in that line, away with you, sir, to the bazaars of Stamboul without delay; and lay out in extensive slave-purchases some of that spare cash you seem at a loss to spend satisfactorily here."

"And what will you do, Janet, while I am bargaining for so many tons of flesh and such an assortment of black eyes?"

"I'll be preparing myself to go out as a missionary to preach liberty to them that are enslaved – your Harem inmates amongst the rest. I'll get admitted there, and I'll stir up mutiny; and you, three-tailed bashaw as you are,[3] sir, shall in a trice find yourself fettered amongst our hands: nor will I, for one, consent to cut your bonds till you have signed a charter,[4] the most liberal that despot ever yet conferred."

"I would consent to be at your mercy, Jane."

"I would have no mercy, Mr. Rochester, if you supplicated for it with an eye like that. While you looked so, I should be certain that whatever charter you might grant under coercion, your first act, when released, would be to violate its conditions."

---

1 Harem.
2 A nymph in the Muslim paradise, and thus by extension any beautiful woman.
3 Turkish governor of the highest rank, who was allowed to display three horse-tails as his battle standard.
4 An allusion to the reform-minded Chartist Movement, which presented its "People's Charter," a petition with over one million signatures, to the British House of Commons in 1839. It was voted on and defeated by a margin of 235 to 46.

"Why, Jane, what would you have? I fear you will compel me to go through a private marriage ceremony, besides that performed at the altar. You will stipulate, I see, for peculiar terms – what will they be?"

"I only want an easy mind, sir; not crushed by crowded obligations. Do you remember what you said of Céline Varens? – of the diamonds, the cashmeres you gave her? I will not be your English Céline Varens. I shall continue to act as Adèle's governess: by that I shall earn my board and lodging, and thirty pounds a year besides. I'll furnish my own wardrobe out of that money, and you shall give me nothing, but —"

"Well, but what?"

"Your regard: and if I give you mine in return, that debt will be quit."

"Well, for cool native impudence, and pure innate pride, you haven't your equal," said he. We were now approaching Thornfield. "Will it please you to dine with me to-day?" he asked, as we re-entered the gates.

"No, thank you, sir."

"And what for, 'no, thank you'? if one may inquire."

"I never have dined with you, sir; and I see no reason why I should now: till —"

"Till what? You delight in half phrases."

"Till I can't help it."

"Do you suppose I eat like an ogre, or a ghoul, that you dread being the companion of my repast?"

"I have formed no suppositions on the subject, sir: but I want to go on as usual for another month."

"You will give up your governessing slavery at once."

"Indeed! begging your pardon, sir, I shall not. I shall just go on with it as usual. I shall keep out of your way all day, as I have been accustomed to do: you may send for me in the evening, when you feel disposed to see me, and I'll come then; but at no other time."

"I want a smoke, Jane, or a pinch of snuff, to comfort me under all this, 'pour me donner une contenance,'[1] as Adèle would say; and unfortunately I have neither my cigar-case, nor my snuff-box. But listen – whisper – it is your time now, little tyrant, but it will be mine

---

1 "To restore my composure."

presently; and when once I have fairly seized you, to have and to hold, I'll just – figuratively speaking – attach you to a chain like this (touching his watch-guard). Yes, bonny wee thing, I'll wear you in my bosom, lest my jewel I should tyne."[1]

He said this as he helped me to alight from the carriage; and while he afterwards lifted out Adèle, I entered the house, and made good my retreat up stairs.

He duly summoned me to his presence in the evening. I had prepared an occupation for him; for I was determined not to spend the whole time in a *tête-à-tête* conversation: I remembered his fine voice; I knew he liked to sing – good singers generally do. I was no vocalist myself, and in his fastidious judgment, no musician, either; but I delighted in listening when the performance was good. No sooner had twilight, that hour of romance, begun to lower her blue and starry banner over the lattice, than I rose, opened the piano, and entreated him, for the love of heaven, to give me a song. He said I was a capricious witch, and that he would rather sing another time; but I averred that no time was like the present.

"Did I like his voice?" he asked.

"Very much." I was not fond of pampering that susceptible vanity of his; but for once, and from motives of expediency, I would e'en soothe and stimulate it.

"Then, Jane, you must play the accompaniment."

"Very well, sir, I will try."

I did try, but was presently swept off the stool and denominated, "a little bungler." Being pushed unceremoniously to one side – which was precisely what I wished – he usurped my place, and proceeded to accompany himself; for he could play as well as sing. I hied me to the window-recess; and while I sat there and looked out on the still trees and dim lawn, to a sweet air was sung in mellow tones, the following strain:-

> The truest love that ever heart
>   Felt at its kindled core
> Did through each vein, in quickened start,
>   The tide of being pour.

---

1 See the song "Bonnie Wee Thing" by Robert Burns (1759-96). To "tyne" something is to lose it.

Her coming was my hope each day,
    Her parting was my pain;
The chance that did her steps delay,
    Was ice in every vein.

I dreamed it would be nameless bliss,
    As I loved, loved to be;
And to this object did I press
    As blind as eagerly.

But wide as pathless was the space
    That lay, our lives, between,
And dangerous as the foamy race
    Of ocean-surges green.

And haunted as a robber-path
    Through wilderness or wood;
For Might and Right, and Woe and Wrath,
    Between our spirits stood.

I dangers dared; I hindrance scorned;
    I omens did defy:
Whatever menaced, harassed, warned,
    I passed impetuous by.

On sped my rainbow, fast as light;
    I flew as in a dream;
For glorious rose upon my sight
    That child of Shower and Gleam.

Still bright on clouds of suffering dim
    Shines that soft, solemn joy;
Nor care I now, how dense and grim
    Disasters gather nigh:

I care not in this moment sweet,
    Though all I have rushed o'er

Should come on pinion, strong and fleet,
    Proclaiming vengeance sore:

Though haughty Hate should strike me down,
    Right, bar approach to me,
And grinding Might, with furious frown,
    Swear endless enmity.

My Love has placed her little hand
    With noble faith in mine,
And vowed that wedlock's sacred band
    Our natures shall entwine.

My Love has sworn, with sealing kiss,
    With me to live – to die;
I have at last my nameless bliss:
    As I love – loved am I!

He rose and came towards me, and I saw his face all kindled, and his full falcon-eye flashing, and tenderness and passion in every lineament. I quailed momentarily – then I rallied. Soft scene, daring demonstration, I would not have; and I stood in peril of both: a weapon of defence must be prepared – I whetted my tongue: as he reached me, I asked with asperity, "whom he was going to marry now?"

"That was a strange question to be put by his darling Jane."

"Indeed! I considered it a very natural and necessary one: he had talked of his future wife dying with him. What did he mean by such a pagan idea? *I* had no intention of dying with him – he might depend on that."

"Oh, all he longed, all he prayed for, was that I might live with him! Death was not for such as I."

"Indeed it was: I had as good a right to die when my time came as he had: but I should bide that time, and not be hurried away in a suttee."[1]

---

1   The custom in which a Hindu widow immolates herself on her husband's funeral pyre.

"Would I forgive him for the selfish idea, and prove my pardon by a reconciling kiss?"

"No: I would rather be excused."

Here I heard myself apostrophized as a "hard little thing;" and it was added, "any other woman would have been melted to marrow at hearing such stanzas crooned in her praise."

I assured him I was naturally hard – very flinty, and that he would often find me so; and that, moreover, I was determined to show him divers rugged points in my character before the ensuing four weeks elapsed: he should know fully what sort of a bargain he had made, while there was yet time to rescind it.

"Would I be quiet, and talk rationally?"

"I would be quiet if he liked; and as to talking rationally, I flattered myself I was doing that now."

He fretted, pished and pshawed. "Very good," I thought; "you may fume and fidget as you please: but this is the best plan to pursue with you, I am certain. I like you more than I can say; but I'll not sink into a bathos of sentiment: and with this needle of repartee I'll keep you from the edge of the gulph too; and, moreover, maintain by its pungent aid that distance between you and myself most conducive to our real mutual advantage."

From less to more, I worked him up to considerable irritation; then, after he had retired, in dudgeon, quite to the other end of the room, I got up, and saying, "I wish you good-night, sir," in my natural and wonted respectful manner, I slipped out by the side-door and got away.

The system thus entered on, I pursued during the whole season of probation; and with the best success. He was kept, to be sure, rather cross and crusty: but on the whole I could see he was excellently entertained; and that a lamb-like submission and turtle-dove sensibility, while fostering his despotism more, would have pleased his judgment, satisfied his common-sense, and even suited his taste, less.

In other people's presence I was, as formerly, deferential and quiet; any other line of conduct being uncalled-for: it was only in the evening conferences I thus thwarted and afflicted him. He continued to send for me punctually the moment the clock struck seven; though when I appeared before him now, he had no such honeyed terms as "love" and "darling" on his lips: the best words at my service were "provoking puppet," "malicious elf," "sprite," "changeling," &c. For caresses too, I now got grimaces; for a pressure of the hand, a pinch on the arm: for a kiss on the cheek, a severe tweak of the ear. It was all right: at present I decidedly preferred these fierce favours to anything more tender. Mrs. Fairfax, I saw approved me: her anxiety on my account vanished; therefore I was certain I did well. Meantime, Mr. Rochester affirmed I was wearing him to skin and bone, and threatened awful vengeance for my present conduct at some period fast coming. I laughed in my sleeve at his menaces: "I can keep you in reasonable check now," I reflected; "and I don't doubt to be able to do it hereafter: if one expedient loses its virtue, another must be devised."

Yet after all my task was not an easy one: often I would rather have pleased than teased him. My future husband was becoming to me my whole world; and, more than the world: almost my hope of heaven. He stood between me and every thought of religion, as an eclipse intervenes between man and the broad sun. I could not, in those days, see God for his creature: of whom I had made an idol.

CHAPTER XXV

THE month of courtship had wasted: its very last hours were being numbered. There was no putting off the day that advanced – the bridal day; and all preparations for its arrival were complete. *I*, at least, had nothing more to do: there were my trunks, packed, locked, corded, ranged in a row along the wall of my little chamber; to-morrow, at this time, they would be far on their road to London: and so should I (D.V.),[1] – or rather, not I, but one Jane Rochester, a person whom as yet I knew not. The cards of address alone remained to nail on: they lay, four little squares, on the drawer. Mr. Rochester had himself written the direction, "Mrs. Rochester, —— Hotel, London," on each: I could not persuade myself to affix them, or to have them affixed. Mrs. Rochester! She did not exist: she would not be born till to-morrow, some time after eight o'clock a.m.; and I would wait to be assured she had come into the world alive, before I assigned to her all that property. It was enough that in yonder closet, opposite my dressing-table, garments said to be hers had already displaced my black stuff Lowood frock and straw bonnet: for not to me appertained that suit of wedding raiment; the pearl-coloured robe, the vapoury veil, pendent from the usurped portmanteau. I shut the closet, to conceal the strange, wraith-like apparel it contained; which, at this evening hour – nine o'clock – gave out certainly a most ghostly shimmer through the shadow of my apartment. "I will leave you by yourself, white dream," I said. "I am feverish: I hear the wind blowing; I will go out of doors and feel it."

It was not only the hurry of preparation that made me feverish; not only the anticipation of the great change – the new life which was to commence to-morrow: both these circumstances had their share, doubtless, in producing that restless, excited mood which hurried me forth at this late hour into the darkening grounds; but a third cause influenced my mind more than they.

I had at heart a strange and anxious thought. Something had happened which I could not comprehend; no one knew of or had seen the event but myself: it had taken place the preceding night. Mr. Rochester that night was absent from home; nor was he yet returned:

---

1 Latin: *Deo volente*: God willing.

business had called him to a small estate of two or three farms he possessed thirty miles off – business it was requisite he should settle in person, previous to his meditated departure from England. I waited now his return; eager to disburthen my mind, and to seek of him the solution of the enigma that perplexed me. Stay till he comes, reader; and, when I disclose my secret to him, you shall share the confidence.

I sought the orchard: driven to its shelter by the wind, which all day had blown strong and full from the south; without, however, bringing a speck of rain. Instead of subsiding as night drew on, it seemed to augment its rush and deepen its roar: the trees blew stedfastly one way, never writhing round, and scarcely tossing back their boughs once in an hour; so continuous was the strain bending their branchy heads northward – the clouds drifted from pole to pole, fast following, mass on mass: no glimpse of blue sky had been visible that July day.

It was not without a certain wild pleasure I ran before the wind, delivering my trouble of mind to the measureless air-torrent thundering through space. Descending the laurel-walk, I faced the wreck of the chestnut tree; it stood up, black and riven: the trunk, split down the centre, gaped ghastly. The cloven halves were not broken from each other, for the firm base and strong roots kept them unsundered below; though community of vitality was destroyed – the sap could flow no more: their great boughs on each side were dead, and next winter's tempests would be sure to fell one or both to earth: as yet, however, they might be said to form one tree – a ruin; but an entire ruin.

"You did right to hold fast to each other," I said: as if the monster-splinters were living things, and could hear me. "I think, scathed as you look, and charred and scorched, there must be a little sense of life in you yet; rising out of that adhesion at the faithful, honest roots: you will never have green leaves more – never more see birds making nests and singing idyls in your boughs; the time of pleasure and love is over with you; but you are not desolate: each of you has a comrade to sympathize with him in his decay." As I looked up at them, the moon appeared momentarily in that part of the sky which filled their fissure; her disk was blood-red and half overcast: she seemed to throw on me one bewildered, dreary glance, and buried herself again instantly in the deep drift of cloud. The wind fell, for a second, round

Thornfield; but far away, over wood and water, poured a wild, melancholy wail: it was sad to listen to, and I ran off again.

Here and there I strayed through the orchard, gathering up the apples with which the grass round the tree roots was thickly strown; then I employed myself in dividing the ripe from the unripe; I carried them into the house and put them away in the store-room. Then I repaired to the library to ascertain whether the fire was lit; for, though summer, I knew, on such a gloomy evening, Mr. Rochester would like to see a cheerful hearth when he came in: yes, the fire had been kindled some time, and burnt well. I placed his arm-chair by the chimney-corner: I wheeled the table near it: I let down the curtain, and had the candles brought in ready for lighting. More restless than ever, when I had completed these arrangements I could not sit still, nor even remain in the house: a little time-piece in the room and the old clock in the hall simultaneously struck ten.

"How late it grows!" I said: "I will run down to the gates: it is moonlight at intervals; I can see a good way on the road. He may be coming now, and to meet him will save some minutes of suspense."

The wind roared high in the great trees which embowered the gates; but the road as far as I could see, to the right hand and the left, was all still and solitary: save for the shadows of clouds crossing it at intervals, as the moon looked out, it was but a long pale line, unvaried by one moving speck.

A puerile tear dimmed my eye while I looked – a tear of disappointment and impatience: ashamed of it, I wiped it away. I lingered; the moon shut herself wholly within her chamber, and drew close her curtain of dense cloud: the night grew dark; rain came driving fast on the gale.

"I wish he would come! I wish he would come!" I exclaimed, seized with hypochondriac foreboding. I had expected his arrival before tea; now it was dark: what could keep him? Had an accident happened? The event of last night again recurred to me. I interpreted it as a warning of disaster. I feared my hopes were too bright to be realized; and I had enjoyed so much bliss lately that I imagined my fortune had passed its meridian, and must now decline.

"Well, I cannot return to the house," I thought; "I cannot sit by the fireside, while he is abroad in inclement weather: better tire my limbs than strain my heart; I will go forward and meet him."

I set out; I walked fast, but not far: ere I had measured a quarter of a mile, I heard the tramp of hoofs; a horseman came on, full gallop, a dog ran by his side. Away with evil presentiment! It was he: here he was, mounted on Mesrour, followed by Pilot. He saw me; for the moon had opened a blue field in the sky, and rode in it watery bright: he took his hat off and waved it round his head. I now ran to meet him.

"There!" he exclaimed, as he stretched out his hand and bent from the saddle: "You can't do without me, that is evident. Step on my boot-toe; give me both hands: mount!"

I obeyed; joy made me agile: I sprang up before him. A hearty kissing I got for a welcome: and some boastful triumph; which I swallowed as well as I could. He checked himself in his exultation to demand, "But is there anything the matter, Janet, that you come to meet me at such an hour? Is there anything wrong?"

"No; but I thought you would never come. I could not bear to wait in the house for you: especially with this rain and wind."

"Rain and wind indeed! Yes, you are dripping like a mermaid; pull my cloak round you: but I think you are feverish, Jane; both your cheek and hand are burning hot. I ask again, is there anything the matter?"

"Nothing, now: I am neither afraid nor unhappy."

"Then you have been both?"

"Rather: but I'll tell you all about it by-and-by, sir; and I daresay you will only laugh at me for my pains."

"I'll laugh at you heartily when to-morrow is past; till then I dare not: my prize is not certain. This is you; who have been as slippery as an eel this last month, and as thorny as a briar-rose? I could not lay a finger anywhere but I was pricked; and now I seem to have gathered up a stray lamb in my arms: you wandered out of the fold to seek your shepherd, did you, Jane?"

"I wanted you: but don't boast. Here we are at Thornfield: now let me get down."

He landed me on the pavement. As John took his horse, and he followed me into the hall, he told me to make haste and put something dry on, and then to return to him in the library; and he stopped me, as I made for the staircase, to extort a promise that I would not be long: nor was I long; in five minutes I rejoined him. I found him at supper.

"Take a seat, and bear me company, Jane: please God, it is the last meal but one you will eat at Thornfield Hall for a long time."

I sat down near him; but told him I could not eat.

"Is it because you have the prospect of a journey before you, Jane? Is it the thoughts of going to London that take away your appetite?"

"I cannot see my prospects clearly to-night, sir; and I hardly know what thoughts I have in my head. Everything in life seems unreal."

"Except me: I am substantial enough: – touch me."

"You, sir, are the most phantom-like of all: you are a mere dream."

He held out his hand, laughing: "Is that a dream?" said he, placing it close to my eyes. He had a rounded, muscular, and vigorous hand, as well as a long, strong arm.

"Yes; though I touch it, it is a dream," said I, as I put it down from before my face. "Sir, have you finished supper?"

"Yes, Jane."

I rang the bell, and ordered away the tray. When we were again alone, I stirred the fire, and then took a low seat at my master's knee.

"It is near midnight," I said.

"Yes: but remember, Jane, you promised to wake with me[1] the night before my wedding."

"I did; and I will keep my promise, for an hour or two at least: I have no wish to go to bed."

"Are all your arrangements complete?"

"All, sir."

"And on my part, likewise," he returned. "I have settled everything; and we shall leave Thornfield to-morrow, within half an hour after our return from church."

"Very well, sir."

"With what an extraordinary smile you uttered that word, – 'very well,' Jane! What a bright spot of colour you have on each cheek! and how strangely your eyes glitter! Are you well?"

"I believe I am."

"Believe! What is the matter? – Tell me what you feel."

"I could not, sir: no words could tell you what I feel. I wish this present hour would never end: who knows with what fate the next may come charged?"

---

1 Keep watch with me.

"This is hypochondria, Jane. You have been over excited, or over fatigued."

"Do you, sir, feel calm and happy?"

"Calm? – no: but happy, – to the heart's core."

I looked up at him to read the signs of bliss in his face: it was ardent and flushed.

"Give me your confidence, Jane," he said: "relieve your mind of any weight that oppresses it, by imparting it to me. What do you fear? – that I shall not prove a good husband?"

"It is the idea farthest from my thoughts."

"Are you apprehensive of the new sphere you are about to enter? – of the new life into which you are passing?"

"No."

"You puzzle me, Jane: your look and tone of sorrowful audacity perplex and pain me. I want an explanation."

"Then, sir, – listen. You were from home last night?"

"I was: I know that; and you hinted a while ago at something which had happened in my absence: – nothing, probably, of consequence; but, in short, it has disturbed you. Let me hear it. Mrs. Fairfax has said something, perhaps? or you have overheard the servants talk? – your sensitive self-respect has been wounded?"

"No, sir." It struck twelve – I waited till the time-piece had concluded its silver chime, and the clock its hoarse, vibrating stroke, and then I proceeded.

"All day, yesterday, I was very busy, and very happy in my ceaseless bustle; for I am not, as you seem to think, troubled by any haunting fears about the new sphere, et cetera: I think it a glorious thing to have the hope of living with you, because I love you. – No, sir, don't caress me now – let me talk undisturbed. Yesterday I trusted well in Providence, and believed that events were working together for your good and mine: it was a fine day, if you recollect – the calmness of the air and sky forbade apprehensions respecting your safety or comfort on your journey. I walked a little while on the pavement after tea, thinking of you; and I beheld you in imagination so near me, I scarcely missed your actual presence. I thought of the life that lay before me – *your* life, sir – an existence more expansive and stirring than my own: as much more so as the depths of the sea to which the brook runs, are than the shallows of its own strait channel. I wondered why moralists call this world a dreary wilderness: for me it blossomed like a rose.[1] Just at sunset, the air turned cold and the sky cloudy: I went in. Sophie called me up stairs to look at my wedding-dress, which they had just brought; and under it in the box I found your present, – the veil which, in your princely extravagance, you sent for from London: resolved, I suppose, since I would not have jewels, to cheat me into accepting something as costly. I smiled as I unfolded it, and devised how I would teaze you about your aristocratic tastes, and your efforts to masque your plebeian bride in the attributes of a peeress. I thought how I would carry down to you the square of unembroidered blonde[2] I had myself prepared as a covering for my low-born head, and ask if that was not good enough for a woman who could bring her husband neither fortune, beauty, nor connections. I saw plainly how you would look; and heard your impetuous republican answers, and your haughty disavowal of any necessity on your part to augment your wealth, or elevate your standing, by marrying either a purse or a coronet."

"How well you read me, you witch!" interposed Mr. Rochester: "but what did you find in the veil besides its embroidery? Did you find poison, or a dagger, that you look so mournful now?"

"No, no, sir; besides the delicacy and richness of the fabric, I found nothing save Fairfax Rochester's pride; and that did not scare me, because I am used to the sight of the demon. But, sir, as it grew dark, the wind rose: it blew yesterday evening, not as it blows now – wild and high – but 'with a sullen, moaning sound'[3] far more eerie. I wished you were at home. I came into this room, and the sight of the empty chair and fireless hearth chilled me. For some time after I went to bed, I could not sleep – a sense of anxious excitement distressed me. The gale, still rising, seemed to my ear to muffle a mournful under-sound; whether in the house or abroad I could not at first tell, but it recurred, doubtful yet doleful at every lull: at last I made out it must be some dog howling at a distance. I was glad when it ceased. On sleeping, I continued in dreams the idea of a dark and gusty night. I continued also the wish to be with you, and experienced a strange, regretful consciousness of some barrier dividing us. During all my first sleep, I was following the windings of an unknown road; total

---

1   See Isaiah 35:1.
2   A kind of lace made with unbleached silk.
3   *The Lay of the Last Minstrel*, I.xiii.1. by Sir Walter Scott (1771-1832).

obscurity environed me; rain pelted me; I was burdened with the charge of a little child: a very small creature, too young and feeble to walk, and which shivered in my cold arms, and wailed piteously in my ear. I thought, sir, that you were on the road a long way before me; and I strained every nerve to overtake you and made effort on effort to utter your name and entreat you to stop – but my movements were fettered; and my voice still died away inarticulate; while you, I felt, withdrew farther and farther every moment."

"And these dreams weigh on your spirits now, Jane, when I am close to you? Little nervous subject! Forget visionary woe, and think only of real happiness! You say you love me, Janet: yes – I will not forget that; and you cannot deny it. *Those* words did not die inarticulate on your lips. I heard them clear and soft: a thought too solemn perhaps, but sweet as music – 'I think it is a glorious thing to have the hope of living with you, Edward, because I love you.' – Do you love me, Jane? repeat it."

"I do, sir – I do, with my whole heart."

"Well," he said, after some minutes' silence, "it is strange: but that sentence has penetrated my breast painfully. Why? I think because you said it with such an earnest, religious energy; and because your upward gaze at me now is the very sublime of faith, truth, and devotion: it is too much as if some spirit were near me. Look wicked, Jane; as you know well how to look; coin one of your wild, shy, provoking smiles; tell me you hate me – teaze me, vex me; do anything but move me: I would rather be incensed than saddened."

"I will teaze you and vex you to your heart's content, when I have finished my tale: but hear me to the end."

"I thought, Jane, you had told me all. I thought I had found the source of your melancholy in a dream."

I shook my head. "What! is there more? But I will not believe it to be anything important. I warn you of incredulity beforehand. Go on."

The disquietude of his air, the somewhat apprehensive impatience of his manner, surprised me: but I proceeded.

"I dreamt another dream, sir: that Thornfield Hall was a dreary ruin, the retreat of bats and owls. I thought that of all the stately front nothing remained but a shell-like wall, very high and very fragile looking. I wandered, on a moonlight night, through the grass-grown enclosure within: here I stumbled over a marble hearth, and there over a fallen fragment of cornice. Wrapped up in a shawl, I still carried the unknown little child: I might not lay it down anywhere, however tired were my arms – however much its weight impeded my progress, I must retain it. I heard the gallop of a horse at a distance on the road: I was sure it was you; and you were departing for many years, and for a distant country. I climbed the thin wall with frantic perilous haste, eager to catch one glimpse of you from the top: the stones rolled from under my feet, the ivy branches I grasped gave way, the child clung round my neck in terror, and almost strangled me: at last I gained the summit. I saw you like a speck on a white track, lessening every moment. The blast blew so strong I could not stand. I sat down on the narrow ledge; I hushed the scared infant in my lap: you turned an angle of the road; I bent forward to take a last look; the wall crumbled; I was shaken; the child rolled from my knee; I lost my balance, fell, and woke."

"Now, Jane, that is all."

"All the preface, sir; the tale is yet to come. On waking, a gleam dazzled my eyes: I thought – oh, it is daylight! But I was mistaken: it was only candle-light. Sophie, I supposed, had come in. There was a light on the dressing-table, and the door of the closet, where, before going to bed, I had hung my wedding dress and veil, stood open: I heard a rustling there. I asked, 'Sophie, what are you doing?' No one answered: but a form emerged from the closet: it took the light, held it aloft and surveyed the garments pendent from the portmanteau. 'Sophie! Sophie!' I again cried: and still it was silent. I had risen up in bed, I bent forward: first, surprise, then bewilderment, came over me; and then my blood crept cold through my veins. Mr. Rochester, this was not Sophie, it was not Leah, it was not Mrs. Fairfax: it was not – no, I was sure of it, and am still – it was not even that strange woman, Grace Poole."

"It must have been one of them," interrupted my master.

"No, sir, I solemnly assure you to the contrary. The shape standing before me had never crossed my eyes within the precincts of Thornfield Hall before: the height, the contour were new to me."

"Describe it, Jane."

"It seemed, sir, a woman, tall and large, with thick and dark hair hanging long down her back. I know not what dress she had on: it was white and straight; but whether gown, sheet, or shroud, I cannot tell."

"Did you see her face?"

"Not at first. But presently she took my veil from its place; she held it up, gazed at it long, and then she threw it over her own head, and turned to the mirror. At that moment I saw the reflection of the visage and features quite distinctly in the dark oblong glass."

"And how were they?"

"Fearful and ghastly to me – oh, sir, I never saw a face like it! It was a discoloured face – it was a savage face. I wish I could forget the roll of the red eyes and the fearful blackened inflation of the lineaments!"

"Ghosts are usually pale, Jane."

"This, sir, was purple: the lips were swelled and dark; the brow furrowed; the black eye-brows wildly raised over the blood-shot eyes. Shall I tell you of what it reminded me?"

"You may."

"Of the foul German spectre – the Vampyre."[1]

"Ah! – What did it do?"

"Sir, it removed my veil from its gaunt head, rent it in two parts, and flinging both on the floor, trampled on them."

"Afterwards?"

"It drew aside the window-curtain and looked out: perhaps it saw dawn approaching, for, taking the candle, it retreated to the door. Just at my bedside, the figure stopped: the fiery eye glared upon me – she thrust up her candle close to my face, and extinguished it under my eyes. I was aware her lurid visage flamed over mine, and I lost consciousness: for the second time in my life – only the second time – I became insensible from terror."

"Who was with you when you revived?"

"No one, sir; but the broad day. I rose, bathed my head and face in water, drank a long draught; felt that though enfeebled I was not ill, and determined that to none but you would I impart this vision. Now, sir, tell me who and what that woman was?"

"The creature of an over-stimulated brain; that is certain. I must be careful of you, my treasure: nerves like yours were not made for rough handling."

---

1   "The Vampyre: A Tale by Lord Byron" first appeared in the *New Monthly Magazine* in 1819, and was an immediate success. Although based on a story begun by Byron, it was actually written by his one-time physician, John William Polidori (1795-1821).

"Sir, depend on it, my nerves were not in fault; the thing was real: the transaction actually took place."

"And your previous dreams: were they real too? Is Thornfield Hall a ruin? Am I severed from you by insuperable obstacles? Am I leaving you without a tear – without a kiss – without a word?"

"Not yet."

"Am I about to do it? – Why the day is already commenced which is to bind us indissolubly; and when we are once united, there shall be no recurrence of these mental terrors: I guarantee that."

"Mental terrors, sir! I wish I could believe them to be only such: I wish it more now than ever; since even you cannot explain to me the mystery of that awful visitant."

"And since I cannot do it, Jane, it must have been unreal."

"But, sir, when I said so to myself on rising this morning, and when I looked round the room to gather courage and comfort from the cheerful aspect of each familiar object in full day-light, there, – on the carpet – I saw what gave the distinct lie to my hypothesis, – the veil, torn from top to bottom in two halves!"

I felt Mr. Rochester start and shudder; he hastily flung his arms round me: "Thank God!" he exclaimed, "that if anything malignant did come near you last night, it was only the veil that was harmed. – Oh, to think what might have happened!"

He drew his breath short, and strained me so close to him I could scarcely pant. After some minutes' silence, he continued, cheerily: –

"Now, Janet, I'll explain to you all about it. It was half dream, half reality: a woman did, I doubt not, enter your room; and that woman was – must have been – Grace Poole. You call her a strange being yourself: from all you know, you have reason so to call her – what did she do to me? what to Mason? In a state between sleeping and waking, you noticed her entrance and her actions; but feverish, almost delirious as you were, you ascribed to her a goblin appearance different from her own: the long dishevelled hair, the swelled black face, the exaggerated stature, were figments of imagination, results of nightmare; the spiteful tearing of the veil was real: and it is like her. I see you would ask why I keep such a woman in my house: when we have been married a year and a day, I will tell you; but not now. Are you satisfied, Jane? Do you accept my solution of the mystery?"

I reflected, and in truth it appeared to me the only possible one:

satisfied I was not, but to please him I endeavoured to appear so – relieved, I certainly did feel; so I answered him with a contented smile. And now, as it was long past one, I prepared to leave him.

"Does not Sophie sleep with Adèle in the nursery?" he asked, as I lit my candle.

"Yes, sir."

"And there is room enough in Adèle's little bed for you. You must share it with her to-night, Jane: it is no wonder that the incident you have related should make you nervous, and I would rather you did not sleep alone: promise me to go to the nursery."

"I shall be very glad to do so, sir."

"And fasten the door securely on the inside. Wake Sophie when you go up stairs, under pretence of requesting her to rouse you in good time to-morrow; for you must be dressed and have finished breakfast before eight. And now, no more sombre thoughts: chase dull care away, Janet. Don't you hear to what soft whispers the wind has fallen? and there is no more beating of rain against the window-panes: look here – (he lifted up the curtain) it is a lovely night!"

It was. Half heaven was pure and stainless: the clouds, now troop-ing before the wind, which had shifted to the west, were filing off eastward in long, silvered columns. The moon shone peacefully.

"Well," said Mr. Rochester, gazing inquiringly into my eyes, "how is my Janet now?"

"The night is serene, sir; and so am I."

"And you will not dream of separation and sorrow to-night; but of happy love and blissful union."

This prediction was but half fulfilled: I did not indeed dream of sorrow, but as little did I dream of joy; for I never slept at all. With little Adèle in my arms, I watched the slumber of childhood – so tranquil, so passionless, so innocent – and waited for the coming day: all my life was awake and astir in my frame; and as soon as the sun rose, I rose too. I remember Adèle clung to me as I left her: I remem-ber I kissed her as I loosened her little hands from my neck; and I cried over her with strange emotion, and quitted her because I feared my sobs would break her still sound repose. She seemed the emblem of my past life; and he, I was now to array myself to meet, the dread, but adored, type of my unknown future day.

CHAPTER XXVI

Sophie came at seven to dress me; she was very long indeed in accomplishing her task: so long that Mr. Rochester, grown, I suppose, impatient of my delay, sent up to ask why I did not come. She was just fastening my veil (the plain square of blond after all) to my hair with a brooch; I hurried from under her hands as soon as I could.

"Stop!" she cried in French. "Look at yourself in the mirror: you have not taken one peep."

So I turned at the door: I saw a robed and veiled figure, so unlike my usual self that it seemed almost the image of a stranger. "Jane!" called a voice, and I hastened down. I was received at the foot of the stairs by Mr. Rochester.

"Lingerer," he said, "my brain is on fire with impatience; and you tarry so long!"

He took me into the dining-room, surveyed me keenly all over, pronounced me "fair as a lily, and not only the pride of his life, but the desire of his eyes," and then telling me he would give me but ten minutes to eat some breakfast, he rang the bell. One of his lately hired servants, a footman, answered it.

"Is John getting the carriage ready?"

"Yes, sir."

"Is the luggage brought down?"

"They are bringing it down now, sir."

"Go you to the church: see if Mr. Wood (the clergyman) and the clerk are there: return and tell me."

The church, as the reader knows, was but just beyond the gates; the footman soon returned.

"Mr. Wood is in the vestry, sir, putting on his surplice."

"And the carriage?"

"The horses are harnessing."

"We shall not want it to go to church; but it must be ready the moment we return: all the boxes and luggage arranged and strapped on, and the coachman in his seat."

"Yes, sir."

"Jane, are you ready?"

I rose. There were no groomsmen, no bridesmaids, no relatives to wait for or marshal: none but Mr. Rochester and I. Mrs. Fairfax stood in the hall as we passed. I would fain have spoken to her, but my hand was held by a grasp of iron: I was hurried along by a stride I could hardly follow; and to look at Mr. Rochester's face was to feel that not a second of delay would be tolerated for any purpose. I wonder what other bridegroom ever looked as he did – so bent up to a purpose, so grimly resolute; or who, under such steadfast brows, ever revealed such flaming and flashing eyes.

I know not whether the day was fair or foul; in descending the drive, I gazed neither on sky nor earth: my heart was with my eyes; and both seemed migrated into Mr. Rochester's frame. I wanted to see the invisible thing on which, as we went along, he appeared to fasten a glance fierce and fell. I wanted to feel the thoughts whose force he seemed breasting and resisting.

At the churchyard wicket he stopped: he discovered I was quite out of breath. "Am I cruel in my love?" he said. "Delay an instant: lean on me, Jane."

And now I can recall the picture of the gray old house of God rising calm before me, of a rook wheeling round the steeple, of a ruddy morning sky beyond. I remember something, too, of the green grave-mounds; and I have not forgotten, either, two figures of strangers, straying amongst the low hillocks, and reading the mementoes graven on the few mossy head-stones. I noticed them, because, as they saw us, they passed round to the back of the church; and I doubted not they were going to enter by the side-aisle door, and witness the ceremony. By Mr. Rochester they were not observed; he was earnestly looking at my face, from which the blood had, I daresay, momentarily fled: for I felt my forehead dewy, and my cheeks and lips cold. When I rallied, which I soon did, he walked gently with me up the path to the porch.

We entered the quiet and humble temple; the priest waited in his white surplice at the lowly altar, the clerk beside him. All was still: two shadows only moved in a remote corner. My conjecture had been correct: the strangers had slipped in before us, and they now stood by the vault of the Rochesters, their backs towards us, viewing through the rails the old, time-stained marble tomb, where a kneeling angel guarded the remains of Damer de Rochester, slain at Marston

Moor[1] in the time of the civil wars; and of Elizabeth, his wife.

Our place was taken at the communion-rails. Hearing a cautious step behind me, I glanced over my shoulder: one of the strangers – a gentleman, evidently – was advancing up the chancel. The service began. The explanation of the intent of matrimony was gone through; and then the clergyman came a step further forward, and bending slightly towards Mr. Rochester, went on.

"I require and charge you both (as ye will answer at the dreadful day of judgment, when the secrets of all hearts shall be disclosed) that if either of you know any impediment why ye may not lawfully be joined together in matrimony, ye do now confess it; for be ye well assured that so many as are coupled together otherwise than God's Word doth allow, are not joined together by God, neither is their matrimony lawful."

He paused, as the custom is. When is the pause after that sentence ever broken by reply? Not, perhaps, once in a hundred years. And the clergyman, who had not lifted his eyes from his book, and had held his breath but for a moment, was proceeding: his hand was already stretched towards Mr. Rochester, as his lips unclosed to ask, "Wilt thou have this woman for thy wedded wife?" – when a distinct and near voice said: –

"The marriage cannot go on: I declare the existence of an impediment."

The clergyman looked up at the speaker, and stood mute; the clerk did the same; Mr. Rochester moved slightly, as if an earthquake had rolled under his feet: taking a firmer footing, and not turning his head or eyes, he said, "Proceed."

Profound silence fell when he had uttered that word, with deep but low intonation. Presently Mr. Wood said: –

"I cannot proceed without some investigation into what has been asserted, and evidence of its truth or falsehood."

"The ceremony is quite broken off," subjoined the voice behind us. "I am in a condition to prove my allegation: an insuperable impediment to this marriage exists."

---

1   Site of a major battle between Royalist and Parliamentary troops on July 2, 1644. The resulting Royalist defeat led to the fall of York and the collapse of Charles I's support in northern England.

Mr. Rochester heard, but heeded not: he stood stubborn and rigid: making no movement, but to possess himself of my hand. What a hot and strong grasp he had! – and how like quarried marble was his pale, firm, massive front at this moment! How his eye shone, still – watchful, and yet wild beneath!

Mr. Wood seemed at a loss. "What is the nature of the impediment?" he asked. "Perhaps it may be got over – explained away?"

"Hardly," was the answer: "I have called it insuperable, and I speak advisedly."

The speaker came forwards, and leaned on the rails. He continued, uttering each word distinctly, calmly, steadily, but not loudly.

"It simply consists in the existence of a previous marriage: Mr. Rochester has a wife now living."

My nerves vibrated to these low-spoken words as they had never vibrated to thunder – my blood felt their subtle violence as it had never felt frost or fire: but I was collected, and in no danger of swooning. I looked at Mr. Rochester: I made him look at me. His whole face was colourless rock: his eye was both spark and flint. He disavowed nothing: he seemed as if he would defy all things. Without speaking; without smiling; without seeming to recognise in me a human being, he only twined my waist with his arm, and riveted me to his side.

"Who are you?" he asked of the intruder.

"My name is Briggs – a solicitor of —street, London."

"And you would thrust on me a wife?"

"I would remind you of your lady's existence, sir: which the law recognises, if you do not."

"Favour me with an account of her – with her name, her parentage, her place of abode."

"Certainly." Mr. Briggs calmly took a paper from his pocket, and read out in a sort of official, nasal voice: –

"'I affirm and can prove that on the 20th of October, A.D. —, (a date of fifteen years back) Edward Fairfax Rochester of Thornfield Hall, in the county of —, and of Ferndean Manor, in —shire, England, was married to my sister, Bertha Antoinetta Mason, daughter of Jonas Mason, merchant, and of Antoinetta his wife, a Creole – at —— church, Spanish-town, Jamaica. The record of the marriage will be found in the register of that church – a copy of it is now in my possession. Signed, Richard Mason.'"

"That – if a genuine document – may prove I have been married, but it does not prove that the woman mentioned therein as my wife is still living."

"She was living three months ago," returned the lawyer.

"How do you know?"

"I have a witness to the fact; whose testimony even you, sir, will scarcely controvert."

"Produce him – or go to hell."

"I will produce him first – he is on the spot: Mr. Mason, have the goodness to step forward."

Mr. Rochester on hearing the name set his teeth; he experienced, too, a sort of strong convulsive quiver: near to him as I was, I felt the spasmodic movement of fury or despair run through his frame. The second stranger, who had hitherto lingered in the background, now drew near; a pale face looked over the solicitor's shoulder – yes, it was Mason himself. Mr. Rochester turned and glared at him. His eye, as I have often said, was a black eye: it had now a tawny, nay a bloody light in its gloom; and his face flushed – olive cheek and hueless forehead received a glow, as from spreading, ascending heart-fire; and he stirred, lifted his strong arm – he could have struck Mason – dashed him on the church-floor – shocked by ruthless blow the breath from his body – but Mason shrank away, and cried faintly, "Good God!" Contempt fell cool on Mr. Rochester – his passion died as if a blight had shrivelled it up: he only asked, "What have *you* to say?"

An inaudible reply escaped Mason's white lips.

"The devil is in it if you cannot answer distinctly. I again demand, what have *you* to say?"

"Sir – sir –" interrupted the clergyman, "do not forget you are in a sacred place." Then addressing Mason, he inquired gently, "Are you aware, sir, whether or not this gentleman's wife is still living?"

"Courage," urged the lawyer, – "speak out."

"She is now living at Thornfield Hall;" said Mason, in more articulate tones: "I saw her there last April. I am her brother."

"At Thornfield Hall!" ejaculated the clergyman. "Impossible! I am an old resident in this neighbourhood, sir, and I never heard of a Mrs. Rochester at Thornfield Hall."

I saw a grim smile contort Mr. Rochester's lip and he muttered: –

"No – by God! I took care that none should hear of it – or of her under that name." He mused – for ten minutes he held counsel with himself: he formed his resolve, and announced it: –

"Enough – all shall bolt out at once, like the bullet from the barrel. – Wood, close your book and take off your surplice; John Green, (to the clerk) leave the church: there will be no wedding to-day:" the man obeyed.

Mr. Rochester continued, hardily and recklessly: "Bigamy is an ugly word! – I meant, however, to be a bigamist: but fate has out-manœuvred me; or Providence has checked me, – perhaps the last. I am little better than a devil at this moment; and, as my pastor there would tell me, deserve no doubt the sternest judgments of God, – even to the quenchless fire and deathless worm.[1] Gentlemen, my plan is broken up! – what this lawyer and his client say is true: I have been married; and the woman to whom I was married lives! You say you never heard of a Mrs. Rochester at the house up yonder, Wood: but I daresay you have many a time inclined your ear to gossip about the mysterious lunatic kept there under watch and ward. Some have whispered to you that she is my bastard half-sister; some, my cast-off mistress; – I now inform you that she is my wife, whom I married fifteen years ago, – Bertha Mason by name; sister of this resolute personage, who is now, with his quivering limbs and white cheeks, showing you what a stout heart men may bear. Cheer up, Dick! – never fear me! – I'd almost as soon strike a woman as you. Bertha Mason is mad; and she came of a mad family: – idiots and maniacs through three generations! Her mother, the Creole, was both a mad woman and a drunkard! – as I found out after I had wed the daughter: for they were silent on family secrets before. Bertha, like a dutiful child, copied her parent in both points. I had a charming partner – pure, wise, modest: you can fancy that I was a happy man. – I went through rich scenes! Oh! my experience has been heavenly, if you only knew it! But I owe you no further explanation. Briggs, Wood, Mason, – I invite you all to come up to the house and visit Mrs. Poole's patient, and *my wife!* – You shall see what sort of a being I was cheated into espousing, and judge whether or not I had a right

1 See Isaiah 66:24.

to break the compact, and seek sympathy with something at least human. This girl," he continued, looking at me, "knew no more than you, Wood, of the disgusting secret: she thought all was fair and legal; and never dreamt she was going to be entrapped into a feigned union with a defrauded wretch, already bound to a bad, mad, and embruted partner! Come, all of you, follow!"

Still holding me fast, he left the church: the three gentlemen came after. At the front door of the hall we found the carriage.

"Take it back to the coach-house, John," said Mr. Rochester, coolly; "it will not be wanted to-day."

At our entrance, Mrs. Fairfax, Adèle, Sophie, Leah, advanced to meet and greet us.

"To the right about – every soul!" cried the master: "away with your congratulations! Who wants them? – Not I! – they are fifteen years too late!"

He passed on and ascended the stairs, still holding my hand, and still beckoning the gentlemen to follow him; which they did. We mounted the first staircase, passed up the gallery, proceeded to the third story: the low, black door, opened by Mr. Rochester's master key, admitted us to the tapestried room, with its great bed, and its pictorial cabinet.

"You know this place, Mason," said our guide; "she bit and stabbed you here."

He lifted the hangings from the wall, uncovering the second door: this, too, he opened. In a room without a window, there burnt a fire, guarded by a high and strong fender, and a lamp suspended from the ceiling by a chain. Grace Poole bent over the fire, apparently cooking something in a saucepan. In the deep shade, at the further end of the room, a figure ran backwards and forwards. What it was, whether beast or human being, one could not, at first sight, tell: it grovelled, seemingly, on all fours; it snatched and growled like some strange wild animal: but it was covered with clothing; and a quantity of dark, grizzled hair, wild as a mane, hid its head and face.

"Good-morrow, Mrs. Poole!" said Mr. Rochester. "How are you? and how is your charge to-day?"

"We're tolerable, sir, I thank you," replied Grace, lifting the boiling mess carefully on to the hob:[1] "rather snappish, but not 'rageous."

---

1 A side-shelf to a fireplace, usually level with the top of the grate

A fierce cry seemed to give the lie to her favourable report: the clothed hyena rose up, and stood tall on its hind feet.

"Ah, sir, she sees you!" exclaimed Grace: "you'd better not stay."

"Only a few moments, Grace: you must allow me a few moments."

"Take care then, sir! – for God's sake, take care!"

The maniac bellowed: she parted her shaggy locks from her visage, and gazed wildly at her visitors. I recognised well that purple face, – those bloated features. Mrs. Poole advanced.

"Keep out of the way," said Mr. Rochester, thrusting her aside: "she has no knife now, I suppose? and I'm on my guard."

"One never knows what she has, sir; she is so cunning: it is not in mortal discretion to fathom her craft."

"We had better leave her," whispered Mason.

"Go to the devil!" was his brother-in-law's recommendation.

"'Ware!" cried Grace. The three gentlemen retreated simultaneously. Mr. Rochester flung me behind him; the lunatic sprang and grappled his throat viciously, and laid her teeth to his cheek: they struggled. She was a big woman, in stature almost equalling her husband, and corpulent besides: she showed virile force in the contest – more than once she almost throttled him, athletic as he was. He could have settled her with a well-planted blow; but he would not strike: he would only wrestle. At last he mastered her arms; Grace Poole gave him a cord, and he pinioned them behind her: with more rope, which was at hand, he bound her to a chair. The operation was performed amidst the fiercest yells, and the most convulsive plunges. Mr. Rochester then turned to the spectators: he looked at them with a smile both acrid and desolate.

"That is *my wife*," said he. "Such is the sole conjugal embrace I am ever to know – such are the endearments which are to solace my leisure hours! And *this* is what I wished to have (laying his hand on my shoulder): this young girl, who stands so grave and quiet at the mouth of hell, looking collectedly at the gambols of a demon. I wanted her just as a change after that fierce ragout.[1] Wood and Briggs, look at the difference! Compare these clear eyes with the red balls yonder – this face with that mask – this form with that bulk;

---

1   A highly-seasoned meat and vegetable stew.

then judge me, priest of the Gospel and man of the law, and remember, with what judgment ye judge ye shall be judged![1] Off with you now. I must shut up my prize."

We all withdrew. Mr. Rochester stayed a moment behind us, to give some further order to Grace Poole. The solicitor addressed me as we descended the stair.

"You, madam," said he, "are cleared from all blame: your uncle will be glad to hear it – if, indeed, he should be still living – when Mr. Mason returns to Madeira."

"My uncle! What of him? Do you know him?"

"Mr. Mason does: Mr. Eyre has been the Funchal[2] correspondent of his house for some years. When your uncle received your letter intimating the contemplated union between yourself and Mr. Rochester, Mr. Mason, who was staying at Madeira to recruit his health, on his way back to Jamaica, happened to be with him. Mr. Eyre mentioned the intelligence; for he knew that my client here was acquainted with a gentleman of the name of Rochester. Mr. Mason, astonished and distressed, as you may suppose, revealed the real state of matters. Your uncle, I am sorry to say, is now on a sickbed; from which, considering the nature of his disease – decline – and the stage it has reached, it is unlikely he will ever rise. He could not then hasten to England himself, to extricate you from the snare into which you had fallen, but he implored Mr. Mason to lose no time in taking steps to prevent the false marriage. He referred him to me for assistance. I used all despatch, and am thankful I was not too late: as you, doubtless, must be also. Were I not morally certain that your uncle will be dead ere you reach Madeira, I would advise you to accompany Mr. Mason back: but as it is, I think you had better remain in England till you can hear further, either from or of Mr. Eyre. Have we anything else to stay for?" he inquired of Mr. Mason.

"No, no – let us be gone," was the anxious reply; and without waiting to take leave of Mr. Rochester, they made their exit at the hall door. The clergyman stayed to exchange a few sentences, either of admonition or reproof, with his haughty parishioner: this duty done, he too departed.

I heard him go as I stood at the half open door of my own room, to which I had now withdrawn. The house cleared, I shut myself

---

1 Matthew 7:1.
2 The capital of Madeira.

in, fastened the bolt that none might intrude, and proceeded – not to weep, not to mourn, I was yet too calm for that, but – mechanically to take off the wedding dress, and replace it by the stuff gown I had worn yesterday, as I thought, for the last time. I then sat down: I felt weak and tired. I leaned my arms on a table, and my head dropped on them. And now I thought: till now I had only heard, seen, moved – followed up and down where I was led or dragged – watched event rush on event, disclosure open beyond disclosure: but *now, I thought.*

The morning had been a quiet morning enough – all except the brief scene with the lunatic: the transaction in the church had not been noisy; there was no explosion of passion, no loud altercation, no dispute, no defiance or challenge, no tears, no sobs: a few words had been spoken, a calmly pronounced objection to the marriage made; some stern, short questions put by Mr. Rochester; answers, explanations given, evidence adduced; an open admission of the truth had been uttered by my master; then the living proof had been seen; the intruders were gone, and all was over.

I was in my own room as usual – just myself, without obvious change: nothing had smitten me, or scathed me, or maimed me. And yet, where was the Jane Eyre of yesterday? – where was her life? – where were her prospects?

Jane Eyre, who had been an ardent, expectant woman – almost a bride – was a cold, solitary girl again: her life was pale; her prospects were desolate. A Christmas frost had come at midsummer: a white December storm had whirled over June; ice glazed the ripe apples, drifts crushed the blowing roses; on hay-field and corn-field lay a frozen shroud: lanes which last night blushed full of flowers, to-day were pathless with untrodden snow; and the woods, which twelve hours since waved leafy and fragrant as groves between the tropics, now spread, waste, wild, and white as pine-forests in wintry Norway. My hopes were all dead – struck with a subtle doom, such as, in one night, fell on all the first-born in the land of Egypt.[1] I looked on my cherished wishes, yesterday so blooming and glowing; they lay stark, chill, livid – corpses that could never revive. I looked at my love: that feeling which was my master's – which he had created; it shivered in my heart, like a suffering child in a cold cradle; sickness and anguish

---

1   See Exodus 12:12 and 12:29.

had seized it: it could not seek Mr. Rochester's arms – it could not derive warmth from his breast. Oh, never more could it turn to him; for faith was blighted – confidence destroyed! Mr. Rochester was not to me what he had been; for he was not what I had thought him. I would not ascribe vice to him; I would not say he had betrayed me: but the attribute of stainless truth was gone from his idea; and from his presence I must go: *that* I perceived well. When – how – whither, I could not yet discern: but he himself, I doubted not, would hurry me from Thornfield. Real affection, it seemed, he could not have for me; it had been only fitful passion: that was balked; he would want me no more. I should fear even to cross his path now: my view must be hateful to him. Oh, how blind had been my eyes! How weak my conduct!

My eyes were covered and closed: eddying darkness seemed to swim round me, and reflection came in as black and confused a flow. Self-abandoned, relaxed and effortless, I seemed to have laid me down in the dried-up bed of a great river; I heard a flood loosened in remote mountains, and felt the torrent come: to rise I had no will, to flee I had no strength. I lay faint; longing to be dead. One idea only still throbbed life-like within me – a remembrance of God: it begot an unuttered prayer: these words went wandering up and down in my rayless mind, as something that should be whispered; but no energy was found to express them: –

"Be not far from me, for trouble is near: there is none to help."[2]

It was near: and as I had lifted no petition to heaven to avert it – as I had neither joined my hands, nor bent my knees, nor moved my lips – it came: in full, heavy swing the torrent poured over me. The whole consciousness of my life lorn, my love lost, my hope quenched, my faith death-struck, swayed full and mighty above me in one sullen mass. That bitter hour cannot be described: in truth, "the waters came into my soul; I sank in deep mire: I felt no standing; I came into deep waters; the floods overflowed me."[2]

END OF VOLUME II.

---

1   Psalms 22:11.
2   See Psalms 69:1-2.

VOLUME III

CHAPTER XXVII

SOME time in the afternoon I raised my head, and looking round and seeing the western sun gilding the sign of its decline on the wall, I asked, "What am I to do?"

But the answer my mind gave – "Leave Thornfield at once" – was so prompt, so dread, that I stopped my ears: I said, I could not bear such words now. "That I am not Edward Rochester's bride, is the least part of my woe," I alleged: "that I have wakened out of most glorious dreams, and found them all void and vain, is a horror I could bear and master; but that I must leave him decidedly, instantly, entirely, is intolerable. I cannot do it."

But, then, a voice within me averred that I could do it; and foretold that I should do it. I wrestled with my own resolution: I wanted to be weak that I might avoid the awful passage of further suffering I saw laid out for me; and conscience, turned tyrant, held passion by the throat, told her, tauntingly, she had yet but dipped her dainty foot in the slough, and swore that with that arm of iron, he would thrust her down to unsounded depths of agony.

"Let me be torn away, then!" I cried. "Let another help me!"

"No; you shall tear yourself away; none shall help you: you shall, yourself, pluck out your right eye; yourself cut off your right hand:[1] your heart shall be the victim; and you, the priest, to transfix it."

I rose up suddenly, terror-struck at the solitude which so ruthless a judge haunted, – at the silence which so awful a voice filled. My head swam as I stood erect: I perceived that I was sickening from excitement and inanition; neither meat nor drink had passed my lips that day, for I had taken no breakfast. And, with a strange pang, I now reflected that, long as I had been shut up here, no message had been sent to ask how I was, or to invite me to come down: not even little Adèle had tapped at the door; not even Mrs. Fairfax had sought me. "Friends always forget those whom fortune forsakes,"[2] I murmured, as I undrew the bolt and passed out. I stumbled over an obstacle: my head was still dizzy, my sight was dim and my limbs were feeble. I could not soon recover myself; I fell, but not on to the ground: an

---

1   See Matthew 5:27-30.
2   Proverbial.

out-stretched arm caught me; I looked up – I was supported by Mr. Rochester, who sat in a chair across my chamber threshold.

"You come out at last," he said. "Well, I have been waiting for you long, and listening; yet not one movement have I heard, nor one sob: five minutes more of that death-like hush, and I should have forced the lock like a burglar. So, you shun me? – you shut yourself up and grieve alone? I would rather you had come and upbraided me with vehemence. You are passionate: I expected a scene of some kind. I was prepared for the hot rain of tears; only I wanted them to be shed on my breast: now a senseless floor has received them, or your drenched handkerchief. But I err: you have not wept at all! I see a white cheek and a faded eye, but no trace of tears. I suppose, then, your heart has been weeping blood?

"Well, Jane; not a word of reproach? Nothing bitter – nothing poignant? Nothing to cut a feeling or sting a passion? You sit quietly where I have placed you, and regard me with a weary, passive look.

"Jane, I never meant to wound you thus. If the man who had but one little ewe lamb that was dear to him as a daughter, that ate of his bread and drank of his cup, and lay in his bosom,[1] had by some mistake slaughtered it at the shambles, he would not have rued his bloody blunder more than I now rue mine. Will you ever forgive me?"

Reader! – I forgave him at the moment, and on the spot. There was such deep remorse in his eye, such true pity in his tone, such manly energy in his manner; and, besides, there was such unchanged love in his whole look and mien – I forgave him all: yet not in words, not outwardly; only at my heart's core.

"You know I am a scoundrel, Jane?" ere long he inquired wistfully – wondering, I suppose, at my continued silence and tameness; the result rather of weakness than of will.

"Yes, sir."

"Then tell me so roundly and sharply – don't spare me."

"I cannot: I am tired and sick. I want some water." He heaved a sort of shuddering sigh, and taking me in his arms, carried me down stairs. At first I did not know to what room he had borne me; all was cloudy to my glazed sight: presently I felt the reviving warmth of a

---

1   See 2 Samuel 12:3.

fire; for, summer as it was, I had become icy cold in my chamber. He put wine to my lips; I tasted it and revived; then I ate something he offered me, and was soon myself. I was in the library — sitting in his chair — he was quite near. "If I could go out of life now, without too sharp a pang, it would be well for me," I thought; "then I should not have to make the effort of cracking my heart-strings in rending them from among Mr. Rochester's. I must leave him, it appears. I do not want to leave him — I cannot leave him."

"How are you now, Jane?"

"Much better, sir: I shall be well soon."

"Taste the wine again, Jane."

I obeyed him; then he put the glass on the table, stood before me, and looked at me attentively. Suddenly he turned away, with an inarticulate exclamation, full of passionate emotion of some kind: he walked fast through the room and came back; he stooped towards me as if to kiss me: but I remembered caresses were now forbidden. I turned my face away, and put his aside.

"What! — How is this?" he exclaimed hastily. "Oh, I know! you won't kiss the husband of Bertha Mason? You consider my arms filled, and my embraces appropriated?"

"At any rate, there is neither room nor claim for me, sir."

"Why, Jane? I will spare you the trouble of much talking: I will answer for you — because I have a wife already, you would reply. — I guess rightly?"

"Yes."

"If you think so, you must have a strange opinion of me; you must regard me as a plotting profligate — a base and low rake who has been simulating disinterested love[1] in order to draw you into a snare deliberately laid, and strip you of honour, and rob you of self-respect. What do you say to that? I see you can say nothing: in the first place, you are faint, still, and have enough to do to draw your breath; in the second place, you cannot yet accustom yourself to accuse and revile me; and, besides, the flood-gates of tears are opened, and they would rush out if you spoke much; and you have no desire to expostulate, to upbraid, to make a scene: you are thinking how *to act — talking*, you consider, is

---

1   i.e., a love not to his social advantage. Rochester worries that Jane will see his declarations and proposal to a governess as coldly premeditated acts of seduction.

of no use. I know you – I am on my guard."

"Sir, I do not wish to act against you," I said; and my unsteady voice warned me to curtail my sentence.

"Not in *your* sense of the word – but in *mine*, you are scheming to destroy me. You have as good as said that I am a married man – as a married man you will shun me, keep out of my way: just now you have refused to kiss me. You intend to make yourself a complete stranger to me; to live under this roof only as Adèle's governess: if ever I say a friendly word to you, if ever a friendly feeling inclines you again to me, you will say, – 'That man had nearly made me his mistress: I must be ice and rock to him;' and ice and rock you will accordingly become."

I cleared and steadied my voice to reply: "All is changed about me, sir; I must change too – there is no doubt of that; and, to avoid fluctuations of feeling, and continual combats with recollections and associations, there is only one way – Adèle must have a new governess, sir."

"Oh, Adèle will go to school – I have settled that already: nor do I mean to torment you with the hideous associations and recollections of Thornfield Hall – this accursed place – this tent of Achan[1] – this insolent vault, offering the ghastliness of living death to the light of the open sky – this narrow stone hell, with its one real fiend, worse than a legion of such as we imagine. – Jane, you shall not stay here, nor will I. I was wrong ever to bring you to Thornfield Hall, knowing as I did how it was haunted. I charged them to conceal from you, before I ever saw you, all knowledge of the curse of the place; merely because I feared Adèle never would have a governess to stay if she knew with what inmate she was housed, and my plans would not permit me to remove the maniac elsewhere – though I possess an old house, Ferndean Manor, even more retired and hidden than this, where I could have lodged her safely enough, had not a scruple about the unhealthiness of the situation, in the heart of a wood, made my conscience recoil from the arrangement. Probably those damp walls would soon have eased me of her charge: but to each villain his own vice; and mine is not a tendency to indirect assassination, even of what I most hate.

---

1   See Joshua 7:19-26.

"Concealing the mad-woman's neighbourhood from you, however, was something like covering a child with a cloak, and laying it down near a upas-tree:[1] that demon's vicinage is poisoned, and always was. But I'll shut up Thornfield Hall: I'll nail up the front door, and board the lower windows; I'll give Mrs. Poole two hundred a year to live here with *my wife,* as you term that fearful hag: Grace will do much for money, and she shall have her son, the keeper at Grimsby Retreat, to bear her company and be at hand to give her aid in the paroxysms, when *my wife* is prompted by her familiar to burn people in their beds at night, to stab them, to bite their flesh from their bones, and so on." –

"Sir," I interrupted him, "you are inexorable for that unfortunate lady: you speak of her with hate – with vindictive antipathy. It is cruel – she cannot help being mad."

"Jane, my little darling, (so I will call you, for so you are), you don't know what you are talking about; you misjudge me again: it is not because she is mad I hate her. If you were mad, do you think I should hate you?"

"I do indeed, sir."

"Then you are mistaken, and you know nothing about me, and nothing about the sort of love of which I am capable. Every atom of your flesh is as dear to me as my own: in pain and sickness it would still be dear. Your mind is my treasure, and if it were broken, it would be my treasure still: if you raved, my arms should confine you, and not a strait waistcoat – your grasp, even in fury, would have a charm for me: if you flew at me as wildly as that woman did this morning, I should receive you in an embrace, at least as fond as it would be restrictive. I should not shrink from you with disgust as I did from her: in your quiet moments you should have no watcher and no nurse but me; and I could hang over you with untiring tenderness, though you gave me no smile in return; and never weary of gazing into your eyes, though they had no longer a ray of recognition for me. – But why do I follow that train of ideas? I was talking of removing you from Thornfield. All, you know, is prepared for prompt departure:

---

1   A Javanese tree whose sap was used to poison arrowheads. The belief in England that the tree was so lethal that it killed plant and animal life for miles around can be traced to a 1783 story in the *London Magazine.*

to-morrow you shall go. I only ask you to endure one more night under this roof, Jane; and then, farewell to its miseries and terrors for ever! I have a place to repair to which will be a secure sanctuary from hateful reminiscences, from unwelcome intrusion – even from falsehood and slander."

"And take Adèle with you, sir," I interrupted; "she will be a companion for you."

"What do you mean, Jane? I told you I would send Adèle to school: and what do I want with a child for a companion? and not my own child, – a French dancer's bastard? Why do you importune me about her? I say, why do you assign Adèle to me for a companion?"

"You spoke of a retirement, sir; and retirement and solitude are dull: too dull for you."

"Solitude! Solitude!" he reiterated, with irritation. "I see I must come to an explanation. I don't know what sphynx-like expression is forming in your countenance. *You* are to share my solitude. Do you understand?"

I shook my head: it required a degree of courage, excited as he was becoming, even to risk that mute sign of dissent. He had been walking fast about the room, and he stopped, as if suddenly rooted to one spot. He looked at me long and hard: I turned my eyes from him, fixed them on the fire, and tried to assume and maintain a quiet, collected aspect.

"Now for the hitch in Jane's character," he said at last, speaking more calmly than from his look I had expected him to speak. "The reel of silk has run smoothly enough so far; but I always knew there would come a knot and a puzzle: here it is. Now for vexation, and exasperation, and endless trouble! By God! I long to exert a fraction of Samson's strength, and break the entanglement like tow!"[1]

He recommenced his walk: but soon again stopped, and this time just before me.

"Jane! will you hear reason?" (he stooped and approached his lips to my ear) "because, if you won't, I'll try violence." His voice was hoarse; his look that of a man who is just about to burst an insufferable bond and plunge headlong into wild licence. I saw that in

---

1   See Judges 16:6–9.

another moment, and with one impetus of frenzy more, I should be able to do nothing with him. The present – the passing second of time – was all I had in which to control and restrain him: a movement of repulsion, flight, fear, would have sealed my doom – and his. But I was not afraid: not in the least. I felt an inward power; a sense of influence, which supported me. The crisis was perilous; but not without its charm: such as the Indian, perhaps, feels when he slips over the rapid in his canoe. I took hold of his clenched hand; loosened the contorted fingers; and said to him, soothingly, –

"Sit down; I'll talk to you as long as you like, and hear all you have to say, whether reasonable or unreasonable."

He sat down: but he did not get leave to speak directly. I had been struggling with tears for some time: I had taken great pains to repress them, because I knew he would not like to see me weep. Now, however, I considered it well to let them flow as freely and as long as they liked. If the flood annoyed him, so much the better. So I gave way, and cried heartily.

Soon I heard him earnestly entreating me to be composed. I said I could not while he was in such a passion.

"But I am not angry, Jane: I only love you too well; and you had steeled your little pale face with such a resolute, frozen look, I could not endure it. Hush, now, and wipe your eyes."

His softened voice announced that he was subdued; so I, in my turn, became calm. Now he made an effort to rest his head on my shoulder: but I would not permit it. Then he would draw me to him: no.

"Jane! Jane!" he said – in such an accent of bitter sadness, it thrilled along every nerve I had; "you don't love me, then? It was only my station, and the rank of my wife, that you valued? Now that you think me disqualified to become your husband, you recoil from my touch as if I were some toad or ape."

These words cut me: yet what could I do or say? I ought probably to have done or said nothing: but I was so tortured by a sense of remorse at thus hurting his feelings, I could not control the wish to drop balm where I had wounded.

"I *do* love you," I said, "more than ever: but I must not show or indulge the feeling; and this is the last time I must express it."

"The last time, Jane! What! do you think you can live with me, and see me daily, and yet, if you still love me, be always cold and distant?"

"No, sir; that I am certain I could not; and therefore I see there is but one way: but you will be furious if I mention it."

"Oh, mention it! If I storm, you have the art of weeping."

"Mr. Rochester, I must leave you."

"For how long, Jane? For a few minutes, while you smooth your hair – which is somewhat dishevelled; and bathe your face – which looks feverish?"

"I must leave Adèle and Thornfield. I must part with you for my whole life: I must begin a new existence amongst strange faces and strange scenes."

"Of course: I told you you should. I pass over the madness about parting from me. You mean you must become a part of me. As to the new existence, it is all right; you shall yet be my wife: I am not married. You shall be Mrs. Rochester – both virtually and nominally. I shall keep only to you so long as you and I live. You shall go to a place I have in the south of France: a white-walled villa on the shores of the Mediterranean. There you shall live a happy, and guarded, and most innocent life. Never fear that I wish to lure you into error – to make you my mistress. Why did you shake your head? Jane, you must be reasonable; or in truth I shall again become frantic."

His voice and hand quivered; his large nostrils dilated; his eye blazed: still, I dared to speak: –

"Sir, your wife is living: that is a fact acknowledged this morning by yourself. If I lived with you as you desire, I should then be your mistress: to say otherwise is sophistical – is false."

"Jane, I am not a gentle-tempered man – you forget that: I am not long-enduring; I am not cool and dispassionate. Out of pity to me and yourself, put your finger on my pulse, feel how it throbs, and – beware!"

He bared his wrist, and offered it to me: the blood was forsaking his cheek and lips, they were growing livid; I was distressed on all hands. To agitate him thus deeply, by a resistance he so abhorred, was cruel: to yield was out of the question. I did what human beings do instinctively when they are driven to utter extremity – looked for aid to one higher than man: the words "God help me!" burst involuntarily from my lips.

"I am a fool!" cried Mr. Rochester, suddenly. "I keep telling her I am not married, and do not explain to her why. I forget she knows nothing of the character of that woman, or of the circumstances attending my infernal union with her. Oh, I am certain Jane will agree with me in opinion, when she knows all that I know! Just put your hand in mine, Janet – that I may have the evidence of touch as well as sight, to prove you are near me – and I will in a few words show you the real state of the case. Can you listen to me?"

"Yes, sir: for hours if you will."

"I ask only minutes. Jane, did you ever hear, or know, that I was not the eldest son of my house: that I had once a brother older than I?"

"I remember Mrs. Fairfax told me so once."

"And did you ever hear that my father was an avaricious, grasping man?"

"I have understood something to that effect."

"Well, Jane, being so, it was his resolution to keep the property together; he could not bear the idea of dividing his estate and leaving me a fair portion: all, he resolved, should go to my brother, Rowland. Yet as little could he endure that a son of his should be a poor man. I must be provided for by a wealthy marriage. He sought me a partner betimes. Mr. Mason, a West India planter and merchant, was his old acquaintance. He was certain his possessions were real and vast: he made inquiries. Mr. Mason, he found, had a son and daughter; and he learned from him that he could and would give the latter a fortune of thirty-thousand pounds: that sufficed. When I left college, I was sent out to Jamaica, to espouse a bride already courted for me. My father said nothing about her money; but he told me Miss Mason was the boast of Spanish Town for her beauty: and this was no lie. I found her a fine woman, in the style of Blanche Ingram; tall, dark, and majestic. Her family wished to secure me, because I was of a good race; and so did she. They showed her to me in parties, splendidly dressed. I seldom saw her alone, and had very little private conversation with her. She flattered me, and lavishly displayed for my pleasure her charms and accomplishments. All the men in her circle seemed to admire her and envy me. I was dazzled, stimulated: my senses were excited; and being ignorant, raw, and inexperienced, I thought I loved her. There is no folly so besotted that the idiotic rivalries of society, the prurience,

the rashness, the blindness of youth, will not hurry a man to its commission. Her relatives encouraged me; competitors piqued me; she
allured me: a marriage was achieved almost before I knew where I
was. Oh – I have no respect for myself when I think of that act! – an
agony of inward contempt masters me. I never loved, I never
esteemed, I did not even know her. I was not sure of the existence of
one virtue in her nature: I had marked neither modesty, nor benevolence, nor candour, nor refinement in her mind or manners – and, I
married her: – gross, grovelling, mole-eyed blockhead that I was!
With less sin I might have – but let me remember to whom I am
speaking.

"My bride's mother I had never seen: I understood she was dead.
The honey-moon over, I learned my mistake: she was only mad; and
shut up in a lunatic asylum. There was a younger brother, too; a complete dumb idiot. The elder one, whom you have seen (and whom I
cannot hate, whilst I abhor all his kindred, because he has some grains
of affection in his feeble mind; shown in the continued interest he
takes in his wretched sister, and also in a dog-like attachment he once
bore me), will probably be in the same state one day. My father, and
my brother Rowland, knew all this; but they thought only of the thirty thousand pounds, and joined in the plot against me.

"These were vile discoveries; but, except for the treachery of concealment, I should have made them no subject of reproach to my
wife: even when I found her nature wholly alien to mine; her tastes
obnoxious to me; her cast of mind common, low, narrow, and singularly incapable of being led to anything higher, expanded to anything
larger – when I found that I could not pass a single evening, nor even
a single hour of the day with her in comfort; that kindly conversation
could not be sustained between us, because, whatever topic I started,
immediately received from her a turn at once coarse and trite,
perverse and imbecile – when I perceived that I should never have
a quiet or settled household, because no servant would bear the continued outbreaks of her violent and unreasonable temper, or the
vexations of her absurd, contradictory, exacting orders – even then
I restrained myself: I eschewed upbraiding, I curtailed remonstrance; I
tried to devour my repentance and disgust in secret; I repressed the
deep antipathy I felt.

"Jane, I will not trouble you with abominable details: some strong words shall express what I have to say. I lived with that woman up-stairs four years, and before that time she had tried me indeed: her character ripened and developed with frightful rapidity; her vices sprung up fast and rank: they were so strong, only cruelty could check them; and I would not use cruelty. What a pigmy intellect she had – and what giant propensities! How fearful were the curses those propensities entailed on me! Bertha Mason, – the true daughter of an infamous mother, – dragged me through all the hideous and degrad-ing agonies which must attend a man bound to a wife at once intem-perate and unchaste.

"My brother in the interval was dead; and at the end of the four years my father died too. I was rich enough now – yet poor to hideous indigence: a nature the most gross, impure, depraved I ever saw, was associated with mine, and called by the law and by society a part of me. And I could not rid myself of it by any legal proceedings; for the doctors now discovered that *my wife* was mad – her excesses had prematurely developed the germs of insanity: – Jane, you don't like my narrative; you look almost sick – shall I defer the rest to another day?"

"No, sir, finish it now; I pity you – I do earnestly pity you."

"Pity, Jane, from some people, is a noxious and insulting sort of tribute, which one is justified in hurling back in the teeth of those who offer it: but that is the sort of pity native to callous, selfish hearts: it is a hybrid; egotistical pain at hearing of woes, crossed with igno-rant contempt for those who have endured them. But that is not your pity, Jane: it is not the feeling of which your whole face is full at this moment – with which your eyes are now almost overflowing – with which your heart is heaving – with which your hand is trembling in mine. Your pity, my darling, is the suffering mother of love: its anguish is the very natal pang of the divine passion. I accept it, Jane: let the daughter have free advent – my arms wait to receive her."

"Now, sir, proceed: what did you do when you found she was mad?"

"Jane – I approached the verge of despair: a remnant of self-respect was all that intervened between me and the gulf. In the eyes of the world I was doubtless covered with grimy dishonour: but I resolved to be clean in my own sight – and to the last I repudiated the contamination of her crimes, and wrenched myself from connexion with her mental defects. Still, society associated my name and person with hers; I yet saw her and heard her daily: something of her breath (faugh!) mixed with the air I breathed; and, besides, I remembered I had once been her husband – that recollection was then, and is now, inexpressibly odious to me: moreover, I knew that while she lived I could never be the husband of another and better wife; and, though five years my senior, (her family and my father had lied to me even in the particular of her age), she was likely to live as long as I, being as robust in frame as she was infirm in mind. Thus, at the age of twenty-six, I was hopeless.

"One night I had been awakened by her yells – (since the medical men had pronounced her mad, she had of course been shut up) – it was a fiery West-Indian night; one of the description that frequently precede the hurricanes of those climates: being unable to sleep in bed, I got up and opened the window. The air was like sulphur-steams – I could find no refreshment anywhere. Mosquitoes came buzzing in and hummed sullenly round the room; the sea, which I could hear from thence, rumbled dull like an earthquake – black clouds were casting up over it; the moon was setting in the waves, broad and red, like a hot cannon-ball – she threw her last bloody glance over a world quivering with the ferment of tempest. I was physically influenced by the atmosphere and scene, and my ears were filled with the curses the maniac still shrieked out; wherein she momentarily mingled my name with such a tone of demon-hate, with such language! – no professed harlot ever had a fouler vocabulary than she: though two rooms off, I heard every word – the thin partitions of the West-India house opposing but slight obstruction to her wolfish cries.

"'This life,' said I at last, 'is hell! this is the air – those are the sounds of the bottomless pit! I have a right to deliver myself from it if I can. The sufferings of this mortal state will leave me with the heavy flesh that now cumbers my soul. Of the fanatic's burning eternity I have no fear: there is not a future state worse than this present one – let me break away, and go home to God!'

"I said this while I knelt down at, and unlocked a trunk which contained a brace of loaded pistols: I meant to shoot myself. I only entertained the intention for a moment; for, not being insane, the crisis of exquisite and unalloyed despair which had originated the wish and design of self-destruction, was past in a second.

"A wind fresh from Europe blew over the ocean and rushed through the open casement: the storm broke, streamed, thundered, blazed, and the air grew pure. I then framed and fixed a resolution. While I walked under the dripping orange-trees of my wet garden, and amongst its drenched pomegranates and pine-apples, and while the refulgent dawn of the tropics kindled round me – I reasoned thus, Jane: – and now listen; for it was true Wisdom that consoled me in that hour, and showed me the right path to follow.

"The sweet wind from Europe was still whispering in the refreshed leaves, and the Atlantic was thundering in glorious liberty: my heart, dried up and scorched for a long time, swelled to the tone, and filled with living blood – my being longed for renewal – my soul thirsted for a pure draught. I saw Hope revive – and felt Regeneration possible. From a flowery arch at the bottom of my garden I gazed over the sea – bluer than the sky: the old world was beyond; clear prospects opened, thus: –

"'Go,' said Hope, 'and live again in Europe: there it is not known what a sullied name you bear, nor what a filthy burden is bound to you. You may take the maniac with you to England; confine her with due attendance and precautions at Thornfield: then travel yourself to what clime you will, and form what new tie you like. That woman, who has so abused your long-suffering – so sullied your name; so outraged your honour; so blighted your youth – is not your wife; nor are you her husband. See that she is cared for as her condition demands, and you have done all that God and humanity require of you. Let her identity, her connection with yourself, be buried in oblivion: you are bound to impart them to no living being. Place her in safety and comfort: shelter her degradation with secrecy, and leave her.'

"I acted precisely on this suggestion. My father and brother had not made my marriage known to their acquaintance; because, in the very first letter I wrote to apprise them of the union – having already begun to experience extreme disgust of its consequences; and from the family character and constitution, seeing a hideous future opening to me – I added an urgent charge to keep it secret: and very soon, the infamous conduct of the wife my father had selected for me, was such as to make him blush to own her as his daughter-in-law. Far from desiring to publish the connection, he became as anxious to conceal it as myself.

"To England, then, I conveyed her: a fearful voyage I had with such a monster in the vessel. Glad was I when I at last got her to Thornfield, and saw her safely lodged in that third story room, of whose secret inner cabinet she has now for ten years made a wild beast's den – a goblin's cell. I had some trouble in finding an attendant for her; as it was necessary to select one on whose fidelity dependence could be placed; for her ravings would inevitably betray my secret: besides, she had lucid intervals of days – sometimes weeks – which she filled up with abuse of me. At last I hired Grace Poole, from the Grimsby Retreat. She and the surgeon, Carter (who dressed Mason's wounds that night he was stabbed and worried), are the only two I have ever admitted to my confidence. Mrs. Fairfax may indeed have suspected something; but she could have gained no precise knowledge as to facts. Grace has, on the whole, proved a good keeper: though, owing partly to a fault of her own, of which it appears nothing can cure her, and which is incident to her harassing profession,[1] her vigilance has been more than once lulled and baffled. The lunatic is both cunning and malignant; she has never failed to take advantage of her guardian's temporary lapses; once to secrete the knife with which she stabbed her brother, and twice to possess herself of the key of her cell, and issue therefrom in the night-time. On the first of these occasions, she perpetrated the attempt to burn me in my bed: on the second she paid that ghastly visit to you. I thank Providence, who watched over you, that she then spent her fury on your wedding apparel; which perhaps brought back vague reminiscences of her own bridal days: but on what might have happened, I cannot endure to reflect. When I think of the thing which flew at my throat this morning, hanging its black and scarlet visage over the nest of my dove, my blood curdles —."

---

1 Grace's "fault" is her tendency to drink too heavily, as we are told more specifically later. This was a characteristic often attributed to both private and public nurses in the nineteenth century.

"And what, sir," I asked, while he paused, "did you do when you had settled her here? Where did you go?"

"What did I do, Jane? I transformed myself into a Will-o'-the-wisp. Where did I go? I pursued wanderings as wild as those of the Marsh-spirit. I sought the Continent, and went devious through all its lands.[1] My fixed desire was to seek and find a good and intelligent woman, whom I could love: a contrast to the fury I left at Thornfield —."

"But you could not marry, sir."

"I had determined and was convinced that I could and ought. It was not my original intention to deceive, as I have deceived you. I meant to tell my tale plainly, and make my proposals openly: and it appeared to me so absolutely rational that I should be considered free to love and be loved, I never doubted some woman might be found willing and able to understand my case and accept me, in spite of the curse with which I was burdened."

"Well, sir?"

"When you are inquisitive, Jane, you always make me smile. You open your eyes like an eager bird, and make every now and then a restless movement; as if answers in speech did not flow fast enough for you, and you wanted to read the tablet of one's heart. But before I go on, tell me what you mean by your 'Well, sir?' It is a small phrase very frequent with you; and which many a time has drawn me on and on through interminable talk: I don't very well know why."

"I mean, – What next? How did you proceed? What came of such an event?"

"Precisely: and what do you wish to know now?"

"Whether you found any one you liked: whether you asked her to marry you; and what she said."

"I can tell you whether I found any one I liked, and whether I asked her to marry me: but what she said is yet to be recorded in the book of Fate. For ten long years I roved about, living first in one capital, then another: sometimes in St. Petersburg; oftener in Paris; occasionally in Rome, Naples, and Florence. Provided with plenty of money, and the passport of an old name, I could choose my own

---

1   Rochester's dark secret and his wanderings through Europe clearly associate him with the Byronic hero so attractive to the Brontës.

society: no circles were closed against me. I sought my ideal of a woman amongst English ladies, French comtesses, Italian signoras, and German Gräfinnen. I could not find her. Sometimes, for a fleeting moment, I thought I caught a glance, heard a tone, beheld a form, which announced the realization of my dream: but I was presently undeceived. You are not to suppose that I desired perfection, either of mind or person. I longed only for what suited me – for the antipodes of the Creole: and I longed vainly. Amongst them all I found not one, whom, had I been ever so free, I – warned as I was of the risks, the horrors, the loathings of incongruous unions – would have asked to marry me. Disappointment made me reckless. I tried dissipation – never debauchery: that I hated, and hate. That was my Indian Messalina's[1] attribute: rooted disgust at it and her restrained me much, even in pleasure. Any enjoyment that bordered on riot seemed to approach me to her and her vices, and I eschewed it.

"Yet I could not live alone: so I tried the companionship of mistresses. The first I chose was Céline Varens – another of those steps which make a man spurn himself when he recalls them. You already know what she was, and how my liaison with her terminated. She had two successors: an Italian, Giacinta, and a German, Clara; both considered singularly handsome. What was their beauty to me in a few weeks? Giacinta was unprincipled and violent: I tired of her in three months. Clara was honest and quiet; but heavy, mindless, unimpressible: not one whit to my taste. I was glad to give her a sufficient sum to set her up in a good line of business, and so get decently rid of her. But, Jane, I see by your face you are not forming a very favourable opinion of me just now. You think me an unfeeling, loose-principled rake: don't you?"

"I don't like you so well as I have done sometimes, indeed, sir. Did it not seem to you in the least wrong to live in that way: first with one mistress and then another? You talk of it as a mere matter of course."

"It was with me; and I did not like it. It was a grovelling fashion of existence: I should never wish to return to it. Hiring a mistress is the

---

1   Valeria Messalina (?25-48 CE) was the wife of the Roman emperor Claudius (10 BCE-54 CE). She became infamous for her lust and infidelity; in her husband's absence she publicly married one of her lovers, and after this affront Claudius had her executed.

next worse thing to buying a slave: both are often by nature, and always by position, inferior; and to live familiarly with inferiors is degrading. I now hate the recollection of the time I passed with Céline, Giacinta, and Clara."

I felt the truth of these words; and I drew from them the certain inference, that if I were so far to forget myself and all the teaching that had ever been instilled into me, as – under any pretext – with any justification – through any temptation – to become the successor of these poor girls, he would one day regard me with the same feeling which now in his mind desecrated their memory. I did not give utterance to this conviction: it was enough to feel it. I impressed it on my heart, that it might remain there to serve me as aid in the time of trial.

"Now, Jane, why don't you say 'Well, sir?' I have not done. You are looking grave. You disapprove of me still, I see. But let me come to the point. Last January, rid of all mistresses – in a harsh, bitter frame of mind, the result of a useless, roving, lonely life – corroded with disappointment, sourly disposed against all man- and especially against all *woman*kind (for I began to regard the notion of an intellectual, faithful, loving woman as a mere dream), recalled by business, I came back to England.

"On a frosty winter afternoon, I rode in sight of Thornfield Hall. Abhorred spot! I expected no peace – no pleasure there. On a stile in Hay-lane I saw a quiet little figure sitting by itself. I passed it as negligently as I did the pollard willow opposite to it: I had no presentiment of what it would be to me; no inward warning that the arbitress of my life – my genius for good or evil – waited there in humble guise. I did not know it, even when, on the occasion of Mesrour's accident, it came up and gravely offered me help. Childish and slender creature! It seemed as if a linnet had hopped to my foot and proposed to bear me on its tiny wing. I was surly; but the thing would not go: it stood by me with strange perseverance, and looked and spoke with a sort of authority. I must be aided, and by that hand: and aided I was.

"When once I had pressed the frail shoulder, something new – a fresh sap and sense – stole into my frame. It was well I had learnt that this elf must return to me – that it belonged to my house down below – or I could not have felt it pass away from under my hand, and seen it vanish behind the dim hedge, without singular regret. I heard you come home that night, Jane: though probably you were not aware that I thought of you, or watched for you. The next day I observed you – myself unseen – for half an hour, while you played with Adèle in the gallery. It was a snowy day, I recollect, and you could not go out of doors. I was in my room; the door was ajar: I could both listen and watch. Adèle claimed your outward attention for a while; yet I fancied your thoughts were elsewhere: but you were very patient with her, my little Jane; you talked to her and amused her a long time. When at last she left you, you lapsed at once into deep reverie: you betook yourself slowly to pace the gallery. Now and then, in passing a casement, you glanced out at the thick-falling snow; you listened to the sobbing wind, and again you paced gently on, and dreamed. I think those day-visions were not dark: there was a pleasurable illumination in your eye occasionally, a soft excitement in your aspect, which told of no bitter, bilious, hypochondriac brooding: your look revealed rather the sweet musings of youth, when its spirit follows on willing wings the flight of Hope, up and on to an ideal heaven. The voice of Mrs. Fairfax speaking to a servant in the hall wakened you: and how curiously you smiled to and at yourself, Janet! There was much sense in your smile: it was very shrewd, and seemed to make light of your own abstraction. It seemed to say – 'My fine visions are all very well, but I must not forget they are absolutely unreal. I have a rosy sky, and a green flowery Eden in my brain; but without, I am perfectly aware, lies at my feet a rough track to travel, and around me gather black tempests to encounter.' You ran downstairs and demanded of Mrs. Fairfax some occupation: the weekly house-accounts to make up, or something of that sort, I think it was. I was vexed with you for getting out of my sight.

"Impatiently I waited for evening, when I might summon you to my presence. An unusual – to me – a perfectly new character I suspected was yours: I desired to search it deeper, and know it better. You entered the room with a look and air at once shy and independent; you were quaintly dressed – much as you are now. I made you talk: ere long I found you full of strange contrasts. Your garb and manner were restricted by rule; your air was often diffident, and altogether that of one refined by nature, but absolutely unused to society, and a good deal afraid of making herself disadvantageously conspicuous by some solecism or blunder; yet, when addressed, you lifted a keen, a daring, and a glowing eye to your interlocutor's face: there was penetration and power in each glance you gave; when plied by close questions, you found ready and round answers. Very soon you seemed to get used to me – I believe you felt the existence of sympathy between you and your grim and cross master, Jane; for it was astonishing to see how quickly a certain pleasant ease tranquillized your manner: snarl as I would, you showed no surprise, fear, annoyance, or displeasure at my moroseness; you watched me, and now and then smiled at me with a simple yet sagacious grace I cannot describe. I was at once content and stimulated with what I saw: I liked what I had seen, and wished to see more. Yet, for a long time, I treated you distantly, and sought your company rarely. I was an intellectual epicure, and wished to prolong the gratification of making this novel and piquant acquaintance: besides, I was for a while troubled with a haunting fear that if I handled the flower freely its bloom would fade – the sweet charm of freshness would leave it. I did not then know that it was no transitory blossom; but rather the radiant resemblance of one, cut in an indestructible gem. Moreover, I wished to see whether you would seek me if I shunned you – but you did not; you kept in the school-room as still as your own desk and easel: if by chance I met you, you passed me as soon, and with as little token of recognition, as was consistent with respect. Your habitual expression in those days, Jane, was a thoughtful look: not despondent, for you were not sickly; but not buoyant, for you had little hope, and no actual pleasure. I wondered what you thought of me – or if you ever thought of me: to find this out, I resumed my notice of you. There was something glad in your glance, and genial in your manner, when you conversed: I saw you had a social heart; it was the silent school-room – it was the tedium of your life that made you mournful. I permitted myself the delight of being kind to you; kindness stirred emotion soon: your face became soft in expression, your tones gentle; I liked my name pronounced by your lips in a grateful, happy accent. I used to enjoy a chance meeting with you, Jane, at this time: there was a curious hesitation in your manner; you glanced at me with a slight trouble – a hovering doubt: you did not know what my caprice might be – whether I was going to play the master and be stern, or the friend, and be benignant. I was now too fond of you often to simulate the first whim; and, when I stretched my hand out cordially, such bloom and light and bliss rose to your young, wistful features, I had much ado often to avoid straining you then and there to my heart."

"Don't talk any more of those days, sir," I interrupted, furtively dashing away some tears from my eyes: his language was torture to me; for I knew what I must do – and do soon – and these reminiscences, and these revelations of his feelings, only made my work more difficult.

"No, Jane," he returned: "what necessity is there to dwell on the Past, when the Present is so much surer – the Future so much brighter?"

I shuddered to hear the infatuated assertion.

"You see now how the case stands – do you not?" he continued. "After a youth and manhood, passed half in unutterable misery and half in dreary solitude, I have for the first time found what I can truly love – I have found *you*. You are my sympathy – my better self – my good angel – I am bound to you with a strong attachment. I think you good, gifted, lovely: a fervent, a solemn passion is conceived in my heart; it leans to you, draws you to my centre and spring of life, wraps my existence about you – and, kindling in pure, powerful flame, fuses you and me in one.

"It was because I felt and knew this, that I resolved to marry you. To tell me that I had already a wife is empty mockery: you know now that I had but a hideous demon. I was wrong to attempt to deceive you; but I feared a stubbornness that exists in your character. I feared early instilled prejudice: I wanted to have you safe before hazarding confidences. This was cowardly: I should have appealed to your nobleness and magnanimity at first, as I do now – opened to you plainly my life of agony – described to you my hunger and thirst after a higher and worthier existence – shown to you, not my *resolution* (that word is weak) but my resistless *bent* to love faithfully and well, where I am faithfully and well loved in return. Then I should have asked you to accept my pledge of fidelity, and to give me yours: Jane – give it me now."

A pause.

"Why are you silent, Jane?"

I was experiencing an ordeal: a hand of fiery iron grasped my vitals. Terrible moment: full of struggle, blackness, burning! Not a human being that ever lived could wish to be loved better than I was loved; and him who thus loved me I absolutely worshipped: and I must renounce love and idol. One drear word comprised my intolerable duty – "Depart!"

"Jane, you understand what I want of you? Just this promise – 'I will be yours, Mr. Rochester.'"

"Mr. Rochester, I will *not* be yours."

Another long silence.

"Jane!" recommenced he, with a gentleness that broke me down with grief, and turned me stone-cold with ominous terror – for this still voice was the pant of a lion rising – "Jane, do you mean to go one way in the world, and to let me go another?"

"I do."

"Jane," (bending towards and embracing me) "do you mean it now?"

"I do."

"And now?" softly kissing my forehead and cheek.

"I do –" extricating myself from restraint rapidly and completely.

"Oh, Jane, this is bitter! This – this is wicked. It would not be wicked to love me."

"It would to obey you."

A wild look raised his brows – crossed his features: he rose; but he forbore yet. I laid my hand on the back of a chair for support: I shook, I feared – but I resolved.

"One instant, Jane. Give one glance to my horrible life when you are gone. All happiness will be torn away with you. What then is left? For a wife I have but the maniac up-stairs: as well might you refer me to some corpse in yonder churchyard. What shall I do, Jane? Where turn for a companion, and for some hope?"

"Do as I do: trust in God and yourself. Believe in heaven. Hope to meet again there."

"Then you will not yield?"

"No."

"Then you condemn me to live wretched, and to die accursed?" His voice rose.

"I advise you to live sinless; and I wish you to die tranquil."

"Then you snatch love and innocence from me? You fling me back on lust for a passion – vice for an occupation?"

"Mr. Rochester, I no more assign this fate to you than I grasp at it for myself. We were born to strive and endure – you as well as I: do so. You will forget me before I forget you."

"You make me a liar by such language: you sully my honour. I declared I could not change: you tell me to my face I shall change soon. And what a distortion in your judgment, what a perversity in your ideas, is proved by your conduct! Is it better to drive a fellow-creature to despair than to transgress a mere human law – no man being injured by the breach? for you have neither relatives nor acquaintances whom you need fear to offend by living with me."

This was true: and while he spoke my very Conscience and Reason turned traitors against me, and charged me with crime in resisting him. They spoke almost as loud as Feeling: and that clamoured wildly. "Oh, comply!" it said. "Think of his misery; think of his danger – look at his state when left alone: remember his head-long nature; consider the recklessness following on despair – soothe him; save him; love him: tell him you love him and will be his. Who in the world cares for *you*? or who will be injured by what you do?"

Still indomitable was the reply – "*I* care for myself. The more solitary, the more friendless, the more unsustained I am, the more I will respect myself. I will keep the law given by God; sanctioned by man. I will hold to the principles received by me when I was sane, and not mad – as I am now. Laws and principles are not for the times when there is no temptation: they are for such moments as this, when body and soul rise in mutiny against their rigour: stringent are they; inviolate they shall be. If at my individual convenience I might break them, what would be their worth? They have a worth – so I have always believed; and if I cannot believe it now, it is because I am insane – quite insane: with my veins running fire, and my heart beating faster than I can count its throbs. Preconceived opinions, foregone determinations, are all I have at this hour to stand by: there I plant my foot."

I did. Mr. Rochester, reading my countenance, saw I had done so. His fury was wrought to the highest: he must yield to it for a moment, whatever followed; he crossed the floor and seized my arm, and grasped my waist. He seemed to devour me with his flaming glance: physically, I felt, at the moment, powerless as stubble exposed to the draught and glow of a furnace – mentally, I still possessed my soul, and with it the certainty of ultimate safety. The soul, fortunately, has an interpreter – often an unconscious, but still a truthful interpreter – in the eye. My eye rose to his; and while I looked in his fierce face, I gave an involuntary sigh: his gripe was painful, and my overtasked strength almost exhausted.

"Never," said he, as he ground his teeth, "never was anything at once so frail and so indomitable. A mere reed she feels in my hand! (and he shook me with the force of his hold.) I could bend her with my finger and thumb: and what good would it do if I bent, if I uptore, if I crushed her? Consider that eye: consider the resolute, wild, free thing looking out of it, defying me, with more than courage – with a stern triumph. Whatever I do with its cage, I cannot get at it – the savage, beautiful creature! If I tear, if I rend the slight prison, my outrage will only let the captive loose. Conqueror I might be of the house; but the inmate would escape to heaven before I could call myself possessor of its clay dwelling-place. And it is you, spirit – with will and energy, and virtue and purity – that I want: not alone your brittle frame. Of yourself, you could come with soft flight and nestle against my heart, if you would: seized against your will, you will elude the grasp like an essence – you will vanish ere I inhale your fragrance. Oh! come, Jane, come!"

As he said this, he released me from his clutch, and only looked at me. The look was far worse to resist than the frantic strain: only an idiot, however, would have succumbed now. I had dared and baffled his fury; I must elude his sorrow: I retired to the door.

"You are going, Jane?"

"I am going, sir."

"You are leaving me?"

"Yes."

"You will not come? – You will not be my comforter, my rescuer? – My deep love, my wild woe, my frantic prayer, are all nothing to you?"

What unutterable pathos was in his voice! How hard it was to reiterate firmly, "I am going."

"Jane!"

"Mr. Rochester."

"Withdraw, then – I consent – but remember, you leave me here in anguish. Go up to your own room; think over all I have said, and, Jane, cast a glance on my sufferings – think of me."

He turned away; he threw himself on his face on the sofa. "Oh, Jane! my hope – my love – my life!" broke in anguish from his lips. Then came a deep, strong sob.

I had already gained the door: but, reader, I walked back – walked back as determinedly as I had retreated. I knelt down by him; I turned his face from the cushion to me; I kissed his cheek; I smoothed his hair with my hand.

"God bless you, my dear master," I said. "God keep you from harm and wrong – direct you, solace you – reward you well for your past kindness to me."

"Little Jane's love would have been my best reward," he answered: "without it, my heart is broken. But Jane will give me her love: yes – nobly, generously."

Up the blood rushed to his face; forth flashed the fire from his eyes; erect he sprang: he held his arms out; but I evaded the embrace, and at once quitted the room.

"Farewell!" was the cry of my heart, as I left him. Despair added, – "Farewell for ever!"

* * * * * *

That night I never thought to sleep: but a slumber fell on me as soon as I lay down in bed. I was transported in thought to the scenes of childhood: I dreamt I lay in the red-room at Gateshead; that the night was dark, and my mind impressed with strange fears. The light that long ago had struck me into syncope,[1] recalled in this vision, seemed glidingly to mount the wall, and tremblingly to pause in the centre of the obscured ceiling. I lifted up my head to look: the roof resolved to clouds, high and dim; the gleam was such as the moon imparts to vapours she is about to sever. I watched her come – watched with the strangest anticipation; as though some word of doom were to be

---

1   Unconsciousness.

written on her disk. She broke forth as never moon yet burst from cloud: a hand first penetrated the sable folds and waved them away; then, not a moon, but a white human form shone in the azure, inclining a glorious brow earthward. It gazed and gazed on me. It spoke, to my spirit: immeasurably distant was the tone, yet so near, it whispered in my heart –

"My daughter, flee temptation!"

"Mother, I will."

So I answered after I had waked from the trance-like dream. It was yet night, but July nights are short: soon after midnight, dawn comes. "It cannot be too early to commence the task I have to fulfil," thought I. I rose: I was dressed; for I had taken off nothing but my shoes. I knew where to find in my drawers some linen, a locket, a ring. In seeking these articles, I encountered the beads of a pearl necklace Mr. Rochester had forced me to accept a few days ago. I left that; it was not mine: it was the visionary bride's who had melted in air. The other articles I made up in a parcel; my purse, containing twenty shillings (it was all I had), I put in my pocket: I tied on my straw bonnet, pinned my shawl, took the parcel and my slippers, which I would not put on yet, and stole from my room.

"Farewell, kind Mrs. Fairfax!" I whispered, as I glided past her door. "Farewell, my darling Adèle!" I said, as I glanced towards the nursery. No thought could be admitted of entering to embrace her. I had to deceive a fine ear: for aught I knew, it might now be listening.

I would have got past Mr. Rochester's chamber without a pause; but my heart momentarily stopping its beat at that threshold, my foot was forced to stop also. No sleep was there: the inmate was walking restlessly from wall to wall; and again and again he sighed while I listened. There was a heaven – a temporary heaven – in this room for me, if I chose: I had but to go in and to say –

"Mr. Rochester, I will love you and live with you through life till death," and a fount of rapture would spring to my lips. I thought of this.

That kind master, who could not sleep now, was waiting with impatience for day. He would send for me in the morning: I should be gone. He would have me sought for: vainly. He would feel himself forsaken; his love rejected: he would suffer; perhaps grow desperate.

I thought of this too. My hand moved towards the lock: I caught it back, and glided on.

Drearily I wound my way down stairs: I knew what I had to do, and I did it mechanically. I sought the key of the side-door in the kitchen; I sought, too, a phial of oil and a feather; I oiled the key and the lock. I got some water, I got some bread: for perhaps I should have to walk far; and my strength, sorely shaken of late, must not break down. All this I did without one sound. I opened the door, passed out, shut it softly. Dim dawn glimmered in the yard. The great gates were closed and locked; but a wicket in one of them was only latched. Through that I departed: it, too, I shut; and now I was out of Thornfield.

A mile off, beyond the fields, lay a road which stretched in the contrary direction to Millcote; a road I had never travelled, but often noticed, and wondered where it led: thither I bent my steps. No reflection was to be allowed now: not one glance was to be cast back; not even one forward. Not one thought was to be given either to the past, or to the future. The first was a page so heavenly sweet – so deadly sad – that to read one line of it would dissolve my courage and break down my energy. The last was an awful blank: something like the world when the deluge was gone by.

I skirted fields, and hedges, and lanes, till after sunrise. I believe it was a lovely summer morning: I know my shoes, which I had put on when I left the house, were soon wet with dew. But I looked neither to rising sun, nor smiling sky, nor wakening nature. He who is taken out to pass through a fair scene to the scaffold, thinks not of the flowers that smile on his road, but of the block and axe-edge; of the dis-severment of bone and vein; of the grave gaping at the end: and I thought of drear flight and homeless wandering – and, oh! with agony I thought of what I left! I could not help it. I thought of him now – in his room – watching the sunrise; hoping I should soon come to say I would stay with him, and be his. I longed to be his; I panted to return: it was not too late; I could yet spare him the bitter pang of bereavement. As yet my flight, I was sure, was undiscovered. I could go back and be his comforter – his pride; his redeemer from misery; perhaps from ruin. Oh, that fear of his self-abandonment – far worse than my abandonment – how it goaded me! It was a barbed arrow-head in my breast: it tore me when I tried to extract it; it sickened me when Remembrance thrust it further in. Birds began singing in brake and copse: birds were faithful to their mates; birds were emblems of love. What was I? In the midst of my pain of heart, and frantic effort of principle, I abhorred myself. I had no solace from self-approbation: none even from self-respect. I had injured – wounded – left my master. I was hateful in my own eyes. Still I could not turn, nor retrace one step. God must have led me on. As to my own will or conscience, impassioned grief had trampled one and stifled the other. I was weeping wildly as I walked along my solitary way: fast, fast I went like one delirious. A weakness, beginning inwardly, extending to the limbs, seized me, and I fell: I lay on the ground some minutes, pressing my face to the wet turf. I had some fear – or hope – that here I should die: but I was soon up; crawling forwards on my hands and knees, and then again raised to my feet – as eager and as determined as ever to reach the road.

When I got there, I was forced to sit to rest me under the hedge; and while I sat, I heard wheels, and saw a coach come on. I stood up and lifted my hand; it stopped. I asked where it was going: the driver named a place a long way off, and where I was sure Mr. Rochester had no connexions. I asked for what sum he would take me there; he said thirty shillings; I answered I had but twenty: well, he would try to make it do. He further gave me leave to get into the inside, as the vehicle was empty: I entered, was shut in, and it rolled on its way.

Gentle reader, may you never feel what I then felt! May your eyes never shed such stormy, scalding, heart-wrung tears as poured from mine. May you never appeal to Heaven in prayers so hopeless and so agonized as in that hour left my lips: for never may you, like me, dread to be the instrument of evil to what you wholly love.

CHAPTER XXVIII

Two days are passed. It is a summer evening; the coachman has set me down at a place called Whitcross: he could take me no farther for the sum I had given, and I was not possessed of another shilling in the world. The coach is a mile off by this time; I am alone. At this moment I discover that I forgot to take my parcel out of the pocket of the coach, where I had placed it for safety: there it remains, there it must remain; and now I am absolutely destitute.

Whitcross is no town, nor even a hamlet; it is but a stone pillar set up where four roads meet: white-washed, I suppose, to be more obvious at a distance and in darkness. Four arms spring from its summit: the nearest town to which these point is, according to the inscription, distant ten miles; the farthest, above twenty. From the well-known names of these towns I learn in what county I have lighted;a north-midland shire, dusk with moorland, ridged with mountain: this I see. There are great moors behind and on each hand of me; there are waves of mountains far beyond that deep valley at my feet. The population here must be thin, and I see no passengers on these roads: they stretch out east, west, north and south – white, broad, lonely; they are all cut in the moor, and the heather grows deep and wild to their very verge. Yet a chance traveller might pass by; and I wish no eye to see me now: strangers would wonder what I am doing, lingering here at the sign-post, evidently objectless and lost. I might be questioned: I could give no answer but what would sound incredible and excite suspicion. Not a tie holds me to human society at this moment – not a charm or hope calls me where my fellow-creatures are – none that saw me would have a kind thought or a good wish for me. I have no relative but the universal mother, Nature: I will seek her breast and ask repose.

I struck straight into the heath; I held on to[1] a hollow I saw deeply furrowing the brown moor-side; I waded knee-deep in its dark growth; I turned with its turnings, and finding a moss-blackened granite crag in a hidden angle, I sat down under it. High banks of moor were about me; the crag protected my head: the sky was over that.

---

1   i.e., "I continued on to."

Some time passed before I felt tranquil even here: I had a vague dread that wild cattle might be near, or that some sportsman or poacher might discover me. If a gust of wind swept the waste, I looked up, fearing it was the rush of a bull; if a plover whistled, I imagined it a man. Finding my apprehensions unfounded, however, and calmed by the deep silence that reigned as evening declined to night-fall, I took confidence. As yet I had not thought; I had only listened, watched, dreaded: now I regained the faculty of reflection.

What was I to do? Where to go? Oh, intolerable questions, when I could do nothing and go nowhere! – when a long way must yet be measured by my weary, trembling limbs before I could reach human habitation – when cold charity must be entreated before I could get a lodging: reluctant sympathy importuned; almost certain repulse incurred; before my tale could be listened to, or one of my wants relieved!

I touched the heath: it was dry, and yet warm with the heat of the summer day. I looked at the sky; it was pure: a kindly star twinkled just above the chasm ridge. The dew fell, but with propitious softness; no breeze whispered. Nature seemed to me benign and good: I thought she loved me, outcast as I was; and I, who from man could anticipate only mistrust, rejection, insult, clung to her with filial fondness. To-night, at least, I would be her guest – as I was her child: my mother would lodge me without money and without price. I had one morsel of bread yet: the remnant of a roll I had bought in a town we passed through at noon with a stray penny – my last coin. I saw ripe bilberries gleaming here and there, like jet beads in the heath: I gathered a handful and eat them with the bread. My hunger, sharp before, was, if not satisfied, appeased by this hermit's meal. I said my evening prayers at its conclusion, and then chose my couch.

Beside the crag, the heath was very deep: when I lay down my feet were buried in it; rising high on each side, it left only a narrow space for the night-air to invade. I folded my shawl double, and spread it over me for a coverlet; a low, mossy swell was my pillow. Thus lodged, I was not, at least at the commencement of the night, cold.

My rest might have been blissful enough, only a sad heart broke it. It plained[1] of its gaping wounds, its inward bleeding, its riven chords.

---

1 Complained.

It trembled for Mr. Rochester and his doom: it bemoaned him with bitter pity; it demanded him with ceaseless longing; and, impotent as a bird with both wings broken, it still quivered its shattered pinions in vain attempts to seek him.

Worn out with this torture of thought, I rose to my knees. Night was come, and her planets were risen: a safe, still night; too serene for the companionship of fear. We know that God is everywhere; but certainly we feel His presence most when His works are on the grandest scale spread before us: and it is in the unclouded night-sky, where His worlds wheel their silent course, that we read clearest His infinitude, His omnipotence, His omnipresence. I had risen to my knees to pray for Mr. Rochester. Looking up, I, with tear-dimmed eyes, saw the mighty milky-way. Remembering what it was – what countless systems there swept space like a soft trace of light – I felt the might and strength of God. Sure was I of His efficiency to save what He had made: convinced I grew that neither earth should perish, nor one of the souls it treasured. I turned my prayer to thanksgiving: the Source of Life was also the Saviour of Spirits. Mr. Rochester was safe: he was God's, and by God would he be guarded. I again nestled to the breast of the hill; and ere long, in sleep, forgot sorrow.

But next day, Want came to me, pale and bare. Long after the little birds had left their nests; long after bees had come in the sweet prime of day to gather the heath honey before the dew was dried – when the long morning shadows were curtailed, and the sun filled earth and sky – I got up, and I looked round me.

What a still, hot, perfect day! What a golden desert this spreading moor! Everywhere sunshine. I wished I could live in it and on it. I saw a lizard run over the crag; I saw a bee busy among the sweet bilberries. I would fain at the moment have become bee or lizard, that I might have found fitting nutriment, permanent shelter here. But I was a human being, and had a human being's wants: I must not linger where there was nothing to supply them. I rose; I looked back at the bed I had left. Hopeless of the future, I wished but this – that my Maker had that night thought good to require my soul of me[1] while I slept; and that this weary frame, absolved by death from further

---

1 See Luke 12:20.

conflict with fate, had now but to decay quietly, and mingle in peace with the soil of this wilderness. Life, however, was yet in my possession; with all its requirements, and pains, and responsibilities. The burden must be carried; the want provided for; the suffering endured; the responsibility fulfilled. I set out.

Whitcross regained, I followed a road which led from the sun, now fervent and high. By no other circumstance had I will to decide my choice. I walked a long time, and when I thought I had nearly done enough, and might conscientiously yield to the fatigue that almost overpowered me — might relax this forced action, and, sitting down on a stone I saw near, submit resistlessly to the apathy that clogged heart and limb — I heard a bell chime — a church bell.

I turned in the direction of the sound, and there, amongst the romantic hills, whose changes and aspect I had ceased to note an hour ago, I saw a hamlet and a spire. All the valley at my right hand was full of pasture-fields, and corn-fields, and wood; and a glittering stream ran zig-zag through the varied shades of green, the mellowing grain, the sombre wood-land, the clear and sunny lea. Recalled by the rumbling of wheels to the road before me, I saw a heavily-laden waggon labouring up the hill; and not far beyond were two cows and their drover. Human life and human labour were near. I must struggle on: strive to live and bend to toil like the rest.

About two o'clock, P.M., I entered the village. At the bottom of its one street, there was a little shop with some cakes of bread in the window. I coveted a cake of bread. With that refreshment I could perhaps regain a degree of energy; without it, it would be difficult to proceed. The wish to have some strength and some vigour returned to me as soon as I was amongst my fellow-beings. I felt it would be degrading to faint with hunger on the causeway of a hamlet. Had I nothing about me I could offer in exchange for one of these rolls? I considered. I had a small silk handkerchief tied round my throat; I had my gloves. I could hardly tell how men and women in extremities of destitution proceeded. I did not know whether either of these articles would be accepted: probably they would not; but I must try.

I entered the shop: a woman was there. Seeing a respectably-dressed person, a lady as she supposed, she came forward with civility. How could she serve me? I was seized with shame: my tongue would not utter the request I had prepared. I dared not offer her the half-worn gloves, the creased handkerchief: besides, I felt it would be absurd. I only begged permission to sit down a moment, as I was tired. Disappointed in the expectation of a customer, she coolly acceded to my request. She pointed to a seat; I sank into it. I felt sorely urged to weep; but conscious how unseasonable such a manifestation would be, I restrained it. Soon I asked her "if there were any dressmaker or plain-work-woman[1] in the village?"

"Yes; two or three. Quite as many as there was employment for."

I reflected. I was driven to the point now. I was brought face to face with Necessity. I stood in the position of one without a resource: without a friend; without a coin. I must do something. What? I must apply somewhere. Where?

"Did she know of any place in the neighbourhood where a servant was wanted?"

"Nay; she couldn't say."

"What was the chief trade in this place? What did most of the people do?"

"Some were farm labourers; a good deal worked at Mr. Oliver's needle-factory, and at the foundry."

"Did Mr. Oliver employ women?"

"Nay; it was men's work."

"And what do the women do?"

"I knaw n't," was the answer. "Some does one thing, and some another. Poor folk mun get on as they can."

She seemed to be tired of my questions: and, indeed, what claim had I to importune her? A neighbour or two came in; my chair was evidently wanted. I took leave.

I passed up the street, looking as I went at all the houses to the right hand and to the left: but I could discover no pretext, nor see an inducement, to enter any. I rambled round the hamlet, going sometimes to a little distance and returning again, for an hour or more. Much exhausted, and suffering greatly now for want of food, I turned aside into a lane and sat down under the hedge. Ere many minutes had elapsed, I was again on my feet, however, and again searching

---

1 A woman hired to do simple sewing, called "plain-work."

something – a resource, or at least an informant. A pretty little house stood at the top of the lane, with a garden before it; exquisitely neat, and brilliantly blooming. I stopped at it. What business had I to approach the white door, or touch the glittering knocker? In what way could it possibly be the interest of the inhabitants of that dwelling to serve me? Yet I drew near and knocked. A mild-looking, cleanly-attired young woman opened the door. In such a voice as might be expected from a hopeless heart and fainting frame – a voice wretchedly low and faltering – I asked if a servant was wanted here?

"No," said she; "we do not keep a servant."

"Can you tell me where I could get employment of any kind?" I continued. "I am a stranger, without acquaintance, in this place. I want some work: no matter what."

But it was not her business to think for me, or to seek a place for me: besides, in her eyes, how doubtful must have appeared my character, position, tale. She shook her head, she "was sorry she could give me no information," and the white door closed, quite gently and civilly: but it shut me out. If she had held it open a little longer, I believe I should have begged a piece of bread; for I was now brought low.

I could not bear to return to the sordid village; where, besides, no prospect of aid was visible. I should have longed rather to deviate to a wood I saw not far off, which appeared in its thick shade to offer inviting shelter; but I was so sick, so weak, so gnawed with nature's cravings, instinct kept me roaming round abodes where there was a chance of food. Solitude would be no solitude – rest no rest – while the vulture, hunger, thus sunk beak and talons in my side.

I drew near houses; I left them, and came back again, and again I wandered away: always repelled by the consciousness of having no claim to ask – no right to expect interest in my isolated lot. Meantime, the afternoon advanced, while I thus wandered about like a lost and starving dog. In crossing a field, I saw the church-spire before me: I hastened towards it. Near the churchyard, and in the middle of a garden, stood a well-built though small house, which I had no doubt was the parsonage. I remembered that strangers who arrive at a place where they have no friends, and who want employment, sometimes apply to the clergyman for introduction and aid. It is the clergyman's function to help – at least with advice – those who wish to help themselves. I seemed to have something like a right to seek counsel here. Renewing then, my courage, and gathering my feeble remains of strength, I pushed on. I reached the house, and knocked at the kitchen-door. An old woman opened; I asked was this the parsonage?

"Yes."

"Was the clergyman in?"

"No."

"Would he be in soon?"

"No, he was gone from home."

"To a distance?"

"Not so far – happen three mile. He had been called away by the sudden death of his father: he was at Marsh End now, and would very likely stay there a fortnight longer."

"Was there any lady of the house?"

"Nay, there was naught but her, and she was housekeeper;" and of her, reader, I could not bear to ask the relief for want of which I was sinking: I could not yet beg; and again I crawled away.

Once more I took off my handkerchief – once more I thought of the cakes of bread in the little shop. Oh, for but a crust! for but one mouthful to allay the pang of famine! Instinctively I turned my face again to the village: I found the shop again, and I went in; and though others were there besides the woman, I ventured the request, "Would she give me a roll for this handkerchief?"

She looked at me with evident suspicion: "Nay, she never sold stuff i' that way."

Almost desperate, I asked for half a cake; she again refused. "How could she tell where I had got the handkerchief?" she said.

"Would she take my gloves?"

"No; what could she do with them?"

Reader, it is not pleasant to dwell on these details. Some say there is enjoyment in looking back to painful experience past; but at this day I can scarcely bear to review the times to which I allude: the moral degradation, blent with the physical suffering, form too distressing a recollection ever to be willingly dwelt on. I blamed none of those who repulsed me. I felt it was what was to be expected, and what could not be helped: an ordinary beggar is frequently an object of suspicion; a well-dressed beggar inevitably so. To be sure, what I begged was employment: but whose business was it to provide me with employment? Not, certainly, that of persons who saw me then for the first time, and who knew nothing about my character. And as to the woman who would not take my handkerchief in exchange for her bread, why, she was right, if the offer appeared to her sinister, or the exchange unprofitable. Let me condense now. I am sick of the subject.

A little before dark I passed a farm-house, at the open door of which the farmer was sitting, eating his supper of bread and cheese: I stopped and said: –

"Will you give me a piece of bread? for I am very hungry." He cast on me a glance of surprise; but without answering, he cut a thick slice from his loaf, and gave it to me. I imagine he did not think I was a beggar, but only an eccentric sort of lady who had taken a fancy to his brown loaf. As soon as I was out of sight of his house, I sat down and ate it.

I could not hope to get a lodging under a roof, and sought it in the wood I have before alluded to. But my night was wretched, my rest broken: the ground was damp, the air cold: besides, intruders passed near me more than once, and I had again and again to change my quarters: no sense of safety or tranquillity befriended me. Towards morning it rained; the whole of the following day was wet. Do not ask me, reader, to give a minute account of that day: as before, I sought work; as before, I was repulsed; as before, I starved: but once did food pass my lips. At the door of a cottage I saw a little girl about to throw a mess of cold porridge into a pig-trough. "Will you give me that?" I asked.

She stared at me. "Mother!" she exclaimed; "there is a woman wants me to give her these porridge."[1]

"Well, lass," replied a voice within, "give it her if she's a beggar. T' pig doesn't want it."

The girl emptied the stiffened mould into my hand, and I devoured it ravenously.

As the wet twilight deepened, I stopped in a solitary bridle-path,

---

1   Dialect. Porridge is here treated as a collective plural.

which I had been pursuing an hour or more.

"My strength is quite failing me," I said, in soliloquy. "I feel I cannot go much further. Shall I be an outcast again this night? While the rain descends so, must I lay my head on the cold, drenched ground? I fear I cannot do otherwise: for who will receive me? But it will be very dreadful: with this feeling of hunger, faintness, chill, and this sense of desolation – this total prostration of hope. In all likelihood, though, I should die before morning. And why cannot I reconcile myself to the prospect of death? Why do I struggle to retain a valueless life? Because I know, or believe, Mr. Rochester is living: and then, to die of want and cold, is a fate to which nature cannot submit passively. Oh, Providence! sustain me a little longer! Aid – direct me!"

My glazed eye wandered over the dim and misty landscape. I saw I had strayed far from the village: it was quite out of sight. The very cultivation surrounding it had disappeared. I had, by cross-ways and by-paths, once more drawn near the tracts of moorland; and now, only a few fields, almost as wild and unproductive as the heath from which they were scarcely reclaimed, lay between me and the dusky hill.

"Well; I would rather die yonder than in a street, or on a frequented road," I reflected. "And far better that crows and ravens – if any ravens there be in these regions – should pick my flesh from my bones, than that they should be prisoned in a workhouse coffin, and moulder in a pauper's grave."

To the hill, then, I turned. I reached it. It remained now only to find a hollow where I could lie down, and feel at least hidden, if not secure: but all the surface of the waste looked level. It showed no variation but of tint: green, where rush and moss overgrew the marshes; black, where the dry soil bore only heath. Dark as it was getting, I could still see these changes; though but as mere alternations of light and shade: for colour had faded with the daylight.

My eye still roved over the sullen swell, and along the moor-edge, vanishing amidst the wildest scenery: when, at one dim point, far in among the marshes and the ridges, a light sprung up. "That is an *ignis fatuus*," was my first thought; and I expected it would soon vanish. It burnt on, however, quite steadily; neither receding nor advancing. "Is it then a bonfire just kindled?" I questioned. I watched to see whether it would spread: but no; as it did not diminish, so it did not enlarge. "It may be a candle in a house," I then conjectured: "but if so, I can never reach it. It is much too far away: and were it within a yard of me, what would it avail? I should but knock at the door to have it shut in my face."

And I sank down where I stood, and hid my face against the ground. I lay still awhile: the night-wind swept over the hill and over me, and died moaning in the distance; the rain fell fast, wetting me afresh to the skin. Could I but have stiffened to the still frost — the friendly numbness of death — it might have pelted on: I should not have felt it; but my yet living flesh shuddered to its chilling influence. I rose ere long.

The light was yet there; shining dim, but constant, through the rain. I tried to walk again: I dragged my exhausted limbs slowly towards it. It led me aslant over the hill, through a wide bog; which would have been impassable in winter, and was splashy and shaking even now, in the height of summer. Here I fell twice; but as often I rose and rallied my faculties. This light was my forlorn hope: I must gain it.

Having crossed the marsh, I saw a trace of white over the moor. I approached it; it was a road or a track: it led straight up to the light, which now beamed from a sort of knoll, amidst a clump of trees — firs, apparently, from what I could distinguish of the character of their forms and foliage through the gloom. My star vanished as I drew near: some obstacle had intervened between me and it. I put out my hand to feel the dark mass before me: I discriminated the rough stones of a low wall — above it, something like palisades, and within, a high and prickly hedge. I groped on. Again a whitish object gleamed before me: it was a gate — a wicket; it moved on its hinges as I touched it. On each side stood a sable bush — holly or yew.

Entering the gate and passing the shrubs, the silhouette of a house rose to view; black, low, and rather long; but the guiding light shone nowhere. All was obscurity. Were the inmates retired to rest? I feared it must be so. In seeking the door, I turned an angle: there shot out the friendly gleam again, from the lozenged panes of a very small latticed window, within a foot of the ground; made still smaller by the growth of ivy or some other creeping plant, whose leaves clustered thick over the portion of the house wall in which it was set. The aperture was so screened and narrow, that curtain or shutter had been deemed un-necessary; and when I stooped down and put aside the spray of foliage shooting over it, I could see all within. I could see clearly a room with a sanded floor, clean scoured; a dresser of walnut, with pewter plates ranged in rows, reflecting the redness and radiance of a glowing peat-fire. I could see a clock, a white deal table,[1] some chairs. The candle, whose ray had been my beacon, burnt on the table; and by its light an elderly woman, somewhat rough-looking, but scrupulously clean, like all about her, was knitting a stocking.

I noticed these objects cursorily only – in them there was nothing extraordinary. A group of more interest appeared near the hearth, sit-ting still amidst the rosy peace and warmth suffusing it. Two young, graceful women – ladies in every point – sat, one in a low rocking-chair, the other on a lower stool; both wore deep mourning of crape and bombazeen,[1] which sombre garb singularly set off their very fair necks and faces: a large old pointer dog rested its massive head on the knee of one girl – in the lap of the other was cushioned a black cat.

A strange place was this humble kitchen for such occupants! Who were they? They could not be the daughters of the elderly person at the table; for she looked like a rustic, and they were all delicacy and cultivation. I had nowhere seen such faces as theirs: and yet, as I gazed on them, I seemed intimate with every lineament. I cannot call them handsome – they were too pale and grave for the word: as they each bent over a book, they looked thoughtful almost to severity. A stand between them supported a second candle and two great volumes, to which they frequently referred; comparing them seemingly with the smaller books they held in their hands, like people consulting a dic-tionary to aid them in the task of translation. This scene was as silent as if all the figures had been shadows, and the fire-lit apartment a pic-ture: so hushed was it, I could hear the cinders fall from the grate, the clock tick in its obscure corner; and I even fancied I could distinguish the click-click of the woman's knitting-needles. When, therefore, a voice broke the strange stillness at last, it was audible enough to me.

"Listen, Diana," said one of the absorbed students; "Franz and old Daniel are together in the night-time, and Franz is telling a dream from which he has wakened in terror – listen!" And in a low voice she

---

1 A table made of sawn fir or pine wood.
2 Twilled material of worsted combined with silk or cotton, often died black.

read something, of which not one word was intelligible to me; for it was in an unknown tongue – neither French nor Latin. Whether it were Greek or German I could not tell.

"That is strong," she said, when she had finished: "I relish it." The other girl, who had lifted her head to listen to her sister, repeated, while she gazed at the fire, a line of what had been read. At a later day, I knew the language and the book; therefore I will here quote the line: though, when I first heard it, it was only like a stroke on sounding brass to me – conveying no meaning:

"'Da trat hervor Einer, anzusehen wie die Sternen Nacht.' Good! good!" she exclaimed, while her dark and deep eye sparkled. "There you have a dim and mighty archangel fitly set before you! The line is worth a hundred pages of fustian. 'Ich wäge die Gedanken in der Schale meines Zornes und die Werke mit dem Gewichte meines Grimms.'[1] I like it!"

Both were again silent.

"Is there ony country where they talk i' that way?" asked the old woman, looking up from her knitting.

"Yes, Hannah – a far larger country than England; where they talk in no other way."

"Well, for sure case, I knawn't how they can understand t' one t' other: and if either o' ye went there, ye could tell what they said, I guess?"

"We could probably tell something of what they said, but not all – for we are not as clever as you think us, Hannah. We don't speak German, and we cannot read it without a dictionary to help us."

"And what good does it do you?"

"We mean to teach it some time – or at least the elements, as they say; and then we shall get more money than we do now."

"Varry like: but give ower studying; ye've done enough for to-night."

"I think we have: at least, I'm tired. Mary, are you?"

"Mortally: after all, it's tough work pegging away at a language with no master but a lexicon."

---

1 A quotation from *Die Räuber* (*The Robbers*), published in 1781 and performed in 1782, the first play written by Friedrich von Schiller (1759-1805). "Then one stepped forth, in appearance like the starry night....I weigh thoughts in the scale of my wrath and deeds with the weight of my fury."

"It is: especially such a language as this crabbed but glorious Deutsch. I wonder when St. John will come home."

"Surely he will not be long now: it is just ten" (looking at a little gold watch she drew from her girdle). "It rains fast. Hannah, will you have the goodness to look at the fire in the parlour?"

The woman rose; she opened a door, through which I dimly saw a passage: soon I heard her stir a fire in an inner room; she presently came back.

"Ah, childer!" said she, "it fair troubles me to go into yond' room now: it looks so lonesome wi' the chair empty and set back in a corner."

She wiped her eyes with her apron: the two girls, grave before, looked sad now.

"But he is in a better place," continued Hannah: "we shouldn't wish him here again. And then, nobody need to have a quieter death nor he had."

"You say he never mentioned us?" inquired one of the ladies.

"He hadn't time, bairn: he was gone in a minute – was your father. He had been a bit ailing like the day before, but naught to signify; and when Mr. St. John asked if he would like either o' ye to be sent for, he fair laughed at him. He began again with a bit of a heaviness in his head the next day – that is, a fortnight sin' – and he went to sleep and niver wakened: he wor a'most stark when your brother went into t' chamber and fand him. Ah, childer! that's t' last o' t' old stock – for ye and Mr. St. John is like of a different soart to them 'at's gone; for all your mother wor mich i' your way, and a'most as book-learned. She wor the pictur' o' ye, Mary: Diana is more like your father."

I thought them so similar I could not tell where the old servant (for such I now concluded her to be) saw the difference. Both were fair complexioned and slenderly made; both possessed faces full of distinction and intelligence. One, to be sure, had hair a shade darker than the other, and there was a difference in their style of wearing it: Mary's pale brown locks were parted and braided smooth; Diana's duskier tresses covered her neck with thick curls.[1] The clock struck ten.

---

1 In a way common to Victorian fiction the sisters' differing style of hair represents their differing personalities. Mary's smooth, braided hair symbolizes her calm and gentle nature, Diana's dark and less constrained curls symbolize her boldness and energy.

"Ye'll want your supper, I am sure," observed Hannah; "and so will Mr. St. John when he comes in."

And she proceeded to prepare the meal. The ladies rose: they seemed about to withdraw to the parlour. Till this moment, I had been so intent on watching them, their appearance and conversation had excited in me so keen an interest, I had half-forgotten my own wretched position: now it recurred to me. More desolate, more desperate than ever, it seemed from contrast. And how impossible did it appear to touch the inmates of this house with concern on my behalf: to make them believe in the truth of my wants and woes – to induce them to vouchsafe a rest for my wanderings! As I groped out the door, and knocked at it hesitatingly, I felt that last idea to be indeed a mere chimera. Hannah opened.

"What do you want?" she inquired, in a voice of surprise, as she surveyed me by the light of the candle she held.

"May I speak to your mistresses?" I said.

"You had better tell me what you have to say to them. Where do you come from?"

"I am a stranger."

"What is your business here at this hour?"

"I want a night's shelter in an out-house[1] or anywhere, and a morsel of bread to eat."

Distrust, the very feeling I dreaded, appeared in Hannah's face. "I'll give you a piece of bread," she said, after a pause; "but we can't take in a vagrant to lodge. It isn't likely."

"Do let me speak to your mistresses."

"No; not I. What can they do for you? You should not be roving about now: it looks very ill."

"But where shall I go if you drive me away? What shall I do?"

"Oh, I'll warrant you know where to go, and what to do. Mind you don't do wrong, that's all. Here is a penny; now go —."

"A penny cannot feed me, and I have no strength to go farther. Don't shut the door! – oh, don't, for God's sake!"

"I must; the rain is driving in —."

"Tell the young ladies. – Let me see them – ."

---

1   i.e., an outlying shed or building.

"Indeed I will not. You are not what you ought to be, or you wouldn't make such a noise. Move off!"

"But I must die if I am turned away."

"Not you. I'm feared you have some ill plans agate,[1] that bring you about folk's houses at this time o' night. If you've any followers – housebreakers or such like – anywhere near, you may tell them we are not by ourselves in the house: we have a gentleman, and dogs, and guns." Here the honest but inflexible servant clapped the door to and bolted it within.

This was the climax. A pang of exquisite suffering – a throe of true despair – rent and heaved my heart. Worn out, indeed, I was: not another step could I stir. I sank on the wet door-step: I groaned – I wrung my hands – I wept in utter anguish. Oh, this spectre of death! Oh, this last hour, approaching in such horror! Alas, this isolation – this banishment from my kind! Not only the anchor of hope, but the footing of fortitude was gone – at least for a moment: but the last I soon endeavoured to regain.

"I can but die," I said, "and I believe in God. Let me try to wait His will in silence."

These words I not only thought, but uttered; and thrusting back all my misery into my heart, I made an effort to compel it to remain there – dumb and still.

"All men must die," said a voice quite close at hand; "but all are not condemned to meet a lingering and premature doom, such as yours would be if you perished here of want."

"Who or what speaks?" I asked, terrified at the unexpected sound, and incapable now of deriving from any occurrence a hope of aid. A form was near – what form, the pitch-dark night and my enfeebled vision prevented me from distinguishing. With a loud, long knock, the newcomer appealed to the door.

"Is it you, Mr. St. John?" cried Hannah.

"Yes – yes; open quickly."

"Well, how wet and cold you must be, such a wild night as it is! Come in – your sisters are quite uneasy about you, and I believe there are bad folks about. There has been a beggar-woman – I declare

---

1 Dialect. Afoot, under way.

she is not gone yet! – laid down there. Get up! for shame! Move off, I say!"

"Hush, Hannah! I have a word to say to the woman. You have done your duty in excluding, now let me do mine in admitting her. I was near, and listened to both you and her. I think this is a peculiar case – I must at least examine into it. Young woman, rise, and pass before me into the house."

With difficulty I obeyed him. Presently I stood within that clean, bright kitchen – on the very hearth – trembling, sickening; conscious of an aspect in the last degree ghastly, wild, and weather-beaten. The two ladies, their brother, Mr. St. John, the old servant, were all gazing at me.

"St. John, who is it?" I heard one ask.

"I cannot tell: I found her at the door," was the reply.

"She does look white," said Hannah.

"As white as clay or death," was responded. "She will fall: let her sit."

And indeed my head swam: I dropped; but a chair received me. I still possessed my senses; though just now I could not speak.

"Perhaps a little water would restore her. Hannah, fetch some. But she is worn to nothing. How very thin, and how very bloodless!"

"A mere spectre!"

"Is she ill, or only famished?"

"Famished, I think. Hannah, is that milk? Give it me, and a piece of bread."

Diana (I knew her by the long curls which I saw drooping between me and the fire as she bent over me) broke some bread, dipped it in milk, and put it to my lips. Her face was near mine: I saw there was pity in it, and I felt sympathy in her hurried breathing. In her simple words, too, the same balm-like emotion spoke: "Try to eat."

"Yes – try," repeated Mary gently; and Mary's hand removed my sodden bonnet and lifted my head. I tasted what they offered me: feebly at first, eagerly soon.

"Not too much at first – restrain her," said the brother; "she has had enough." And he withdrew the cup of milk and the plate of bread.

"A little more, St. John – look at the avidity in her eyes."

"No more at present, sister. Try if she can speak now – ask her her name."

I felt I could speak, and I answered – "My name is Jane Elliott." Anxious as ever to avoid discovery, I had before resolved to assume an *alias*.

"And where do you live? Where are your friends?"

I was silent.

"Can we send for any one you know?"

I shook my head.

"What account can you give of yourself?"

Somehow, now that I had once crossed the threshold of this house, and once was brought face to face with its owners, I felt no longer outcast, vagrant, and disowned by the wide world. I dared to put off the mendicant – to resume my natural manner and character. I began once more to know myself; and when Mr. St. John demanded an account – which at present I was far too weak to render – I said, after a brief pause –

"Sir, I can give you no details to-night."

"But what, then," said he, "do you expect me to do for you?"

"Nothing," I replied. My strength sufficed for but short answers. Diana took the word:

"Do you mean," she asked, "that we have now given you what aid you require? and that we may dismiss you to the moor and the rainy night?"

I looked at her. She had, I thought, a remarkable countenance; instinct both with power and goodness. I took sudden courage. Answering her compassionate gaze with a smile, I said: "I will trust you. If I were a masterless and stray dog, I know that you would not turn me from your hearth to-night: as it is, I really have no fear. Do with me and for me as you like; but excuse me from much discourse – my breath is short – I feel a spasm when I speak." All three surveyed me, and all three were silent.

"Hannah," said Mr. St. John, at last, "let her sit there at present, and ask her no questions; in ten minutes more, give her the remainder of that milk and bread. Mary and Diana, let us go into the parlour and talk the matter over."

They withdrew. Very soon one of the ladies returned – I could not tell which. A kind of pleasant stupor was stealing over me as I sat by the genial fire. In an undertone, she gave some directions to Hannah. Ere long, with the servant's aid, I contrived to mount a staircase: my dripping clothes were removed; soon a warm, dry bed received me. I thanked God – experienced amidst unutterable exhaustion a glow of grateful joy – and slept.

CHAPTER XXIX

THE recollection of about three days and nights succeeding this is very dim in my mind. I can recall some sensations felt in that interval; but few thoughts framed, and no actions performed. I knew I was in a small room, and in a narrow bed. To that bed I seemed to have grown: I lay on it motionless as a stone; and to have torn me from it would have been almost to kill me. I took no note of the lapse of time – of the change from morning to noon, from noon to evening. I observed when any one entered or left the apartment; I could even tell who they were; I could understand what was said when the speaker stood near me; but I could not answer: to open my lips or move my limbs was equally impossible. Hannah, the servant, was my most frequent visitor. Her coming disturbed me. I had a feeling that she wished me away; that she did not understand me or my circumstances; that she was prejudiced against me. Diana and Mary appeared in the chamber once or twice a day. They would whisper sentences of this sort at my bedside: –

"It is very well we took her in."

"Yes; she would certainly have been found dead at the door in the morning had she been left out all night. I wonder what she has gone through?"

"Strange hardships, I imagine – poor, emaciated, pallid wanderer!"

"She is not an uneducated person, I should think, by her manner of speaking: her accent was quite pure; and the clothes she took off, though splashed and wet, were little worn, and fine."

"She has a peculiar face; fleshless and haggard as it is, I rather like it; and when in good health and animated, I can fancy her physiognomy would be agreeable."

Never once in their dialogues did I hear a syllable of regret at the hospitality they had extended to me; or of suspicion of, or aversion to, myself. I was comforted.

Mr. St. John came but once: he looked at me, and said my state of lethargy was the result of reaction from excessive and protracted fatigue. He pronounced it needless to send for a doctor: nature, he was sure, would manage best, left to herself. He said every nerve had been overstrained in some way, and the whole system must sleep torpid awhile. There was no disease. He imagined my recovery would be rapid enough when once commenced. These opinions he delivered in few words, in a quiet, low voice; and added, after a pause, in the tone of a man little accustomed to expansive comment, "rather an unusual physiognomy: certainly, not indicative of vulgarity or degradation."

"Far otherwise," responded Diana. "To speak truth, St. John, my heart rather warms to the poor little soul. I wish we may be able to benefit her permanently."

"That is hardly likely," was the reply. "You will find she is some young lady who has had a misunderstanding with her friends, and has probably injudiciously left them. We may, perhaps, succeed in restoring her to them, if she is not obstinate: but I trace lines of force in her face which make me sceptical of her tractability." He stood considering me some minutes; then added, "She looks sensible, but not at all handsome."

"She is so ill, St. John."

"Ill or well, she would always be plain. The grace and harmony of beauty are quite wanting in those features."

On the third day, I was better; on the fourth, I could speak, move, rise in bed, and turn. Hannah had brought me some gruel and dry toast, about, as I supposed, the dinner hour. I had eaten with relish: the food was good – void of the feverish flavour which had hitherto poisoned what I had swallowed. When she left me, I felt comparatively strong and revived; ere long satiety of repose and desire for action stirred me. I wished to rise: but what could I put on? Only my damp and bemired apparel; in which I had slept on the ground and fallen in the marsh. I felt ashamed to appear before my benefactors so clad. I was spared the humiliation.

On a chair by the bedside were all my own things, clean and dry. My black silk frock hung against the wall. The traces of the bog were removed from it; the creases left by the wet, smoothed out: it was quite decent. My very shoes and stockings were purified and rendered presentable. There were the means of washing in the room, and a comb and brush to smooth my hair. After a weary process, and resting every five minutes, I succeeded in dressing myself. My clothes hung loose on me; for I was much wasted: but I covered deficiencies with a shawl, and once more clean and respectable-looking – no speck of the dirt, no trace of the disorder I so hated, and which seemed so to degrade me, left – I crept down a stone staircase, with the aid of the banisters, to a narrow, low passage, and found my way presently to the kitchen.

It was full of the fragrance of new bread, and the warmth of a generous fire. Hannah was baking. Prejudices, it is well known, are most difficult to eradicate from the heart whose soil has never been loosened or fertilized by education: they grow there, firm as weeds among stones. Hannah had been cold and stiff, indeed, at the first: latterly, she had begun to relent a little; and when she saw me come in tidy and well-dressed, she even smiled.

"What, you have got up?" she said. "You are better, then. You may sit you down in my chair on the hearthstone, if you will."

She pointed to the rocking chair: I took it. She bustled about, examining me every now and then with the corner of her eye. Turning to me, as she took some loaves from the oven, she asked, bluntly, –

"Did you ever go a-begging afore you came here?"

I was indignant for a moment: but remembering that anger was out of the question, and that I had indeed appeared as a beggar to her, I answered quietly; but still not without a certain marked firmness, –

"You are mistaken, in supposing me a beggar. I am no beggar; any more than yourself or your young ladies."

After a pause she said, "I dunnut understand that: you've like no house, nor no brass, I guess?"

"The want of house or brass (by which I suppose you mean money) does not make a beggar in your sense of the word."

"Are you book-learned?" she inquired, presently.

"Yes, very."

"But you've never been to boarding-school?"

"I was at a boarding-school eight years."

She opened her eyes wide. "Whatever cannot ye keep yourseln for, then?"

"I have kept myself; and, I trust, shall keep myself again. What are you going to do with these gooseberries?" I inquired, as she brought out a basket of the fruit.

"Mak' 'em into pies."

"Give them to me and I'll pick them."

"Nay; I dunnut want ye to do nought."

"But I must do something. Let me have them."

She consented; and she even brought me a clean towel to spread over my dress, "lest," as she said, "I should mucky it."

"Ye've not been used to sarvant's wark, I see by your hands," she remarked. "Happen ye've been a dressmaker?"

"No, you are wrong. And now, never mind what I have been: don't trouble your head further about me; but tell me the name of the house where we are."

"Some calls it Marsh-End, and some calls it Moor House."

"And the gentleman who lives here is called Mr. St. John?"

"Nay; he doesn't live here: he is only staying awhile. When he is at home, he is in his own parish at Morton."

"That village a few miles off?"

"Aye."

"And what is he?"

"He is a parson."

I remembered the answer of the old housekeeper at the parsonage, when I had asked to see the clergyman. "This, then, was his father's residence?"

"Aye; old Mr. Rivers lived here, and his father, and grandfather, and gurt (great) grandfather afore him."

"The name, then, of that gentleman, is Mr. St. John Rivers?"

"Aye; St. John is like his kirstened name."

"And his sisters are called Diana and Mary Rivers?"

"Yes."

"Their father is dead?"

"Dead three weeks sin', of a stroke."

"They have no mother?"

"The mistress has been dead this mony a year."

"Have you lived with the family long?"

"I've lived here thirty year. I nursed them all three."

"That proves you must have been an honest and faithful servant. I will say so much for you, though you have had the incivility to call me a beggar."

She again regarded me with a surprised stare. "I believe," she said, "I was quite mista'en in my thoughts of you: but there is so mony cheats goes about, you mun forgie me."

"And though," I continued, rather severely, "you wished to turn me from the door, on a night when you should not have shut out a dog."

"Well, it was hard: but what can a body do? I thought more o' th' childer nor of mysel: poor things! They've like nobody to tak' care on 'em but me. I'm like to look sharpish."[1]

I maintained a grave silence for some minutes.

"You munnut think too hardly of me," she again remarked.

"But I do think hardly of you," I said; "and I'll tell you why – not so much because you refused to give me shelter, or regarded me as an impostor, as because you just now made it a species of reproach that I had no 'brass' and no house. Some of the best people that ever lived have been as destitute as I am; and if you are a Christian, you ought not to consider poverty a crime."

"No more I ought," said she: "Mr. St. John tells me so too; and I see I wor wrang – but I've clear a different notion on you now to what I had. You look a raight down dacent little crater."

"That will do – I forgive you now. Shake hands."

She put her floury and horny hand into mine; another and heartier smile illumined her rough face: and from that moment we were friends.

Hannah was evidently fond of talking. While I picked the fruit, and she made the paste for the pies, she proceeded to give me sundry details about her deceased master and mistress, and "the childer," as she called the young people.

Old Mr. Rivers, she said, was a plain man enough; but a gentleman, and of as ancient a family as could be found. Marsh-End had belonged to the Rivers' ever since it was a house: and it was, she affirmed, "aboon two hundred year old – for all it looked but a small, humble place, naught to compare wi' Mr. Oliver's grand hall down i' Morton Vale. But she could remember Bill Oliver's father a journeyman needle-maker; and th' Rivers' wor gentry i' th' owd days o' th' Henrys, as onybody might see by looking into th' registers i' Morton Church vestry." Still, she allowed, "the owd maister was like other folk – naught mich out o' t' common way: stark mad o' shooting, and

---

1   Dialect. "I'm obliged to be on guard."

farming, and sich like." The mistress was different. She was a great reader, and studied a deal; and the "bairns" had taken after her. There was nothing like them in these parts, nor ever had been: they had liked learning, all three, almost from the time they could speak; and they had always been "of a mak' of their own." Mr.St. John, when he grew up, would go to college and be a parson; and the girls, as soon as they left school, would seek places as governesses: for they had told her their father had some years ago lost a great deal of money, by a man he had trusted turning bankrupt; and as he was now not rich enough to give them fortunes, they must provide for themselves. They had lived very little at home for a long while, and were only come now to stay a few weeks on account of their father's death: but they did so like Marsh-End and Morton, and all these moors and hills about. They had been in London, and many other grand towns; but they always said there was no place like home: and then they were so agreeable with each other – never fell out nor "threaped."[1] She did not know where there was such a family for being united.

Having finished my task of gooseberry picking, I asked where the two ladies and their brother were now.

"Gone over to Morton for a walk; but they would be back in half an hour to tea."

They returned within the time Hannah had allotted them: they entered by the kitchen door. Mr. St. John, when he saw me, merely bowed and passed through; the two ladies stopped: Mary, in a few words, kindly and calmly expressed the pleasure she felt in seeing me well enough to be able to come down; Diana took my hand: she shook her head at me.

"You should have waited for my leave to descend," she said. "You still look very pale – and so thin! Poor child! – poor girl!"

Diana had a voice toned, to my ear, like the cooing of a dove. She possessed eyes whose gaze I delighted to encounter. Her whole face seemed to me full of charm. Mary's countenance was equally intelligent – her features equally pretty: but her expression was more reserved; and her manners, though gentle, more distant. Diana looked and spoke with a certain authority: she had a will evidently. It was my

---

1 Dialect. "Quarrelled."

nature to feel pleasure in yielding to an authority supported like hers; and to bend, where my conscience and self-respect permitted, to an active will.

"And what business have you here?" she continued. "It is not your place. Mary and I sit in the kitchen sometimes, because at home we like to be free, even to license – but you are a visitor, and must go into the parlour."

"I am very well here."

"Not at all – with Hannah bustling about and covering you with flour."

"Besides, the fire is too hot for you," interposed Mary.

"To be sure," added her sister. "Come, you must be obedient." And still holding my hand, she made me rise, and led me into the inner room.

"Sit there," she said, placing me on the sofa, "while we take our things off and get the tea ready: it is another privilege we exercise in our little moorland home – to prepare our own meals when we are so inclined; or when Hannah is baking, brewing, washing, or ironing."

She closed the door, leaving me solus with Mr. St. John, who sat opposite; a book or newspaper in his hand. I examined, first, the parlour, and then its occupant.

The parlour was rather a small room, very plainly furnished; yet comfortable, because clean and neat. The old-fashioned chairs were very bright, and the walnut-wood table was like a looking-glass. A few strange, antique portraits of the men and women of other days decorated the stained walls; a cupboard with glass doors contained some books and an ancient set of china. There was no superfluous ornament in the room – not one modern piece of furniture, save a brace of work-boxes and a lady's desk in rosewood, which stood on a side-table: everything – including the carpet and curtains – looked at once well worn and well saved.

Mr. St. John – sitting as still as one of the dusty pictures on the walls; keeping his eyes fixed on the page he perused, and his lips mutely sealed – was easy enough to examine. Had he been a statue instead of a man, he could not have been easier. He was young – perhaps from twenty-eight to thirty – tall, slender; his face riveted the eye: it was like a Greek face, very pure in outline; quite a straight, classic nose; quite an Athenian mouth and chin. It is seldom, indeed, an English face comes so near the antique models as did his. He might well be a little shocked at the irregularity of my lineaments, his own being so harmonious. His eyes were large and blue, with brown lashes; his high forehead, colourless as ivory, was partially streaked over by careless locks of fair hair.

This is a gentle delineation, is it not, reader? Yet he whom it describes scarcely impressed one with the idea of a gentle, a yielding, an impressible, or even of a placid nature. Quiescent as he now sat, there was something about his nostril, his mouth, his brow, which, to my perceptions, indicated elements within either restless, or hard, or eager. He did not speak to me one word, nor even direct to me one glance, till his sisters returned. Diana, as she passed in and out, in the course of preparing tea, brought me a little cake, baked on the top of the oven.

"Eat that now," she said: "you must be hungry. Hannah says you have had nothing but some gruel since breakfast."

I did not refuse it, for my appetite was awakened and keen. Mr. Rivers now closed his book, approached the table, and, as he took a seat, fixed his blue, pictorial-looking eyes full on me. There was an unceremonious directness, a searching, decided steadfastness in his gaze now, which told that intention, and not diffidence, had hitherto kept it averted from the stranger.

"You are very hungry," he said.

"I am, sir." It is my way – it always was my way, by instinct – ever to meet the brief with brevity, the direct with plainness.

"It is well for you that a low fever has forced you to abstain for the last three days: there would have been danger in yielding to the cravings of your appetite at first. Now you may eat; though still not immoderately."

"I trust I shall not eat long at your expense, sir," was my very clumsily-contrived, unpolished answer.

"No," he said coolly: "when you have indicated to us the residence of your friends, we can write to them, and you may be restored to home."

"That, I must plainly tell you, is out of my power to do; being absolutely without home and friends."

The three looked at me: but not distrustfully. I felt there was no suspicion in their glances: there was more of curiosity. I speak particularly of the young ladies. St. John's eyes, though clear enough in a literal sense, in a figurative one were difficult to fathom. He seemed to use them rather as instruments to search other people's thoughts, than as agents to reveal his own: the which combination of keenness and reserve was considerably more calculated to embarrass than to encourage.

"Do you mean to say," he asked, "that you are completely isolated from every connection?"

"I do. Not a tie links me to any living thing: not a claim do I possess to admittance under any roof in England."

"A most singular position at your age!"

Here I saw his glance directed to my hands, which were folded on the table before me. I wondered what he sought there: his words soon explained the quest.

"You have never been married? You are a spinster?"

Diana laughed. "Why, she can't be above seventeen or eighteen years old, St. John," said she.

"I am near nineteen: but I am not married. No."

I felt a burning glow mount to my face; for bitter and agitating recollections were awakened by the allusion to marriage. They all saw the embarrassment, and the emotion. Diana and Mary relieved me by turning their eyes elsewhere than to my crimsoned visage; but the colder and sterner brother continued to gaze, till the trouble he had excited forced out tears as well as colour.

"Where did you last reside?" he now asked.

"You are too inquisitive, St. John," murmured Mary, in a low voice: but he leaned over the table and required an answer, by a second firm and piercing look.

"The name of the place where, and of the person with whom I lived, is my secret," I replied, concisely.

"Which, if you like, you have, in my opinion, a right to keep, both from St. John and every other questioner," remarked Diana.

"Yet if I know nothing about you or your history, I cannot help you," he said. "And you need help: do you not?"

"I need it, and I seek it, so far, sir – that some true philanthropist will put me in the way of getting work which I can do, and the remuneration for which will keep me: if but in the barest necessaries of life."

"I know not whether I am a true philanthropist; yet I am willing to aid you to the utmost of my power, in a purpose so honest. First, then, tell me what you have been accustomed to do, and what you *can* do."

I had now swallowed my tea. I was mightily refreshed by the beverage; as much so as a giant with wine: it gave new tone to my unstrung nerves, and enabled me to address this penetrating young judge steadily.

"Mr. Rivers," I said, turning to him, and looking at him as he looked at me, openly and without diffidence, "you and your sisters have done me a great service – the greatest man can do his fellow-being: you have rescued me, by your noble hospitality, from death. This benefit conferred gives you an unlimited claim on my gratitude; and a claim, to a certain extent, on my confidence. I will tell you as much of the history of the wanderer you have harboured, as I can tell without compromising my own peace of mind – my own security, moral and physical, and that of others.

"I am an orphan; the daughter of a clergyman. My parents died before I could know them. I was brought up a dependent; educated in a charitable institution. I will even tell you the name of the establishment, where I passed six years as a pupil, and two as a teacher – Lowood Orphan Asylum, —shire: you will have heard of it, Mr. Rivers? – the Rev. Robert Brocklehurst is the treasurer."

"I have heard of Mr. Brocklehurst, and I have seen the school."

"I left Lowood nearly a year since to become a private governess. I obtained a good situation, and was happy. This place I was obliged to leave four days before I came here. The reason of my departure I cannot and ought not to explain: it would be useless – dangerous; and would sound incredible. No blame attached to me: I am as free from culpability as any one of you three. Miserable I am, and must be for a time; for the catastrophe which drove me from a house I had found a paradise was of a strange and direful nature. I observed but two points in planning my departure – speed, secrecy: to secure these, I had to leave behind me everything I possessed, except a small parcel; which, in my hurry and trouble of mind, I forgot to take out of the coach that brought me to Whitcross. To this neighbourhood, then, I came, quite destitute. I slept two nights in the open air, and wandered about two days without crossing a threshold: but[1] twice in that space of time did I taste food; and it was when brought by hunger, exhaustion, and despair, almost to the last gasp, that you, Mr. Rivers, forbade me to perish of want at your door, and took me under the shelter of your roof. I know all your sisters have done for me since – for I have not been insensible during my seeming torpor – and I owe to their spontaneous, genuine, genial compassion, as large a debt as to your evangelical charity."

"Don't make her talk any more now, St. John," said Diana as I paused; "she is evidently not yet fit for excitement. Come to the sofa, and sit down now, Miss Elliott."

I gave an involuntary half-start at hearing the *alias*: I had forgotten my new name. Mr. Rivers, whom nothing seemed to escape, noticed it at once.

"You said your name was Jane Elliott?" he observed.

"I did say so; and it is the name by which I think it expedient to be called at present: but it is not my real name, and when I hear it, it sounds strange to me."

"Your real name you will not give?"

"No: I fear discovery above all things; and whatever disclosure would lead to it I avoid."

"You are quite right, I am sure," said Diana. "Now, do, brother, let her be at peace a while."

But when St. John had mused a few moments, he recommenced, as imperturbably, and with as much acumen as ever.

"You would not like to be long dependent on our hospitality – you would wish, I see, to dispense as soon as may be with my sisters' compassion; and, above all, with my *charity* (I am quite sensible of the distinction drawn, nor do I resent it – it is just): you desire to be independent of us?"

"I do: I have already said so. Show me how to work, or how to seek work: that is all I now ask; then let me go, if it be but to the

---

1 Only.

meanest cottage – but *till then*, allow me to stay here: I dread another essay of the horrors of homeless destitution."

"Indeed, you *shall* stay here," said Diana, putting her white hand on my head. "You *shall*," repeated Mary, in the tone of undemonstrative sincerity, which seemed natural to her.

"My sisters, you see, have a pleasure in keeping you," said Mr. St. John, "as they would have a pleasure in keeping and cherishing a half-frozen bird, some wintry wind might have driven through their casement. *I* feel more inclination to put you in the way of keeping yourself; and shall endeavour to do so: but observe, my sphere is narrow. I am but the incumbent of a poor country parish: my aid must be of the humblest sort. And if you are inclined to despise the day of small things,[1] seek some more efficient succour than such as I can offer."

"She has already said that she is willing to do anything honest she *can* do," answered Diana, for me; "and you know, St. John, she has no choice of helpers: she is forced to put up with such crusty people as you."

"I will be a dressmaker: I will be a plain-work-woman; I will be a servant, a nurse-girl, if I can be no better," I answered.

"Right," said Mr. St. John, quite coolly. "If such is your spirit, I promise to aid you; in my own time and way."

He now resumed the book with which he had been occupied before tea. I soon withdrew; for I had talked as much, and sat up as long, as my present strength would permit.

---

1   See Zechariah 4:10.

CHAPTER XXX

THE more I knew of the inmates of Moor-House, the better I liked them. In a few days I had so far recovered my health that I could sit up all day, and walk out sometimes. I could join with Diana and Mary in all their occupations; converse with them as much as they wished, and aid them when and where they would allow me. There was a reviving pleasure in this intercourse, of a kind now tasted by me for the first time – the pleasure arising from perfect congeniality of tastes, sentiments, and principles.

I liked to read what they liked to read: what they enjoyed, delighted me; what they approved, I reverenced. They loved their sequestered home. I, too, in the gray, small, antique structure, with its low roof, its latticed casements, its mouldering walls, its avenue of aged firs – all grown aslant under the stress of mountain winds; its garden, dark with yew and holly – and where no flowers but of the hardiest species would bloom – found a charm, both potent and permanent. They clung to the purple moors behind and around their dwelling – to the hollow vale into which the pebbly bridle-path leading from their gate descended; and which wound between fern-banks first, and then amongst a few of the wildest little pasture-fields that ever bordered a wilderness of heath, or gave sustenance to a flock of grey moorland sheep, with their little mossy-faced lambs: – they clung to this scene, I say, with a perfect enthusiasm of attachment. I could comprehend the feeling, and share both its strength and truth. I saw the fascination of the locality. I felt the consecration of its loneliness: my eye feasted on the outline of swell and sweep – on the wild colouring communicated to ridge and dell, by moss, by heath-bell, by flower-sprinkled turf, by brilliant bracken, and mellow granite crag. These details were just to me what they were to them – so many pure and sweet sources of pleasure. The strong blast and the soft breeze; the rough and the halcyon day; the hours of sunrise and sunset; the moonlight and the clouded night, developed for me, in these regions, the same attraction as for them – wound round my faculties the same spell that entranced theirs.

In-doors we agreed equally well. They were both more accomplished and better read than I was: but with eagerness I followed in the path of knowledge they had trodden before me. I devoured the books they lent me: then it was full satisfaction to discuss with them in the evening what I had perused during the day. Thought fitted thought; opinion met opinion: we coincided, in short, perfectly.

If in our trio there was a superior and a leader, it was Diana. Physically, she far excelled me: she was handsome; she was vigorous. In her animal spirits, there was an affluence of life, and certainty of flow, such as excited my wonder, while it baffled my comprehension. I could talk a while when the evening commenced: but the first gush of vivacity and fluency gone, I was fain to sit on a stool at Diana's feet, to rest my head on her knee, and listen alternately to her and Mary; while they sounded thoroughly the topic on which I had but touched. Diana offered to teach me German. I liked to learn of her: I saw the part of instructress pleased and suited her; that of scholar pleased and suited me no less. Our natures dovetailed: mutual affection – of the strongest kind – was the result. They discovered I could draw: their pencils and colour-boxes were immediately at my service. My skill, greater in this one point than theirs, surprised and charmed them. Mary would sit and watch me by the hour together: then she would take lessons; and a docile, intelligent, assiduous pupil, she made. Thus occupied, and mutually entertained, days passed like hours, and weeks like days.

As to Mr. St. John, the intimacy which had arisen so naturally and rapidly between me and his sisters, did not extend to him. One reason of the distance yet observed between us was, that he was comparatively seldom at home: a large proportion of his time appeared devoted to visiting the sick and poor among the scattered population of his parish.

No weather seemed to hinder him in these pastoral excursions: rain or fair, he would, when his hours of morning study were over, take his hat, and, followed by his father's old pointer, Carlo, go out on his mission of love, or duty – I scarcely know in which light he regarded it. Sometimes, when the day was very unfavourable, his sisters would expostulate. He would then say, with a peculiar smile, more solemn than cheerful, –

"And if I let a gust of wind or a sprinkling of rain turn me aside from these easy tasks, what preparation would such sloth be for the future I propose to myself?"

Diana and Mary's general answer to this question was a sigh, and some minutes of apparently mournful meditation.

But besides his frequent absences, there was another barrier to friendship with him: he seemed of a reserved, an abstracted, and even of a brooding nature. Zealous in his ministerial labours, blameless in his life and habits, he yet did not appear to enjoy that mental serenity, that inward content, which should be the reward of every sincere Christian and practical philanthropist. Often, of an evening, when he sat at the window, his desk and papers before him, he would cease reading or writing, rest his chin on his hand, and deliver himself up to I know not what course of thought: but that it was perturbed and exciting might be seen in the frequent flash and changeful dilation of his eye.

I think, moreover, that Nature was not to him that treasury of delight it was to his sisters. He expressed once, and but once in my hearing, a strong sense of the rugged charm of the hills, and an inborn affection for the dark roof and hoary walls he called his home: but there was more of gloom than pleasure in the tone and words in which the sentiment was manifested; and never did he seem to roam the moors for the sake of their soothing silence − never seek out or dwell upon the thousand peaceful delights they could yield.

Incommunicative as he was, some time elapsed before I had an opportunity of gauging his mind. I first got an idea of its calibre when I heard him preach in his own church at Morton. I wish I could describe that sermon: but it is past my power. I cannot even render faithfully the effect it produced on me.

It began calm − and indeed, as far as delivery and pitch of voice went, it was calm to the end: an earnestly felt, yet strictly restrained zeal breathed soon in the distinct accents, and prompted the nervous[1] language. This grew to force − compressed, condensed, controlled. The heart was thrilled, the mind astonished, by the power of the preacher: neither were softened. Throughout there was a strange bitterness; an absence of consolatory gentleness: stern allusions to Calvinistic doctrines[2] − election, predestination, reprobation[3] − were

---

1 Vigorous.
2 Doctrines developed by John Calvin (1509-64), French theologian and Protestant reformer.
3 Election and predestination describe the Calvinist position that God's mercy is a mystery offered only to a predestined, "elect" group of individuals. Reprobation is

frequent; and each reference to these points sounded like a sentence pronounced for doom. When he had done, instead of feeling better, calmer, more enlightened by his discourse, I experienced an inexpressible sadness; for it seemed to me – I know not whether equally so to others – that the eloquence to which I had been listening had sprung from a depth where lay turbid dregs of disappointment – where moved troubling impulses of insatiate yearnings and disquieting aspirations. I was sure St. John Rivers – pure-lived, conscientious, zealous as he was – had not yet found that peace of God which passeth all understanding:[1] he had no more found it, I thought, than had I; with my concealed and racking regrets for my broken idol and lost elysium[2] – regrets to which I have latterly avoided referring; but which possessed me and tyrannized over me ruthlessly.

Meantime, a month was gone. Diana and Mary were soon to leave Moor-House, and return to the far different life and scene which awaited them, as governesses in a large, fashionable, south-of-England city; where each held a situation in families, by whose wealthy and haughty members they were regarded only as humble dependants, and who neither knew nor sought one of their innate excellences, and appreciated only their acquired accomplishments as they appreciated the skill of their cook, or the taste of their waiting woman. Mr. St. John had said nothing to me yet about the employment he had promised to obtain for me: yet it became urgent that I should have a vocation of some kind. One morning, being left alone with him a few minutes in the parlour, I ventured to approach the window-recess – which his table, chair, and desk consecrated as a kind of study – and I was going to speak; though not very well knowing in what words to frame my inquiry – for it is at all times difficult to break the ice of reserve glassing over such natures as his – when he saved me the trouble, by being the first to commence a dialogue.

Looking up as I drew near – "You have a question to ask of me?" he said.

"Yes; I wish to know whether you have heard of any service I can offer myself to undertake."

---

the other side of this doctrine, which argues that "reprobates," or the non-elect, are predestined to damnation.

1 Philippians 4:7.

2 In Greek mythology, the realm of the blessed after death; i.e., paradise.

"I found or devised something for you three weeks ago; but as you seemed both useful and happy here – as my sisters had evidently become attached to you, and your society gave them unusual pleasure – I deemed it inexpedient to break in on your mutual comfort, till their approaching departure from Marsh-End should render yours necessary."

"And they will go in three days now?" I said.

"Yes; and when they go, I shall return to the parsonage at Morton: Hannah will accompany me; and this old house will be shut up."

I waited a few moments, expecting he would go on with the subject first broached; but he seemed to have entered another train of reflection: his look denoted abstraction from me and my business. I was obliged to recall him to a theme which was of necessity one of close and anxious interest to me.

"What is the employment you had in view, Mr. Rivers? I hope this delay will not have increased the difficulty of securing it."

"Oh, no; since it is an employment which depends only on me to give, and you to accept."

He again paused: there seemed a reluctance to continue. I grew impatient: a restless movement or two, and an eager and exacting glance fastened on his face, conveyed the feeling to him as effectually as words could have done, and with less trouble.

"You need be in no hurry to hear," he said: "let me frankly tell you, I have nothing eligible or profitable to suggest. Before I explain, recall, if you please, my notice, clearly given, that if I helped you, it must be as the blind man would help the lame. I am poor; for I find that, when I have paid my father's debts, all the patrimony remaining to me will be this crumbling grange, the row of scathed firs behind, and the patch of moorish soil, with the yew-trees and holly-bushes in front. I am obscure: Rivers is an old name; but of the three sole descendants of the race, two earn the dependant's crust among strangers, and the third considers himself an alien from his native country – not only for life, but in death. Yes, and deems, and is bound to deem himself honoured by the lot; and aspires but after the day when the cross of separation from fleshly ties shall be laid on his shoulders, and when the Head of that church-militant of whose humblest members he is one, shall give the word, 'Rise, follow me!'"

St. John said these words as he pronounced his sermons, with a quiet, deep voice; with an unflushed cheek, and a coruscating radiance of glance. He resumed: –

"And since I am myself poor and obscure, I can offer you but a service of poverty and obscurity. *You* may even think it degrading – for I see now your habits have been what the world calls refined: your tastes lean to the ideal; and your society has at least been amongst the educated – but *I* consider that no service degrades which can better our race. I hold that the more arid and unreclaimed the soil where the Christian labourer's task of tillage is appointed him – the scantier the meed his toil brings – the higher the honour. His, under such circumstances, is the destiny of the pioneer: and the first pioneers of the Gospel were the Apostles – their captain was Jesus, the Redeemer, himself."

"Well?" I said, as he again paused – "proceed."

He looked at me before he proceeded: indeed, he seemed leisurely to read my face, as if its features and lines were characters on a page. The conclusions drawn from this scrutiny he partially expressed in his succeeding observations.

"I believe you will accept the post I offer you," said he; "and hold it for a while: not permanently, though: any more than I could permanently keep the narrow and narrowing – the tranquil, hidden office of English country incumbent: for in your nature is an alloy as detrimental to repose as that in mine; though of a different kind."

"Do explain," I urged, when he halted once more.

"I will; and you shall hear how poor the proposal is – how trivial – how cramping. I shall not stay long at Morton, now that my father is dead, and that I am my own master. I shall leave the place probably in the course of a twelvemonth: but while I *do* stay, I will exert myself to the utmost for its improvement. Morton, when I came to it two years ago, had no school: the children of the poor were excluded from every hope of progress. I established one for boys: I mean now to open a second school for girls. I have hired a building for the purpose, with a cottage of two rooms attached to it for the mistress's house. Her salary will be thirty pounds a year: her house is already furnished, very simply, but sufficiently, by the kindness of a lady, Miss Oliver; the only daughter of the sole rich man in my parish – Mr.

Oliver, the proprietor of a needle-factory and iron-foundry in the valley. The same lady pays for the education and clothing of an orphan from the workhouse; on condition that she shall aid the mistress in such menial offices connected with her own house and the school, as her occupation of teaching will prevent her having time to discharge in person. Will you be this mistress?"

He put the question rather hurriedly; he seemed half to expect an indignant, or at least a disdainful rejection of the offer: not knowing all my thoughts and feelings, though guessing some, he could not tell in what light the lot would appear to me. In truth it was humble – but then it was sheltered, and I wanted a safe asylum: it was plodding – but then, compared with that of a governess in a rich house, it was independent; and the fear of servitude with strangers entered my soul like iron: it was not ignoble – not unworthy – not mentally degrading. I made my decision.

"I thank you for the proposal, Mr. Rivers; and I accept it with all my heart."

"But you comprehend me?" he said. "It is a village-school: your scholars will be only poor girls – cottagers' children – at the best, farmers' daughters. Knitting, sewing, reading, writing, cyphering,[1] will be all you will have to teach. What will you do with your accomplishments? What, with the largest portion of your mind – sentiments – tastes?"

"Save them till they are wanted. They will keep."

"You know what you undertake, then?"

"I do."

He now smiled: and not a bitter or a sad smile; but one well pleased and deeply gratified.

"And when will you commence the exercise of your function?"

"I will go to my house to-morrow, and open the school, if you like, next week."

"Very well: so be it."

He rose and walked through the room. Standing still, he again looked at me. He shook his head.

"What do you disapprove of, Mr. Rivers?" I asked.

---

1   Arithmetic.

"You will not stay at Morton long: no, no!"

"Why? What is your reason for saying so?"

"I read it in your eye: it is not of that description which promises the maintenance of an even tenor in life."

"I am not ambitious."

He started at the word "ambitious." He repeated, "No. What made you think of ambition? Who is ambitious? I know I am: but how did you find it out?"

"I was speaking of myself."

"Well, if you are not ambitious, you are —." He paused.

"What?"

"I was going to say, impassioned: but perhaps you would have misunderstood the word, and been displeased. I mean, that human affections and sympathies have a most powerful hold on you. I am sure you cannot long be content to pass your leisure in solitude, and to devote your working hours to a monotonous labour wholly void of stimulus; any more than I can be content," he added, with emphasis, "to live here buried in morass, pent in with mountain – my nature, that God gave me, contravened; my faculties, heaven-bestowed, paralyzed – made useless. You hear now how I contradict myself. I, who preached contentment with a humble lot, and justified the vocation even of hewers of wood, and drawers of water,[1] in God's service – I, His ordained minister, almost rave in my restlessness. Well, propensities and principles must be reconciled by some means."

He left the room. In this brief hour I had learnt more of him than in the whole previous month: yet still he puzzled me.

Diana and Mary Rivers became more sad and silent as the day approached for leaving their brother, and their home. They both tried to appear as usual; but the sorrow they had to struggle against was one that could not be entirely conquered or concealed. Diana intimated that this would be a different parting from any they had ever yet known. It would probably, as far as St. John was concerned, be a parting for years: it might be a parting for life.

"He will sacrifice all to his long-framed resolves," she said: "natural affection and feelings more potent still. St. John looks quiet, Jane,

---

1   Joshua 9:21.

but he hides a fever in his vitals. You would think him gentle, yet in some things he is inexorable as death; and the worst of it is, my conscience will hardly permit me to dissuade him from his severe decision: certainly, I cannot for a moment blame him for it. It is right, noble, Christian: yet it breaks my heart." And the tears gushed to her fine eyes. Mary bent her head low over her work.

"We are now without father: we shall soon be without home and brother," she murmured.

At that moment a little incident supervened, which seemed decreed by fate, purposely to prove the truth of the adage, that "misfortunes never come singly,"[1] and to add to their distresses the vexing one of the slip between the cup and the lip. St. John passed the window reading a letter. He entered.

"Our uncle John is dead," said he.

Both the sisters seemed struck: not shocked or appalled: the tidings appeared in their eyes rather momentous than afflicting.

"Dead?" repeated Diana.

"Yes."

She riveted a searching gaze on her brother's face. "And what then?" she demanded, in a low voice.

"What then, Die?" he replied, maintaining a marble immobility of feature. "What then? Why – nothing. Read."

He threw the letter into her lap. She glanced over it, and handed it to Mary. Mary perused it in silence, and returned it to her brother. All three looked at each other, and all three smiled – a dreary, pensive smile enough.

"Amen! We can yet live," said Diana, at last.

"At any rate, it makes us no worse off than we were before," remarked Mary.

"Only it forces rather strongly on the mind the picture of what *might have been*," said Mr. Rivers, "and contrasts it somewhat too vividly with what *is*."

He folded the letter, locked it in his desk, and again went out.

For some minutes no one spoke. Diana then turned to me.

"Jane, you will wonder at us and our mysteries," she said; "and

---

1 Proverbial.

think us hard-hearted beings not to be more moved at the death of so near a relation as an uncle: but we have never seen him or known him. He was my mother's brother. My father and he quarrelled long ago. It was by his advice that my father risked most of his property in the speculation that ruined him. Mutual recriminations passed between them: they parted in anger, and were never reconciled. My uncle engaged afterwards in more prosperous undertakings: it appears he realised a fortune of twenty thousand pounds. He was never married, and had no near kindred but ourselves, and one other person, not more closely related than we. My father always cherished the idea that he would atone for his error, by leaving his possessions to us: that letter informs us that he has bequeathed every penny to the other relation; with the exception of thirty guineas, to be divided between St. John, Diana, and Mary Rivers, for the purchase of three mourning rings. He had a right, of course, to do as he pleased: and yet a momentary damp is cast on the spirits by the receipt of such news. Mary and I would have esteemed ourselves rich with a thousand pounds each; and to St. John such a sum would have been valuable, for the good it would have enabled him to do."

This explanation given, the subject was dropped, and no further reference made to it, by either Mr. Rivers or his sisters. The next day, I left Marsh End for Morton. The day after, Diana and Mary quitted it for distant B—. In a week, Mr. Rivers and Hannah repaired to the parsonage: and so the old grange was abandoned.

CHAPTER XXXI

MY home, then – when I at last find a home, – is a cottage: a little room with white-washed walls, and a sanded floor; containing four painted chairs and a table, a clock, a cupboard, with two or three plates and dishes, and a set of tea-things in delf.[1] Above, a chamber of the same dimensions as the kitchen, with a deal bedstead, and chest of drawers; small, yet too large to be filled with my scanty wardrobe: though the kindness of my gentle and generous friends has increased that, by a modest stock of such things as are necessary.

It is evening. I have dismissed, with the fee of an orange, the little orphan who serves me as a handmaid. I am sitting alone on the hearth. This morning, the village school opened. I had twenty scholars. But three of the number can read: none write or cypher. Several knit, and a few sew a little. They speak with the broadest accent of the district. At present, they and I have a difficulty in understanding each other's language. Some of them are unmannered, rough, intractable, as well as ignorant; but others are docile, have a wish to learn, and evince a disposition that pleases me. I must not forget that these coarsely-clad little peasants are of flesh and blood as good as the scions of gentlest genealogy; and that the germs of native excellence, refinement, intelligence, kind feeling, are as likely to exist in their hearts as in those of the best-born. My duty will be to develop these germs: surely I shall find some happiness in discharging that office. Much enjoyment I do not expect in the life opening before me: yet it will, doubtless, if I regulate my mind, and exert my powers as I ought, yield me enough to live on from day to day.

Was I very gleeful, settled, content, during the hours I passed in yonder bare, humble school-room this morning and afternoon? Not to deceive myself, I must reply – No: I felt desolate to a degree. I felt – yes, idiot that I am – I felt degraded. I doubted I had taken a step which sank instead of raising me in the scale of social existence. I was weakly dismayed at the ignorance, the poverty, the coarseness of all I heard and saw round me. But let me not hate and despise myself too much for these feelings: I know them to be wrong – that is a great step gained; I shall strive to overcome them. To-morrow, I trust, I shall

---

1   More properly "delft," a glazed earthenware crockery made at Delft in Holland.

get the better of them partially; and in a few weeks, perhaps, they will be quite subdued. In a few months, it is possible, the happiness of seeing progress, and a change for the better in my scholars, may substitute gratification for disgust.

Meantime, let me ask myself one question – Which is better? – To have surrendered to temptation; listened to passion; made no painful effort – no struggle; – but to have sunk down in the silken snare; fallen asleep on the flowers covering it; wakened in a southern clime, amongst the luxuries of a pleasure-villa: to have been now living in France, Mr. Rochester's mistress; delirious with his love half my time – for he would – oh, yes, he would have loved me well for a while. He *did* love me – no one will ever love me so again. I shall never more know the sweet homage given to beauty, youth, and grace – for never to any one else shall I seem to possess these charms. He was fond and proud of me – it is what no man besides will ever be. – But where am I wandering, and what am I saying: and, above all, feeling? Whether is it better, I ask, to be a slave in a fool's paradise at Marseilles – fevered with delusive bliss one hour – suffocating with the bitterest tears of remorse and shame the next – or to be a village-schoolmistress, free and honest, in a breezy mountain nook in the healthy heart of England?

Yes; I feel now that I was right when I adhered to principle and law, and scorned and crushed the insane promptings of a frenzied moment. God directed me to a correct choice: I thank His providence for the guidance!

Having brought my eventide musings to this point, I rose, went to my door, and looked at the sunset of the harvest-day, and at the quiet fields before my cottage; which, with the school, was distant half a mile from the village. The birds were singing their last strains –

"The air was mild, the dew was balm."[1]

While I looked, I thought myself happy, and was surprised to find myself ere long weeping – and why? For the doom which had reft me from adhesion to my master: for him I was no more to see; for the desperate grief and fatal fury – consequences of my departure –

---

1 See Scott's *The Lay of the Last Minstrel* (1805), III.xxiv.3-4.

which might now, perhaps, be dragging him from the path of right, too far to leave hope of ultimate restoration thither. At this thought, I turned my face aside from the lovely sky of eve and lonely vale of Morton – I say *lonely*, for in that bend of it visible to me, there was no building apparent save the church and the parsonage, half-hid in trees; and, quite at the extremity, the roof of Vale-Hall, where the rich Mr. Oliver and his daughter lived. I hid my eyes, and leant my head against the stone frame of my door: but soon a slight noise near the wicket which shut in my tiny garden from the meadow beyond it, made me look up. A dog – old Carlo, Mr. Rivers' pointer, as I saw in a moment – was pushing the gate with his nose, and St. John himself leant upon it with folded arms; his brow knit, his gaze, grave almost to displeasure, fixed on me. I asked him to come in.

"No, I cannot stay: I have only brought you a little parcel my sisters left for you. I think it contains a colour-box, pencils, and paper."

I approached to take it: a welcome gift it was. He examined my face, I thought, with austerity, as I came near: the traces of tears were doubtless very visible upon it.

"Have you found your first day's work harder than you expected?" he asked.

"Oh, no! On the contrary, I think in time I shall get on with my scholars very well."

"But perhaps your accommodations – your cottage – your furniture – have disappointed your expectations? They are, in truth, scanty enough; but" — I interrupted:

"My cottage is clean and weather-proof; my furniture sufficient and commodious. All I see has made me thankful, not despondent. I am not absolutely such a fool and sensualist as to regret the absence of a carpet, a sofa, and silver plate: besides, five weeks ago I had nothing – I was an outcast, a beggar, a vagrant; now I have acquaintance, a home, a business. I wonder at the goodness of God; the generosity of my friends; the bounty of my lot. I do not repine."

"But you feel solitude an oppression? The little house there behind you is dark and empty?"

"I have hardly had time yet to enjoy a sense of tranquillity, much less to grow impatient under one of loneliness."

"Very well; I hope you feel the content you express: at any rate, your good sense will tell you that it is too soon yet to yield to the vacillating fears of Lot's wife.[1] What you had left before I saw you, of course I do not know; but I counsel you to resist, firmly, every temptation which would incline you to look back: pursue your present career steadily, for some months at least."

"It is what I mean to do," I answered. St. John continued: —

"It is hard work to control the workings of inclination, and turn the bent of nature: but that it may be done, I know from experience. God has given us, in a measure, the power to make our own fate; and when our energies seem to demand a sustenance they cannot get — when our will strains after a path we may not follow — we need neither starve from inanition, nor stand still in despair: we have but to seek another nourishment for the mind, as strong as the forbidden food it longed to taste — and perhaps purer; and to hew out for the adventurous foot a road as direct and broad as the one Fortune has blocked up against us, if rougher than it.

"A year ago, I was myself intensely miserable, because I thought I had made a mistake in entering the ministry: its uniform duties wearied me to death. I burnt for the more active life of the world — for the more exciting toils of a literary career — for the destiny of an artist, author, orator; anything, rather than that of a priest: yes, the heart of a politician, of a soldier, of a votary of glory, a lover of renown, a luster after power, beat under my curate's surplice. I considered; my life was so wretched, it must be changed, or I must die. After a season of darkness and struggling, light broke and relief fell: my cramped existence all at once spread out to a plain without bounds — my powers heard a call from heaven to rise, gather their full strength, spread their wings and mount beyond ken. God had an errand for me; to bear which afar, to deliver it well, skill and strength, courage and eloquence, the best qualifications of soldier, statesman and orator, were all needed: for these all centre in the good missionary.

"A missionary I resolved to be. From that moment my state of mind changed: the fetters dissolved and dropped from every faculty, leaving nothing of bondage but its galling soreness — which time only can heal. My father, indeed, opposed the determination; but since his death, I have not a legitimate obstacle to contend with: some affairs settled, a successor for Morton provided, an entanglement or two of

---

1   See Genesis 19:26. When fleeing the destruction of Sodom and Gomorrah, Lot's wife looked back in regret, and was turned into a pillar of salt.

the feelings broken through or cut asunder – a last conflict with human weakness, in which I know I shall overcome, because I have vowed that I *will* overcome – and I leave Europe for the East."

He said this in his peculiar, subdued yet emphatic voice; looking, when he had ceased speaking, not at me, but at the setting sun: at which I looked too. Both he and I had our backs towards the path leading up the field to the wicket. We had heard no step on the grass-grown track; the water running in the vale was the one lulling sound of the hour and scene: we might well then start when a gay voice, sweet as a silver bell, exclaimed: –

"Good evening, Mr. Rivers. And good evening, old Carlo. Your dog is quicker to recognize his friends than you are, sir: he pricked his ears and wagged his tail when I was at the bottom of the field, and you have your back towards me now."

It was true. Though Mr. Rivers had started at the first of those musical accents, as if a thunderbolt had split a cloud over his head, he stood yet, at the close of the sentence, in the same attitude in which the speaker had surprised him: his arm resting on the gate, his face directed towards the west. He turned at last, with measured delibera-tion. A vision, as it seemed to me, had risen at his side. There appeared, within three feet of him, a form clad in pure white – a youthful, graceful form: full, yet fine in contour; and when, after bending to caress Carlo, it lifted up its head, and threw back a long veil, there bloomed under his glance a face of perfect beauty. Perfect beauty is a strong expression; but I do not retract or qualify it: as sweet features as ever the temperate clime of Albion[1] moulded; as pure hues of rose and lily as ever her humid gales and vapoury skies generated and screened, justified, in this instance, the term. No charm was want-ing, no defect was perceptible: the young girl had regular and delicate lineaments; eyes shaped and coloured as we see them in lovely pic-tures, large, and dark, and full; the long and shadowy eyelash which encircles a fine eye with so soft a fascination; the pencilled brow which gives such clearness; the white, smooth forehead, which adds such repose to the livelier beauties of tint and ray; the cheek, oval, fresh and smooth; the lips fresh too, ruddy, healthy, sweetly formed; the even and gleaming teeth without flaw; the small, dimpled chin;

---

1 Britain.

the ornament of rich, plenteous tresses, – all advantages, in short, which combined, realize the ideal of beauty, were fully hers. I wondered, as I looked at this fair creature: I admired her with my whole heart. Nature had surely formed her in a partial mood; and forgetting her usual stinted step-mother dole of gifts, had endowed this, her darling, with a granddame's bounty.

What did St. John Rivers think of this earthly angel? I naturally asked myself that question as I saw him turn to her and look at her; and, as naturally, I sought the answer to the inquiry in his countenance. He had already withdrawn his eye from the Peri,[1] and was looking at a humble tuft of daisies which grew by the wicket.

"A lovely evening; but late for you to be out alone," he said, as he crushed the snowy heads of the closed flowers with his foot.

"Oh, I only came home from S—— (she mentioned the name of a large town some twenty miles distant) this afternoon. Papa told me you had opened your school, and that the new mistress was come; and so I put on my bonnet after tea, and ran up the valley to see her: this is she?" pointing to me.

"It is," said St. John.

"Do you think you shall like Morton?" she asked of me; with a direct and naïve simplicity of tone and manner, pleasing, if child-like.

"I hope I shall. I have many inducements to do so."

"Did you find your scholars as attentive as you expected?"

"Quite."

"Do you like your house?"

"Very much."

"Have I furnished it nicely?"

"Very nicely indeed."

"And made a good choice of an attendant for you in Alice Wood?"

"You have indeed. She is teachable and handy." (This, then, I thought, is Miss Oliver, the heiress: favoured, it seems, in the gifts of fortune, as well as in those of nature! What happy combination of the planets presided over her birth, I wonder?)

"I shall come up and help you to teach sometimes," she added. "It will be a change for me to visit you now and then: and I like a change. Mr. Rivers, I have been *so* gay during my stay at S——. Last

---

1   In Persian mythology, a beautiful spirit.

night, or rather this morning, I was dancing till two o'clock. The —th regiment are stationed there, since the riots;[1] and the officers are the most agreeable men in the world: they put all our young knife-grinders and scissar merchants to shame."

It seemed to me that Mr. St. John's under lip protruded, and his upper lip curled a moment. His mouth certainly looked a good deal compressed, and the lower part of his face unusually stern and square, as the laughing girl gave him this information. He lifted his gaze, too, from the daisies, and turned it on her. An unsmiling, a searching, a meaning gaze it was. She answered it with a second laugh: and laughter well became her youth, her roses, her dimples, her bright eyes.

As he stood, mute and grave, she again fell to caressing Carlo. "Poor Carlo loves me," said she. "*He* is not stern and distant to his friends; and if he could speak, he would not be silent."

As she patted the dog's head, bending with native grace before his young and austere master, I saw a glow rise to that master's face. I saw his solemn eye melt with sudden fire, and flicker with resistless emotion. Flushed and kindled thus, he looked nearly as beautiful for a man as she for a woman. His chest heaved once, as if his large heart, weary of despotic constriction, had expanded, despite the will, and made a vigorous bound for the attainment of liberty. But he curbed it, I think, as a resolute rider would curb a rearing steed. He responded neither by word nor movement to the gentle advances made him.

"Papa says you never come to see us now," continued Miss Oliver, looking up. "You are quite a stranger at Vale Hall. He is alone this evening, and not very well: will you return with me and visit him?"

"It is not a seasonable hour to intrude on Mr. Oliver," answered St. John.

"Not a seasonable hour! But, I declare, it is. It is just the hour when papa most wants company: when the works are closed, and he has no business to occupy him. Now, Mr. Rivers, *do* come. Why are you so very shy, and so very sombre?" She filled up the hiatus his silence left by a reply of her own.

"I forgot!" she exclaimed, shaking her beautiful curled head, as if shocked at herself. "I am so giddy and thoughtless! *Do* excuse me. It

---

1   Probably a reference to the anti-industrialization Luddite riots of 1812; the dating of the action of *Jane Eyre* is not consistent throughout the text. Brontë returned to the topic of these riots in her next novel, *Shirley* (1849).

had slipped my memory that you have good reasons to be indisposed for joining in my chatter. Diana and Mary have left you, and Moor House is shut up, and you are so lonely. I am sure I pity you. Do come and see papa."

"Not to-night, Miss Rosamond, not to-night."

Mr. St. John spoke almost like an automaton: himself only knew the effort it cost him thus to refuse.

"Well, if you are so obstinate, I will leave you; for I dare not stay any longer: the dew begins to fall. Good-evening!"

She held out her hand. He just touched it. "Good-evening!" he repeated, in a voice low and hollow as an echo. She turned; but in a moment returned.

"Are you well?" she asked. Well might she put the question: his face was blanched as her gown.

"Quite well," he enunciated; and, with a bow, he left the gate. She went one way; he another. She turned twice to gaze after him, as she tripped fairy-like down the field; he, as he strode firmly across, never turned at all.

This spectacle of another's suffering and sacrifice, rapt my thoughts from exclusive meditation on my own. Diana Rivers had designated her brother "inexorable as death." She had not exaggerated.

CHAPTER XXXII

I CONTINUED the labours of the village school as actively and faithfully as I could. It was truly hard work at first. Some time elapsed
before, with all my efforts, I could comprehend my scholars and their
nature. Wholly untaught, with faculties quite torpid, they seemed to
me hopelessly dull; and, at first sight, all dull alike: but I soon found I
was mistaken. There was a difference amongst them as amongst the
educated; and when I got to know them, and they me, this difference
rapidly developed itself. Their amazement at me, my language, my
rules and ways, once subsided, I found some of these heavy-looking,
gaping rustics wake up into sharp-witted girls enough. Many showed
themselves obliging, and amiable too; and I discovered amongst them
not a few examples of natural politeness, and innate self-respect, as
well as of excellent capacity, that won both my good will and my
admiration. These soon took a pleasure in doing their work well; in
keeping their persons neat; in learning their tasks regularly; in acquiring quiet and orderly manners. The rapidity of their progress, in some
instances, was even surprising; and an honest and happy pride I took
in it: besides, I began personally to like some of the best girls; and they
liked me. I had amongst my scholars several farmers' daughters: young
women grown, almost. These could already read, write, and sew; and
to them I taught the elements of grammar, geography, history, and the
finer kinds of needlework. I found estimable characters amongst them
– characters desirous of information, and disposed for improvement –
with whom I passed many a pleasant evening hour in their own
homes. Their parents then (the farmer and his wife) loaded me with
attentions. There was an enjoyment in accepting their simple kindness, and in repaying it by a consideration – a scrupulous regard to
their feelings – to which they were not, perhaps, at all times accustomed, and which both charmed and benefited them; because, while
it elevated them in their own eyes, it made them emulous to merit
the deferential treatment they received.

I felt I became a favourite in the neighbourhood. Whenever I
went out, I heard on all sides cordial salutations, and was welcomed
with friendly smiles. To live amidst general regard, though it be but
the regard of working-people, is like "sitting in sunshine, calm and

sweet:"[1] serene inward feelings bud and bloom under the ray. At this period of my life, my heart far oftener swelled with thankfulness than sunk with dejection: and yet, reader, to tell you all, in the midst of this calm, this useful existence – after a day passed in honourable exertion amongst my scholars, an evening spent in drawing or reading contentedly alone – I used to rush into strange dreams at night: dreams many-coloured, agitated, full of the ideal, the stirring, the stormy – dreams where, amidst unusual scenes, charged with adventure, with agitating risk and romantic chance, I still again and again met Mr. Rochester, always at some exciting crisis; and then the sense of being in his arms, hearing his voice, meeting his eye, touching his hand and cheek, loving him, being loved by him – the hope of passing a lifetime at his side, would be renewed, with all its first force and fire. Then I awoke. Then I recalled where I was, and how situated. Then I rose up on my curtainless bed, trembling and quivering; and then the still, dark night witnessed the convulsion of despair, and heard the burst of passion. By nine o'clock the next morning, I was punctually opening the school; tranquil, settled, prepared for the steady duties of the day.

Rosamond Oliver kept her word in coming to visit me. Her call at the school was generally made in the course of her morning ride. She would canter up to the door on her pony, followed by a mounted livery servant. Anything more exquisite than her appearance, in her purple habit, with her Amazon's cap of black velvet placed gracefully above the long curls that kissed her cheek and floated to her shoulders, can scarcely be imagined: and it was thus she would enter the rustic building, and glide through the dazzled ranks of the village children. She generally came at the hour when Mr. Rivers was engaged in giving his daily catechising lesson. Keenly, I fear, did the eye of the visitress pierce the young pastor's heart. A sort of instinct seemed to warn him of her entrance, even when he did not see it; and when he was looking quite away from the door, if she appeared at it, his cheek would glow, and his marble-seeming features, though they refused to relax, changed indescribably; and in their very quiescence

---

1   From Thomas Moore's *Lalla Rookh*, Third Day, 346. The poem was published in 1817.

became expressive of a repressed fervour, stronger than working muscle or darting glance could indicate.

Of course, she knew her power: indeed, he did not, because he could not, conceal it from her. In spite of his Christian stoicism, when she went up and addressed him, and smiled gaily, encouragingly, even fondly in his face, his hand would tremble, and his eye burn. He seemed to say, with his sad and resolute look, if he did not say it with his lips, "I love you, and I know you prefer me. It is not despair of success that keeps me dumb. If I offered my heart, I believe you would accept it. But that heart is already laid on a sacred altar: the fire is arranged round it. It will soon be no more than a sacrifice consumed."

And then she would pout like a disappointed child; a pensive cloud would soften her radiant vivacity; she would withdraw her hand hastily from his, and turn in transient petulance from his aspect, at once so heroic and so martyr-like. St. John, no doubt, would have given the world to follow, recall, retain her, when she thus left him: but he would not give one chance of Heaven; nor relinquish, for the elysium of her love, one hope of the true, eternal Paradise. Besides, he could not bound all that he had in his nature – the rover, the aspirant, the poet, the priest – in the limits of a single passion. He could not – he would not – renounce his wild field of mission warfare for the parlours and the peace of Vale Hall. I learnt so much from himself, in an inroad I once, despite his reserve, had the daring to make on his confidence.

Miss Oliver already honoured me with frequent visits to my cottage. I had learnt her whole character; which was without mystery or disguise: she was coquettish, but not heartless; exacting, but not worthlessly selfish. She had been indulged from her birth, but was not absolutely spoilt. She was hasty, but good-humoured; vain (she could not help it, when every glance in the glass showed her such a flush of loveliness), but not affected; liberal-handed; innocent of the pride of wealth; ingenuous; sufficiently intelligent; gay, lively, and unthinking: she was very charming, in short, even to a cool observer of her own sex like me; but she was not profoundly interesting or thoroughly impressive. A very different sort of mind was hers from that, for instance, of the sisters of St. John. Still, I liked her almost as I liked my pupil Adèle: except that, for a child whom we have watched over and taught, a closer affection is engendered than we can give an equally attractive adult acquaintance.

She had taken an amiable caprice to me. She said I was like Mr. Rivers (only, certainly, she allowed, "not one-tenth so handsome; though I was a nice, neat little soul enough: but he was an angel"). I was, however, good, clever, composed, and firm, like him. I was a *lusus naturë*,[1] she affirmed, as a village-schoolmistress: she was sure my previous history, if known, would make a delightful romance.

One evening, while with her usual child-like activity, and thoughtless yet not offensive inquisitiveness, she was rummaging the cupboard and the table-drawer of my little kitchen, she discovered first two French books, a volume of Schiller, a German grammar and dictionary; and then my drawing-materials and some sketches, including a pencil-head of a pretty little cherub-like girl, one of my scholars, and sundry views from nature, taken in the Vale of Morton and on the surrounding moors. She was first transfixed with surprise, and then electrified with delight.

"Had I done these pictures? Did I know French and German? What a love – what a miracle I was! I drew better than her master in the first school in S——. Would I sketch a portrait of her to show to papa?"

"With pleasure," I replied; and I felt a thrill of artist-delight at the idea of copying from so perfect and radiant a model. She had then on a dark-blue silk dress; her arms and her neck were bare; her only ornament was her chestnut tresses, which waved over her shoulders with all the wild grace of natural curls. I took a sheet of fine card-board, and drew a careful outline. I promised myself the pleasure of colouring it; and, as it was getting late then, I told her she must come and sit another day.

She made such a report of me to her father, that Mr. Oliver him-self accompanied her next evening – a tall, massive-featured, middle-aged, and grey-headed man, at whose side his lovely daughter looked like a bright flower near a hoary turret. He appeared a taciturn, and perhaps a proud personage; but he was very kind to me. The sketch of

---

1   Latin. A freak of nature. An unusual specimen.

Rosamond's portrait pleased him highly: he said I must make a finished picture of it. He insisted, too, on my coming the next day to spend the evening at Vale-Hall.

I went. I found it a large, handsome residence, showing abundant evidences of wealth in the proprietor. Rosamond was full of glee and pleasure all the time I stayed. Her father was affable; and when he entered into conversation with me after tea, he expressed in strong terms his approbation of what I had done in Morton school; and said he only feared, from what he saw and heard, I was too good for the place, and would soon quit it for one more suitable.

"Indeed!" cried Rosamond, "she is clever enough to be a governess in a high family, papa."

I thought – I would far rather be where I am than in any high family in the land. Mr. Oliver spoke of Mr. Rivers – of the Rivers' family – with great respect. He said it was a very old name in that neighbourhood; that the ancestors of the house were wealthy; that all Morton had once belonged to them; that even now he considered the representative of that house might, if he liked, make an alliance with the best. He accounted it a pity that so fine and talented a young man should have formed the design of going out as a missionary: it was quite throwing a valuable life away. It appeared, then, that her father would throw no obstacle in the way of Rosamond's union with St. John. Mr. Oliver evidently regarded the young clergyman's good birth, old name, and sacred profession, as sufficient compensation for the want of fortune.

It was the fifth of November, and a holiday.[1] My little servant, after helping me to clean my house, was gone; well satisfied with the fee of a penny for her aid. All about me was spotless and bright – scoured floor, polished grate, and well-rubbed chairs. I had also made myself neat, and had now the afternoon before me to spend as I would.

The translation of a few pages of German occupied an hour; then I got my palette and pencils, and fell to the more soothing, because easier occupation, of completing Rosamond Oliver's miniature. The head was finished already: there was but the background to tint, and the drapery to shade off; a touch of carmine, too, to add to the ripe

---

1   Guy Fawkes Day, the anniversary of the failed Gunpowder Plot in 1605.

lips – a soft curl here and there to the tresses – a deeper tinge to the shadow of the lash under the azured eyelid. I was absorbed in the execution of these nice details, when, after one rapid tap, my door unclosed, admitting St. John Rivers.

"I am come to see how you are spending your holiday," he said. "Not, I hope, in thought? No, that is well: while you draw you will not feel lonely. You see, I mistrust you still: though you have borne up wonderfully so far. I have brought you a book for evening solace," and he laid on the table a new publication – a poem: one of those genuine productions so often vouchsafed to the fortunate public of those days – the golden age of modern literature. Alas! the readers of our era are less favoured. But, courage! I will not pause either to accuse or repine. I know poetry is not dead, nor genius lost; nor has Mammon[1] gained power over either, to bind or slay: they will both assert their existence, their presence, their liberty, and strength again one day. Powerful angels, safe in heaven! they smile when sordid souls triumph, and feeble ones weep over their destruction. Poetry destroyed? Genius banished? No! Mediocrity, no: do not let envy prompt you to the thought. No; they not only live, but reign, and redeem: and without their divine influence spread everywhere, you would be in hell – the hell of your own meanness.

While I was eagerly glancing at the bright pages of Marmion[2] (for Marmion it was), St. John stooped to examine my drawing. His tall figure sprang erect again with a start: he said nothing. I looked up at him: he shunned my eye. I knew his thoughts well, and could read his heart plainly; at the moment I felt calmer and cooler than he: I had then temporarily the advantage of him; and I conceived an inclination to do him some good, if I could.

"With all his firmness and self-control," thought I, "he tasks himself too far: locks every feeling and pang within – expresses, confesses, imparts nothing. I am sure it would benefit him to talk a little about this sweet Rosamond, whom he thinks he ought not to marry: I will make him talk."

I said first: "Take a chair, Mr. Rivers." But he answered, as he

---

1   The demon of materialism and covetousness. Jane uses the name here to represent money and the desire for wealth.
2   Scott's long narrative poem *Marmion* was published in 1808.

always did, that he could not stay. "Very well," I responded, mentally, "stand, if you like; but you shall not go just yet, I am determined: solitude is at least as bad for you as it is for me. I'll try if I cannot discover the secret spring of your confidence, and find an aperture in that marble breast through which I can shed one drop of the balm of sympathy."

"Is this portrait like?" I asked, bluntly.

"Like! Like whom? I did not observe it closely."

"You did, Mr. Rivers."

He almost started at my sudden and strange abruptness: he looked at me astonished. "Oh, that is nothing yet," I muttered within. "I don't mean to be baffled by a little stiffness on your part: I'm prepared to go to considerable lengths." I continued, "You observed it closely and distinctly: but I have no objection to your looking at it again," and I rose and placed it in his hand.

"A well-executed picture," he said; "very soft, clear colouring; very graceful and correct drawing."

"Yes, yes; I know all that. But what of the resemblance? Who is it like?"

Mastering some hesitation, he answered, "Miss Oliver, I presume."

"Of course. And now, sir, to reward you for the accurate guess, I will promise to paint you a careful and faithful duplicate of this very picture, provided you admit that the gift would be acceptable to you. I don't wish to throw away my time and trouble on an offering you would deem worthless."

He continued to gaze at the picture: the longer he looked, the firmer he held it, the more he seemed to covet it. "It is like!" he murmured; "the eye is well managed: the colour, light, expression, are perfect. It smiles!"

"Would it comfort, or would it wound you to have a similar painting? Tell me that. When you are at Madagascar, or at the Cape, or in India, would it be a consolation to have that memento in your possession; or would the sight of it bring recollections calculated to enervate and distress?"

He now furtively raised his eyes: he glanced at me irresolute, disturbed: he again surveyed the picture.

"That I should like to have it is certain: whether it would be judicious or wise is another question."

Since I had ascertained that Rosamond really preferred him, and that her father was not likely to oppose the match, I – less exalted in my views than St. John – had been strongly disposed in my own heart to advocate their union. It seemed to me that, should he become the possessor of Mr. Oliver's large fortune, he might do as much good with it as if he went and laid his genius out to wither, and his strength to waste, under a tropical sun. With this persuasion, I now answered: –

"As far as I can see, it would be wiser and more judicious if you were to take to yourself the original at once."

By this time he had sat down: he had laid the picture on the table before him, and, with his brow supported on both hands, hung fondly over it. I discerned he was now neither angry nor shocked at my audacity. I saw even that to be thus frankly addressed on a subject he had deemed unapproachable – to hear it thus freely handled – was beginning to be felt by him as a new pleasure – an unhoped-for relief. Reserved people often really need the frank discussion of their sentiments and griefs more than the expansive. The sternest-seeming stoic is human after all; and to "burst" with boldness and good will into "the silent sea"[1] of their souls, is often to confer on them the first of obligations.

"She likes you, I am sure," said I, as I stood behind his chair, "and her father respects you. Moreover, she is a sweet girl – rather thoughtless; but you would have sufficient thought for both yourself and her. You ought to marry her."

"*Does* she like me?" he asked.

"Certainly; better than she likes any one else. She talks of you continually: there is no subject she enjoys so much, or touches upon so often."

"It is very pleasant to hear this," he said – "very: go on for another quarter of an hour." And he actually took out his watch and laid it upon the table to measure the time.

"But where is the use of going on," I asked, "when you are probably preparing some iron blow of contradiction, or forging a fresh chain to fetter your heart?"

"Don't imagine such hard things. Fancy me yielding and melting,

---

1 A quotation from "The Rime of the Ancient Mariner," II.105-106, by Samuel Taylor Coleridge (1772-1834). The poem originally appeared in the collection *Lyrical Ballads*, which Coleridge published with Wordsworth in 1798.

as I am doing: human love rising like a freshly opened fountain in my mind, and overflowing with sweet inundation all the field I have so carefully, and with such labour, prepared – so assiduously sown with the seeds of good intentions, of self-denying plans. And now it is deluged with a nectarous flood – the young germs swamped – delicious poison[1] cankering them: now I see myself stretched on an ottoman in the drawing-room at Vale Hall, at my bride Rosamond Oliver's feet: she is talking to me with her sweet voice – gazing down on me with those eyes your skilful hand has copied so well – smiling at me with these coral lips. She is mine – I am hers – this present life and passing world suffice to me. Hush! say nothing – my heart is full of delight – my senses are entranced – let the time I marked pass in peace."

I humoured him: the watch ticked on: he breathed fast and low: I stood silent. Amidst this hush the quarter sped: he replaced the watch, laid the picture down, rose, and stood on the hearth.

"Now," said he, "that little space was given to delirium and delusion. I rested my temples on the breast of temptation, and put my neck voluntarily under her yoke of flowers; I tasted her cup. The pillow was burning: there is an asp in the garland: the wine has a bitter taste: her promises are hollow – her offers false: I see and know all this."

I gazed at him in wonder.

"It is strange," pursued he, "that while I love Rosamond Oliver so wildly – with all the intensity, indeed, of a first passion, the object of which is exquisitely beautiful, graceful, and fascinating – I experience at the same time a calm, unwarped consciousness, that she would not make me a good wife; that she is not the partner suited to me; that I should discover this within a year after marriage; and that to twelve months' rapture would succeed a lifetime of regret. This I know."

"Strange, indeed!" I could not help ejaculating.

"While something in me," he went on, "is acutely sensible to her charms, something else is as deeply impressed with her defects: they are such that she could sympathize in nothing I aspired to – co-operate in nothing I undertook. Rosamond a sufferer, a labourer, a female apostle? Rosamond a missionary's wife? No!"

---

1   See *Antony and Cleopatra*, I.v.27.

"But you need not be a missionary. You might relinquish that scheme."

"Relinquish! What – my vocation? My great work? My foundation laid on earth for a mansion in heaven?[1] My hopes of being numbered in the band who have merged all ambitions in the glorious one of bettering their race – of carrying knowledge into the realms of ignorance – of substituting peace for war – freedom for bondage – religion for superstition – the hope of heaven for the fear of hell? Must I relinquish that? It is dearer than the blood in my veins. It is what I have to look forward to, and to live for."

After a considerable pause, I said – "And Miss Oliver? Are her disappointment and sorrow of no interest to you?"

"Miss Oliver is ever surrounded by suitors and flatterers: in less than a month, my image will be effaced from her heart. She will forget me; and will marry, probably, some one who will make her far happier than I should do."

"You speak coolly enough; but you suffer in the conflict. You are wasting away."

"No. If I get a little thin, it is with anxiety about my prospects, yet unsettled – my departure, continually procrastinated. Only this morning, I received intelligence that the successor, whose arrival I have been so long expecting, cannot be ready to replace me for three months to come yet: and perhaps the three months may extend to six."

"You tremble and become flushed whenever Miss Oliver enters the schoolroom."

Again the surprised expression crossed his face. He had not imagined that a woman would dare to speak so to a man. For me, I felt at home in this sort of discourse. I could never rest in communication with strong, discreet, and refined minds, whether male or female, till I had passed the outworks of conventional reserve, and crossed the threshold of confidence, and won a place by their heart's very hearthstone.

"You *are* original," said he, "and not timid. There is something brave in your spirit, as well as penetrating in your eye: but allow me to

---

1   See 1 Timothy 6:19.

assure you that you partially misinterpret my emotions. You think them more profound and potent than they are. You give me a larger allowance of sympathy than I have a just claim to. When I colour, and when I shake before Miss Oliver, I do not pity myself. I scorn the weakness. I know it is ignoble; a mere fever of the flesh: not, I declare, the convulsion of the soul. *That* is just as fixed as a rock, firm set in the depths of a restless sea. Know me to be what I am – a cold, hard man."

I smiled incredulously.

"You have taken my confidence by storm," he continued; "and now it is much at your service. I am simply, in my original state – stripped of that blood-bleached robe with which Christianity covers human deformity – a cold, hard, ambitious man. Natural affection only, of all the sentiments, has permanent power over me. Reason, and not Feeling, is my guide: my ambition is unlimited; my desire to rise higher, to do more than others, insatiable. I honour endurance, perseverance, industry, talent; because these are the means by which men achieve great ends, and mount to lofty eminence. I watch your career with interest, because I consider you a specimen of a diligent, orderly, energetic woman: not because I deeply compassionate what you have gone through, or what you still suffer."

"You would describe yourself as a mere pagan philosopher," I said.

"No. There is this difference between me and deistic philosophers: I believe; and I believe the Gospel. You missed your epithet. I am not a pagan, but a Christian philosopher – a follower of the sect of Jesus. As his disciple I adopt his pure, his merciful, his benignant doctrines. I advocate them: I am sworn to spread them. Won in youth to religion, she has cultivated my original qualities thus: – From the minute germ, natural affection, she has developed the overshadowing tree, philanthropy. From the wild, stringy root of human uprightness, she has reared a due sense of the Divine justice. Of the ambition to win power and renown for my wretched self, she has formed the ambition to spread my Master's kingdom; to achieve victories for the standard of the cross. So much has religion done for me; turning the original materials to the best account: pruning and training nature. But she could not eradicate nature: nor will it be eradicated 'till this mortal shall put on immortality.'"[1]

---

1 See 1 Corinthians 15:53.

Having said this, he took his hat, which lay on the table beside my palette. Once more he looked at the portrait.

"She *is* lovely," he murmured. "She is well named the Rose of the World,[1] indeed!"

"And may I not paint one like it for you?"

"*Cui bono?*[2] No."

He drew over the picture the sheet of thin paper on which I was accustomed to rest my hand in painting to prevent the card-board from being sullied. What he suddenly saw on this blank paper, it was impossible for me to tell: but something had caught his eye. He took it up with a snatch; he looked at the edge; then shot a glance at me, inexpressibly peculiar, and quite incomprehensible: a glance that seemed to take and make note of every point in my shape, face, and dress; for it traversed all, quick, keen as lightning. His lips parted, as if to speak: but he checked the coming sentence, whatever it was.

"What is the matter?" I asked.

"Nothing in the world," was the reply; and, replacing the paper, I saw him dexterously tear a narrow slip from the margin. It disappeared in his glove; and, with one hasty nod and "good-afternoon," he vanished.

"Well!" I exclaimed, using an expression of the district; "that caps the globe, however!"[3]

I, in my turn, scrutinized the paper; but saw nothing on it, save a few dingy stains of paint, where I had tried the tint in my pencil. I pondered the mystery a minute or two; but finding it insolvable, and being certain it could not be of much moment, I dismissed, and soon forgot it.

---

1 The name Rosamond literally means "rose of the world."
2 Latin. "Who would benefit?"
3 i.e., "that tops everything."

CHAPTER XXXIII

WHEN Mr. St. John went, it was beginning to snow: the whirling storm continued all night. The next day a keen wind brought fresh and blinding falls: by twilight the valley was drifted up and almost impassable. I had closed my shutter, laid a mat to the door to prevent the snow from blowing in under it, trimmed my fire, and after sitting nearly an hour on the hearth listening to the muffled fury of the tempest, I lit a candle, took down Marmion and beginning –

> "Day set on Norham's castled steep,
>   And Tweed's fair river broad and deep,
>   And Cheviot mountains lone;
>   The massive towers, the donjon keep,
>   The flanking walls that round them sweep,
>   In yellow lustre shone."[1]

I soon forgot storm in music.

I heard a noise: the wind, I thought, shook the door. No; it was St. John Rivers, who, lifting the latch, came in out of the frozen hurricane – the howling darkness – and stood before me; the cloak that covered his tall figure all white as a glacier. I was almost in consternation; so little had I expected any guest from the blocked-up vale that night.

"Any ill news?" I demanded. "Has anything happened?"

"No. How very easily alarmed you are!" he answered, removing his cloak and hanging it up against the door: towards which he again

---

1 The novel somewhat misquotes *Marmion*'s opening lines, which actually read:

> "Day set on Norham's castled steep,
>   And Tweed's fair river, broad and deep,
>   And Cheviot's mountains lone:
>   The battled towers, the donjon keep,
>   The loophole grates, where captives weep,
>   The flanking walls that round it sweep,
>   In yellow lustre shone."

Brontë substitutes "massive towers" for "battled towers" in line 4, deletes line 5, and has line 6 read "that round them sweep" rather than the original "then round it sweep."

coolly pushed the mat which his entrance had deranged. He stamped the snow from his boots.

"I shall sully the purity of your floor," said he, "but you must excuse me for once." Then he approached the fire: "I have had hard work to get here, I assure you," he observed, as he warmed his hands over the flame. "One drift took me up to the waist: happily the snow is quite soft yet."

"But why are you come?" I could not forbear saying.

"Rather an inhospitable question to put to a visitor; but since you ask it, I answer, simply to have a little talk with you: I got tired of my mute books and empty rooms. Besides, since yesterday, I have experienced the excitement of a person to whom a tale has been half-told, and who is impatient to hear the sequel."

He sat down. I recalled his singular conduct of yesterday, and really I began to fear his wits were touched. If he were insane, however, his was a very cool and collected insanity: I had never seen that handsome-featured face of his look more like chiselled marble than it did just now; as he put aside his snow-wet hair from his forehead and let the fire-light shine free on his pale brow and cheek as pale: where it grieved me to discover the hollow trace of care or sorrow now so plainly graved.[1] I waited, expecting he would say something I could at least comprehend; but his hand was now at his chin, his finger on his lip: he was thinking. It struck me that his hand looked wasted like his face. A perhaps uncalled-for gush of pity came over my heart: I was moved to say: –

"I wish Diana or Mary would come and live with you: it is too bad that you should be quite alone; and you are recklessly rash about your own health."

"Not at all," said he: "I care for myself when necessary: I am well now. What do you see amiss in me?"

This was said with a careless, abstracted indifference, which showed that my solicitude was, at least in his opinion, wholly superfluous. I was silenced.

He still slowly moved his finger over his upper lip, and still his eye dwelt dreamily on the glowing grate: thinking it urgent to say some-

---

1 Engraved.

thing, I asked him presently if he felt any cold draught from the door, which was behind him.

"No, no;" he responded shortly and somewhat testily.

"Well," I reflected; "if you won't talk, you may be still: I'll let you alone now and return to my book."

So I snuffed the candle, and resumed the perusal of Marmion. He soon stirred; my eye was instantly drawn to his movements: he only took out a morocco pocket-book, thence produced a letter which he read in silence, folded it, put it back, relapsed into meditation. It was vain to try to read with such an inscrutable fixture before me; nor could I, in my impatience, consent to be dumb: he might rebuff me if he liked, but talk I would.

"Have you heard from Diana and Mary lately?"

"Not since the letter I showed you a week ago."

"There has not been any change made about your own arrangements? You will not be summoned to leave England sooner than you expected?"

"I fear not, indeed: such chance is too good to befall me." Baffled so far, I changed my ground – I bethought myself to talk about the school and my scholars.

"Mary Garrett's mother is better, and Mary came back to the school this morning, and I shall have four new girls next week from the Foundry Close – they would have come to-day but for the snow."

"Indeed?"

"Mr. Oliver pays for two."

"Does he?"

"He means to give the whole school a treat at Christmas."

"I know."

"Was it your suggestion?"

"No."

"Whose then?"

"His daughter's, I think."

"It is like her: she is so good-natured."

"Yes."

Again came the blank of a pause: the clock struck eight strokes. It aroused him; he uncrossed his legs, sat erect, turned to me.

"Leave your book a moment, and come a little nearer the fire," he said.

Wondering, and of my wonder finding no end, I complied.

"Half an hour ago," he pursued, "I spoke of my impatience to hear the sequel of a tale: on reflection, I find the matter will be better managed by my assuming the narrator's part, and converting you into a listener. Before commencing, it is but fair to warn you that the story will sound somewhat hackneyed in your ears: but stale details often regain a degree of freshness when they pass through new lips. For the rest, whether trite or novel, it is short.

"Twenty years ago, a poor curate — never mind his name at this moment — fell in love with a rich man's daughter: she fell in love with him, and married him, against the advice of all her friends; who consequently disowned her immediately after the wedding. Before two years passed, the rash pair were both dead, and laid quietly side by side under one slab. (I have seen their grave; it formed part of the pavement of a huge churchyard surrounding the grim, soot-black old cathedral of an overgrown manufacturing town in —shire.) They left a daughter, which, at its very birth, Charity received in her lap — cold as that of the snow-drift I almost stuck fast in to-night. Charity carried the friendless thing to the house of its rich, maternal relations; it was reared by an aunt-in-law, called (I come to names now) Mrs. Reed of Gateshead — you start — did you hear a noise? I daresay it is only a rat scrambling along the rafters of the adjoining schoolroom: it was a barn before I had it repaired and altered, and barns are generally haunted by rats. To proceed. Mrs. Reed kept the orphan ten years: whether it was happy or not with her, I cannot say, never having been told; but at the end of that time she transferred it to a place you know — being no other than Lowood school, where you so long resided yourself. It seems her career there was very honourable: from a pupil, she became a teacher, like yourself — really it strikes me there are parallel points in her history and yours — she left it to be a governess: there, again, your fates were analogous; she undertook the education of the ward of a certain Mr. Rochester."

"Mr. Rivers!" I interrupted.

"I can guess your feelings," he said, "but restrain them for a while: I have nearly finished; hear me to the end. Of Mr. Rochester's character I know nothing but the one fact that he professed to offer honourable marriage to this young girl, and that at the very altar she discovered he had a wife yet alive, though a lunatic. What his subsequent conduct and proposals were is a matter of pure conjecture; but when an event transpired which rendered inquiry after the governess necessary, it was discovered she was gone – no one could tell when, where, or how. She had left Thornfield Hall in the night; every research after her course had been vain: the country had been scoured far and wide; no vestige of information could be gathered respecting her. Yet that she should be found is become a matter of serious urgency: advertisements have been put in all the papers; I myself have received a letter from one Mr. Briggs, a solicitor, communicating the details I have just imparted. Is it not an odd tale?"

"Just tell me this," said I, "and since you know so much, you surely *can* tell it me – what of Mr. Rochester? How and where is he? What is he doing? Is he well?"

"I am ignorant of all concerning Mr. Rochester: the letter never mentions him but to narrate the fraudulent and illegal attempt I have adverted to. You should rather ask the name of the governess – the nature of the event which requires her appearance."

"Did no one go to Thornfield Hall then? Did no one see Mr. Rochester?"

"I suppose not."

"But they wrote to him?"

"Of course."

"And what did he say? Who has his letters?"

"Mr. Briggs intimates that the answer to his application was not from Mr. Rochester but from a lady: it is signed 'Alice Fairfax.'"

I felt cold and dismayed; my worst fears then were probably true: he had in all probability left England and rushed in reckless desperation to some former haunt on the continent. And what opiate for his severe sufferings – what object for his strong passions – had he sought there? I dared not answer the question. Oh, my poor master – once almost my husband – whom I had often called "my dear Edward"!

"He must have been a bad man," observed Mr. Rivers.

"You don't know him – don't pronounce an opinion upon him," I said with warmth.

"Very well," he answered quietly; "and indeed my head is otherwise occupied than with him: I have my tale to finish. Since you won't ask the governess's name, I must tell it of my own accord – stay

– I have it here – it is always more satisfactory to see important points written down, fairly committed to black and white."

And the pocket-book was again deliberately produced, opened, sought through; from one of its compartments was extracted a shabby slip of paper, hastily torn off: I recognised in its texture and its stains of ultra-marine, and lake,[1] and vermilion, the ravished margin of the portrait-cover. He got up, held it close to my eyes; and I read, traced in Indian ink, in my own handwriting, the words "JANE EYRE" – the work doubtless of some moment of abstraction.

"Briggs wrote to me of a Jane Eyre;" he said, "the advertisements demanded a Jane Eyre: I knew a Jane Elliott. – I confess I had my suspicions, but it was only yesterday afternoon they were at once resolved into certainty. You own the name and renounce the *alias*?"

"Yes – yes – but where is Mr. Briggs? He perhaps knows more of Mr. Rochester than you do."

"Briggs is in London; I should doubt his knowing anything at all about Mr. Rochester: it is not in Mr. Rochester he is interested. Meantime, you forget essential points in pursuing trifles: you do not inquire why Mr. Briggs sought after you – what he wanted with you."

"Well, what did he want?"

"Merely to tell you that your uncle, Mr. Eyre of Madeira, is dead; that he has left you all his property, and that you are now rich – merely that – nothing more."

"I! rich?"

"Yes, you, rich – quite an heiress."

Silence succeeded.

"You must prove your identity of course," resumed St. John presently: "a step which will offer no difficulties; you can then enter on immediate possession. Your fortune is vested in the English funds: Briggs has the will and the necessary documents."

Here was a new card turned up! It is a fine thing, reader, to be lifted in a moment from indigence to wealth – a very fine thing: but not a matter one can comprehend, or consequently enjoy, all at once. And then there are other chances in life far more thrilling and rapture-

---

1 A reddish pigment.

giving: *this* is solid, an affair of the actual world, nothing ideal about it: all its associations are solid and sober, and its manifestations are the same. One does not jump, and spring, and shout hurrah! at hearing one has got a fortune; one begins to consider responsibilities, and to ponder business: on a base of steady satisfaction rise certain grave cares – and we contain ourselves, and brood over our bliss with a solemn brow.

Besides, the words Legacy, Bequest, go side by side with the words Death, Funeral. My uncle I had heard was dead – my only relative; ever since being made aware of his existence, I had cherished the hope of one day seeing him: now, I never should. And then this money came only to me: not to me and a rejoicing family, but to my isolated self. It was a grand boon doubtless; and independence would be glorious – yes, I felt that – *that* thought swelled my heart.

"You unbend your forehead at last," said Mr. Rivers: "I thought Medusa had looked at you, and that you were turning to stone – perhaps now you will ask how much you are worth?"

"How much am I worth?"

"Oh, a trifle! Nothing of course to speak of – twenty thousand pounds, I think they say – but what is that?"

"Twenty thousand pounds!"

Here was a new stunner – I had been calculating on four or five thousand. This news actually took my breath for a moment: Mr. St. John, whom I had never heard laugh before, laughed now.

"Well," said he, "if you had committed a murder, and I had told you your crime was discovered, you could scarcely look more aghast."

"It is a large sum – don't you think there is a mistake?"

"No mistake at all."

"Perhaps you have read the figures wrong – it may be 2000?"

"It is written in letters, not figures, – twenty thousand."

I again felt rather like an individual of but average gastronomical powers sitting down to feast alone at a table spread with provisions for a hundred. Mr. Rivers rose now and put his cloak on.

"If it were not such a very wild night," he said, "I would send Hannah down to keep you company: you look too desperately miserable to be left alone. But Hannah, poor woman! could not stride the drifts so well as I; her legs are not quite so long: so I must e'en leave you to your sorrows. Good-night."

He was lifting the latch: a sudden thought occurred to me.

"Stop one minute!" I cried.

"Well?"

"It puzzles me to know why Mr. Briggs wrote to you about me; or how he knew you, or could fancy that you, living in such an out-of-the-way place, had the power to aid in my discovery."

"Oh! I am a clergyman," he said; "and the clergy are often appealed to about odd matters." Again the latch rattled.

"No: that does not satisfy me!" I exclaimed: and indeed, there was something in the hasty and unexplanatory reply, which, instead of allaying, piqued my curiosity more than ever.

"It is a very strange piece of business," I added: "I must know more about it."

"Another time."

"No; to-night! – to-night!" and as he turned from the door, I placed myself between it and him. He looked rather embarrassed.

"You certainly shall not go till you have told me all!" I said.

"I would rather not, just now."

"You shall! – you must!"

"I would rather Diana or Mary informed you."

Of course these objections wrought my eagerness to a climax: gratified it must be, and that without delay; and I told him so.

"But I apprised you that I was a hard man," said he; "difficult to persuade."

"And I am a hard woman, – impossible to put off."

"And then," he pursued, "I am cold: no fervour infects me."

"Whereas I am hot, and fire dissolves ice. The blaze there has thawed all the snow from your cloak; by the same token, it has streamed on to my floor, and made it like a trampled street. As you hope ever to be forgiven, Mr. Rivers, the high crime and misdemeanour of spoiling a sanded kitchen, tell me what I wish to know."

"Well, then," he said, "I yield; if not to your earnestness, to your perseverance: as stone is worn by continual dropping. Besides, you must know some day, – as well now as later. Your name is Jane Eyre?"

"Of course: that was all settled before."

"You are not, perhaps, aware that I am your namesake? – that I was christened St. John Eyre Rivers?"

"No, indeed! I remember now seeing the letter E comprised in your initials written in books you have at different times lent me; but I never asked for what name it stood. But what then? Surely —"

I stopped: I could not trust myself to entertain, much less to express, the thought that rushed upon me – that embodied itself, – that, in a second, stood out a strong, solid probability. Circumstances knit themselves, fitted themselves, shot into order: the chain that had been lying hitherto a formless lump of links, was drawn out straight, – every ring was perfect, the connection complete. I knew, by instinct, how the matter stood, before St. John had said another word: but I cannot expect the reader to have the same intuitive perception, so I must repeat his explanation.

"My mother's name was Eyre: she had two brothers; one a clergyman, who married Miss Jane Reed, of Gateshead; the other, John Eyre, Esq., merchant, late of Funchal, Madeira. Mr. Briggs, being Mr. Eyre's solicitor, wrote to us last August to inform us of our uncle's death; and to say that he had left his property to his brother the clergyman's orphan daughter; overlooking us, in consequence of a quarrel, never forgiven, between him and my father. He wrote again a few weeks since, to intimate that the heiress was lost; and asking if we knew anything of her. A name casually written on a slip of paper has enabled me to find her out. You know the rest." Again he was going, but I set my back against the door.

"Do let me speak," I said; "let me have one moment to draw breath and reflect." I paused – he stood before me, hat in hand, looking composed enough. I resumed: –

"Your mother was my father's sister?"

"Yes."

"My aunt, consequently?"

He bowed.

"My uncle John was your uncle John? You, Diana, and Mary, are his sister's children; as I am his brother's child?"

"Undeniably."

"You three, then, are my cousins: half our blood on each side flows from the same source?"

"We are cousins: yes."

I surveyed him. It seemed I had found a brother: one I could be proud of, – one I could love; and two sisters, whose qualities were such, that when I knew them but as mere strangers, they had inspired me with genuine affection and admiration. The two girls, on whom, kneeling down on the wet ground, and looking through the low, latticed window of Moor House kitchen, I had gazed with so bitter a mixture of interest and despair, were my near kinswomen; and the young and stately gentleman who had found me almost dying at his threshold, was my blood relation. Glorious discovery to a lonely wretch! This was wealth indeed! – wealth for the heart! – a mine of pure, genial affections. This was a blessing, bright, vivid, and exhilarating! – not like the ponderous gift of gold: rich and welcome enough in its way, but sobering from its weight. I now clapped my hands in sudden joy – my pulse bounded, my veins thrilled.

"Oh, I am glad! – I am glad!" I exclaimed.

St. John smiled. "Did I not say you neglected essential points to pursue trifles?" he asked. "You were serious when I told you you had got a fortune; and now, for a matter of no moment, you are excited."

"What *can* you mean? It may be of no moment to you: you have sisters, and don't care for a cousin; but I had nobody; and now three relations, – or two, if you don't choose to be counted, – are born into my world, full grown. I say again, I am glad!"

I walked fast through the room: I stopped, half suffocated with the thoughts that rose faster than I could receive, comprehend, settle them: – thoughts of what might, could, would, and should be, and that ere long. I looked at the blank wall: it seemed a sky, thick with ascending stars, – every one lit me to a purpose or delight. Those who had saved my life, whom, till this hour, I had loved barrenly, I could now benefit. They were under a yoke: I could free them; they were scattered, – I could reunite them – the independence, the affluence which was mine, might be theirs too. Were we not four? Twenty thousand pounds shared equally, would be five thousand each, – enough and to spare: justice would be done, – mutual happiness secured. Now the wealth did not weigh on me: now it was not a mere bequest of coin, – it was a legacy of life, hope, enjoyment.

How I looked while these ideas were taking my spirit by storm, I cannot tell; but I perceived soon that Mr. Rivers had placed a chair behind me, and was gently attempting to make me sit down on it. He also advised me to be composed. I scorned the insinuation of helplessness and distraction, shook off his hand, and began to walk about again.

"Write to Diana and Mary to-morrow," I said, "and tell them to come home directly: Diana said they would both consider themselves rich with a thousand pounds, so with five thousand, they will do very well."

"Tell me where I can get you a glass of water," said St. John; "you must really make an effort to tranquillize your feelings."

"Nonsense! and what sort of an effect will the bequest have on you? Will it keep you in England, induce you to marry Miss Oliver, and settle down like an ordinary mortal?"

"You wander: your head becomes confused. I have been too abrupt in communicating the news: it has excited you beyond your strength."

"Mr. Rivers! you quite put me out of patience; I am rational enough; it is you who misunderstand; or rather, who affect to misunderstand."

"Perhaps if you explained yourself a little more fully, I should comprehend better."

"Explain! What is there to explain? You cannot fail to see that twenty thousand pounds, the sum in question, divided equally between the nephew and three nieces of our uncle, will give five thousand to each? What I want is, that you should write to your sisters and tell them of the fortune that has accrued to them."

"To you, you mean."

"I have intimated my view of the case: I am incapable of taking any other. I am not brutally selfish, blindly unjust, or fiendishly ungrateful. Besides, I am resolved I will have a home and connections. I like Moor-House, and I will live at Moor-House; I like Diana, and Mary, and I will attach myself for life to Diana and Mary. It would please and benefit me to have five thousand pounds; it would torment and oppress me to have twenty thousand: which, moreover, could never be mine in justice, though it might in law. I abandon to you, then, what is absolutely superfluous to me. Let there be no opposition, and no discussion about it: let us agree amongst each other, and decide the point at once."

"This is acting on first impulses: you must take days to consider such a matter, ere your word can be regarded as valid."

"Oh! if all you doubt is my sincerity, I am easy: you see the justice of the case?"

"I *do* see a certain justice; but it is contrary to all custom. Besides the entire fortune is your right: my uncle gained it by his own efforts; he was free to leave it to whom he would: he left it to you. After all, justice permits you to keep it: you may, with a clear conscience, consider it absolutely your own."

"With me," said I, "it is fully as much a matter of feeling as of conscience: I must indulge my feelings; I so seldom have had an opportunity of doing so. Were you to argue, object, and annoy me for a year, I could not forego the delicious pleasure of which I have caught a glimpse – that of repaying, in part, a mighty obligation, and winning to myself lifelong friends."

"You think so now," rejoined St. John; "because you do not know what it is to possess, nor consequently to enjoy wealth: you cannot form a notion of the importance twenty thousand pounds would give you; of the place it would enable you to take in society; of the prospects it would open to you: you cannot —"

"And you," I interrupted, "cannot at all imagine the craving I have for fraternal and sisterly love. I never had a home, I never had brothers or sisters; I must and will have them now: you are not reluctant to admit me and own me, are you?"

"Jane: I will be your brother – my sisters will be your sisters – without stipulating for this sacrifice of your just rights."

"Brother? Yes; at the distance of a thousand leagues! Sisters? Yes; slaving amongst strangers! I, wealthy – gorged with gold I never earned and do not merit! You, pennyless! Famous equality and fraternization! Close union! Intimate attachment!"

"But, Jane, your aspirations after family ties and domestic happiness may be realized otherwise than by the means you contemplate: you may marry."

"Nonsense again! Marry! I don't want to marry, and never shall marry."

"That is saying too much: such hazardous affirmations are a proof of the excitement under which you labour."

"It is not saying too much: I know what I feel, and how averse are my inclinations to the bare thought of marriage. No one would take me for love; and I will not be regarded in the light of a mere money-speculation. And I do not want a stranger – unsympathizing, alien, different from me; I want my kindred: those with whom I have full fellow-feeling. Say again you will be my brother: when you uttered the words I was satisfied, happy; repeat them, if you can repeat them sincerely."

"I think I can. I know I have always loved my own sisters; and I know on what my affection for them is grounded, – respect for their worth, and admiration of their talents. You too have principle and mind: your tastes and habits resemble Diana's and Mary's; your presence is always agreeable to me; in your conversation I have already for some time found a salutary solace. I feel I can easily and naturally make room in my heart for you, as my third and youngest sister."

"Thank you: that contents me for to-night. Now you had better go; for if you stay longer, you will perhaps irritate me afresh by some mistrustful scruple."

"And the school, Miss Eyre? It must now be shut up, I suppose?"

"No. I will retain my post of mistress till you get a substitute."

He smiled approbation: we shook hands, and he took leave.

I need not narrate in detail the further struggles I had, and arguments I used, to get matters regarding the legacy settled as I wished. My task was a very hard one: but, as I was absolutely resolved – as my cousins saw at length that my mind was really and immutably fixed on making a just division of the property – as they must in their own hearts have felt the equity of the intention; and must, besides, have been innately conscious that in my place they would have done precisely what I wished to do – they yielded at length so far as to consent to put the affair to arbitration. The judges chosen were Mr. Oliver and an able lawyer: both coincided in my opinion: I carried my point. The instruments of transfer were drawn out: St. John, Diana, Mary, and I, each became possessed of a competency.

CHAPTER XXXIV

It was near Christmas by the time all was settled: the season of general holiday approached. I now closed Morton-school: taking care that the parting should not be barren on my side. Good fortune opens the hand as well as the heart wonderfully; and to give somewhat when we have largely received, is but to afford a vent to the unusual ebullition of the sensations. I had long felt with pleasure that many of my rustic scholars liked me, and when we parted, that consciousness was confirmed: they manifested their affection plainly and strongly. Deep was my gratification to find I had really a place in their unsophisticated hearts: I promised them that never a week should pass in future that I did not visit them, and give them an hour's teaching in their school.

Mr. Rivers came up, as – having seen the classes, now numbering sixty girls, file out before me, and locked the door – I stood with the key in my hand, exchanging a few words of special farewell with some half-dozen of my best scholars: as decent, respectable, modest, and well-informed young women as could be found in the ranks of the British peasantry. And that is saying a great deal; for after all, the British peasantry are the best taught, best mannered, most self-respecting of any in Europe: since those days I have seen paysannes and Bäuerinnen;[1] and the best of them seemed to me ignorant, coarse, and besotted, compared with my Morton girls.

"Do you consider you have got your reward for a season of exertion?" asked Mr. Rivers when they were gone. "Does not the consciousness of having done some real good in your day and generation give pleasure?"

"Doubtless."

"And you have only toiled a few months! Would not a life devoted to the task of regenerating your race be well spent?"

"Yes," I said; "but I could not go on for ever so: I want to enjoy my own faculties as well as to cultivate those of other people. I must enjoy them now: don't recall either my mind or body to the school; I am out of it and disposed for full holiday."

---

1   French and German peasant women. Brontë demonstrates, not for the first or last time in the novel, a certain chauvinism in favour of English values.

He looked grave. "What now? What sudden eagerness is this you evince? What are you going to do?"

"To be active: as active as I can. And first I must beg you to set Hannah at liberty, and get somebody else to wait on you."

"Do you want her?"

"Yes, to go with me to Moor-House: Diana and Mary will be at home in a week, and I want to have everything in order against their arrival."

"I understand: I thought you were for flying off on some excursion. It is better so: Hannah shall go with you."

"Tell her to be ready by to-morrow then; and here is the school-room key: I will give you the key of my cottage in the morning."

He took it. "You give it up very gleefully," said he: "I don't quite understand your light-heartedness; because I cannot tell what employment you propose to yourself as a substitute for the one you are relinquishing. What aim, what purpose, what ambition in life have you now?"

"My first aim will be to *clean down* (do you comprehend the full force of the expression?) – to *clean down* Moor-House from chamber to cellar; my next to rub it up with bees-wax, oil, and an indefinite number of cloths, till it glitters again; my third, to arrange every chair, table, bed, carpet, with mathematical precision; afterwards I shall go near to ruin you in coals and peat to keep up good fires in every room; and lastly, the two days preceding that on which your sisters are expected, will be devoted by Hannah and me to such a beating of eggs, sorting of currants, grating of spices, compounding of Christmas cakes, chopping up of materials for mince-pies, and solemnizing of other culinary rites, as words can convey but an inadequate notion of to the uninitiated like you. My purpose, in short, is to have all things in an absolutely perfect state of readiness for Diana and Mary, before next Thursday; and my ambition is to give them a beau ideal of a welcome[1] when they come."

St. John smiled slightly: still he was dissatisfied.

"It is all very well for the present," said he: "but seriously, I trust that when the first flush of vivacity is over, you will look a little higher than domestic endearments and household joys."

---

1   i.e., a welcome of the highest excellence.

"The best things the world has!" I interrupted.

"No, Jane, no: this world is not the scene of fruition; do not attempt to make it so: nor of rest; do not turn slothful."

"I mean, on the contrary, to be busy."

"Jane, I excuse you for the present: two months' grace I allow you for the full enjoyment of your new position, and for pleasing yourself with this late-found charm of relationship; but *then*, I hope you will begin to look beyond Moor-House and Morton, and sisterly society, and the selfish calm and sensual comfort of civilized affluence. I hope your energies will then once more trouble you with their strength."

I looked at him with surprise. "St. John," I said, "I think you are almost wicked to talk so. I am disposed to be as content as a queen, and you try to stir me up to restlessness! To what end?"

"To the end of turning to profit the talents which God has committed to your keeping; and of which he will surely one day demand a strict account. Jane, I shall watch you closely and anxiously – I warn you of that – and try to restrain the disproportionate fervour with which you throw yourself into common-place home pleasures. Don't cling so tenaciously to ties of the flesh; save your constancy and ardour for an adequate cause: forbear to waste them on trite transient objects. Do you hear, Jane?"

"Yes; just as if you were speaking Greek. I feel I have adequate cause to be happy, and I *will* be happy. Good-bye!"

Happy at Moor-House I was, and hard I worked; and so did Hannah: she was charmed to see how jovial I could be amidst the bustle of a house turned topsy-turvy – how I could brush, and dust, and clean, and cook. And really after a day or two of confusion worse confounded,[1] it was delightful, by degrees, to invoke order from the chaos ourselves had made. I had previously taken a journey to S——, to purchase some new furniture: my cousins having given me carte blanche to effect what alterations I pleased, and a sum having been set aside for that purpose. The ordinary sitting-room and bed-rooms I left much as they were; for I knew Diana and Mary would derive more pleasure from seeing again the old homely tables, and chairs, and beds, than from the spectacle of the smartest innovations. Still some novelty was necessary, to give to their return the piquancy with

---

1 *Paradise Lost*, II.996.

which I wished it to be invested. Dark handsome new carpets and curtains, an arrangement of some carefully selected antique ornaments in porcelain and bronze, new coverings, and mirrors, and dressing-cases for the toilet-tables, answered the end: they looked fresh without being glaring. A spare parlour and bed-room I refurnished entirely, with old mahogany and crimson upholstery: I laid canvass on the passage, and carpets on the stairs. When all was finished, I thought Moor-House as complete a model of bright modest snugness within, as it was, at this season, a specimen of wintry waste and desert dreariness without.

The eventful Thursday at length came. They were expected about dark, and ere dusk; fires were lit up stairs and below; the kitchen was in perfect trim; Hannah and I were dressed, and all was in readiness.

St. John arrived first. I had entreated him to keep quite clear of the house till everything was arranged: and, indeed, the bare idea of the commotion, at once sordid and trivial, going on within its walls sufficed to scare him to estrangement. He found me in the kitchen, watching the progress of certain cakes for tea, then baking. Approaching the hearth, he asked, "If I was at last satisfied with house-maid's work?" I answered by inviting him to accompany me on a general inspection of the result of my labours. With some difficulty, I got him to make the tour of the house. He just looked in at the doors I opened; and when he had wandered up stairs and down stairs, he said I must have gone through a great deal of fatigue and trouble to have effected such considerable changes in so short a time: but not a syllable did he utter indicating pleasure in the improved aspect of his abode.

This silence damped me. I thought perhaps the alterations had disturbed some old associations he valued. I inquired whether this was the case: no doubt in a somewhat crest-fallen tone.

"Not at all; he had, on the contrary, remarked that I had scrupulously respected every association: he feared, indeed, I must have bestowed more thought on the matter than it was worth. How many minutes, for instance, had I devoted to studying the arrangement of this very room? – By-the-bye, could I tell him where such a book was?"

I showed him the volume on the shelf: he took it down; and withdrawing to his accustomed window recess, he began to read it.

Now, I did not like this, reader. St. John was a good man; but I began to feel he had spoken truth of himself, when he said he was hard and cold. The humanities and amenities of life had no attraction for him – its peaceful enjoyments no charm. Literally, he lived only to aspire – after what was good and great, certainly: but still he would never rest; nor approve of others resting round him. As I looked at his lofty forehead, still and pale as a white stone – at his fine lineaments fixed in study – I comprehended all at once that he would hardly make a good husband: that it would be a trying thing to be his wife. I understood, as by inspiration, the nature of his love for Miss Oliver: I agreed with him that it was but a love of the senses. I comprehended how he should despise himself for the feverish influence it exercised over him; how he should wish to stifle and destroy it; how he should mistrust its ever conducing permanently to his happiness, or hers. I saw he was of the material from which nature hews her heroes – Christian and Pagan – her lawgivers, her statesmen, her conquerors: a steadfast bulwark for great interests to rest upon; but, at the fireside, too often a cold cumbrous column, gloomy and out of place.

"This parlour is not his sphere," I reflected: "the Himalayan ridge, or Caffre[1] bush, even the plague-cursed Guinea coast swamp, would suit him better. Well may he eschew the calm of domestic life; it is not his element: there his faculties stagnate – they cannot develope or appear to advantage. It is in scenes of strife and danger – where courage is proved, and energy exercised, and fortitude tasked – that he will speak and move, the leader and superior. A merry child would have the advantage of him on this hearth. He is right to choose a missionary's career – I see it now."

"They are coming! they are coming!" cried Hannah, throwing open the parlour door. At the same moment old Carlo barked joyfully. Out I ran. It was now dark; but a rumbling of wheels was audible. Hannah soon had a lantern lit. The vehicle had stopped at the wicket; the driver opened the door: first one well-known form, then another, stepped out. In a minute I had my face under their bonnets, in contact, first with Mary's soft cheek, then with Diana's flowing curls. They laughed – kissed me – then Hannah: patted Carlo, who was half wild with delight, asked eagerly if all was well; and being assured in the affirmative, hastened into the house.

1   African.

They were stiff with their long and jolting drive from Whitcross, and chilled with the frosty night air; but their pleasant countenances expanded to the cheering fire light. While the driver and Hannah brought in the boxes, they demanded St. John. At this moment he advanced from the parlour. They both threw their arms round his neck at once. He gave each one quiet kiss, said in a low tone a few words of welcome, stood awhile to be talked to, and then, intimating that he supposed they would soon rejoin him in the parlour, withdrew there as to a place of refuge.

I had lit their candles to go up stairs, but Diana had first to give hospitable orders respecting the driver; this done, both followed me. They were delighted with the renovation and decorations of their rooms; with the new drapery, and fresh carpets, and rich tinted china vases: they expressed their gratification ungrudgingly. I had the pleasure of feeling that my arrangements met their wishes exactly; and that what I had done added a vivid charm to their joyous return home.

Sweet was that evening. My cousins, full of exhilaration, were so eloquent in narrative and comment, that their fluency covered St. John's taciturnity: he was sincerely glad to see his sisters; but in their glow of fervour and flow of joy he could not sympathize. The event of the day – that is, the return of Diana and Mary – pleased him; but the accompaniments of that event, the glad tumult, the garrulous glee of reception, irked him: I saw he wished the calmer morrow was come. In the very meridian[1] of the night's enjoyment, about an hour after tea, a rap was heard at the door. Hannah entered, with the intimation that "a poor lad was come, at that unlikely[2] time, to fetch Mr. Rivers to see his mother, who was drawing away."[3]

"Where does she live, Hannah?"

"Clear up at Whitcross Brow, almost four miles off; and moor and moss all the way."

"Tell him I will go."

"I'm sure, sir, you had better not. It's the worst road to travel after dark that can be: there's no track at all over the bog. And then it is

---

1   Zenith, height.
2   Dialect. Inconvenient.
3   Dialect. Dying.

such a bitter night – the keenest wind you ever felt. You had better send word, sir, that you will be there in the morning."

But he was already in the passage, putting on his cloak; and without one objection, one murmur, he departed. It was then nine o'clock: he did not return till midnight. Starved[1] and tired enough he was: but he looked happier than when he set out. He had performed an act of duty; made an exertion; felt his own strength to do and deny, and was on better terms with himself.

I am afraid the whole of the ensuing week tried his patience. It was Christmas week: we took to no settled employment, but spent it in a sort of merry domestic dissipation. The air of the moors, the freedom of home, the dawn of prosperity, acted on Diana's and Mary's spirits like some life-giving elixir: they were gay from morning till noon, and from noon till night. They could always talk; and their discourse, witty, pithy, original, had such charms for me, that I preferred listening to, and sharing in it, to doing anything else. St. John did not rebuke our vivacity; but he escaped from it: he was seldom in the house: his parish was large, the population scattered, and he found daily business in visiting the sick and poor in its different districts.

One morning, at breakfast, Diana, after looking a little pensive for some minutes, asked him "If his plans were yet unchanged."

"Unchanged and unchangeable," was the reply. And he proceeded to inform us that his departure from England was now definitely fixed for the ensuing year.

"And Rosamond Oliver?" suggested Mary: the words seeming to escape her lips involuntarily; for no sooner had she uttered them, than she made a gesture as if wishing to recall them. St. John had a book in his hand – it was his unsocial custom to read at meals – he closed it, and looked up.

"Rosamond Oliver," said he, "is about to be married to Mr. Granby; one of the best connected and most estimable residents in S——, grandson and heir to Sir Frederic Granby: I had the intelligence from her father yesterday."

His sisters looked at each other, and at me; we all three looked at him: he was serene as glass.

---

1   Numb with cold.

"The match must have been got up hastily," said Diana: "they cannot have known each other long."

"But two months: they met in October at the county ball at S——. But where there are no obstacles to a union, as in the present case, where the connection is in every point desirable, delays are unnecessary: they will be married as soon as S—— Place, which Sir Frederic gives up to them, can be refitted for their reception."

The first time I found St. John alone after this communication, I felt tempted to inquire if the event distressed him: but he seemed so little to need sympathy, that, so far from venturing to offer him more, I experienced some shame at the recollection of what I had already hazarded. Besides, I was out of practice in talking to him: his reserve was again frozen over, and my frankness was congealed beneath it. He had not kept his promise of treating me like his sisters; he continually made little, chilling differences between us, which did not at all tend to the development of cordiality: in short, now that I was acknowledged his kinswoman, and lived under the same roof with him, I felt the distance between us to be far greater than when he had known me only as the village schoolmistress. When I remembered how far I had once been admitted to his confidence, I could hardly comprehend his present frigidity.

Such being the case, I felt not a little surprised when he raised his head suddenly from the desk over which he was stooping, and said:

"You see, Jane, the battle is fought and the victory won."

Startled at being thus addressed, I did not immediately reply; after a moment's hesitation I answered: –

"But are you sure you are not in the position of those conquerors whose triumphs have cost them too dear? Would not such another ruin you?"

"I think not; and if I were, it does not much signify: I shall never be called upon to contend for such another. The event of the conflict is decisive: my way is now clear; I thank God for it!" So saying, he returned to his papers and his silence.

As our mutual happiness (*i.e.* Diana's, Mary's, and mine) settled into a quieter character, and we resumed our usual habits and regular studies, St. John stayed more at home: he sat with us in the same room, sometimes for hours together. While Mary drew, Diana pursued a course of Encyclopëdic reading she had (to my awe and amazement) undertaken, and I fagged away at German, he pondered a mystic lore of his own: that of some Eastern tongue, the acquisition of which he thought necessary to his plans.

Thus engaged, he appeared, sitting in his own recess, quiet and absorbed enough; but that blue eye of his had a habit of leaving the outlandish-looking grammar, and wandering over, and sometimes fixing upon us, his fellow-students, with a curious intensity of observation: if caught, it would be instantly withdrawn; yet ever and anon, it returned searchingly to our table. I wondered what it meant: I wondered, too, at the punctual satisfaction he never failed to exhibit on an occasion that seemed to me of small moment, namely – my weekly visit to Morton school; and still more was I puzzled when, if the day was unfavourable, if there was snow, or rain, or high wind, and his sisters urged me not to go, he would invariably make light of their solicitude, and encourage me to accomplish the task without regard to the elements.

"Jane is not such a weakling as you would make her," he would say; "she can bear a mountain blast, or a shower, or a few flakes of snow, as well as any of us. Her constitution is both sound and elastic; – better calculated to endure variations of climate than many more robust."

And when I returned, sometimes a good deal tired, and not a little weather-beaten, I never dared complain, because I saw that to murmur would be to vex him: on all occasions fortitude pleased him; the reverse was a special annoyance.

One afternoon, however, I got leave to stay at home, because I really had a cold. His sisters were gone to Morton in my stead: I sat reading Schiller; he, deciphering his crabbed Oriental scrolls. As I exchanged a translation for an exercise, I happened to look his way: there I found myself under the influence of the ever-watchful blue eye. How long it had been searching me through and through, and over and over, I cannot tell: so keen was it, and yet so cold, I felt for the moment superstitious – as if I were sitting in the room with something uncanny.

"Jane, what are you doing?"

"Learning German."

"I want you to give up German, and learn Hindostanee."

"You are not in earnest?"

"In such earnest that I must have it so: and I will tell you why."

He then went on to explain that Hindostanee was the language he was himself at present studying; that as he advanced, he was apt to forget the commencement; that it would assist him greatly to have a pupil with whom he might again and again go over the elements, and so fix them thoroughly in his mind; that his choice had hovered for some time between me and his sisters; but that he had fixed it on me, because he saw I could sit at a task the longest of the three. Would I do him this favour? I should not, perhaps, have to make the sacrifice long; as it wanted now barely three months to his departure.

St. John was not a man to be lightly refused: you felt that every impression made on him, either for pain or pleasure, was deep-graved and permanent. I consented. When Diana and Mary returned, the former found her scholar transferred from her to her brother: she laughed; and both she and Mary agreed that St. John should never have persuaded them to such a step. He answered, quietly: –

"I knew it."

I found him a very patient, very forbearing, and yet an exacting master: he expected me to do a great deal; and when I fulfilled his expectations he, in his own way, fully testified his approbation. By degrees, he acquired a certain influence over me that took away my liberty of mind: his praise and notice were more restraining than his indifference. I could no longer talk or laugh freely when he was by; because a tiresomely importunate instinct reminded me that vivacity (at least in me) was distasteful to him. I was so fully aware that only serious moods and occupations were acceptable, that in his presence every effort to sustain or follow any other, became vain: I fell under a freezing spell. When he said "go," I went; "come," I came; "do this," I did it. But I did not love my servitude: I wished, many a time, he had continued to neglect me.

One evening when, at bed-time, his sisters and I stood round him, bidding him good-night, he kissed each of them, as was his custom; and, as was equally his custom, he gave me his hand. Diana, who chanced to be in a frolicksome humour (*she* was not painfully controlled by his will; for hers, in another way, was as strong), exclaimed: –

"St. John! you used to call Jane your third sister, but you don't treat her as such: you should kiss her too."

She pushed me towards him. I thought Diana very provoking, and felt uncomfortably confused; and while I was thus thinking and feeling, St. John bent his head, his Greek face was brought to a level with mine, his eyes questioned my eyes piercingly – he kissed me. There are no such things as marble kisses, or ice kisses, or I should say, my ecclesiastical cousin's salute belonged to one of these classes; but there may be experiment kisses, and his was an experiment kiss. When given, he viewed me to learn the result; it was not striking: I am sure I did not blush; perhaps I might have turned a little pale, for I felt as if this kiss were a seal affixed to my fetters. He never omitted the ceremony afterwards, and the gravity and quiescence with which I underwent it, seemed to invest it for him with a certain charm.

As for me, I daily wished more to please him: but to do so, I felt daily more and more that I must disown half my nature, stifle half my faculties, wrest my tastes from their original bent, force myself to the adoption of pursuits for which I had no natural vocation. He wanted to train me to an elevation I could never reach: it racked me hourly to aspire to the standard he uplifted. The thing was as impossible as to mould my irregular features to his correct and classic pattern, to give to my changeable green eyes the sea blue tint and solemn lustre of his own.

Not his ascendancy alone, however, held me in thrall at present. Of late it had been easy enough for me to look sad: a cankering evil sat in my heart and drained my happiness at its source – the evil of suspense.

Perhaps you think I had forgotten Mr. Rochester, reader, amidst these changes of place and fortune. Not for a moment. His idea was still with me; because it was not a vapour sunshine could disperse; nor a sand-traced effigy storms could wash away: it was a name graven on a tablet, fated to last as long as the marble it inscribed. The craving to know what had become of him followed me everywhere: when I was at Morton, I re-entered my cottage every evening to think of that; and now at Moor-House, I sought my bedroom each night to brood over it.

In the course of my necessary correspondence with Mr. Briggs about the will, I had inquired if he knew anything of Mr. Rochester's present residence and state of health; but, as St. John had conjectured, he was quite ignorant of all concerning him. I then wrote to Mrs. Fairfax, entreating information on the subject. I had calculated with certainty on this step answering my end: I felt sure it would elicit an early answer. I was astonished when a fortnight passed without reply; but when two months wore away, and day after day the post arrived and brought nothing for me, I fell a prey to the keenest anxiety.

I wrote again: there was a chance of my first letter having missed. Renewed hope followed renewed effort; it shone like the former for some weeks, then, like it, it faded, flickered: not a line, not a word reached me. When half a year wasted in vain expectancy, my hope died out; and then I felt dark indeed.

A fine spring shone round me, which I could not enjoy. Summer approached; Diana tried to cheer me: she said I looked ill, and wished to accompany me to the sea-side. This St. John opposed; he said I did not want dissipation, I wanted employment: my present life was too purposeless, I required an aim; and, I suppose by way of supplying deficiencies, he prolonged still further my lessons in Hindostanee, and grew more urgent in requiring their accomplishment: and I, like a fool, never thought of resisting him – I could not resist him.

One day I had come to my studies in lower spirits than usual; the ebb was occasioned by a poignantly felt disappointment: Hannah had told me in the morning there was a letter for me, and when I went down to take it, almost certain that the long looked-for tidings were vouchsafed me at last, I found only an unimportant note from Mr. Briggs on business. The bitter check had wrung from me some tears; and now as I sat poring over the crabbed characters and flourishing tropes of an Indian scribe, my eyes filled again.

St. John called me to his side to read; in attempting to do this my voice failed me: words were lost in sobs. He and I were the only occupants of the parlour: Diana was practising her music in the draw-ing-room, Mary was gardening – it was a very fine May-day, clear, sunny, and breezy. My companion expressed no surprise at this emotion, nor did he question me as to its cause; he only said: –

"We will wait a few minutes, Jane, till you are more composed." And while I smothered the paroxysm with all haste, he sat calm and patient, leaning on his desk and looking like a physician watching with the eye of science an expected and fully-understood crisis in a patient's malady. Having stifled my sobs, wiped my eyes, and muttered something about not being very well that morning, I resumed my task, and succeeded in completing it. St. John put away my books and his, locked his desk, and said: –

"Now, Jane, you shall take a walk; and with me."

"I will call Diana and Mary."

"No. I want only one companion this morning, and that must be you: put on your things; go out by the kitchen door; take the road towards the head of Marsh-Glen: I will join you in a moment."

I know no medium: I never in my life have known any medium in my dealings with positive, hard characters, antagonistic to my own, between absolute submission and determined revolt. I have always faithfully observed the one, up to the very moment of bursting, sometimes with volcanic vehemence, into the other; and as neither present circumstances warranted, nor my present mood inclined me to mutiny, I observed careful obedience to St. John's directions; and in ten minutes I was treading the wild track of the glen, side by side with him.

The breeze was from the west: it came over the hills, sweet with scents of heath and rush; the sky was of stainless blue; the stream descending the ravine, swelled with past spring rains, poured along plentiful and clear, catching golden gleams from the sun, and sapphire tints from the firmament. As we advanced and left the track, we trod a soft turf, mossy fine and emerald green, minutely enamelled with a tiny white flower, and spangled with a star-like yellow blossom: the hills, meantime, shut us quite in; for the glen, towards its head, wound to their very core.

"Let us rest here," said St. John, as we reached the first stragglers of a battalion of rocks, guarding a sort of pass, beyond which the beck rushed down, a waterfall; and where, still a little further, the mountain shook off turf and flower, had only heath for raiment, and crag for gem – where it exaggerated the wild to the savage, and exchanged the fresh for the frowning – where it guarded the forlorn hope of solitude, and a last refuge for silence.

I took a seat: St. John stood near me. He looked up the pass and down the hollow; his glance wandered away with the stream, and returned to traverse the unclouded heaven which coloured it: he removed his hat, let the breeze stir his hair and kiss his brow. He seemed in communion with the genius of the haunt: with his eye he bade farewell to something.

"And I shall see it again," he said aloud, "in dreams, when I sleep by the Ganges:[1] and again, in a more remote hour – when another slumber overcomes me – on the shore of a darker stream."

Strange words of a strange love! An austere patriot's passion for his fatherland! He sat down: for half an hour we never spoke; neither he to me nor I to him: that interval past, he recommenced: –

"Jane, I go in six weeks; I have taken my berth in an East Indiaman which sails on the twentieth of June."

"God will protect you; for you have undertaken his work," I answered.

"Yes," said he, "there is my glory and joy. I am the servant of an infallible master. I am not going out under human guidance, subject to the defective laws and erring control of my feeble fellow-worms: my king, my lawgiver, my captain, is the All-perfect. It seems strange to me that all round me do not burn to enlist under the same banner – to join in the same enterprise."

"All have not your powers; and it would be folly for the feeble to wish to march with the strong."

"I do not speak to the feeble, or think of them: I address only such as are worthy of the work, and competent to accomplish it."

"Those are few in number, and difficult to discover."

"You say truly: but when found, it is right to stir them up – to urge and exhort them to the effort – to show them what their gifts are, and why they were given – to speak Heaven's message in their ear, – to offer them, direct from God, a place in the ranks of his chosen."

"If they are really qualified for the task, will not their own hearts be the first to inform them of it?"

I felt as if an awful charm was framing round and gathering over me: I trembled to hear some fatal word spoken which would at once declare and rivet the spell.

---

1   A major river in India, sacred to Hinduism.

"And what does *your* heart say?" demanded St. John.

"My heart is mute, – my heart is mute," I answered, struck and thrilled.

"Then I must speak for it," continued the deep, relentless voice. "Jane, come with me to India: come as my help-meet and fellow-labourer."

The glen and sky spun round: the hills heaved! It was as if I had heard a summons from Heaven – as if a visionary messenger, like him of Macedonia, had enounced "Come over and help us!"[1] But I was no apostle, – I could not behold the herald, – I could not receive his call.

"Oh, St. John!" I cried, "have some mercy!"

I appealed to one who, in the discharge of what he believed his duty, knew neither mercy nor remorse. He continued: –

"God and nature intended you for a missionary's wife. It is not personal, but mental endowments they have given you: you are formed for labour, not for love. A missionary's wife you must – shall be. You shall be mine: I claim you – not for my pleasure, but for my Sovereign's service."

"I am not fit for it: I have no vocation," I said.

He had calculated on these first objections: he was not irritated by them. Indeed, as he leaned back against the crag behind him, folded his arms on his chest, and fixed his countenance, I saw he was prepared for a long and trying opposition, and had taken in a stock of patience to last him to its close – resolved, however, that that close should be conquest for him.

"Humility, Jane," said he, "is the ground-work of Christian virtues: you say right that you are not fit for the work. Who is fit for it? Or who, that ever was truly called, believed himself worthy of the summons? I, for instance, am but dust and ashes. With St. Paul I acknowledge myself the chiefest of sinners:[2] but I do not suffer this sense of my personal vileness to daunt me. I know my Leader: that He is just as well as mighty; and while He has chosen a feeble instrument to perform a great task, He will, from the boundless stores of His providence, supply the inadequacy of the means to the end. Think like me,

---

1   See Acts 16:9.
2   See 1 Timothy 1:15

Jane – trust like me. It is the Rock of Ages I ask you to lean on: do not doubt but it will bear the weight of your human weakness."

"I do not understand a missionary life: I have never studied missionary labours."

"There I, humble as I am, can give you the aid you want: I can set you your task from hour to hour; stand by you always; help you from moment to moment. This I could do in the beginning: soon (for I know your powers) you would be as strong and apt as myself, and would not require my help."

"But my powers – where are they for this undertaking? I do not feel them. Nothing speaks or stirs in me while you talk. I am sensible of no light kindling – no life quickening – no voice counselling or cheering. Oh, I wish I could make you see how much my mind is at this moment like a rayless dungeon, with one shrinking fear fettered in its depths – the fear of being persuaded by you to attempt what I cannot accomplish!"

"I have an answer for you – hear it. I have watched you ever since we first met: I have made you my study for ten months. I have proved you in that time by sundry tests: and what have I seen and elicited? In the village school I found you could perform well, punctually, uprightly, labour uncongenial to your habits and inclinations; I saw you could perform it with capacity and tact: you could win while you controlled. In the calm with which you learnt you had become suddenly rich, I read a mind clear of the vice of Demas:[1] – lucre had no undue power over you. In the resolute readiness with which you cut your wealth into four shares, keeping but one to yourself, and relinquishing the three others to the claim of abstract justice, I recognised a soul that revelled in the flame and excitement of sacrifice. In the tractability with which, at my wish, you forsook a study in which you were interested, and adopted another, because it interested me; in the untiring assiduity with which you have since persevered in it – in the unflagging energy and unshaken temper with which you have met its difficulties – I acknowledge the complement of the qualities I seek. Jane, you are docile, diligent, disinterested, faithful, constant, and courageous; very gentle, and very heroic: cease to mistrust yourself –

---

1   See 2 Timothy 4:10. Demas' "vice" was to abandon Paul for the attractions of the material world.

I can trust you unreservedly. As a conductress of Indian schools, and a helper amongst Indian women, your assistance will be to me invaluable."

My iron shroud contracted round me:[1] persuasion advanced with slow sure step. Shut my eyes as I would, these last words of his succeeded in making the way, which had seemed blocked up, comparatively clear. My work, which had appeared so vague, so hopelessly diffuse, condensed itself as he proceeded, and assumed a definite form under his shaping hand. He waited for an answer. I demanded a quarter of an hour to think, before I again hazarded a reply.

"Very willingly," he rejoined; and rising, he strode a little distance up the pass, threw himself down on a swell of heath, and there lay still.

"I *can* do what he wants me to do: I am forced to see and acknowledge that," I meditated – " that is, if life be spared me. But I feel mine is not the existence to be long protracted under an Indian sun. – What then? He does not care for that: when my time came to die he would resign me, in all serenity and sanctity, to the God who gave me. The case is very plain before me. In leaving England, I should leave a loved but empty land – Mr. Rochester is not there: and if he were, what is, what can that ever be to me? My business is to live without him now: nothing so absurd, so weak as to drag on from day to day, as if I were waiting some impossible change in circumstances, which might reunite me to him. Of course (as St. John once said) I must seek another interest in life to replace the one lost: is not the occupation he now offers me truly the most glorious man can adopt or God assign? Is it not, by its noble cares and sublime results, the one best calculated to fill the void left by uptorn affections and demolished hopes? I believe I must say, yes – and yet I shudder. Alas! If I join St. John, I abandon half myself: if I go to India, I go to premature death. And how will the interval between leaving England for India, and India for the grave, be filled? Oh, I know well! That, too, is very clear to my vision. By straining to satisfy St. John till my sinews ache, I *shall* satisfy him – to the finest central point and farthest outward circle of his expectations. If I *do* go with him – if I *do* make the sacri-

---

1 An allusion to the short story "The Iron Shroud," which appeared in *Blackwood's Magazine* in August 1830.

fice he urges, I will make it absolutely: I will throw all on the altar – heart, vitals, the entire victim. He will never love me; but he shall approve me: I will show him energies he has not yet seen, resources he has never suspected. Yes: I can work as hard as he can; and with as little grudging.

"Consent, then, to his demand is possible: but for one item – one dreadful item. It is – that he asks me to be his wife, and has no more of a husband's heart for me than that frowning giant of a rock, down which the stream is foaming in yonder gorge. He prizes me as a soldier would a good weapon; and that is all. Unmarried to him, this would never grieve me; but can I let him complete his calculations – coolly put into practice his plans – go through the wedding ceremony? Can I receive from him the bridal ring, endure all the forms of love (which I doubt not he would scrupulously observe) and know that the spirit was quite absent? Can I bear the consciousness that every endearment he bestows is a sacrifice made on principle? No: such a martyrdom would be monstrous. I will never undergo it. As his sister, I might accompany him – not as his wife: I will tell him so."

I looked towards the knoll: there he lay, still as a prostrate column; his face turned to me: his eye beaming watchful, and keen. He started to his feet and approached me.

"I am ready to go to India, if I may go free."

"Your answer requires a commentary," he said; "it is not clear."

"You have hitherto been my adopted brother: I, your adopted sister; let us continue as such: you and I had better not marry."

He shook his head. "Adopted fraternity will not do in this case. If you were my real sister it would be different: I should take you, and seek no wife. But, as it is, either our union must be consecrated and sealed by marriage, or it cannot exist: practical obstacles oppose themselves to any other plan. Do you not see it, Jane? Consider a moment – your strong sense will guide you."

I did consider: and still my sense, such as it was, directed me only to the fact that we did not love each other as man and wife should; and therefore it inferred we ought not to marry. I said so. "St. John," I returned, "I regard you as a brother – you, me as a sister: so let us continue."

"We cannot – we cannot," he answered, with short, sharp determination: "it would not do. You have said you will go with me to India: remember – you have said that."

"Conditionally."

"Well – well. To the main point – the departure with me from England, the co-operation with me in my future labours – you do not object. You have already as good as put your hand to the plough:[1] you are too consistent to withdraw it. You have but one end to keep in view – how the work you have undertaken can best be done. Simplify your complicated interests, feelings, thoughts, wishes, aims; merge all considerations in one purpose: that of fulfilling with effect – with power – the mission of your great Master. To do so, you must have a coadjutor – not a brother; that is a loose tie: but a husband. I, too, do not want a sister: a sister might any day be taken from me. I want a wife: the sole helpmeet I can influence efficiently in life, and retain absolutely till death."

I shuddered as he spoke: I felt his influence in my marrow – his hold on my limbs.

"Seek one elsewhere than in me, St. John: seek one fitted to you."

"One fitted to my purpose, you mean – fitted to my vocation. Again I tell you it is not the insignificant private individual – the mere man, with the man's selfish senses – I wish to mate: it is the missionary."

"And I will give the missionary my energies – it is all he wants – but not myself: that would be only adding the husk and shell to the kernel. For them he has no use: I retain them."

"You cannot – you ought not. Do you think God will be satisfied with half an oblation?[2] Will He accept a mutilated sacrifice? It is the cause of God I advocate: it is under His standard I enlist you. I cannot accept on His behalf a divided allegiance: it must be entire."

"Oh! I will give my heart to God," I said. "*You* do not want it."

I will not swear, reader, that there was not something of repressed sarcasm both in the tone in which I uttered this sentence, and in the feeling that accompanied it. I had silently feared St. John till now, because I had not understood him. He had held me in awe,[3] because

---

1   See Luke 9:62.
2   Offering.
3   i.e., St. John's personality had created awe in Jane.

he had held me in doubt. How much of him was saint, how much mortal, I could not heretofore tell; but revelations were being made in this conference: the analysis of his nature was proceeding before my eyes. I saw his fallibilities: I comprehended them. I understood that, sitting there where I did, on the bank of heath, and with that handsome form before me, I sat at the feet of a man, erring as I. The veil fell from his hardness and despotism. Having felt in him the presence of these qualities, I felt his imperfection, and took courage. I was with an equal – one with whom I might argue – one whom, if I saw good, I might resist.

He was silent after I had uttered the last sentence, and I presently risked an upward glance at his countenance. His eye, bent on me, expressed at once stern surprise and keen inquiry. "Is she sarcastic, and sarcastic to *me?*" it seemed to say. "What does this signify?"

"Do not let us forget that this is a solemn matter," he said, ere long; "one of which we may neither think nor talk lightly without sin. I trust, Jane, you are in earnest when you say you will give your heart to God: it is all I want. Once wrench your heart from man, and fix it on your Maker, the advancement of that Maker's spiritual kingdom on earth will be your chief delight and endeavour: you will be ready to do at once whatever furthers that end. You will see what impetus would be given to your efforts and mine by our physical and mental union in marriage: the only union that gives a character of permanent conformity to the destinies and designs of human beings; and, passing over all minor caprices – all trivial difficulties and delicacies of feeling – all scruple about the degree, kind, strength, or tenderness of mere personal inclination – you will hasten to enter into that union at once."

"Shall I?" I said briefly; and I looked at his features, beautiful in their harmony, but strangely formidable in their still severity: at his brow, commanding but not open; at his eyes, bright, and deep, and searching, but never soft; at his tall, imposing figure; and fancied myself in idea, *his wife*. Oh! it would never do! As his curate, his comrade, all would be right: I would cross oceans with him in that capacity; toil under eastern suns, in Asian deserts with him in that office; admire and emulate his courage, and devotion, and vigour; accommodate quietly to his masterhood; smile undisturbed at his ineradicable ambition; discriminate the Christian from the man; profoundly esteem the one, and freely forgive the other. I should suffer often, no doubt, attached to him only in this capacity: my body would be under rather a stringent yoke, but my heart and mind would be free. I should still have my unblighted self to turn to: my natural unenslaved feelings with which to communicate in moments of loneliness. There would be recesses in my mind which would be only mine, to which he never came; and sentiments growing there fresh and sheltered, which his austerity could never blight, nor his measured warrior-march trample down: but as his wife – at his side always, and always restrained, and always checked – forced to keep the fire of my nature continually low, to compel it to burn inwardly and never utter a cry, though the imprisoned flame consumed vital after vital – *this* would be unendurable.

"St. John!" I exclaimed, when I had got so far in my meditation.

"Well?" he answered, icily.

"I repeat: I freely consent to go with you as your fellow-missionary; but not as your wife: I cannot marry you and become a part of you."

"A part of me you must become," he answered, steadily; "otherwise the whole bargain is void. How can I, a man not yet thirty, take out with me to India a girl of nineteen, unless she be married to me? How can we be for ever together – sometimes in solitudes, sometimes amidst savage tribes – and unwed?"

"Very well," I said shortly; "under the circumstances, quite as well as if I were either your real sister; or a man and a clergyman, like yourself."

"It is known that you are not my sister; I cannot introduce you as such: to attempt it would be to fasten injurious suspicions on us both. And for the rest, though you have a man's vigorous brain, you have a woman's heart, and – it would not do."

"It would do," I affirmed, with some disdain, "perfectly well. I have a woman's heart; but not where you are concerned; for you I have only a comrade's constancy; a fellow-soldier's frankness, fidelity, fraternity, if you like; a neophyte's respect and submission to his hierophant: nothing more – don't fear."

"It is what I want," he said, speaking to himself; "it is just what I want. And there are obstacles in the way: they must be hewn down.

Jane, you would not repent marrying me; be certain of that: we *must* be married. I repeat it: there is no other way; and undoubtedly enough of love would follow upon marriage to render the union right even in your eyes."

"I scorn your idea of love," I could not help saying, as I rose up and stood before him, leaning my back against the rock. "I scorn the counterfeit sentiment you offer: yes, St. John, and I scorn you when you offer it."

He looked at me fixedly: compressing his well-cut lips while he did so. Whether he was incensed or surprised, or what, it was not easy to tell: he could command his countenance thoroughly.

"I scarcely expected to hear that expression from you," he said: "I think I have done and uttered nothing to deserve scorn."

I was touched by his gentle tone, and overawed by his high, calm mien.

"Forgive me the words, St. John: but it is your own fault that I have been roused to speak so unguardedly. You have introduced a topic on which our natures are at variance – a topic we should never discuss: the very name of love is an apple of discord[1] between us – if the reality were required, what should we do? How should we feel? My dear cousin, abandon your scheme of marriage – forget it."

"No," said he; "it is a long-cherished scheme, and the only one which can secure my great end: but I shall urge you no further at present. To-morrow I leave home for Cambridge: I have many friends there to whom I should wish to say farewell. I shall be absent a fortnight – take that space of time to consider my offer: and do not forget that if you reject it, it is not me you deny, but God. Through my means, He opens to you a noble career: as my wife only can you enter upon it. Refuse to be my wife, and you limit yourself for ever to a track of selfish ease and barren obscurity. Tremble, lest in that case you should be numbered with those who have denied the faith and are worse than infidels!"

He had done. Turning from me, he once more –

---

1   An apple, inscribed "For the fairest," which Eris (goddess of discord) threw among the Olympian goddesses. The resulting conflict between Hera, Athena, and Aphrodite led Zeus to appoint the Trojan prince Paris to judge the contest. His award of the apple to Aphrodite resulted in his elopement with Helen, and the subsequent destruction of Troy.

"Looked to river, looked to hill."[1]

But this time his feelings were all pent in his heart: I was not worthy to hear them uttered. As I walked by his side homeward, I read well in his iron silence all he felt towards me: the disappointment of an austere and despotic nature, which has met resistance where it expected submission – the disapprobation of a cool, inflexible judgment, which has detected in another feelings and views in which it has no power to sympathize: in short, as a man, he would have wished to coerce me into obedience: it was only as a sincere Christian he bore so patiently with my perversity, and allowed so long a space for reflection and repentance.

That night, after he had kissed his sisters, he thought proper to forget even to shake hands with me; but left the room in silence. I – who, though I had no love, had much friendship for him – was hurt by the marked omission: so much hurt that tears started to my eyes.

"I see you and St. John have been quarrelling, Jane," said Diana, "during your walk on the moor. But go after him; he is now lingering in the passage, expecting you – he will make it up."

I have not much pride under such circumstances: I would always rather be happy than dignified; and I ran after him – he stood at the foot of the stairs.

"Good-night, St. John," said I.

"Good-night, Jane," he replied, calmly.

"Then shake hands," I added.

What a cold, loose touch he impressed on my fingers! He was deeply displeased by what had occurred that day: cordiality would not warm, nor tears move him. No happy reconciliation was to be had with him – no cheering smile or generous word: but still the Christian was patient and placid; and when I asked him if he forgave me, he answered that he was not in the habit of cherishing the remembrance of vexation; that he had nothing to forgive; not having been offended.

And with that answer, he left me. I would much rather he had knocked me down.

---

1   From Scott's *The Lay of the Last Minstrel*, V.xxvi.1.

CHAPTER XXXV

HE did not leave for Cambridge the next day, as he had said he would. He deferred his departure a whole week; and during that time he made me feel what severe punishment a good, yet stern, a conscientious, yet implacable man can inflict on one who has offended him. Without one overt act of hostility, one upbraiding word, he contrived to impress me momently[1] with the conviction that I was put beyond the pale of his favour.

Not that St. John harboured a spirit of unchristian vindictiveness – not that he would have injured a hair of my head, if it had been fully in his power to do so. Both by nature and principle he was superior to the mean gratification of vengeance: he had forgiven me for saying I scorned him and his love, but he had not forgotten the words; and as long as he and I lived he never would forget them. I saw by his look, when he turned to me, that they were always written on the air between me and him: whenever I spoke, they sounded in my voice to his ear; and their echo toned every answer he gave me.

He did not abstain from conversing with me: he even called me as usual each morning to join him at his desk; and I fear the corrupt man within him had a pleasure unimparted to, and unshared by, the pure Christian, in evincing with what skill he could, while acting and speaking apparently just as usual, extract from every deed and every phrase the spirit of interest and approval which had formerly communicated a certain austere charm to his language and manner. To me, he was in reality become no longer flesh, but marble: his eye was a cold, bright, blue gem; his tongue, a speaking instrument – nothing more.

All this was torture to me – refined, lingering torture. It kept up a slow fire of indignation, and a trembling trouble of grief, which harassed and crushed me altogether. I felt how – if I were his wife – this good man, pure as the deep sunless source, could soon kill me; without drawing from my veins a single drop of blood, or receiving on his own crystal conscience the faintest stain of crime. Especially I felt this, when I made any attempt to propitiate him. No ruth met my ruth. *He* experienced no suffering from estrangement – no yearning

---

1   Moment by moment.

after reconciliation; and though, more than once, my fast falling tears blistered the page over which we both bent, they produced no more effect on him than if his heart had been really a matter of stone or metal. To his sisters, meantime, he was somewhat kinder than usual: as if afraid that mere coldness would not sufficiently convince me how completely I was banished and banned, he added the force of contrast; and this I am sure he did, not by malice, but on principle.

The night before he left home, happening to see him walking in the garden about sunset, and remembering, as I looked at him, that this man, alienated as he now was, had once saved my life, and that we were near relations, I was moved to make a last attempt to regain his friendship. I went out and approached him, as he stood leaning over the little gate: I spoke to the point at once.

"St. John, I am unhappy, because you are still angry with me. Let us be friends."

"I hope we are friends," was the unmoved reply; while he still watched the rising of the moon, which he had been contemplating as I approached.

"No, St. John, we are not friends as we were. You know that."

"Are we not? That is wrong. For my part, I wish you no ill and all good."

"I believe you, St. John; for I am sure you are incapable of wishing any one ill: but, as I am your kinswoman, I should desire somewhat more of affection than that sort of general philanthropy you extend to mere strangers."

"Of course," he said. "Your wish is reasonable; and I am far from regarding you as a stranger."

This, spoken in a cool, tranquil tone, was mortifying and baffling enough. Had I attended to the suggestions of pride and ire, I should immediately have left him: but something worked within me more strongly than those feelings could. I deeply venerated my cousin's talent and principle. His friendship was of value to me: to lose it tried me severely. I would not so soon relinquish the attempt to reconquer it.

"Must we part in this way, St. John? And when you go to India, will you leave me so, without a kinder word than you have yet spoken?"

He now turned quite from the moon, and faced me.

"When I go to India, Jane, will I leave you? What! do you not go to India?"

"You said I could not, unless I married you."

"And you will not marry me? You adhere to that resolution?"

Reader, do you know, as I do, what terror those cold people can put into the ice of their questions? How much of the fall of the avalanche is in their anger? of the breaking up of the frozen sea in their displeasure?

"No, St. John, I will not marry you. I adhere to my resolution."

The avalanche had shaken and slid a little forward; but it did not yet crash down.

"Once more, why this refusal?" he asked.

"Formerly" I answered, "because you did not love me; now I reply, because you almost hate me. If I were to marry you, you would kill me. You are killing me now."

His lips and cheeks turned white – quite white.

"*I should kill – I am killing you?* Your words are such as ought not to be used: violent, unfeminine, and untrue. They betray an unfortunate state of mind: they merit severe reproof: they would seem inexcusable; but that it is the duty of man to forgive his fellow, even until seventy-and-seven times."[1]

I had finished the business now. While earnestly wishing to erase from his mind the trace of my former offence, I had stamped on that tenacious surface, another and far deeper impression: I had burnt it in.

"Now you will indeed hate me," I said. "It is useless to attempt to conciliate you: I see I have made an eternal enemy of you."

A fresh wrong did these words inflict: the worse, because they touched on the truth. That bloodless lip quivered to a temporary spasm. I knew the steely ire I had whetted. I was heart-wrung.

"You utterly misinterpret my words," I said, at once seizing his hand: "I have no intention to grieve or pain you – indeed, I have not."

Most bitterly he smiled – most decidedly he withdrew his hand from mine. "And now you recall your promise, and will not go to India at all, I presume?" said he, after a considerable pause.

---

1   Matthew 18:22.

"Yes I will, as your assistant," I answered.

A very long silence succeeded. What struggle there was in him between Nature and Grace in this interval, I cannot tell: only singular gleams scintillated in his eyes, and strange shadows passed over his face. He spoke at last.

"I before proved to you the absurdity of a single woman of your age proposing to accompany abroad a single man of mine. I proved it to you in such terms as, I should have thought, would have prevented your ever again alluding to the plan. That you have done so, I regret – for your sake."

I interrupted him. Anything like a tangible reproach gave me courage at once. "Keep to common sense, St. John: you are verging on nonsense. You pretend to be shocked by what I have said. You are not really shocked; for, with your superior mind, you cannot be either so dull or so conceited as to misunderstand my meaning. I say again, I will be your curate, if you like, but never your wife."

Again he turned lividly pale; but, as before, controlled his passion perfectly. He answered emphatically, but calmly: –

"A female curate, who is not my wife, would never suit me. With me, then, it seems, you cannot go: but if you are sincere in your offer, I will, while in town, speak to a married missionary, whose wife needs a coadjutor. Your own fortune will make you independent of the Society's aid; and thus you may still be spared the dishonour of break-ing your promise, and deserting the band you engaged to join."

Now I never had, as the reader knows, either given any formal promise, or entered into any engagement; and this language was all much too hard, and much too despotic for the occasion. I replied: –

"There is no dishonour; no breach of promise; no desertion in the case. I am not under the slightest obligation to go to India: especially with strangers. With you, I would have ventured much; because I admire, confide in, and, as a sister, I love you: but I am convinced that, go when and with whom I would, I should not live long in that cli-mate."

"Ah! you are afraid of yourself," he said, curling his lip.

"I am. God did not give me my life to throw away; and to do as you wish me, would, I begin to think, be almost equivalent to committing suicide. Moreover, before I definitely resolve on quitting

England, I will know for certain, whether I cannot be of greater use by remaining in it than by leaving it."

"What do you mean?"

"It would be fruitless to attempt to explain: but there is a point on which I have long endured painful doubt; and I can go nowhere till by some means that doubt is removed."

"I know where your heart turns, and to what it clings. The interest you cherish is lawless and unconsecrated. Long since you ought to have crushed it: now you should blush to allude to it. You think of Mr. Rochester?"

It was true. I confessed it by silence.

"Are you going to seek Mr. Rochester?"

"I must find out what is become of him."

"It remains for me, then," he said, "to remember you in my prayers; and to entreat God for you, in all earnestness, that you may not indeed become a castaway. I had thought I recognised in you one of the chosen. But God sees not as man sees:[1] *His* will be done."

He opened the gate, passed through it, and strayed away down the glen. He was soon out of sight.

On re-entering the parlour, I found Diana standing at the window, looking very thoughtful. Diana was a great deal taller than I: she put her hand on my shoulder, and, stooping, examined my face.

"Jane," she said, "you are always agitated and pale now. I am sure there is something the matter. Tell me what business St. John and you have on hands. I have watched you this half hour from the window: you must forgive my being such a spy, but for a long time I have fancied I hardly know what. St. John is a strange being —"

She paused – I did not speak: soon she resumed: –

"That brother of mine cherishes peculiar views of some sort respecting you, I am sure: he has long distinguished you by a notice and interest he never showed any one else – to what end? I wish he loved you – does he, Jane?"

I put her cool hand to my hot forehead: "No, Die, not one whit."

"Then why does he follow you so with his eyes – and get you so frequently alone with him, and keep you so continually at his side? Mary and I had both concluded he wished you to marry him."

---

1   1 Samuel 16:7.

"He does – he has asked me to be his wife."

Diana clapped her hands. "That is just what we hoped and thought! And you will marry him, Jane, won't you? And then he will stay in England."

"Far from that Diana; his sole idea in proposing to me is to procure a fitting fellow-labourer in his Indian toils."

"What! He wishes you to go to India?"

"Yes."

"Madness!" she exclaimed. "You would not live three months there, I am certain. You never shall go: you have not consented – have you, Jane?"

"I have refused to marry him —"

"And have consequently displeased him?" she suggested.

"Deeply: he will never forgive me, I fear: yet I offered to accompany him as his sister."

"It was frantic folly to do so, Jane. Think of the task you undertook – one of incessant fatigue: where fatigue kills even the strong; and you are weak. St. John – you know him – would urge you to impossibilities: with him there would be no permission to rest during the hot hours; and unfortunately, I have noticed, whatever he exacts, you force yourself to perform. I am astonished you found courage to refuse his hand. You do not love him then, Jane?"

"Not as a husband."

"Yet he is a handsome fellow."

"And I am so plain you see, Die. We should never suit."

"Plain! You? Not at all. You are much too pretty, as well as too good, to be grilled alive in Calcutta." And again she earnestly conjured me to give up all thoughts of going out with her brother.

"I must, indeed," I said; "for when just now I repeated the offer of serving him for a deacon, he expressed himself shocked at my want of decency. He seemed to think I had committed an impropriety in proposing to accompany him unmarried: as if I had not from the first hoped to find in him a brother; and habitually regarded him as such."

"What makes you say he does not love you, Jane?"

"You should hear himself on the subject. He has again and again explained that it is not himself, but his office he wishes to mate. He has told me I am formed for labour – not for love: which is true, no doubt. But, in my opinion, if I am not formed for love, it follows that I am not formed for marriage. Would it not be strange, Die, to be chained for life to a man who regarded one but as a useful tool?"

"Insupportable – unnatural – out of the question!"

"And then," I continued; "though I have only sisterly affection for him now, yet, if forced to be his wife, I can imagine the possibility of conceiving an inevitable, strange, torturing kind of love for him: because he is so talented; and there is often a certain heroic grandeur in his look, manner, and conversation. In that case, my lot would become unspeakably wretched. He would not want me to love him; and if I showed the feeling, he would make me sensible that it was a superfluity, unrequired by him, unbecoming in me. I know he would."

"And yet, St. John is a good man," said Diana.

"He is a good and a great man: but he forgets, pitilessly, the feelings and claims of little people, in pursuing his own large views. It is better, therefore, for the insignificant to keep out of his way; lest, in his progress, he should trample them down. Here he comes! I will leave you, Diana." And I hastened up stairs as I saw him entering the garden.

But I was forced to meet him again at supper. During that meal he appeared just as composed as usual. I had thought he would hardly speak to me, and I was certain he had given up the pursuit of his matrimonial scheme: the sequel showed I was mistaken on both points. He addressed me precisely in his ordinary manner; or what had, of late, been his ordinary manner: one scrupulously polite. No doubt he had invoked the help of the Holy Spirit to subdue the anger I had roused in him, and now believed he had forgiven me once more.

For the evening reading before prayers, he selected the twenty-first chapter of Revelations. It was at all times pleasant to listen, while from his lips fell the words of the Bible: never did his fine voice sound at once so sweet and full – never did his manner become so impressive in its noble simplicity, as when he delivered the oracles of God; and to-night that voice took a more solemn tone – that manner a more thrilling meaning – as he sat in the midst of his household circle (the May moon shining in through the uncurtained window, and rendering almost unnecessary the light of the candle on the table): as he sat there, bending over the great old Bible, and described from its page the vision of the new heaven and the new earth – told how God would come to dwell with men, how he would wipe away all tears from their eyes, and promised that there should be no more death, neither sorrow nor crying, nor any more pain, because the former things were passed away.

The succeeding words thrilled me strangely as he spoke them: especially as I felt, by the slight, indescribable alteration in sound, that in uttering them, his eye had turned on me.

"He that overcometh shall inherit all things; and I will be his God, and he shall be my son. But," was slowly, distinctly read, "the fearful, the unbelieving, &c., shall have their part in the lake which burneth with fire and brimstone, which is the second death."[1]

Henceforward, I knew what fate St. John feared for me.

A calm, subdued triumph, blent with a longing earnestness, marked his enunciation of the last glorious verses of that chapter. The reader believed his name was already written in the Lamb's book of life, and he yearned after the hour which should admit him to the city to which the kings of the earth bring their glory and honour; which has no need of sun or moon to shine in it, because the glory of God lightens it, and the Lamb is the light thereof.

In the prayer following the chapter, all his energy gathered – all his stern zeal woke: he was in deep earnest, wrestling with God, and resolved on a conquest. He supplicated strength for the weak-hearted; guidance for wanderers from the fold: a return, even at the eleventh hour, for those whom the temptations of the world and the flesh were luring from the narrow path. He asked, he urged, he claimed the boon of a brand snatched from the burning.[2] Earnestness is ever deeply solemn: first, as I listened to that prayer, I wondered at his; then, when it continued and rose, I was touched by it, and at last awed. He felt the greatness and goodness of his purpose so sincerely: others who heard him plead for it, could not but feel it too.

The prayer over, we took leave of him: he was to go at a very early hour in the morning. Diana and Mary having kissed him, left the room – in compliance, I think, with a whispered hint from him: I tendered my hand, and wished him a pleasant journey.

---

1 Revelation 21:7-8.
2 See Amos 4:11.

"Thank you, Jane. As I said, I shall return from Cambridge in a fortnight: that space, then, is yet left you for reflection. If I listened to human pride, I should say no more to you of marriage with me; but I listen to my duty, and keep steadily in view my first aim – to do all things to the glory of God. My Master was long-suffering: so will I be. I cannot give you up to perdition as a vessel of wrath: repent – resolve; while there is yet time. Remember, we are bid to work while it is day – warned that 'the night cometh when no man shall work.'[1] Remember the fate of Dives, who had his good things in this life.[2] God give you strength to choose that better part which shall not be taken from you!"[3]

He laid his hand on my head as he uttered the last words. He had spoken earnestly, mildly: his look was not, indeed, that of a lover beholding his mistress; but it was that of a pastor recalling his wandering sheep – or better, of a guardian angel watching the soul for which he is responsible. All men of talent, whether they be men of feeling or not; whether they be zealots, or aspirants, or despots – provided only they be sincere – have their sublime moments: when they subdue and rule. I felt veneration for St. John – veneration so strong that its impetus thrust me at once to the point I had so long shunned. I was tempted to cease struggling with him – to rush down the torrent of his will into the gulf of his existence, and there lose my own. I was almost as hard beset by him now as I had been once before, in a different way, by another. I was a fool both times. To have yielded then would have been an error of principle; to have yielded now would have been an error of judgment. So I think at this hour, when I look back to the crisis through the quiet medium of time: I was unconscious of folly at the instant.

I stood motionless under my hierophant's touch. My refusals were forgotten – my fears overcome – my wrestlings paralyzed. The Impossible – *i.e.* my marriage with St. John – was fast becoming the Possible. All was changing utterly, with a sudden sweep. Religion called – Angels beckoned – God commanded – life rolled together like a

---

1 John 9:4.
2 See Luke 16:19-31. "Dives," which means "rich man," is the name usually given to the wealthy man in the parable of Lazarus which appears in these verses. His fate is to burn in hell without respite.
3 See Luke 10:42.

scroll[1] – death's gates opening, shewed eternity beyond: it seemed, that for safety and bliss there, all here might be sacrificed in a second. The dim room was full of visions.

"Could you decide now?" asked the missionary. The inquiry was put in gentle tones: he drew me to him as gently. Oh, that gentleness! how far more potent is it than force! I could resist St. John's wrath: I grew pliant as a reed under his kindness. Yet I knew all the time, if I yielded now, I should not the less be made to repent, some day, of my former rebellion. His nature was not changed by one hour of solemn prayer: it was only elevated.

"I could decide if I were but certain," I answered: "were I but convinced that it is God's will I should marry you, I could vow to marry you here and now – come afterwards what would!"

"My prayers are heard!" ejaculated St. John. He pressed his hand firmer on my head, as if he claimed me: he surrounded me with his arm, *almost* as if he loved me (I say *almost* – I knew the difference – for I had felt what it was to be loved; but, like him, I had now put love out of the question, and thought only of duty): I contended with my inward dimness of vision, before which clouds yet rolled. I sincerely, deeply, fervently longed to do what was right; and only that. "Shew me – shew me the path!" I entreated of Heaven. I was excited more than I had ever been; and whether what followed was the effect of excitement, the reader shall judge.

All the house was still; for I believe all, except St. John and myself, were now retired to rest. The one candle was dying out: the room was full of moonlight. My heart beat fast and thick: I heard its throb. Suddenly it stood still to an inexpressible feeling that thrilled it through, and passed at once to my head and extremities. The feeling was not like an electric shock; but it was quite as sharp, as strange, as startling: it acted on my senses as if their utmost activity hitherto had been but torpor; from which they were now summoned, and forced to wake. They rose expectant: eye and ear waited, while the flesh quivered on my bones.

"What have you heard? What do you see?" asked St. John. I saw nothing: but I heard a voice somewhere cry –

---

1   See Isaiah 34:4.

"Jane! Jane! Jane!" Nothing more.

"Oh, God! what is it?" I gasped.

I might have said, "Where is it?" for it did not seem in the room – nor in the house – nor in the garden: it did not come out of the air – nor from under the earth – nor from overhead. I had heard it – where, or whence, for ever impossible to know! And it was the voice of a human being – a known, loved, well-remembered voice – that of Edward Fairfax Rochester; and it spoke in pain and woe – wildly, eerily, urgently.

"I am coming!" I cried. "Wait for me! Oh, I will come!" I flew to the door, and looked into the passage: it was dark. I ran out into the garden: it was void.

"Where are you?" I exclaimed.

The hills beyond Marsh-Glen sent the answer faintly back – "Where are you!" I listened. The wind sighed low in the firs: all was moorland loneliness and midnight hush.

"Down superstition!" I commented, as that spectre rose up black by the black yew at the gate. "This is not thy deception, nor thy witchcraft: it is the work of nature. She was roused, and did – no miracle – but her best."

I broke from St. John; who had followed, and would have detained me. It was *my* turn to assume ascendancy. *My* powers were in play, and in force. I told him to forbear question or remark; I desired him to leave me: I must, and would be alone. He obeyed at once. Where there is energy to command well enough, obedience never fails. I mounted to my chamber; locked myself in; fell on my knees; and prayed in my way – a different way to St. John's, but effective in its own fashion. I seemed to penetrate very near a Mighty Spirit; and my soul rushed out in gratitude at His feet. I rose from the thanksgiving – took a resolve – and lay down, unscared, enlightened – eager but for the daylight.

CHAPTER XXXVI

THE daylight came. I rose at dawn. I busied myself for an hour or two with arranging my things in my chamber, drawers and wardrobe, in the order wherein I should wish to leave them during a brief absence. Meantime, I heard St. John quit his room. He stopped at my door: I feared he would knock – no, but a slip of paper was passed under the door. I took it up. It bore these words: –

"You left me too suddenly last night. Had you stayed but a little longer, you would have laid your hand on the Christian's cross and the angel's crown. I shall expect your clear decision when I return this day fortnight. Meantime, watch and pray that you enter not into temptation: the spirit, I trust, is willing, but the flesh, I see, is weak.[1] I shall pray for you hourly. – Yours, St. John."

"My spirit," I answered mentally, "is willing to do what is right; and my flesh, I hope, is strong enough to accomplish the will of Heaven, when once that will is distinctly known to me. At any rate, it shall be strong enough to search – inquire – to grope an outlet from this cloud of doubt, and find the open day of certainty."

It was the first of June; yet the morning was overcast and chilly: rain beat fast on my casement. I heard the front-door open, and St. John pass out. Looking through the window, I saw him traverse the garden. He took the way over the misty moors in the direction of Whitcross – there he would meet the coach.

"In a few more hours I shall succeed you on that track, cousin," thought I: "I too have a coach to meet at Whitcross. I too have some to see and ask after in England, before I depart for ever."

It wanted yet two hours of breakfast-time. I filled the interval in walking softly about my room, and pondering the visitation which had given my plans their present bent. I recalled that inward sensation I had experienced: for I could recall it, with all its unspeakable strangeness. I recalled the voice I had heard; again I questioned whence it came, as vainly as before: it seemed in *me* – not in the external world. I asked, was it a mere nervous impression – a delusion? I could not conceive or believe it: it was more like an inspiration. The wondrous shock of feeling had come like the earthquake

---

1 See Matthew 26:41 and Mark 14:38.

which shook the foundations of Paul and Silas's prison: it had opened the doors of the soul's cell, and loosed its bands[1] – it had wakened it out of its sleep, whence it sprang trembling, listening, aghast; then vibrated thrice a cry on my startled ear, and in my quaking heart, and through my spirit; which neither feared nor shook, but exulted as if in joy over the success of one effort it had been privileged to make, independent of the cumbrous body.

"Ere many days," I said, as I terminated my musings, "I will know something of him whose voice seemed last night to summon me. Letters have proved of no avail – personal inquiry shall replace them."

At breakfast, I announced to Diana and Mary that I was going a journey, and should be absent at least four days.

"Alone, Jane?" they asked.

"Yes; it was to see, or hear news of, a friend about whom I had for some time been uneasy."

They might have said, as I have no doubt they thought, that they had believed me to be without any friends save them: for, indeed, I had often said so; but with their true, natural delicacy, they abstained from comment: except that Diana asked me if I was sure I was well enough to travel. I looked very pale, she observed. I replied that nothing ailed me save anxiety of mind, which I hoped soon to alleviate.

It was easy to make my further arrangements; for I was troubled with no inquiries – no surmises. Having once explained to them that I could not now be explicit about my plans, they kindly and wisely acquiesced in the silence with which I pursued them; according to me the privilege of free action I should, under similar circumstances, have accorded them.

I left Moor-House at three o'clock, P.M., and soon after four, I stood at the foot of the signpost of Whitcross, waiting the arrival of the coach which was to take me to distant Thornfield. Amidst the silence of those solitary roads and desert hills, I heard it approach from a great distance. It was the same vehicle whence, a year ago, I had alighted one summer evening on this very spot – how desolate, and hopeless, and objectless! It stopped as I beckoned. I entered – not now obliged to part with my whole fortune as the price of its accommo-

---

1   See Acts 16:25-26.

dation. Once more on the road to Thornfield, I felt like the messenger-pigeon flying home.

It was a journey of six-and-thirty hours. I had set out from Whitcross on a Tuesday afternoon, and early on the succeeding Thursday morning the coach stopped to water the horses at a wayside inn, situated in the midst of scenery whose green hedges and large fields, and low, pastoral hills (how mild of feature and verdant of hue compared with the stern north-midland moors of Morton!) met my eye like the lineaments of a once familiar face. Yes, I knew the character of this landscape: I was sure we were near my bourne.

"How far is Thornfield-Hall from here?" I asked of the ostler.[1]

"Just two miles, ma'am, across the fields."

"My journey is closed," I thought to myself. I got out of the coach, gave a box I had into the ostler's charge, to be kept till I called for it; paid my fare; satisfied the coachman, and was going: the brightening day gleamed on the sign of the inn, and I read in gilt letters "The Rochester Arms." My heart leapt up: I was already on my master's very lands. It fell again: the thought struck it: –

"Your master himself may be beyond the British Channel, for aught you know: and then, if he is at Thornfield-Hall, towards which you hasten, who besides him is there? His lunatic wife; and you have nothing to do with him: you dare not speak to him or seek his presence. You have lost your labour – you had better go no farther," urged the monitor. "Ask information of the people at the inn; they can give you all you seek: they can solve your doubts at once. Go up to that man, and inquire if Mr. Rochester be at home."

The suggestion was sensible; and yet I could not force myself to act on it. I so dreaded a reply that would crush me with despair. To prolong doubt was to prolong hope. I might yet once more see the Hall under the ray of her star. There was the stile before me – the very fields through which I had hurried, blind, deaf, distracted, with a revengeful fury tracking and scourging me, on the morning I fled from Thornfield: ere I well knew what course I had resolved to take, I was in the midst of them. How fast I walked! How I ran sometimes! How I looked forward to catch the first view of the well-known

---

1 The stableman at an inn.

woods! With what feelings I welcomed single trees I knew, and familiar glimpses of meadow and hill between them!

At last the woods rose; the rookery clustered dark; a loud cawing
broke the morning stillness. Strange delight inspired me: on I hastened. Another field crossed – a lane threaded – and there were the
court-yard walls – the back-offices: the house itself, the rookery still
hid.

"My first view of it shall be in front," I determined, "where its
bold battlements will strike the eye nobly at once, and where I can
single out my master's very window: perhaps he will be standing at it
– he rises early: perhaps he is now walking in the orchard, or on the
pavement in front. Could I but see him! – but a moment! Surely, in
that case, I should not be so mad as to run to him? I cannot tell – I am
not certain. And if I did – what then? God bless him! What then?
Who would be hurt by my once more tasting the life his glance can
give me? – I rave: perhaps at this moment he is watching the sun rise
over the Pyrenees,[1] or on the tideless sea of the south."

I had coasted along the lower wall of the orchard – turned its
angle: there was a gate just there, opening into the meadow, between
two stone pillars, crowned by stone balls. From behind one pillar I
could peep round quietly at the full front of the mansion. I advanced
my head with precaution, desirous to ascertain if any bedroom win-
dow-blinds were yet drawn up: battlements, windows, long front – all
from this sheltered station were at my command.

The crows sailing overhead perhaps watched me while I took this
survey. I wonder what they thought: they must have considered I was
very careful and timid at first, and that gradually I grew very bold and
reckless. A peep, and then a long stare; and then a departure from my
niche and a straying out into the meadow; and a sudden stop full in
front of the great mansion, and a protracted, hardy gaze towards it.
"What affectation of diffidence was this at first?" they might have
demanded; "What stupid regardlessness now?"

Hear an illustration, reader.

A lover finds his mistress asleep on a mossy bank; he wishes to
catch a glimpse of her fair face without waking her. He steals softly
over the grass, careful to make no sound; he pauses – fancying she has

---

1   The range of mountains which separates France and Spain.

stirred: he withdraws; not for worlds would he be seen. All is still: he again advances: he bends above her; a light veil rests on her features: he lifts it, bends lower; now his eyes anticipate the vision of beauty – warm and blooming and lovely in rest. How hurried was their first glance! But how they fix! How he starts! How he suddenly and vehemently clasps in both arms the form he dared not, a moment since, touch with his finger! How he calls aloud a name, and drops his burden, and gazes on it wildly! He thus grasps and cries, and gazes, because he no longer fears to waken by any sound he can utter – by any movement he can make. He thought his love slept sweetly: he finds she is stone-dead.

I looked with timorous joy towards a stately house: I saw a blackened ruin.

No need to cower behind a gate-post, indeed! – to peep up at chamber lattices, fearing life was astir behind them! No need to listen for doors opening – to fancy steps on the pavement or the gravel-walk! The lawn, the grounds were trodden and waste: the portal yawned void. The front was, as I had once seen it in a dream, but a shell-like wall, very high and very fragile looking, perforated with paneless windows: no roof, no battlements, no chimneys – all had crashed in.

And there was the silence of death about it: the solitude of a lonesome wild. No wonder that letters addressed to people here had never received an answer: as well despatch epistles to a vault in a church-aisle. The grim blackness of the stones told by what fate the Hall had fallen – by conflagration: but how kindled? What story belonged to this disaster? What loss, besides mortar, and marble, and woodwork, had followed upon it? Had life been wrecked, as well as property? If so, whose? Dreadful question: there was no one here to answer it – not even dumb sign, mute token.

In wandering round the shattered walls and through the devastated interior, I gathered evidence that the calamity was not of late occurrence. Winter snows, I thought, had drifted through that void arch, winter rains beaten in at those hollow casements; for, amidst the drenched piles of rubbish, spring had cherished vegetation: grass and weed grew here and there between the stones and fallen rafters. And, oh! where, meantime, was the hapless owner of this wreck? In what land? Under what auspices? My eye involuntarily wandered to the grey church tower near the gates, and I asked, "Is he with Damerde Rochester, sharing the shelter of his narrow marble house?"

Some answer must be had to these questions. I could find it nowhere but at the inn; and thither, ere long, I returned. The host himself brought my breakfast into the parlour. I requested him to shut the door and sit down: I had some questions to ask him. But when he complied, I scarcely knew how to begin; such horror had I of the possible answers. And yet the spectacle of desolation I had just left, prepared me in a measure for a tale of misery. The host was a respectable-looking, middle-aged man.

"You know Thornfield Hall, of course?" I managed to say at last.

"Yes, ma'am; I lived there once."

"Did you?" Not in my time, I thought: you are a stranger to me.

"I was the late Mr. Rochester's butler," he added.

The late! I seemed to have received with full force the blow I had been trying to evade.

"The late!" I gasped. "Is he dead?"

"I mean the present gentleman, Mr. Edward's father," he explained. I breathed again: my blood resumed its flow. Fully assured by these words that Mr. Edward – *my* Mr. Rochester (God bless him, wherever he was!) – was at least alive: was, in short, "the present gentleman," (gladdening words!) it seemed I could hear all that was to come – whatever the disclosures might be – with comparative tranquillity. Since he was not in the grave, I could bear, I thought, to learn that he was at the Antipodes.[1]

"Is Mr. Rochester living at Thornfield Hall now?" I asked: knowing, of course, what the answer would be, but yet desirous of deferring the direct question as to where he really was.

"No, ma'am – oh, no! No one is living there. I suppose you are a stranger in these parts, or you would have heard what happened last autumn. Thornfield Hall is quite a ruin: it was burnt down just about harvest-time – A dreadful calamity! such an immense quantity of valuable property destroyed: hardly any of the furniture could be saved. The fire broke out at dead of night, and before the engines arrived from Millcote, the building was one mass of flame. It was a terrible spectacle: I witnessed it myself."

---

1   A word often used to describe Australia, and signifying the other side of the world from England.

"At dead of night!" I muttered. Yes, that was ever the hour of fatality at Thornfield. "Was it known how it originated?" I demanded.

"They guessed, ma'am: they guessed. Indeed, I should say it was ascertained beyond a doubt. You are not perhaps aware," he continued, edging his chair a little nearer the table, and speaking low, "that there was a lady, – a – a lunatic, kept in the house?"

"I have heard something of it."

"She was kept in very close confinement, ma'am: people even for some years were not absolutely certain of her existence. No one saw her: they only knew by rumour that such a person was at the Hall; and who or what she was it was difficult to conjecture. They said Mr. Edward had brought her from abroad; and some believed she had been his mistress. But a queer thing happened a year since – a very queer thing."

I feared now to hear my own story. I endeavoured to recall him to the main fact.

"And this lady?"

"This lady, ma'am," he answered, "turned out to be Mr. Rochester's wife! The discovery was brought about in the strangest way. There was a young lady, a governess at the Hall, that Mr. Rochester fell in –"

"But the fire?" I suggested.

"I'm coming to that, ma'am – that Mr. Edward fell in love with. The servants say they never saw anybody so much in love as he was: he was after her continually. They used to watch him – servants will, you know, ma'am – and he set store on her past everything: for all, nobody but him thought her so very handsome. She was a little small thing, they say, almost like a child. I never saw her myself; but I've heard Leah, the housemaid, tell of her. Leah liked her well enough. Mr. Rochester was about forty, and this governess not twenty; and, you see, when gentlemen of his age fall in love with girls, they are often like as if they were bewitched: well, he would marry her."

"You shall tell me this part of the story another time," I said; "but now I have a particular reason for wishing to hear all about the fire. Was it suspected that this lunatic, Mrs. Rochester, had any hand in it?"

"You've hit it, ma'am: it's quite certain that it was her, and nobody but her, that set it going. She had a woman to take care of her called Mrs. Poole – an able woman in her line, and very trustworthy; but for one fault – a fault common to a deal of them nurses and matrons – *she kept a private bottle of gin by her*, and now and then took a drop over much. It's excusable, for she had a hard life of it: but still it was dangerous; for, when Mrs. Poole was fast asleep, after the gin and water, the mad lady, who was as cunning as a witch, would take the keys out of her pocket, let herself out of her chamber, and go roaming about the house, doing any wild mischief that came into her head. They say she had nearly burnt her husband in his bed once: but I don't know about that. However, on this night, she set fire first to the hangings of the room next her own; and then she got down to a lower story, and made her way to the chamber that had been the governess's – (she was like as if she knew somehow how matters had gone on, and had a spite at her) – and she kindled the bed there: but there was nobody sleeping in it, fortunately. The governess had run away two months before; and for all Mr. Rochester sought her as if she had been the most precious thing he had in the world, he could never hear a word of her; and he grew savage – quite savage on his disappointment: he never was a mild man, but he got dangerous after he lost her. He would be alone, too. He sent Mrs. Fairfax, the housekeeper, away to her friends at a distance; but he did it handsomely, for he settled an annuity on her for life: and she deserved it – she was a very good woman. Miss Adèle, a ward he had, was put to school. He broke off acquaintance with all the gentry, and shut himself up, like a hermit, at the Hall."

"What! did he not leave England?"

"Leave England? Bless you, no! He would not cross the door-stones of the house; except at night, when he walked just like a ghost about the grounds and in the orchard as if he had lost his senses – which it is my opinion he had; for a more spirited, bolder, keener gentleman than he was before that midge of a governess crossed him, you never saw, ma'am. He was not a man given to wine, or cards, or racing, as some are, and he was not so very handsome; but he had a courage and a will of his own, if ever man had. I knew him from a boy, you see: and for my part I have often wished that Miss Eyre had been sunk in the sea before she came to Thornfield Hall."

"Then Mr. Rochester was at home when the fire broke out?"

"Yes, indeed was he; and he went up to the attics when all was burning above and below, and got the servants out of their beds and helped them down himself – and went back to get his mad wife out of her cell. And then they called out to him that she was on the roof; where she was standing, waving her arms, above the battlements, and shouting out till they could hear her a mile off: I saw her and heard her with my own eyes.[1] She was a big woman, and had long black hair: we could see it streaming against the flames as she stood. I witnessed, and several more witnessed Mr. Rochester ascend through the skylight on to the roof: we heard him call 'Bertha!' We saw him approach her; and then, ma'am, she yelled, and gave a spring, and the next minute she lay smashed on the pavement."

"Dead?"

"Dead? Ay, dead as the stones on which her brains and blood were scattered."

"Good God!"

"You may well say so, ma'am: it was frightful!"

He shuddered.

"And afterwards?" I urged.

"Well, ma'am, afterwards the house was burnt to the ground: there are only some bits of walls standing now."

"Were any other lives lost?"

"No – perhaps it would have been better if there had."

"What do you mean?"

"Poor Mr. Edward!" he ejaculated, "I little thought ever to have seen it! Some say it was a just judgment on him for keeping his first marriage secret, and wanting to take another wife while he had one living: but I pity him, for my part."

"You said he was alive?" I exclaimed.

"Yes, yes: he is alive; but many think he had better be dead."

"Why? How?" My blood was again running cold.

"Where is he?" I demanded. "Is he in England?"

"Aye – aye – he's in England; he can't get out of England, I fancy – he's a fixture now."

What agony was this? And the man seemed resolved to protract it!

"He is stone-blind," he said at last. "Yes – he is stone-blind – is Mr. Edward."

---

1   Brontë revised this sentence but failed to make the revision consistent with its original form. That is why the landlord claims he "heard her with his own eyes."

I had dreaded worse. I had dreaded he was mad. I summoned strength to ask what had caused this calamity.

"It was all his own courage, and a body may say, his kindness, in a way, ma'am: he wouldn't leave the house till every one else was out before him. As he came down the great stair-case at last, after Mrs. Rochester had flung herself from the battlements, there was a great crash – all fell. He was taken out from under the ruins, alive, but sadly hurt: a beam had fallen in such a way as to protect him partly; but one eye was knocked out, and one hand so crushed that Mr. Carter, the surgeon, had to amputate it directly. The other eye inflamed: he lost the sight of that also. He is now helpless, indeed – blind and a cripple."

"Where is he? Where does he now live?"

"At Ferndean, a manor-house on a farm he has, about thirty miles off: quite a desolate spot."

"Who is with him?"

"Old John and his wife: he would have none else. He is quite broken down, they say."

"Have you any sort of conveyance?"

"We have a chaise, ma'am, a very handsome chaise."

"Let it be got ready instantly; and if your post-boy can drive me to Ferndean before dark this day, I'll pay both you and him twice the hire you usually demand."

CHAPTER XXXVII

THE manor-house of Ferndean was a building of considerable antiquity, moderate size, and no architectural pretensions, deep buried in a wood. I had heard of it before. Mr. Rochester often spoke of it, and sometimes went there. His father had purchased the estate for the sake of the game covers. He would have let the house; but could find no tenant, in consequence of its ineligible and insalubrious site. Ferndean then remained uninhabited and unfurnished; with the exception of some two or three rooms fitted up for the accommodation of the squire when he went there in the season to shoot.

To this house I came, just ere dark, on an evening marked by the characteristics of sad sky, cold gale, and continued small, penetrating rain. The last mile I performed on foot, having dismissed the chaise and driver with the double remuneration I had promised. Even when within a very short distance of the manor-house, you could see nothing of it; so thick and dark grew the timber of the gloomy wood about it. Iron gates between granite pillars showed me where to enter, and passing through them, I found myself at once in the twilight of close-ranked trees. There was a grass-grown track descending the forest-aisle, between hoar and knotty shafts and under branched arches. I followed it, expecting soon to reach the dwelling; but it stretched on and on, it wound far and farther: no sign of habitation or grounds was visible.

I thought I had taken a wrong direction and lost my way. The darkness of natural as well as of sylvan dusk, gathered over me: I looked round in search of another road. There was none: all was interwoven stem, columnar trunk, dense, summer foliage – no opening anywhere.

I proceeded: at last my way opened, the trees thinned a little; presently I beheld a railing, then the house – scarce, by this dim light, distinguishable from the trees, so dank and green were its decaying walls. Entering a portal, fastened only by a latch, I stood amidst a space of enclosed ground, from which the wood swept away in a semicircle. There were no flowers, no garden-beds; only a broad gravel-walk girdling a grass-plat, and this set in the heavy frame of the forest. The house presented two pointed gables in its front; the windows were latticed and narrow: the front-door was narrow too, one step led up to it. The whole looked, as the host of the Rochester Arms had said, "quite a desolate spot." It was as still as a church on a week-day: the pattering rain on the forest leaves was the only sound audible in its vicinage.

"Can there be life here?" I asked.

Yes: life of some kind there was; for I heard a movement – that narrow front-door was unclosing, and some shape was about to issue from the grange.

It opened slowly: a figure came out into the twilight and stood on the step; a man without a hat: he stretched forth his hand as if to feel whether it rained. Dusk as it was, I had recognised him; – it was my master, Edward Fairfax Rochester, and no other.

I stayed my step, almost my breath, and stood to watch him – to examine him, myself unseen, and alas! to him invisible. It was a sudden meeting, and one in which rapture was kept well in check by pain. I had no difficulty in restraining my voice from exclamation, my step from hasty advance.

His form was of the same strong and stalwart contour as ever: his port was still erect, his hair was still raven-black; nor were his features altered or sunk: not in one year's space, by any sorrow, could his athletic strength be quelled, or his vigorous prime blighted. But in his countenance, I saw a change: that looked desperate and brooding – that reminded me of some wronged and fettered wild-beast or bird, dangerous to approach in his sullen woe. The caged eagle, whose gold-ringed eyes cruelty has extinguished, might look as looked that sightless Samson.[1]

And, reader, do you think I feared him in his blind ferocity? – if you do, you little know me. A soft hope blent with my sorrow that soon I should dare to drop a kiss on that brow of rock, and on those lids so sternly sealed beneath it: but not yet. I would not accost him yet.

He descended the one step, and advanced slowly and gropingly towards the grass-plat. Where was his daring stride now? Then he paused, as if he knew not which way to turn. He lifted his head and

---

1   See Judges 16:21. After Delilah betrays the secret of Samson's strength he is captured by the Philistines and blinded by them.

opened his eyelids; gazed blank, and with a straining effort, on the sky, and toward the amphitheatre of trees: one saw that all to him was void darkness. He stretched his right hand (the left arm, the mutilated one, he kept hidden in his bosom); he seemed to wish by touch to gain an idea of what lay round him: he met but vacancy still; for the trees were some yards off where he stood. He relinquished the endeavour, folded his arms, and stood quiet and mute in the rain, now falling fast on his uncovered head. At this moment John approached him from some quarter.

"Will you take my arm, sir?" he said; "there is a heavy shower coming on: had you not better go in?"

"Let me alone," was the answer.

John withdrew, without having observed me. Mr. Rochester now tried to walk about: vainly, – all was too uncertain. He groped his way back to the house, and, re-entering it, closed the door.

I now drew near and knocked: John's wife opened for me. "Mary," I said, "how are you?"

She started as if she had seen a ghost: I calmed her. To her hurried "Is it really you, Miss, come at this late hour to this 'only[1] place?" I answered by taking her hand; and then I followed her into the kitchen, where John now sat by a good fire. I explained to them, in a few words, that I had heard all which had happened since I left Thornfield, and that I was come to see Mr. Rochester. I asked John to go down to the turnpike-house, where I had dismissed the chaise, and bring my trunk, which I had left there; and then, while I removed my bonnet and shawl, I questioned Mary as to whether I could be accommodated at the Manor House for the night; and finding that arrangements to that effect, though difficult, would not be impossible, I informed her I should stay. Just at this moment the parlour-bell rang.

"When you go in," said I, "tell your master that a person wishes to speak to him: but do not give my name."

"I don't think he will see you," she answered; "he refuses everybody."

When she returned, I inquired what he had said.

---

1   Dialect. Lonely.

"You are to send in your name and your business," she replied. She then proceeded to fill a glass with water, and place it on a tray, together with candles.

"Is that what he rang for?" I asked.

"Yes: he always has candles brought in at dark, though he is blind."

"Give the tray to me: I will carry it in."

I took it from her hand: she pointed me out the parlour door. The tray shook as I held it; the water spilt from the glass; my heart struck my ribs loud and fast. Mary opened the door for me, and shut it behind me.

This parlour looked gloomy: a neglected handful of fire burnt low in the grate; and, leaning over it, with his head supported against the high, old-fashioned mantel-piece, appeared the blind tenant of the room. His old dog, Pilot, lay on one side, removed out of the way, and coiled up as if afraid of being inadvertently trodden on. Pilot pricked up his ears when I came in; then he jumped up with a yelp and a whine, and bounded towards me: he almost knocked the tray from my hands. I set it on the table; then patted him, and said softly, "Lie down!" Mr. Rochester turned mechanically to *see* what the commotion was: but as he *saw* nothing, he returned and sighed.

"Give me the water, Mary," he said.

I approached him with the now only half-filled glass: Pilot followed me, still excited.

"What is the matter?" he inquired.

"Down, Pilot!" I again said. He checked the water on its way to his lips, and seemed to listen: he drank, and put the glass down. "This is you, Mary, is it not?"

"Mary is in the kitchen," I answered.

He put out his hand with a quick gesture, but not seeing where I stood, he did not touch me. "Who is this? Who is this?" he demanded, trying, as it seemed, to *see* with those sightless eyes, – unavailing and distressing attempt! "Answer me – speak again!" he ordered, imperiously and aloud.

"Will you have a little more water, sir? I spilt half of what was in the glass," I said.

"*Who* is it? *What* is it? Who speaks?"

"Pilot knows me, and John and Mary know I am here: I came only this evening," I answered.

"Great God! – what delusion has come over me? What sweet madness has seized me?"

"No delusion – no madness: your mind, sir, is too strong for delusion – your health too sound for frenzy."

"And where is this speaker? Is it only a voice? Oh! I *cannot* see, but I must feel, or my heart will stop and my brain burst. Whatever – whoever you are – be perceptible to the touch or I cannot live!"

He groped: I arrested his wandering hand, and prisoned it in both mine.

"Her very fingers!" he cried; "her small, slight fingers! If so, there must be more of her."

The muscular hand broke from my custody; my arm was seized, my shoulder – neck – waist – I was entwined and gathered to him.

"Is it Jane? *What* is it? This is her shape – this is her size —"

"And this her voice," I added. "She is all here: her heart, too. God bless you, sir! I am glad to be so near you again."

"Jane Eyre! – Jane Eyre!" was all he said.

"My dear master," I answered, "I am Jane Eyre: I have found you out – I am come back to you."

"In truth? – in the flesh? My living Jane?"

"You touch me, sir – you hold me, and fast enough: I am not cold like a corpse, nor vacant like air, am I?"

"My living darling! These are certainly her limbs, and these her features: but I cannot be so blest after all my misery. It is a dream: such dreams as I have had at night when I have clasped her once more to my heart, as I do now; and kissed her, as thus – and felt that she loved me, and trusted that she would not leave me."

"Which I never will, sir, from this day."

"Never will, says the vision? But I always woke and found it an empty mockery; and I was desolate and abandoned – my life dark, lonely, hopeless – my soul athirst and forbidden to drink – my heart famished and never to be fed. Gentle, soft dream, nestling in my arms now, you will fly, too; as your sisters have all fled before you: but kiss me before you go – embrace me, Jane."

"There, sir – and there!"

I pressed my lips to his once brilliant and now rayless eyes – I swept his hair from his brow, and kissed that too. He suddenly seemed to rouse himself: the conviction of the reality of all this seized him.

"It is you – is it Jane? You are come back to me then?"

"I am."

"And you do not lie dead in some ditch, under some stream? And you are not a pining outcast amongst strangers?"

"No, sir; I am an independent woman now."

"Independent! What do you mean, Jane?"

"My uncle in Madeira is dead, and he left me five thousand pounds."

"Ah! this is practical – this is real!" he cried: "I should never dream that. Besides, there is that peculiar voice of hers, so animating and piquant, as well as soft: it cheers my withered heart; it puts life into it. – What, Janet! Are you an independent woman? A rich woman?"

"Quite rich, sir. If you won't let me live with you, I can build a house of my own close up to your door, and you may come and sit in my parlour when you want company of an evening."

"But as you are rich, Jane, you have now, no doubt, friends who will look after you, and not suffer you to devote yourself to a blind lameter[1] like me?"

"I told you I am independent, sir, as well as rich: I am my own mistress."

"And you will stay with me?"

"Certainly – unless you object. I will be your neighbour, your nurse, your housekeeper. I find you lonely: I will be your companion – to read to you, to walk with you, to sit with you, to wait on you, to be eyes and hands to you. Cease to look so melancholy, my dear Master; you shall not be left desolate, so long as I live."

He replied not: he seemed serious – abstracted: he sighed; he half-opened his lips as if to speak; he closed them again. I felt a little embarrassed. Perhaps I had been too officious in my offers of companionship and aid: perhaps I had too rashly overleaped conventionalities; and he, like St. John, saw impropriety in my inconsiderateness. I had indeed made my proposal from the idea that he wished and would ask me to be his wife: an expectation, not the less certain because unexpressed, had buoyed me up, that he would claim me at once as his own. But no hint to that effect escaping him, and his

---

1 i.e., someone lame or disabled.

countenance becoming more overcast, I suddenly remembered that I might have been all wrong, and was perhaps playing the fool unwittingly; and I began gently to withdraw myself from his arms – but he eagerly snatched me closer.

"No – no – Jane; you must not go. No – I have touched you, heard you, felt the comfort of your presence – the sweetness of your consolation: I cannot give up these joys. I have little left in myself – I must have you. The world may laugh – may call me absurd, selfish – but it does not signify. My very soul demands you: it will be satisfied; or it will take deadly vengeance on its frame."

"Well, sir, I will stay with you: I have said so."

"Yes – but you understand one thing by staying with me; and I understand another. You, perhaps, could make up your mind to be about my hand and chair – to wait on me as a kind little nurse (for you have an affectionate heart and a generous spirit, which prompt you to make sacrifices for those you pity), and that ought to suffice for me no doubt. I suppose I should now entertain none but fatherly feelings for you: do you think so? Come – tell me."

"I will think what you like, sir: I am content to be only your nurse, if you think it better."

"But you cannot always be my nurse, Janet: you are young – you must marry one day."

"I don't care about being married."

"You should care Janet: if I were what I once was, I would try to make you care – but – a sightless block!"

He relapsed again into gloom. I, on the contrary, became more cheerful and took fresh courage: these last words gave me an insight as to where the difficulty lay; and as it was no difficulty with me, I felt quite relieved from my previous embarrassment. I resumed a livelier vein of conversation.

"It is time some one undertook to re-humanize you," said I, parting his thick and long-uncut locks; "for I see you are being metamorphosed into a lion, or something of that sort. You have a 'faux air'[1] of Nebuchadnezzar in the fields about you, that is certain: your hair reminds me of eagles' feathers; whether your nails are grown like

---

1 Resemblance to.

birds' claws or not,[1] I have not yet noticed."

"On this arm, I have neither hand nor nails;" he said, drawing the mutilated limb from his breast, and shewing it to me. "It is a mere stump – a ghastly sight! Don't you think so, Jane?"

"It is a pity to see it; and a pity to see your eyes – and the scar of fire on your forehead: and the worst of it is, one is in danger of loving you too well for all this; and making too much of you."

"I thought you would be revolted, Jane, when you saw my arm, and my cicatrized visage."

"Did you? Don't tell me so – lest I should say something disparaging to your judgment. Now, let me leave you an instant, to make a better fire and have the hearth swept up. Can you tell when there is a good fire?"

"Yes; with the right eye I see a glow – a ruddy haze."

"And you see the candles?"

"Very dimly – each is a luminous cloud."

"Can you see me?"

"No, my fairy: but I am only too thankful to hear and feel you."

"When do you take supper?"

"I never take supper."

"But you shall have some to-night. I am hungry: so are you, I dare say, only you forget."

Summoning Mary, I soon had the room in more cheerful order: I prepared him, likewise, a comfortable repast. My spirits were excited, and with pleasure and ease I talked to him during supper, and for a long time after. There was no harassing restraint, no repressing of glee and vivacity with him; for with him I was at perfect ease, because I knew I suited him: all I said or did seemed either to console or revive him. Delightful consciousness! It brought to life and light my whole nature: in his presence I thoroughly lived; and he lived in mine. Blind as he was, smiles played over his face, joy dawned on his forehead: his lineaments softened and warmed.

After supper, he began to ask me many questions, of where I had been, what I had been doing, how I had found him out; but I gave him only very partial replies: it was too late to enter into particulars that night. Besides, I wished to touch no deep-thrilling chord – to

---

1   See Daniel 4:33.

open no fresh well of emotion in his heart: my sole present aim was to cheer him. Cheered, as I have said, he was: and yet but by fits. If a moment's silence broke the conversation, he would turn restless, touch me, then say, "Jane."

"You are altogether a human being, Jane? You are certain of that?"

"I conscientiously believe so, Mr. Rochester."

"Yet how, on this dark and doleful evening, could you so suddenly rise on my lone hearth? I stretched my hand to take a glass of water from a hireling, and it was given me by you: I asked a question, expecting John's wife to answer me, and your voice spoke at my ear."

"Because I had come in, in Mary's stead, with the tray."

"And there is enchantment in the very hour I am now spending with you. Who can tell what a dark, dreary, hopeless life I have dragged on for months past? Doing nothing, expecting nothing; merging night in day; feeling but the sensation of cold when I let the fire go out, of hunger when I forgot to eat: and then a ceaseless sorrow, and, at times, a very delirium of desire to behold my Jane again. Yes: for her restoration I longed, far more than for that of my lost sight. How can it be, that Jane is with me and says she loves me? Will she not depart as suddenly as she came? To-morrow, I fear, I shall find her no more."

A common-place, practical reply, out of the train of his own disturbed ideas, was, I was sure, the best and most re-assuring for him in this frame of mind. I passed my finger over his eyebrows, and remarked that they were scorched, and that I should apply something which would make them grow as broad and black as ever.

"Where is the use of doing me good in any way, beneficent spirit, when, at some fatal moment, you will again desert me – passing like a shadow, whither and how, to me unknown; and for me, remaining afterwards undiscoverable?"

"Have you a pocket-comb about you, sir?"

"What for, Jane?"

"Just to comb out this shaggy black mane. I find you rather alarming, when I examine you close at hand: you talk of my being a fairy; but, I am sure, you are more like a brownie."[1]

"Am I hideous, Jane?"

---

1 In folklore a brownie was a benevolent, although rather ugly, goblin.

"Very, sir: you always were, you know."

"Humph! The wickedness has not been taken out of you, wherever you have sojourned."

"Yet I have been with good people; far better than you: a hundred times better; people possessed of ideas and views you never entertained in your life: quite more refined and exalted."

"Who the deuce have you been with?"

"If you twist in that way, you will make me pull the hair out of your head; and then I think you will cease to entertain doubts of my substantiality."

"Who have you been with, Jane?"

"You shall not get it out of me to-night, sir; you must wait till to-morrow: to leave my tale half-told, will, you know, be a sort of security that I shall appear at your breakfast-table to finish it. By-the-by, I must mind not to rise on your hearth with only a glass of water, then: I must bring an egg at the least, to say nothing of fried ham."

"You mocking changeling – fairy-born and human-bred! You make me feel as I have not felt these twelve months. If Saul could have had you for his David, the evil spirit would have been exorcised without the aid of the harp."[1]

"There, sir, you are redd up[2] and made decent. Now I'll leave you: I have been travelling these last three days, and I believe I am tired. Good-night!"

"Just one word, Jane: were there only ladies in the house where you have been?"

I laughed and made my escape, still laughing as I ran up stairs. "A good idea!" I thought, with glee. "I see I have the means of fretting him out of his melancholy for some time to come."

Very early the next morning, I heard him up and astir, wandering from one room to another. As soon as Mary came down, I heard the question: "Is Miss Eyre here?" Then: "Which room did you put her into? Was it dry? Is she up? Go and ask if she wants anything; and when she will come down."

I came down as soon as I thought there was a prospect of break-fast. Entering the room very softly, I had a view of him before he

---

1   See 1 Samuel 16:23.
2   Dialect. Tidied up.

discovered my presence. It was mournful, indeed, to witness the sub-jugation of that vigorous spirit to a corporeal infirmity. He sat in his chair, – still, but not at rest: expectant evidently; the lines of now habitual sadness marking his strong features. His countenance reminded one of a lamp quenched, waiting to be relit – and alas! it was not himself that could now kindle the lustre of animated expres-sion: he was dependent on another for that office! I had meant to be gay and careless, but the powerlessness of the strong man touched my heart to the quick: still I accosted him with what vivacity I could: –

"It is a bright, sunny morning, sir," I said. "The rain is over and gone,[1] and there is a tender shining after it: you shall have a walk soon."

I had wakened the glow: his features beamed.

"Oh, you are indeed there, my sky-lark! Come to me. You are not gone: not vanished? I heard one of your kind an hour ago, singing high over the wood: but its song had no music for me, any more than the rising sun had rays. All the melody on earth is concentrated in my Jane's tongue to my ear (I am glad it is not naturally a silent one): all the sunshine I can feel is in her presence."

The water stood in my eyes to hear this avowal of his dependence: just as if a royal eagle, chained to a perch, should be forced to entreat a sparrow to become its purveyor. But I would not be lachrymose: I dashed off the salt-drops, and busied myself with preparing breakfast.

Most of the morning was spent in the open air. I led him out of the wet and wild wood into some cheerful fields: I described to him how brilliantly green they were; how the flowers and hedges looked refreshed; how sparklingly blue was the sky. I sought a seat for him in a hidden and lovely spot: a dry stump of a tree; nor did I refuse to let him, when seated, place me on his knee: why should I, when both he and I were happier near than apart? Pilot lay beside us: all was quiet. He broke out suddenly while clasping me in his arms: –

"Cruel, cruel deserter! Oh, Jane, what did I feel when I discovered you had fled from Thornfield, and when I could nowhere find you; and, after examining your apartment, ascertained that you had taken no money, nor anything which could serve as an equivalent! A pearl

---

1   Song of Solomon 2:11.

necklace I had given you lay untouched in its little casket; your trunks were left corded and locked as they had been prepared for the bridal tour. What could my darling do, I asked, left destitute and pennyless? And what did she do? Let me hear now."

Thus urged, I began the narrative of my experience for the last year. I softened considerably what related to the three days of wandering and starvation, because to have told him all would have been to inflict unnecessary pain: the little I did say lacerated his faithful heart deeper than I wished.

I should not have left him thus, he said, without any means of making my way: I should have told him my intention. I should have confided in him: he would never have forced me to be his mistress. Violent as he had seemed in his despair, he, in truth, loved me far too well and too tenderly to constitute himself my tyrant: he would have given me half his fortune, without demanding so much as a kiss in return, rather than I should have flung myself friendless on the wide world. I had endured, he was certain, more than I had confessed to him.

"Well, whatever my sufferings had been they were very short," I answered: and then I proceeded to tell him how I had been received at Moor-House; how I had obtained the office of schoolmistress, &c. The accession of fortune, the discovery of my relations, followed in due order. Of course, St. John Rivers' name came in frequently in the progress of my tale. When I had done, that name was immediately taken up.

"This St. John, then, is your cousin?"

"Yes."

"You have spoken of him often: did you like him?"

"He was a very good man, sir; I could not help liking him."

"A good man? Does that mean a respectable, well-conducted man of fifty? Or what does it mean?"

"St. John was only twenty-nine, sir."

"'*Jeune encore*,'[1] as the French say. Is he a person of low stature, phlegmatic, and plain? A person whose goodness consists rather in his guiltlessness of vice, than in his prowess in virtue?"

---

1   Still young.

"He is untiringly active. Great and exalted deeds are what he lives to perform."

"But his brain? That is probably rather soft? He means well: but you shrug your shoulders to hear him talk?"

"He talks little, sir: what he does say is ever to the point. His brain is first rate, I should think: not impressible, but vigorous."

"Is he an able man, then?"

"Truly able."

"A thoroughly educated man?"

"St. John is an accomplished and profound scholar."

"His manners, I think you said, are not to your taste? – priggish and parsonic?"

"I never mentioned his manners; but, unless I had a very bad taste, they must suit it: they are polished, calm, and gentlemanlike."

"His appearance, – I forget what description you gave of his appearance; – a sort of raw curate, half strangled with his white neck-cloth, and stilted up on his thick-soled high-lows,[1] eh?"

"St. John dresses well. He is a handsome man: tall, fair, with blue eyes, and a Grecian profile."

(*Aside.*) "Damn him!" – (*To me*) "Did you like him, Jane?"

"Yes, Mr. Rochester, I liked him: but you asked me that before."

I perceived, of course, the drift of my interlocutor. Jealousy had got hold of him: she stung him; but the sting was salutary: it gave him respite from the gnawing fang of melancholy. I would not, therefore, immediately charm the snake.

"Perhaps you would rather not sit any longer on my knee, Miss Eyre?" was the next somewhat unexpected observation.

"Why not, Mr. Rochester?"

"The picture you have just drawn is suggestive of a rather too overwhelming contrast. Your words have delineated very prettily a graceful Apollo: he is present to your imagination, – 'tall, fair, blue-eyed, and with a Grecian profile.' Your eyes dwell on a Vulcan,[2] – a

---

1 An unfashionable boot reaching above the ankle and laced in front.

2 Apollo was the Greek god of music and poetry; he was famous for his youth and beauty. Vulcan, the Roman name for Hephaestus, was the god of fire and metalwork. He was blackened by standing at his forge, and walked lame because as a child his leg was broken when his father Zeus hurled him from Olympus during a quarrel.

real blacksmith, brown, broad-shouldered; and blind and lame into the bargain."

"I never thought of it before; but you certainly are rather like Vulcan, sir."

Well, – you can leave me, ma'am: but before you go (and he retained me by a firmer grasp than ever), you will be pleased just to answer me a question or two." He paused.

"What questions, Mr. Rochester?"

Then followed this cross-examination: –

"St. John made you school-mistress of Morton before he knew you were his cousin?"

"Yes."

"You would often see him? He would visit the school sometimes?"

"Daily."

"He would approve of your plans, Jane? – I know they would be clever; for you are a talented creature?"

"He approved of them – yes."

"He would discover many things in you he could not have expected to find? Some of your accomplishments are not ordinary."

"I don't know about that."

"You had a little cottage near the school, you say: did he ever come there to see you?"

"Now and then."

"Of an evening?"

"Once or twice."

A pause.

"How long did you reside with him and his sisters after the cousinship was discovered?"

"Five months."

"Did Rivers spend much time with the ladies of his family?"

"Yes; the back parlour was both his study and ours: he sat near the window, and we by the table."

"Did he study much?"

"A good deal."

"What?"

"Hindostanee."

"And what did you do meantime?"

"I learnt German, at first."

"Did he teach you?"

"He did not understand German."

"Did he teach you nothing?"

"A little Hindostanee."

"Rivers taught you Hindostanee?"

"Yes, sir."

"And his sisters also?"

"No."

"Only you?"

"Only me."

"Did you ask to learn?"

"No."

"He wished to teach you?"

"Yes."

A second pause.

"Why did he wish it? Of what use could Hindostanee be to you?"

"He intended me to go with him to India."

"Ah! here I reach the root of the matter. He wanted you to marry him?"

"He asked me to marry him."

"That is a fiction – an impudent invention to vex me."

"I beg your pardon, it is the literal truth: he asked me more than once, and was as stiff about urging his point as ever you could be."

"Miss Eyre, I repeat it, you can leave me. How often am I to say the same thing? Why do you remain pertinaciously perched on my knee, when I have given you notice to quit?"

"Because I am comfortable there."

"No, Jane, you are not comfortable there: because your heart is not with me: it is with this cousin – this St. John. Oh, till this moment, I thought my little Jane was all mine! I had a belief she loved me even when she left me: that was an atom of sweet in much bitter. Long as we have been parted, hot tears as I have wept over our separation, I never thought that while I was mourning her, she was loving another! But it is useless grieving. Jane, leave me: go and marry Rivers."

"Shake me off, then, sir – push me away; for I'll not leave you of my own accord."

"Jane, I ever like your tone of voice: it still renews hope, it sounds so truthful. When I hear it, it carries me back a year. I forget that you have formed a new tie. But I am not a fool – go —."

"Where must I go, sir?"

"Your own way – with the husband you have chosen."

"Who is that?"

"You know – this St. John Rivers."

"He is not my husband, nor ever will be. He does not love me: I do not love him. He loves (as he *can* love, and that is not as you love) a beautiful young lady called Rosamond. He wanted to marry me only because he thought I should make a suitable missionary's wife, which she would not have done. He is good and great, but severe; and, for me, cold as an iceberg. He is not like you, sir: I am not happy at his side, nor near him, nor with him. He has no indulgence for me – no fondness. He sees nothing attractive in me: not even youth – only a few useful mental points. Then must I leave you, sir, to go to him?"

I shuddered involuntarily, and clung instinctively closer to my blind but beloved master. He smiled.

"What, Jane! Is this true? Is such really the state of matters between you and Rivers?"

"Absolutely, sir. Oh, you need not be jealous! I wanted to teaze you a little to make you less sad: I thought anger would be better than grief. But if you wish me to love you, could you but see how much I *do* love you, you would be proud and content. All my heart is yours, sir: it belongs to you; and with you it would remain, were fate to exile the rest of me from your presence for ever."

Again, as he kissed me, painful thoughts darkened his aspect.

"My seared vision! My crippled strength!" he murmured regret-fully.

I caressed, in order to soothe him. I knew of what he was thinking, and wanted to speak for him; but dared not. As he turned aside his face a minute, I saw a tear slide from under the sealed eyelid, and trickle down the manly cheek. My heart swelled.

"I am no better than the old, lightning-struck chestnut tree in Thornfield orchard;" he remarked, ere long. "And what right would

that ruin have to bid a budding woodbine cover its decay with freshness?"

"You are no ruin, sir – no lightning-struck tree: you are green and
vigorous. Plants will grow about your roots, whether you ask them or
not, because they take delight in your bountiful shadow; and as they
grow they will lean towards you, and wind round you, because your
strength offers them so safe a prop."

Again he smiled: I gave him comfort.

"You speak of friends, Jane?" he asked.

"Yes; of friends," I answered rather hesitatingly: for I knew I meant
more than friends, but could not tell what other word to employ. He
helped me.

"Ah! Jane. But I want a wife."

"Do you, sir?"

"Yes: is it news to you?"

"Of course: you said nothing about it before."

"Is it unwelcome news?"

"That depends on circumstances, sir – on your choice."

"Which you shall make for me, Jane. I will abide by your decision."

"Choose then, sir – *her who loves you best.*"

"I will at least choose – *her I love best.* Jane, will you marry me?"

"Yes, sir."

"A poor blind man, whom you will have to lead about by the
hand?"

"Yes, sir."

"A crippled man, twenty years older than you, whom you will
have to wait on?"

"Yes, sir."

"Truly, Jane?"

"Most truly, sir."

"Oh! my darling! God bless you and reward you!"

"Mr. Rochester, if ever I did a good deed in my life – if ever I
thought a good thought – if ever I prayed a sincere and blameless
prayer – if ever I wished a righteous wish, – I am rewarded now. To be
your wife is, for me, to be as happy as I can be on earth."

"Because you delight in sacrifice."

"Sacrifice! What do I sacrifice? Famine for food, expectation for content. To be privileged to put my arms round what I value – to press my lips to what I love – to repose on what I trust: is that to make a sacrifice? If so, then certainly I delight in sacrifice."

"And to bear with my infirmities, Jane: to overlook my deficiencies."

"Which are none, sir, to me. I love you better now, when I can really be useful to you, than I did in your state of proud independence, when you disdained every part but that of the giver and protector."

"Hitherto I have hated to be helped – to be led: henceforth, I feel, I shall hate it no more. I did not like to put my hand into a hireling's, but it is pleasant to feel it circled by Jane's little fingers. I preferred utter loneliness to the constant attendance of servants; but Jane's soft ministry will be a perpetual joy. Jane suits me: do I suit her?"

"To the finest fibre of my nature, sir."

"The case being so, we have nothing in the world to wait for: we must be married instantly."

He looked and spoke with eagerness: his old impetuosity was rising.

"We must become one flesh without any delay, Jane: there is but the licence to get – then we marry —."

"Mr. Rochester, I have just discovered the sun is far declined from its meridian, and Pilot is actually gone home to his dinner. Let me look at your watch."

"Fasten it into your girdle, Janet, and keep it henceforward: I have no use for it."

"It is nearly four o'clock in the afternoon, sir. Don't you feel hungry?"

"The third day from this must be our wedding-day, Jane. Never mind fine clothes and jewels, now: all that is not worth a fillip."

"The sun has dried up all the rain-drops, sir. The breeze is still: it is quite hot."

"Do you know, Jane, I have your little pearl necklace at this moment fastened round my bronze scrag[1] under my cravat? I have worn it since the day I lost my only treasure: as a memento of her."

---

1 Slang. Neck.

"We will go home through the wood: that will be the shadiest way."

He pursued his own thoughts without heeding me.

"Jane! you think me, I daresay, an irreligious dog: but my heart swells with gratitude to the beneficent God of this earth just now. He sees not as man sees, but far clearer: judges not as man judges, but far more wisely. I did wrong: I would have sullied my innocent flower – breathed guilt on its purity: the Omnipotent snatched it from me. I, in my stiff-necked rebellion, almost cursed the dispensation: instead of bending to the decree, I defied it. Divine justice pursued its course; disasters came thick on me: I was forced to pass through the valley of the shadow of death.[1] *His* chastisements are mighty; and one smote me which has humbled me for ever. You know I was proud of my strength: but what is it now, when I must give it over to foreign guidance, as a child does its weakness? Of late, Jane – only of late – I began to see and acknowledge the hand of God in my doom. I began to experience remorse, repentance; the wish for reconcilement to my Maker. I began sometimes to pray: very brief prayers they were, but very sincere.

"Some days since: nay, I can number them – four: it was last Monday night – a singular mood came over me: one in which grief replaced frenzy – sorrow, sullenness. I had long had the impression that since I could nowhere find you, you must be dead. Late that night – perhaps it might be between eleven and twelve o'clock – ere I retired to my dreary rest, I supplicated God, that, if it seemed good to Him, I might soon be taken from this life, and admitted to that world to come, where there was still hope of rejoining Jane.

"I was in my own room, and sitting by the window, which was open: it soothed me to feel the balmy night-air; though I could see no stars, and only by a vague, luminous haze, knew the presence of a moon. I longed for thee, Janet! Oh, I longed for thee both with soul and flesh! I asked of God, at once in anguish and humility, if I had not been long enough desolate, afflicted, tormented; and might not soon taste bliss and peace once more. That I merited all I endured, I acknowledged – that I could scarcely endure more, I pleaded; and the alpha and omega[1] of my heart's wishes broke involuntarily from my

---

1   Psalm 23:4.

lips, in the words – 'Jane! Jane! Jane!'"

"Did you speak these words aloud?"

"I did, Jane. If any listener had heard me, he would have thought me mad: I pronounced them with such frantic energy."

"And it was last Monday night: somewhere near midnight?"

"Yes; but the time is of no consequence: what followed is the strange point. You will think me superstitious – some superstition I have in my blood, and always had: nevertheless, this is true – true at least it is that I heard what I now relate.

"As I exclaimed 'Jane! Jane! Jane!' a voice – I cannot tell whence the voice came, but I know whose voice it was – replied, 'I am coming: wait for me!' and a moment after, went whispering on the wind, the words – 'Where are you?'

"I'll tell you, if I can, the idea, the picture these words opened to my mind: yet it is difficult to express what I want to express. Ferndean is buried, as you see, in a heavy wood, where sound falls dull, and dies unreverberating. 'Where are you?' seemed spoken amongst mountains; for I heard a hill-sent echo repeat the words. Cooler and fresher at the moment the gale seemed to visit my brow: I could have deemed that in some wild, lone scene, I and Jane were meeting. In spirit, I believe, we must have met. You no doubt were, at that hour, in unconscious sleep, Jane: perhaps your soul wandered from its cell to comfort mine; for those were your accents – as certain as I live – they were yours!"

Reader, it was on Monday night – near midnight – that I too had received the mysterious summons: those were the very words by which I had replied to it. I listened to Mr. Rochester's narrative; but made no disclosure in return. The coincidence struck me as too awful and inexplicable to be communicated or discussed. If I told anything, my tale would be such as must necessarily make a profound impression on the mind of my hearer; and that mind, yet from its sufferings too prone to gloom, needed not the deeper shade of the supernatural. I kept these things, then, and pondered them in my heart.[2]

"You cannot now wonder," continued my master, "that when you

---

1   The first and last letters of the Greek alphabet; in this case meaning the beginning and the end. See also Revelation 21:6.

2   See Luke 2:19.

rose upon me so unexpectedly last night, I had difficulty in believing you any other than a mere voice and vision: something that would melt to silence and annihilation, as the midnight whisper and mountain echo had melted before. Now, I thank God! I know it to be otherwise. Yes, I thank God!"

He put me off his knee, rose, and reverently lifting his hat from his brow, and bending his sightless eyes to the earth, he stood in mute devotion. Only the last words of the worship were audible.

"I thank my Maker, that in the midst of judgment he has remembered mercy. I humbly entreat my Redeemer to give me strength to lead henceforth a purer life than I have done hitherto!"

Then he stretched his hand out to be led. I took that dear hand, held it a moment to my lips, then let it pass round my shoulder: being so much lower of stature than he, I served both for his prop and guide. We entered the wood, and wended homeward.

CHAPTER XXXVIII

CONCLUSION.

READER, I married him. A quiet wedding we had: he and I, the parson and clerk, were alone present. When we got back from church, I went into the kitchen of the manor-house, where Mary was cooking the dinner, and John cleaning the knives, and I said: –

"Mary, I have been married to Mr. Rochester this morning." The housekeeper and her husband were both of that decent phlegmatic order of people, to whom one may at any time safely communicate a remarkable piece of news without incurring the danger of having one's ears pierced by some shrill ejaculation, and subsequently stunned by a torrent of wordy wonderment. Mary did look up, and she did stare at me: the ladle with which she was basting a pair of chickens roasting at the fire, did for some three minutes hang suspended in air; and for the same space of time John's knives also had rest from the polishing process: but Mary, bending again over the roast, said only: –

"Have you, miss? Well, for sure!"

A short time after she pursued: "I seed you go out with the master, but I didn't know you were gone to church to be wed;" and she basted away. John, when I turned to him, was grinning from ear to ear.

"I telled Mary how it would be," he said: "I knew what Mr. Edward" (John was an old servant, and had known his master when he was the cadet[1] of the house, therefore, he often gave him his christian name) – "I knew what Mr. Edward would do; and I was certain he would not wait long neither: and he's done right, for aught I knaw. I wish you joy, miss!" and he politely pulled his forelock.

"Thank you, John. Mr. Rochester told me to give you and Mary this." I put into his hand a five-pound note. Without waiting to hear more, I left the kitchen. In passing the door of that sanctum some time after, I caught the words: –

"She'll happen do better for him nor ony o' t' grand ladies."[2] And again, "If she ben't one o' th' handsomest, she's noan faâl[3] and varry

---

1   Younger son.
2   Dialect. "She'll perhaps do better for him than any of the grand ladies."
3   Dialect. Not "foul;" i.e., not ugly.

good-natured; and i' his een[1] she's fair beautiful, onybody may see that."

I wrote to Moor-House and to Cambridge immediately, to say what I had done: fully explaining also why I had thus acted. Diana and Mary approved the step unreservedly. Diana announced that she would just give me time to get over the honey-moon, and then she would come and see me.

"She had better not wait till then, Jane," said Mr. Rochester, when I read her letter to him; "if she does, she will be too late, for our honey-moon will shine our life-long: its beams will only fade over your grave or mine."

How St. John received the news, I don't know; he never answered the letter in which I communicated it: yet six months after, he wrote to me; without, however, mentioning Mr. Rochester's name or alluding to my marriage. His letter was then calm; and, though very serious, kind. He has maintained a regular, though not frequent correspondence ever since: he hopes I am happy, and trusts I am not of those who live without God in the world, and only mind earthly things.

You have not quite forgotten little Adèle, have you, reader? I had not; I soon asked and obtained leave of Mr. Rochester, to go and see her at the school where he had placed her. Her frantic joy at beholding me again moved me much. She looked pale and thin: she said she was not happy. I found the rules of the establishment were too strict, its course of study too severe, for a child of her age: I took her home with me. I meant to become her governess once more; but I soon found this impracticable: my time and cares were now required by another – my husband needed them all. So I sought out a school conducted on a more indulgent system; and near enough to permit of my visiting her often, and bringing her home sometimes. I took care she should never want for anything that could contribute to her comfort: she soon settled in her new abode, became very happy there, and made fair progress in her studies. As she grew up, a sound, English education corrected in a great measure her French defects; and when she left school, I found in her a pleasing and obliging companion:

---

1   Dialect. In his eyes.

docile, good-tempered and well-principled. By her grateful attention to me and mine, she has long since well repaid any little kindness I ever had it in my power to offer her.

My tale draws to its close: one word respecting my experience of married life, and one brief glance at the fortunes of those whose names have most frequently recurred in this narrative, and I have done.

I have now been married ten years. I know what it is to live entirely for and with what I love best on earth. I hold myself supremely blest – blest beyond what language can express; because I am my husband's life as fully as he is mine. No woman was ever nearer to her mate than I am: ever more absolutely bone of his bone, and flesh of his flesh.[1] I know no weariness of my Edward's society: he knows none of mine, any more than we each do of the pulsation of the heart that beats in our separate bosoms; consequently, we are ever together. To be together is for us to be at once as free as in solitude, as gay as in company. We talk, I believe, all day long: to talk to each other is but a more animated and an audible thinking. All my confidence is bestowed on him; all his confidence is devoted to me: we are precisely suited in character; perfect concord is the result.

Mr. Rochester continued blind the first two years of our union: perhaps it was that circumstance that drew us so very near – that knit us so very close; for I was then his vision, as I am still his right hand. Literally, I was (what he often called me) the apple of his eye.[2] He saw nature – he saw books through me; and never did I weary of gazing for his behalf, and of putting into words the effect of field, tree, town, river, cloud, sunbeam – of the landscape before us; of the weather round us – and impressing by sound on his ear what light could no longer stamp on his eye. Never did I weary of reading to him; never did I weary of conducting him where he wished to go: of doing for him what he wished to be done. And there was a pleasure in my services, most full, most exquisite, even though sad – because he claimed these services without painful shame or damping humiliation. He loved me so truly, that he knew no reluctance in profiting by my attendance: he felt I loved him so fondly, that to yield that attendance was to indulge my sweetest wishes.

---

1 Genesis 2:23.
2 The pupil of his eye.

One morning at the end of the two years, as I was writing a letter to his dictation, he came and bent over me, and said –

"Jane, have you a glittering ornament round your neck?"

I had a gold watch-chain: I answered, "Yes."

"And have you a pale blue dress on?"

I had. He informed me then, that for some time he had fancied the obscurity clouding one eye was becoming less dense; and that now he was sure of it.

He and I went up to London. He had the advice of an eminent oculist; and he eventually recovered the sight of that one eye. He cannot now see very distinctly: he cannot read or write much; but he can find his way without being led by the hand: the sky is no longer a blank to him – the earth no longer a void. When his first-born was put into his arms, he could see that the boy had inherited his own eyes, as they once were – large, brilliant, and black. On that occasion, he again, with a full heart, acknowledged that God had tempered judgment with mercy.

My Edward and I, then, are happy: and the more so, because those we most love are happy likewise. Diana and Mary Rivers are both married: alternately, once every year, they come to see us, and we go to see them. Diana's husband is a captain in the navy: a gallant officer, and a good man. Mary's is a clergyman: a college friend of her brother's; and, from his attainments and principles, worthy of the connexion. Both Captain Fitzjames and Mr. Wharton love their wives, and are loved by them.

As to St. John Rivers, he left England: he went to India. He entered on the path he had marked for himself; he pursues it still. A more resolute, indefatigable pioneer never wrought amidst rocks and dangers. Firm, faithful, and devoted; full of energy, and zeal, and truth, he labours for his race: he clears their painful way to improvement; he hews down like a giant the prejudices of creed and caste that encumber it. He may be stern; he may be exacting; he may be ambitious yet: but his is the sternness of the warrior Greatheart, who guards his pilgrim-convoy from the onslaught of Apollyon.[1] His is the exaction of

---

1   Both Greatheart and Apollyon are characters in *The Pilgrim's Progress* by John Bunyan (1628-88). However, Apollyon, a demon, appears in the first part of the work, published in 1678, while Greatheart appears in the second, published in 1684. They therefore never directly encounter each other.

the apostle, who speaks but for Christ, when he says – "Whosoever will come after me, let him deny himself, and take up his cross and follow me."[1] His is the ambition of the high master-spirit, which aims to fill a place in the first rank of those who are redeemed from the earth – who stand without fault before the throne of God; who share the last mighty victories of the lamb; who are called, and chosen, and faithful.[2]

St. John is unmarried: he never will marry now. Himself has hitherto sufficed to the toil; and the toil draws near its close: his glorious sun hastens to its setting. The last letter I received from him drew from my eyes human tears, and yet filled my heart with Divine joy: he anticipated his sure reward, his incorruptible crown.[3] I know that a stranger's hand will write to me next, to say that the good and faithful servant[4] has been called at length into the joy of his Lord. And why weep for this? No fear of death will darken St. John's last hour: his mind will be unclouded; his heart will be undaunted; his hope will be sure; his faith steadfast. His own words are a pledge of this: –

"My Master," he says, "has forewarned me. Daily he announces more distinctly, – 'Surely I come quickly;' and hourly I more eagerly respond, – 'Amen; even so come, Lord Jesus!'"[5]

FINIS.

1   Mark 8:34.
2   See Revelation 15:4-5.
3   See 1 Corinthians 9:25.
4   Matthew 25:21.
5   Revelation 22:20, the second-last verse in the Bible.

Appendix A: Prefatory Material to Subsequent Editions of Jane Eyre

1. Preface to the Second Edition of *Jane Eyre*, Charlotte Brontë

PREFACE

A PREFACE to the first edition of 'Jane Eyre' being unnecessary, I gave none: this second edition demands a few words both of acknowledgement and miscellaneous remark.

My thanks are due in three quarters.

To the Public, for the fair field its honest suffrage has opened to an obscure aspirant.

To my Publishers, for the aid their tact, their energy, their practical sense, and frank liberality have afforded an unknown and unrecommended Author.

The Press and the Public are but vague personifications for me, and I must thank them in vague terms; but my Publishers are definite: so are certain generous critics who have encouraged me as only large-hearted and high-minded men know how to encourage a struggling stranger; to them, *i.e.* to my Publishers and the select Reviewers, I say cordially, Gentlemen, I thank you from my heart.

Having thus acknowledged what I owe those who have aided and approved me, I turn to another class; a small one, so far as I know, but not, therefore, to be overlooked. I mean the timorous or carping few who doubt the tendency of such books as 'Jane Eyre': in whose eyes whatever is unusual is wrong; whose ears detect in each protest against bigotry – that parent of crime – an insult to piety, that regent of God on earth. I would suggest to such doubters certain obvious distinctions; I would remind them of certain simple truths.

Conventionality is not morality. Self-righteousness is not religion. To attack the first is not to assail the last. To pluck the mask from the face of the Pharisee, is not to lift an impious hand to the Crown of Thorns.

These things and deeds are diametrically opposed: they are as distinct as is vice from virtue. Men too often confound them; they should not be confounded: appearance should not be mistaken for truth; narrow human doctrines, that only tend to elate and magnify a few, should not be substituted for the world-redeeming creed of Christ. There is – I repeat it – a difference; and it is a good, and not a bad action to mark broadly and clearly the line of separation between them.

The world may not like to see these ideas dissevered, for it has been accustomed to blend them; finding it convenient to make external show pass for sterling worth – to let white-washed walls vouch for clean shrines. It may hate him who dares to scrutinize and expose – to rase the gilding, and show base metal under it – to penetrate the sepulchre, and reveal charnel relics:[1] but, hate as it will, it is indebted to him.

Ahab did not like Micaiah, because he never prophesied good concerning him, but evil: probably he liked the sycophant son of Chenaanah better; yet might Ahab have escaped a bloody death, had he but stopped his ears to flattery, and opened them to faithful counsel.[2]

There is a man in our own days whose words are not framed to tickle delicate ears: who, to my thinking, comes before the great ones of society, much as the son of Imlah came before the throned Kings of Judah and Israel; and who speaks truth as deep, with a power as prophet-like and as vital – a mien as dauntless and as daring. Is the satirist of 'Vanity Fair'[3] admired in high places? I cannot tell; but I think if some of those amongst whom he hurls the Greek fire[4] of his sarcasm, and over whom he flashes the levin-brand[5] of his denunciation, were to take his warnings in time – they or their seed might yet escape a fatal Ramoth-Gilead.

Why have I alluded to this man? I have alluded to him, Reader, because I think I see in him an intellect profounder and more unique

---

1 For Christ's comments on the hypocrisy of the Pharisees, and his comparison of them to "whited sepulchres," see Matthew 23: 23-27.

2 See 2 Chronicles 18.

3 William Makepeace Thackeray (1811-63) published *Vanity Fair* in monthly numbers from January 1847 to July 1848.

4 An inflammable liquid, first used by the Greeks to set enemy ships on fire.

5 "Levin" is a flash of lightning, while "brand" is an archaic word for the blade of a sword. Thackeray's satire is described as a weapon he flashes over the heads of those he criticizes.

than his contemporaries have yet recognised; because I regard him as the first social regenerator of the day – as the very master of that working corps who would restore to rectitude the warped system of things; because I think no commentator on his writings has yet found the comparison that suits him, the terms which rightly characterize his talent. They say he is like Fielding:[1] they talk of his wit, humour, comic powers. He resembles Fielding as an eagle does a vulture: Fielding could stoop on carrion, but Thackeray never does.[2] His wit is bright, his humour attractive, but both bear the same relation to his serious genius, that the mere lambent sheet-lightning playing under the edge of the summer-cloud, does to the electric death-spark hid in its womb. Finally; I have alluded to Mr. Thackeray, because to him – if he will accept the tribute of a total stranger – I have dedicated this second edition of 'Jane Eyre'.[3]

CURRER BELL.
Dec. 21st, 1847.

2. Note to the Third Edition of *Jane Eyre*, Charlotte Brontë

NOTE TO THE THIRD EDITION

I AVAIL myself of the opportunity which a third edition of 'Jane Eyre' affords me, of again addressing a word to the public, to explain that my claim to the title of novelist rests on this one work alone. If, therefore, the authorship of other works of fiction has been attributed to me, an honour is awarded where it is not merited; and consequently, denied where it is justly due.[4]

This explanation will serve to rectify mistakes which may already have been made, and to prevent future errors.

CURRER BELL.
April 13th, 1848.

---

1 Henry Fielding (1707-54), English novelist and satirist.
2 Brontë is apparently offended by the sometimes scurrilous nature of Fielding's satire.
3 For the unfortunate consequences of this dedication see the present edition's A Note on the Text.
4 See the present edition's A Note on the Text for an explanation of Brontë's comments here.

Appendix B: Charlotte Brontë: Correspondence on Being a Governess

To Emily Brontë

June 8, 1839
Stonegappe[1]

Dearest Lavinia,[2]

I am most exceedingly obliged to you for the trouble you have taken in seeking up my things and sending them all right. The box and its contents were most acceptable. I only wish I had asked you to send me some letter-paper. This is my last sheet but two. When you can send the other articles of raiment now manufacturing, I shall be right down glad of them.

I have striven hard to be pleased with my new situation.[3] The country, the house, and the grounds are, as I have said, divine. But, alack-a-day! there is such a thing as seeing all beautiful around you – pleasant woods, winding white paths, green lawns, and blue sunshine sky – and not having a free moment or a free thought left to enjoy them in. The children are constantly with me, and more riotous, perverse, unmanageable cubs never grew. As for correcting them, I soon quickly found that was entirely out of the question: they are to do as they like. A complaint to Mrs. Sidgwick brings only black looks upon oneself, and unjust, partial excuses to screen the children. I have tried that plan once. It succeeded so notably that I shall try it no more. I said in my last letter that Mrs. Sidgwick did not know me. I now begin to find that she does not intend to know me, that she cares nothing in the world about me except to contrive how the greatest possible quantity of labour may be squeezed out of me, and to that end she overwhelms me with oceans of needlework, yards of

---

1 The name of the house in which Brontë was governess.
2 A nickname for Emily Brontë.
3 Brontë had temporarily taken on the position of governess in the household of John Benson Sidgwick (1800-72) and his wife Sarah Hannah (1803-87), the "Mrs. Sidgwick" referred to in the rest of the letter.

cambric[1] to hem, muslin nightcaps to make, and, above all things, dolls to dress. I do not think she likes me at all, because I can't help being shy in such an entirely novel scene, surrounded as I have hitherto been by strange and constantly changing faces. [I used to think I should like to be in the stir of grand folks' society but I have had enough of it – it is dreary work to look on and listen.][2] I see now more clearly than I have ever done before that a private governess has not existence, is not considered a living and rational being except as connected with the wearisome duties she has to fulfil. While she is teaching the children, working for them, amusing them, it is all right. If she steals a moment for herself she is a nuisance. Nevertheless, Mrs. Sidgwick is universally considered an amiable woman. Her manners are fussily affable. She talks a great deal, but as it seems to me not much to the purpose. Perhaps I may like her better after a while. At present I have no call to her. Mr. Sidgwick is in my opinion a hundred times better – less profession, less bustling condescension, but a far kinder heart. It is very seldom that he speaks to me, but when he does I always feel happier and more settled for some minutes after. He never asks me to wipe the children's smutty noses or tie their shoes or fetch their pinafores[3] or set them a chair. One of the pleasantest afternoons I have spent here – indeed, the only one at all pleasant – was when Mr. Sidgwick walked out with the children, and I had orders to follow a little behind. As he strolled on through his fields with his magnificent Newfoundland dog at his side, he looked very like what a frank, wealthy, Conservative gentleman ought to be. He spoke freely and unaffectedly to the people he met, and though he indulged his children and allowed them to tease himself far too much, he would not suffer them grossly to insult others.

I am getting quite to have a regard for the Carter family.[4] At home I should not care for them, but here they are friends. Mr. Carter was

---

1 A fine white linen.
2 This section of text appears in the version of the letter reproduced in Elizabeth Gaskell's *The Life of Charlotte Brontë*.
3 Washable coverings worn over clothing to protect it from dirt.
4 The Reverend Edward Carter and his family were residing on the Stonegappe estate. He was serving as curate of the nearby church at Lothersdale, the living for which was under the patronage of John Sidgwick. As curate of Mirfield he had known Brontë as a child, and it is likely that she obtained her position with the Sidgwicks through his recommendation.

at Mirfield yesterday and saw Anne.[1] He says she was looking uncommonly well. Poor girl, *she* must indeed wish to be at home. As to Mrs. Collins'[2] report that Mrs. Sidgwick intended to keep me permanently, I do not think that such was ever her design. Moreover, I would not stay without some alterations. For instance, this burden of sewing would have to be removed. It is too bad for anything. I never in my whole life had my time so fully taken up. Next week we are going to Swarcliffe, Mr. Greenwood's place near Harrogate,[3] to stay three weeks or a month. After that time I hope Miss Hoby[4] will return. Don't show this letter to papa or aunt, only to Branwell.[5] They will think I am never satisfied wherever I am. I complain to you because it is a relief, and really I have had some unexpected mortifications to put up with. However, things may mend, but Mrs. Sidgwick expects me to do things that I cannot do – to love her children and be entirely devoted to them. I am really very well. I am so sleepy that I can write no more. I must leave off. Love to all. – Goodbye.

Direct your next dispatch – J. Greenwood, Esq., Swarcliffe, near Harrogate.

C. Brontë

2. To Ellen Nussey

[January 24, 1840]
[Haworth]

My Dear Ellen[6]

I have given Mrs. Edward Halliley her coup de grace – that is to

---

1 Anne Brontë was serving as governess in the Ingham family of Blake Hall, near Mirfield.
2 Not definitely identified.
3 John Greenwood (1763-1846) was Sarah Sidgwick's father. He purchased Swarcliffe House, which was about five miles from Harrogate, in 1805.
4 Not definitely identified.
5 Brontë is concerned that Emily only show this letter to their brother Branwell. She does not want her aunt Elizabeth Branwell (1776-1842), who had been living at Haworth since 1821, or her father Patrick Brontë (1777-1861) to hear about her discontent.
6 Brontë met Ellen Nussey (1817-97) when they were pupils together at Roe Head School, and their friendship developed into a life-long relationship.

say I have relinquished the idea of becoming an inmate of her family[1] – I have no doubt she will be very cross with me especially as when I first declined going she pressed me to take a trial of a month – I am now therefore again adrift, without an object – I am sorry for this but something may turn up erelong[.]

I know not whether to encourage you in your plan of going out or not[2] – your health seems to me the great obstacle – if you could obtain a situation like Mary Brooke[3] you might do very well – But you could never live in an unruly, violent family of Modern children such for instance as those at Blake Hall – Anne is not to return[4] – Mrs. Ingham is a placid mild woman – but as for the children it was one struggle of life-wearing exertion to keep them in anything like decent order.

I am miserable when I allow myself to dwell on the necessity of spending my life as a Governess. The chief requisite for that station seems to me to be the power of taking things easily as they come and of making oneself comfortable and at home wherever we may chance to be – qualities in which all our family are singularly deficient. I know I cannot live with a person like Mrs Sidgwick – but I hope all women are not like her – and my motto is "Try again"[.]

Mary Taylor[5] – I am sorry to hear is ill – have you seen her or heard anything of her lately – Sickness seems very general and Death too at least in this neighbourhood. Mr. Price is dead[6] – he had fallen into a state of delicate health for sometime and the rupture of a blood-vessel carried him off. He was a strong athletic-looking man when I saw him and that is scarcely six months ago. Though I knew

---

1 The Halliley family, relatives of some friends of Brontë's father, had offered her a position as governess. After vacillating over whether or not to accept, Brontë finally turned them down.

2 Ellen Nussey was considering becoming a governess herself. Unsurprisingly, Brontë is not very encouraging.

3 Not definitely identified.

4 See note 1, p. 562. Anne Brontë had been dismissed from Blake Hall at the end of 1839.

5 Mary Taylor (1817-93) was another pupil at Roe Head with whom Brontë developed a close friendship.

6 The Reverend David Pryce (1811-40) had proposed to Brontë by letter, after a single visit to Haworth, in August 1839. Although Brontë turned him down, and tended to treat his proposal as comical, she is clearly upset by his unexpected death.

so little of him, and of course could not be deeply or permanently interested in what concerned him – I confess when I suddenly heard he was dead, I felt both shocked and saddened. It was no shame to feel so, was it?

I scold you Ellen for writing illegibly and badly, but I think you may repay the compliment with cent per cent interest – I am not in the humour for writing a long letter so good bye. God – bless you[.]

[Signature cut off]

3. To Ellen Nussey

[?March 3, 1841]
[Upperwood House, Rawdon]

My dear Ellen,[1]

I told you some time since, that I meant to get a situation, and when I said so my resolution was quite fixed. I felt that however often I was disappointed, I had no intention of relinquishing my efforts. After being severely baffled two or three times, – after a world of trouble in the way of correspondence and interviews, – I have at length succeeded, and am fairly established in my new place. It is in the family of Mr. White of Upperwood House, Rawdon.[2]

The house is not very large, but exceedingly comfortable, and well regulated; the grounds are fine and extensive. In taking this place I have made a large sacrifice in the way of salary, in the hope of securing comfort, by which word I do not mean to express good eating and drinking, or warm fire, or a soft bed, but the society of cheerful faces, and minds and hearts not dug out of a lead-mine, or cut from a marble quarry. My salary is not really more than £16. per annum, though it is nominally £20., but the expense of washing will be deducted therefrom. My pupils are two in number, a girl of eight and a boy of six. As to my employers, you will not expect me to say much respecting their characters when I tell you that I only arrived here yesterday. I have not the faculty of telling an individual's disposition at

---

1   See note 6, p. 562.
2   Brontë's next, and last, position as governess was in the household of John White (?1790–1860).

first sight. Before I can venture to pronounce on a character, I must see it first under various lights, and from various points of view. All I can say therefore is, both Mr. and Mrs. White seem to me good sort of people. I have as yet had no cause to complain of want of considerateness or civility. My pupils are wild and unbroken, but apparently well disposed. I wish I may be able to say as much next time I write to you. My earnest wish and endeavour will be to please them. If I can but feel that I am giving satisfaction, and if at the same time I can keep my health, I shall, I hope, be moderately happy. But no one but myself can tell how hard a governess' work is to me – for no one but myself is aware how utterly averse my whole mind and nature are to the employment. Do not think that I fail to blame myself for this, or that I leave any means unemployed to conquer this feeling. Some of my greatest difficulties lie in things that would appear to you comparatively trivial. I find it so hard to repel the rude familiarity of children. I find it so difficult to ask either servants or mistress for anything I want, however much I want it. It is less pain to me to endure the greatest inconvenience than to go into the kitchen to request its removal. I am a fool. Heaven knows I cannot help it!

Now can you tell me whether it is considered improper for governesses to ask their friends to come and see them. I do not mean, of course, to stay, but just for a call of an hour or two? If it is not absolute treason, I do fervently request that you will contrive, in some way or other, to let me have a sight of your face. Yet I feel at the same time, that I am making a very foolish and almost impracticable demand; yet Rawdon is only four miles from Bradford!

I dare say you have received a valentine this year from our bonny-faced friend the curate of Haworth.[1] I got a precious specimen a few days before I left home, but I knew better how to treat it than I did those we received a year ago. I am up to the dodges and artifices of his lordship's character, he knows I know him, and you cannot conceive how quiet and respectful he has long been. Mind I am not writing against him, I never *will* do that. I like him very much. I honour and admire his generous, open disposition, and sweet temper, – but

---

1   William Weightman became curate under Patrick Brontë in 1839. A handsome and amorous man, he apparently paid court at one time or another to all the unattached women around Haworth.

for all the tricks, wiles, and insincerities of love, the gentleman has not his match for twenty miles round. He would fain persuade every woman under thirty whom he sees that he is desperately in love with her. I have a great deal more to say, but I have not a moment's time to write it in. My dear Ellen, *do* write to me soon, don't forget. Good bye

[Unsigned]

Appendix C: Jane Eyre *and the Governess Question*

1. "Hints on the Modern Governess System," Unsigned

Fraser's Magazine,[1] November 1844

"Society is full of abuses. Women complain of being brutally enslaved, badly brought up, badly educated, badly treated, and badly defended. All this is, unfortunately, true. These complaints are just, and do not doubt but that before long a thousand voices will be uplifted to remedy the evil." – *Lettres à Marcie*.[2]

The cry has gone forth. The plaint in the drawing-room has been echoed by groans from the work-room. All reflecting womankind from Lady Emmeline[3] to the milliner's apprentice[4] who wrote touchingly to Lord Ashley,[5] make their moan. Thoughtful women in all ages have bewailed the cramping pressure of ignorance and jealous thraldom. 'Tis an old cry, though the note is now changed. Lady Mary Wortley[6] charged her grand-daughter to hide the learning she might acquire; a wise woman of to-day might, with equal justice, caution her child to acquire her knowledge before she sports it. 'Tis an age of teaching. The craving mind may no longer feed where it lists.

---

1 *Fraser's Magazine*, founded in London in 1830, was an influential literary and intellectual journal. It ceased publication in 1882.

2 A series of fictional letters by George Sand (Armandine Aurore Lucile Dupin, 1804-76) which were first published in *Le Monde* in 1837.

3 Not definitely identified. The name is probably fictional, and used to denote an aristocratic woman in contrast to the milliner's apprentice who follows. This sentence thus echoes the preceding one, which suggests female discontent spreads from the top to the bottom of the social hierarchy.

4 A milliner is a person, usually a woman, who makes lady's hats. Young girls were often apprenticed to them to learn this trade, for which their families paid a premium, and although the girls themselves received room and board, they did not receive a salary. They thus represented the lowest level of "proper" female society.

5 Anthony Ashley Cooper, 7th Earl of Shaftesbury (1801-85), elected to parliament in 1826, quickly made his reputation as a social reformer.

6 Lady Mary Wortley Montague (1689-1762) was famous for her extensive correspondence and for her leadership of eighteenth-century London society.

A system of "cramming" bears sway, from Bell's school[1] to the senate-house. No woman can complain of lack of teaching, nowadays; she may though still with reason sigh after *education*....

To trace the growth of woman's desire after knowledge would be the task of a philosopher; for us, it suffices to see that it is, that is has been from all ages. The barter of Paradise for the means of knowledge is the first recorded act of woman's life; she tempted man to forego all tried blessings, for the untried boon of "knowing good and evil."[2] Thenceforth, man wreaked his vengeance upon woman, for the loss of ease and plenty, by keeping her ignorant, and, consequently, help-less. But since the day that Christianity dawned on the world, an emancipation of the weak out of the power of the strong has been silently progressing. The faint cry, uplifted at intervals, swelled into a chorus; there was a sudden rush; all the world clamoured for a better education for women; no wonder, in such a struggle, that the greater number mistook chaff and husks for bread. The movement was all too sudden. Education, in as far as it implies intellectual and moral growth, is the work of life; its operations are as secret and as self-derived as the gradual shooting of the green blade into the wheat-ear.

Now, when that cry of women after knowledge pierced the air, a thousand sprang up, mushroomwise, in a night, to answer it. Mothers who had only read their bibles and receipt-books found themselves unprepared for the emergency – we have so little patience, so little foresight. Then, teaching, that holy vocation of a woman, became a trade. An universal demand creates its own supply. Here was a tempt-ing opening to all aspiring women, who were free to try a new field; the unmarried daughters of the gentry left with scanty portions, had, till now, been content to eke out their small incomes in trade; many

---

1   A reference to the Rev. Andrew Bell, who introduced a system of schooling into India that promoted the education of the poor. It was based on the idea that stu-dents would be grouped by ability; the top group would learn from the teacher, and then divide to teach the lesson to students in the lower classes. This kept costs down, because one teacher could instruct large numbers of pupils. A modified ver-sion of the concept was later introduced to parochial schools throughout England, and is essentially the system used at Lowood Institution in *Jane Eyre*. The mechani-cal, hierarchical nature of the learning imparted was seen as an advantage, because it instilled respect and orderliness, thus reducing the risk that education might breed discontent in those destined to lower-class occupations.

2   See Genesis 3:1-7.

were the gentlewomen, in our great-grandmothers' days, who lived in honoured independence, though they kept small shops, to which their old friends resorted. They did not lose caste because they sat for part of the day behind the counter. However, this refuge grew insecure from the outward pressure of public opinion in favour of refinement. The vast spread of colonisation at this juncture drew many bold spirits among the men from the warehouse. Women shared in the growing distaste for the ell-wand and the steel-yard.[1] Many left their quiet homes for the school-rooms of halls and castles. As they mounted the stair, others came from a lower rank, and filled the vacant steps. The restless rage to push on had stirred all classes. Those who, disappointed in their new stand, looked wistfully back to the old, found that when they would return they could not. There was no place left for them but that which they had chosen. Like much else, it looked best from a distance. Here, then, was a whole class of women driven into a new line, for which they had received no fitting preparation. As America and the Indies were filled by swarms of adventurers, marriage necessarily decreased. There was such an over-plus of single women that the old order of things was subversed. Women must have bread to eat as well as men. If they have no husbands to toil for them, they must win food for themselves. They found, if they would not sink in the scale, they must work with their heads, and not with their hands. Must! oh the ruthlessness of necessity! We know the fate of the weed when mighty waters rush together. The new generation, thirsting to be taught, found teachers at their mercy, hanging between two ranks. Do the weak desire to learn what they may expect from the strong? Let them ponder deeply the governess system of the present day. This was the watch-word, "Teach us on our own terms, or work, and cease to be gentlewomen." To the newly risen race of governesses, even such equivocal gentility was preferable to a second change, though it was to be gained at the price of isolation. Time was when the daughters of poor clergymen, with pedigrees longer than their purses, found secure and honourable service as housekeepers and ladies'-maids. A new order of things had come round. The still-room[2]

---

1   An ell-wand is a measuring rod approximately 45 inches long. A steel-yard is a type of weighing apparatus or scale. Both would have been used in shops to measure merchandise.

2   The housekeeper's storeroom in a mansion or country house.

was no longer a safe retreat to decayed gentlewomen. A love of show kept pace with the desire of knowledge. A profligate adept in confectionary[1] was preferred before a respectable woman, who knew the business of preserving order and decency better than the mysteries of the stew-pan and the ice-pail.[2]

The policy of the world is to take advantage of want. It became apparent that a whole family of daughters might be taught by one of these single women, struggling for bread, for less than it formerly cost to send one girl to school. Where competition was so great, there was no difficulty in driving a bargain. The means of instruction might be had so cheaply, that the grocer's daughters could be taught to read *Paul and Virginia*[3] in the original tongue, and to strum *the Fall of Paris*.[4] In process of time, therefore, a governess became a necessary appanage in every family.

Whether it be right or wrong, as a general rule, for mothers to delegate their most sacred trust to hired strangers, we are not here to discuss. The fact exists. Is the system carried out fairly for all parties? Is there any question astir as to its abuse? Philanthropic eyes are scanning many social evils. Is it yet considered how far a whole race of women are dragging out weary lives under a mass of trials, the detail of which would fill a "blue book"[5] by themselves? True, if the case were known, "a thousand voices" would be "uplifted."[6] The miseries of the governess may even swell that sickening clamour about the "rights of women,"[7] which would never have been raised had women been true to themselves. But that trite saying in this case has its point.

---

1   i.e., a woman of improper character but skillful at concocting sweets and pastries, as well as fashionable articles of dress.

2   Utensils for making confectionary. The author is playing on the idea of "preserving order and decency" as opposed to simply cooking up "preserves" and other sweets.

3   *Paul et Virginie*, a popular and extremely sentimental French romance, was first published in 1787 by Jacques-Henri Bernadin de St.-Pierre (1737-1814).

4   A popular sentimental song of the period. In this case to "strum" means to play (unskillfully) on the piano; Anne Brontë uses the word in this way in *Agnes Grey* (1847).

5   An official Parliamentary or Privy-Council report. They were issued in blue paper covers.

6   See epigraph to this article.

7   Controversy over what came to be called "the woman question" began growing in the 1820s and 1830s. Arguments for female equality, and particularly for giving women the vote, were generally viewed as destructive of the social order.

The modern governess system is a case between woman and woman. Before one sex demands its due from the other, let it be just to itself.

Punch has ably pleaded in the cause of salaries and qualifications.[1] The statistics touching lunatic asylums give a frightful proportion of governesses in the list of the insane.[2] But has the whole life in home schoolrooms ever been investigated? We ask this with a real wish to be informed, with a hope of directing eyes to this unknown page of human life. Have kind, ladylike, cultivated women ever reflected on the relation which subsists between themselves and others of like minds, and, perhaps, formerly in similar circumstances? Have they every tried to put themselves in the position of the young women devoting themselves to the education of their children, who yet live as strangers in the midst of homes?...

One cannot conceive of a greater anomaly than that which makes a woman responsible for children, and their exemplar in all things, whose mother treats her as if she were unfit to associate with herself and her guests. Children, who only look to the outside of things, must draw the inference that their governess is a mere machine for teaching. To their eyes, she appears wholly cut off from the links in their chain of sympathies. She, with all the exuberance of a youthful heart, fresh from the warmth and common interests of a family, is suddenly thrust into a post whose conscientious fulfilment requires a discretion and reticence not natural to youth. New difficulties and responsibilities meet her every day; she is hourly tried by all those childish follies and perversities which need a mother's instinctive love to make them tolerable; yet a forbearance and spring of spirits is claimed from the

---

1 Because competition for positions was so fierce, governesses' salaries were often extremely low. It became a popular argument that governesses could command better pay and improve their economic condition if they were taught to be better teachers. The satirical magazine *Punch* became an advocate for improving the conditions for governesses. See the appendix article following this one.

2 Although there is some statistical evidence supporting a higher proportion of governesses in asylums than other occupational groups, the reasons for this are complex. For example, a private asylum often provided the cheapest "respectable" accommodation available to a woman without family, and between positions. The belief that governesses were mentally unstable due to the stresses of their situation became a commonplace well into the late 1860s. The most famous literary representation of this idea, which also demonstrates its longevity, is Henry James' *The Turn of the Screw* (1898).

stranger, in spite of the frets she endures, which He who made the heart knew that maternal affection only could supply, under the perpetual contradictions of wilful childhood. This strength of instinct has been given to every mother. It enables her to walk lightly under a load which, without it, she could not sustain. But should not women think twice, before they expect from strangers who have not even the natural affection of kindred, a mother's conduct to their children? Day by day the governess is worn by the disappointments the most promising child must inflict upon its teacher; but to whom can she, in her weariness, turn for sympathy? Not one mother in a thousand can bear to hear her child's faults spoken of by a third person, however quick-sighted she is to them herself, without some resentment towards the speaker. A very young woman would probably fear to venture on such delicate ground with the parents.

If she is indiscreet, she writes to her family about her pupils, and is taught hereafter by bitter experience the fruits of incaution; some, perhaps, go on all their lives betraying a holy trust. The lips of a conscientious teacher would be sealed, by the awe of looking in upon a child's soul and seeing all its struggles. For no relief to herself could she dare to expose to others what she has learned by a trust implicit as that placed in a confessor. She must live daily amidst the trials of a home without its blessings; she must bear about on her heart the sins she witnesses and the responsibilities that crush her; without any consent of her will, she is made the *confidante* of many family secrets; she must live in a familiar circle as if her eyes did not perceive the tokens of bitterness; she must appear not to hear sharp sayings and *mal-à-propos*[1] speeches; kindly words of courtesy must be always on her lips; she must be ever on her guard; let her relax her self-restraint for one moment, and who shall say what mischief and misery might ensue to all from one heedless expression of hers? Wholesome discipline, no doubt! It were well, perhaps, if it were made the groundwork of all home intercourse; but who amongst the young, unaided and without counsel, is sufficient for these things? Is not caution the fruit of experience? Ay, and these young creatures, if they have high moral principles, learn enough bitter experience in a year to give them the sorrows of maturity, without its strength and safety.

---

1   Out of place; inappropriate.

The consequences to themselves? They spring up suddenly in premature development, like plants in a hot-house, – old in heart, aged in appearance, before the bloom of youth is brushed from their years, drawn upwards by the insufferable light, from which in their glass-houses, there is no shelter. It is no exaggeration to say that hundreds snap yearly from the stalk, or prolong a withered, sickly life, till they, too, sink, and are carried out to die miserably in the by-ways of the world.

This is but one instance of the unnatural state of isolation to which women are exposed who prefer honest exertion to inaction and dependence....But when the lesson-books are closed, and the little ones have capered out of the school-room, what becomes of the teacher, who has not exchanged a thought or a word with any one of congenial mind all day? Hour after hour she has *bent down her* mind, and *raised* the children's to given points, which, however interesting, are exhausting. A young thing, perhaps, still herself, ready to spring up again at one kindly touch. Do not even fond mothers, who teach their own children, feel that after the labours of the day they need some interchange of *mind*? They have often felt refreshed when husband or friend has given them a new thought, or understood an articulated feeling, after the repression of the day, necessary in fulfilling the duty of teaching. Who is there that has not know the dryness of spending time with people of more limited capacities and interests than one's own? The governess has a better lot than this, inasmuch as she may hope to expand the germs given into her fostering care; whereas the uncongenial companion can only expect less and less of bud and blossom as years roll on. Let mothers ask if they would not expect their own daughters to languish in spirits and energy, if they had no intercourse with older companions. Whilst the children are with their parents and their guests, the governess, quite as often as not, is expected to remain in the school-room, unless specially invited to join the circle. This is peculiarly the case in large establishments, where the school-room arrangements are distinct from the rest of the family. We believe that most young women of delicate perceptions would prefer their desolate apartment to feeling themselves clogs upon the family party. But do people know what they are about when they leave young creatures alone, long evening after evening, following days of seclusion and exhaustion? Factory-girls, shop-women, teachers of accomplishments, return to their homes at night. The servants gather round the work-table or the hall-fire. Prisoners in gaol may collect together in knots in their yards, look in each other's faces, hear the sound of human voices, tell their troubles and joys, and listen to their neighbours. Solitary confinement, even for felons, is reserved to punish some special offence. It is only the governess, and a certain class of private tutors, who must hear the echoes from the drawing-room and the offices, feeling that, in a house full of people, they dwell alone. Nervous irritability, dejection, loss of energy, are the inevitable results which follow a too solitary life in youth. Yet, without elasticity in her own frame, how can the governess be a fitting companion and teacher of such gay, volatile creatures as children, – so easily cowed and spirit-broken by harshness or settled sadness in those who live with them? Would not querulous temper of depression of spirits in the governess be complained of by the parents? Do they consider, when they expect cheerfulness and an even composure of spirits from one fretted with children's restless waywardness, and chilled by the frosty indifference and neglect of the grown-up members of the family, that they ask an impossible thing? There may be some phlegmatic exceptions, but, merely to judge by common parlance, governesses are usually a fretful, discontented race. Why? They are the weak, they are trampled upon; if they turn upon their oppressors they must starve....We have sometimes been astonished at comparing the qualifications required in letters of inquiry touching governesses with the remuneration offered, – such a catalogue of literary, ornamental, and moral acquirements as one would think no ordinary mortal would lay claim to; and all these demands on body and mind to be paid by a paltry 40l. a-year! It is not a fair interest upon the capital invested in the girl's education. One cannot learn French, German, Italian, Latin, music, dancing, and drawing, to say nothing of history, globes, and arithmetic, for nothing. It may be asked, Why does the girl close with such an offer? Let the old proverb reply, "Better half a loaf than no bread." The market is over-stocked; governess are much at a discount. Many ladies would not dare to treat their maids as they behave to the teacher of their children. Why? The maid has a broad field before her; she can afford to turn upon her mistress. The governess must endure all things, or perish. A low marriage or a slow death are her only loopholes of escape. Oh, shame on us who make a gain of the pressing miseries of others!...

The most direct remedy for all these evils would appear to be to induce governesses to measure themselves by a higher rule. If they were raised in their own eyes, they would be more looked up to by others. In order to this, it is necessary that they should better understand the nature of their calling. If they saw more clearly the end of their vocation, and strove to fulfil it, they would make the way plainer for their successors. Pupils who have been carefully trained in habits of self-culture, and with a right appreciation of education, will, in their turn, be better able to do the like office to their children. If circumstances oblige such pupils hereafter to hire instructors for their families, we may be sure that such mothers will have a truer sympathy, and would more justly value the governesses of their children, than those who have been brought up by women, who, whilst they taught, despised themselves for teaching. It is not too much to say, that governesses of the present day have it in their power to remedy the abuse of the system under which they groan far more than their superiors can do. They can train the mother that will be, to teach her own child, not yet in existence. But this working for the future may be too much to be expected from the people of to-day.

There are other ways, more immediate in their result, of ameliorating the condition of female teachers. The market is glutted. If the supply were lessened, the demand would be greater. Let women labour in other fields, and thus diminish the superabundant stock of teachers. New tracks are beginning to open. The female school of design for the improvement of manufactures might profitably occupy much time and skill,[1] now wasted in copying monstrous Arabs and gaudy Corsairs.[2] There are many women as capable of discharging the office of clerk and book-keeper as men; besides, the will finds the

---

1   The Victorian period saw a surge of interest in technical education, particularly involving the application of mechanical drawing and design to industry. By the middle of the nineteenth century independent schools teaching such skills began to open.
2   Examples of inappropriately romantic, and thus valueless, subjects for a drawing or sketch. See Blanche Ingram's self-declared infatuation with such "outlaws" in the text of *Jane Eyre*.

way. What may not determined perseverance achieve? If, by such diversion, the services of the remaining governesses were enhanced in worth, they would necessarily fetch a higher price. This change would lead to another. Mothers who are now tempted by low salaries to transfer the instruction of their children to strangers would find that they must return to the old plan of putting the young ones in the way of teaching themselves. Professional men's wives of small means, the wives of the poor clergy, of the tradesmen and yeomen, would find a governess too expensive a luxury for short purses. Some present inconvenience might result, but who can doubt that the daughters of poor men would receive instruction more befitting their future lots if they learned of their mothers the lore that makes skilful housewives, instead of being crammed by a hireling, who was brought up in a second-rate school? They would become fitted to be good wives and good mothers, should such be their appointed lot. If they do not marry, it is from this class that ladies amongst the gentry should seek assistance, not to teach their children, but to rule their households....If mothers would obey their highest calling, many who now fill their places would be safer and happier in their lower vocation. Those tradespeople and yeomen who now send their daughters to bad schools, in order to fit them to be ill-paid governesses, would bring them up for housekeepers, were this office restored to respectability. The time which ladies now spend in ordering their establishment might be better devoted to their children, whereas a woman who has her own self-respect to keep up would, for the same salary now given to the lowest order of governesses, be better able than the mistress to check fraud, and guard against peculation amongst the servants. It may be, under such a system, that the families of the gentry would be less accomplished; but they would be more reasonable. And those who desire to give their daughters such pleasant resources as music, drawing, or languages, can call in the aid of masters. Surely it must be acknowledged that women whose lesson of life has been learned at mothers' knees, over infants' cradles, will be more earnest and genuine than those taught by a stranger, however well qualified. Who would seriously set the backwardness resulting from home interruptions against the depth and breadth of character, which would be the consequence if girls shared in the cares and joys of their mothers? Where can the truth of life be studied to greater advantage than in a mother's sick-room or by a baby-brother's cot?

There is yet another class who have availed themselves of hired services for their children because they were to be had so cheaply. Mothers in frugal parsonages have learned to think that their girls must be taught. The wives of country apothecaries and lawyers will give their girls the shreds and patches of those acquirements which become the daughters of wealthy patients and clients. Every miss must grind a waltz, daub a piece of paper, and chatter bad French. As a matter of necessity, then, they must have a governess. The mother, with her yearly increasing nursery, and all the manifold cares of a small income, must be unequal to the task. But oh, the folly of such a plan! It is cutting the ground from under their children's feet; it is dooming them to the same wretched lot as the poor governess drags who teaches them. Nowhere do the abuses of the governess system glare out so hideously as in such establishments as these. Mothers in this station, who give their daughters a false refinement, are unfitting them to be the honoured wives of working men, or to gain their own bread independently if they remain unmarried....

We live in a hard, work-a-day world. Women of to-day, in as far as they are self-dependent, will win its respect and their own repose. Yet a few words more. *Self-dependence* is not *independence*; strength and softness are not incompatible with each other. If women who have vigorously used their faculties have thereby lost their distinctive womanly graces, it is not that such activity must needs foster a masculine temper. There have hitherto been only rare instances of women who dare to use their energies, except as wives and mothers. Singularity of position is apt to lead to eccentricity of conduct. But let the world's eye be used to contemplate female labour, and the single woman will toil in her chosen path with as much of a womanly reserve and gentleness as marks the matron in her sphere of activity.

2. "Governesses' Benevolent Institution,"[1] Unsigned

Punch[2] 10 (1846)

In furtherance of the objects of this most useful charity, it is in contemplation to establish a School, for the purpose of preparing young ladies destined to be governesses, for the situations they are intended to fill. The necessity of teaching those who are to be teachers, and of instructing the governess how to govern, is obvious; the pupils, accordingly, will learn all the modern languages and accomplishments – geography, astronomy, the use of the globes, and so much of moral philosophy as includes the true principles of education. But as the social position of a governess is a peculiar one, being, as a novelty, rather uncomfortable, though, like a certain process to which eels are subjected,[3] nothing when anybody is used to it. One great object of this School will be to familiarise the pupils with the life they may expect to lead. Its arrangements will therefore comprise a system of training calculated for the inculcation of an amount of practical as well as moral philosophy adequate to this purpose.

To the Institution will be attached a Servants' Hall, wherein, at state times, will attend a number of footmen and other menials, to intercourse with whom the future governess may be habituated, and whose insults and impertinences she may learn betimes to put up with. A nursery will also be connected with it, in order to exercise her patience in the management of refractory children, at which probation the students will take turns. The children will be selected from the most purse-proud families, and their mammas will drop in every now and then, daily, and reprimand and find fault capriciously and unjustly with their preceptress, so as to inure her to such treatment. Some charitable ladies of great style, in the vicinity of Russell Square,[4] have volunteered their services in this particular. One of

---

1   An organization established in 1843 to provide some relief from the harsh conditions faced by governesses. It conducted a registry for employment and later became a resource for the old and infirm.
2   *Punch, or the London Charivari* was founded in 1841 as an illustrated weekly comic/satiric periodical.
3   After being caught on a line eels were skinned before being cooked.
4   A wealthy residential area in London, Russell Square was built on the lands of the Dukes of Bedford in the early nineteenth century.

these ladies will, moreover, preside regularly at dinner to teach the language of looks, that the learner may understand, from a glance, when she is to refuse wine, or to decline another helping.

Evening parties will be given occasionally, in the schoolroom, and to them will be invited a number of agreeable men, that the "young persons" may know how to behave in society; that is, to hold their tongues and sit still. For the due enforcement of these proprieties, one of the ladies aforesaid will also be present, accompanied by her daughters, by whom the scholars are to be studiously snubbed, by way of a lesson to them in meekness under contumely. The novices, during leisure hours, are to sit in separate apartments, accessible to all the servants, who, however, will not be allowed to wait upon them, or bring them any refreshment, if hungry from the insufficiency of their meals. Their dresses are to be such as a young lady can afford upon twenty pounds a year, finding herself in everything but her victuals, and not having, by half, as much of those as she can eat.

Thus, it may be hoped, will governesses be provided with qualifications high enough, wants few enough, and spirit humble enough, to meet the views of any lady in the land.

3. "On the Social Position of Governesses" By the Author of 'Woman's Mission.'[1] Unsigned [Sarah Lewis]

Fraser's Magazine, April 1848

The following remarks, on a subject of some public importance, were originally called forth by an application from a distinguished friend of the writer, who requested assistance for the bazar about to be held in aid of the 'Governesses' Benevolent Institution.' Some friends to whom they were communicated urged their publication, as placing the claims of governesses on grounds more consistent with their truth and value, than public opinion, or even public benevolence, has yet attained to respecting that important body. It is hoped that they may have some interest from the novelty, and some weight from the fact, of their coming from one *within*, and not *without* the 'pale.'

---

1   A very popular female conduct book published by Sarah Lewis, anonymously, in 1839. Lewis had served as a governess herself.

However difficult, if not impossible it may be, to put the public in possession of the real motives of an author, it is highly desirable to prevent the imputation of such as are false. This is especially the case with respect to all statements of abuses: it *is* of importance to know that public censures are not provoked by private grievances. The writer, then, has no wrongs of any kind to resent. A long professional career has, by a rare felicity, shewn her her profession only under its brightest aspect; and her professional relations with individuals have been marked by a liberality, a courtesy, a high consideration, worthy of all gratitude, and which have left nothing to be desired by the most jealous personal or professional self-respect.

In treating, therefore, of the wrongs, or what she conceives to be the wrongs, of governesses, she is actuated by none of the asperity of adversity, and none of the bitterness of wounded self-love. But a personal exemption from great 'class evils,' ought not to blind the understanding to their existence, or shut the heart to the misery which they produce. Even the perception of these evils, however, would not have sufficed to urge her to a public declaration of her sentiments, but that she feels some of the highest interests of society to be thereby compromised, and that society is even more unjust to itself than to her profession in suffering their existence.

The frequent appeals to public compassion made in behalf of governesses – the 'fancy fairs,' 'shilling subscription cards,'[1] got up with a view to their benefit, are calculated to fill a thinking mind with painful reflections, and a cynical mind with bitter ones. There must be some great wrong – something very 'rotten in the state of Denmark,'[2] before society would venture to offer, or respectable individuals could be induced to accept, such compensation for social prejudice and social injustice!

It is difficult to speak of benevolent intentions, even when one thinks them ill-directed, with any thing approaching to harshness; but it remains a matter of grave consideration whether the tendency of

---

1 Both fancy fairs and subscription cards were charity methods for raising money. The first consisted of the sale of such "fancy" goods as wrist warmers, ornamented slippers, and various knitted goods. The second committed the signer to donating the amount, in this case a small one, recorded on the card. Lewis sees them as humiliating to the professional aspirations of governesses.
2 *Hamlet* I.iv.90.

the above-mentioned charities be not, like many of the efforts of merely impulsive benevolence, to relieve in individual distress at the expense of general good.

It is too true that governesses can rarely provide for old age or contingencies. But why? Because the emolument received by governesses (however superior) is not sufficient to enable a person, required to keep up the appearances of a gentlewoman, to do so – because the general notions on this subject are notoriously such, as to have been made the subject of more than one popular burlesque! The salary of a first-rate governess is scarcely more than the interest of money which her education *ought* to have cost; and those of all under 'first-rate' are not more than is given to the upper servants of good families. The profession of a private governess is the only profession which offers no premium to distinguished abilities, and we see the results, unhappily, every day. Would it not be better to pay governesses a little more, and to pity them a little less? The prejudices which would degrade, and the injustice which inadequately remunerates, the members of an honourable and useful profession, are ill compensated by a tardy and patronising compassion. The writer knows not how the members of her profession feel *generally*, but, for her own part, she would prefer having recourse to that legal provision which the laws of her country allow all to claim, – to receiving in the form of *alms* that which had been denied in the form of *wages*. Nor can it be wondered at if the high-minded amongst the body should reject, rather than be grateful for, that form of compensation which arises from public charity, and is to be sued for *in formâ pauperis*.[1]

But this is not the only, nor, in the writer's opinion, the gravest, aspect of the subject. That individuals should suffer humiliation is a light thing in comparison of a great cause suffering injury.

Education is a great cause. The public think it so; they talk of it, at least, as such! The progress of society permits no one now to *say*, whatever he may *think*, that ours is a degrading occupation. We have essays on education, essays on educators; how the tone of the one and the character of the other may be raised. Can the tone of education, or the character of educators, be raised, while society continues to offer to the members of this profession for their services – the wages

---

1   Latin. In the guise of a pauper.

and social position of a domestic, and for their distresses and old age – the provision of a pauper?

Their knowledge of human nature must be very small who do not perceive that a class, the distresses and necessities of which are thus constantly made the theme of public commiseration and the object of public charity, can never attain (as a class) to that position of social respectability which the members of so influential a profession ought to occupy; and education can never be what it ought to be, till educators do fill such a place in public estimation. How is society to learn to look up with respect to those on whom it has been first taught to look down with pity? It is impossible!

But there are two sides to every question; and where there is blame it is never altogether on one; nor is it here. Candour compels the acknowledgement, that while the respectable and meritorious are often grievously underpaid, there are but too many in our profession who would be overpaid *at any price*. And the same candour compels also the humiliating confession, that the inadequate remuneration and low social position of governesses may be greatly attributed to the assumption of the office by those whose necessities are their only title to employment. Is it not monstrous, that while a lady will not give her dress to be made to any one but a first-rate dress-maker, she will give her children to be educated by a second or third-rate governess? That she will commit their training for this world and the next to a woman whose only qualification for the task is, that she has had a twelvemonth's apprenticeship in an inferior boarding-school, or – that her father failed last week?[1] One has really very little right to complain of the want of respect shewn by society to a profession which respects itself so little as to have allowed this state of things to continue without a grand simultaneous effort to remedy it. But such an effort being, it is to be feared, hopeless, some other remedy must be found. This remedy appears to lie, not in public *charity* but in public *institutions*. That governesses may be more respected, they must be better qualified; that they may be better qualified, they must be better paid; that they may be both, they must be better chosen; that they may be better chosen, there must be somebody to choose them. *That*

---

1 Young middle-class women whose fathers went bankrupt often had no choice but to take positions as governesses to support themselves.

somebody should be the Government; for the Church, which *ought* to be the curator of public education, does not sufficiently represent the people to take up its office. The Government, then, in our own, as in other countries, ought to take upon itself the office of securing the public interests by excluding the half-educated or simply necessitous from the rank of public instructors, thus giving respectability to the office and security to the public.

The public feeling on this subject has already found representatives in two bodies, – the 'Queen's College,' and the 'College of Preceptors.'[1] To both – and especially to the latter, as organised by the Education body itself – much gratitude is due for their endeavours after a great moral and national good. But the writer (with diffidence) suggests that they are both deficient in a most important respect, – viz. they are not armed with a competent and efficient weight of authority. The power needed is a power of *exclusion*, – a power which can say, 'You shall not take up this vocation unless you shew testimonials of ability.' No privately organised body would, or could, assume to itself the power of such exclusion; and the assumption, that the diploma granted to the capable would amount to a virtual exclusion of the incapable, seems to be based on an insufficient consideration of the peculiar difficulties of the case.

Some of these difficulties the writer (also with diffidence) ventures to suggest. It appears to her, that while the ignorant and incapable might (by accepting low salaries) evade the requisite examination, the *very superior* – those of acknowledged merit and talent – might neglect it, not from contempt, but because nothing but a Government diploma, absolutely indispensable, and giving to the educator the dignity of a recognised public functionary, could be to such persons a sufficient desideratum to induce them to submit to the ordeal of a public examination. Now these are the very persons whom it would be desirable to tempt into that profession to which society entrusts its dearest interests. It appears also to her, that no amount of fairness or impartiality could secure the members of those bodies

---

1   Both institutions were established to formalize the education of teachers. Queen's College, which opened in 1848, offered potential governesses lectures and examinations to improve their skills, and provided certification of their proficiency upon graduation.

from the suspicion of partisanship in the exercise of their self-constituted functions; and that the clamour of injustice – first raised, perhaps, by disappointed incapacity – would soon find an echo in the public mind, and nullify the benefits expected. A Government sanction, then, appears to be the principal means by which the object so laudably attempted by these bodies can be attained; and the *only* means by which full security can be given, either to the profession or to the public, that the highest of all tasks may not often be assigned to the lowest of all minds!

But, waiting these better times, there is much misery waiting also for relief. And that Charity should stay her hand till Justice has done *her* work is not to be expected, – not even to be wished. It is, however, to be desired, that this relief could be afforded in a manner which would maintain the dignity of the profession, while it solaces the distress of the individual; that some regard (as to ways and means) be had to the feelings of those, who are many of the *in reality*, and all of them *by courtesy*, gentlewomen; that still more regard be had to the public interests, which are deeply compromised by any further degradation of a body so important to the moral interests of the community.

If these remarks prove suggestive of any useful thoughts to the public in general, the writer will be well content; but her chief object is to rouse the attention of those of her own sex and profession, who may not yet have considered the subject in its full bearings, on their own position and interests, as well as on the public good. *To* them she looks for sympathy; *from* them must come the efforts (whether pecuniary or otherwise) that are to overcome the evils which all must deplore. Why should not the heads of prosperous and respectable ladies' schools come to the rescue of their less fortunate sisters? An annual subscription of comparatively moderate amount from all such would effect much good in this cause. To be the pensioners of a fund having (at least for its basis) a professional combination is one thing; to be the pauperised claimants of eleemosynary[1] public charity is another. To rescue the less fortunate members of our noble common profession from so degrading a necessity would seem to be an object needing no other recommendation than its own merits. And if this

---

1   Unearned, gratuitous.

appeal rouse a few thinking heads and noble hearts (there are some such amongst us) to consideration and consequent action, it will not have been made in vain.

4. Review of *Vanity Fair*,[1] *Jane Eyre*, *Governesses' Benevolent Institution – Report for 1847*, Unsigned [Elizabeth Rigby (later Lady Eastlake)][2]

Quarterly Review,[3] December 1848

A remarkable novel is a great event for English society. It is a kind of common friend, about whom people can speak the truth without fear of being compromised, and confess their emotions without being ashamed. We are a particularly shy and reserved people, and set about nothing so awkwardly as the simple art of getting really acquainted with each other. We meet over and over again in what is conventionally called 'easy society,' with the tacit understanding to go so far and no farther; to be as polite as we ought to be, and as intellectual as we can; but mutually and honourably to forbear lifting those veils which each spreads over his inner sentiments and sympathies. For this purpose a host of devices have been contrived by which all the forms of friendship may be gone through, without committing ourselves to one spark of the spirit. We fly with eagerness to some common ground in which each can take the liveliest interest, without taking the slightest in the world in his companion. Our various fashionable manias, for charity one season, for science the next, are only so many clever contrivances for keeping our neighbour at arm's length. We can attend committees, and canvass for subscribers, and archæologise, and geologise, and take ether with our fellow Christians for a twelve-month, as we might sit cross-legged and smoke the pipe of fraternity with a Turk for the same period – and know at the end of the time as

---

1   See Preface to the Second Edition of *Jane Eyre*, Appendix A.1.

2   Elizabeth Rigby (1809–93), writer and art historian, was from 1842 on the sole female contributor to the *Quarterly Review*. This scathing attack on *Jane Eyre* is arguably her most famous piece for the magazine.

3   The *Quarterly Review*, founded in 1809, was an influential Tory journal established specifically to counter the liberal political position of the *Edinburgh Review* (est. 1802). The *Quarterly* ceased publication in 1967.

little of the real feelings of the one as we should about the domestic relations of the other. But there are ways and means for lifting the veil which equally favour our national idiosyncrasy; and a new and remarkable novel is one of them – especially the nearer it comes to real life. We invite our neighbour to a walk with the deliberate and malicious object of getting thoroughly acquainted with him. We ask no impertinent questions – we proffer no indiscreet confidences – we do not even sound him, ever so delicately, as to his opinion of a common friend, for he would be sure not to say, lest we should go and tell; but we simply discuss Becky Sharp,[1] or Jane Eyre, and our object is answered at once.

There is something about these two new and noticeable characters which especially compels everybody to speak out. They are not to be dismissed with a few commonplace moralities and sentimentalities. They do not fit any ready-made criticism. They give the most stupid something to think of, and the most reserved something to say; the most charitable too are betrayed into home comparisons which they usually condemn, and the most ingenious stumble into paradoxes which they can hardly defend. Becky and Jane also stand well side by side both in their analogies and their contrasts. Both the ladies are governesses, and both make the same move in society; the one, in Jane Eyre phraseology, marrying her 'master,' and the other her master's son. Neither starts in life with more than a moderate capital of good looks – Jane Eyre with hardly that – for it is the fashion now-a-days with novelists to give no encouragement to the insolence of mere beauty, but rather to prove to all whom it may concern how little a sensible woman requires to get on with in the world. Both have also an elfish kind of nature, with which they divine the secrets of other hearts, and conceal those of their own; and both rejoice in that peculiarity of feature which Mademoiselle de Luzy has not contributed to render popular, viz., green eyes. Beyond this, however, there is no similarity either in the minds, manners, or fortunes of the two heroines. They think and act upon diametrically opposite principles – at least so the author of 'Jane Eyre' intends us to believe – and each, were they to meet, which we should of all things enjoy to see them do,

---

1   One of the main characters in *Vanity Fair*.

would cordially despise and abominate the other. Which of the two, however, would most successfully *dupe* the other is a different question, and one not so easy to decide; though we have our own ideas upon the subject....

'Jane Eyre,' as a work, and one of equal popularity, is, in almost every respect, a total contrast to 'Vanity Fair.' The characters and events, though some of them masterly in conception, are coined expressly for the purpose of bringing out great effects. The hero and heroine are beings both so singularly unattractive that the reader feels they can have no vocation in the novel but to be brought together; and they do things which, though not impossible, lie utterly beyond the bounds of probability. On this account a short sketch of the plan seems requisite; not but what it is a plan familiar enough to all readers of novels – especially those of the old school and those of the lowest school of our own day. For Jane Eyre is merely another Pamela,[1] who, by the force of her character and the strength of her principles, is carried victoriously through great trials and temptations from the man she loves. Nor is she even a Pamela adapted and refined to modern notions; for though the story is conducted without those derelictions of decorum which we are to believe had their excuse in the manners of Richardson's time, yet it is stamped with a coarseness of language and laxity of tone which have certainly no excuse in ours. It is a very remarkable book: we have no remembrance of another combining such genuine power with such horrid taste. Both together have equally assisted to gain the great popularity it has enjoyed; for in these days of extravagant adoration of all that bears the stamp of novelty and originality, sheer rudeness and vulgarity have come in for a most mistaken worship [a synopsis of *Jane Eyre* follows]....

Such is the outline of a tale in which, combined with great materials for power and feeling, the reader may trace gross inconsistencies and improbabilities, and chief and foremost that highest moral offence a novel writer can commit, that of making an unworthy character interesting in the eyes of the reader. Mr. Rochester is a man

---

1   A reference to the novel *Pamela, or Virtue Rewarded*, published by Samuel Richardson (1689-1761) in 1740. Pamela is relentlessly pursued by a man of superior social status, who attempts to take advantage of his position to seduce her. Her virtue is so strong, however, that he finally decides to marry her.

who deliberately and secretly seeks to violate the laws both of God and man, and yet we will be bound half our lady readers are enchanted with him for a model of generosity and honour. We would have thought that such a hero had had no chance, in the purer taste of the present day; but the popularity of Jane Eyre is a proof how deeply the love for illegitimate romance is implanted in our nature. Not that the author is strictly responsible for this. Mr. Rochester's character is tolerably consistent. He is made as coarse and as brutal as can in all conscience be required to keep our sympathies at a distance. In point of literary consistency the hero is at all events impugnable, though we cannot say as much for the heroine.

As to Jane's character – there is none of that harmonious unity about it which made little Becky so grateful a subject of analysis – nor are the discrepancies of that kind which have their excuse and their response in our nature. The inconsistencies of Jane's character lie mainly not in her own imperfections, though of course she has her share, but in the author's. There is that confusion in the relations between cause and effect, which is not so much untrue to human nature as to human art. The error in Jane Eyre is, not that her character is this or that, but that she is made one thing in the eyes of her imaginary companions, and another in that of the actual reader. There is a perpetual disparity between the account she herself gives of the effect she produces, and the means shown us by which she brings that effect about. We hear nothing but self-eulogiums on the perfect tact and wondrous penetration with which she is gifted, and yet almost every word she utters offends us, not only with the absence of these qualities, but with the positive contrasts of them, in either her pedantry, stupidity, or gross vulgarity. She is one of those ladies who put us in the unpleasant predicament of undervaluing their very virtues for dislike of the person in whom they are represented. One feels provoked as Jane Eyre stands before us – for in the wonderful reality of her thoughts and descriptions, she seems accountable for all done in her name – with principles you must approve in the main, and yet with language and manners that offend you in every particular. Even in that *chef-d'oeuvre*[1] of brilliant retrospective sketching, the

---

1   Masterpiece.

description of her early life, it is the childhood and not the child that interests you. The little Jane, with her sharp eyes and dogmatic speeches, is a being you neither could fondle nor love. There is a hardness in her infantine earnestness, and a spiteful precocity in her reasoning, which repulses all our sympathy. One sees that she is of nature to dwell upon and treasure up every slight and unkindness, real or fancied, and such natures we know are surer than any others to meet with plenty of this sort of thing. As the child, so also the woman – an uninteresting, sententious, pedantic thing; with no experience of the world, and yet with no simplicity or freshness in its stead. What are her first answers to Mr. Rochester but such as would have quenched all interest, even for a prettier woman, in any man of common knowledge of what was nature – and especially in a *blasé*[1] monster like him? A more affected governessy effusion we never read....Most lover's play is wearisome and nonsensical to the lookers on – but the part Jane assumes is one which could only be efficiently sustained by the substitution of Sam for her master. Coarse as Mr. Rochester is, one winces for him under the infliction of this housemaid beau idéal[2] of the arts of coquetry. A little more, and we should have flung the book aside to lie for ever among the trumpery with which such scenes ally it; but it were a pity to have halted here, for wonderful things lie beyond – scenes of suppressed feeling, more fearful to witness than the most violent tornados of passion – struggles with such intense sorrow and suffering as it is sufficient misery to know that any one should have conceived, far less passed through; and yet with that stamp of truth which takes precedence in the human heart before actual experience. The flippant, fifth-rate, plebeian actress has vanished, and only a noble, high-souled woman, bound to us by the reality of her sorrow, and yet raised above us by the strength of her will, stands in actual life before us. If this be Jane Eyre, the author has done her injustice hitherto, not we. Let us look at her in the first recognition of her sorrow after the discomfiture of the marriage. True, it is not the attitude of a Christian, who knows that all things work together for good to those who love God, but it is a splendidly drawn picture of a natural heart, of high power, intense feeling, and

---

1 Bored; weary through over-indulgence.
2 Idealization.

fine religious instinct, falling prostrate, but not grovelling, before the tremendous blast of sudden affliction....We have said that this was the picture of a natural heart. This, to our view, is the great and crying mischief of the book. Jane Eyre is throughout the personification of an unregenerate and undisciplined spirit, the more dangerous to exhibit from that prestige of principles and self-control which is liable to dazzle the eye too much for it to observe the inefficient and unsound foundation on which it rests. It is true Jane does right, and exerts great moral strength, but it is the strength of a mere heathen mind which is a law unto itself. No Christian grace is perceptible upon her. She has inherited in fullest measure the worst sin of our fallen nature – the sin of pride. Jane Eyre is proud, and therefore she is ungrateful too. It pleased God to make her an orphan, friendless, and penniless – yet she thanks nobody, and least of all Him, for the food and raiment, the friends, companions, and instructors of her helpless youth – for the care and education vouchsafed to her till she was capable in mind as fitted in years to provide for herself. On the contrary, she looks upon all that has been done for her not only as her undoubted right, but as falling far short of it. The doctrine of humility is not more foreign to her mind than it is repudiated by her heart. It is by her own talents, virtues, and courage that she is made to attain the summit of human happiness, and, as far as Jane Eyre's own statement is concerned, no one would think that she owed anything either to God above or to man below. She flees from Mr. Rochester, and has not a being to turn to. Why was this? The excellence of the present institutions at Casterton, which succeeded that of Cowan Bridge near Kirkby Lonsdale – these being distinctly, as we hear, the original and the reformed Lowoods of the book – is pretty generally known.[1] Jane had lived there for eight years with 110 girls and fifteen teachers. Why had she formed no friendships among them? Other orphans have left the same and similar institutions, furnished with friends for life, and puzzled with homes to choose from. How comes it that Jane had acquired neither? Among that number of associates there were surely some exceptions to what she so presumptuously stigmatises as 'the society of inferior minds.' Of course it suited the

---

1   See the note on Lowood Institution which appears in Chapter IV of *Jane Eyre*.

author's end to represent the heroine as utterly destitute of the common means of assistance, in order to exhibit both her trials and her powers of self-support – the whole book rests on this assumption – but it is one which, under the circumstances, is very unnatural and very unjust.

Altogether the auto-biography of Jane Eyre is pre-eminently an anti-Christian composition. There is throughout it a murmuring against the comforts of the rich and against the privations of the poor, which, as far as each individual is concerned, is a murmuring against God's appointment – there is a proud and perpetual assertion of the rights of man, for which we find no authority either in God's word or in God's providence – there is that pervading tone of ungodly discontent which is at once the most prominent and most subtle evil which the law and the pulpit, which all civilized society in fact has at the present day to contend with. We do not hesitate to say that the tone of mind and thought which has overthrown authority and violated every code human and divine abroad,[1] and fostered Chartism and rebellion at home,[2] is the same which has also written Jane Eyre.

Still we say again this is a very remarkable book. We are painfully alive to the moral, religious, and literary deficiencies of the picture, and such passages of beauty and power as we have quoted cannot redeem it, but it is impossible not to be spellbound with the freedom of the touch. It would be mere hackneyed courtesy to call it 'fine writing.' It bears no impress of being written at all, but is poured out rather in the heat and hurry of an instinct, which flows ungovernably on to its object, indifferent by what means it reaches it, and unconscious too. As regards the author's chief object, however, it is a failure – that, namely, of making a plain, odd woman, destitute of all the conventional features of feminine attraction, interesting in our sight. We

---

1 The wave of revolutionary movements which swept through Europe in 1848 and 1849 caused severe insecurity in Britain, especially among conservative Tory circles such as those catered to by the *Quarterly Review*.

2 Chartism was a radical labour movement of the 1830s and 1840s aimed at eliminating social and economic injustices through political reform. Its last great expression occurred in 1848, fuelled by the revolutions across the channel and high unemployment in Britain. Rigby is reacting to riots which occurred in March in Glasgow, and to a mass demonstration which took place in London in April. Brontë provides a passing allusion to the movement in Chapter XXIV of *Jane Eyre*.

deny that he has succeeded in this. Jane Eyre, in spite of some grand things about her, is a being totally uncongenial to our feelings from beginning to end. We acknowledge her firmness – we respect her determination – we feel for her struggles; but, for all that, and setting aside higher considerations, the impression she leaves on our mind is that of a decidedly vulgar-minded woman – one whom we should not care for as an acquaintance, whom we should not seek as a friend, whom we should not desire for a relation, and whom we should scrupulously avoid for a governess.

There seem to have arisen in the novel-reading world some doubts as to who really wrote this book; and various rumours, more or less romantic, have been current in Mayfair,[1] the metropolis of gossip, as to the authorship....For our parts, we see no great interest in the question at all. The first edition of 'Jane Eyre' purports to be edited by Currer Bell, one of a trio of brothers, or sisters, or cousins, by names Currer, Acton, and Ellis Bell, already known as the joint-authors of a volume of poems.[2] The second edition the same – dedicated, however, 'by the author,' to Mr. Thackeray; and the dedication (itself an indubitable *chip* of Jane Eyre) signed Currer Bell. Author and editor therefore are one, and we are as much satisfied to accept this double individual under the name of 'Currer Bell,' as under any other, more or less euphonious. Whoever it be, it is a person who, with great mental powers, combines a total ignorance of the habits of society, a great coarseness of taste, and a heathenish doctrine of religion. And as these characteristics appear more or less in the writings of all three, Currer, Acton, and Ellis alike, for their poems differ less in degree of power than in kind, we are ready to accept the fact of their identity or of their relationship with equal satisfaction. At all events there can be no interest attached to the writer of 'Wuthering Heights' – a novel succeeding 'Jane Eyre,' and purporting to be written by Ellis Bell – unless it were for the sake of more individual reprobation. For though there is a decided family likeness between the two, yet the aspect of the Jane and Rochester animals in their native state, as Catherine and Heathfield [sic], is too odiously and abominably pagan to be palatable even

---

1   A fashionable district in London between Oxford Street and Piccadilly, occupying the site of the old fairground.
2   See *A Note on the Text* to the present edition.

to the most vitiated class of English readers. With all the unscrupulousness of the French school of novels it combines that repulsive vulgarity in the choice of its vice which supplies its own antidote.[1] The question of authorship, therefore, can deserve a moment's curiosity only as far as 'Jane Eyre' is concerned, and though we cannot pronounce that it appertains to a real Mr. Currer Bell and to no other, yet that it appertains to a man, and not, as many assert, to a woman, we are strongly inclined to affirm. Without entering into the question whether the power of the writing be above her, or the vulgarity below her, there are, we believe, minutië of circumstantial evidence which at once acquit the feminine hand. No woman – a lady friend, whom we are always happy to consult, assures us – makes mistakes in her own *métier*[2] – no woman *trusses game* and garnishes dessert-dishes with the same hands, or talks of so doing in the same breath. Above all, no woman attires another in such fancy dresses as Jane's ladies assume – Miss Ingram coming down, irresistible, 'in a *morning* robe of sky-blue crape, a gauze azure scarf twisted in her hair!!' No lady, we understand, when suddenly roused in the night, would think of hurrying on '*a frock*.' They have garments more convenient for such occasions, and more becoming too. This evidence seems incontrovertible. Even granting that these incongruities were purposely assumed, for the sake of disguising the female pen, there is nothing gained; for if we ascribe the book to a woman at all, we have no alternative but to ascribe it to one who has, for some sufficient reason, long forfeited the society of her own sex.[3]

And if by no woman, it is certainly also by no artist. The Thackeray eye has had no part there. There is not more disparity between the art of drawing Jane assumes and her evident total ignorance of its first principles, than between the report she gives of her own character and the conclusions we form for ourselves. Not but what, in another sense, the author may be classed as an artist of very high grade. Let him describe the simplest things in nature – a rainy landscape, a

---

1   Emily Brontë's novel *Wuthering Heights* received almost universally bad reviews when it was published in 1847.
2   Realm.
3   Brontë was, understandably, particularly insulted by these kinds of comments. She wrote a bitter and sarcastic response to this attack in her preface to *Shirley*, but it was so extreme Smith, Elder refused to publish it.

cloudy sky, or a bare moorside, and he shows the hand of a master; but the moment he talks of the art itself, it is obvious that he is a complete ignoramus.

We cannot help feeling that this work must be far from beneficial to that class of ladies whose cause it affects to advocate. Jane Eyre is not precisely the mouthpiece one would select to plead the cause of governesses, and it is therefore the greater pity that she has chosen it: for there is none we are convinced which, at the present time, more deserves and demands an earnest and judicious befriending. If these times puzzle us how to meet the claims and wants of the lower classes of our dependants, they puzzle and shame us too in the case of that highest dependant of all, the governess – who is not only entitled to our gratitude and respect by her position, but, in nine cases out of ten, by the circumstances which reduced her to it. For the case of the governess is so much the harder than that of any other class of the community, in that they are not only quite as liable to all the vicissitudes of life, but are absolutely supplied by them. There may be, and are, exceptions to this rule, but the real definition of a governess, in the English sense, is a being who is our equal in birth, manners, and education, but our inferior in worldly wealth. Take a lady, in every meaning of the word, born and bred, and let her father pass through the gazette, and she wants nothing more to suit our highest *beau idéal* of a guide and instructress to our children. We need the imprudencies, extravagancies, mistakes, or crimes of a certain number of fathers, to sow that seed from which we reap the harvest of governesses. There is no other class of labourers for hire who are thus systematically supplied by the misfortunes of our fellow-creatures. There is no other class which so cruelly requires its members to be, in birth, mind, and manners, above their station, in order to fit them for their station. From this peculiarity in their very qualifications for office result all the peculiar and most painful anomalies of their professional existence. The line which severs the governess from her employers is not one which will take care of itself, as in the case of a servant. If she sits at table she does not shock you – if she opens her mouth she does not distress you – her appearance and manners are likely to be as good as your own – her education rather better; there is nothing upon the face of the thing to stamp her as having been called to a different state of life from that in which it has pleased God to place you; and there-fore the distinction has to be kept up by a fictitious barrier which presses with cruel weight upon the mental strength or constitutional vanity of a woman. People talk of the prevailing vanity of governesses, and we grant it in one sense fully – but how should it not be so? If a governess have a grain of vanity in her composition, it is sought and probed for by every species of slight and mortification, intentional or not, till it starts into unnatural life beneath the irritation. She must be a saint, or no woman at all, who can rise above those perpetual little dropping-water trials to which the self-love of an averagely-placed governess is exposed. That fearful fact that the lunatic asylums of this country are supplied with a larger proportion of their inmates from the ranks of young governesses than from any other class of life,[1] is a sufficient proof how seldom she can. But it is not her vanity which sends her there, but her *wounded* vanity – the distinction is great – and wounded vanity, as all medical men will tell us, is the rock on which most minds go to pieces.

Man cannot live by the head alone, far less woman. A governess has no equals, and therefore can have no sympathy. She is a burden and restraint in society, as all must be who are placed ostensibly at the same table and yet are forbidden to help themselves or to be helped to the same viands. She is a bore to almost any gentleman, as a tabooed woman, to whom he is interdicted from granting the usual privileges of the sex, and yet who is perpetually crossing his path. She is a bore to most ladies by the same rule, and a reproach too – for her dull, fagging, bread-and-water life is perpetually putting their pampered listlessness to shame. The servants invariably detest her, for she is a dependant like themselves, and yet, for all that, as much their superior in other respects as the family they both serve. Her pupils may love her, and she may take the deepest interest in them, but they cannot be her friends. She must, to all intents and purposes, live alone, or she transgresses that invisible but rigid line which alone establishes the distance between herself and her employers.

We do not deny that there are exceptions to this statement – that there are many governesses who are treated with an almost undue

---

1   See the note on this topic in Appendix C.1.

equality and kindness – that there are many who suffer from slights which they entirely make for themselves, and affect a humility which is never needed – and also that there is no class in which there are women so encroaching, so *exigeantes*,[1] and so disagreeable. But still these are exceptions, let them be ever so numerous. The broad and real characteristics of the governess's qualifications, position, and trials are such as we have described, and must be such. Nor have we brought them forward with any view, or hope, or even with any wish to see them remedied, for in the inherent constitution of English habits, feelings, and prejudices, there is no possibility that they should be....all this cannot be altered with us. We shall ever prefer to place those immediately about our children who have been born and bred with somewhat of the same refinement as ourselves. We must ever keep them in a sort of isolation, for it is the only means for maintaining that distance which the reserve of English manners and the decorum of English families exact. That true justice and delicacy in the employer which would make a sunshine even in a barren schoolroom must ever be too rare to be depended upon. That familiarity which should level all distinction a right-thinking governess would scorn to attempt; – all this must be continued as it is. But there *is* one thing, the absence of which need not be added to the other drawbacks of her lot; which would go far to compensate to her for the misfortunes which reduced her to this mode of life, and for the trials attendant upon it – for the years of chilly solitude through which the heart is kept shivering upon a diet that can never sufficiently warm it, and that in the longing season of youth – for the nothing less than maternal cares and solicitudes for which she reaps no maternal reward – for a life spent in harness from morning till night, and from one year's end to another – for the old age and incapacity creeping on and threatening to deprive her even of that mode of existence which habit has made endurable – there is something that would compensate for all this, and that is *better pay*....

There is something positively usurious in the manner with which the misfortunes of the individual or the general difficulty of the times is now-a-days constantly taken advantage of to cut the stipend of the

---

1 Demanding.

governess down to the lowest ratio that she will accept.... 'And they are very glad to get that, I can tell you,' is the cold-hearted rejoinder, if you expostulate on the injustice of throwing all the labour of the teacher and many of the chief duties of a parent upon the shoulders of a young woman, for the remuneration of thirty or even twenty pounds a-year. It may be quite true that she is glad to get even this; and if so, it is very deplorable: but this has no relation to the services exacted and the assistance given; and these should be more especially the standard where the plaintiff, as in the case of the governess, possesses no means of resistance. Workmen may rebel, and tradesmen may combine, not to let you have their labour or their wares under a certain rate; but the governess has no refuge – no escape; she is a needy *lady*, whose services are of far too precious a kind to have any stated market value, and is therefore left to the mercy, or what they call the *means*, of the family that engages here....

Women, whose husbands leave them in peace from morning till night, for counting-houses or lawyers' offices – certainly leave them with nothing better to do than to educate and attend to their children – must now, forsooth, be keeping ill-paid governesses for those duties which one would hope a peeress only unwillingly relinquishes. Women, from whom society requires nothing but that they should quietly and unremittingly do that for which their station offers them the happy leisure, must now treat themselves to one of those *pro-mammas* who, owing to various causes, more or less distressing, have become so plentiful that they may be had *cheap!* If more governesses find a penurious maintenance by these means, more mothers are encouraged to neglect those duties, which, one would have thought, they would have been as jealous of as of that first duty of all that infancy requires from them. It is evident, too, that by this unfair demand the supply has been suddenly increased. Farmers and tradespeople are now educating their daughters for governesses as a mode of advancing them a step in life, and thus a number of underbred young women have crept into the profession who have brought down the value of salaries and interfered with the rights of those whose birth and misfortunes leave them no other refuge....

While we therefore applaud heartily the efforts for their comfort and relief which have been made within the last few years, in the establishment of the Governesses' Benevolent Institution, we look with sorrow, and almost with horror, at the disclosures which those efforts have brought to light. There is no document which more painfully exposes the peculiar tyranny of our present state of civilization than those pages in the Report of this Society containing the list of candidates for the few and small annuities which the Institution is as yet in the condition to give. We know of nothing, in truth or fiction, more affecting than the sad and simple annals of these afflicted and destitute ladies, many of them with their aristocratic names, who, having passed through that course of servitude which, as we have shown, is peculiarly and inevitable deprived of most of those endearing sympathies which gladden this life, are now left in their old age or sickness without even the absolute necessaries for existence. With minds also which, from their original refinement and constant cultivation, have the keener sense of the misery and injustice of their lot; for the delicate and well-bred lady we at first congratulated ourselves on having engaged in our family is equally the same when we cast her off to shift for herself. What a mockery must all this thankless acquisition of knowledge, which has been the object of her study and the puff in her credentials, appear to her now!...

The 'Queen's College for Female Education, and for granting Certificates of Qualification to Governesses'[1] is another new establishment which promises very essentially to promote the interest of this class of ladies. We have not space to enter into its many merits: we would only observe, that, as the real and highest responsibility and recommendation of an *English* governess must ever rest more upon her moral than her literary qualifications, the plan of subjecting her to an examination upon the latter appears to us neither wise nor fair. This plan, it is true, has been pursued with tolerable success abroad, but it must be kept in mind that the foreign governess is a mere teacher, whose duties cease with the school-room hours, who has her three-months' holiday in the year, and who has, in short, little or nothing to do with the moral guidance of her pupils. What we, on the contrary, require and seek for our children is not a learned machine stamped and ticketed with credentials like a piece of patent goods, but

---

1   See note on this college in Appendix C.4.

rather a woman endowed with that sound principle, refinement, and sense, which no committee of education in the world could ascertain or certify. At the best, all parents of sense must be aware that no governess can teach an art or accomplishment like a regular professor, and that her vocation is rather the encouraging and directing her pupils in such pursuits, than the positive imparting of them. We perceive that the submission to this examination is, for the present, nominally optional; but it is easy to foresee that if some ladies, in order to obtain the promised certificate, go through it, it will soon be made a necessary condition with all. This we consider unfair. As it is, the advantage is already sufficiently on the English mother's side in the balance. If she wishes for the same system as that pursued on the continent in one respect, she should adopt it in all, and she would soon discover how greatly she was the loser.

Appendix D: Jane Eyre and the Proper Young Woman

The Daughters of England: Their Position in Society, Character and Responsibilities, Sarah Stickney Ellis,[1] 1842

If it were possible for a human being to be suddenly, and for the first time, awakened to consciousness, with the full possession of all its reasoning faculties, the natural inquiry of such a being would be, "What am I? – how am I to act? – and, what are my capabilities for action?"

The sphere upon which a young woman enters on first leaving school, or, to use a popular phrase, on "completing her education," is so entirely new to her, her mind is so often the subject of new impressions, and her attention so frequently absorbed by new motives for exertion, that, if at all accustomed to reflect, we cannot doubt but she will make these, or similar questions, the subject of serious inquiry – "What is my position in society? What do I aim at? And what means do I intend to employ for the accomplishment of my purpose?" And it is to assist any of the daughters of England, who may be making these inquires in sincerity of heart, that I would ask their attention to the following pages; just as an experienced traveller, who had himself often stepped aside from the safest path, and found the difficulty of returning, would be anxious to leave directions for others who might follow, in order that they might avoid the dangers with which he had already become acquainted, and pursue their course with greater certainty of attaining the end desired.

First, then, What is your position in society? For, until this point is clearly settled in your own mind, it would be vain to attempt any description of the plan to be pursued. The settlement of this point, however, must depend upon yourselves. Whether you are rich, or poor, an orphan, or the child of watchful parents – one of a numerous family, or comparatively alone – filling an exalted or an humble position – of highly gifted mind, or otherwise – all these points must be clearly ascertained before you can properly understand the kind of

---

1   Sarah Stickney Ellis (1799-1872), influential writer of advice manuals and conduct books for women. Her other works include *The Women of England* (1838), *The Wives of England* (1843), and *The Mothers of England* (1843).

duty required of you. How these questions might be answered, is of no importance to the writer, in the present stage of this work. The importance of their being clearly and faithfully answered to yourselves, is all she would enforce.

For my own purpose, it is not necessary to go further into your particular history or circumstances, than to regard you as women, and, as I hope, Christian women. As Christian women, then, I address you. This is placing you on high ground; yet surely there are few of my young country women who would be willing to take lower.

As women, then, the first thing of importance is to be content to be inferior to men – inferior in mental power, in the same proportion that you are inferior in bodily strength. Facility of movement, aptitude, and grace, the bodily frame of woman may possess in a higher degree than that of man; just as in the softer touches of mental and spiritual beauty, her character may present a lovelier page than his. Yet, as the great attribute of power must still be wanting there, it becomes more immediately her business to inquire how this want may be supplied.

An able and eloquent writer on "Woman's Mission,"[1] has justly observed, that woman's strength is in her influence. And, in order to render this influence more complete, you will find on examination, that you are by nature endowed with peculiar faculties – with a quickness of perception, facility of adaptation, and acuteness of feeling, which fit you especially for the part you have to act in life; and which, at the same time, render you, in a higher degree than men, susceptible both of pain and pleasure.

These are your qualifications as mere women. As Christians, how wide is the prospect which opens before you – how various the claims upon your attention – how vast your capabilities – how deep the responsibility which those capabilities involve! In the first place, you are not alone; you are one of a family – of a social circle – of a community – of a nation. You are a being whose existence will never terminate, who *must* live for ever, and whose happiness or misery through that endless future which lies before you, will be influenced by the choice you are now in the act of making.

1   Sarah Lewis. See Appendix C.3.

What, then, is the great object of your life? "To be good and happy," you will probably say; or, "To be happy and good." Which is it? For there is an important difference in giving precedence to one or the other of these two words. In one case, your aim is to secure to yourself all the advantages you can possibly enjoy, and wait for the satisfaction they produce, before you begin the great business of self-improvement. In the other, you look at your duties first, examine them well, submit yourself without reserve to their claims, and, having made them habitual, reap your reward in that happiness of which no human being can deprive you, and which no earthly event can entirely destroy....Again, is your aim to live for this world only, or for eternity? This is the question of supreme importance, which all who profess to be Christians, and who think seriously, must ask and answer to themselves. There can be no delay here. Time is silently deciding this question for you. Before another day has passed, you will be so much nearer to the kingdom of heaven, or so much farther from it. Another day, another, and another, of this fearful indecision, will be adding to your distance from the path of peace, and rendering your task more difficult if you should afterwards seek to return.

If it be your deliberate desire to live for this world only, all the highest faculties of your nature may then lie dormant, for there is no field of exercise here, to make the cultivation of them worth the pains. If it is your deliberate desire to live for this world only, the improvement of the bodily senses becomes more properly the object of primary interest, in order that you may taste, smell, feel, hear, and see, with more acuteness. A little invention, a little calculation, a little observation of cause and effect, may be necessary, in order that the senses may be gratified in a higher degree; but beyond this, all would indeed by worse than vanity, that would tend to raise the human mind to knowledge of its own capabilities, and yet leave it to perish with the frail tenement it inhabits.

I cannot, however, suppose it possible that any daughter of Christian parents, in this enlightened country, would deliberately make so blind, so despicable a choice. And if your aim be to live for eternity; if you would really make this an object, not merely to read or to talk about, but to strive after, as the highest good you are capable of conceiving, then is the great mystery of your being unravelled – then is a field of exercise laid open for the noblest faculties of your soul – then has faith its true foundation, hope its unextinguishable beacon, and charity its sure reward.[1]

I must now take it for granted, that the youthful reader of these pages has reflected seriously upon her position in society as a woman, has acknowledged her inferiority to man, has examined her own nature, and found there a capability of feeling, a quickness of perception, and a facility of adaptation, beyond what he possesses, and which, consequently, fit her for a distinct and separate sphere; and I would also gladly persuade myself, that the same individual, as a Christian woman, has made her decision not to live for herself, so much as for others; but, above all, not live for this world, so much as for eternity. The question then arises – What means are to be adopted in the pursuit of this most desirable end? Some of my young readers will perhaps be disposed to exclaim, "Why, this is but the old story of giving up the world, and all its pleasures!" But let them not be too hasty in their conclusions. It is not a system of giving up which I am about to recommend to them, so much as one of attaining. My advice is rather to advance than to retreat, yet to be sure that you advance in the right way.

★ ★ ★ ★

I have already stated, that women, in their position in life, must be content to be inferior to men; but as their inferiority consists chiefly in their want of power, this deficiency is abundantly made up to them by their capability of exercising influence; it is made up to them also in other ways, incalculable in their number and extent; but in none so effectually as by that order of Divine Providence which places them, in a moral and religious point of view, on the same level with man; nor can it be a subject of regret to any right-minded woman, that they are not only exempt from the most laborious occupations both of mind and body, but also from the necessity of engaging in those eager pecuniary speculations, and in that fierce conflict of worldly interests by which men are so deeply occupied as to be in a manner

---

1   See 1 Corinthians 13:13.

compelled to stifle their best feelings, until they become in reality the characters they at first only assumed. Can it be a subject of regret to any kind and feeling woman, that her sphere of action is one adapted to the exercise of the affections, where she may love, and trust, and hope, and serve, to the utmost of her wishes? Can it be a subject of regret that she is not called upon, so much as man, to calculate, to compete, to struggle, but rather to occupy a sphere in which the elements of discord cannot with propriety be admitted – in which beauty and order are expected to denote her presence, and where the exercise of benevolence is the duty she is most frequently called upon to perform.

Women almost universally consider themselves, and wish to be considered by others, as extremely affectionate; scarcely can a more severe libel be pronounced upon a woman than to say that she is not so. Now the whole law of woman's life is a law of love. I propose, therefore, to treat the subject in this light – to try whether the neglect of their peculiar duties does not imply an absence of love, and whether the principle of love, thoroughly carried out, would not so influence their conduct and feelings as to render them all which their best friends could desire.

Let us, however, clearly understand each other at the outset. To love, is a very different thing from a desire to be beloved. To love, is woman's nature – to be beloved is the consequence of her having properly exercised and controlled that nature. To love, is a woman's duty – to be beloved, is her reward.

★ ★ ★ ★

Of all kinds of knowledge, that of our own ignorance, is the first to be acquired. It is an humbling lesson for those to learn, who are built up on the foundation of what is called a good education; yet, such is the fact, that the knowledge which young ladies bring home with them from school, forms but a very small part of that which they will be expected to possess. Indeed, such is the illimitable nature of knowledge, that persons can only be said to know much or little by comparison. It is by comparing ourselves with others, and especially with those who are more advanced in life, that we first learn the important secret of our own deficiencies. And it is good to keep the mind open to this truth, for without having clearly ascertained our own inferiority, we should always be liable to make the most egregious mistakes, not only by telling those around us what they already know, and wearying our acquaintance with the most tedious common-place; but by the worst kind of false assumption – by placing ourselves in exalted positions, and thereby rendering our ignorance more conspicuous.

★　★　★　★

Another form which the love of distinction assumes, is that of singularity. I have already said much on the subject of good taste, to show that it holds an important place among the excellencies of woman, so much so, as almost to supply the want of judgement, where that quality is deficient. Nothing, however, can more effecutally prove the absence of good taste in women, than to be singular by design. Many are so constituted as to be unavoidably singular; but even this is only reconciled by their friends on the ground that they would lose much in originality and strength of character, by studying to be more like the generality of women.

. . . .

There is yet another flight of female ambition, another course which the love of distinction is apt to make, more product of folly, and of disappointment, perhaps, than all the rest. It is the ambition of the female author who writes for fame. Could those young aspirants know how little real dignity there is connected with the *trade* of authorship, their harps would be exchanged for distaffs, their rose-tinted paper would be converted into ashes, and their Parnassus[1] would dwindle to a molehill....The same want of sympathy which so often inspires the first effort of female authorship, might often find a sweet and abundant interchange of kindness in many a faithful heart beside the homely hearth. And after all, there is more true poetry in the fire-side affections of early life, than in all those sympathetic associations with unknown and untried developments of mind, which ever have existed either amongst the sons or the daughters of men.

1　A mountain in Greece sacred to the Muses. It thus represents artistic aspiration.

Taking a more sober view of the case, there are, unquestionably, subjects of deep interest with which women have opportunities peculiar to themselves of becoming acquainted, and thus of benefiting their fellow creatures through the medium of their writings. But, after all, literature is not the natural channel for a woman's feelings; and pity not envy, ought to be the meed of her who writes for the public. How much of what with other women is reserved for the select and chosen intercourse of affection, with her must be laid bare to the coarse cavillings, and coarser commendations, of amateur or professional critics. How much of what no woman loves to say, except to the listening ear of domestic affection, by her must be told – nay, blazoned to the world. And then, in her season of depression, or of wounded feeling, when her spirit yearns to sit in solitude, or even in darkness, so that it may be still; to know and feel that the very essence of that spirit, now embodied in a palpable form, has become an article of sale and bargain, tossed over from the hands of one workman to another, free alike to the touch of the prince and the peasant, and no longer to be reclaimed at will by the original possessor, let the world receive it as it may.

Is such, I ask, an enviable distinction?

Appendix E: Race, Empire, and the West Indies

1. "Occasional Discourse on the Negro Question," Unsigned [Thomas Carlyle][1]

Fraser's Magazine, December 1849

The following Occasional Discourse, delivered by we know not whom, and of date seemingly above a year back, may perhaps be welcome to here and there a speculative reader. It comes to us, – no speaker named, no time or place assigned, no commentary of any sort given, – in the handwriting of the so-called 'Doctor,' properly 'Absconded Reporter,' Dr. Phelim M'Quirk, whose singular powers of reporting, and also whose debts, extravagances, and sorrowful insidious finance-operations, now winded up by a sudden disappearance, to the grief of many poor tradespeople, are making too much noise in the police-offices at present! Of M'Quirk's composition we by no means suppose it to be; but from M'Quirk, as the last traceable source, it comes to us; – offered, in fact, by his respectable unfortunate landlady, desirous to make up part of her losses in this way.

To absconded reporters who bilk their lodgings, we have of course no account to give; but if the Speaker be of any eminence or substantiality, and feel himself aggrieved by the transaction, let him understand that such, and such only, is our connexion with him or his affairs. As the Colonial and Negro question is still alive, and likely to grow livelier for some time,[2] we have accepted the Article, at a cheap market-rate; and give it publicity, without in the least committing ourselves to the strange doctrines and notions shadowed forth in it. Doctrines and notions which, we rather suspect, are pretty much in a

---

1 Thomas Carlyle (1795-1881), influential Scottish essayist and historian. Although published anonymously this piece was immediately identifiable as his, due to its distinctive style and narrative voice. He later expanded the article and published it as a pamphlet under the title "Occasional Discourse on the Nigger Question" (1853).
2 The Act ending British participation in the slave trade was passed in 1807, while slavery itself was abolished throughout the British Empire in 1833. The political, economic, ethical, and racial issues surrounding slavery, however, continued to be controversial throughout the century.

'minority of one,' in the present era of the world! Here, sure enough, are peculiar views of the Rights of Negroes; involving, it is probable, peculiar ditto of innumerable other rights, duties, expectations, wrongs and disappointments, much argued of, by logic and by grape-shot, in these emancipated epochs of the human mind! – Silence now, however; and let the Speaker himself enter.

My Philanthropic Friends, – It is my painful duty to address some words to you, this evening, on the Rights of Negroes. Taking, as we hope we do, an extensive survey of social affairs, which we find all in a state of the frightfullest embroilment, and as it were, of inextricable final bankruptcy, just at present; and being desirous to adjust ourselves in that huge upbreak, and unutterable welter of tumbling ruins, and to see well that our grand proposed Association of Associations, the UNIVERSAL ABOLITION-OF-PAIN ASSOCIATION, which is meant to be the consummate golden flower and summary of modern Philan-thropisms all in one, do *not* issue us a universal 'Sluggard-and-Scoundrel Protection Society,' – we have judged that, before constituting ourselves, it would be very proper to commune earnestly with one another, and discourse together on the leading elements of our great Problem, which surely is one of the greatest. With this view the Council has decided both that the Negro Question, as lying at the bottom, was to be the first handled, and if possible the first settled; and then also, what was of much more questionable wisdom, that – that, in short, I was to be Speaker on the occasion. An honourable duty; yet, as I said, a painful one! – Well, you shall hear what I have to say on the matter; and you will not in the least like it.

West-Indian affairs, as we all know, and some of us know to our cost, are in a rather troublous condition this good while.[1] In regard to West Indian affairs, however, Lord John Russell[2] is able to comfort us with one fact, indisputable where so many are dubious, That the

---

1   The British West Indies, which depended on slave labour to harvest sugarcane and other plantation crops, was particularly hard hit by abolition. Although white planters were allotted twenty million pounds in compensation for loss of labour and property, a series of bankruptcies and financial failures occurred throughout the 1840s. This situation was exacerbated by the growing movement towards free trade from 1842 on.

2   Lord John Russell (1792-1878), author, orator, and influential Whig politician. He held the position of colonial secretary, foreign secretary, and was prime minister of England 1846-52 and 1865-66.

Negroes are all very happy and doing well. A fact very comfortable indeed. West Indian Whites, it is admitted, are far enough from happy; West Indian Colonies not unlike sinking wholly into ruin: at home too, the British Whites are rather badly off; several millions of them hanging on the verge of continual famine; and in single towns, many thousands of them very sore put to it, at this time, not to live 'well,' or as a man should, in any sense temporal or spiritual, but to live at all: – these, again, are uncomfortable facts; and they are extremely extensive and important ones. But, thank Heavens, our interesting Black population, – equalling almost in number of heads one of the Ridings of Yorkshire,[1] and in *worth* (in quantity of intellect, faculty, docility, energy, and available human valour and value) perhaps one of the streets of Seven Dials,[2] – are all doing remarkably well. 'Sweet blighted lilies,' – as the American epitaph on the Nigger child has it, – sweet blighted lilies, they are holding up their heads again! How pleasant, in the universal bankruptcy abroad, and dim dreary stagnancy at home, as if for England too there remained nothing but to suppress Chartist riots, banish unfed Irishmen, vote the supplies,[3] and *wait* with arms crossed till black Anarchy and Social Death devoured us also, as it has done the others; how pleasant to have always this fact to fall back upon; Our beautiful Black darlings are at last happy; with little labour except to the teeth, *which* surely, in those excellent horse-jaws of theirs, will not fail!

Exeter Hall,[4] my philanthropic friends, has had its way in this matter. The Twenty Millions, a mere trifle despatched with a single dash of the pen, are paid;[5] and far over the sea, we have a few black persons rendered extremely 'free' indeed. Sitting yonder with their

---

1   Yorkshire, the largest of the northern counties of England, consisted of three relatively sparsely populated "ridings," or administrative districts.

2   A slum district in London.

3   For "Chartist riots" see the note on Chartism in Appendix D.4. The Irish potato famine of 1845 caused a crisis emigration to England which panicked many middle-class observers. "Vote the supplies" describes the procedure by which Parliament grants the ruling government a sum of money for expenses not covered by revenue. This type of emergency funding would obviously be needed to deal with riots and famine.

4   A large auditorium which opened in London in 1831. It was the headquarters for various charitable and philanthropic societies, as well as such dissenting religious groups as Methodists, Quakers, and Unitarians.

5   See note 1, p. 608.

beautiful muzzles up to the ears in pumpkins, imbibing sweet pulps and juices; the grinder and incisor teeth ready for every new work, and the pumpkins cheap as grass in those rich climates: while the sugar-crops rot round them uncut, because labour cannot be hired, so cheap are the pumpkins: – and at home we are but required to rasp from the breakfast loaves of our own English labourers some slight 'differential sugar-duties,' and lend a poor half-million or a few poor millions now and then, to keep that beautiful state of matters going on.[1] A state of matters lovely to contemplate, in these emancipated epochs of the human mind; which has earned us not only the praises of Exeter Hall, and loud long-eared hallelujahs of laudatory psalmody from the Friends of Freedom everywhere, but lasting favour (it is hoped) from the Heavenly Powers themselves: – which may at least justly appeal to the Heavenly Powers, and ask them, If ever in terrestrial procedure they saw the match of it? Certainly in the past history of the human species it has no parallel; nor, one hopes, will it have in the future.

Sunk in deep froth-oceans of 'Benevolence,' 'Fraternity,' 'Emancipation-principle,' 'Christian Philanthropy,' and other most amiable-looking, but most baseless and in the end baleful and all-bewildering jargon, – sad product of a sceptical Eighteenth Century, and of poor human hearts left *destitute* of any earnest guidance, and disbelieving that there ever was any, Christian or Heathen, and reduced to believe in rosepink Sentimentalism alone, and to cultivate the same under its Christian, Antichristian, Broad-brimmed,[2] Brutus-headed[3] and other forms, – has not the human species gone strange roads, during that period? and poor Exeter Hall, cultivating the Broadbrimmed form of Christian Sentimentalism, and long talking and bleating and braying in that strain, has it not worked out results? Our West Indian Legislatings, with their spoutings, anti-spoutings and interminable jangle and babble; our Twenty millions down on the nail for Blacks of our own; Thirty gradual millions more, and many brave British lives to boot, in

---

1 At the time Carlyle is writing the duty on slave-grown sugar cane was higher than that on sugar cane grown by freemen. He is suggesting that (white) English labourers are subsidizing this situation and suffering because of it.

2 A reference to the broad-brimmed hats worn by Quakers.

3 A reference to a kind of wig known as a "Brutus," often worn by early nineteenth-century republicans and reformers.

watching Blacks of other people's;[1] and now at last our ruined sugar-estates, differential sugar-duties, 'immigration loan,'[2] and beautiful Blacks sitting there up to the ears in pumpkins, and doleful Whites sitting here without potatoes to eat:[3] never till now, I think, did the sun look down on such a jumble of human nonsenses; – of which, with the two hot nights of the Missing-Despatch Debate, God grant that the measure might now at last be full![4] But no, it is not yet full; we have a long way to travel back, and terrible founderings to make, and in fact an immense load of nonsense to dislodge from our poor heads, and manifold cobwebs to rend from our poor eyes, before we get into the road again, and can begin to act as serious men that have work to do in this Universe, and no longer as windy sentimentalists that merely have speeches to deliver and despatches to write. Oh Heaven, in West-Indian matters, and in all manner of matters, it is so with us: the more is the sorrow! –

The West Indies, it appears, are short of labour; as indeed is very conceivable in those circumstances: where a Black man by working about half an hour a-day (such is the calculation) can supply himself, by aid of sun and soil, with as much pumpkin as will suffice, he is likely to be a little stiff to raise into hard work! Supply and demand, which, science says, should be brought to bear on him, have an uphill task of it with such a man. Strong sun supplies itself gratis, rich soil in those unpeopled or half-peopled regions almost gratis; those are *his* 'supply;' and half an hour a-day, directed upon these, will produce pumpkin, which is his 'demand.' The fortunate Black man, very swiftly does he settle *his* account with supply and demand: – not so swiftly the less fortunate White man of these tropical localities. He himself cannot work; and his black neighbour, rich in pumpkin, is in no haste to help him. Sunk to the ears in pumpkin, imbibing saccharine juices,

---

1 Carlyle is probably referring to the costs of the Royal Navy anti-slavery squadrons which patrolled the coasts of East and West Africa to inhibit the slave trade of other countries. He specifically mocks this strategy later in the essay.

2 A Parliamentary loan meant to encourage immigration to the West Indies.

3 See note 3, p. 609.

4 The Missing-Despatch Debate took place in the Parliamentary session of 1847–48. It involved a dispatch from the governor of Jamaica which was not received by the chair of the West India Committee. This was either a simple oversight or a deliberate withholding of the dispatch from him by the government, and the argument within the House of Commons on the issue became heated.

and much at his ease in the Creation, he can listen to the less fortunate white man's 'demand,' and take his own time in supplying it. Higher wages, massa;[1] higher; for your cane-crop cannot wait; still higher, – till no conceivable opulence of cane-crop will cover such wages! In Demerara,[2] as I read in the blue book[3] of last year, the cane-crop, far and wide, stands rotting; the fortunate black gentlemen, strong in their pumpkins, having all struck till the 'demand' rise a little, Sweet blighted lilies, now getting up their heads again!

Science, however, has a remedy still. Since the demand is so pressing, and the supply so inadequate (equal in fact to *nothing* in some places, as appears), increase the supply; bring more Blacks into the labour market, then will the rate fall, says science. Not the least surprising part of our West Indian policy is this recipe of 'immigration;' of keeping down the labour-market in those islands by importing new Africans to labour and live there. If the Africans that are already there could be made to lay down their pumpkins and labour for their living, there are already Africans enough. If the new Africans, after labouring a little, take to pumpkins like the others, what remedy is there? To bring in new and ever new Africans, say you, till pumpkins themselves grow dear; till the country is crowded with Africans; and black men there, like white men here, are forced by hunger to labour for their living? That will be a consummation. To have 'emancipated' the West Indies into *Black Ireland*; 'free' indeed, but an Ireland, and black! The world may yet see prodigies; and reality be stranger than a nightmare dream.

Our own white or sallow Ireland, sluttishly starving from age to age on its net-of-parliament 'freedom,' was hitherto the flower of mismanagement among the nations: but what will this be to a Negro Ireland, with pumpkins themselves fallen scarce like potatoes! Imagination cannot fathom such an object; the belly of Chaos never held the like. The human mind, in its wide wanderings, has not dreamt yet of such a 'freedom' as that will be. Towards that, if Exeter Hall and science of supply and demand are to continue our guides in the matter, we are daily travelling, and even struggling, with loans of

---

1   Dialect. Master.
2   A county in British Guiana.
3   See the note on blue books in Appendix C.1.

half-a-million and such-like, to accelerate ourselves.

Truly, my philanthropic friends, Exeter Hall Philanthropy is wonderful; and the Social Science — not a 'gay science,' but a rueful — which finds the secret of this universe in 'supply-and-demand,' and reduces the duty of human governors to that of letting men alone, is also wonderful. Not a 'gay science,' I should say, like some we have heard of; no, a dreary, desolate, and indeed quite abject and distressing one; what we might call, by way of eminence, the *dismal science.* These two, Exeter Hall Philanthropy and the Dismal Science, led by any sacred cause of Black Emancipation, or the like to, fall in love and make a wedding of it, – will give birth to progenies and prodigies; dark extensive moon-calves,[1] unnameable abortions, wide-coiled monstrosities, such as the world has not seen hitherto!

In fact, it will behoove us of this English nation to overhaul our West Indian procedure from top to bottom; and ascertain a little better what it is that Fact and Nature demand of us, and what only Exeter Hall wedded to the Dismal Science demands. To the former set of demands we will endeavour, at our peril, – and worse peril than our purse's, at our soul's peril, – to give all obedience. To the latter we will very frequently demur; and try if we cannot stop short where they contradict the former, – and especially *before* arriving at the black throat of ruin, whither they appear to be leading us. Alas, in many other provinces besides the West Indian, that unhappy wedding of Philanthropic Liberalism and the Dismal Science has engendered such all-enveloping delusions of the mooncalf sort; and wrought huge woe for us, and for the poor civilized world, in these days! And sore will be the battle with said mooncalves; and terrible the struggle to return out of our delusions, floating rapidly on which, not the West Indies alone, but Europe generally is near the Niagara Falls.[2] [*Here various persons, in an agitated manner, with an air of indignation, left the room; especially one very tall gentleman in white trousers, whose boots creaked much. The President, in a resolved voice, with a look of official rigour, whatever his own private feelings might be, enjoined 'Silence, Silence!' The meeting again sat motionless.*]

---

1 Imbeciles.
2 Carlyle uses Niagara Falls as an image of social and political chaos. See his essay "Shooting Niagara: And After?" (1867).

My philanthropic friends, can you discern no fixed headlands in this wide-weltering deluge of benevolent twaddle and revolutionary grape-shot that has burst forth on us; no sure bearings at all? Fact and Nature, it seems to me, say a few words to us, if happily we have still an ear for Fact and Nature. Let us listen a little, and try.

And first, with regard to the West Indies, it may be laid down as a principle, which no eloquence in Exeter Hall, or Westminster Hall,[1] or elsewhere, can invalidate or hide, except for a short time only, That no Black man who will not work according to what ability the gods have given him for working, has the smallest right to eat pumpkin, or to any fraction of land that will grow pumpkin, however plentiful such land may be; but has an indisputable and perpetual *right* to be compelled, by the real proprietors of said land, to do competent work for his living. This is the everlasting duty of all men, black or white, who are born into this world. To do competent work, to labour honestly according to the ability given them; for that and for no other purpose was each one of us sent into this world; and woe is to every man who, by friend or by foe, is prevented from fulfilling this the end of his being. That is the 'unhappy' lot; lot equally unhappy cannot otherwise be provided for man. Whatsoever prohibits or prevents a man from this his sacred appointment to labour while he lives on earth, – that, I say, is the man's deadliest enemy; and all men are called upon to do what is in their power or opportunity towards delivering him from it. If it be his own indolence that prevents and prohibits him, then his own indolence is the enemy he must be delivered from: and the first 'right' he has, – poor indolent blockhead, black or white, is, That every unprohibited man, whatsoever wiser, more industrious person may be passing that way, shall endeavour to 'emancipate' him from his indolence, and by some wise means, as I said, compel him to do the work he is fit for. This is the eternal law of nature for a man, my beneficent Exeter Hall friends; this, that he shall be permitted, encouraged, and if need be compelled to do what work the Maker of him has intended by the making of him for this world! Not that he should eat pumpkin with never such felicity in the West India Islands is, or can be, the blessedness of our black friend; but that he should do

---

1 Probably a reference to Parliament, but possibly to Westminster as a court of justice.

useful work there, according as the gifts have been bestowed on him for that. And his own happiness, and that of others round him, will alone be possible by his and their getting into such a relation that this can be permitted him, and in case of need that this can be compelled him. I beg you to understand this; for you seem to have a little forgotten it, and there lie a thousand inferences in it, not quite useless for Exeter Hall, at present. The idle black man in the West Indies had not long since the right, and will again under better form, if it please Heaven, have the right (actually the first 'right of man' for an indolent person) to be *compelled* to work as he was fit, and to *do* the Maker's will who had constructed him with such and such prefigurements of capability. And I incessantly pray Heaven, all men, the whitest alike and the blackest, the richest and the poorest, in other regions of the world, had attained precisely the same right, the divine right of being compelled (if 'permitted' will not answer) to do what work they are appointed for, and not to go idle another minute, in a life so short! Alas, we had then a perfect world; and the Millennium, and true 'Organization of Labour,' and reign of complete blessedness, for all workers and men, had then arrived, – which in these our own poor districts of the Planet, as we all lament to know, it is very far from having yet done.

Let me suggest another consideration withal. West India Islands, still full of waste fertility, produce abundant pumpkins; pumpkins, however, you will please to observe, are not the sole requisite for human wellbeing. No: for a pig they are the one thing needful; but for a man they are only the first of several things needful. And now, as to the right of chief management in cultivating those West India lands; as to the 'right of property' so-called, and of doing what you like with your own? The question is abstruse enough. Who it may be that has a right to raise pumpkins and other produce on those Islands, perhaps none can, except temporarily, decide. The Islands are good withal for pepper, for sugar, for sage, arrowroot, for coffee, perhaps for cinnamon and precious spices; things far nobler than pumpkins; and leading towards commerces, arts, politics, and social developments, which alone are the noble product, where men (and not pigs with pumpkins) are the parties concerned! Well, all this fruit too, fruit spicy and commercial, fruit spiritual and celestial, so far beyond the merely pumpkinish and grossly terrene, lies in the West India lands; and the ultimate 'proprietorship' of them, – why, I suppose, it will vest in him who can the *best* educe from them whatever of noble produce they were created fit for yielding. He, I compute, is the real 'Vicegerent of the Maker' there; in him, better and better chosen, and not in another, is the 'property' vested by decree of Heaven's chancery itself!

Up to this time it is the Saxon British mainly; they hitherto have cultivated with some manfulness; and when a manfuller class of culti-vators, stronger, worthier to have such land, abler to bring fruit from it, shall make their appearance, – they, doubt it not, by fortune of war and other confused negotiations and vicissitude, will be declared by Nature and Fact to *be* the worthier, and will become proprietors, – perhaps also only for a time. That is the law, I take it; ultimate, supreme, for all lands in all countries under this sky. The one perfect eternal proprietor is the Maker who created them: the temporary better or worst proprietor is he whom the Maker has sent on that mission; he who the best hitherto can educe from said lands the beneficent gifts the Maker endowed them with; or, which is but another definition of the same person, he who leads hitherto the manfullest life on that bit of soil, doing, better than another yet found can do, the Eternal Purpose and Supreme Will there.

And now observe, my friends, it was not Black Quashee[1] or those he represents that made those West India Islands what they are, or can by any hypothesis be considered to have the right of growing pump-kins there. For countless ages, since they first mounted oozy, on the back of earthquakes, from their dark bed in the Ocean deeps, and reeking saluted the tropical Sun, and ever onwards till the European white man first saw them some three short centuries ago, those Islands had produced mere jungle, savagery, poison-reptiles and swamp-malaria: till the white European first saw them, they were as if not yet created, – their noble elements of cinnamon, sugar, coffee, pepper black and grey, lying all asleep, waiting the white Enchanter who should say to them, Awake! Till the end of human history and the sounding of the Trump of Doom,[2] they might have lain so, had

---

1   Quashee was a standard name used to represent the stereotype of both African and West Indian blacks.
2   See 1 Corinthians 15:52.

Quashee and the like of him been the only artists in the game. Swamps, fever-jungles, man-eating Caribs,[1] rattle-snakes, and reeking waste and putrefaction, this had been the produce of them under the incompetent Caribal (what we call Cannibal) possessors till that time; and Quashee knows, himself, whether ever he could have introduced an improvement. Him, had he by a miraculous chance been wafted thither, the Caribals would have eaten, rolling him as a fat morsel under their tongue; for him, till the sounding of the Trump of Doom, the rattle-snakes and savageries would have held on their way. It was not he, then; it was another than he! Never by art of his could one pumpkin have grown there to solace any human throat; nothing but savagery and reeking putrefaction could have grown there. These plentiful pumpkins, I say therefore, are not his: no, they are another's; they are his only under conditions; conditions which Exeter Hall, for the present, has forgotten; but which Nature and the Eternal Powers have by no manner of means forgotten, but do at all moments keep in mind; and, at the right moment, will, with the due impressiveness, perhaps in a rather terrible manner, bring again to our mind also!

If Quashee will not honestly aid in bringing out those sugars, cinnamons, and nobler products of the West Indian Islands, for the benefit of all mankind, then I say neither will the Powers permit Quashee to continue growing pumpkins there for his own lazy benefit; but will sheer him out, by and by, like a lazy gourd overshadowing rich ground; him and all that partake with him, – perhaps in a very terrible manner. For, under favour of Exeter Hall, the 'terrible manner' is not yet quite extinct with the Destinies in this Universe; nor will it quite cease, I apprehend, for soft sawder[2] or philanthropic stump-oratory[3] now or henceforth. No; the gods wish besides pumpkins, that spices and valuable products be grown in their West Indies; thus much they have declared in so making the West Indies: – infinitely more they wish, that manful industrious men occupy their West Indies, not indolent two-legged cattle, however 'happy' over their abundant pumpkins! Both these things, we may be assured, the

---

1   Inhabitants of South America and parts of the Caribbean.
2   Flattery.
3   Political speech making. Stumps were sometimes used as platforms from which to deliver addresses to a crowd.

immortal gods have decided upon, passed their eternal act of parliament for: and both of them, though all terrestrial Parliaments and entities oppose to the death, shall be done. Quashee, if he will not help in bringing out the spices, will get himself made a slave again (which state will be a little less ugly than his present one), and with beneficent whip, since other methods avail not, will be compelled to work. Or, alas, let him look across to Haiti, and trace a far sterner prophecy![1] Let him, by his ugliness, idleness, rebellion, banish all White men from the West Indies, and make it all one Haiti, – with little or no sugar growing, black Peter exterminating black Paul, and where a garden of the Hesperides might be, nothing but a tropical dog-kennel and pestiferous jungle, – does he think that will for ever continue pleasant to gods and men? I see men, the rose-pink cant all peeled away from them, land one day on those black coasts; men *sent* by the Laws of this Universe and the inexorable Course of Things; men hungry for gold, remorseless, fierce as old Buccaneers were; – and a doom for Quashee which I had rather not contemplate! The gods are long-suffering; but the law from the beginning was, He that will not work shall perish from the earth, and the patience of the gods has limits!

Before the West Indies could grow a pumpkin for any Negro, how much European heroism had to spend itself in obscure battle; to sink, in mortal agony, before the jungles, the putrescences and waste savageries could become arable, and the Devils be in some measure chained there! The West Indies grow pine-apples, and sweet fruits, and spices; we hope they will one day grow beautiful Heroic human Lives too, which is surely the ultimate object they were made for: beautiful souls and brave; sages, poets, what not; making the Earth nobler round them, as their kindred from of old have been doing; true 'splinters of the old Harz Rock;' heroic white men, worthy to be called old Saxons,[2] browned with a mahogany tint in those new climates and conditions. But under the soil of Jamaica, before it could even produce spices or any pumpkin, the bones of many thousand British men had

---

1   Haiti won its independence from white colonial rule in 1804. Its subsequent history was sometimes turbulent.
2   Carlyle suggests that the Anglo-Saxon ancestors of the English originally came from the Harz Mountain region of Germany. He is mistaken.

to be laid. Brave Colonel Fortescue, brave Colonel Sedgwick, brave Colonel Brayne,[1] – the dust of many thousand strong old English hearts lies there; worn down swiftly in frightful travail, chaining the Devils, which were manifold. Heroic Blake[2] contributed a bit of his life to that Jamaica. A bit of the great Protector's[3] own life lies there; beneath those pumpkins lies a bit of the life that was Oliver Cromwell's. How the great Protector would have rejoiced to think, that all this was to issue in growing pumpkins to keep Quashee in a comfortably idle condition! No; that is not the ultimate issue; not that.

The West Indian Whites, so soon as this bewilderment of philan-thropic and other jargon abates from them, and their poor eyes get to discern a little what the Facts are and what the Laws are, will strike into another course, I apprehend! I apprehend they will, as a prelimi-nary, resolutely *refuse* to permit the Black man any privilege whatever of pumpkins till he agree for work in return. Not a square inch of soil in those fruitful Isles, purchased by British blood, shall any Black man hold to grow pumpkins for him, except on terms that are fair towards Britain. Fair; see that they be not unfair, not towards ourselves, and still more, not towards him. For injustice is *forever* accursed: and pre-cisely our unfairness towards the enslaved black man has, – by inevitable revulsion and fated turn of the wheel, – brought about these present confusions. Fair towards Britain it will be, that Quashee give work for privilege to grow pumpkins. Not a pumpkin, Quashee, not a square yard of soil, till you agree to do the State so many days of service. Annually that soil will grow you pumpkins; but annually also without fail shall you, for the owner thereof, do your appointed days of labour. The State has plenty of waste soil; but the State will

---

1   Richard Fortescue (?-1655), Robert Sedgwick (?-1656), and William Brayne (?-1657) served as commanders of Oliver Cromwell's forces in Jamaica, and each was briefly governor of the island.

2   Robert Blake (1599-1657), British admiral whose forces destroyed the Spanish West Indian fleet in 1657. He died shortly afterwards.

3   Oliver Cromwell (1599-1658), Puritan general and politician, held the position of Lord Protector of England 1653-58. It was under his rule that England colonized the West Indies. In his series of lectures entitled "On Heroes, Hero-Worship, and the Heroic in History," delivered in 1840 and published in 1841, Carlyle identifies Cromwell as his ideal of the Hero-King.

religiously give you none of it on other terms. The State wants sugar from these Islands, and means to have it; wants virtuous industry in these Islands, and must have it. The State demands of you such service as will bring these results, this latter result which includes all. Not a Black Ireland, by immigration, and boundless black supply for the demand; not that, – may the gods forbid! – but a regulated West Indies, with black working population in adequate numbers; all 'happy,' if they find it possible and *not* entirely unbeautiful to gods and men, which latter result they *must* find possible! All 'happy' enough; that is to say, all working according to the faculty they have got, making a little more divine this earth which the gods have given them. Is there any other 'happiness,' – if it be not that of pigs fattening daily to the slaughter? So will the State speak by and by.

Any poor idle Black man, any idle White man, rich or poor, is a mere eye-sorrow to the State; a perpetual blister on the skin of the State. The State is taking measures, some of them rather extensive in Europe at this very time, and already as in Paris, Berlin, and elsewhere, rather tremendous measures, to *get* its rich white men set to work; for alas, they also have long sat Negro-like up to the ears in pumpkin, regardless of 'work,' and of a world all going to waste for their idleness! Extensive measures, I say; and already (as, in all European lands, this scandalous Year of street-barricades and fugitive sham-kings exhibits) *tremendous* measures; for the thing is instant to be done.[1]

The thing must be done everywhere; *must* is the word. Only it is so terribly difficult to do; and will take generations yet, this of getting our rich European white men 'set to work!' But yours in the West Indies, my obscure Black friends, your work, and the getting of you set to it, is a simple affair; and by diligence, the West Indian legislatures, and Royal governors, setting their faces fairly to the problem, will get it done. You are not 'slaves' now; nor do I wish, if it can be avoided, to see you slaves again: but decidedly you will have to be servants to those that are born *wiser* than you, that are born lords of you, – servants to the whites, if they *are* (as what mortal can doubt they

---

1   A reference to contemporary revolutionary movements taking place in France and Germany. The "sham-king" Carlyle has in mind is probably Louis Philippe, the so-called "citizen king," who accepted the French crown as the elect sovereign of the people in 1830. He was forced to abdicate, and fled to England under the name "Mr. Smith" in 1848.

are?) born wiser than you. That, you may depend on it, my obscure Black friends, is and was always the Law of the World, for you and for all men: To *be* servants, the more foolish of us to the more wise; and only sorrow, futility and disappointment will betide both, till both in some approximate degree get to conform to the same. Heaven's laws are not repealable by Earth, however Earth may try, – and it has been trying hard, in some directions, of late! I say, no well-being, and in the end no being at all, will be possible for you or us, if the law of Heaven is not complied with. And if 'slave' mean essentially 'servant hired for life,' – for life, or by a contract of long continuance and not easily dissoluble, – I ask, Whether, in all human things, the 'contract of long continuance' is not precisely the contract to be desired, were the right terms once found for it? Servant hired for life, were the right terms once found, which I do not pretend they are, seems to me much preferable to servant hired for the month, or by contract dissoluble in a day. An ill-situated servant, that; – servant grown to be *nomadic*; between whom and his master a good relation *cannot* easily spring up!

To state articulately, and put into practical Lawbooks, what on all sides is *fair* from the West India White to the West India Black; what relations the Eternal Maker *has* established between these two creatures of His; what He has written down, with intricate but ineffaceable record, legible to candid human insight, in the respective qualities, strengths, necessities and capabilities of each of the two: this will be a long problem; only to be solved by continuous human endeavour, and earnest effort gradually perfecting itself as experience successively yields new light to it. This will be to '*find* the right terms' of a contract that will endure, and be sanctioned by Heaven, and obtain prosperity on Earth, between the two. A long problem, terribly neglected hitherto; – whence these West-Indian sorrows, and Exeter-Hall monstrosities, just now! But a problem which must be entered upon, and by degrees be completed. A problem which, I think, the English People, if they mean to retain human Colonies, and not Black Irelands in addition to the white, cannot begin too soon! What are the true relations between Negro and White, their mutual duties under the sight of the Maker of them both; what human laws will assist both to comply more and more with these? The solution only to be gained by earnest endeavour and sincere experience, such as have never yet been bestowed on it, is not yet here; the solution is perhaps still distant: but some approximation to it, various real approximations, could be made, and must be made: – this of declaring that Negro and white are *un*related, loose from one another, on a footing of perfect equality, and subject to no law but that of Supply and Demand according to the Dismal Science; this, which contradicts the palpablest facts, is clearly no solution, but a cutting of the knot asunder; and every hour we persist in this is leading us towards *disso*lution instead of solution!

What then is practically to be done? Much, very much, my friends, to which it hardly falls to me to allude at present: but all this of perfect equality, of cutting quite loose from one another; all this, with 'immigration loan,' 'happiness of black peasantry,' and the other melancholy stuff that has followed from it, will first of all require to be *un*done, and have the ground cleared of it, by way of preliminary to 'doing!' –

Already one hears of Black *Adscripti glebæ*;[1] which seems a promising arrangement, one of the first to suggest itself in such a compliency. It appears the Dutch Blacks, in Java, are already a kind of *Adscripts*, after the manner of the old European serfs; bound, by royal authority, to give so many days of work a year.[2] Is not this something like a real approximation; the first step towards all manner of such? Wherever, in British territory, there exists a Black man, and needful work to the just extent is not to be got out of him, such a law, in defect of better, should be brought to bear upon said Black man! How may laws of like purport, conceivable some of them, might be brought to bear upon the Black man and the White, with all despatch, by way of solution instead of dissolution to their complicated case just now! On the whole it ought to be rendered possible, ought it not, for White men to live beside Black men, and in some just manner to command Black men, and produce West-Indian fruitfulness by means of them? West-Indian fruitfulness will need to be produced. If the English cannot

---

1   Latin. Bound to the soil; i.e., a feudal arrangement in which agricultural workers have no choice but to work for the landowner.

2   The Dutch, after a revolt in Java, instituted a system in which blacks were forced to devote part of their land to export crops such as sugar cane and coffee. They then had to deliver them to the government as a form of taxation.

find the method for that, they may rest assured there will another come (Brother Jonathan[1] or still another) who can. He it is whom the gods will bid continue in the West Indies; bidding us ignominiously, Depart ye quack-ridden, incompetent! –

One other remark, as to the present Trade in Slaves, and to our suppression of the same. If buying of black war-captives in Africa, and bringing them over to the Sugar Islands for sale again be, as I think it is, a contradiction of the Laws of this Universe, let us heartily pray Heaven to end the practice; let us ourselves help Heaven to end it, wherever the opportunity is given. If it be the most flagrant and alarming contradiction to the said Laws which is now witnessed on this Earth; so flagrant and alarming that a just man cannot exist, and follow his affairs, in the same Planet with it; why, then indeed – But is it, quite certainly, such? Alas, look at that group of *un*sold, unbought, unmarketable Irish 'free' citizens, dying there in the ditch, whither my Lord of Rackrent[2] and the constitutional sheriffs have evicted them; or at those 'divine missionaries,' of the same free country, now traversing, with rags on back and child on each arm, the principal thoroughfares of London, to tell men what 'freedom' really is; – and admit that there may be doubts on that point! But if it *is*, I say, the most alarming contradiction to the said Laws which is now witnessed on this earth; so flagrant a contradiction that a just man cannot exist, and follow his affairs, in the same Planet with it, then, sure enough, let us, in God's name, fling aside all our affairs, and hasten to put an end to it, as the first thing the Heavens want us to do. By all manner of means; this thing done, the Heavens will prosper all other things with us! Not a doubt of it, – provided your premiss be not doubtful.

But now further more give me leave to ask, Whether the way of doing it is this somewhat surprising one, of trying to blockade the Continent of Africa itself, and to watch slave-ships along that

---

1 British name for Americans. The nineteenth-century equivalent of "Uncle Sam."

2 Name used to describe Irish landlords who rented tenant cottages to the highest bidder, thus ensuring the greatest possible income for themselves. If the tenant failed to pay the rent they were evicted both from the cottage and the land, as Carlyle describes in the rest of this sentence. For a satirical picture of Irish landlords see Maria Edgeworth's novel *Castle Rackrent* (1800).

extremely extensive and unwholesome coast? The enterprize is very gigantic; and proves hitherto as futile as any enterprize has lately done. Certain wise men once, before this, set about confining the cuckoo by a big circular wall; but they could not manage it![1] – Watch the Coast of Africa, good part of the Coast of the terraqueous Globe? And the living centres of this slave mischief, the live-coals that produce all this world-wide smoke, it appears, be simply in two points, Cuba and Brazil, which *are* perfectly accessible and manageable.

If the Laws of Heaven do authorize you to keep the whole word in a pother about this question; if you really can appeal to the Almighty God upon it, and set common interests, and terrestrial considerations, and common sense, at defiance in behalf of it, – why, in Heaven's name not go to Cuba and Brazil with a sufficiency of 74-gun ships; and signify to those nefarious countries: That their procedure on the Negro Question is too bad; that, of all the solecisms now submitted to on Earth, it is the most alarming and transcendent, and, in fact, is such that a just man cannot follow his affairs any longer in the same Planet with it; that they clearly will not, the nefarious populations will not, for love or fear, watching or entreaty, respect the rights of the Negro enough: – wherefore you here, with your Seventy-fours, are come to be King over them, and will on the spot henceforth see for yourselves that they do it! Why not, if Heaven do send you? The thing can be done; easily, if you are sure of that proviso. It can be done: it is the way to 'suppress the Slave-trade;' and so far as yet appears, the one way.

Most thinking people! – If hen-stealing prevail to a plainly unendurable extent, will you station police-officers at every henroost; and keep them watching and cruizing incessantly to and fro over the Parish, in the unwholesome dark, at enormous expense, with almost no effect; or will you not try rather to discover where the fox's den is, and kill the fox? Most thinking people, you know the fox and his den;

---

1 An apocryphal story about the village of Gotham, located in Nottinghamshire, whose inhabitants had a reputation for foolishness. The town supposedly believed it could create an eternal summer by trapping a cuckoo, and in order to achieve this built a hedge around it. Obviously enough, the bird simply flew away. Carlyle suggests attempting to blockade Africa will have roughly the same effectiveness. See note 1, p. 611.

there he is, – kill him, and discharge your cruizers and police-watchers!

Oh, my friends, I feel there is an immense fund of Human Stupidity circulating among us, and much clogging our affairs for some time past! A certain man has called us, 'of all peoples the wisest in action;' but he added, 'the stupidest in speech;'[1] – and it is a sore thing in these constitutional times, times mainly of universal Parliamentary and other Eloquence, that the 'speakers' have all first to emit, in such tumultuous volumes, their human stupor, as the indispensable preliminary, and everywhere we must first see that and its results *out* before beginning any business! (*Explicit MS.*)

2. "The Negro Question," Unsigned [John Stuart Mill][2]

Fraser's Magazine, January 1850

[IF all the meetings at Exeter Hall be not presided over by strictly impartial chairmen, they ought to be. We shall set an example to our pious brethren in this respect, by giving publicity to the following letter. Our readers have now both sides of the question before them, and can form their own opinions upon it. – EDITOR.]

To the Editor of *Fraser's Magazine*.
Sir,

Your last month's Number contains a speech against the 'rights of Negroes,' the doctrines and spirit of which ought not to pass without remonstrance. The author issues his opinions, or rather ordinances, under imposing auspices; no less than those of the 'immortal gods.' 'The Powers,' 'the Destinies,' announce through him, not only what *will* be, but what *shall* be done; what they 'have decided upon, passed their eternal act of parliament for.' This is speaking 'as one having

---

1 Carlyle quotes his own opinion in *Past and Present* (1843): "Of all the Nations in the world at present the English are the stupidest in speech, the wisest in action."

2 John Stuart Mill (1806–73), writer, philosopher, and M.P. for Westminster 1865–68. He and Thomas Carlyle had at one point been good friends, but by the 1840s their political and philosophical positions had diverged widely. This piece, a direct rebuttal and rejection of "Occasional Discourse on the Negro Question," signalled the end of whatever friendship remained.

authority;' but authority from whom? If by the quality of the message we may judge of those who sent it, *not* from any powers to whom just or good men acknowledge allegiance. This so-called 'eternal Act of Parliament' is no new law, but the old law of the strongest, – a law against which the great teachers of mankind have in all ages protested: – it is the law of force and cunning; the law that whoever is more powerful than another, is 'born lord' of that other, the other being born his 'servant,' who must be 'compelled to work' for him by 'beneficent whip,' if 'other methods avail not.' I see nothing divine in this injunction. If 'the gods' will this, it is the first duty of human beings to resist such gods. Omnipotent these 'gods' are *not*, for powers which demand *human* tyranny and injustice cannot accomplish their purpose unless human beings cooperate. The history of human improvement is the record of a struggle by which inch after inch of ground has been wrung from these maleficent powers, and more and more of human life rescued from the iniquitous dominion of the law of might. Much, very much of this work still remains to do; but the progress made in it is the best and greatest achievement yet performed by mankind, and it was hardly to be expected at this period of the world that we should be enjoined, by way of a great reform in human affairs, to begin *un*doing it.

The age, it appears, is ill with a most pernicious disease, which infects all its proceedings, and of which the conduct of this country in regard to the Negroes is a prominent symptom – the Disease of Philanthropy. 'Sunk in deep froth-oceans of Benevolence, Fraternity, Emancipation-principle, Christian Philanthropy, and other most amiable-looking, but most baseless, and, in the end, baleful and all-bewildering jargon,' the product of 'hearts left destitute of any earnest guidance, and disbelieving that there ever was any, Christian or heathen,' the 'human species' is 'reduced to believe in rose-pink sentimentalism alone.' On this alleged condition of the human species I shall have something to say presently. But I must first set my anti-philanthropic opponent right on a matter of fact. He entirely misunderstands the great national revolt of the conscience of this country against slavery and the slave-trade, if he supposes it to have been an affair of sentiment. It depended no more on humane feelings than any cause which so irresistibly appealed to them must necessarily do. Its first victories were gained while the lash yet ruled uncontested in the barrack-yard and the rod in schools, and while men were still hanged by dozens for stealing to the value of forty shillings. It triumphed because it was the cause of justice; and, in the estimation of the great majority of its supporters, of religion. Its originators and leaders were persons of a stern sense of moral obligation, who, in the spirit of the religion of their time, seldom spoke much of benevolence and philanthropy, but often of duty, crime, and sin. For nearly two centuries had negroes, many thousands annually, been seized by force or treachery and carried off to the West Indies to be worked to death, literally to death, for it was the received maxim, the acknowledged dictate of good economy, to wear them out quickly and import more. In this fact every other possible cruelty, tyranny, and wanton oppression was by implication included. And the motive on the part of the slave-owners was the love of gold; or, to speak more truly, of vulgar and puerile ostentation. I have yet to learn that anything more detestable than this has been done by human beings towards human beings in any part of the earth. It is a mockery to talk of comparing it with Ireland. And this went on, not, like Irish beggary, because England had not the skill to prevent it, – not merely by the sufferance, but by the laws of the English nation. At last, however, there were found men, in growing number, who determined not to rest until the iniquity was extirpated; who made the destruction of it as much the business and end of their lives, as ordinary men make their private interests; who would not be content with softening its hideous features, and making it less intolerable to the sight, but would stop at nothing short of its utter and irrevocable extinction. I am so far from seeing anything contemptible in this resolution, that, in my sober opinion, the persons who formed and executed it deserve to be numbered among those, not numerous in any age, who have led noble lives according to their lights, and laid on mankind a debt of permanent gratitude.

After fifty years of toil and sacrifice, the object was accomplished,[1] and the negroes, freed from despotism of their fellow-beings, were left to themselves, and to the chances which the arrangements of

---

1   The British abolitionist movement, although begun by Quakers in the late seventeenth century, reached its greatest influence in the late eighteenth and early nineteenth centuries, culminating in the freeing of all British slaves in 1833.

existing society provide for those who have no resource but their labour. These chances proved favourable to them, and, for the last ten years, they afford the unusual spectacle of a labouring class whose labour bears so high a price that they can exist in comfort on the wages of a comparatively small quantity of work. This, to the ex-slave-owners, is an inconvenience; but I have not yet heard that any of them has been reduced to beg his bread, or even to dig for it, as the negro, however scandalously he enjoys himself, still must: a carriage or some other luxury the less, is in most cases, I believe, the limit of their privations – no very hard measure of retributive justice; those who have had tyrannical power taken away from them, may think themselves fortunate if they come so well off; at all events, it is an embarrassment out of which the nation is not called on to help them: if they cannot continue to realize their large incomes without more labourers, let them find them, and bring them from where they can best be procured, only not by force. Not so thinks your anti-philanthropic contributor. That negroes should exist, and enjoy existence, on so little work is a scandal in his eyes, worse than their former slavery. It must be put a stop to at any price. He does not 'wish to see' them slaves again 'if it can be avoided;' but 'decidedly' they 'will have to be servants,' 'servants to the whites,' 'compelled to labour,' and 'not to go idle another minute.' 'Black Quashee,' 'up to the ears in pumpkins,' and 'working about half an hour a day,' is to him the abomination of abominations. I have so serious a quarrel with him about principles, that I have no time to spare for his facts; but let me remark, how easily he takes for granted those which fit his case. Because he reads in some blue-book of a strike for wages in Demerara, such as he may read of any day in Manchester,[1] he draws a picture of negro inactivity, copied from the wildest prophecies of the slavery party before emancipation. If the negroes worked no more than 'half an hour a day,' would the sugar crops, in all except notoriously bad seasons, be so considerable, so little diminished from what they were in the time of slavery, as is proved by the Customhouse returns? But it is not the facts of the question, so much as the moralities of it, that I care to dispute with your contributor.

---

1   Manchester, one of the major northern industrial cities in England, was often the scene of labour unrest.

A black man working no more than your contributor affirms that they work, is, he says, 'an eye-sorrow,' a 'blister on the skin of the state,' and many other things equally disagreeable; to *work* being the grand duty of man. 'To do competent work, to labour honestly according to the ability given them; for that, and for no other purpose, was each one of us sent into this world.' Whoever prevents him from his 'sacred appointment to labour while he lives on earth' is 'his deadliest enemy.' If it be 'his own indolence' that prevents him, 'the first *right* he has' is that all wiser and more industrious persons shall, 'by some wise means, compel him to do the work he is fit for.' Why not at once say that, by 'some wise means,' every thing should be made right in the world? While we are about it, wisdom may as well be suggested as the remedy for all evils, as for one only. Your contributor incessantly prays Heaven that all persons, black and white, may be put in possession of this 'divine right of being compelled, if permitted will not serve, to do what work they are appointed for.' But as this cannot be conveniently managed just yet, he will begin with the blacks, and will make them work *for* certain whites, those whites *not* working at all; that so 'the eternal purpose and supreme will' may be fulfilled, and 'injustice,' which is 'for ever accursed,' may cease.

This pet theory of your contributor about work, we all know well enough, though some persons might not be prepared for so bold an application of it. Let me say a few words on this 'gospel of work' – which, to my mind, as justly deserves the name of a cant as any of those which he has opposed, while the truth it contains is immeasurably farther from being the whole truth than that contained in the words Benevolence, Fraternity, or any other of his catalogue of contemptibilities. To give it a rational meaning, it must first be known what he means by work. Does work mean every thing which people *do*? No; or he would not reproach people with doing no work. Does it mean laborious exertion? No; for many a day spent in killing game, includes more muscular fatigue than a day's ploughing. Does it mean *useful* exertion? But your contributor always scoffs at the idea of utility. Does he mean that all persons ought to earn their living? But some earn their living by doing nothing, and some by doing mischief; and the negroes, whom he despises, still do earn by labour the 'pumpkins' they consume and the finery they wear.

Work, I imagine, is not a good in itself. There is nothing laudable in work for work's sake. To work voluntarily for a worthy object is laudable; but what constitutes a worthy object? On this matter, the oracle of which your contributor is the prophet has never yet been prevailed on to declare itself. He revolves in an eternal circle round the idea of work, as if turning up the earth, or driving a shuttle or a quill, were ends in themselves, and the ends of human existence. Yet, even in the case of the most sublime service to humanity, it is not because it is work that it is worthy; the worth lies in the service itself, and in the will to render it – the noble feelings of which it is the fruit; and if the nobleness of will is proved by other evidence than work, as for instance by danger or sacrifice, there is the same worthiness. While we talk only of work, and not of its object, we are far from the root of the matter; or if it may be called the root, it is a root without flower or fruit.

In the present case, it seems, a noble object means 'spices.' 'The gods wish, besides pumpkins, that spices and valuable products be grown in their West Indies' – the 'noble elements of cinnamon, sugar, coffee, pepper black and grey,' 'things far nobler than pumpkins.' Why so? Is what supports life, inferior in dignity to what merely gratifies the sense of taste? Is it the verdict of the 'immortal gods' that pepper is noble, freedom (even freedom from the lash) contemptible? But spices lead 'towards commerces, arts, politics, and social developments.' Perhaps so; but of what sort? When they must be produced by slaves, the 'politics and social developments' they lead to are such as the world, I hope, will not choose to be cursed with much longer.

The worth of work does not surely consist in its leading to other work, and so on to work upon work without end. On the contrary, the multiplication of work, for purposes not worth caring about, is one of the evils of our present condition. When justice and reason shall be the rule of human affairs, one of the first things to which we may expect them to be applied is the question, How many of the so-called luxuries, conveniences, refinements, and ornaments of life, are *worth* the labour which must be undergone as the condition of producing them? The beautifying of existence is as worthy and useful an object as the sustaining of it; but only a vitiated taste can see any such result in those fopperies of so-called civilization, which myriads of hands are now occupied and lives wasted in providing. In opposition to the 'gospel of work,' I would assert the gospel of leisure, and maintain that human beings *cannot* rise to the finer attributes of their nature compatibly with a life filled with labour. I do not include under the name labour such work, if work it be called, as is done by writers and afforders of 'guidance,' an occupation which, let alone the vanity of the thing, cannot be called by the same name with the real labour, the exhausting, stiffening, stupefying toil of many kinds of agricultural and manufacturing labourers. To reduce very greatly the quantity of work required to carry on existence, is as needful as to distribute it more equally; and the progress of science, and the increasing ascendancy of justice and good sense, tend to this result.

There is a portion of work rendered necessary by the fact of each person's existence: no one could exist unless work, to a certain amount, were done either by or for him. Of this each is bound, in justice, to perform his share; and society has an incontestable right to declare to every one, that if he work not, at this work of necessity, neither shall he eat. Society has not enforced this right, having in so far postponed the rule of justice to other considerations. But there is an ever-growing demand that it be enforced, so soon as any endurable plan can be devised for the purpose. If this experiment is to be tried in the West Indies, let it be tried impartially; and let the whole produce belong to those who do the work which produces it. We would not have black labourers compelled to grow spices which they do not want, and white proprietors who do not work at all exchanging the spices for houses in Belgrave Square.[1] We would not withhold from the whites, any more than from the blacks, the 'divine right' of being compelled to labour. Let them have exactly the same share in the produce that they have in the work. If they do not like this, let them remain as they are, so long as they are permitted, and make the best of supply and demand.

Your contributor's notions of justice and proprietary right are of another kind than these. According to him, the whole West Indies belong to the whites: the negroes have no claim there, to either land or food, but by their sufferance. 'It was not Black Quashee, or those

---

1   A fashionable residential area in the West End of London.

he represents, that made those West India islands what they are.' I submit, that those who furnished the thews and sinews really had something to do with the matter. 'Under the soil of Jamaica the bones of many thousand British men' – 'brave Colonel Fortescue, brave Colonel Sedgwick, brave Colonel Brayne,' and divers others, 'had to be laid.' How many hundred thousand African men laid their bones there, after having had their lives pressed out by slow or fierce torture? They could have better done without Colonel Fortescue, than Colonel Fortescue could have done without them. But he was the stronger, and could 'compel;' what they did and suffered therefore goes for nothing. Not only they did not, but it seems they *could* not have cultivated those islands. 'Never by art of his' (the negro) 'could one pumpkin have grown there to solace any human throat.' They grow pumpkins, however, and more than pumpkins, in a very similar country, their native Africa. We are told to look at Haiti: what does your contributor know of Haiti? 'Little or no sugar growing, black Peter exterminating black Paul, and where a garden of the Hesperides might be, nothing but a tropical dog-kennel and pestiferous jungle.' Are we to listen to arguments grounded on hearsays like these? In what is black Haiti worse than white Mexico? If the truth were known, how much worse is it than white Spain?[1]

But the great ethical doctrine of the Discourse, than which a doctrine more damnable, I should think, never was propounded by a professed moral reformer, is, that one kind of human beings are born servants to another kind. 'You will have to be servants,' he tells the negroes, 'to those that are born *wiser* than you, that are born lords of you – servants to the whites, if they are (as what mortal can doubt that they are?) born wiser than you.' I do not hold him to the absurd letter of his dictum; it belongs to the mannerism in which he is enthralled like a child in swaddling clothes. By 'born wiser,' I will suppose him to mean, born more capable of wisdom: a proposition which, he says, no mortal can doubt, but which I will make bold to say, that a full moiety[2] of all thinking persons, who have attended to

---

1 After achieving independence from Spain in 1821, Mexico experienced fifty years of civil war and revolution. Spain itself, throughout the 1840s, went through significant political turmoil.

2 Half.

the subject, either doubt or positively deny. Among the things for which your contributor professes entire disrespect, is the analytical examination of human nature. It is by analytical examination that we have learned whatever we know of the laws of external nature; and if he had not disdained to apply the same mode of investigation to the laws of the formation of character, he would have escaped the vulgar error of imputing every difference which he finds among human beings to an original difference of nature. As well might it be said, that of two trees, sprung from the same stock, one cannot be taller than another but from greater vigour in the original seeding. Is nothing to be attributed to soil, nothing to climate, nothing to difference of exposure – has no storm swept over the one and not the other, no lightning scathed it, no beast browsed on it, no insects preyed on it, no passing stranger stript off its leaves or its bark? If the trees grew near together, may not the one which, by whatever accident, grew up first, have retarded the other's development by its shade? Human beings are subject to an infinitely greater variety of accidents and external influences than trees, and have infinitely more operation in impairing the growth of one another; since those who begin by being strongest, have almost always hitherto used their strength to keep the others weak. What the original differences are among human beings, I know no more than your contributor, and no less; it is one of the questions not yet satisfactorily answered in the natural history of the species. This, however, is well known – that spontaneous improvement, beyond a very low grade, – improvement by internal development, without aid from other individuals or peoples – is one of the rarest phenomena in history; and whenever known to have occurred, was the result of an extraordinary combination of advantages; in addition doubtless to many accidents of which all trace is now lost. No argument against the capacity of negroes for improvement, could be drawn from their not being one of these rare exceptions. It is curious withal, that the earliest known civilization was, we have the strongest reason to believe, a negro civilization. The original Egyptians are inferred, from the evidence of their sculptures, to have been a negro race: it was from negroes, therefore, that the Greeks learnt their first lessons in civilization; and to the records and traditions of these negroes did the Greek philosophers to the very end of their career resort (I do not say with much fruit) as a treasury of mysterious wisdom. But I again renounce all advantage from facts: were the whites born ever so superior in intelligence to the blacks, and competent by nature to instruct and advise them, it would not be the less monstrous to assert that they had therefore a right either to subdue them by force, or circumvent them by superior skill; to throw upon them the toils and hardships of life, reserving for themselves, under the misapplied name of work, its agreeable excitements.

Were I to point out, even in the highest terms, every vulnerable point in your contributor's Discourse, I should produce a longer dissertation than his. One instance more most suffice. If labour is wanted, it is a very obvious idea to import labourers; and if negroes are best suited to the climate, to import negroes. This is a mode of adjusting the balance between work and labourers, quite in accordance with received principles: it is neither before nor behind the existing moralities of the world: and since it would accomplish the object of making the negroes work more, your contributor at least, it might have been supposed, would have approved of it. On the contrary, this prospect is to him the most dismal of all; for either 'the new Africans, after labouring a little,' will 'take to pumpkins like the others,' or if so many of them come that they will be obliged to work for their living, there will be 'a black Ireland.' The labour market admits of three possible conditions, and not, as this would imply, of only two. Either, first, the labourers can live almost without working, which is said to be the case in Demerara; or, secondly, which is the common case, they can live by working, but must work in order to live; or, thirdly, they cannot by working get a sufficient living, which is the case in Ireland. Your contributor sees only the extreme cases, but no possibility of the medium. If Africans are imported, he thinks there must either be so few of them, that they will not need to work, or so many, that although they work, they will not be able to live.

Let me say a few words on the general quarrel of your contributor with the present age. Every age has its faults, and is indebted to those who point them out. Our own age needs this service as much as others; but it is not to be concluded that it has degenerated from former ages, because its faults are different. We must beware, too, of mistaking its virtues for faults, merely because, as is inevitable, its faults mingle with its virtues and colour them. Your contributor thinks that the age has too much humanity, is too anxious to abolish pain. I affirm, on the contrary, that it has too little humanity – is most culpably indifferent to the subject; and I point to any day's police reports as the proof. I am not now accusing the brutal portion of the population, but the humane portion; if they were humane *enough*, they would have contrived long ago to prevent these daily atrocities. It is not by excess of a good quality that the age is in fault, but by deficiency – deficiency even of philanthropy, and still more of other qualities wherewith to balance and direct what philanthropy it has. An 'Universal Abolition of Pain Association' may serve to point a sarcasm, but can any worthier object of endeavour be pointed out than that of diminishing pain? Is the labour which ends in growing spices noble, and not that which lessens the pangs of suffering? We are told, with a triumphant air, as if it were a thing to be glad of, that 'the Destinies' proceed in a 'terrible manner;' and this manner will not cease 'for soft sawder or philanthropic stump-oratory;' but whatever the means may be, it *has* ceased in no inconsiderable degree, and is ceasing more and more: every year the 'terrible manner,' in some department or other, is made a little less terrible. Is our cholera comparable to the old pestilence – our hospitals to the old lazar-houses[1] – our workhouses to the hanging of vagrants – our prisons to those visited by Howard?[2] It is precisely *because* we have succeeded in abolishing so much pain, because pain and its infliction are no longer familiar as our daily bread, that we are so much more shocked by what remains of it than our ancestors were, or than in your contributor's opinion we ought to be.

But (however it be with pain in general) the abolition of the infliction of pain by the mere will of a human being, the abolition, in short, of despotism, seems to be, in no peculiar degree, the occupation of this age; and it would be difficult to show that any age had undertaken a worthier. Though we cannot extirpate all pain, we can, if we

---

1   Houses which took in beggars or paupers afflicted with diseases such as leprosy. They were infamous for their squalor and lack of hygiene.
2   John Howard (1726-90), English traveller and prison reformer. He was instrumental in bringing about two Parliamentary acts which introduced sanitary standards into British prisons and reformed the ways in which jailers were paid. He was the author of *The State of Prisons in England and Wales, with an Account of some Foreign Prisons* (1777) and *An Account of the Principal Lazarettos in Europe* (1780).

are sufficiently determined upon it, abolish all tyranny; one of the greatest victories yet gained over that enemy is slave-emancipation, and all Europe is struggling, with various success, towards further conquests over it. If, in the pursuit of this, we lose sight of any object equally important; if we forget that freedom is not the only thing necessary for human beings, let us be thankful to any one who points out what is wanting; but let us not consent to turn back.

That this country should turn back, in the matter of negro slavery, I have not the smallest apprehension. There is, however, another place where that tyranny still flourishes, but now for the first time finds itself seriously in danger. At this crisis of American slavery, when the decisive conflict between right and iniquity seems about to commence, your contributor steps in, and flings this missile, loaded with the weight of his reputation, into the abolitionist camp. The words of English writers of celebrity are words of power on the other side of the ocean; and the owners of human flesh, who probably thought they had not an honest man on their side between the Atlantic and the Vistula,[1] will welcome such an auxiliary. Circulated as his dissertation will probably be, by those whose interests profit by it, from one end of the American Union to the other, I hardly know of an act by which one person could have done so much mischief as this may possibly do; and I hold that by thus acting, he has made himself an instrument of what an able writer in the *Inquirer* justly calls 'a true work of the devil.'[2]

---

1   A river in Poland.
2   A quotation from an anonymous article, "Mr. Carlyle on the Negroes," which appeared in the *Inquirer* of December 8, 1849.

Appendix F: Jamaica and Governor Eyre

1. "The Insurrection in Jamaica"[1]
Despatch from Edward John Eyre,[2] Governor of Jamaica

Reprinted in *The Times*, November 20, 1865

King's-house, Oct. 20, 1865

Sir, – It is my very painful duty to inform you that a most serious and alarming insurrection of the negro population has taken place in this colony, and been attended with great loss of life and destruction of property. The outbreak commenced at Morant Bay, in St. Thomas-in-the-East, and rapidly spread through the contiguous parishes.

2. A succinct statement of the occurrence will, perhaps, best enable you to comprehend the very imminent jeopardy in which the colony has been placed, and the nature of the steps taken to put down the rebellion.

3. I may promise that there were three principal objects to be attained.

---

1 The events leading up to the rebellion in Jamaica occurred in the rural area of Morant Bay. On October 11, 1865, a crowd of three to five hundred blacks and "coloureds" gathered in front of the village court house to protest an attempted arrest, and confronted the thirty-seven volunteer guards who had been assembled to protect the building. The Riot Act was read, but the crowd ignored this and began throwing stones. The Volunteers responded by firing a volley into the protestors, killing seven of them. The crowd then rushed the Volunteers, drove them back into the court house, and set the building on fire. Eighteen people, including the district's chief magistrate, were killed in the attack, and for the next few days the rioters controlled the area. During the insurrection a total of twenty-one people were killed. On October 13 the Governor of Jamaica, Edward John Eyre, declared martial law in the district, and sent in troops to quell the uprising. Within a week the rebellion had been ended, but reprisals under martial law went on for another month. In that time 439 blacks were killed either by being court-martialed and hanged or simply shot without trial. Approximately 600 men and women were flogged, and over 1,000 huts and houses were destroyed. The colonial troops suffered no casualties.

2 Edward John Eyre (1815-1901) emigrated to Australia at the age of 17, and eventually became a magistrate. He was appointed governor of New Zealand in 1847, and of St. Vincent in 1854. He became governor of Jamaica in 1862. After the rebellion he was suspended from his post and recalled to England. Although he never held another colonial position, he was awarded a government pension in 1872.

First. To save the lives of the ladies, children, and other isolated and unprotected persons in the districts where the rebellion existed.

Secondly. To head the insurrectionary movement and prevent the further spread of the rebellion in its progress along and around the east end of the island.

Thirdly. To punish the rebels and restore peace to the disturbed districts.

4. On the morning of Wednesday, the 11th inst., at 8 a.m., I received at Spanish Town, a letter from the Baron von Ketelhodt,[1] Custos[2] of St. Thomas in the East, written the previous evening from Morant Bay, to inform me that serious disturbances were apprehended and to request that troops might be sent.

5. The circumstances stated in the Baron's letters were to the effect that on Saturday, the 7th of October, while a black man was being brought up for trial before the justices, a large number of the peasantry, armed with bludgeons and preceded by a band of music, came into the town, and leaving the music at a little distance surrounded the Court-house, openly expressing their determination to rescue the man about to be tried, if convicted. One of their party, having created a considerable disturbance in the Court-house, was ordered into custody, whereupon the mob rushed in, rescued the prisoner, and maltreated the policemen in attendance.

No further injury appears to have been done at this time, and the magistrates seem to have thought so little of the occurrence, that no steps were taken to communicate with the Executive.

6. On Monday, the 9th of October, the justices issued a warrant for the apprehension of 28 of the principal persons concerned in the disturbance of Saturday, and confided it to six policemen for execution.

Upon the arrival of the police at the settlement where the parties lived (called "Stoney Gut," and about three or four miles from Morant Bay), a shell was blown,[3] and the negroes collected in large numbers, armed with guns, cutlasses, pikes, and bayonets.

---

1 A German who had married an Englishwoman with property in Jamaica, von Ketelhodt was the leader of the planter party in Jamaica. He was also a close friend and political supportor of Governor Eyre.

2 Literally a guardian or custodian. In this case the Chief Magistrate of a colonial Parish.

3 i.e., a conch shell used as a horn.

They caught and ill-treated three of the policemen, putting them in handcuffs, and administering to them an oath upon a Bible which they had ready, binding them to desert the whites and join their (that is the black) party.

8. Upon receiving this communication at 8 a.m., I immediately sent for the Executive Committee, and after a hurried consultation with them and with the Attorney-General, an express was sent over to Kingston, requesting the General commanding Her Majesty's troops to get ready 100 men for immediate embarcation, and an express was also sent off to Captain De Horsey, of Her Majesty's ship Wolverene, and senior naval officer at Port Royal, to request that, if possible, a man-of-war might at once be sent up to Kingston, to receive the troops and take them to their destination.

9. Unfortunately the only man-of-war besides the Wolverene had left Port Royal for Vera Cruz on this very morning.

Captain de Horsey, however, at once got ready his own ship, the Wolverene, took her up to Kingston by 5 o'clock, and by 6 p.m. the troops were embarked, and away to Port Royal, where the ship was to anchor till daylight, and then run down to Morant Bay.

10. Having thus done all in my power at the time and without the least delay, I returned to my temporary residence at Flamstead, in the Mountains, to be present at a dinner party which was to meet there the next day.

11. On that day (Thursday, the 12th), about half-past 4 p.m. I received a private letter from a Mr. Davidson, a magistrate of St. David's, which had been sent across the country, stating that it was reported the blacks had risen and murdered the Baron, two sons of the rector of the parish (Mr. Cooke), and several other persons, and stating that it was expected the rebels were coming along the line of the Blue Mountain Valley to destroy the properties contiguous thereto and to murder the white and coloured inhabitants.

12. Upon receiving this communication, I wrote a hasty application to the General for 200 more troops, and then at once got upon my horse, and set off for Kingston. When about half way down the mountain, I met a messenger from the Custos of Kingston, corroborating the intelligence I had already received. Upon arriving at the residence of General O'Connor about 7 p.m., I found the news of the

massacre had reached Kingston about 2 p.m.

....

14. The Executive Committee met me in consultation at the residence of General O'Connor, and expresses were sent out to collect the Privy Council, which was assembled a little before midnight.

The result of the deliberation was that it was considered expedient at once to declare martial law, and notices were forthwith sent out to the members of the Privy Council and members of Assembly to meet at 8 a.m. next morning, to hold a Council of War, this being the legal formality required by the 9th Victoria, cap. 35, sec. 95, 6, 7, and 8.

15. Considering the extreme urgency of the case and the magnitude of the interests at stake, I considered it my duty to make preparations for proceeding in person to the scene of disturbance, to superintend and direct the operations which might be necessary, and as there was no man-of-war in port or English steamer I chartered the Caravelle, one of the French line of packet ships, which fortunately happened to be in port, and was most considerately placed at my service by Captain Burat.

16. About half an hour after midnight I got away with my aide-de-camp, Colonel Hunt, and drove over to Spanish Town. Here I had the Governor's secretary and his clerk at once called up, and the requisite proclamation for establishing martial law prepared. By half-past 6 a.m. on Friday, the 13th, I had completed my arrangements and returned to Kingston by 8 a.m., where I met the Council of War, and with their concurrence at once declared the county of Surrey, except Kingston, to be under martial law.

....

The most frightful atrocities were perpetrated [by the rebels]. The Island Curate of Bath, the Rev. V. Herschell, is said to have had his tongue cut out while still alive, and an attempt is said to have been made to skin him. One person (Mr. Charles Price, a black gentleman, formerly a member of Assembly) was ripped open and his entrails taken out. One gentleman (Lieutenant Hall, of the Volunteers) is said to have been pushed into an outbuilding, which was then set on fire, and kept there until he was literally roasted alive. Many are said to have had their eyes scooped out; heads were cleft open and the brains taken out. The Baron's fingers were cut off and carried away as trophies by the murderers. Some bodies were half burst, others horribly battered. Indeed, the whole outrage could only be paralleled by the atrocities of the Indian mutiny.[1] The women, as usual on such occasions, were even more brutal and barbarous than the men; the only redeeming trait being that, so far as we could learn, no ladies or children had as yet been injured.

20. I append a narrative by Mr. Stephen Cooke, clerk of the peace and magistrates, one of the survivors, of the circumstances immediately preceding the massacre, and so far as he knows of the occurrences of the massacre itself; but it is obvious from the nature of the case that it can only be a most imperfect and incomplete account. The true and full story can never be hoped for. All the principal inhabitants of the district had been killed, and the entire Volunteer force (with the exception of a few who escaped), consisting of 22 officers and men, nobly died at their posts, gallantly doing their duty.

. . . .

23. Having landed the 50 men brought in the Caravelle, orders were issued for 50 blue jackets and Marines to start at daylight on the 14th for Easington, in St. David's, to meet and co-operate with the party of the 2d battalion 6th Regiment, which had been detached from Newcastle, as already stated, to work up along the line of the Blue Mountain Valley to the same locality (Easington).

24. It was now about 9 o'clock p.m., but Brigadier Nelson and myself at once embarked on board the gunboat Onyx, Lieutenant Brand, for Port Morant, where we arrive a little after midnight.

25. Here we learnt that Captain Luke, the officer in charge of the party from Morant Bay, had again sent on in advance as far as Bath a detachment of 35 men, under Ensign Cullen, for the purpose of protecting women and children. We ascertained also that some of the rebels were in the immediate vicinity of our camp, and a party of 25 men was sent out at 2 a.m. in the morning to try and surprise some in their huts. Two men and some women were thus captured. One of

---

1   A serious rebellion, led by Indian troops or "Sepoys," which occurred in 1857. The British did not regain control of India until mid-1858, and the spectre of this uprising continued to haunt colonial administrators. The "atrocities" committed by Indian soldiers were wildly exaggerated in England, and Eyre's association of the Jamican rebellion with this earlier one serves to justify his actions. The mutilations described here were later attributed to the work of vultures and dogs.

the men was a principal in the disturbances of the name of Fleming. He was tried by court-martial and at once hung. The second, quite a young man, was flogged. The women were released.

. . . .

27. Soon after we reached Morant Bay the Wolverene came in sight, having on board another company of the 2d battalion 6th Regiment. The day was intensely wet, and, as the encampment was not very well protected from the weather, the troops and sailors were subjected to much discomfort and exposure.

28. The prisoners on board the Wolverene were landed, and five of them tried by court-martial, four of whom were hung on the stone archway of the burnt Court-house, near to which all the massacres had taken place on the 11th. One prisoner was flogged. The Attorney-General of the colony, in his capacity as a captain in the militia, sat as a member of the court.

. . . .

37. I personally inspected the Maroons,[1] a fine body of about 150 men, who, in the most loyal spirit, had come down on the day preceding our arrival, ill-armed as they were, determined to protect Port Antonio. They were unbounded in their devotion and loyalty, and were beyond measure delighted to see again their former captain, the Honourable A. G. Fyfe, whom I had brought with me in the Wolverene, and under whose orders they at once placed themselves.

A party of Maroons had already been of great service in protecting Bath, and the fact of this singular and isolated people proving faithful is one of incalculable value to the Government in the emergency which exists. I shall address you separately in reference to the Maroons when I am less pressed for time.

38. It was now clear that by the rapidity of our movements we had got ahead of the rebellion, which, breaking out at Morant Bay, had proceeded rapidly along the south-east, east and north corner of the island.

By occupying Port Antonio in time, we not only saved that district

---

1   Originally fugitive slaves who had escaped into the mountains and forests of Jamaica. After emancipation many of them continued to live outside of the towns and plantations. Their willingness to aid colonial troops in hunting down and capturing alleged rebels created long-lasting bitterness.

from destruction, but we met and stopped the further progress of the rebellion 12 miles east of it.

We had indeed accomplished some most important results in a singularly brief space of time.

A military post was established at Morant Bay, and another at Port Antonio, while the centre of a line connecting the two was occupied by the friendly Maroons.

39. The greater portion of the rebels were therefore hemmed in within the country east of this line. The spread of the rebellion westward was stopped, and if no independent outbreak occurs in any other part of the island, we shall have the disturbed districts under control, and can at leisure deal with and punish the insurgents.

At the same time, all the helpless and unprotected ladies, children, and other refugees, have been got in and saved.

40. All our most important work being thus done, and the troops comfortably established in their barracks, we had for the first time a night of quiet and rest, on the night of Sunday, the 15 of October.

41. At daybreak on Monday, the 16 of October, a court-martial sat to try prisoners, and 27 were found guilty and hung.

. . . .

48. There was one very important point to be decided upon. Throughout my tour in the Wolverene and Onyx, I found everywhere the most unmistakable evidence that Mr. George William Gordon,[1] a coloured member of the House of Assembly, had not only been mixed up in the matter, but was himself, through his own misrepresentation and seditious language addressed to the ignorant black people, the chief cause and origin of the whole rebellion. Mr. Gordon was now in Kingston, and it became necessary to decide what action should be taken with regard to him. Having obtained a deposition on oath that certain seditious printed notices had been sent through the post-office directed in his hand-writing to the parties who have been leaders in the rebellion, I at once called upon the Custos to issue a warrant and capture him. For some little time he managed to evade capture, but, finding that sooner or later it was inevitable, he proceed-

---

1 George William Gordon (?–1865) was a prominent opponent of Governor Eyre's colonial policies in Jamaica. The son of a white planter and a slave-woman, he had become a landowner and had served as a member of the Jamaican House of Assembly.

ed to the house of General O'Connor and there gave himself up, I at once had him placed on board the Wolverene for safe custody and conveyance to Morant-bay.[1]

49. Great difference of opinion prevailed in Kingston as to the policy of taking Mr. Gordon. Nearly all coincided in believing him to be the occasion of the rebellion, and that he ought to be taken, but many of the inhabitants were under considerable apprehension that his capture might lead to an immediate outbreak in Kingston itself. I did not share in this feeling. Moreover, considering it right in the abstract, and desirable as a matter of policy, that while the poor black men who had been misled were undergoing condign punishment, the chief instigator of all the evil should not go unpunished, I at once took upon myself the responsibility of his capture.

. . . .

57. All was going on well at the camp. The parties from Stoney Gut had returned; more rebels had been captured or shot, and a report had also been received from Colonel Hobbs, who, after reaching Stoney Gut, and finding it occupied by the Morant-bay detachment, had retired again towards Mocklands – a position some distance inland, on the line of the Blue Mountain Valley.

Colonel Hobbs had seen and shot a good many rebels as well as captured some prisoners.

On the morning of the 20th of October, having landed Brigadier Nelson and the Militia officers who aided as members of courts-martial, and having put on shore the prisoners including G. W. Gordon, I again proceeded in the Wolverene to Kingston, reaching that city about 2 p.m.

. . . .

63. I cannot myself doubt that it is in a great degree due to Dr.

---

1   This was Eyre's most controversial, and arguably most improper, action during the rebellion. By arresting Gordon in Kingston, where martial law did not apply, and transporting him to Morant Bay, where it did, Eyre all but ensured that Gordon would be found guilty and executed. Subsequent investigations found very little evidence directly linking Gordon to the insurrection, and serious irregularities in the court martial which condemned him, so the suspicion that Eyre had taken advantage of the situation to permanently remove a troublesome political enemy was aroused. It was this "judicial murder" which became the centre of efforts to indict Eyre after he was recalled to England.

Underhill's letter and the meetings held in connexion with that letter,[1] where the people were told that they were tyrannized over and ill-treated, were over-taxed, were denied political rights, had no just tribunals, were misrepresented to Her Majesty's Government by the authorities and by the planters, and where, in fact, language of the most exciting and seditious kind was constantly used, and the people told plainly to right themselves, to be up and doing, to put their shoulders to the wheel, to do as the Haytians had done,[2] and other similar advice.

64. The parties who have more immediately taken part in these nefarious proceedings are: – firstly, G. W. Gordon, a member of the Assembly and a Baptist preacher; secondly, several black persons, chiefly of the Baptist persuasion, connected with him; thirdly, various political demagogues and agitators, who, having no character or property to lose, make a trade of exciting the ignorant people; fourthly, a few persons of better information and education, who find their interest in acquiring an influence among the black people by professing to advise them, while in reality they are but exciting and stimulating their evil passions; fifthly, a few Baptist missionaries,[3] who like —— endorse at public meetings or otherwise all the untruthful statements or innuendos propagated in Dr. Underhill's letter; and, lastly a section of the press, which, like the *Watchman* and the *County*

---

1 Edward Bean Underhill was the Joint Secretary of the Baptist Missionary Society (see note below). In 1859 he had visited Jamaica and studied the conditions of the black population. After returning to England he continued to receive reports from Baptist missionaries on the island, and in 1865 he became so disturbed by what he was being told that he wrote a letter to the Secretary of State for the Colonies listing the colonial administration's failures. When Eyre was asked to respond to this letter he became violently angry at what he saw as interference with his governorship. Blacks throughout the island celebrated the appearance of someone to champion their cause in England, and held a series of mass meetings to demonstrate their support for Underhill's position.

2 In 1791 a slave revolt broke out in Haiti, and by 1804, after the island had successfully repelled both French and British attempts to reimpose colonial control, it was ruled exclusively by blacks. See Carlyle and Mill's comments on the event in Appendix E. This rebellion, along with the Indian Mutiny, was often used to justify the need for a "firm" (not to say severe) response to potential uprisings.

3 Baptist preachers and missionaries had been instrumental in abolishing slavery in the West Indies. After emancipation they contined to aggressively support the black population, which brought them into direct conflict with colonial administrators and white planters.

Union,[1] is always disseminating seditious doctrines, and endeavouring to bring into contempt the representative of the Sovereign and all constituted authority.

63. While it is my duty to point out how mischievous has been the influence of a few of the Baptist ministers, and of various members of that persuasion, it is equally my duty and a pleasure to me to state that I believe the large majority of the Baptist ministers have been most anxious to support the authorities, to teach their people to be loyal and industrious, and to endorse the advice given to the peasantry by Her Most Gracious Majesty.

66. In reporting the occurrences of the outbreak of the rebellion, and the steps taken to put it down, it is my duty to state most unequivocally my opinion that Jamaica has been, and to a certain extent still is, in the greatest jeopardy.

67. Humanly speaking, I believe that the promptitude and vigour of action which has at once grappled with and punished the rebellion has been the saving of Jamaica. The whole colony has been upon a mine, which required but a spark to ignite it. Disaffection and disloyalty still exist in nearly all the parishes of the island, and had there been the least hesitation or delay in dealing with them in the parishes where they became developed in rebellion I confidently believe that the insurrection would have been universal throughout the entire island, and that either the colony would have been lost to the mother country, or an almost interminable war and an unknown expense have had to be incurred in suppressing it.

. . . .

77. We have been singularly fortunate in capturing or shooting a large number of the principal ringleaders in the rebellion, and many of whom were personally concerned in the atrocious butcheries on the 12th of October at the Morant Bay Courthouse, or in the subsequent destruction of life and property further to the eastward, as the rebellion extended in that direction. Very many acknowledged their guilt before execution.

78. It is a remarkable fact that, so far as we can ascertain, the rebels at Morant Bay did not proceed in any considerable numbers to the

---

1   Jamaican newspapers which supported reform within the island's government.

adjacent districts; but the people of each district rose and committed the deeds of violence and destruction that were done within it. This fact shows how widespread the feeling of disaffection is, and how prepared the people of each parish were to catch the spirit and follow the example of their neighbours. It shows, to, the extreme insecurity which yet exists in nearly all the other parishes of Jamaica, where the same bad spirit prevails. In the lately disturbed districts the rebellion is crushed, in the others it is only kept under for the present, but might at any moment burst into fury.

79. I append various military reports and some other papers, bearing upon the rebellion or upon the state of other parishes.

It has been impracticable to obtain a correct list of all the European or coloured persons who have been killed or wounded.

80. I append the names of those at present known, but there were some burnt in the Court-house, and others are missing, and nothing certain known about them. Even thus, however, the list is a very long and sad one, and comprises many persons of station, education, and weight in the community, whose loss is irreparable in a colony like Jamaica.

81. Copies of a letter taken at Stoney Gut, and of threatening letters which have since been received, either here or at Kingston, are attached.

I also add copies of the local newspapers
I have the honour to be, Sir, your most obedient humble servant,
E. EYRE

P.S., October 23. – Having kept my despatch open, I am enabled to add that Mr. George William Gordon has been tried by court-martial at Morant Bay, and sentenced to be hung. The execution was to take place this morning at 8 a.m.

I have seen the proceedings of the court, and concur both in the justice of the sentence and in the policy of carrying it into effect. It is absolutely necessary for the future security of Jamaica that condign punishment should be inflicted upon those through whose seditious acts and language the rebellion has been originated.

2. "The Outbreak in Jamaica"

The Times, November 28, 1865

Yesterday a meeting of the citizens of Manchester[1] was held in the large room of the Town-hall, having been convened by the Mayor, in compliance with a requisition to which about 600 signatures were attached, for the purpose of adopting a memorial to the Government to inquire into the outbreak and repression of the recent disturbances in Jamaica. The room was well filled with an audience of several hundreds in number and of influential composition.

The MAYOR (Mr. Bowker) took the chair, and opened the proceedings by expressing a desire that the discussion would be of an impartial character, and calculated to elicit the truth. (Applause.)

Mr. T. B. Potter, M.P., moved the first resolution: –

"That, in the opinion of this meeting, the circumstances of the late deplorable events in Jamaica are such as to call for a strict and impartial investigation on the part of the Government of this country into the origin and causes of the outbreak, and especially into the legality and necessity of the severe measures adopted for its suppression."

He said he never attended a town's meeting in Manchester under a more strong conviction of the necessity of appealing to public opinion, nor did he ever attend one with more regret, because he believed that the circumstances into which an investigation was now sought was such as appeared to the world something like a disgrace and dishonour to the English name. (Applause.) The honour of England belonged not merely to the Government but to all her citizens. England could not afford to do any great wrong. Perhaps we over-esteemed ourselves, but certainly we stood before the nations of the world in such a position that, as a free people, we could not afford to do anything that was a disgrace to the name of freemen. In the present case it was desired to call upon the Government to investigate not merely the original causes of the outbreak in Jamaica, but also the conduct of the Governor. It was impossible to doubt from his antecedents that Governor Eyre was a brave and gallant man. His

---

1 Manchester was a centre of Radical and Reform politics throughout the nineteenth century.

conduct in South Australia was marked by the most signal acts of bravery and self-sacrifice. (Hear, hear.) He was the protector of the Blacks on the Murray River, and so conducted himself as to gain the confidence of all. It could hardly, therefore, have been absolute prejudice against the Blacks or the coloured people of Jamaica which led to the circumstances that seemed to require investigation; but it seemed as if Governor Eyre had been panic-stricken and "lost his head" in the recent disturbances – outbreaks they could scarcely be called. Undoubtedly great dissatisfaction existed among the coloured people; injudicious steps were taken by the authorities, with a very small force at their command, to interfere by physical force; and it must be remembered, however unfortunate the after occurrences, the people were first fired upon by the Volunteers. (Hear, hear.) No doubt the law was broken when a legal arrest was interfered with, but we all know how dangerous it was to fire upon the people. Such things had been known even in England, and in Manchester, and in one case the attack upon the people by the authorities gave the signal for great changes in this country.[1] (Hear.) It could scarcely be imagined that, had a formidable outbreak in Jamaica been anticipated, the Volunteers would not have had a sufficient supply of ammunition to hold their own; but when the thing burst upon them the authorities seemed quite to lose their presence of mind. When one looked at the case of Mr. Gordon he (Mr. Potter) confessed it made his blood run cold to think than an Englishman – for though coloured men, these were Englishmen (cheers), our fellow subjects, whose rights were our rights, as ours were theirs (renewed cheers) – a political opponent of the policy of the planter party should have surrendered himself when a civil warrant was issued against him, and been the placed on board the Wolverene, the Governor sailing with him in that ship to Morant Bay, there to hand him over to the tender mercies of a court-martial. If nothing further came out to palliate the circumstances, there were great doubts whether Governor Eyre and the officers composing that court-martial had not been guilty of murder. (Continuous cheers.) It

---

1 A reference to the so-called "Peterloo" massacre. On August 16, 1819, a reform meeting held in St. Peter's Field, Manchester, was charged by a force of cavalry and yeomanry. Eleven people were killed and about 600 injured. Public outrage gave added impetus to the Reform movement.

was not asked by this meeting that governor Eyre, like poor Gordon, should be punished without a hearing, but that a full and fair investigation by the Government should be instituted at once. To see the names of military officers attached to such despatches as had been sent to this country must awake a general feeling of regret. He (Mr. Potter) had heard men speak with deep regret of the atrocities they had themselves witnessed during the Indian mutiny, when coloured people who had no more to do with the Sepoys or the mutiny than gentlemen in this room were massacred with the greatest cruelty because the authorities and the soldiery had been worked up to a feeling almost of barbarity by the dreadful accounts of Indian crimes, many of which turned out to be entirely false.[1] The accounts we now heard of the horrible intentions of the Blacks when this rising in Jamaica took place, – that they meant to seize the lands of the planters and divide them among themselves; to exterminate the male population and appropriate the females – how like all this was to the story we heard from India at the commencement of the mutiny. And what proof was there of all this? It appeared to him that there was none. (Hear, hear.) He must refer for a moment to the articles which had appeared in one of the leading journals of England. (A hiss.) He did not blame that journal so much, because its articles would not appear unless they paid – unless there was demand for them, but he did regret most sincerely that there should be any class of the community which delighted in them. However much the bigotry and intolerance of *The Times'* articles on the subject of the coloured people might please a certain section and small class of English society, they did not please the true heart of England. (Applause.) It was all very well for *The Times* to say of the working classes who heard Mr. Gladstone[2] that they were not fitted for the trust of the franchise[3] (hisses); that there

---

1   See the note on this topic in Appendix F.1. Here the speaker associates the idea of "atrocities" with the colonial authorities, rather than with the rebels.

2   William Ewart Gladstone (1809–98), Liberal statesman, held a number of important governmental posts throughout his long political career. He became leader of the House of Commons in 1865, and proposed an extension of voting rights which was defeated in 1866. He was returned as Prime Minister in 1868, 1880, 1886, and 1892.

3   A great deal of the tension generated by the Eyre controversy can be connected to contemporary British politics. The agitation to extend the franchise to the working class, which resulted in the passing of the Second Reform Bill in 1867, was causing

should be ignorance among the working classes was, indeed, very much to be regretted, but it was still more disgraceful that there should be such an amount of ignorance and bigotry in the upper classes that it could answer the purpose of *The Times* to insert in that paper such articles as had appeared there.

The Rev. G. W. CONDER (Independent) seconded the resolution . . . .

Mr. JACOB BRIGHT,[1] who was received with repeated cheering, proposed the adoption of a memorial to Lord Russell,[2] and its presentation by a deputation....The memorial was as follows: –

"TO THE RIGHT HON. THE EARL RUSSELL, FIRST LORD OF HER MAJESTY'S TREASURY.

"The memorial of the citizens of Manchester, in public meeting assembled, showeth, – "That your memorialists have heard with deep regret of the recent lamentable occurrences in the island of Jamaica, whereby the lives of many of their fellow subjects have been sacrificed in an alleged insurrection, and in the means adopted for its suppression. That your memorialists have seen it stated that the outbreak was only part of a wide-spread plan for the subversion of Her Majesty's Government in the island; and also, on the other hand, that it was immediately provoked by the authorities themselves commencing hostilities by ordering the Volunteers to fire on the multitude....That your memorialists have observed it stated in the despatch of the Governor that a Mr. George Gordon, who was suspected of complicity in the outbreak, and for whose apprehension a warrant had been issued by the civil Government, which had failed to secure his capture, was transferred from a district under civil law to one which was under martial law, after he had surrendered himself to the civil authorities, and there tried by a court-martial, condemned, and executed – a proceeding which your memorialists believe to be a violation of British law and subversive of the rights of British subjects."

---

serious social unrest. Fears about potential anarchy in England found expression in Conservative support for Eyre's restoration of order in Jamaica, while Liberal and Radical leaders saw his actions as glaring examples of autocratic excess.

1 The less prominent, but no less fervent, brother of John Bright (1811-98), Radical politician and driving force behind the Second Reform Bill.

2 See note to Appendix E.1.

. . . .

The facts which justified the course adopted by those who had convened the meeting were few, but they were prominent – nay, ghastly and astounding. A condition of feeling which often existed previous to a riot rendered it extremely probable that riotous proceedings would take place at Morant Bay; and, as had happened very often in this and other countries, extreme mismanagement brought about this riot. The riot became a very serious one and many lives had been lost. A few Volunteers fired upon a large crowd, and as the crowd outnumbered the Volunteers nothing was more likely than that those firing should be overwhelmed. The Volunteers retreated into the court-house, where they were attacked, the court-house was set on fire, and in their endeavours to escape the mob killed some 16 or 18 people and injured a number of others. That was on the Wednesday. That terminated everything that could be called a fight. It might have been thought, seeing that after this the Government maintained its authority, seeing that the population was cowed and that no further resistance was made, that if there had been just a moderate amount of head or heart in the official class, those who killed the Volunteers would have been apprehended, put upon their trial, and received the reward of their crimes according to the laws of the island. But instead of taking this common-sense, just, and humane course there was a positive massacre; there were hundreds of men and women massacred when the strife was over and the riot had been put down. And this could only have been a petty insurrection or riot, for only a few policemen were employed to apprehend the prisoners, and but about 20 Volunteers were employed to fire upon the 600 people. But Governor Eyre and his wretched associates were not satisfied to employ the soldiery of the Government in order to over-awe the population or massacre it; they associated themselves in their bloody work with the aboriginal and barbarous Maroon population from the mountains of Jamaica, and these Maroons very much contributed to the horrors of the affair. These Maroons, of course, would with equal avidity have hunted down General Eyre and his associates if they had been employed to do so by the opposite party.[1] (Cheers.) All were familiar

---

1 Bright presents a very different picture of the Maroons than did Eyre in his despatch.

with the story of Gordon, a member of the Jamaica Parliament, a man of property and education, the son of an Englishman who married an English lady, a religious man, and a Reformer in the island; and if there could be 50 such men there might be a Government in Jamaica. (Applause.) But it was nothing now that these accidents attached to Mr. Gordon. Gordon was a man and a British subject, and a British subject, no matter what his colour, his extraction, his position in society, merely because he was a British subject, had inalienable rights, the first of which was that he could never be punished for any crime for which he had not been legally tried and convicted. It was but truth to say that the killing of Gordon ("No, murder"), and the manner in which he had been killed had stirred the profoundest patriotic feeling of the British heart. (Hear, hear.) The Englishman loved his country, but he loved it because it was the country of law, and because in it he was never subject to the caprices of a despotic will. But we begin to ask now whether we were secure in the possession of these rights, which had been guaranteed to us by institutions, and had come down from the remotest times, and which had stood every attempt to destroy them, whether those attempts had been made by wearers of coronets or wearers of crowns. (Cheers.)

. . . .

It had been said that Governor Eyre was a pious man. (A laugh.) Piety united to knowledge and strength was a great addition to a man's character and enabled him better to perform his duty. But he (Mr. Bright) did not much value piety in a Government or a man holding a responsible position, united only with ignorance and weakness; it made a man in such a position the more dangerous, when it brought him much credit and disarmed suspicion. Some people had urged that a total change of Government should take place in Jamaica, but that was a matter upon which an opinion could not be pronounced without much information. Seeing that such a governor could be put in such a position he should be extremely afraid of having a government simply by a Governor in council; he should prefer that a large suffrage should exist in Jamaica, and that those men who had been so much trampled upon, and in whose way so many difficulties had been placed, should have a greater control in the Parliament by being able to send members of their own class to sit there.[1] (Applause.) This meeting asked for an inquiry, not merely for an act which was downright unconstitutional; they asked for an inquiry into those acts, too, which would seek to shelter themselves under the plea of martial law. Though when martial law was proclaimed the civil law was silent, yet human feelings should still be there, and human judgment should not be overthrown. Even if these men who had been guilty of the atrocities described could claim that they were acting under martial law, if it was found that they had acted without justice, with cruelty, and an utter abandonment of reason, the least thing we could demand was that they should be removed from their places, and never again put in positions of responsibility. (Cheers.) But if it were found that a British Governor had in one single case annihilated all law, and left a man shelterless to the malignant hatred of his enemies, and that that man had been murdered, then the sentiment of this country would never be appeased until that governor be put upon his trial (loud applause); and if so tried he be found guilty of that highest offence known to the British people, he should receive the reward due to so great a crime. (Loud cheers.)

Dr. JOHN WATTS[2] seconded the resolution. He said these deplorable results in Jamaica had been caused by the passing of judgment without trial....The grave charge was made against Governor Eyre of removing a man from a place where civil law prevailed, where no doubt an impartial jury could have been empanelled, and a good Judge found – the charge was that the Governor removed a man from this safe custody, and took him away from the means of a safe trial, and handed him over to the semi-military authority of a militia; that under this authority he was hanged, and that up to this moment there had not come evidence that this man had any complicity in this riot, or was proved to have been in any plan of rebellion. Mr. Gordon appeared to have been a very temperate man....He was also an Englishman, and it was peculiarly appropriate this meeting should be held in Manchester, for Mr. Gordon was a Manchester citizen, who for years was a corresponding clerk in a Manchester house, where he

---

1 This is a clear allusion to the issue of voting reform, and demonstrates the way events in Jamaica were used to echo the situation in England.

2 John Watts (1818-87), educational and social reformer. He took up residence in Manchester in 1841, and lived there until his death.

gave great satisfaction. Here was a man who had learnt his Radicalism in their own city, who had emigrated to one of our colonies, and had risen to be a member of Parliament there, who had endeavoured to do the best possible for the people to whom he was connected by blood, and whom he saw oppressed, and who had become a martyr for their benefit. It was therefore appropriate the meeting should demand an inquiry into the loss of life of one of their own citizens.

The motion was supported by the Rev. A. S. STEINTHAL and passed *nem. con.*,[1] after a suggestion had been adopted adding the mayor to the deputation as its head.

A vote of thanks to the mayor was passed, and

Mr. POTTER, M.P., then stated that the deputation would have an interview with Earl Russell to-day (Tuesday) at half-past 1.

3. Editorial

The Times, November 30, 1865

The speech of Governor EYRE to the Jamaica Legislature[2] may convince our readers that we did not speak at random when we declared that in the opinion of the best-informed persons in the island there had been a conspiracy among the negroes, with no less an object than the murder and despoiling of the white people, and those of the coloured who sided with them. That opinion may, of course, be entirely erroneous. It is possible that Mr. EYRE, the Council, the House of Assembly, the General in command, the Custodes, Magistrates, and other people in authority in the colony, have all gone stark mad, and have been in that state for months. It is equally possible that there has been no rebellion at all, and that the outrages committed in the eastern part of the island are a pure illusion. These two propositions will have to be established by those who have constituted themselves the apologists of the negroes and the denouncers of the Colonial Government. The second sight which can give them a

---

1   "Without dissenting voice"; unanimously.
2   On November 7, 1865, while reprisals for the rebellion were continuing, Eyre made a speech defending his actions. He was hailed as a hero by the colony's administrators and by the white population in general.

better knowledge of the events in Jamaica than the people who are on the spot we do not affect to share; our own course has simply been to take the best information which was to be obtained, to compare it with what was known of the state and past history of the island, and to judge accordingly. The result is that there is not a single statement we made which has not been confirmed on the highest authority. The dangerous designs of the negroes, the treasonable spirit that prevailed, the pernicious influence of certain politicians and preachers, and the necessity for a strong Government for some considerable time, if life and property were to be saved and civilization upheld, have now been positively announced by the QUEEN's representative amid the assent and applause of the Legislature. So strong is the conviction that the only hope for the island is to place full authority in a few hands and to prevent an ignorant and barbarous race from being excited by the machinations of demagogues, that it seems almost likely the ancient institutions of the island will be abolished, and the chief British settlement in the West Indies revert to the condition of a CROWN colony.[1]

Governor EYRE opened the Session of the Legislature on the 7th inst. At that time order had been restored in the disturbed districts, but it seems that Kingston was still crowded with the white inhabitants, that the estates were deserted, and apprehension continued to prevail....His Excellency having been personally on the scene of the disturbances, having full information of all that had passed and was passing in the island, reiterates, in the strongest manner, the opinions expressed in his late despatch, and in the presence of the Commander-in-Chief, the Commodore, and the principal officers engaged against the negroes, declares the colony to be in serious danger. He speaks of the "wicked and unprovoked rebellion." As to the effect of it, he declares that "a large amount of property has been destroyed, an immense expense has been entailed on the country, and one of the

---

[1] In the same speech Eyre argued that the rebellion indicated the black population's desire to control the island, and that they might achieve this if they won suffrage. He therefore recommended that the Jamaican Assembly be abolished, and that Jamaica petition London to become a Crown Colony under the authority of the governor. His recommendation was accepted, the Assembly was voted out of existence, and Jamaican self-government ended.

richest and most productive districts of the colony has been left without a resident proprietor or manager to reap the abundant crops now ready for the harvest." As to the nature of it, he says further on, – "To this prompt and decisive action I firmly believe we owe it, under God's Providence, that we are able to meet here this day. One moment's hesitation, one single reverse, might have lit the torch which would have blazed in rebellion from one end of the island to the other." "There is scarcely a district or a parish in the island where disloyalty, sedition, and murderous intentions are not widely disseminated, and in many instances openly expressed." Nor does the Governor hesitate to speak of "this most diabolical conspiracy to murder the white and coloured inhabitants of this colony." The speech from which we have made these extracts was delivered on a solemn occasion a fortnight after the rising had been virtually suppressed; it was addressed to the Legislature, in the presence of the chief military and naval officers on the station, and was immediately published. Are we to believe that a man in his senses would in this formal manner utter a tissue of absurdities, or make statements which any one of the many present could contradict? Moreover, we find that the Legislature was entirely in accord with the Governor; his address was praised in the highest terms by several members, and Mr. WESTMORELAND, a member of the Executive Committee, at once introduced a Bill to carry out the principal of its recommendations.

With regard to the proposed amendment of the Constitution, we can only regret that it should be necessary, and we trust that so far as it curtails the free institutions of the island its provisions will not be permanent.[1] Jamaica, like several of the other islands, had a legislative system which, under judicious management, might have been made an efficient engine of civilization to the coloured race. It seems to us that if that race is ever to be raised to self-government, it must be, under the leadership of the whites, by such machinery as the British colonies afford. Equal rights to white and black, but such a moderately high property qualification as will sift the black race, and give the electoral franchise only to that minority which is at present, and must be for a generation or two, all that is fitted to use it, present the best

---

1 Jamaica was granted a new constitution in 1884.

means of raising up a respectable and steady class of coloured men through whom civilization may descend to the lower levels. In the British colonies, where the coloured man has had every advantage, where every one of the race who distinguishes himself is studiously favoured by the Governors, there is a much better field for the experiment than among the proud and jealous Americans of the South. The abrogation of the Jamaican Constitution is so far a subject for regret, and is a signal instance of the evils which unscrupulous agitators may bring upon the cause of freedom. But if the colony be ungovernable under the present system, there is nothing but to submit to the change. Governor EYRE speaks the simple truth when he says that he know of no general grievance under which the negroes of Jamaica laboured. "They are less taxed, can live more easily and cheaply, and are less under an obligation to work for subsistence than any peasantry in the world. The same laws as to the imposition of taxes, the administration of justice, and the enjoyment of political rights, apply to them and to the white and coloured inhabitants alike. They ought to be better off, more comfortable, and more independent than the labourers of any other country. If it is not so, it is due to their own indolence, improvidence, and vice." This is precisely what has been said in this journal, and gives a complete and satisfactory contradiction to the mischievous statements which helped to raise the late agitation.

We repeat that we hope the day will soon return when the negro population may be intrusted with free institutions, and may meet and speak and vote without any danger to anybody. But for their sake, as well as that of the whites, it is the duty of the Home Government to support to the utmost the authorities in the island. We regret as much as any one can do the recent severities, the accounts of which, however, have evidently been preposterously exaggerated. But for some time to come there must be a firm Government. There is, we fully believe, a good deal more to be learnt about the purposes of the Jamaica negroes. From all parts of the island it is reported that their language, behaviour, and bearing indicate the deepest animosity to the whites, and their belief that a day of triumph is at hand. The confessions of some of the prisoners bear witness to a definite conspiracy. Doubtless, among the great majority of them the purpose is of the vaguest and wildest kind, but it is not the less dangerous. The late convulsions in America, the vibration of which has extended to Ireland,[1] have also been felt in the West India islands, where the negro has been most independent and most ill-advised. Maroon wars,[2] slave insurrections, and the St. Domingo revolution[3] make up the historical learning of the Jamaica peasant, and antagonism to the white man is his only political conception. On such a nature the tales of conquering negro armies, dividing Louisiana estates,[4] and dispersing white men's meetings, join with the influence of the agitators of the island in producing the worst effects. For the benefit of all the Government should be administered for a time with a strong hand.

4. Letter to the Editor, Charles Buxton[5]

The Times, December 7, 1865

TO THE EDITOR OF THE TIMES

Sir, – I have been waiting in hopes that some abler advocate would defend the character of the negroes from the heavy charges that have been made against them; but as no one else has undertaken the task in your columns, I feel it to be my plain duty to step forward on their behalf.

---

1 The American Civil War (1861-65) had ended on April 9. It seriously divided English society, and there seemed an obvious danger that rights granted to ex-slaves in the South might cause unrest among ex-slaves in the West Indies. As well, England feared Fenian uprisings in Ireland might be encouraged by this example of freedom achieved through armed conflict. The nationalist Irish Republican Brotherhood (Fenians for short) had been founded in New York in 1857. The association of blacks with the Irish as two "inferior" colonized peoples was common in nineteenth-century England.

2 There were two main Maroon Wars in Jamaica, the first occurring in 1734-8 and the second in 1795-96. The Maroons also, however, made sporadic raids on British plantations throughout the colony's history.

3 Another reference to the Haitian slave rebellion of 1791-1804.

4 A reference to the rumour that Louisiana plantations would be divided up and given to the freed slaves and black Union soldiers.

5 Charles Buxton (1823-71), Liberal politician. He was the original chair of the Jamaica Committee (see Appendix E.7 below), and was elected MP for Newport in 1857, for Maidstone in 1859, and for East Surrey in 1865.

I only ask you to allow me to restate the dry bare facts of the case, as told us by Governor Eyre himself and his subordinates. I will not draw a single inference; I will make no comment; I will not utter one word of abuse or of indignation. All I ask is that you will allow me to clear the simple facts from all extraneous matter.

Sir Roderick Murchison[1] says that we ought to believe what Governor Eyre tells us. Most heartily do I agree with him. All I want is that the public should grapple with and vividly realize the truth of Governor Eyre's own statements.

We are told, indeed, that we ought not to say a word until we get further information; but I am merely going to quote Governor Eyre's own words against those who, like the Tory press, have all rushed forward to condemn the negro unheard. Now, the charge against him is stated with great clearness in the letter which you publish to-day.[2] It is that the "diabolical plan" of the negroes was "simply the destruction of the whites and browns, and the confiscation of their property for the benefit of the blacks. Murder, cold-blooded, cowardly, indiscriminate, was the means adopted to effect the designed end." To this it has usually been added that the plan of Mr. Gordon and his friends was to get possession of the persons of the white women and children.

Very well. I simply ask the reader to give his mind to the following facts: –

What immediately led to the outbreak was the attempt of the whites to turn the negroes out of certain lands which they had occupied. This caused immense excitement. There was a riot. Six policemen were afterwards sent to arrest 27 of the leading rioters; they were resisted, but were sent back unharmed.

The capture was afterwards quietly effected. When the prisoners were tried the negroes surrounded the Court-house with clamour and tumult, but not one single act of violence of any sort or kind is attributed to them until the Riot Act was read, and a volley was fired into them by the Volunteers, doing, we are told, great execution, and we afterwards hear of their carrying away their dead. Upon this the

---

1   Roderick Impey Murchison (1792-1871), Scottish geologist, explorer, and president of the Royal Geographical Society. He had known Eyre in Australia, and defended his character when he came under attack by the English press.

2   i.e., the letter to which this writer is responding, published on December 6.

mob attacked those who had fired upon them; but – mark this, it is a point of vital importance – we are told that the negroes rushed to the police station and seized the arms and ammunition there contained, and commenced firing upon the Court-house. This demonstrates that they had not come armed with any intention of massacre. Mad as they were with excitement after being fired upon, they yet deliberately spared Dr. Major and Dr. Gerard. Mr. Cook was saved by a black man, who "sat watching over and protecting him;" young Alberga was also spared, and several wounded who escaped.

But the most vital point of all is this – that except a Custom-house officer, who was killed directly afterwards, and a mulatto bookkeeper, not one single act of violence towards any white man, woman, or child is related as having occurred after the attack on the Court-house. And this although the negroes rose in various districts and plundered the plantations, and we hear of hundreds of white people coming in from those plantations. Yet not one white person on the plantations was either killed or wounded.

These are the plain, bald facts. God forbid that for one moment I should defend the cruel murder of two Volunteers in the Court-house, or the subsequent plundering and burning of the plantations; but I do ask your readers to weigh these facts, and to ask themselves whether they square with the notion that the negroes were intending a general massacre and rape.

Next, I wish in the same dry way, to put before your readers the facts of which General Eyre and his subordinates inform us, with regard to the flogging, hanging, and shooting of which we have heard so much. As to the mere fact that terrible severity has been exercised there is no dispute. It is, I fear, indisputable that, as the letter from Jamaica states which you yesterday published, upwards of 1,000 (other accounts say 2,000) negroes have been shot or hanged, besides an immense number who have been "severely lashed." The plea on which these doings are justified is that, in Mr. Eyre's own words "the just severity which has been exercised is but a merciful substitute for the much larger measure of punishment which would have had to be executed had the rebellion been allowed time to gather head and extend itself," or, as you put it with more point on Saturday, we surely ought not to blame Mr. Eyre for steps taken "in an hour of extreme peril."

Now there lies the gist of the matter. That is the vital question. Were these things done "in an hour of extreme peril?" If they were, I, for one, will not breathe a word against Mr. Eyre. In that case I would cordially agree with you that it would be shameful for us, sitting at ease at home, to condemn a man for acts done under the dire necessity of suddenly confronting a fearful peril, not to himself, but to others.

But here is the plain fact. We have it on Mr. Eyre's own authority that before these "just severities were exercised" the rebellion was at an end, the disaffected districts were in the hands of the military, order was restored, the moment of peril was gone by.

This, be it observed, is a mere question of dates. Here are Mr. Eyre's own words: – "Within three days from the first intelligence of the rebellion reaching Kingston it was headed, checked, and hemmed in. Within a week it was fairly crushed," – mark these important words – "and arrangements were made for scouring the entire district, to capture and punish the guilty."

Even had we not his words, Mr. Eyre's own conduct would demonstrate this to have been the case. The massacre of Morant Bay took place on October 11. By October 15, his despatch says, "our most important work being done, we had for the first time a night of quiet and rest." And he adds that as there was no pressing necessity for his stay at Port Antonio he returned to Kingston, which, be it remembered, was so undisturbed that martial law was never proclaimed there.

Now, it was on the 16th of October, after "the night of rest and quiet," that what I may call the work of regular slaughter began. It was on that day, October 16, the court-martial sat for the first time....Such was the position of affairs when the following incidents took place. I will not sicken your readers by repeating the long and awful catalogue of punishments and executions which are detailed by the Jamaica newspapers – not, I fear, that we can disbelieve them. Those unanimous accounts, not written by the sufferers or their friends, but by the actors and bystanders themselves, bear the stamp of truth upon them. But the essential point to observe is that these deeds went on, seemingly without check, for three weeks and more after the first outbreak – long after even the faintest shadow of insurrection had disappeared. These things, I say, were done in deliberate cold blood, when there was no longer so much as the shadow of a shade of danger. Here, for example is one extract from Lieutenant Adcock's despatch to General Nelson.[1] I quote it because it describes what he did on the day of his return to headquarters from his expedition, 13 days after the outbreak. "In the morning," he says, "I first flogged four and hung six rebels. At Leith-hall there were a few prisoners, all of whom I flogged." And then he burned 11 houses and one meeting-house. On the previous evening he mentions that he found 67 prisoners at Golden Grove, and "disposed" of as many as possible, but was too tired to continue after dark. But now mark this. In the same official despatch he says, "I consider the state of the country quiet throughout this district," demonstrating that he at least was not hanging and flogging as a precautionary measure. Again, at the end of October, Captain Ford states, "This morning we made a raid with 30 men; back at 4 p.m., bringing prisoners. Having flogged nine men and burnt three negro houses, then had a court-martial on the prisoners, who amounted to about 50 or 60. Several were flogged without court-martial on a simple examination. One man, John Anderson, a kind of parson or schoolmaster, got 50 lashes; one man got 100; the other eight were hanged or shot." The same man writes, "The black troops shot about 160 people on their march from Port Antonio to Manchioneel. Hanged seven in Manchioneel, and shot three on our way to Port Morant. This is a picture of martial law. The soldiers enjoy it; the inhabitants have to dread it; if they run on their approach they are shot for running away." Now, the very paper which inserts Captain Ford's letter states that "in the neighbouring parishes the greatest order prevails." Well may the Saturday Review[2] say of this Captain Ford, – "if Ford escapes hanging, except on full proof that he is a shameless liar, there is no justice in Jamaica."...On October 31, 20 days from the outbreak, we are informed by the papers that "at 6 o'clock this morning" the 15 condemned to death on the previous

---

1 Colonel Alexander Abercrombie Nelson (1816–93) acted as commander-in-chief of the military forces dispatched to Morant Bay. Eyre promoted him to Brigadier-General at the time of the rebellion.

2 The Saturday Review was a Tory newspaper which largely supported Eyre, but it acknowledged that troop actions subsequent to the rebellion were excessive.

day were hanged, except two, who received 100 and 140 lashes respectively. On that day "the court-martial resumed its sittings," and 13 more were sentenced to be hanged. "The sentences were carried out the same evening, in the presence of the untried rebels."...On the 1st of November this court-martial hanged seven more, while, unless the newspapers tell lies, 99 prisoners "against whom there was no proof that they were ever in arms or present at any murder, &c.," were, "with some exceptions, catted and sent adrift."[1]

But without trusting to any newspaper reports, I assert, and I defy contradiction, that the illustrations I have extracted from the official despatches prove that these doings were not done in a moment of panic, from a providential care to stay the spreading of insurrection, but were retrospective and vindictive only.

Now, Sir, I will not utter one word to express my own feeling beyond asking the reader to reflect whether, if we had heard instead that the Russians went on for three weeks, on account of an *émeute*[2] with the Poles, flogging, shooting, and hanging them, or if the Hungarians had been thus treated by the Austrians, or the Algerian Arabs by the French, or even the Taepings by the Chinese, we should speak of this as "just severity?"

I am, Sir, your obedient servant.

---

1   i.e., flogged and turned loose. "Catted" means to be repeatedly struck on the back with a cat-o-nine-tails, a whip with nine knotted lashes. It was the authorized instrument of punishment in the British army and navy until 1881.
2   French. Riot.

5. *Punch*, The Jamaica Question

THE JAMAICA QUESTION.

White Planter. "AM NOT *I* A MAN AND BROTHER. TOO, MR. STIGGINS?"

Punch's cartoonist turns the abolitionist slogan "Am I not a man and a brother?", which was used to emphasize the dehumanizing effects of slavery, against those who continue to support the rights of blacks. He implies that "Mr. Stiggins," representing the evangelical interests of Exeter Hall, has no concern for the white planters who must deal with the economic and political repercussions of emancipation.

6. "The Bold Governor Eyre and the Bulls of Exeter Hall"[1] (A Song for the Streets)

Punch, February 10, 1866

On the right of the Strand,[2] as you walk to the West,
The street of all London the finest and best,
You'll see a Greek word on a portico tall:[3]
The building behind it is Exeter Hall.

There people resort to hear spouters abuse
Mahommedans, Catholics, Pagans, and Jews,[4]
Ex-drunkards talk cant, Irish clergymen brawl,[5]
And fanatics howl nonsense in Exeter Hall.

The victim, just now, of its blather and blare,
Is a brave British gentleman, GOVERNOR EYRE,
Who, for saving Jamaica with powder and ball,
Has roused all the malice of Exeter Hall.

The Hall has its Pets, whom you must not attack,
And chiefly it pets QUASHI-BUNGO[6] the black:
And if QUASHI-BUNGO quotes words from ST. PAUL,[7]
It's ready to kiss him, is Exeter Hall.

At times QUASHI-BUNGO from scripture refrains,
And chops up white people, and scoops out their brains:

---

1 For Exeter Hall see the note to Appendix E.1.
2 The Strand is on the north side of the Thames. It begins at Trafalgar Square, and connects Westminster to the City.
3 The word inscribed above Exeter Hall, in Greek script, is "Philadelphon," which translates approximately as "Brotherly Love."
4 *Punch* emphasizes what it sees as Evangelical intolerance, in ironic contrast to the "Greek word" of the first stanza.
5 The Irish clergy were stereotypically presented as pugnacious. See Brontë's characterization of the curate Mr. Malone in *Shirley* (1849).
6 A derogatory term for both African and West Indian blacks. See Carlyle's use of the name "Quashee" in Appendix E.1.
7 Evangelical, dissenting missionaries were considerably more effective at converting blacks to Christianity than were their Anglican "competitors."

Uprises at once the philanthropist squall,
"Of course you provoked him," says Exeter Hall.

For some horrible murders performed by the Pet,
EYRE gave him a lesson he'll never forget,
"You monster, you wretch! QUASHI-BUNGO to maul;
"We'll hang you at Newgate,"[1] cries Exeter Hall.

"We'll hear," says JOHN BULL,[2] "hold your jabber and row,
I've known my old friend MR. EYRE before now."
"He's a NERO, a JEFFREYS, a GOVERNOR WALL,"[3]
Cries, screaming with passion, mad Exeter Hall.

Now John stops his ears to fanatical spite,
And suspects QUASHI-BUNGO was served very right,
But he'll hear the whole story, not told in the drawl
And spasmodic bewailings of Exeter Hall.

But if, when the tale of Jamaica is told,
The QUEEN gives her thanks to the Governor bold,
What a bellow will burst from the favourite stall
Of the big bulls of Bashan[4] in Exeter Hall!

---

1   Newgate was the principal west gate of London. Its gatehouse was used as a prison
    from the twelfth century until it was demolished in 1902.
2   A character used to represent the national personality of England. He first appeared
    in a collection of pamphlets published by John Arbuthnot (1667-1735) entitled *The
    History of John Bull* (1712). Throughout the Eyre controversy both sides claimed to
    represent "true" English feeling.
3   For Nero see the note to Chapter I in *Jane Eyre*, where Jane uses this epithet to
    describe John Reed. George Jeffreys, 1st Baron Jeffreys (1648-89) was an infamous
    London judge who rose to favour with James II by willingly finding guilty and exe-
    cuting his political enemies. He is most notorious for the "Bloody Assizes" in 1685,
    during which he had hanged 150 of the Duke of Monmouth's followers, and had
    800 others transported to the West Indies. Joseph Wall (1737-1802) was made lieu-
    tenant-governor of Senegal in 1779. On the voyage to assume his post he had a man
    named Paterson flogged so severely that he died. Just as Wall was preparing to give
    up his position in 1782, and without holding a court martial, he ordered a sergeant
    named Benjamin Armstrong to receive 800 lashes. Armstrong died and, on his
    return to England, Wall was charged with murder. He fled to France, but returned
    in 1797, and offered to stand trial in 1801. He was found guilty and executed on
    January 28, 1802.
4   See Psalm 22:12-13.

7. "Statement of the Jamaica Committee"[1]

The Daily News, July 30, 1866

The Jamaica Committee wish to explain to the public the motives by which they are actuated, and the objects which they have in view.

When there is reason to believe that a British subject has been illegally put to death, or otherwise illegally punished by a person in authority, it is the duty of the Government to inquire into the case; and if it appears that the offence has been committed, to vindicate the law by bringing the offender to public justice.

From the facts recorded in the Report of the Royal Commissioners of Inquiry,[2] and in other documents relating to the late disturbances in Jamaica, coupled with the legal opinion of Mr. Edward James and Mr. Fitzjames Stephen,[3] published by the Committee, there appeared strong reason to believe that George William Gordon, Samuel Clarke, Edward Fleming, Charles Mitchell, William Grant, Henry Lawrence, and many other subjects of Her Majesty, both male and female, had been illegally put to death, or flogged, and in some cases flogged and afterwards put to death, and that the houses of many others had been illegally burnt, by Ex-Governor Eyre, Brigadier Nelson, and their subordinates and coadjutors. The attention of the Government was therefore called to these cases in Parliament by Mr. Mill, the Chairman of the Committee.[4]

The Government not only declined to take any steps for the

---

1   A committee formed in December 1865 to defend black interests in Jamaica, and to bring about the prosecution of Governor Eyre for his actions there. Its original Chair, Charles Buxton, was replaced by John Stuart Mill in July 1866. It could claim as members and supporters such prominent figures as Herbert Spencer, Leslie Stephen, and Charles Darwin.

2   This Royal Commission arrived in Jamaica on January 20, 1866, and began gathering evidence on January 25. It heard 730 witnesses, and completed its report on April 9, 1866. In general it praised Eyre for his prompt reaction to the rebellion, but criticized the excessive punishments which took place under martial law afterwards. Eyre was reprimanded and dismissed from his position.

3   Two lawyers retained by the Jamaica Committee to analyze the legality of Eyre's actions.

4   Mill delivered this speech to Parliament on July 19, 1866, and argued that legal proceedings should be initiated against Eyre by the Government.

vindication of the law, but declined on grounds and in a tone which appear to the Committee to aggravate the dangerous aspect of the proceedings in question as infractions of the constitutional liberty of the subject.[1]

The duty now devolves upon private citizens of taking such measures as the constitution may point out for the defence of those legal and chartered rights which protect the lives and liberties of all.

In undertaking to discharge this duty, so far as circumstances and the means placed at their disposal may permit, the Committee are not, any more than the ordinary ministers of public justice, actuated by vindictive feelings towards those whom they believe to have violated the law. Their aim, besides upholding the obligation of justice and humanity towards all races beneath the Queen's sway, is to vindicate, by an appeal to judicial authority, the great legal and constitutional principles which have been violated in the late proceedings, and deserted by the Government

They desire in the first instance to establish, by judicial sentence, the principle that the illegal execution of a British subject by a person in authority is not merely an error which superiors in office may at their discretion visit with displeasure or condone, but a crime which will certainly be punished by the law. The condition of a British subject will be altered if, for the offence of taking his life without law, a public functionary is to be responsible only to a Minster of the Crown who, in the case most dangerous to public liberty, would obviously be not the censor of his subordinate but his abettor.

. . . .

In the second place, the Committee desire to challenge in a Court of Justice the jurisdiction of courts of martial law, which, as the late evens show, may be made engines of indiscriminate butchery and torture; to obtain a judicial answer to the question whether military and naval officers, untrained to judicial investigation, and inflamed, probably, by the passions of the crisis, can legally torture or put to death the

---

1 Benjamin Disraeli (see below), speaking for the Tory government, responded to Mill's speech by rejecting his argument for prosecution, and asserting that the Government, having dismissed Eyre, could do nothing further.

subjects of Her Majesty for high treason and other civil offences without a jury or any adequate security for justice, and without necessarily keeping even a record of the proceedings; and to have it determined by authority whether the law which these courts assume to administer is really law at all, or sanguinary licence which the law will repress and punish.

The mere refusal of Mr. Eyre's superiors in office to reinstate him in his government affords little satisfaction to the community as regards the first of these objects, and none at all as regards the second....The execution of Mr. Gordon is condemned in more positive terms; but it is condemned as a stretch of severity uncalled for in the particular case, not as an infraction of public rights and principles of justice sacred in all cases alike. The practice of trying British subjects for high treason and other civil offences by court-martial is not repudiated in this Dispatch; while the language of Mr. Disraeli,[1] in his reply to Mr. Mill's questions, admits the proclamation of martial law is the suspension of all law, and exposes the lives of British subjects to irresponsible butchery.

. . . .

When indeed the Committee consider the circumstances of such a case as that of Mr. Gordon – the political antagonism which previously subsisted between him and Governor Eyre – the apparent absence of any ground of military necessity for taking the life of a man who was a helpless captive in the hands of the authorities – the eagerness with which the Governor personally interposed to arrest him and carry him in a war ship from the place where he was living under the protection of the common law to one where it was supposed that his life might with impunity be taken without a regular trial – the voice of warning raised in vain by a member of the Council, who, seeing the Governor's intention, suggested that Mr. Gordon should be tried before a civil court – the composition of the court, which, by its

---

1   Benjamin Disraeli, 1st Earl of Beaconsfield (1804-81), Tory statesman and novelist. He was elected MP for Maidstone in 1837, and became Chancellor of the Exchequer and leader of the House of Commons in 1852. He was again Chancellor of the Exchequer when the Second Reform Bill passed in 1867. He was elected Prime Minster in 1868, and held the position again from 1874 to 1880.

combined incompetence and ruthlessness, cut off all hope alike of justice and of mercy – the pitiless manner in which the accused was deprived all legal advice and assistance, and of the benefit of evidence which might have been given in his favour – the interception and destruction of the letter of advice sent openly to the Brigadier-General for the guidance of the prisoner in pleading, and the refusal of the brief delay necessary to call a most important witness who resided almost on the spot – the evidence on which the conviction was founded, and the total insufficiency of which to support the charge must have been palpable to any man of common understanding – the warm approval of the sentence upon that evidence by the Governor after the date at which, by his own account, the insurrection had been got under, and when, consequently, the plea of military necessity could no longer have any force – they must confess that this is not a case which they would particularly shrink from submitting to the investigation of a court of justice.

If the execution of Mr. Gordon was illegal, and, in the eye of the law, a murder, it was a murder of which Mr. Eyre was not only constructively but personally guilty; which was committed not only under his authority, but, to all intents and purposes, with his own hand.

To lay it down that proof of private malice is indispensable in order to make an illegal execution a murder, would be to hold out impunity to the crime which is the most dangerous of all to the community – the crime of a public functionary who abuses the power entrusted to him to compass, under the forms of justice, the death of a citizen obnoxious to the Government. To lay it down that the plea of good intentions is sufficient to divest an act of criminality would be, in like manner, to hold out impunity to all political homicide: since all who commit political homicide, whether the agents of a Government or its opponents, believe that the political object which they have in view is good.

. . . .

In attempting to vindicate the law against the violence of persons in authority, the Committee will take care to give no pretence for the charge that they are showing sympathy with disorder....They have no desire to abet resistance to lawful authority or to weaken the arm of the magistrate in preserving public order. But, on the other hand, they would remind their fellow-citizens that hopeless wrong is the sure parent of rebellion, and that its best antidote is the hope of constitutional redress.

The Committee, then, submit that they are endeavouring to defend public liberty against aggression from public motives, and by the means pointed out by law; and that they may justly claim the sympathy and support of all to whom public liberty is dear.

Signed, on behalf of the Committee,

J. S. Mill, Chairman.

P. A. Taylor, Treasurer.[1]

F. W. Chesson, Hon. Sec.[2]

8. Letter from Thomas Carlyle to Hamilton Hume[3]

Ripple Court
Ringwould, Dover
August 23, 1866

SIR, – The clamour raised against Governor Eyre appears to me to be disgraceful to the good sense of England; and if it rested on any depth of conviction, and were not rather (as I always flatter myself it is) a thing of rumour and hearsay, of repetition and reverberation, mostly from the teeth outward, I should consider it of evil omen to

---

1 Peter A. Taylor (1819–1891), Radical politician. He was MP for Leicester from 1862 to 1884, and served as the Committee's Treasurer from its inception.

2 F. W. Chesson had also served as Secretary for the British Emancipation Society, and therefore it was natural that he should hold the same position for the Jamaica Committee.

3 Hamilton Hume (1797–1873), Australian explorer. He quickly came to Eyre's defense, and helped organize what came to be called the Eyre Defence and Aid Fund Committee. Its purpose was to block the Jamaica Committee's attempts to prosecute the ex-governor. Hume approached Carlyle for support, and Carlyle acted as Chair for a few of the Committee's meetings. His official position, however, was Vice-President. Hume also asked Carlyle for permission to publish this letter, and it was widely read and debated. In his journal entry of September 26, 1866, Carlyle notes that a "small letter of mine — has been raging through all the newspapers of the empire."

the country, and to its highest interests, in these times. For my own share, all the light that has yet reached me on Mr. Eyre and his history in the world goes steadily to establish the conclusion that he is a just, humane, and valiant man, faithful to his trusts everywhere, and with no ordinary faculty of executing them; that his late services in Jamaica were of great, perhaps of incalculable value, as certainly they were of perilous and appalling difficulty, – something like the case of 'fire,' suddenly reported, 'in the ship's powder room' in mid ocean, where the moments mean the ages, and life and death hang on your use or your misuse of the moments; and, in short, that penalty and clamour are not the thing this Governor merits from any of us, but honour and thanks, and wise *imitation* (I will farther say), should similar emergencies rise, on the great scale or on the small, in whatever *we* are governing.

The English nation never loved anarchy; nor was wont to spend its sympathy on miserable mad seditions, especially of this inhuman and half-brutish type; but always loved order, and the prompt suppression of seditions; and reserved its tears for something worthier than promoters of such delirious and fatal enterprises who had got their wages for their sad industry.[1] Has the English nation changed, then, altogether? I flatter myself *it* has not, not yet quite; but only that certain loose superficial portions of it have become a great deal louder, and not any wiser, than they formerly used to be.

At any rate, though much averse, at any time, and at this time in particular,[2] to figure on committees, or run into public noises without call, I do at once, and feel that as a British citizen I should, and must make you welcome to my name for your committee, and to whatever good it can do you. With the hope only that many other British men, of far more significance in such a matter, will at once or gradually do the like; and that, in fine, by wise effort and persistence, a blind and disgraceful act of public injustice may be prevented;[3] and an egregious folly as well, – not to say, for none can say or compute, what a vital detriment throughout the British empire, in such an example set to all the colonies and governors the British Empire has!

---

1   An allusion to George William Gordon.
2   Carlyle's wife, Jane Welsh Carlyle (1801-66), had died in April.
3   Carlyle is referring to the attempt to indict Eyre.

Farther service, I fear, I am not in a state to promise; but the whole weight of my conviction and good wishes is with you; and if other service possible to me do present itself, I shall not want for willingness in case of need. Enclosed is my mite of contribution to your fund.

I have the honour to be, yours truly.

9. A Speech in London, John Ruskin[1]

The Daily Telegraph, September 8, 1866

MR. RUSKIN said it was as difficult to account for the violence of the attack upon Mr. Eyre, as for the narrowness of temper which had given it special direction. He had joined the committee,[2] as he doubted not every member composing that committee had joined it, in the simple desire of obtaining justice, not for black men only, nor for white, but for men of every race and colour. He detested all cruelty and all injustice by whomsoever inflicted or suffered; he would sternly reprobate the crime which dragged a black family from their home to dig your fields; and more sternly the crime which turned a white family out of their home that you might drive by a shorter road over their hearth. But whatever might be the motive or the temper of the accusations brought against Mr. Eyre, the ground of them was, under any circumstances, untenable.

His accusers were under the radical mistake of confusing the office of a governor with that of a judge. The duty of a judge was only to declare and enforce law. That of a governor is to do what law cannot do, and to deal with such immediate events, and necessities arising out of them, as may be beyond the scope of existing law. Now, so far as the so-call "Governor" Eyre was not a governor, nor intended to be one, by those who so styled him, but only an administrator of British law in Jamaica, he (Mr. Ruskin) was not there either to defend or accuse him. None but those who knew all his acts, and their consistency or inconsistency with written statute, had any right to do so. To

---

1 John Ruskin (1819-1900), influential prose writer, particularly on aesthetic and social issues.
2 Other prominent Victorian authors who supported the Eyre Defence Committee included Charles Kingsley, Alfred Lord Tennyson, and Charles Dickens.

the arbiter of law in a criminal court, it is no matter what insurrection is imminent in the street outside, or what will be the probable consequences of the criminal's acquittal or condemnation. He must calmly acquit or condemn according to law. But it was to be held in mind that if Mr. Eyre, though called a governor, was in reality only a law officer, there was at the time of impending outbreak no governor of Jamaica. And Mr. Eyre, though being called one, had clearly no alternative but instantly to take upon himself the responsibility of the higher office, and, as an English gentleman should, do, as indeed he did, at his own peril, that which needed to be done. The first thing needing to be done in a crisis of imminent rebellion was to seize the ringleaders of it, and bring them, if time and circumstances admit, to legal trial; but if the enemy to be dealt with is likely to mistake legal delay for infirmity of purpose or hand, all forms of law were by that fact effete and inapplicable, and they were so in all cases as soon as the question became definitely one of time and of instant danger.

It would be advisable to take an instance of this, in a minor matter, intelligible to every one, and close at our doors. It was alleged (Mr. Ruskin supposed) by Mr. Mill and the party he led that to hang a man on suspicion amounted to murder. If that were so, he presumed that to shoot a man on suspicion would be no less murder. Now, in the course of the past year, a drunken workman staggered, late at night, inside the garden gate of a gentleman living in London. The gentleman looked out of his window, saw the drunken man in his garden, and then and there, on suspicion, shot him dead. The jury did not even bring him in guilty of manslaughter. That being the present state of the home law respecting human life, Mr. Mill's beautifully logical position might be expressed in these terms: "For the protection of your own person, and of a few feet of your own property, it is lawful for you to take life, on so much suspicion as may arise from a shadow cast on the wrong side of your wall. But for the safety, not of your own poor person, but of sixteen thousand men, women, and children, confiding in your protection, and entrusted to it; and for the guardianship, not of your own stairs and plate-chest, but of a province involving in its safety that of all English possessions in the West Indies, — for these minor ends it is not lawful for you to take a single life on suspicion, though the suspicion rest, not on a shadow on the wall, but on experience of the character and conduct of the accused during many previous years." That was Mr. Mill's position, which he would contentedly leave him to develop.

For the question now to be brought home to the English people was, not whether Mr. Eyre had erred in this act or the other, nor whether the circumstances required less than he did or more. They might just as well bring any general who had won a decisive battle to trial because it was alleged that he had lost five or six men in unnecessarily occupying a dangerous position, or had shot a peasant by mistake for a spy. The question put at issue by the adverse prosecution was in fact this, and nothing else than this, whether Mr. Eyre, under circumstances of instant public danger, did, or did not, do to the best of his power and ability what he believed to be his duty? To this question, fairly put, he doubted not that the hearts of all true and brave Englishmen would make but one answer – namely, that Mr. Eyre did his duty to the uttermost, with no bye-fears or base motives; and that he was rewarded by being enabled to save the State entrusted to him. How otherwise rewarded it would be for England now to determine. Had he, after all efforts bravely made, failed of his purpose – had he lost Jamaica instead of saving it – if then, after unquelled insurrection, there had been question of government at all, he might justly and advisedly have been superseded; but not even then brought to trial on such grounds.[1] But as the matter stands, the official removal of him from his place was an act of national imbecility which had not hitherto its parallel in history.

It was the act – as this threat of prosecution was the cry – of a nation blinded by its avarice to all true valour and virtue, and haunted, therefore, by phantoms of both; it was the suicidal act of a people which, for the sake of filling its pockets, would pour mortal venom into all its air and all its streams; would shorten the lives of its labourers by thirty years a life, that it might get its needle-packets twopence each cheaper;[2] would communicate its liberty to foreign nations by

---

1   The Jamaica Committee never managed to bring a successful indictment against Eyre.

2   Ruskin and Carlyle positioned themselves as defenders of British workers, and argued that their plight was more important than that of "foreign" blacks. In an earlier letter about the controversy Ruskin wrote "Not that I like slavery, or object to

forcing them to buy poison at the cannon's mouth,[1] and prove its chivalry to them by shrinking in panic from the side of a people being slaughtered, though a people who had given them their daughter for their future Queen;[2] and then would howl in the frantic collapse of their decayed consciences, that they might be permitted righteously to reward with ruin the man who had dared to strike down one seditious leader, and rescue the lives of a population. Whether this cry, and the feeling which it represented, were indeed the voice and the thought of the English people it was now to be asked. That was the simple duty for which they were that day met together. He believed it was not the voice of the whole English people, and that there was another opinion of theirs yet to be taken on the matter. But if not, and this proved to be indeed the English mind, the condemnation or acquittal of Mr. Eyre were matters of very little moment; for the time would then assuredly have come for the bringing of the English people themselves to a trial, in which judgment would not require to be petitioned for.

---

the emancipation of any kind or number of blacks in due place and time. But I ... believe that white emancipation not only ought to precede, but must by law of all fate precede, black emancipation" (*Daily Telegraph*, December 20, 1865). See Dickens' attack on "telescopic philanthropy" in *Bleak House* (1853).

1 A reference to the Opium Wars fought in 1839-42 and 1856-60. In both cases the British were victorious and managed to impose their trading rights on China.

2 A reference to the Belgian Revolution of 1830, in which the southern provinces of the Netherlands broke away from the Dutch and formed their own country. After a series of riots and armed conflicts the Dutch were finally forced to acknowledge the new state. Although England recognized Belgium in 1831, it did not materially support its succession. Victoria's mother, Maria Louisa of Saxe-Coburg, was the sister of Leopold I, the first king of Belgium.

Select Bibliography

1. On *Jane Eyre*

Azim, Firdous. "Rereading Feminism's Texts: *Jane Eyre* and *Shirley*." *The Colonial Rise of the Novel*. London: Routledge, 1993. 172-213.

Beattie, Valerie. "The Mystery at Thornfield: Representations of Madness in *Jane Eyre*." *Studies in the Novel* 28.4 (Winter 1996): 493-505.

Boumelha, Penny. "'And What Do the Women Do?': Jane Eyre, Jamaica, and the Gentleman's House." *Southern Review* 21.2 (1988): 111-22.

Donaldson, Laura E. "The Miranda Complex: Colonialism and the Question of Feminist Reading." *Diacritics* 18.3 (1988): 65-77.

Eagleton, Terry. "*Jane Eyre*." *Myths of Power: A Marxist Study of the Brontës*. 2nd ed. London: Macmillan, 1988.

Federico, Annette. "'A Cool Observer of Her Own Sex Like Me': Girl-Watching in *Jane Eyre*." *Victorian Newsletter* 80 (Fall 1991): 29-33.

Gilbert, Sandra M. and Susan Gubar. "A Dialogue of Self and Soul: Plain Jane's Progress." *The Madwoman in the Attic: The Woman Writer and the Nineteenth-Century Literary Imagination*. New Haven: Yale UP, 1979. 336-371.

Griffin, Gail B. "Once More to the Attic: Bertha Rochester and the Pattern of Redemption in *Jane Eyre*." *Nineteenth-Century Women Writers of the English-Speaking World*. Ed. Rhoda B. Nathan. New York: Greenwood P, 1986. 89-97.

Hoeveler, Diane Long and Beth Lau, eds. *Approaches to Teaching Brontë's Jane Eyre*. New York: MLA, 1993.

Marcus, Sharon. "The Profession of the Author: Abstraction, Advertising, and *Jane Eyre*." *PMLA* 110.2 (March 1995): 206-19.

Meyers, Susan L. "Colonialism and the Figurative Strategy of *Jane Eyre*." *Victorian Studies* 33.2 (1990): 247-268.

Michie, Elsie B. "'The Yahoo, Not the Demon': Heathcliff, Rochester, and the Simianization of the Irish." *Outside the Pale: Cultural Exclusion, Gender Difference, and the Victorian Woman Writer*. Ithaca: Cornell UP, 1993. 46-78.

Peters, John G. "Inside and Outside: *Jane Eyre* and Marginalization through Labeling." *Studies in the Novel* 28:1 (Spring 1996): 57-75.

Poovey, Mary. "The Anathematized Race: The Governess and *Jane Eyre*." *Uneven Developments: The Ideological Work of Gender in Mid-Victorian England*. Chicago: U of Chicago P, 1988. 126-63.

Rich, Adrienne. "Jane Eyre: The Temptations of a Motherless Woman." *On Lies, Secrets and Silence: Selected Prose, 1966-1978*. New York: Norton, 1979. 89-106.

Schwartz, Nina. "No Place Like Home: The Logic of the Supplement in *Jane Eyre*." *Jane Eyre*. Ed. Beth Newman. Boston: Bedford Books, 1996.

Showalter, Elaine. "Feminine Heroes: Charlotte Brontë and George Eliot." *A Literature of Their Own: British Women Novelists from Brontë to Lessing*. Princeton: Princeton UP, 1977. 100-152.

Spivak, Gayatri Chakravorty. "Three Women's Texts and a Critique of Imperialism." *Critical Inquiry* 12.1 (1985): 243-261.

Witt, Amanda B. "'I Read It in Your Eye': Spiritual Vision in *Jane Eyre*." *Victorian Newsletter* 85 (Spring 1994): 29-34.

Woolf, Virginia. "'Jane Eyre' and 'Wuthering Heights.'" *The Common Reader* (First Series). London: Hogarth Press, 1948. 196-204.

Zonana, Joyce. "The Sultan and the Slave: Feminist Orientalism and the Structure of *Jane Eyre*." *Signs* 18:3 (Spring 1993): 592-617.

2. *Jane Eyre*: Nineteenth-Century Reviews

[Chorley, H. F.]. *Athenaeum*, 23 October 1847, 1100-1.

[Eagles, John]. *Blackwood's Magazine*, October 1848, 459-74.

[Lewes, G. H.]. *Fraser's Magazine*, December 1847, 686-95.

———. *Westminster Review*, January 1848, 581-4.

[Lorimer, James]. *North British Review*, August 1849, 455-93.

[Rigby, Elizabeth]. *Quarterly Review*, December 1848, 153-85.

Unsigned Review. *Spectator*, 6 November 1847, 1074-75.

Unsigned Review. *Christian Remembrancer*, April 1848, 396-409.

3. Brontë Biographies

Barker, Juliet. *The Brontës*. New York: St. Martin's, 1994.

Fraser, Rebecca. *Charlotte Brontë*. London: Methuen, 1988.

Gaskell, Elizabeth. *The Life of Charlotte Brontë*. Harmondsworth: Penguin, 1975.

Gérin, Winifred. *Charlotte Brontë: The Evolution of Genius*. Oxford: OUP, 1967.

Peters, Margot. *Unquiet Soul: A Biography of Charlotte Brontë*. Garden City: Doubleday, 1975.

4. Background

Armstrong, Nancy. *Desire and Domestic Fiction: A Political History of the Novel.* Oxford: OUP, 1987.

Hall, Catherine. *White, Male and Middle Class: Explorations in Feminism and History.* New York: Routledge, 1992.

Helsinger, Elizabeth K., Robin Lauterbach Sheets, and William Veeder. *The Woman Question: Society and Literature in Britain and America, 1837-1883.* New York: Garland, 1983.

Hughes, Kathryn. *The Victorian Governess.* London: Hambledon Press, 1993.

Langland, Elizabeth. *Nobody's Angels: Middle-Class Women and Domestic Ideology in Victorian Culture.* Ithaca: Cornell UP, 1995.

McClintock, Anne. *Imperial Leather: Race, Gender and Sexuality in the Colonial Context.* New York: Routledge, 1995.

Peterson, M. Jeanne. "The Victorian Governess: Status Incongruence in Family and Society." *Suffer and Be Still: Women in the Victorian Age.* Ed. Martha Vicinus. Bloomington: Indiana UP, 1972.

Pinion, F. B. *A Brontë Companion.* London: Macmillan, 1975.

Qualls, Barry V. *The Secular Pilgrims of Victorian Fiction: The Novel as Book of Life.* Cambridge: Cambridge UP, 1982.

Semmel, Bernard. *The Governor Eyre Controversy.* London: MacGibbon and Kee, 1962.

Sharpe, Jenny. *Allegories of Empire: The Figure of the Woman in the Colonial Text.* Minneapolis: U of Minnesota P, 1993.

broadview literary texts

"This is a series in which the editing is something of an art form."
The Washington Post

"Broadview's format is inviting. Clearly printed on good paper, with distinctive photographs on the covers, the books provide the physical pleasure that is so often a component of enticing one to pick up a book in the first place.... And, by providing a broad context, the editors have done us a great service."
Eighteenth-Century Fiction

"These editions *[Frankenstein, Hard Times, Heart of Darkness]* are top-notch—far better than anything else in the market today."
Craig Keating, Langara College

The Broadview Literary Texts series represents an important effort to see the ever-changing canon of English literature from new angles. The series brings together texts that have long been regarded as classics with lesser-known texts that offer a fresh light—and that in many cases may also claim to be of real importance in our literary tradition.

Each volume in the series presents the text together with a variety of documents from the period, enabling readers to get a fuller, richer sense of the world out of which it emerged. Samples of the science available for Mary Shelley to draw on in writing *Frankenstein,* stark reports from the Congo in the late nineteenth century that help to illuminate Conrad's *Heart of Darkness;* late eighteenth-century statements on the proper roles for women and men that help contextualize the feminist themes of the late eighteenth-century novels *Millenium Hall* and *Something New*—these are the sorts of fascinating background materials that round out each Broadview Literary Texts edition.

Each volume also includes a full introduction, chronology, bibliography, and explanatory notes. Newly typeset and produced on high-quality paper in an attractive Trade paperback format, Broadview Literary Texts are a delight to handle as well as to read.

The distinctive cover images for the series are also designed (like the duotone process itself) to combine two slightly different perspectives. Early photographs inevitably evoke a sense of pastness, yet the images for most volumes in the series involve a conscious use of anachronism. The covers are thus designed to draw attention to social and temporal context, while suggesting that the works themselves may also relate to periods other than that from which they emerged—including our own era.